Calamity Jane

The Calamitous Life of Martha Jane Cannary, 1852–1903

Written by **Christian Perrissin**

Illustrated by **Matthieu Blanchin**

Lettered by **Frank Cvetkovic**

Translated by **Diana Schutz & Brandon Kander**

Facebook: **facebook.com/idwpublishing**
Twitter: **@idwpublishing**
YouTube: **youtube.com/idwpublishing**
Tumblr: **tumblr.idwpublishing.com**
Instagram: **instagram.com/idwpublishing**

ISBN: 978-1-63140-869-4   20 19 18 17   1 2 3 4

COLLECTION EDITOR
JUSTIN EISINGER

EDITORIAL ASSISTANCE
by ALONZO SIMON
and LESLIE MANES

COLLECTION DESIGNER
CLYDE GRAPA

PUBLISHER
TED ADAMS

Ted Adams, CEO & Publisher
Greg Goldstein, President & COO
Robbie Robbins, EVP/Sr. Graphic Artist
Chris Ryall, Chief Creative Officer/Editor-in-Chief
David Hedgecock, Editor-in-Chief
Laurie Windrow, Senior VP of Sales & Marketing
Matthew Ruzicka, CPA, Chief Financial Officer
Lorelei Bunjes, VP of Digital Services
Jerry Bennington, VP of New Product Development

Thank you to the sky, the earth, the Bear, and the White Buffalo...

-Mathieu Blanchin

Martha Jane Cannary
(1852~1869)

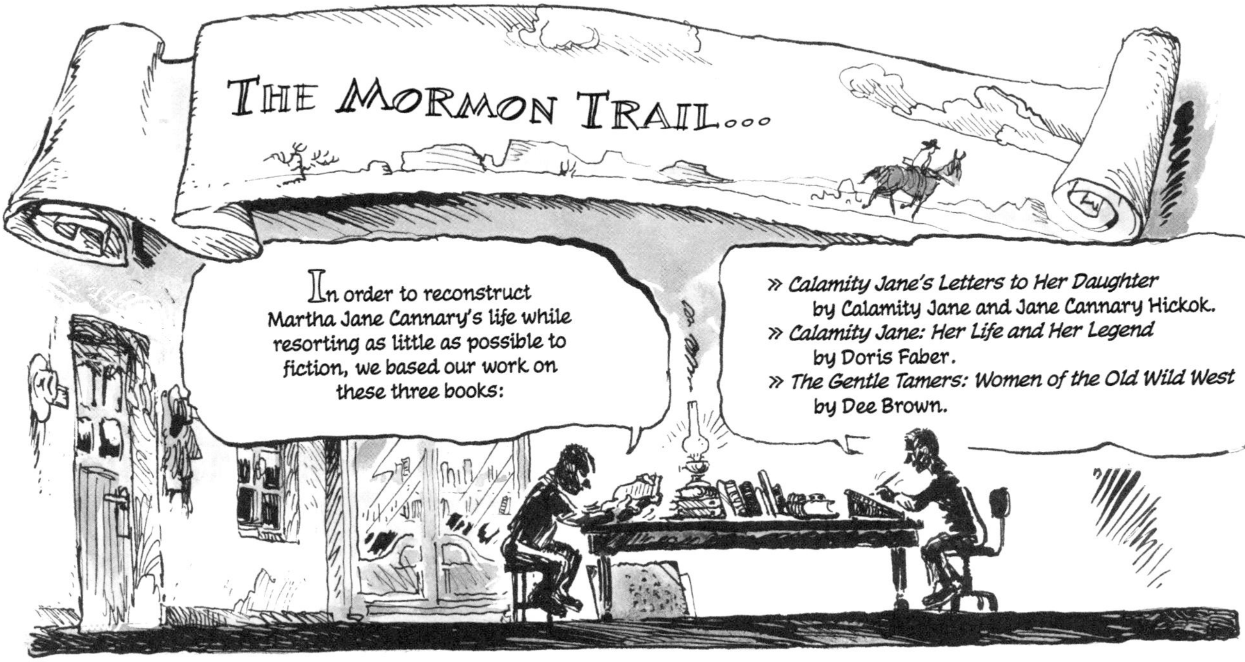
THE MORMON TRAIL...
In order to reconstruct Martha Jane Cannary's life while resorting as little as possible to fiction, we based our work on these three books:
» *Calamity Jane's Letters to Her Daughter* by Calamity Jane and Jane Cannary Hickok.
» *Calamity Jane: Her Life and Her Legend* by Doris Faber.
» *The Gentle Tamers: Women of the Old Wild West* by Dee Brown.

What's indisputable is that Calamity Jane was born May 1, 1852, near Princeton, Missouri. Her parents -- Robert and Charlotte Cannary -- were broke, so tried their luck with farming... But they were better at making children! Martha Jane's birth was followed by five more:

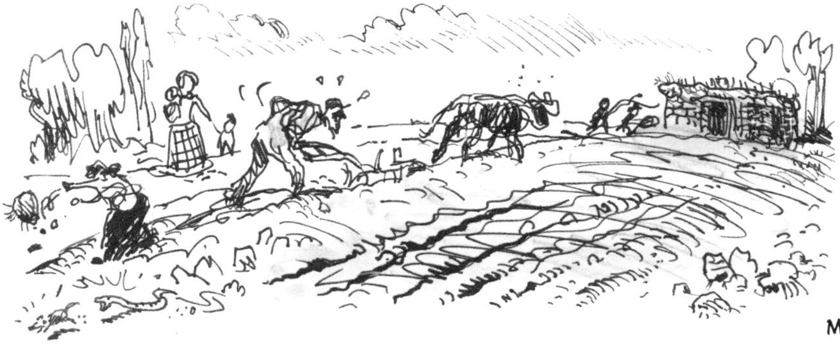

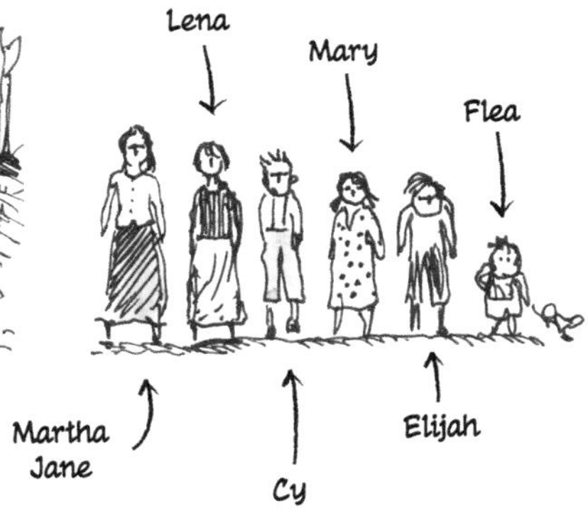
Lena
Mary
Flea
Martha Jane
Cy
Elijah

We also know that Martha Jane had very little schooling. But sporadic lessons allowed her to decipher the Bible and to learn enough penmanship that she later was able to write her *Letters to Her Daughter*.

The isolation of the family farm no doubt led to such spotty education, but it's also pretty likely that, at an early age, Martha Jane was stuck taking care of her siblings while her parents toiled in the fields.

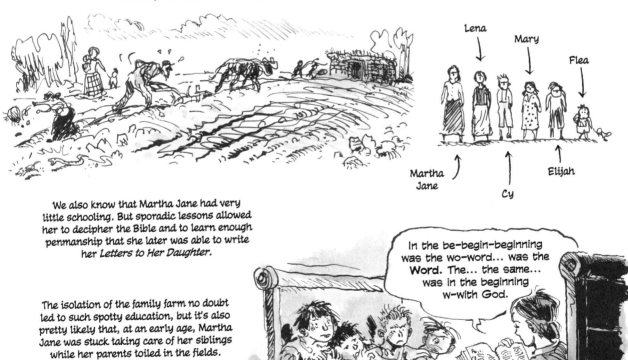

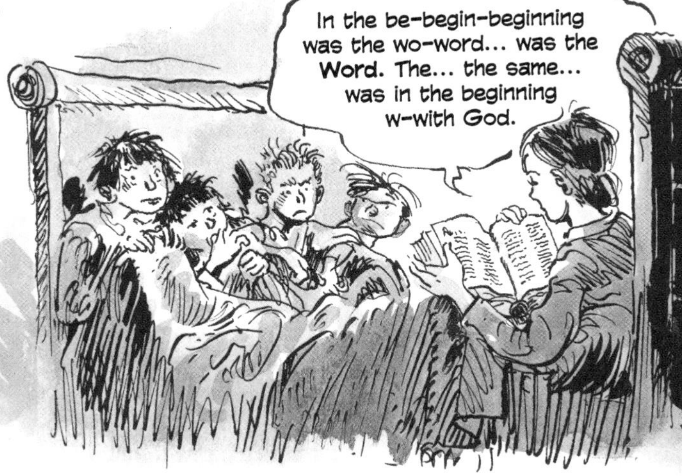
In the be-begin-beginning was the wo-word... was the **Word**. The... the same... was in the beginning w-with God.

When Martha Jane was 13 years old, an embittered Robert and Charlotte Cannary, now much the worse for wear, decided to leave it all behind and head west. They sold everything they could -- which wasn't much -- to invest in a small wagon team...

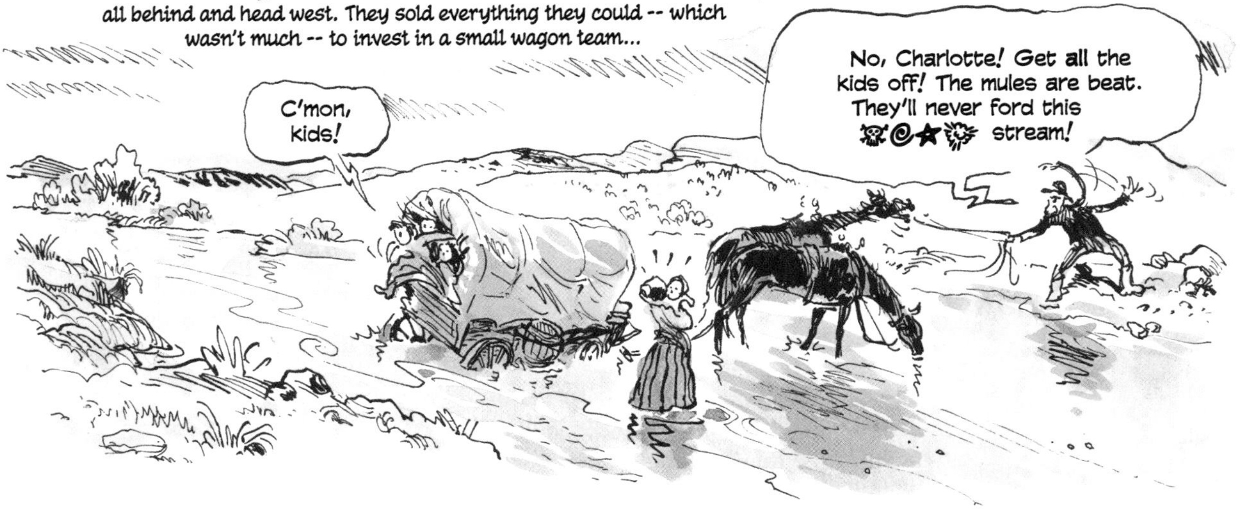
C'mon, kids!
No, Charlotte! Get all the kids off! The mules are beat. They'll never ford this stream!

They made it to **Independence,** at a bend of the **Missouri River.** This was the point of departure for homesteader wagon trains.
(See map on facing page »)

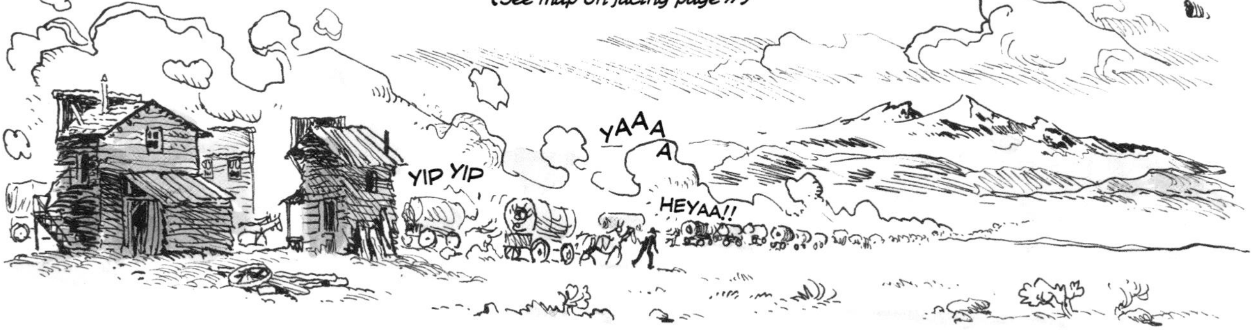
YIP YIP
YAAAA
HEYAA!!

Springtime 1865. The Civil War had ended April 9 with the surrender of General Lee, followed by Lincoln's assassination just a few days later: on April 14, while at the theater, the President was shot by John Wilkes Booth, a pro-Confederate actor.

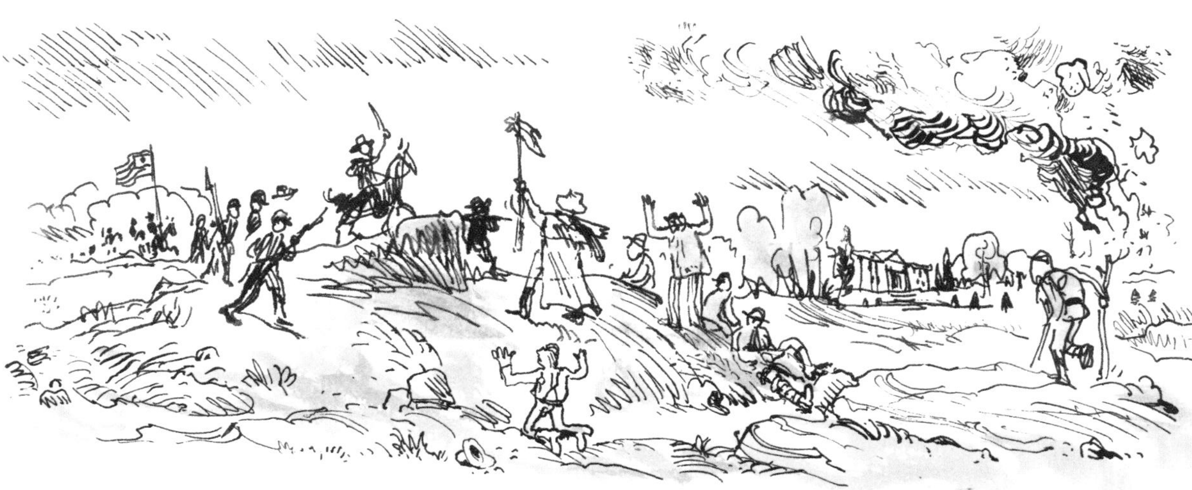

At the time, and up until **1876**, the American nation was divided in **two**. The **East** consisted of very populous states (by 1876 there were 42 million in 31 states) filled with cities, roads, and railways, while the **West**...

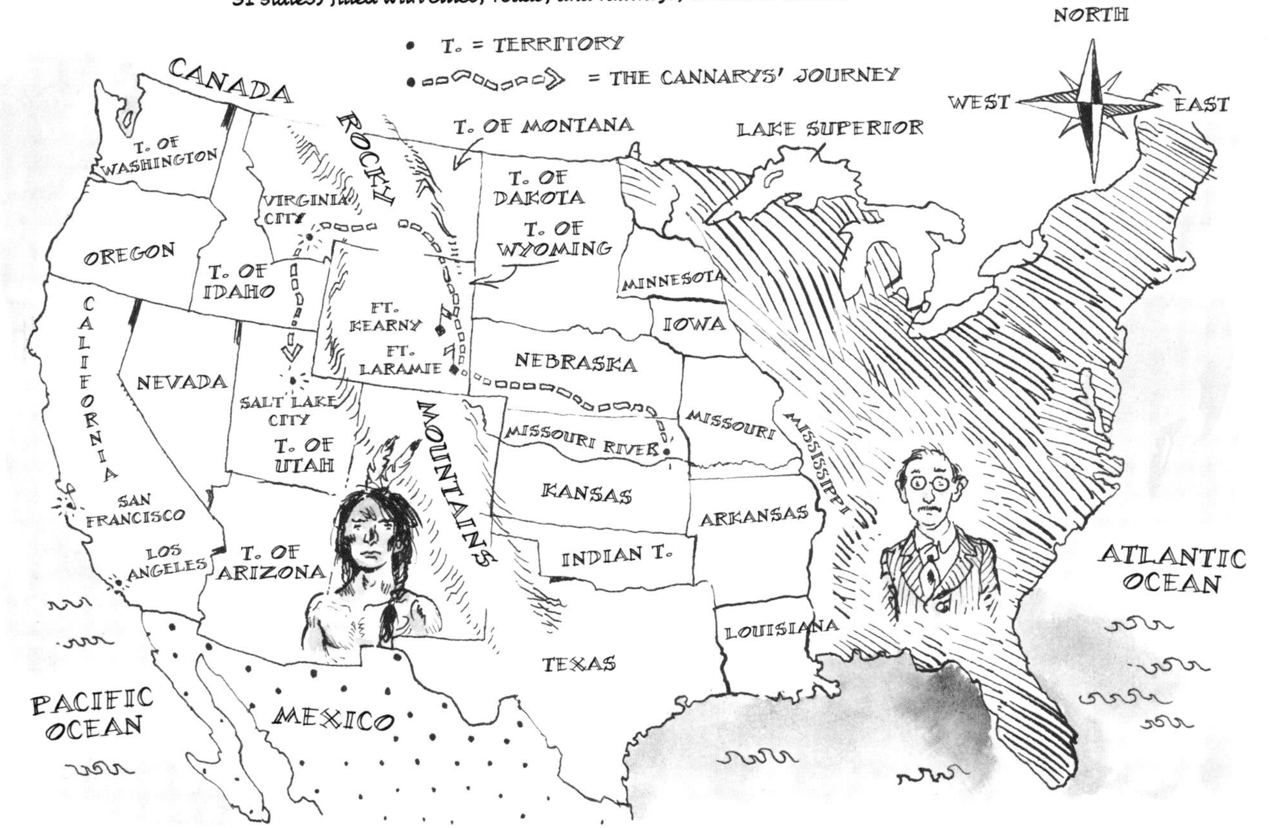

NORTH
WEST
EAST
• T. = TERRITORY
= THE CANNARYS' JOURNEY
CANADA
T. OF WASHINGTON
ROCKY
MOUNTAINS
T. OF MONTANA
LAKE SUPERIOR
VIRGINIA CITY
T. OF DAKOTA
T. OF WYOMING
OREGON
T. OF IDAHO
MINNESOTA
IOWA
FT. KEARNY
FT. LARAMIE
NEBRASKA
CALIFORNIA
NEVADA
SALT LAKE CITY
T. OF UTAH
MISSOURI
MISSISSIPPI
MISSOURI RIVER
KANSAS
SAN FRANCISCO
ARKANSAS
LOS ANGELES
T. OF ARIZONA
INDIAN T.
ATLANTIC OCEAN
LOUISIANA
TEXAS
PACIFIC OCEAN
MEXICO

...In **1865** the West was still carving out vast territories. Only scattered forts and mail outposts along the trails testified to the white man's presence. By 1876, just two million white settlers, consistently scorned by Easterners, were dispersed throughout this part of the continent, a land dominated by Indian tribes. The West was still a region ruled by the forces of nature and by the Indians, who intended to keep it that way!

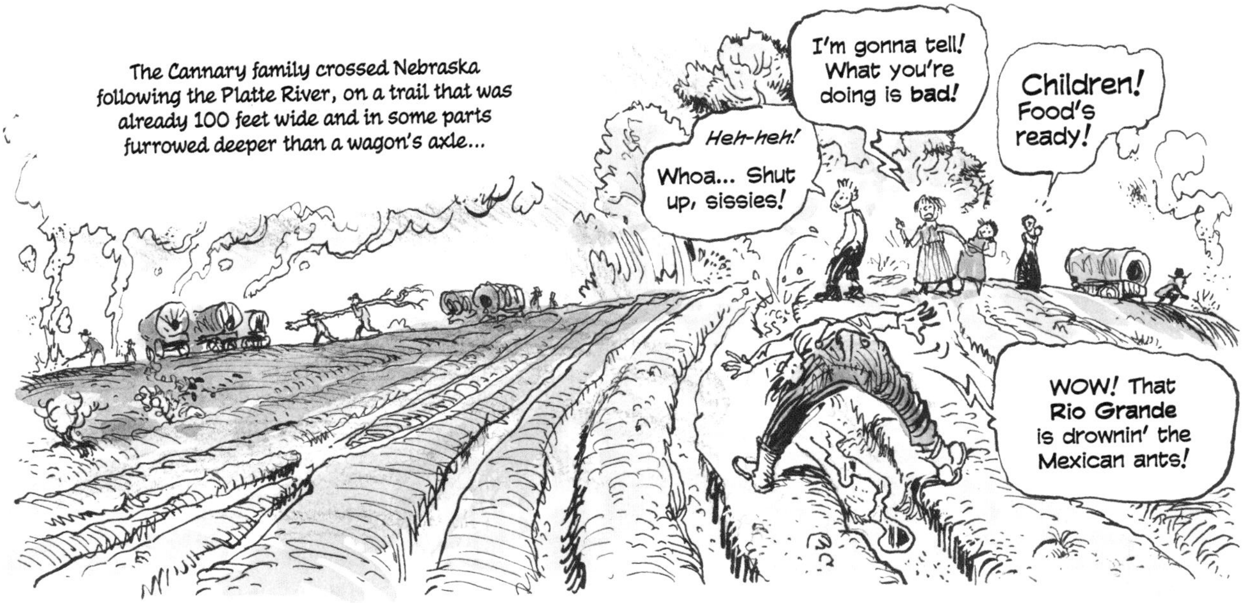

The Cannary family crossed Nebraska following the Platte River, on a trail that was already 100 feet wide and in some parts furrowed deeper than a wagon's axle...
I'm gonna tell! What you're doing is **bad!**
Children! Food's ready!
Heh-heh!
Whoa... Shut up, sissies!
WOW! That **Rio Grande** is drownin' the Mexican ants!

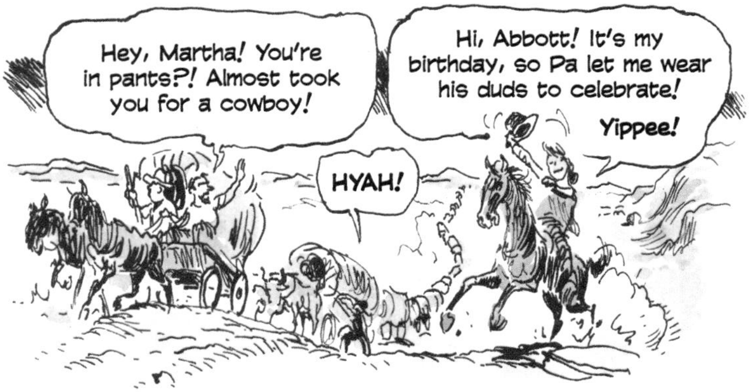
Hey, Martha! You're in pants?! Almost took you for a cowboy!
Hi, Abbott! It's my birthday, so Pa let me wear his duds to celebrate!
Yippee!
HYAH!

All we know about the Cannary family's trek is that Martha couldn't hold still and spent the time on her pony, riding up and down the half-mile length of the convoy.

After five months on the trail, the settlers reached **FORT LARAMIE,** the last stop before crossing the **ROCKY MOUNTAINS.**

The Rockies: backbone of the entire continent, running all the way from Canada to Mexico... After Laramie, the trail split: California to the south, and Oregon due west. The Cannarys took the western fork towards **Oregon** but left the wagon train at **Virginia City, Montana,** then a Rocky Mountain gold-mining camp.

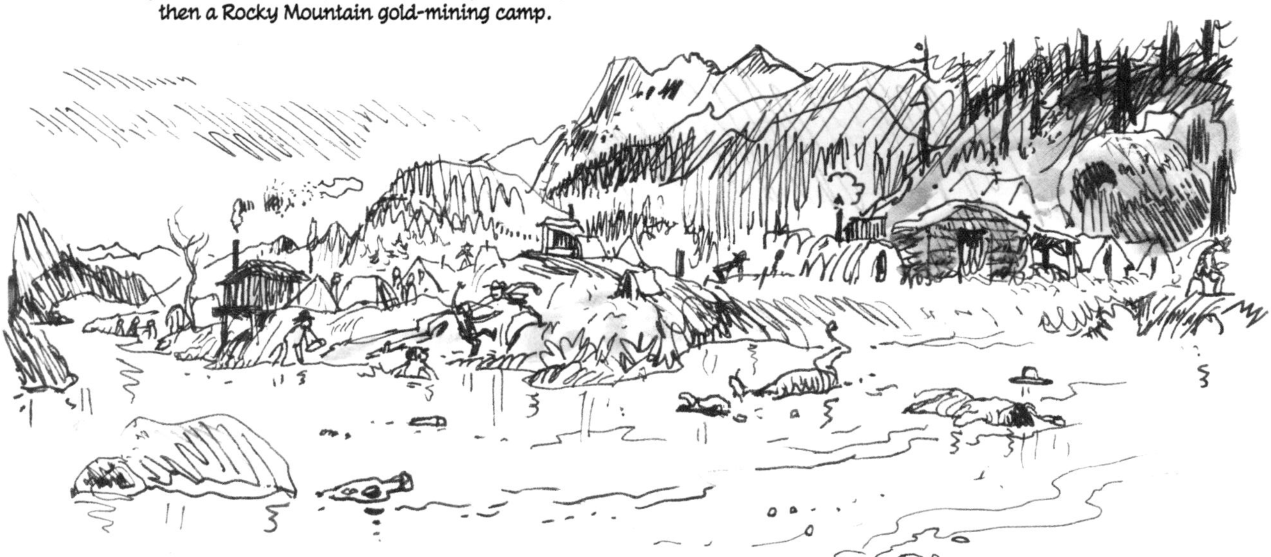

Virginia City consisted of 15,000 people crammed into huts or tents, living only in the hope of striking a rich vein. Alcohol, prostitution, brawls, and murder were rampant... We know that the Cannarys spent the winter there before heading south again, as broke as ever, Robert having had no more luck as a prospector than as a farmer.

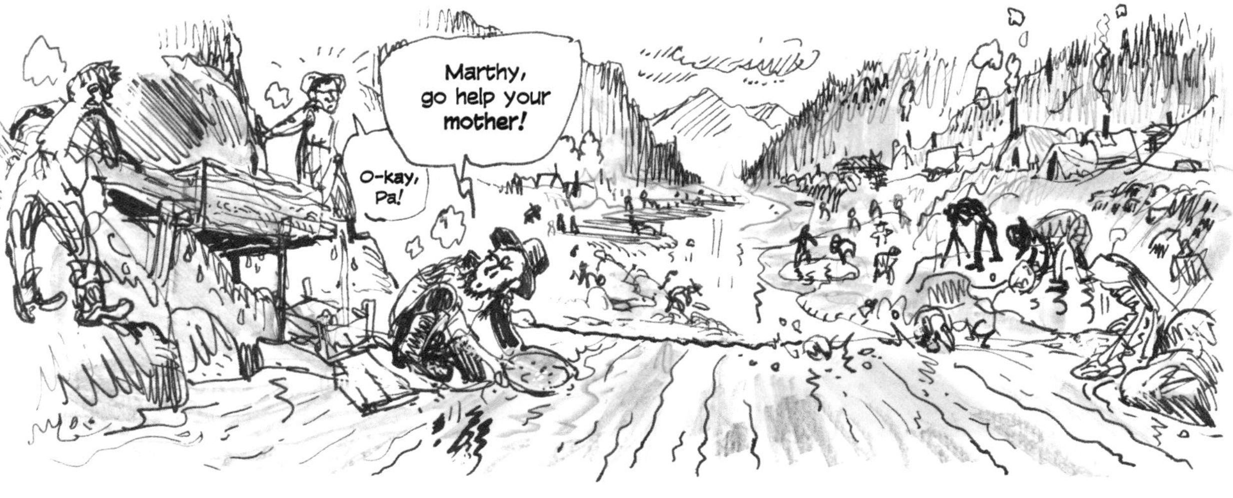
Marthy, go help your **mother!**
O-kay, Pa!

We know that Charlotte Cannary died on the road, somewhere in Montana. A fatal accident? Pleurisy? Crossing the Grim Reaper's path was all too common in the Old West.

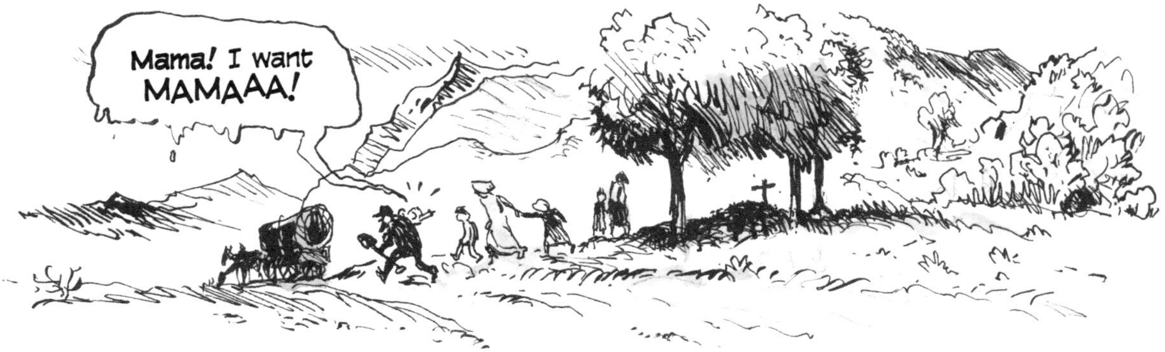
Mama! I want MAMAAA!

We next pick up the trail of Robert and his six children 100 miles farther south, in the **Utah** desert near **Salt Lake City,** which was founded by Mormon homesteaders.

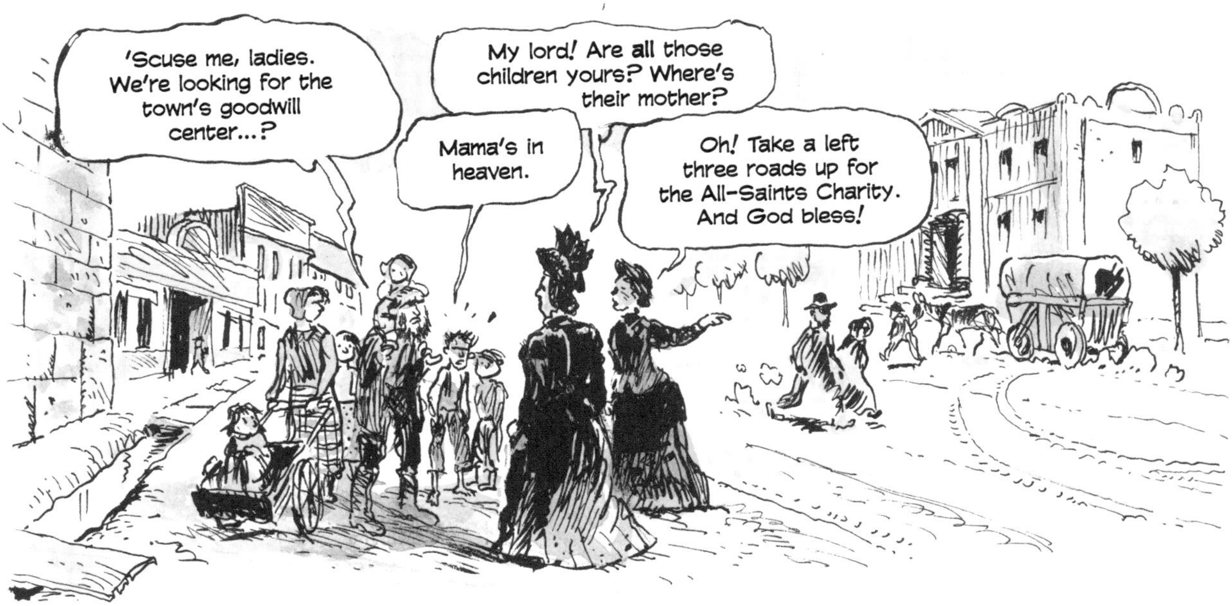
'Scuse me, ladies. We're looking for the town's goodwill center...?
My lord! Are **all** those children yours? Where's their mother?
Mama's in heaven.
Oh! Take a left three roads up for the All-Saints Charity. And God bless!

Salt Lake City was already a flourishing spot, with sun-baked brick houses and mountain streams coursing along its streets, irrigating the many orchards and flower gardens. Without the means to rent one of these fine houses, the Cannarys had to settle for more modest accommodation on the outskirts of town...

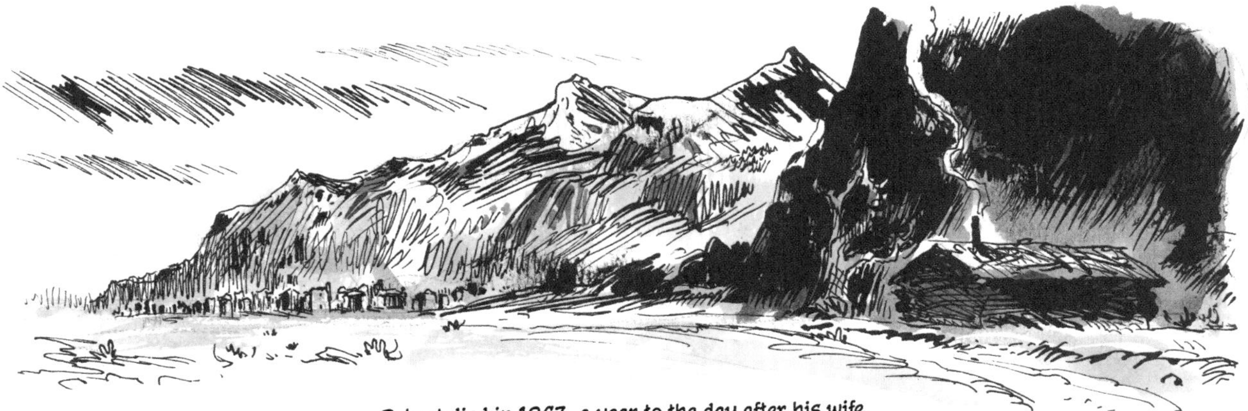

Robert died in 1867, a year to the day after his wife. Martha Jane, only 15 years old, was now saddled with the job of caring for her brothers and sisters, all by herself!

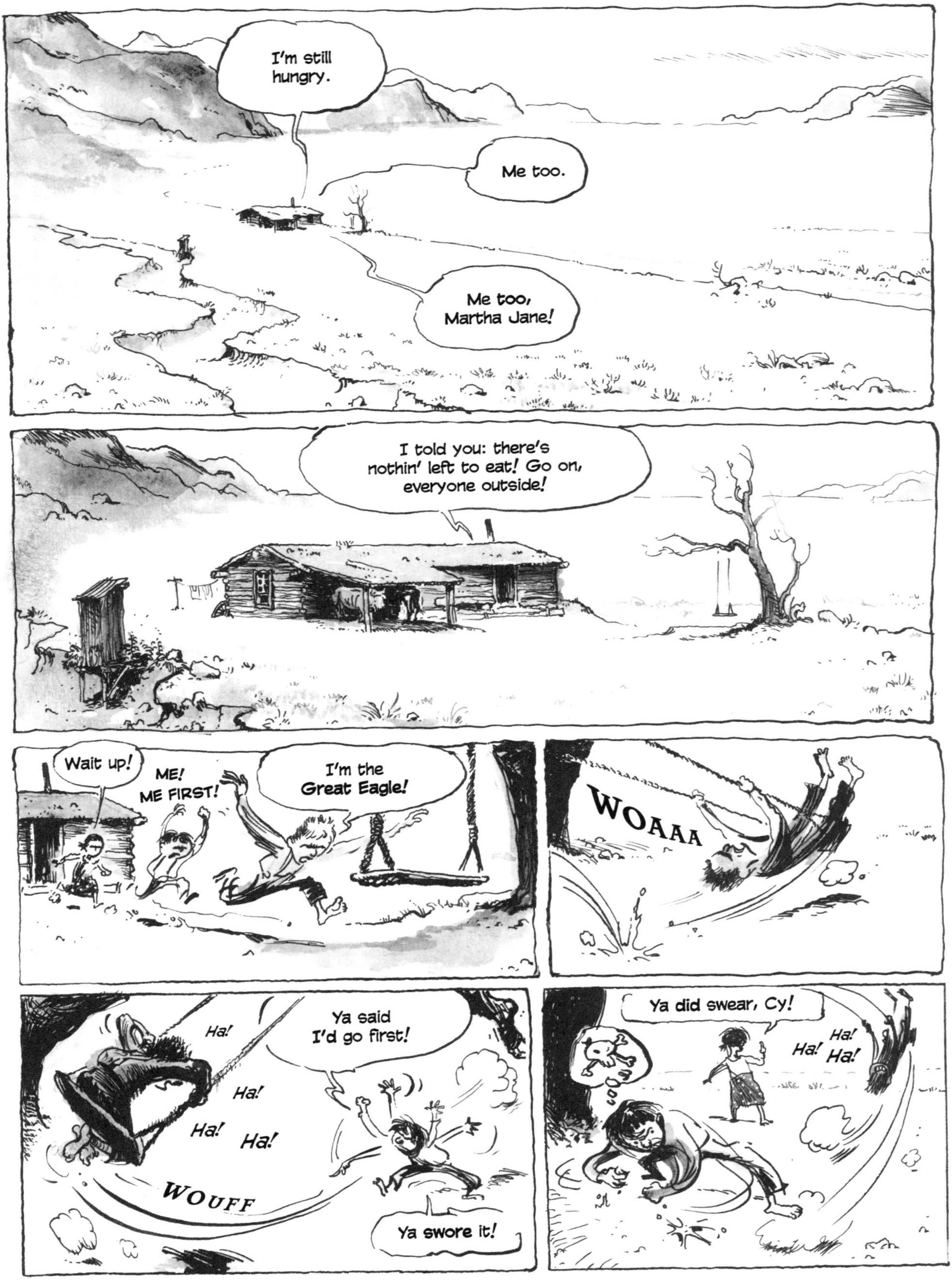
I'm still hungry.
Me too.
Me too, Martha Jane!
I told you: there's nothin' left to eat! Go on, everyone outside!
Wait up!
ME! ME FIRST!
I'm the Great Eagle!
WOAAA
Ha!
Ya said I'd go first!
Ha!
Ha!
Ha!
WOUFF
Ya swore it!
Ya did swear, Cy!
Ha!
Ha!
Ha!

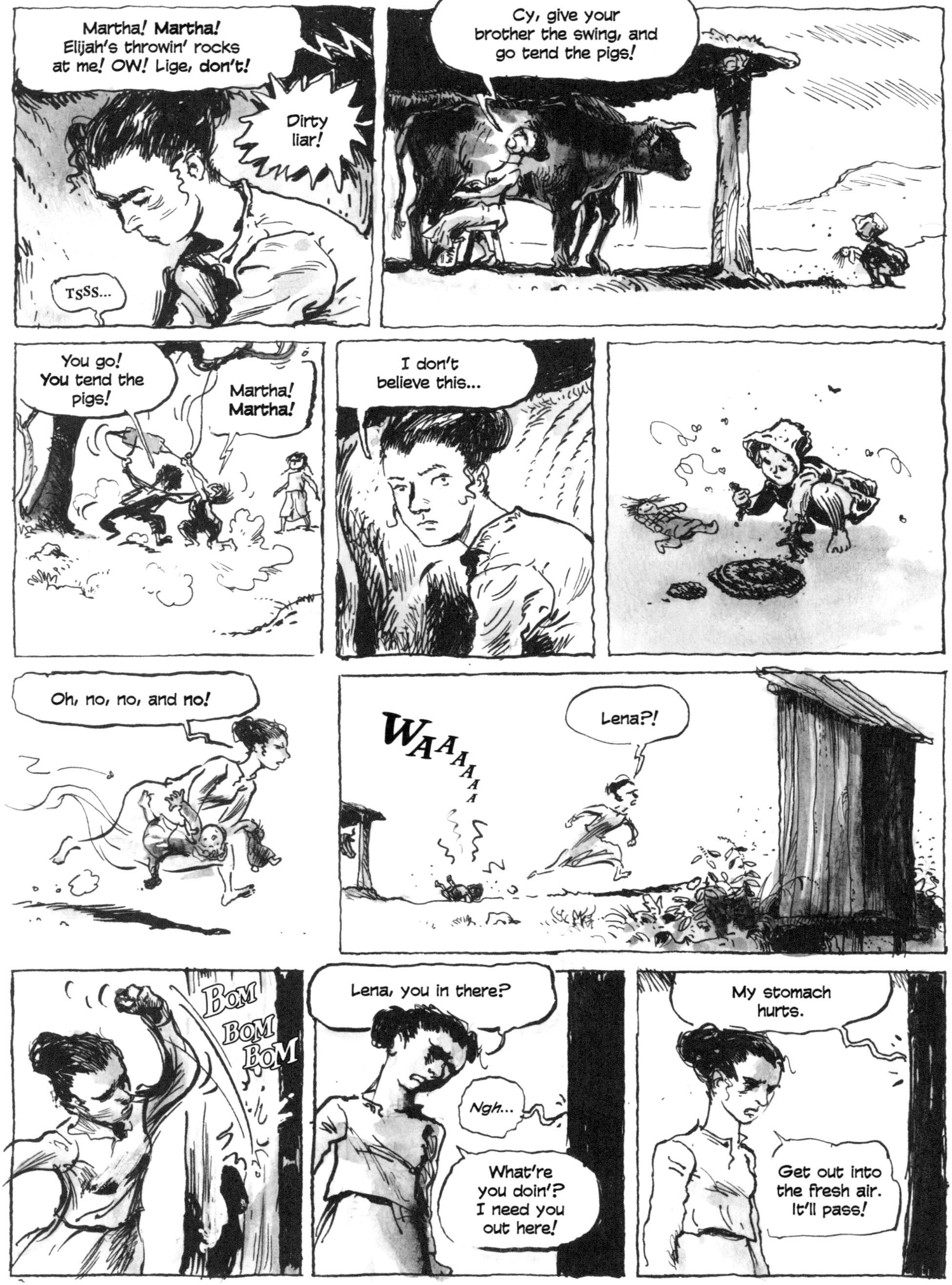
Martha! Martha! Elijah's throwin' rocks at me! OW! Lige, don't!
Dirty liar!
Tsss...
Cy, give your brother the swing, and go tend the pigs!
You go! You tend the pigs!
Martha! Martha!
I don't believe this...
Oh, no, no, and no!
WAAAAAAA
Lena?!
BOM BOM BOM
Lena, you in there?
Ngh...
What're you doin'? I need you out here!
My stomach hurts.
Get out into the fresh air. It'll pass!

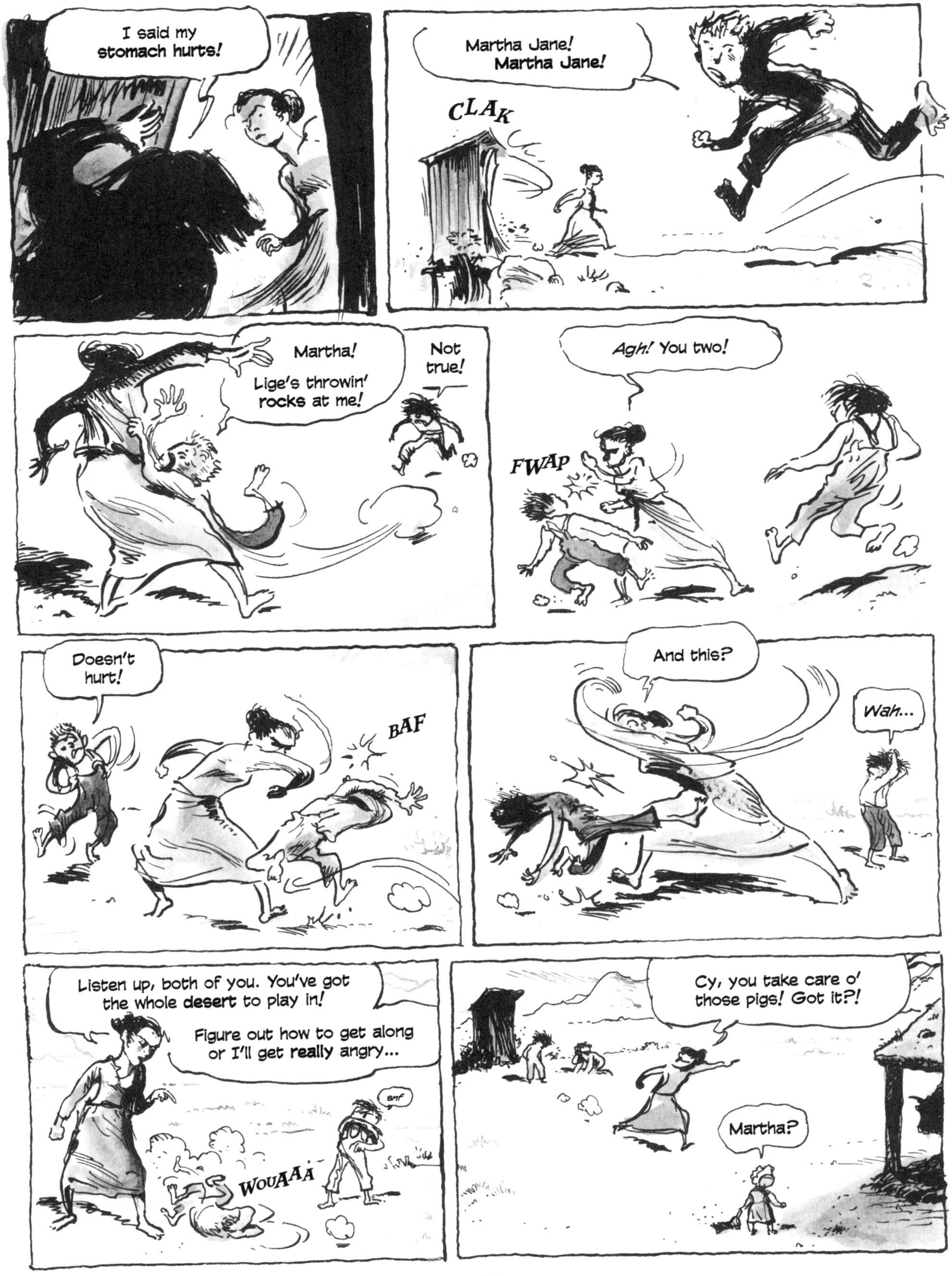
I said my stomach hurts!
Martha Jane! Martha Jane!
CLAK
Martha! Lige's throwin' rocks at me!
Not true!
Agh! You two!
FWAP
Doesn't hurt!
BAF
And this?
Wah...
Listen up, both of you. You've got the whole desert to play in!
Figure out how to get along or I'll get really angry...
WOUAAA
Cy, you take care o' those pigs! Got it?!
Martha?

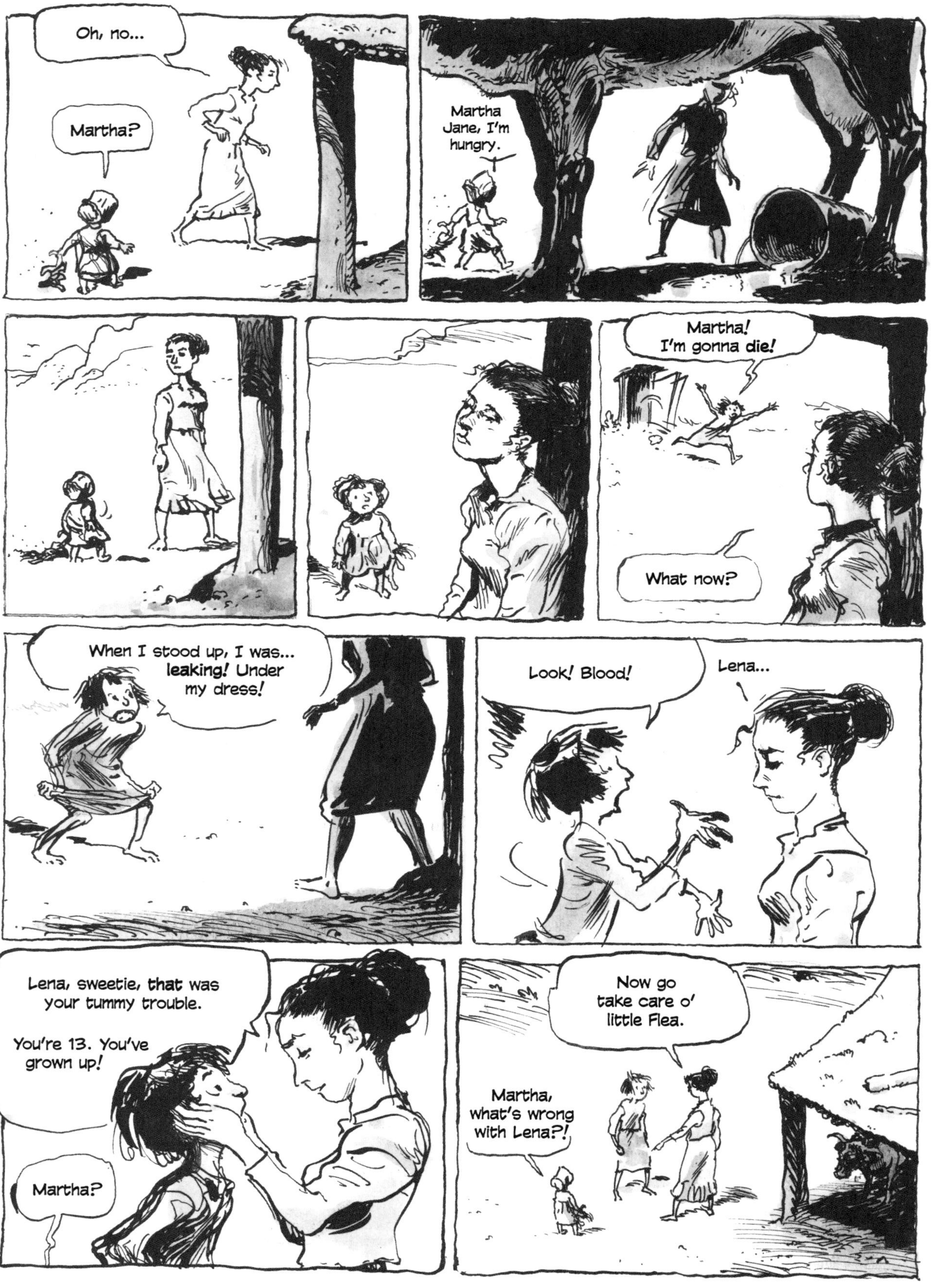
Oh, no...
Martha?
Martha Jane, I'm hungry.
Martha! I'm gonna die!
What now?
When I stood up, I was... leaking! Under my dress!
Look! Blood!
Lena...
Lena, sweetie, that was your tummy trouble.
You're 13. You've grown up!
Martha?
Now go take care o' little Flea.
Martha, what's wrong with Lena?!

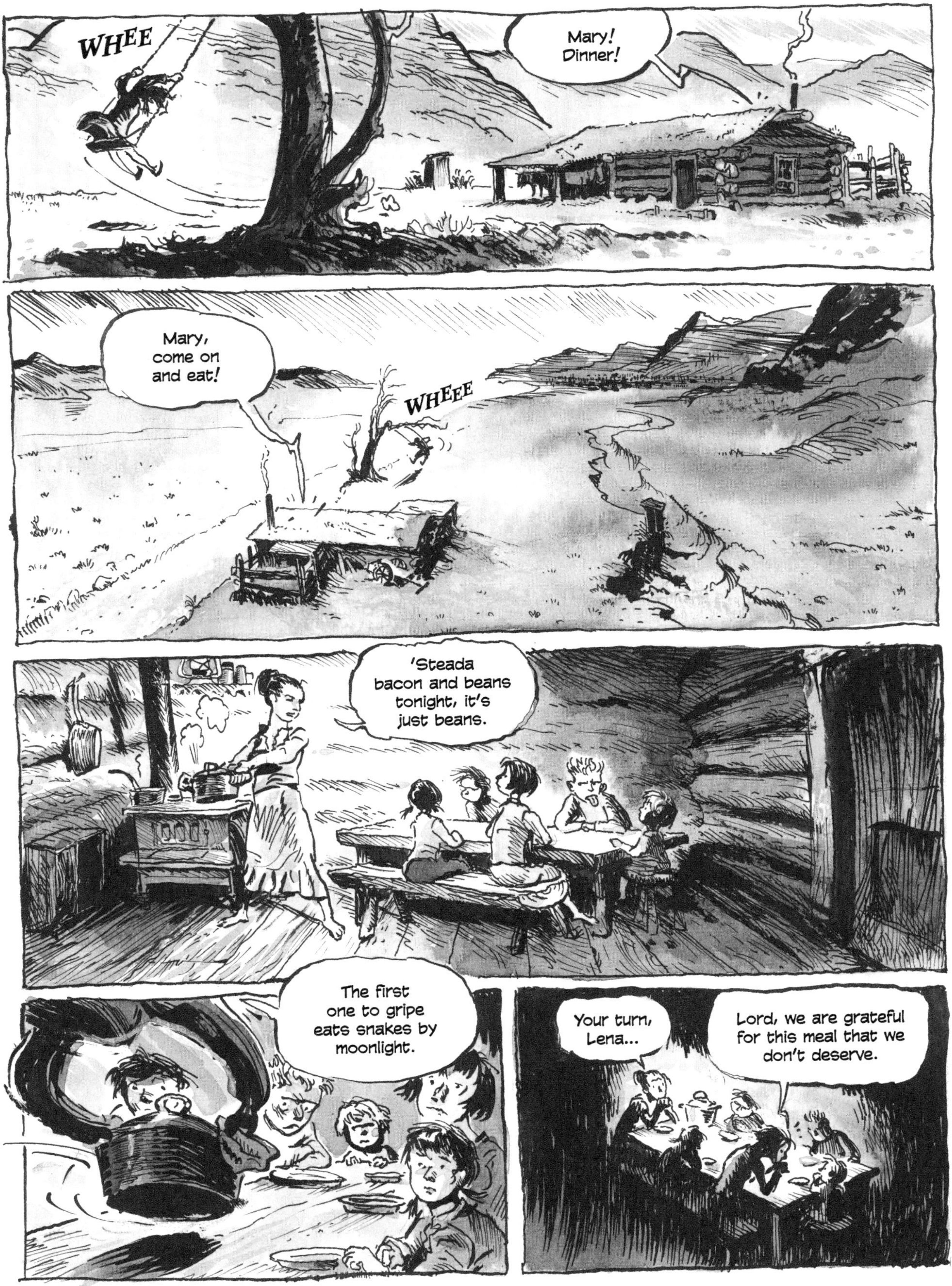
WHEE
Mary! Dinner!
Mary, come on and eat!
WHEEE
'Steada bacon and beans tonight, it's just beans.
The first one to gripe eats snakes by moonlight.
Your turn, Lena...
Lord, we are grateful for this meal that we don't deserve.

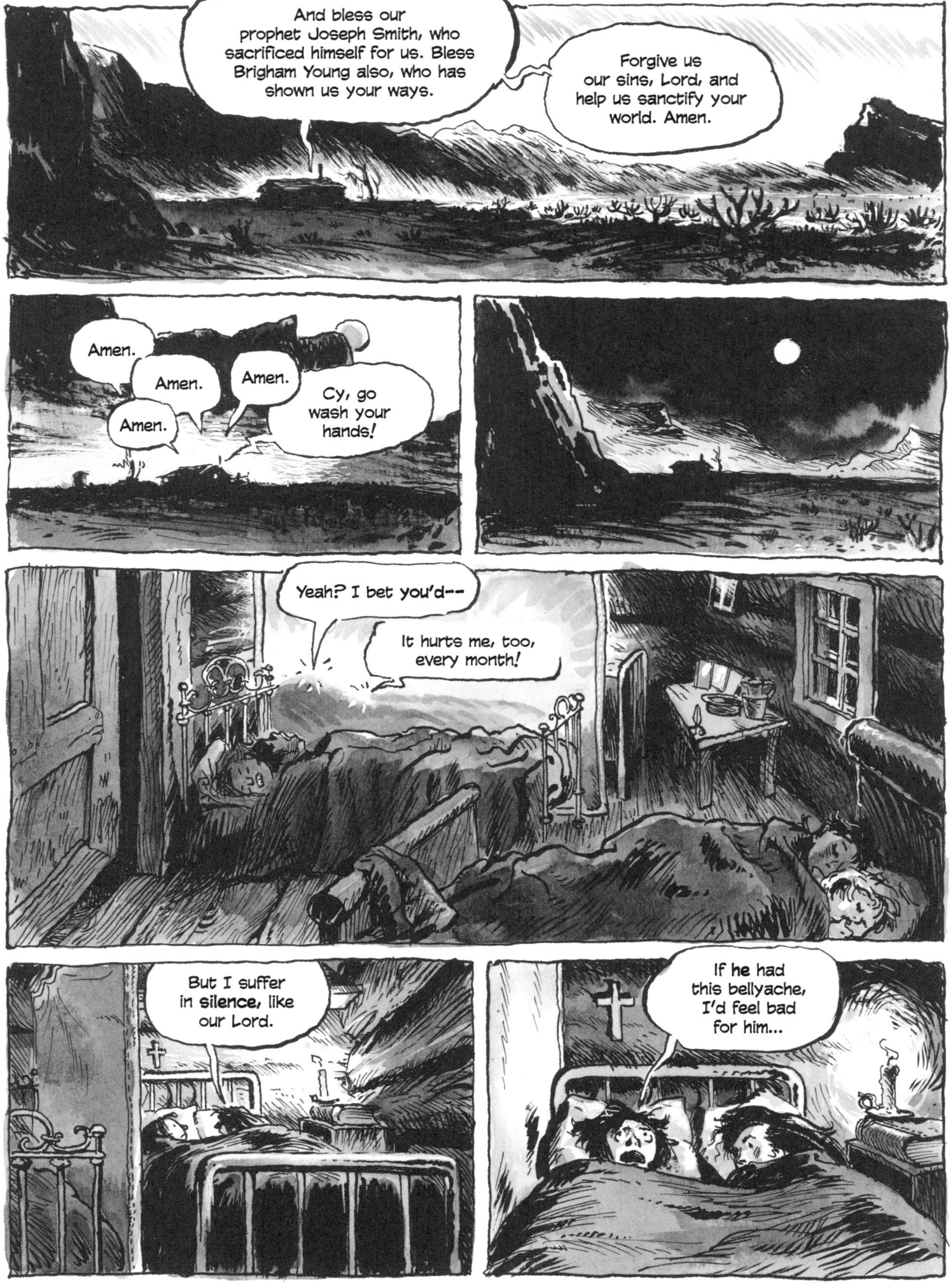

And bless our prophet Joseph Smith, who sacrificed himself for us. Bless Brigham Young also, who has shown us your ways.
Forgive us our sins, Lord, and help us sanctify your world. Amen.
Amen.
Amen.
Amen.
Amen.
Cy, go wash your hands!
Yeah? I bet you'd--
It hurts me, too, every month!
But I suffer in silence, like our Lord.
If he had this bellyache, I'd feel bad for him...

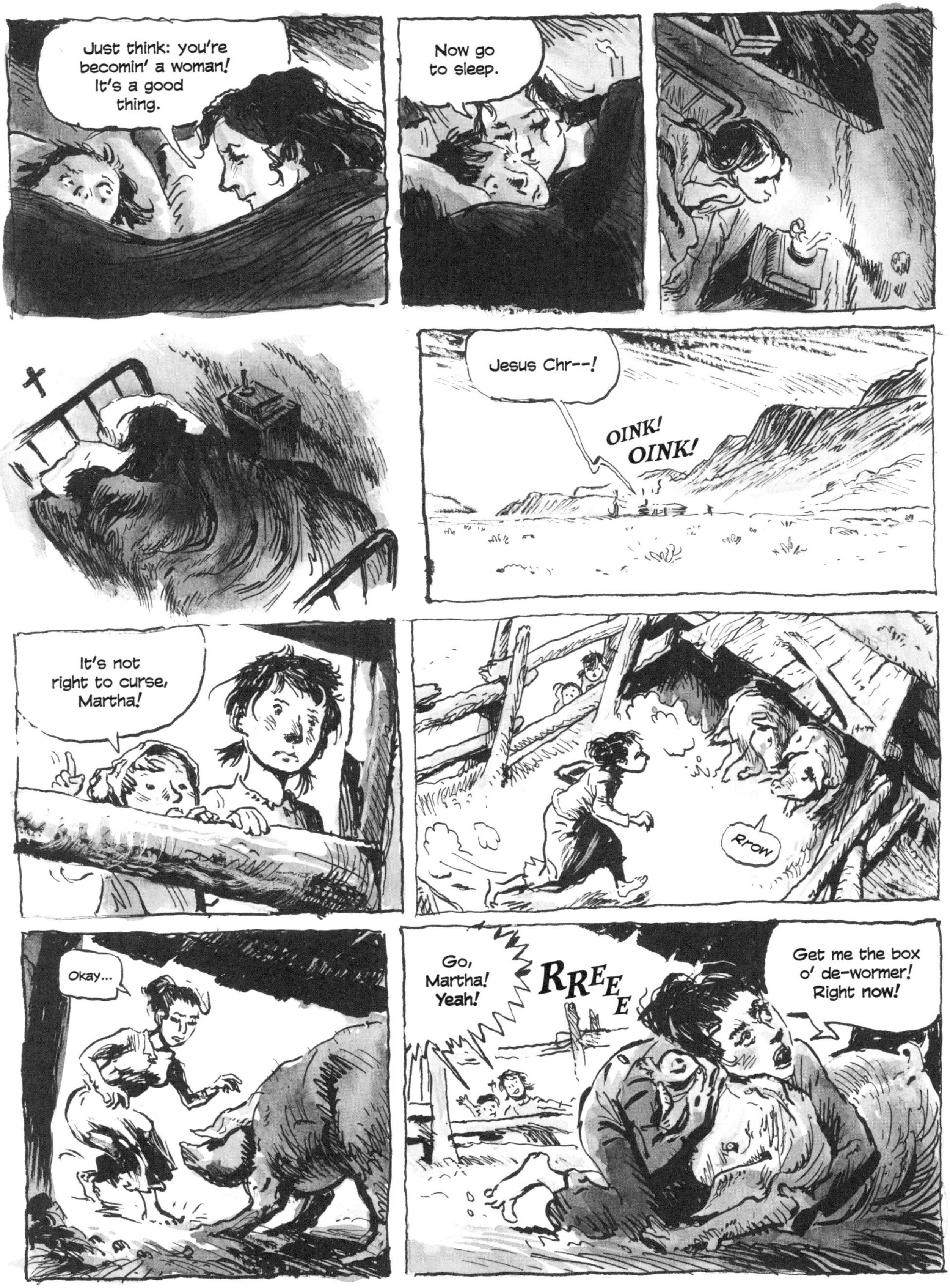
Just think: you're becomin' a woman! It's a good thing.
Now go to sleep.
Jesus Chr--!
OINK! OINK!
It's not right to curse, Martha!
Rrow
Okay...
Go, Martha! Yeah!
RREEE
Get me the box o' de-wormer! Right now!

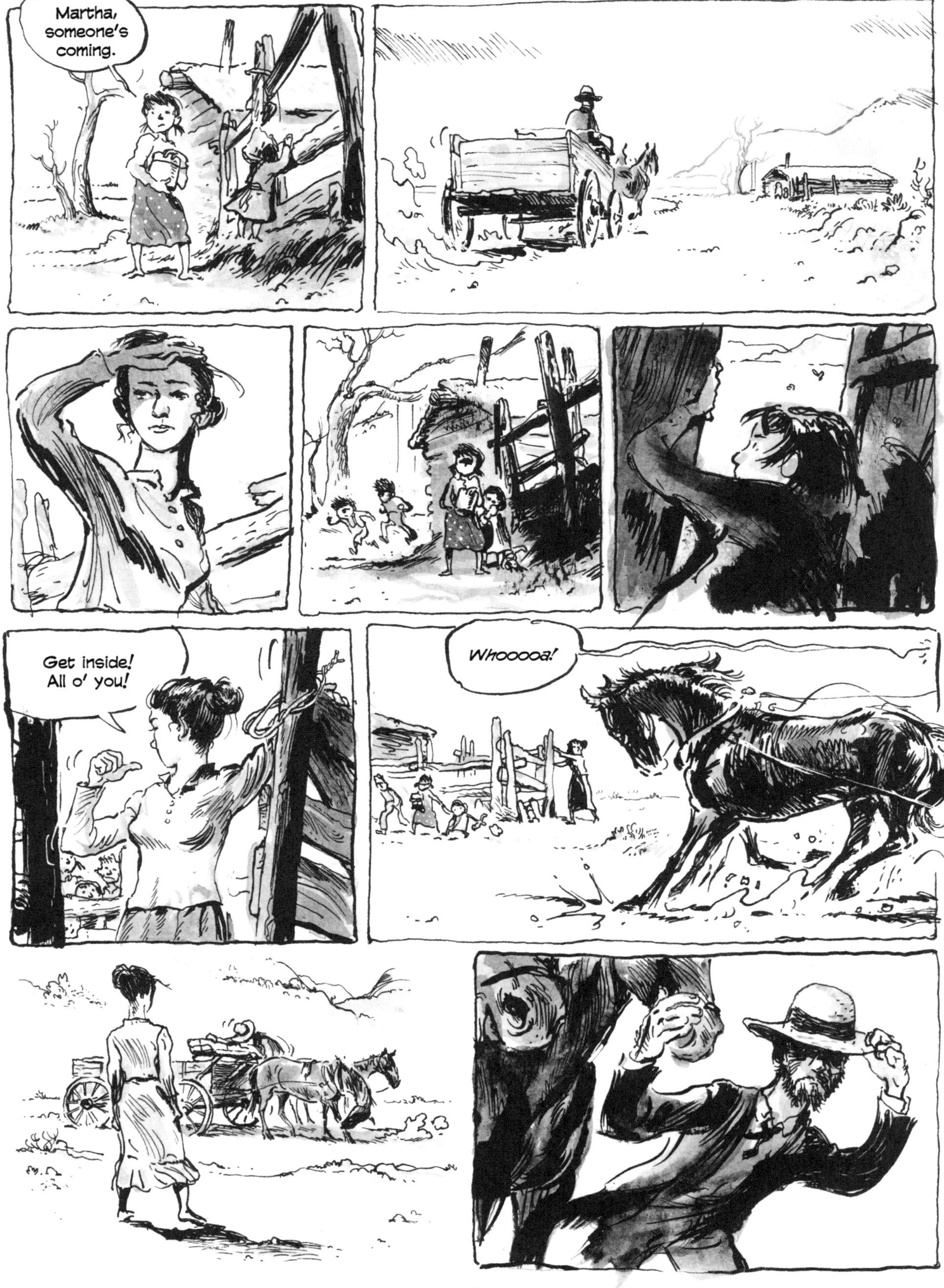
Martha, someone's coming.
Get inside! All o' you!
Whoooa!

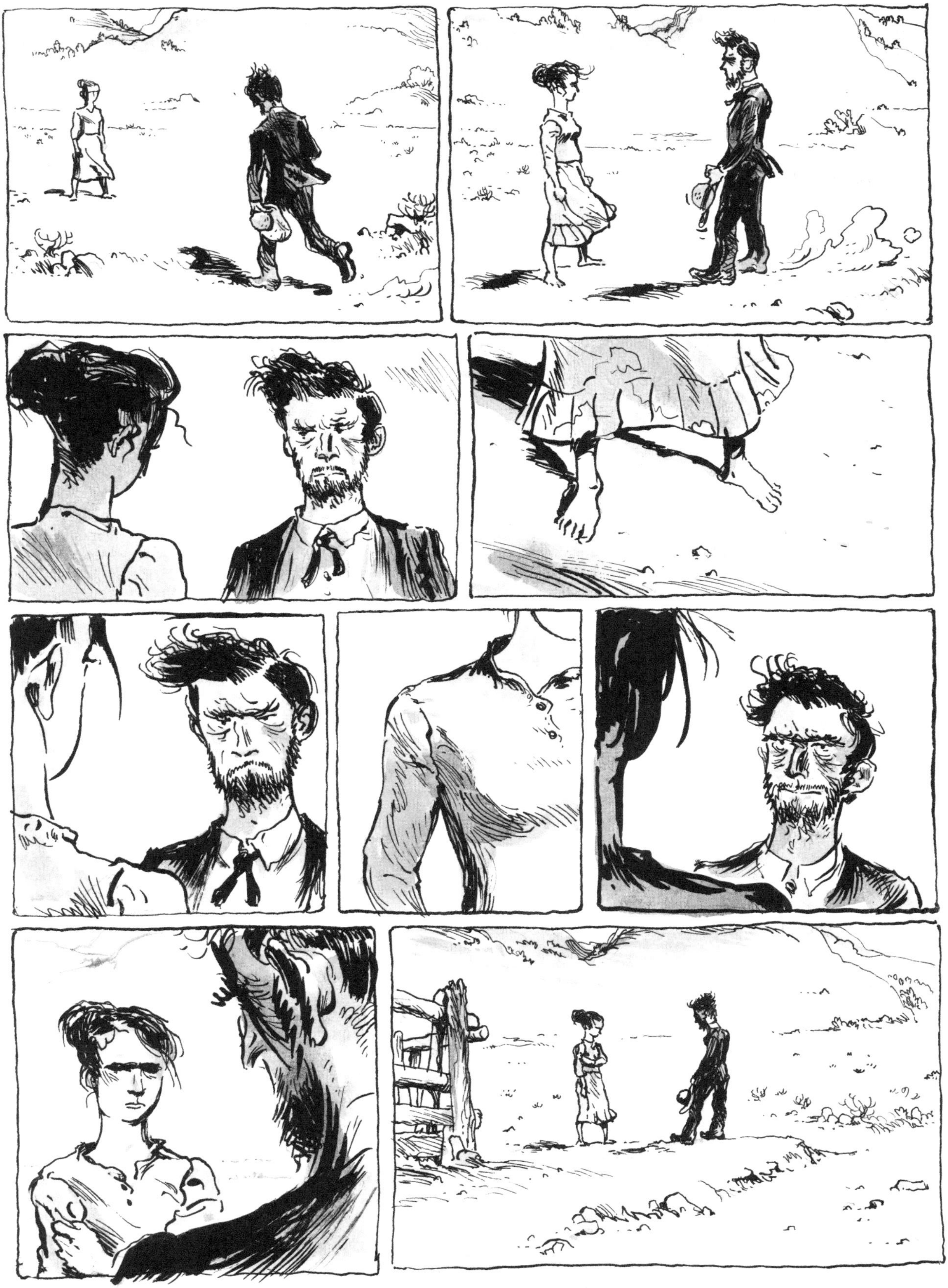

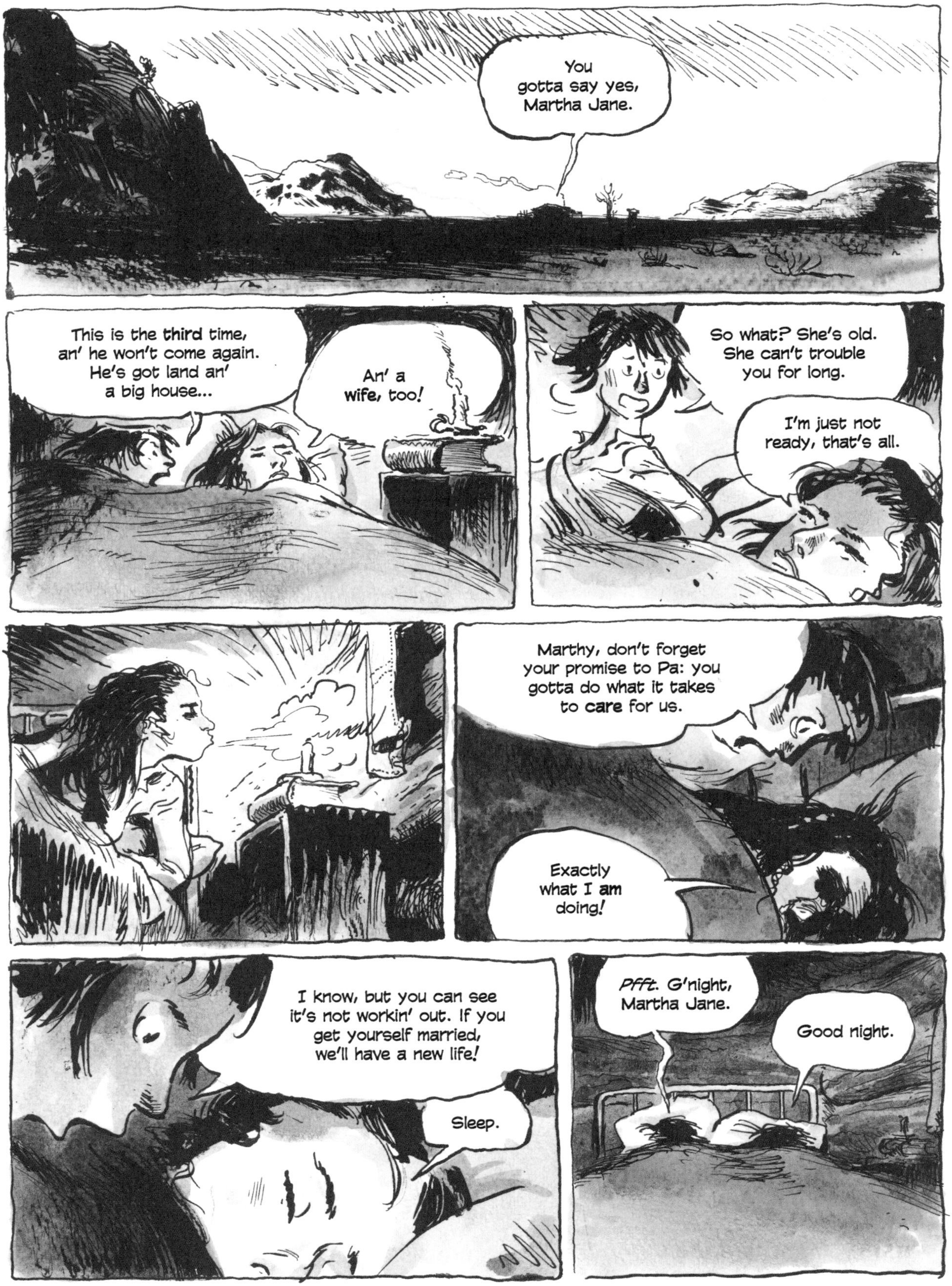

You gotta say yes, Martha Jane.
This is the third time, an' he won't come again. He's got land an' a big house...
An' a wife, too!
So what? She's old. She can't trouble you for long.
I'm just not ready, that's all.
Marthy, don't forget your promise to Pa: you gotta do what it takes to care for us.
Exactly what I am doing!
I know, but you can see it's not workin' out. If you get yourself married, we'll have a new life!
Sleep.
Pfft. G'night, Martha Jane.
Good night.

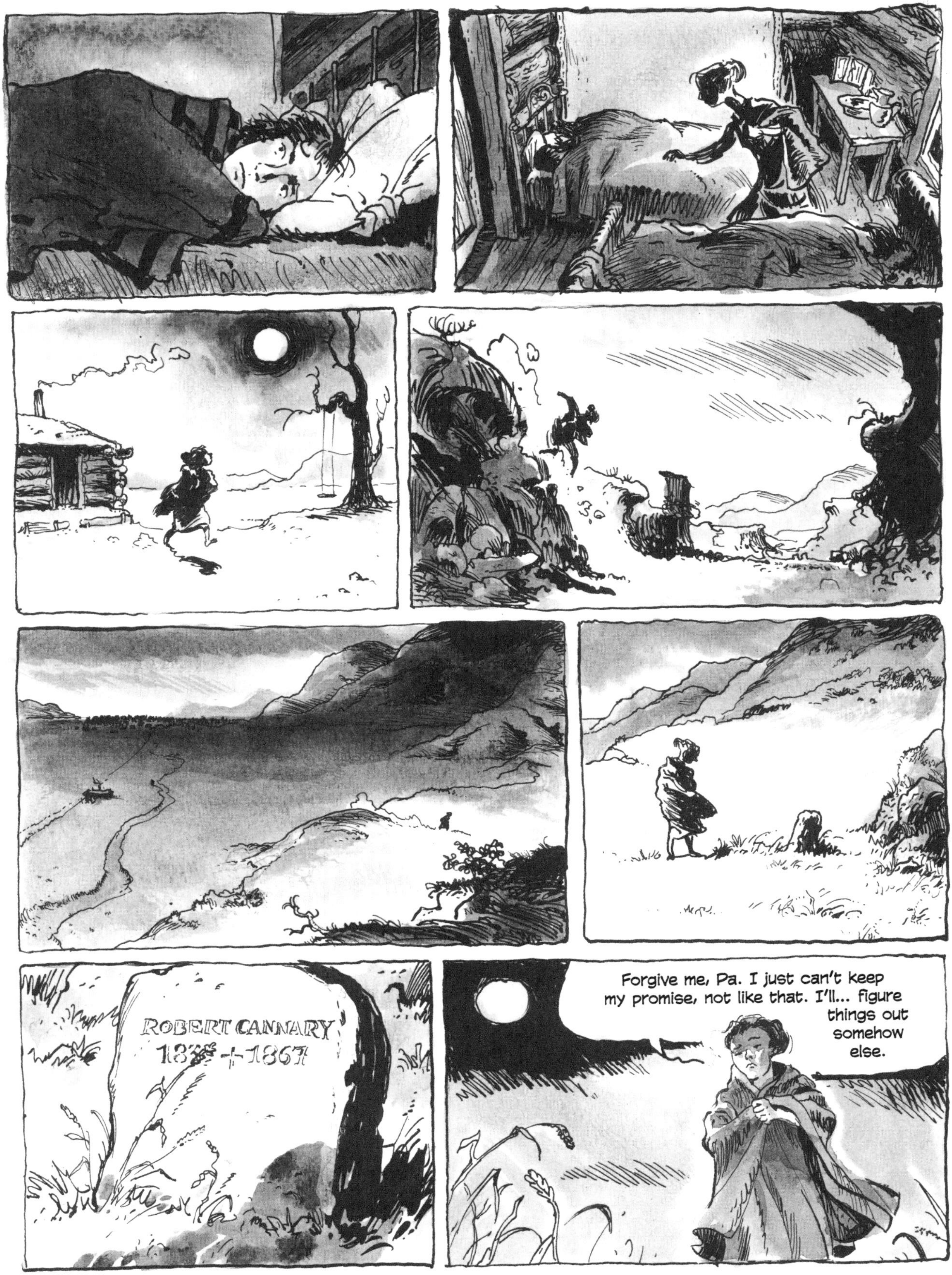
ROBERT CANNARY
Forgive me, Pa. I just can't keep my promise, not like that. I'll... figure things out somehow else.

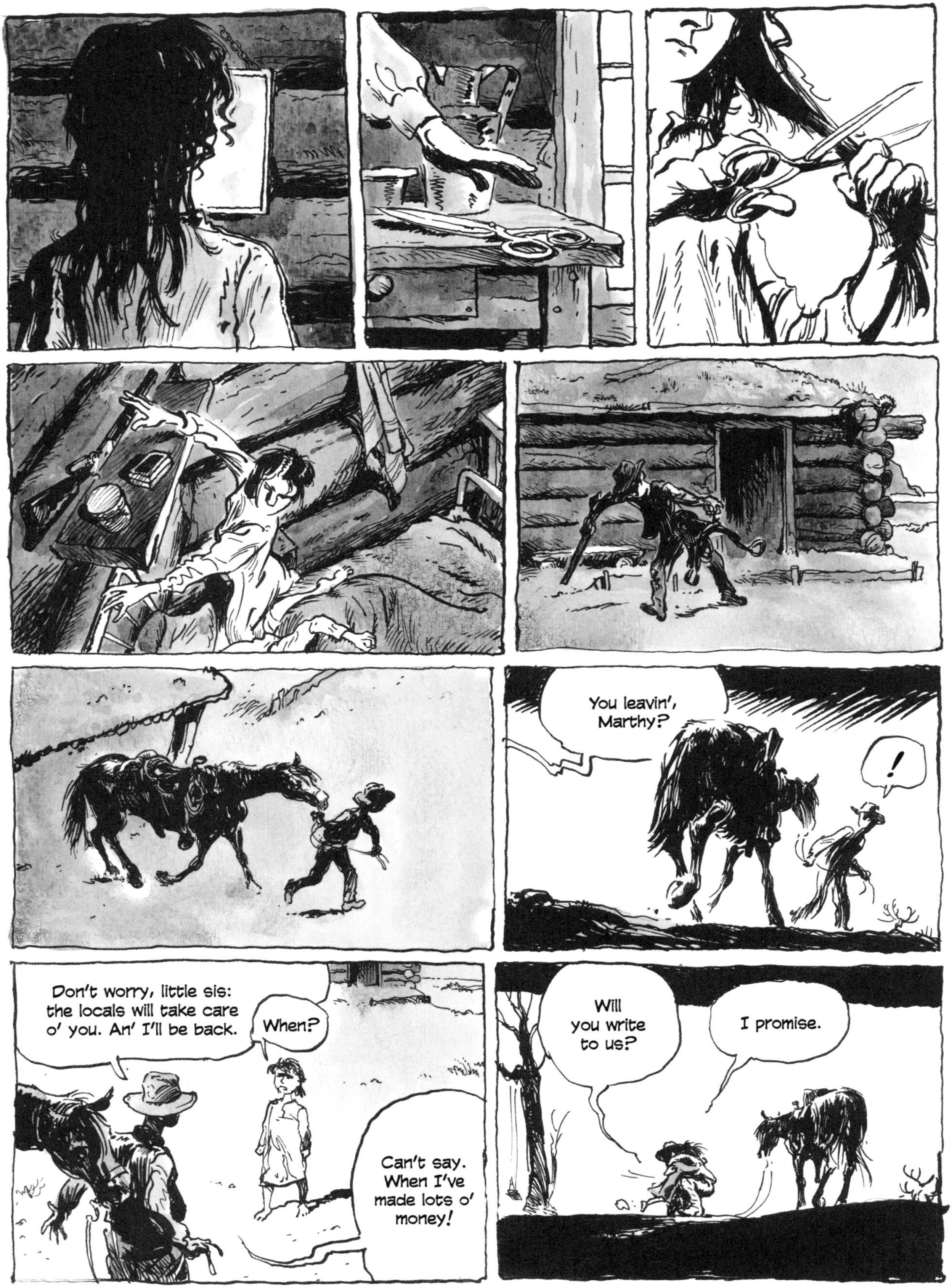
You leavin', Marthy?
!
Don't worry, little sis: the locals will take care o' you. An' I'll be back.
When?
Can't say. When I've made lots o' money!
Will you write to us?
I promise.

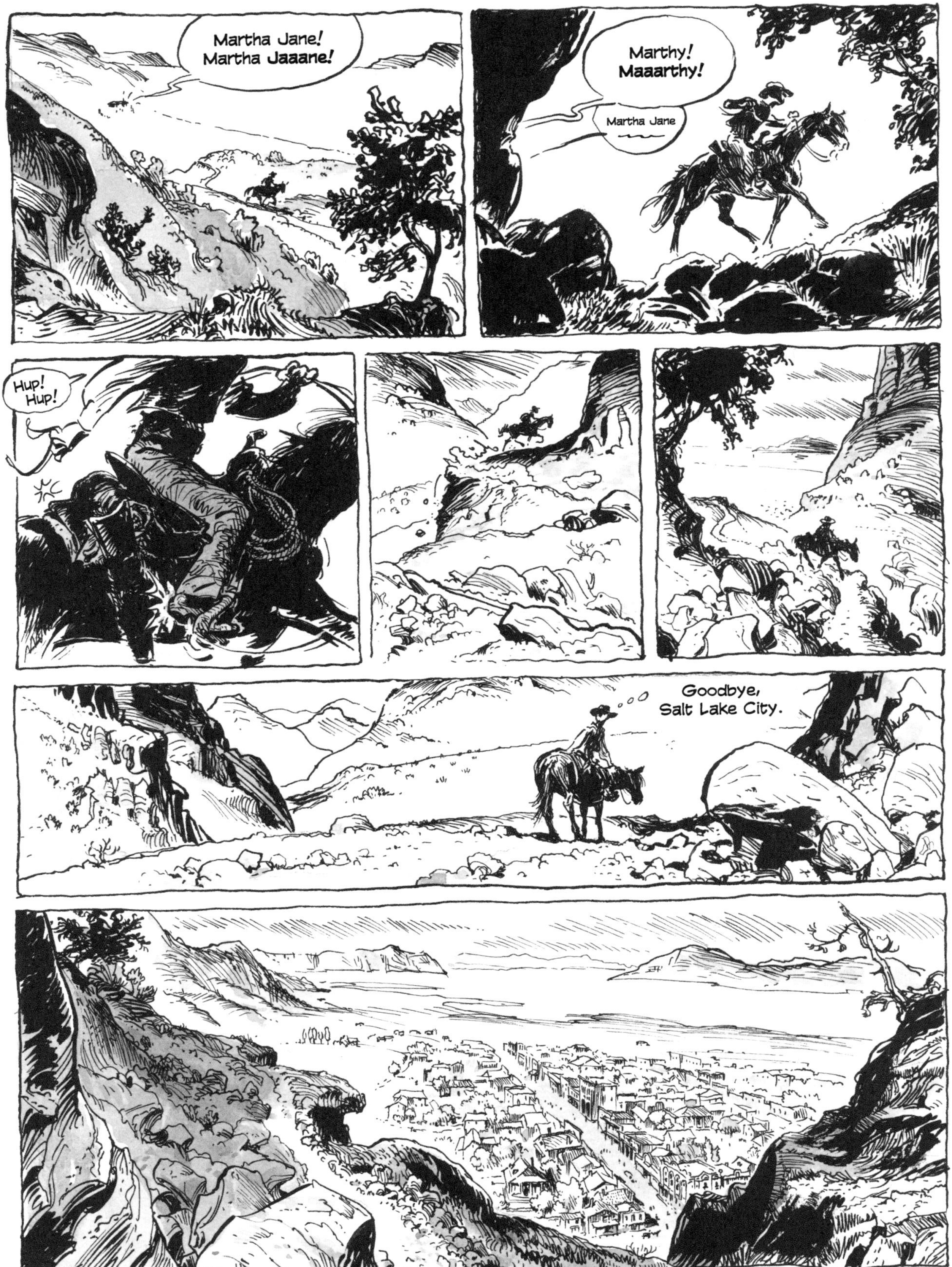
Martha Jane!
Martha Jaaane!
Marthy!
Maaarthy!
Martha Jane
Hup!
Hup!
Goodbye,
Salt Lake City.

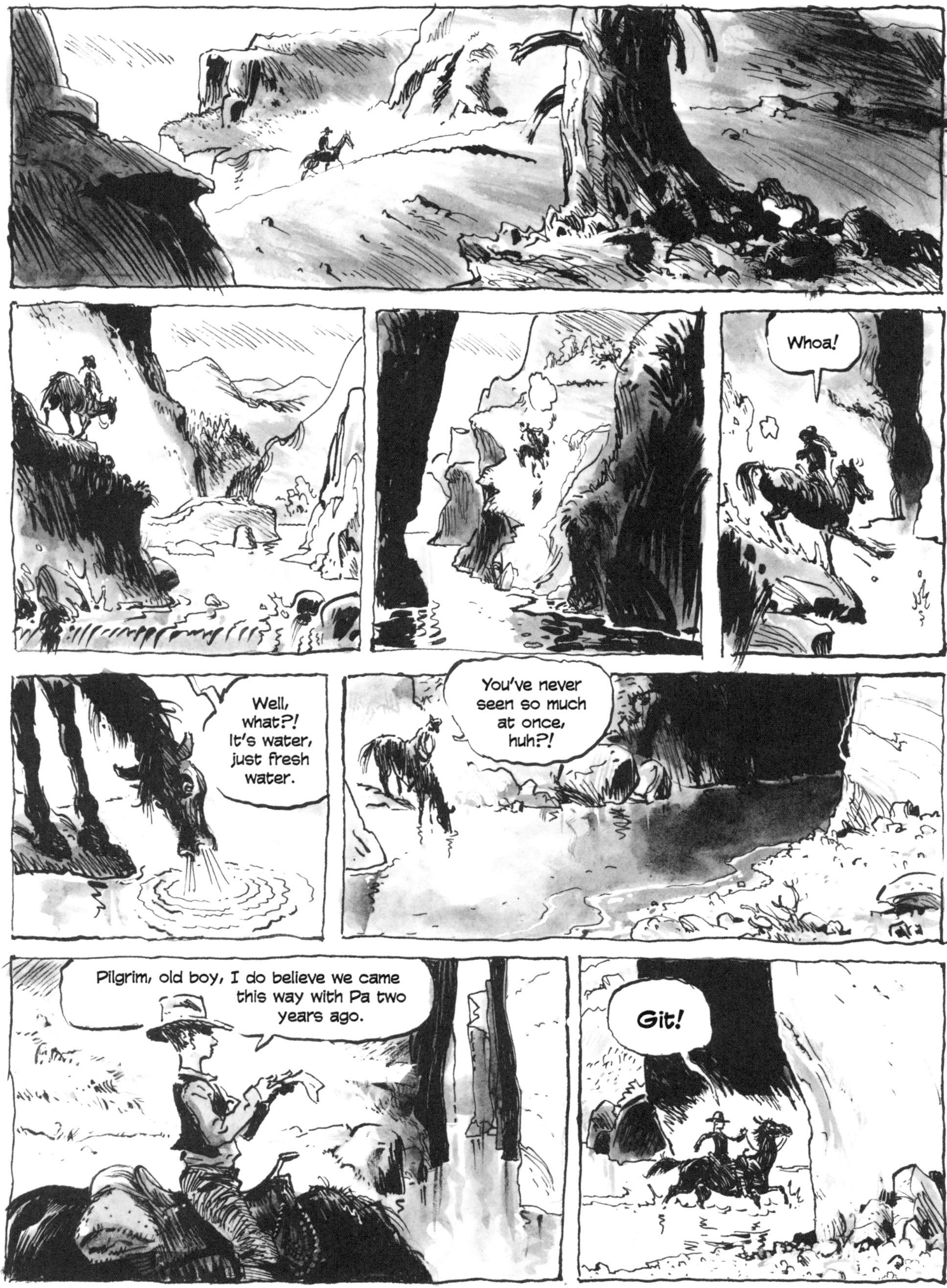
Whoa!
Well, what?! It's water, just fresh water.
You've never seen so much at once, huh?!
Pilgrim, old boy, I do believe we came this way with Pa two years ago.
Git!

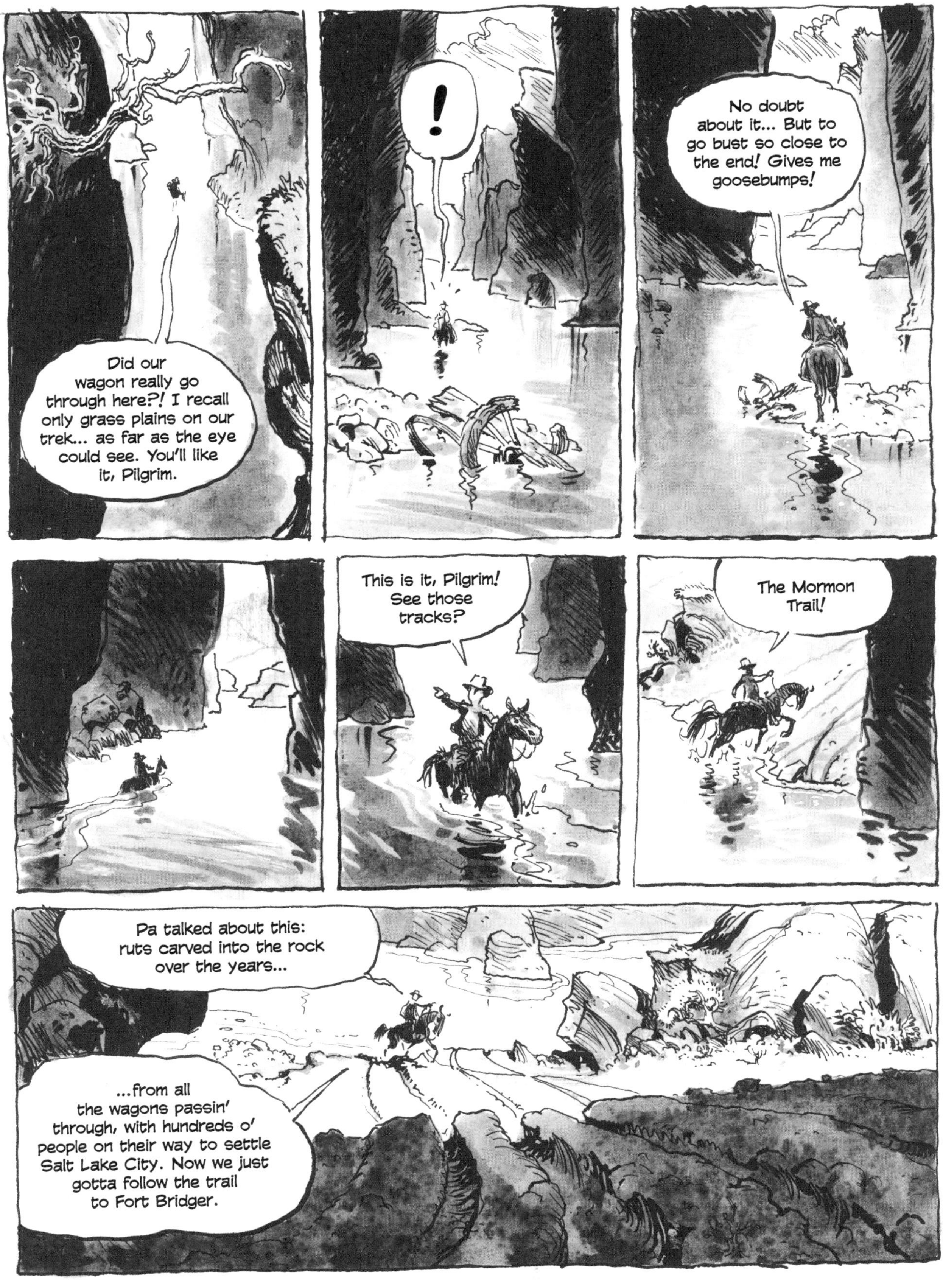
Did our wagon really go through here?! I recall only grass plains on our trek... as far as the eye could see. You'll like it, Pilgrim.
!
No doubt about it... But to go bust so close to the end! Gives me goosebumps!
This is it, Pilgrim! See those tracks?
The Mormon Trail!
Pa talked about this: ruts carved into the rock over the years...
...from all the wagons passin' through, with hundreds o' people on their way to settle Salt Lake City. Now we just gotta follow the trail to Fort Bridger.

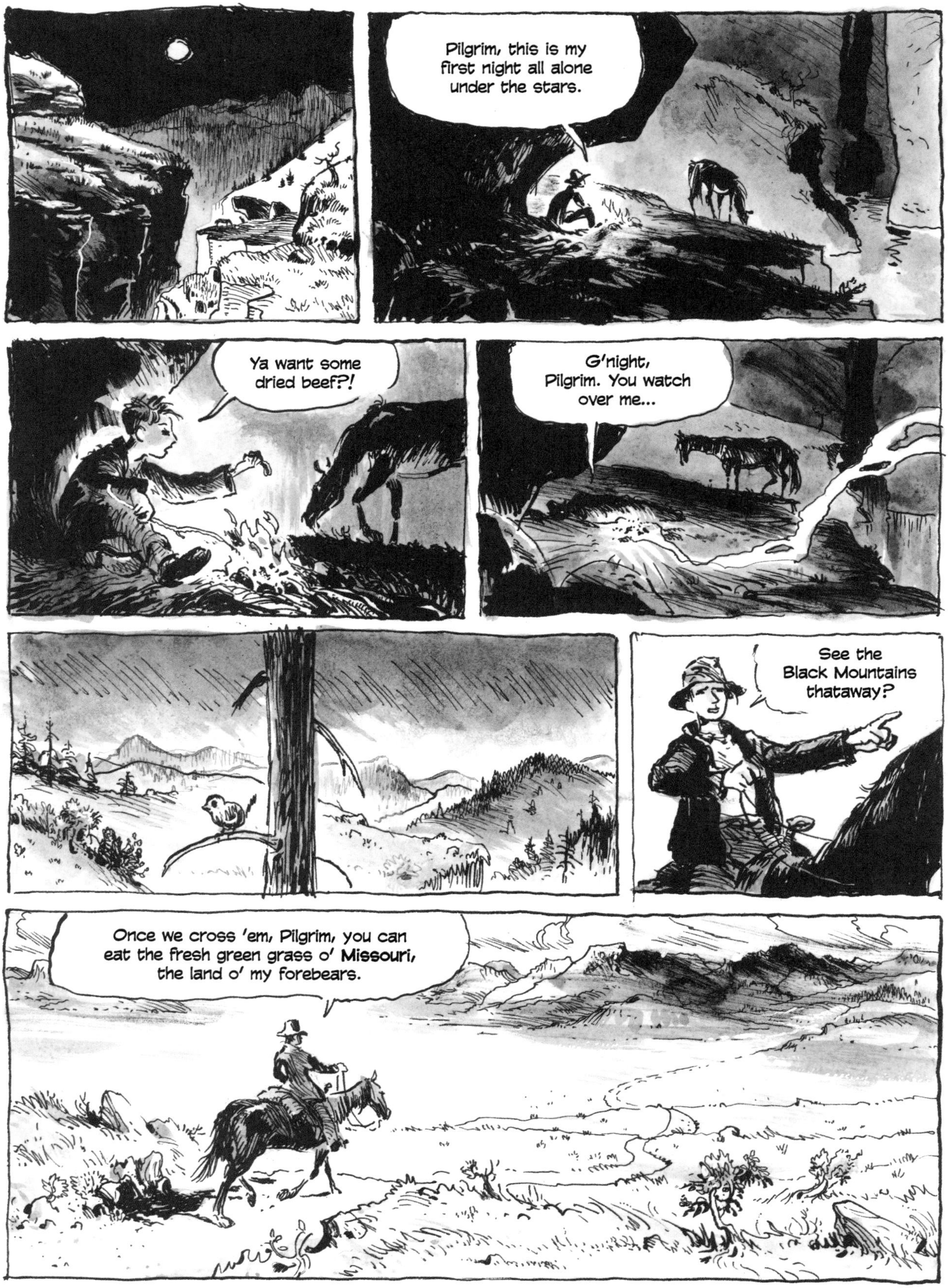
Pilgrim, this is my first night all alone under the stars.
Ya want some dried beef?!
G'night, Pilgrim. You watch over me...
See the Black Mountains thataway?
Once we cross 'em, Pilgrim, you can eat the fresh green grass o' **Missouri**, the land o' my forebears.

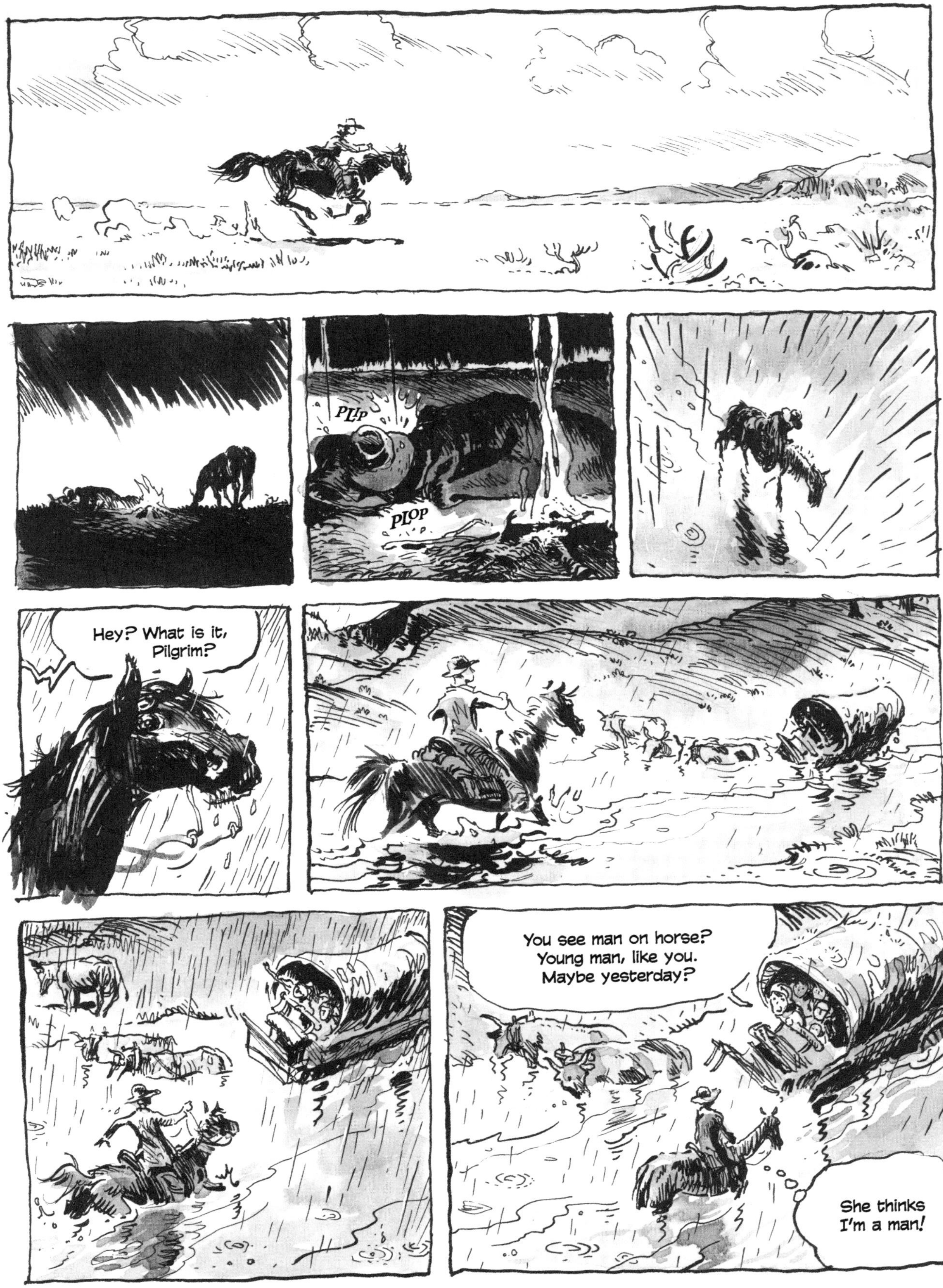
PLIP
PLOP
Hey? What is it, Pilgrim?
You see man on horse? Young man, like you. Maybe yesterday?
She thinks I'm a man!

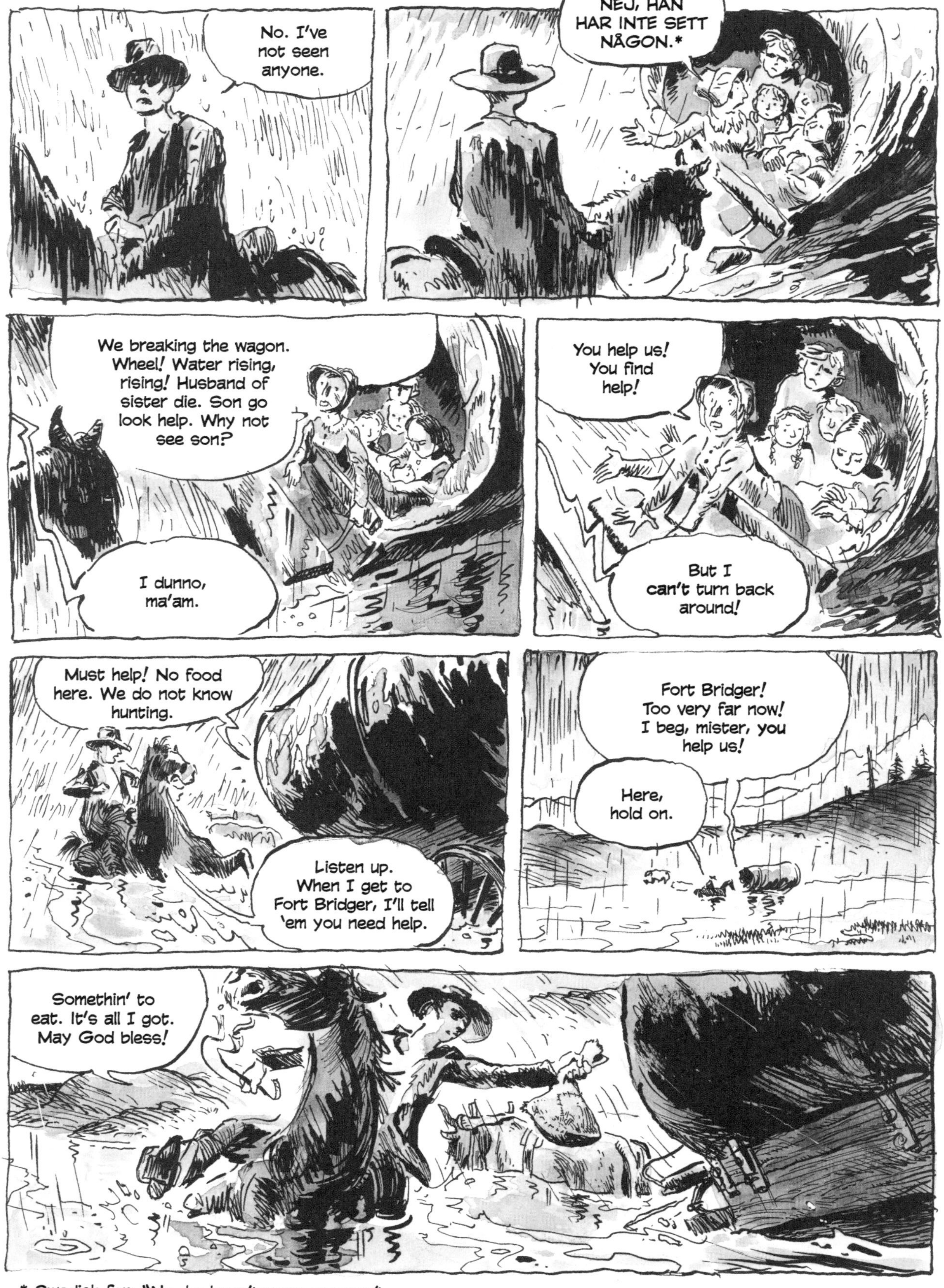
No. I've not seen anyone.
NEJ, HAN HAR INTE SETT NÅGON.*
We breaking the wagon. Wheel! Water rising, rising! Husband of sister die. Son go look help. Why not see son?
I dunno, ma'am.
You help us! You find help!
But I **can't** turn back around!
Must help! No food here. We do not know hunting.
Listen up. When I get to Fort Bridger, I'll tell 'em you need help.
Fort Bridger! Too very far now! I beg, mister, **you** help us!
Here, hold on.
Somethin' to eat. It's all I got. May God bless!

* Swedish for: "No, he hasn't seen anyone."

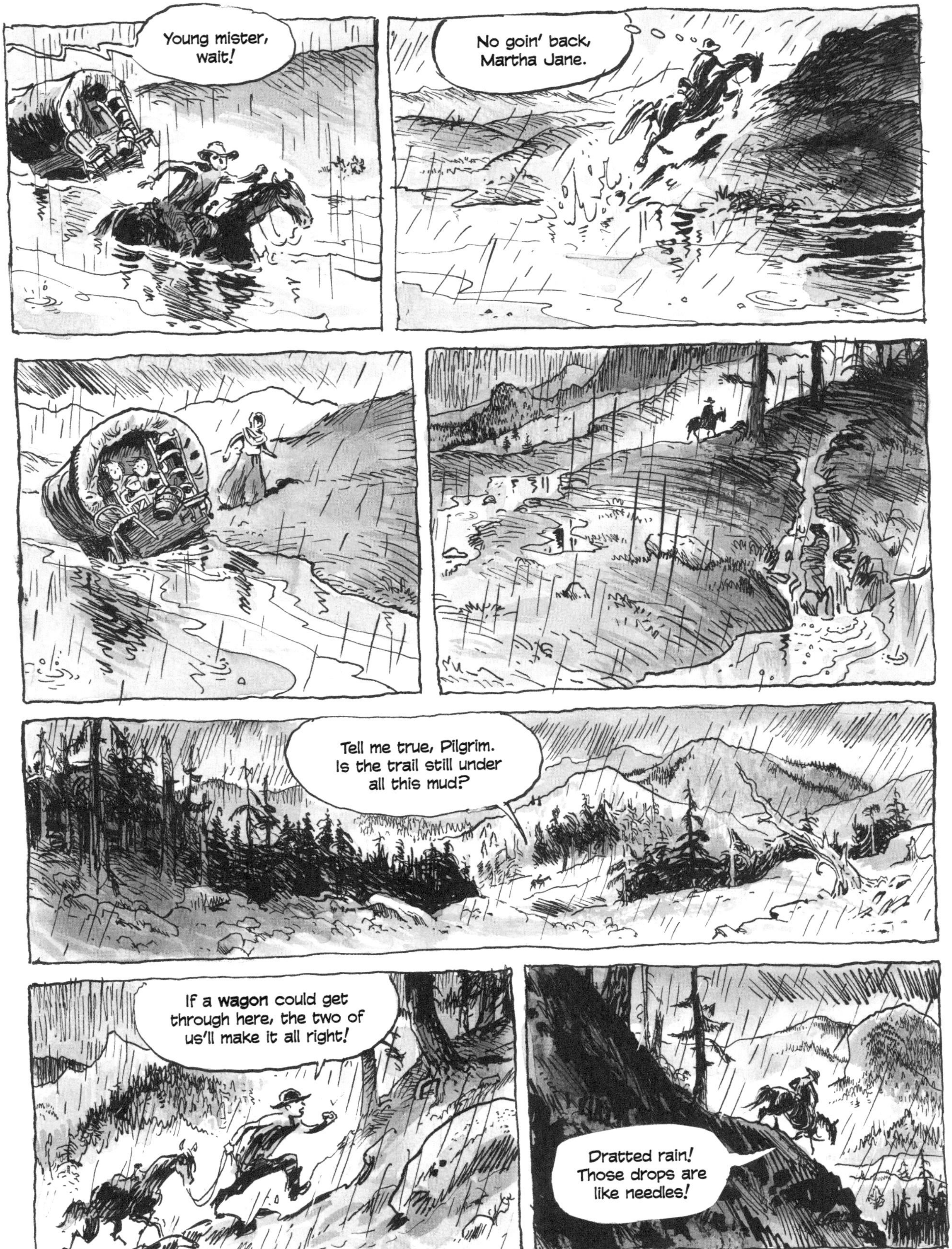
Young mister,
wait!
No goin' back,
Martha Jane.
Tell me true, Pilgrim.
Is the trail still under
all this mud?
If a wagon could get
through here, the two of
us'll make it all right!
Dratted rain!
Those drops are
like needles!

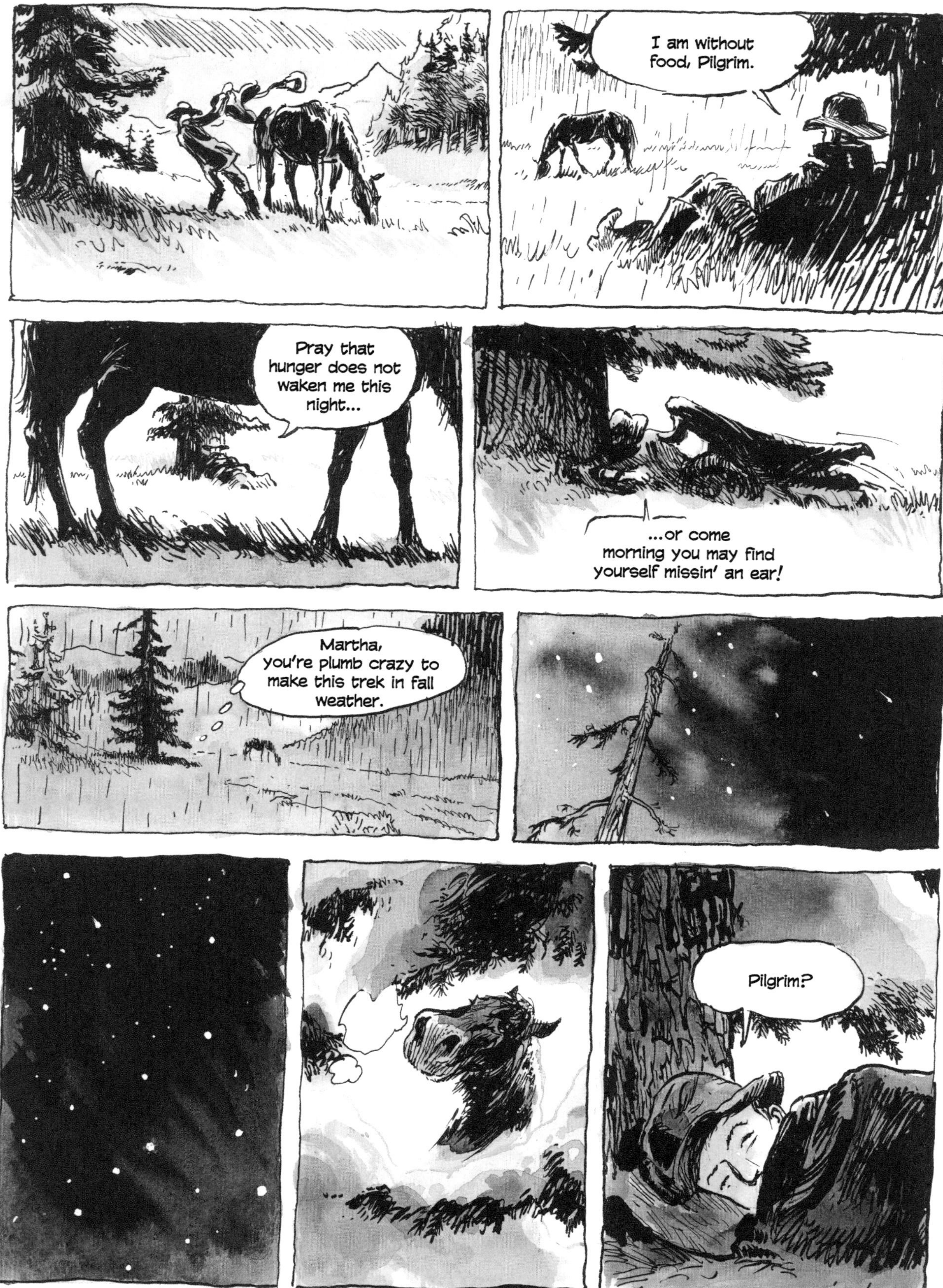
I am without food, Pilgrim.
Pray that hunger does not waken me this night...
...or come morning you may find yourself missin' an ear!
Martha, you're plumb crazy to make this trek in fall weather.
Pilgrim?

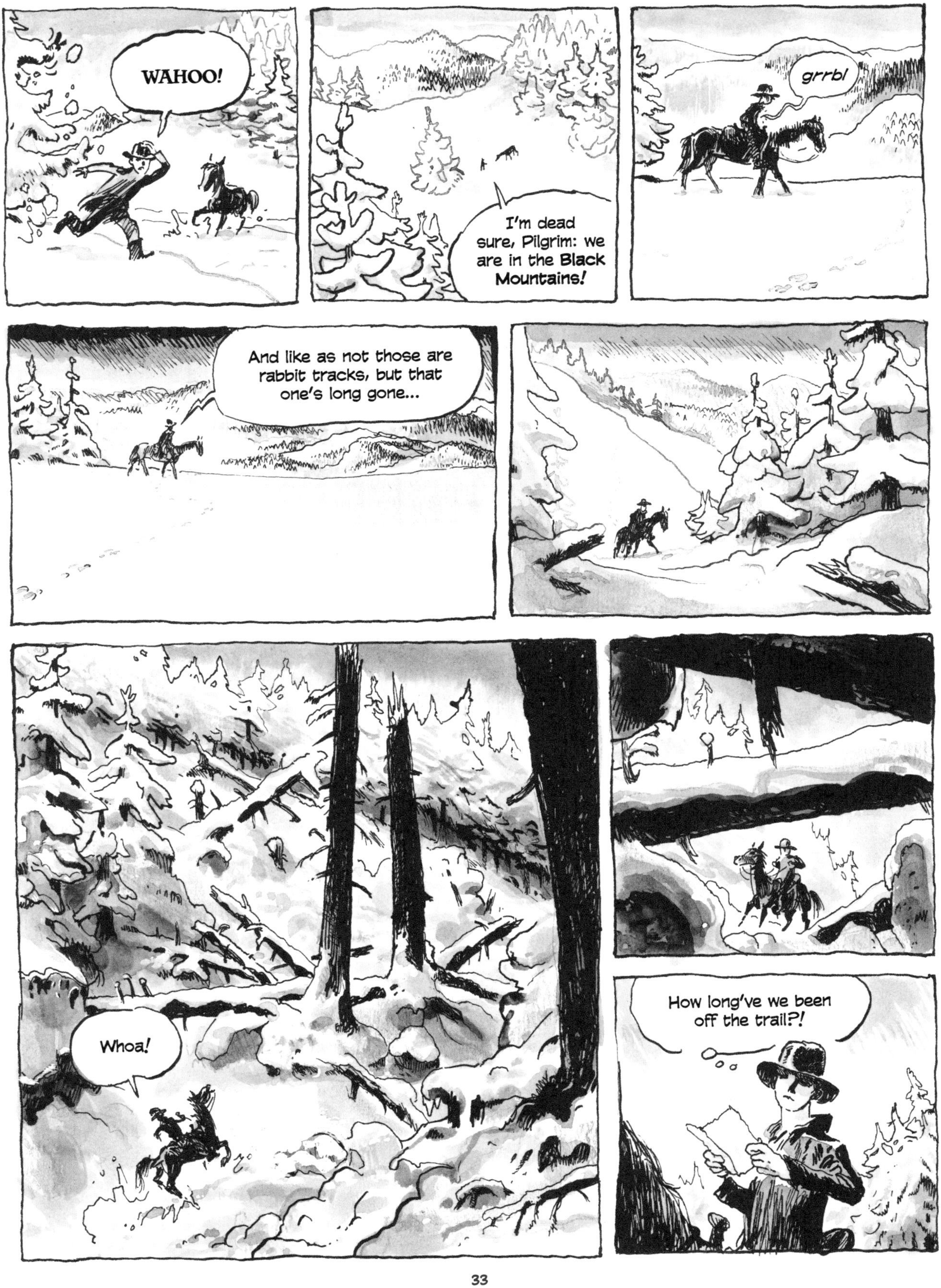
WAHOO!
I'm dead sure, Pilgrim: we are in the Black Mountains!
grrbl
And like as not those are rabbit tracks, but that one's long gone...
Whoa!
How long've we been off the trail?!

I don't know if Pa's map can help us anymore.

We oughtta be almost to Fort Bridger after the last three days. So we should be right around **here**...

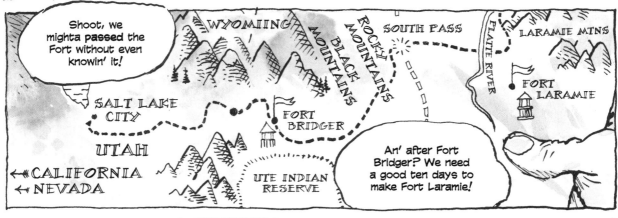

Shoot, we mighta **passed** the Fort without even knowin' it!

WYOMIING

BLACK MOUNTAINS

ROCKY MOUNTAINS

SOUTH PASS

PLATTE RIVER

LARAMIE MTNS

FORT LARAMIE

SALT LAKE CITY

FORT BRIDGER

UTAH

←CALIFORNIA

← NEVADA

UTE INDIAN RESERVE

An' after Fort Bridger? We need a good ten days to make Fort Laramie!

But we'll be **prepared** this time, Pilgrim. Promise. I'll even try to ride with a wagon train...

But for now, we **haveta** find the trail again... Which means we need some luck!

Ho!

That's it... we are truly lost!

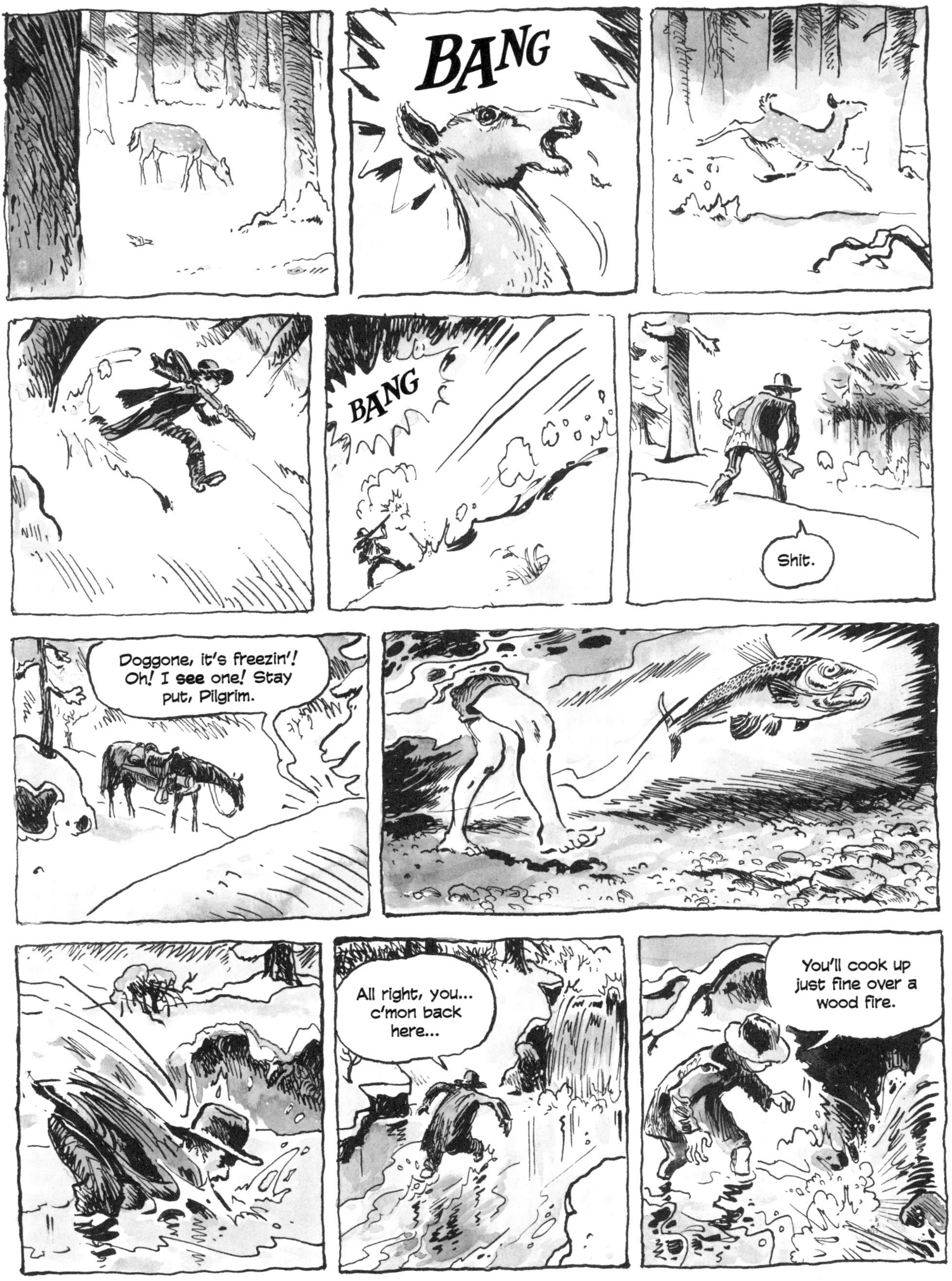
BANG
BANG
Shit.
Doggone, it's freezin'! Oh! I see one! Stay put, Pilgrim.
All right, you... c'mon back here...
You'll cook up just fine over a wood fire.

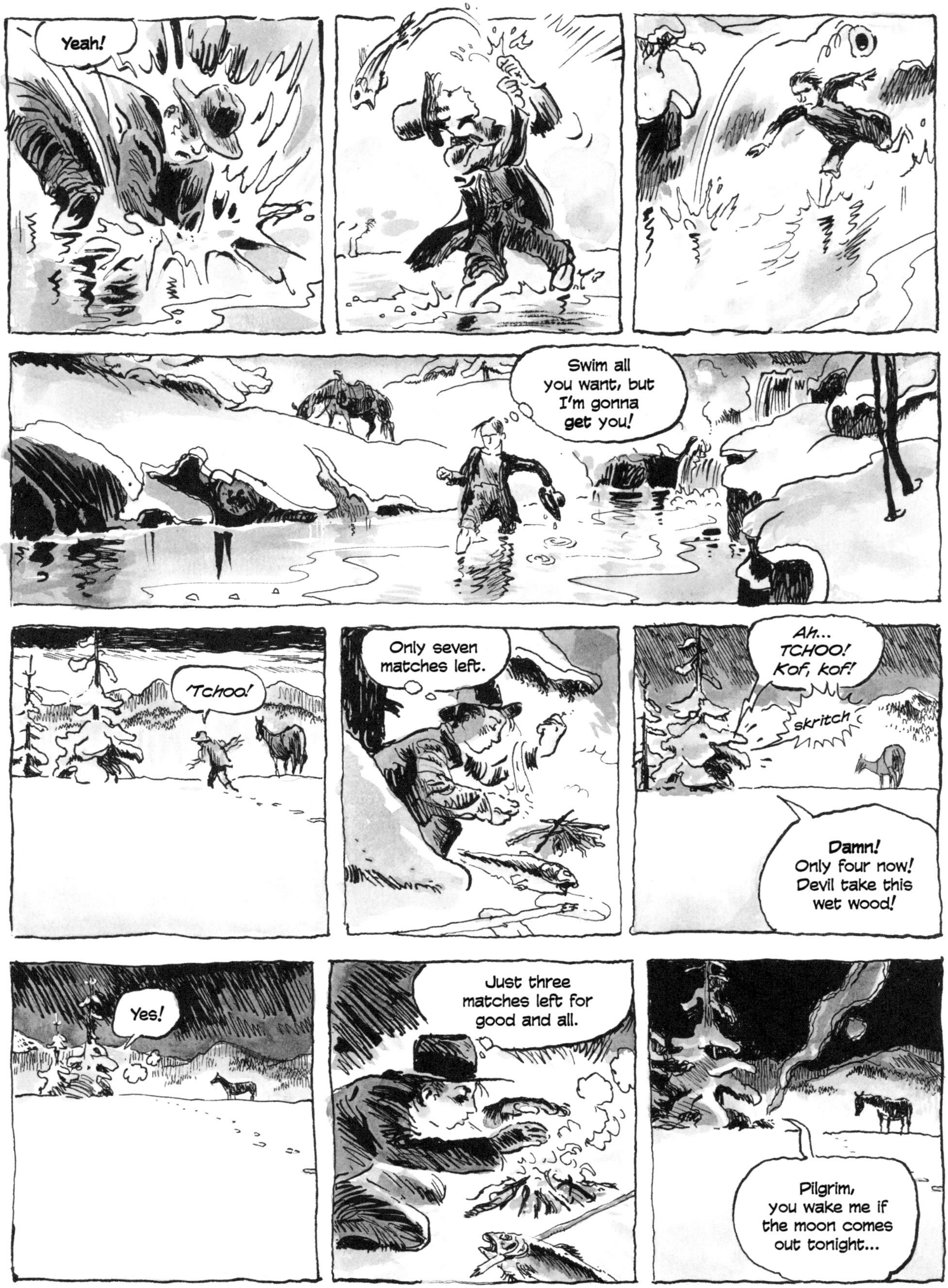
Yeah!
Swim all you want, but I'm gonna get you!
'Tchoo!
Only seven matches left.
Ah... TCHOO! Kof, kof!
skritch
Damn! Only four now! Devil take this wet wood!
Yes!
Just three matches left for good and all.
Pilgrim, you wake me if the moon comes out tonight...

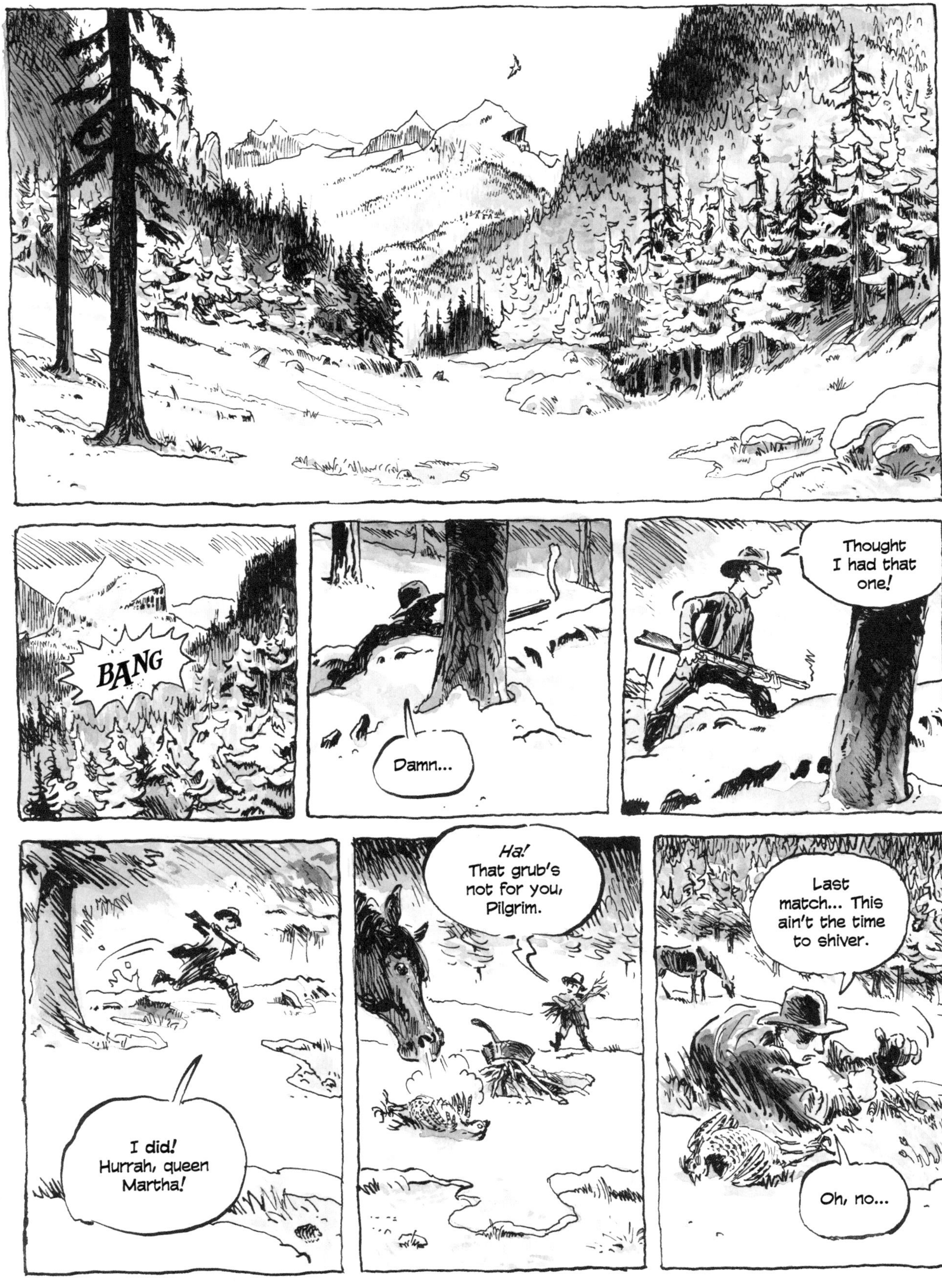
BANG
Damn...
Thought I had that one!
I did! Hurrah, queen Martha!
Ha! That grub's not for you, Pilgrim.
Last match... This ain't the time to shiver.
Oh, no...

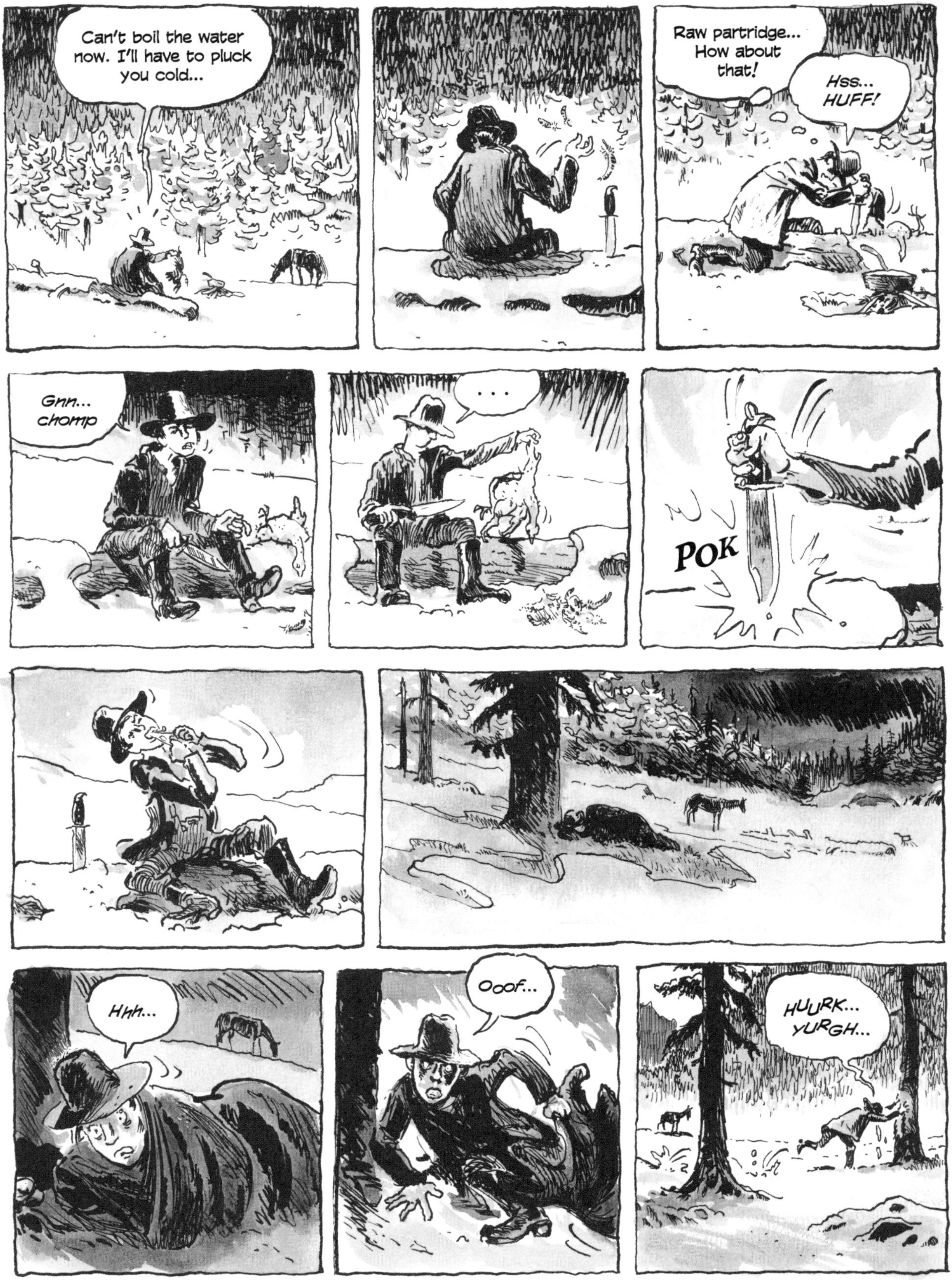
Can't boil the water now. I'll have to pluck you cold...
Raw partridge... How about that!
Hss... HUFF!
Gnn... chomp
. . .
POK
Hhh...
Ooof...
HUURK... YURGH...

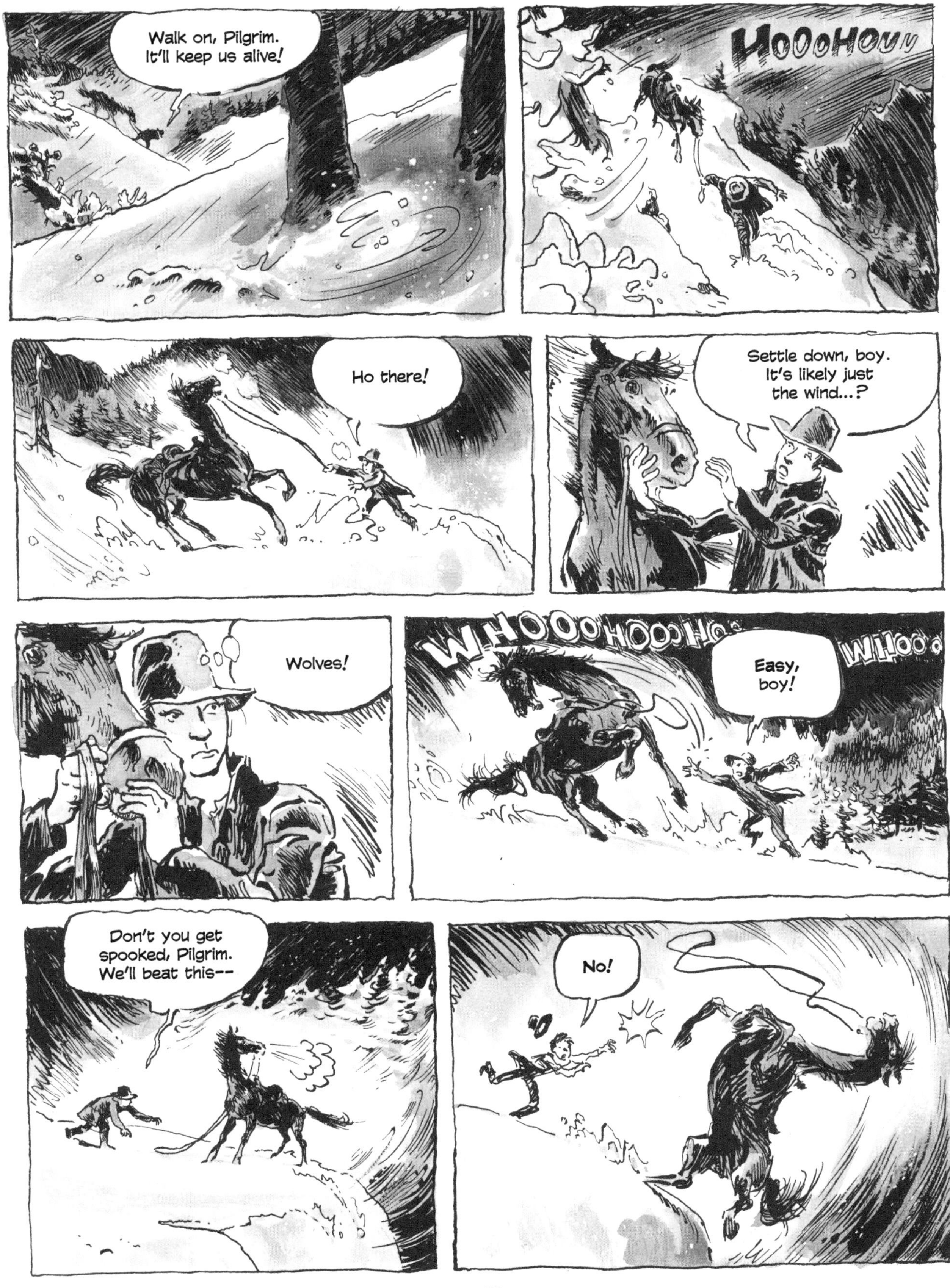
Walk on, Pilgrim. It'll keep us alive!
HOOOHOU
Ho there!
Settle down, boy. It's likely just the wind...?
Wolves!
Easy, boy!
Don't you get spooked, Pilgrim. We'll beat this--
No!

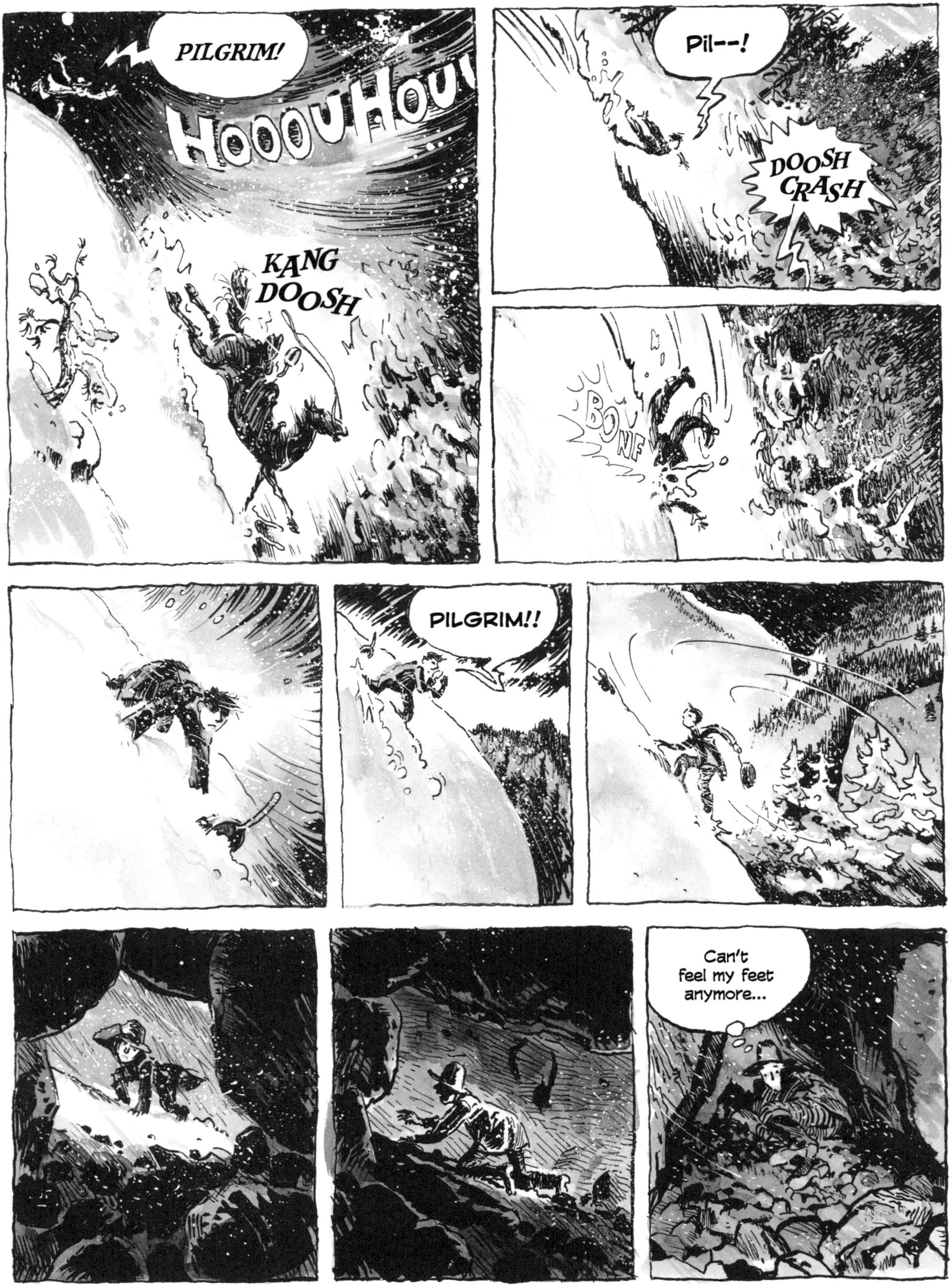
PILGRIM!
HOOOUHOU
KANG DOOSH
Pil--!
DOOSH CRASH
BONF
PILGRIM!!
Can't feel my feet anymore...

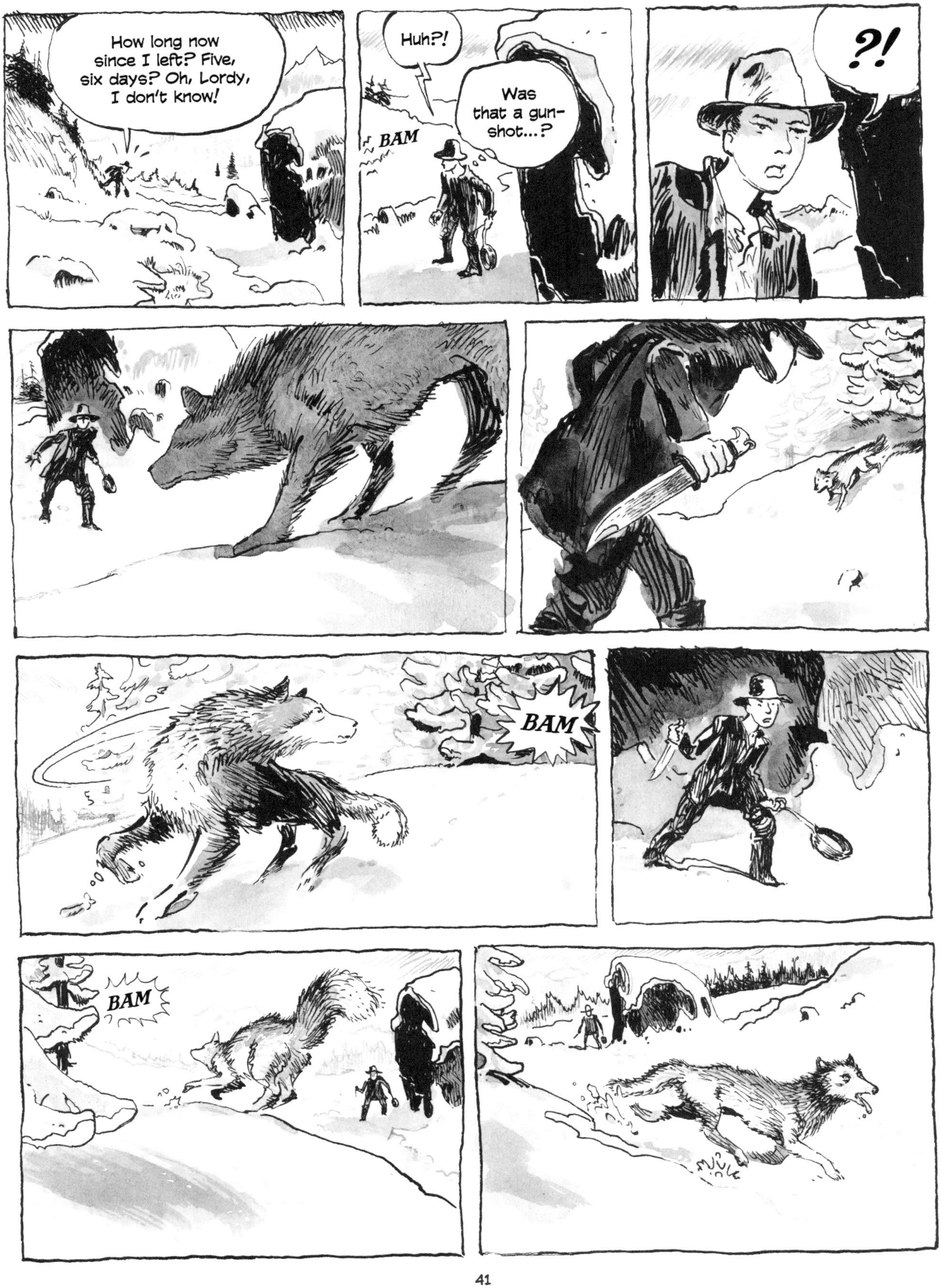
How long now since I left? Five, six days? Oh, Lordy, I don't know!
Huh?!
BAM
Was that a gun-shot...?
?!
BAM
BAM

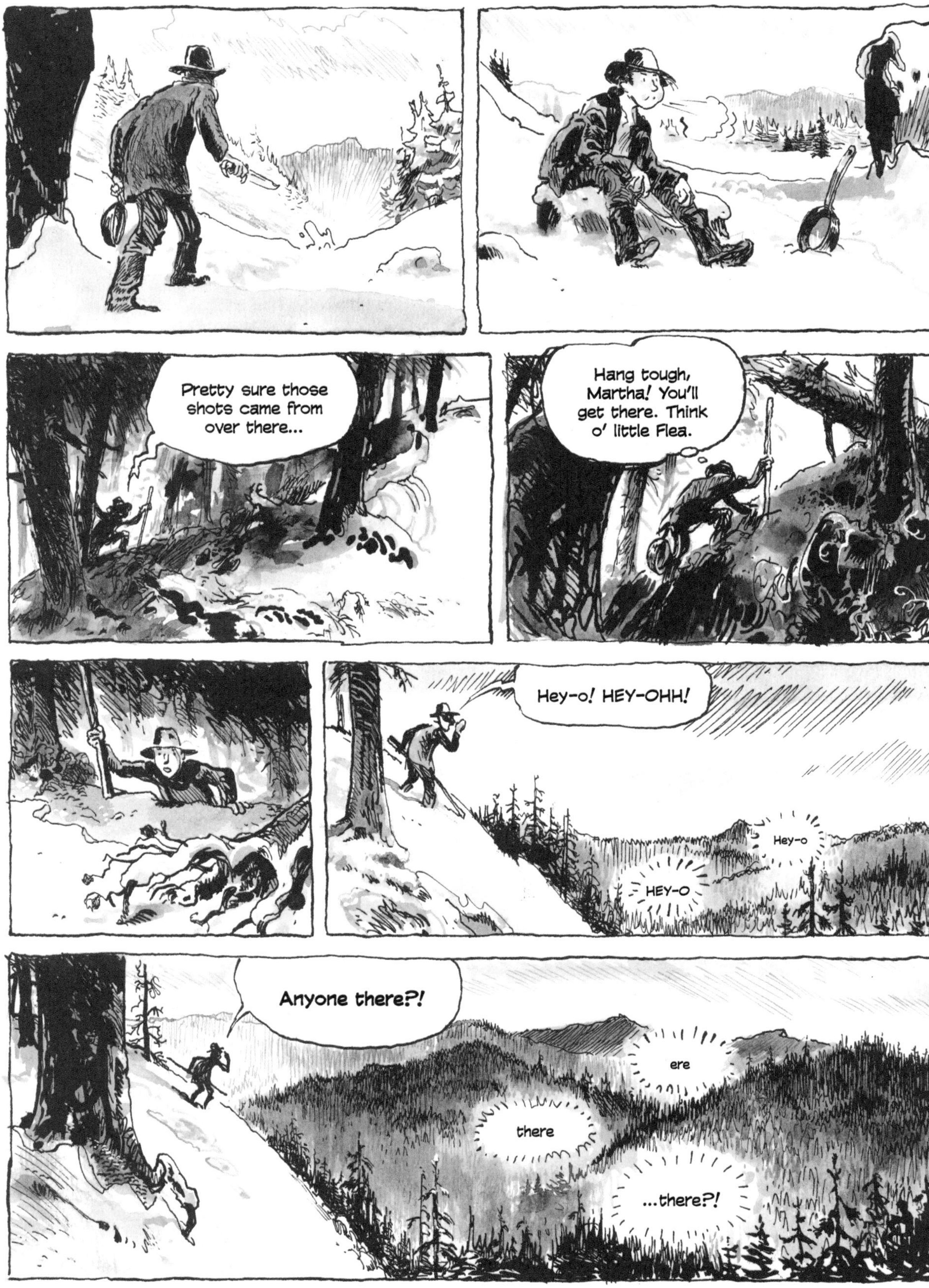
Pretty sure those shots came from over there...
Hang tough, Martha! You'll get there. Think o' little Flea.
Hey-o! HEY-OHH!
Hey-o
HEY-O
Anyone there?!
ere
there
...there?!

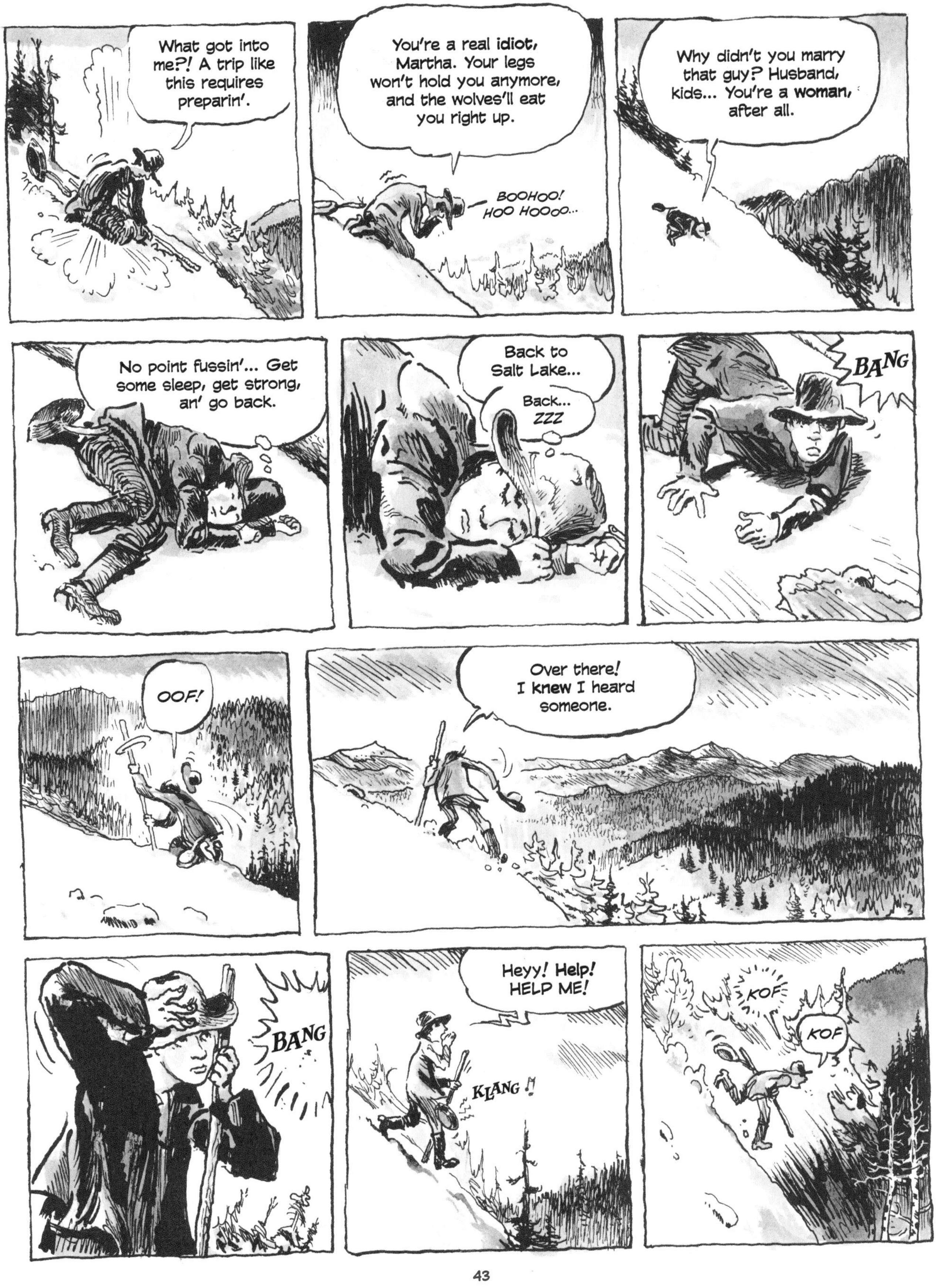
What got into me?! A trip like this requires preparin'.
You're a real idiot, Martha. Your legs won't hold you anymore, and the wolves'll eat you right up.
BOOHOO! HOO HOOOO...
Why didn't you marry that guy? Husband, kids... You're a woman, after all.
No point fussin'... Get some sleep, get strong, an' go back.
Back to Salt Lake...
Back... ZZZ
BANG
OOF!
Over there! I knew I heard someone.
BANG
Heyy! Help! HELP ME!
KLANG
KOF
KOF

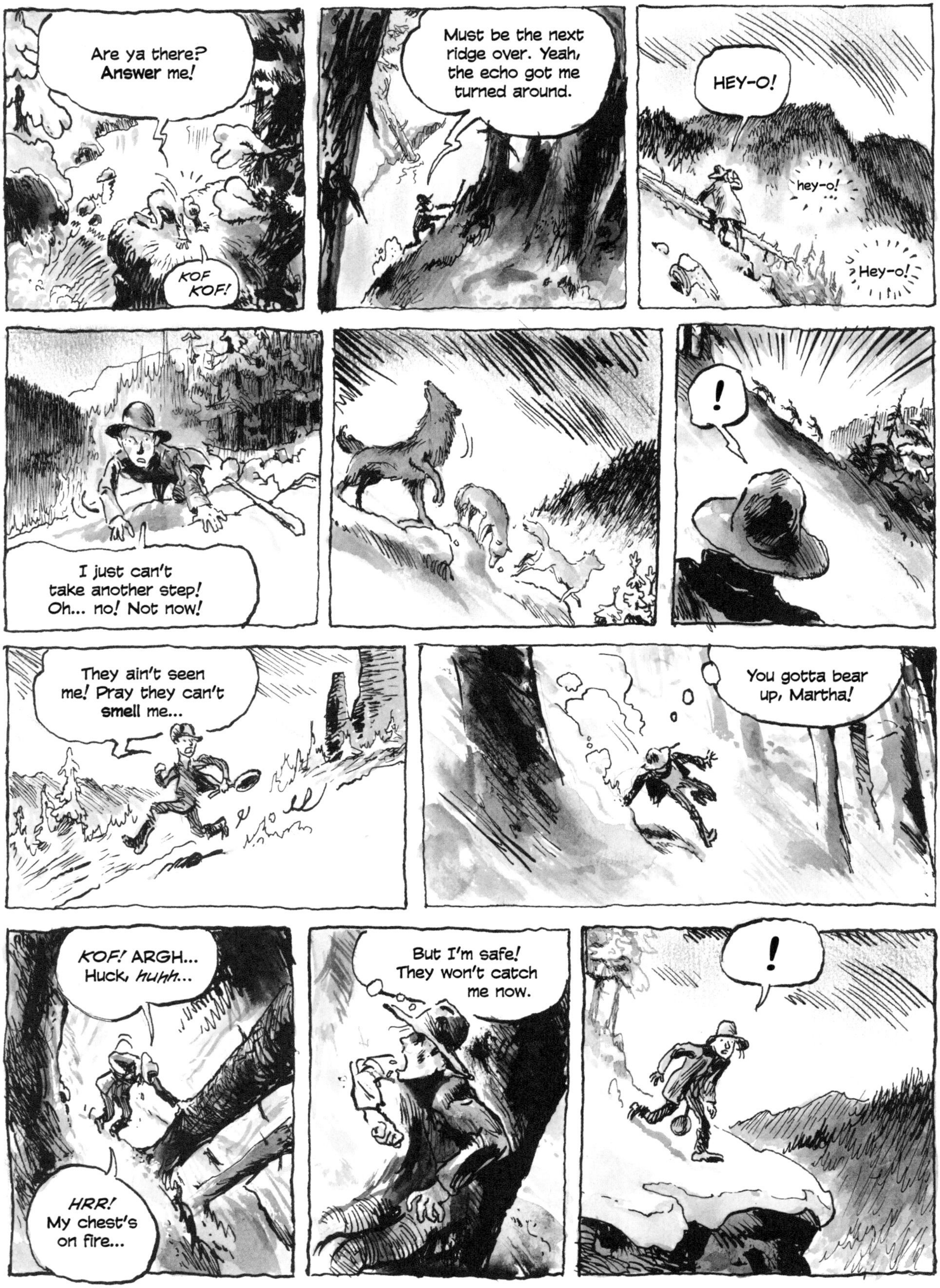

Are ya there? Answer me!
KOF KOF!
Must be the next ridge over. Yeah, the echo got me turned around.
HEY-O!
hey-o!
Hey-o!
I just can't take another step! Oh... no! Not now!
!
They ain't seen me! Pray they can't smell me...
You gotta bear up, Martha!
KOF! ARGH... Huck, huhh...
HRR! My chest's on fire...
But I'm safe! They won't catch me now.
!

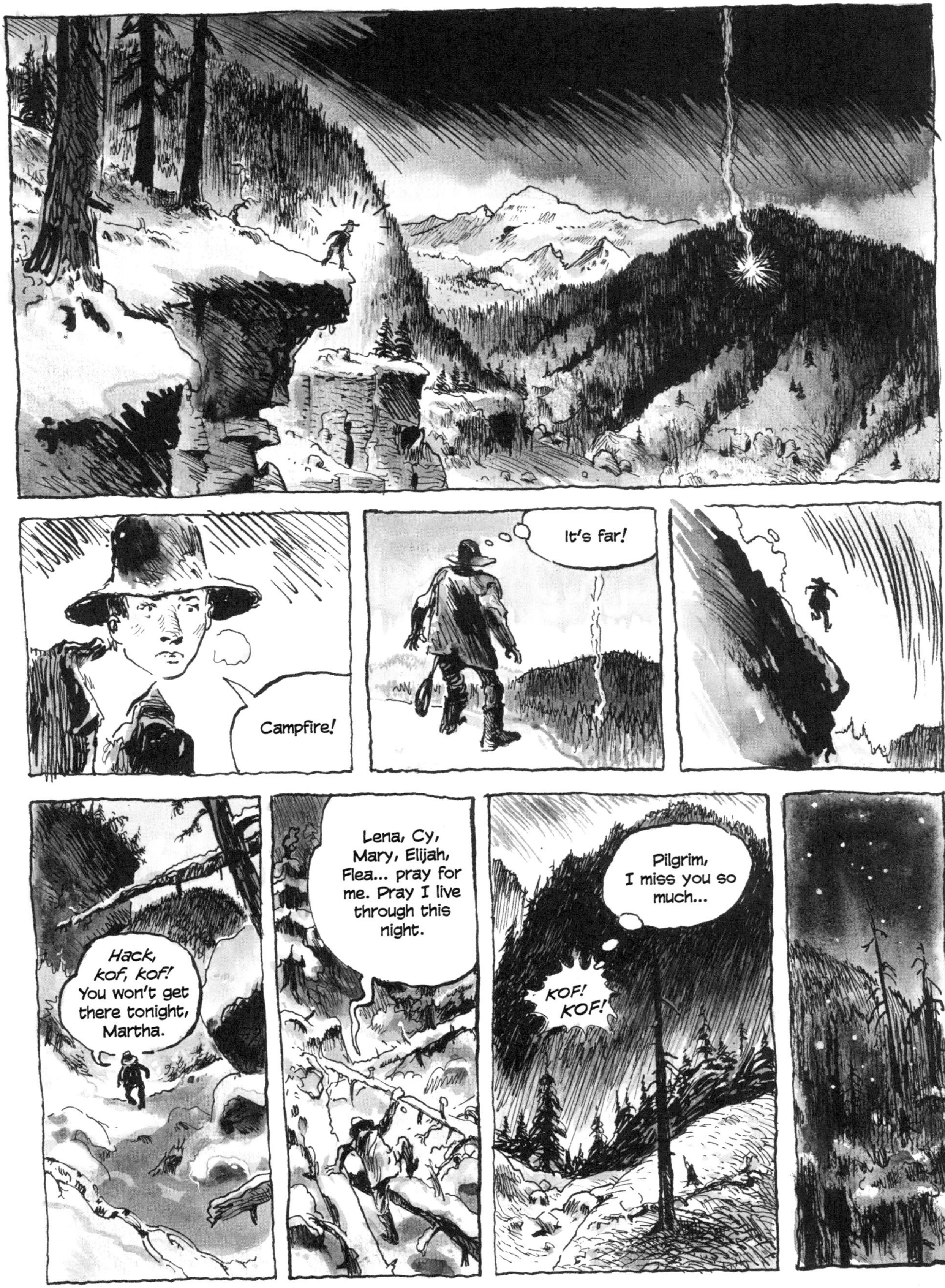
Campfire!
It's far!
Hack, kof, kof! You won't get there tonight, Martha.
Lena, Cy, Mary, Elijah, Flea... pray for me. Pray I live through this night.
Pilgrim, I miss you so much...
KOF! KOF!

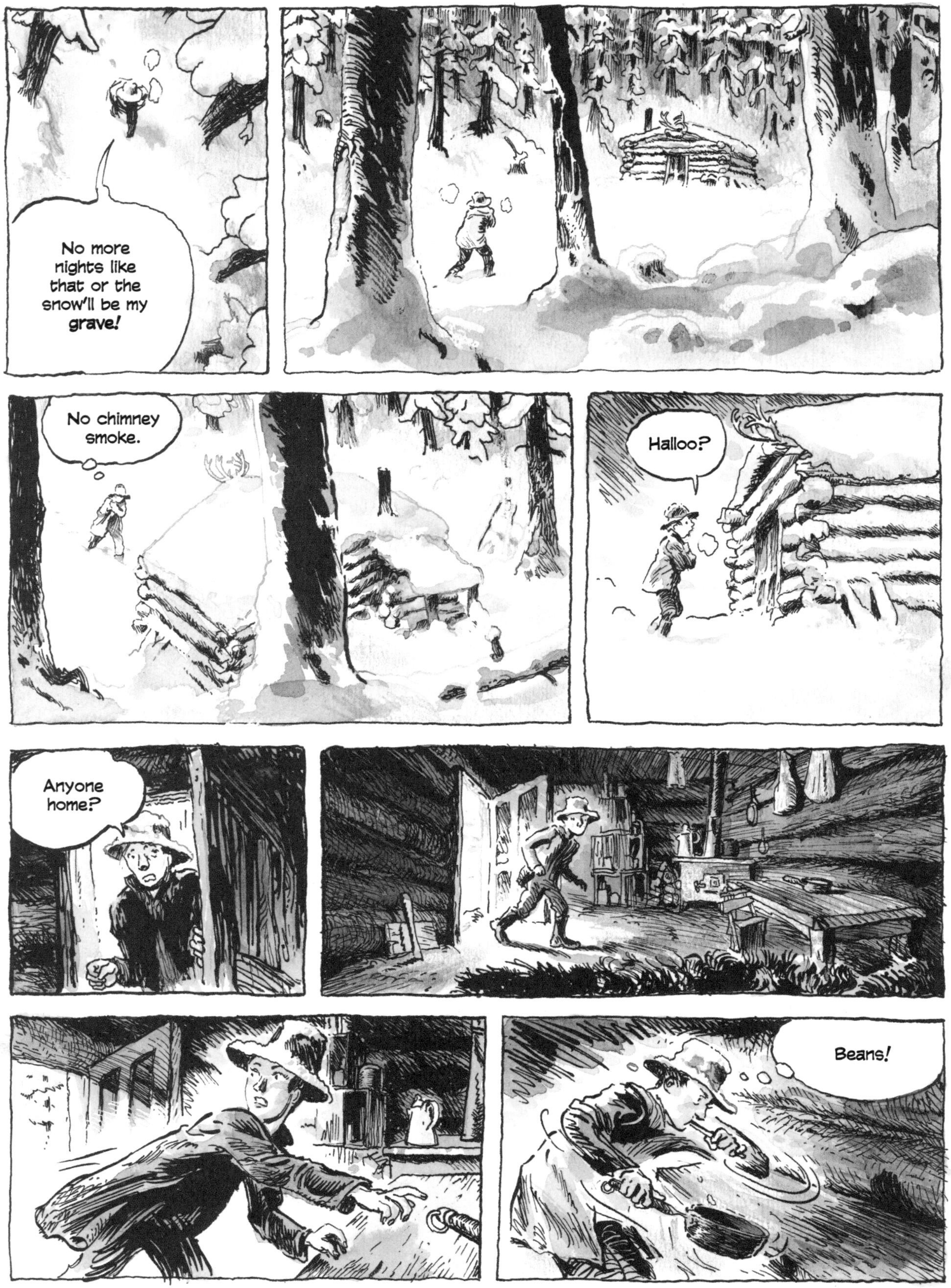
No more nights like that or the snow'll be my **grave!**
No chimney smoke.
Halloo?
Anyone home?
Beans!

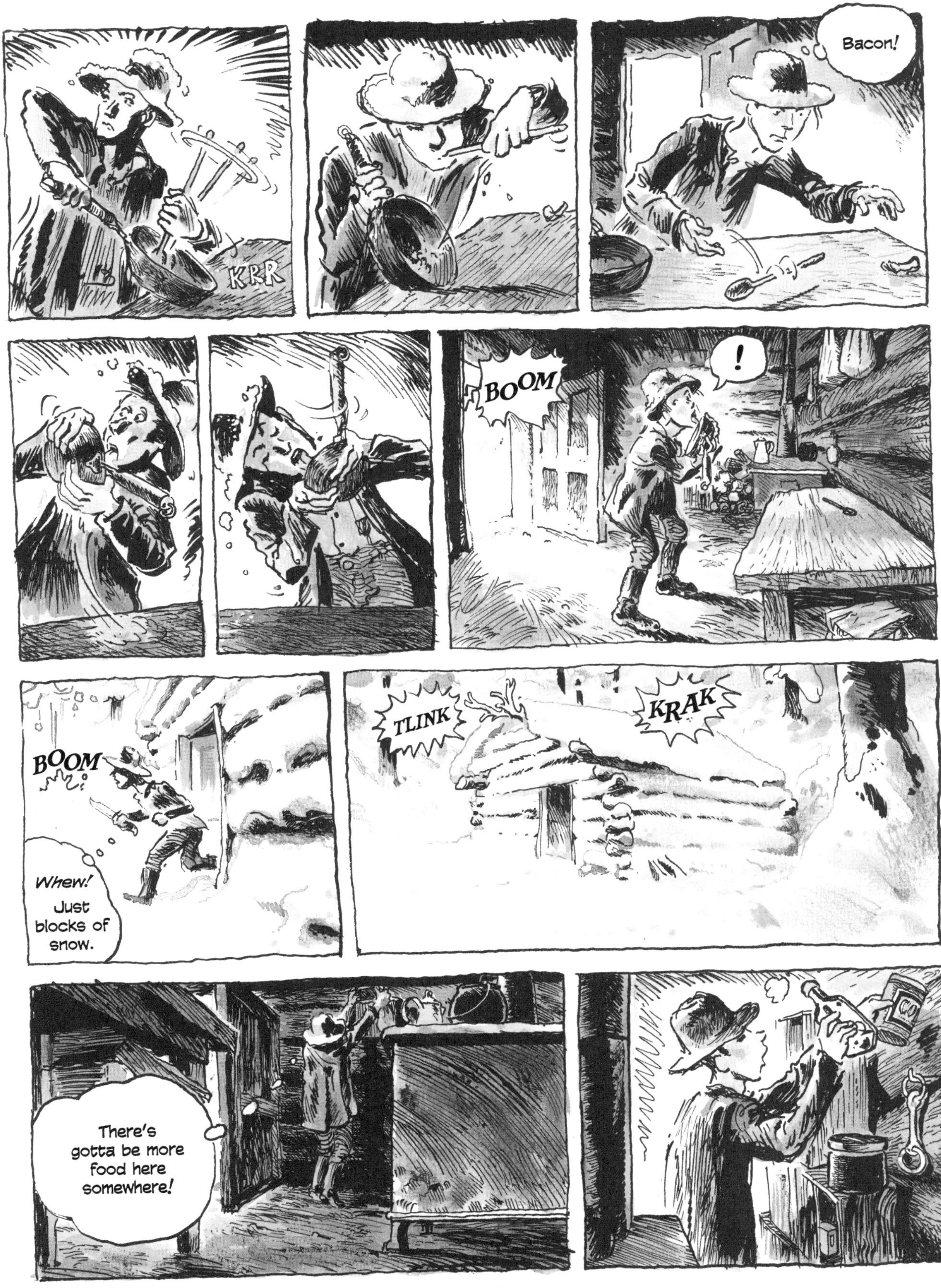
KRR
Bacon!
BOOM
!
BOOM
Whew! Just blocks of snow.
TLINK
KRAK
There's gotta be more food here somewhere!

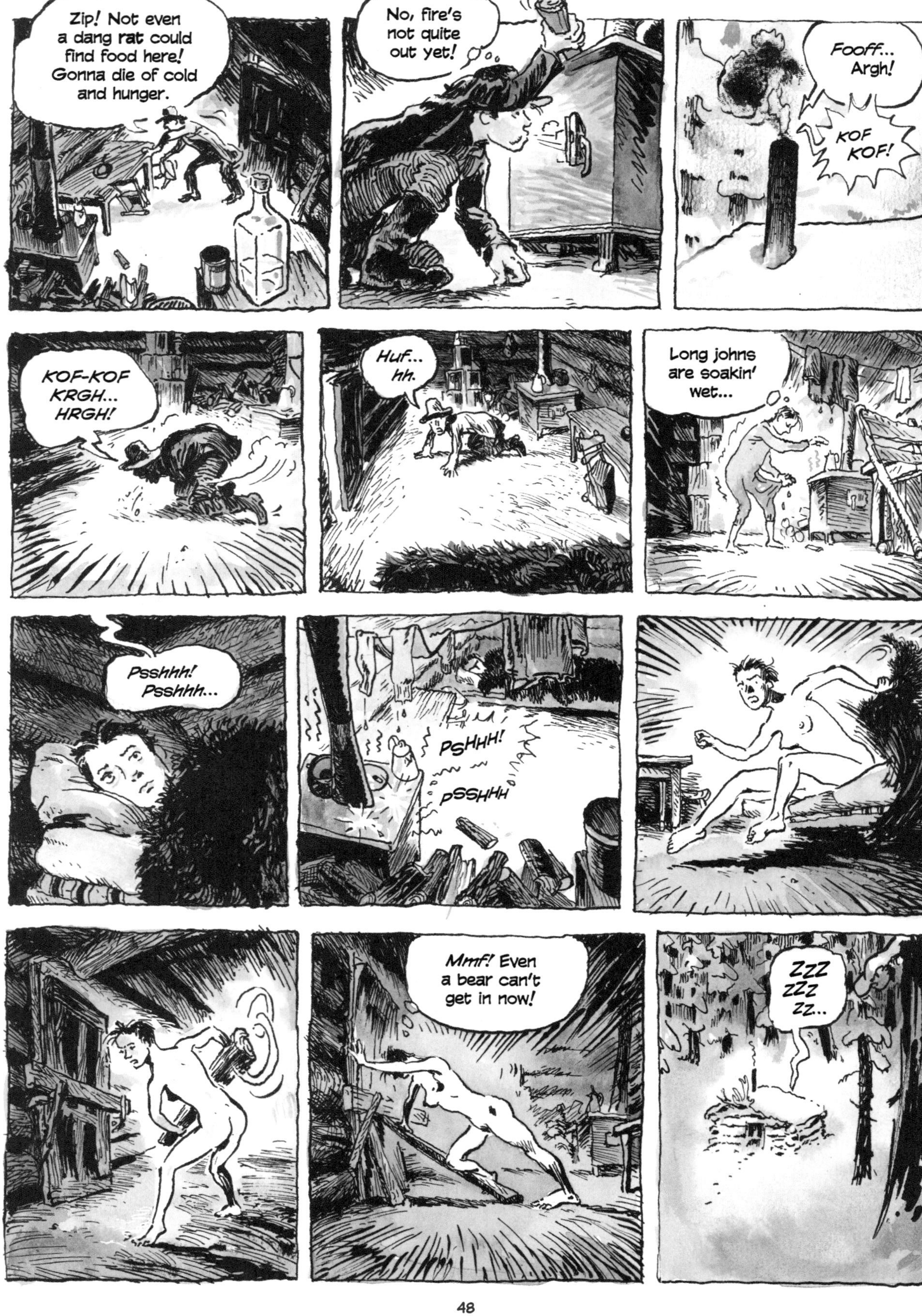

Zip! Not even a dang rat could find food here! Gonna die of cold and hunger.
No, fire's not quite out yet!
Fooff... Argh!
KOF KOF!
KOF-KOF KRGH... HRGH!
Huf... hh.
Long johns are soakin' wet...
Psshhh! Psshhh...
PSHHH!
PSSHHH
Mmf! Even a bear can't get in now!
ZZZ ZZZ ZZ...

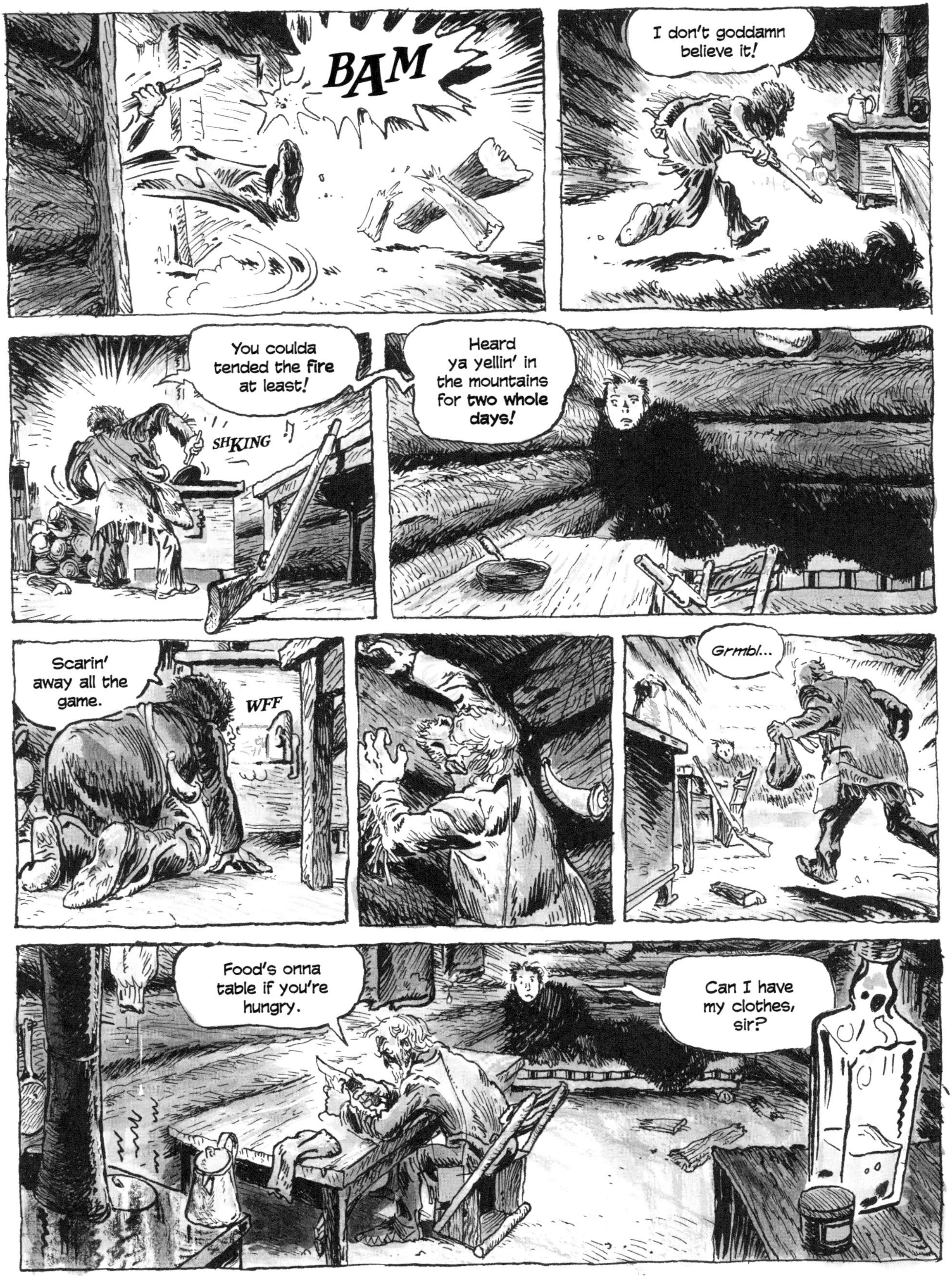
BAM
I don't goddamn believe it!
You coulda tended the fire at least!
SHKING
Heard ya yellin' in the mountains for two whole days!
Scarin' away all the game.
WFF
Grmbl...
Food's onna table if you're hungry.
Can I have my clothes, sir?

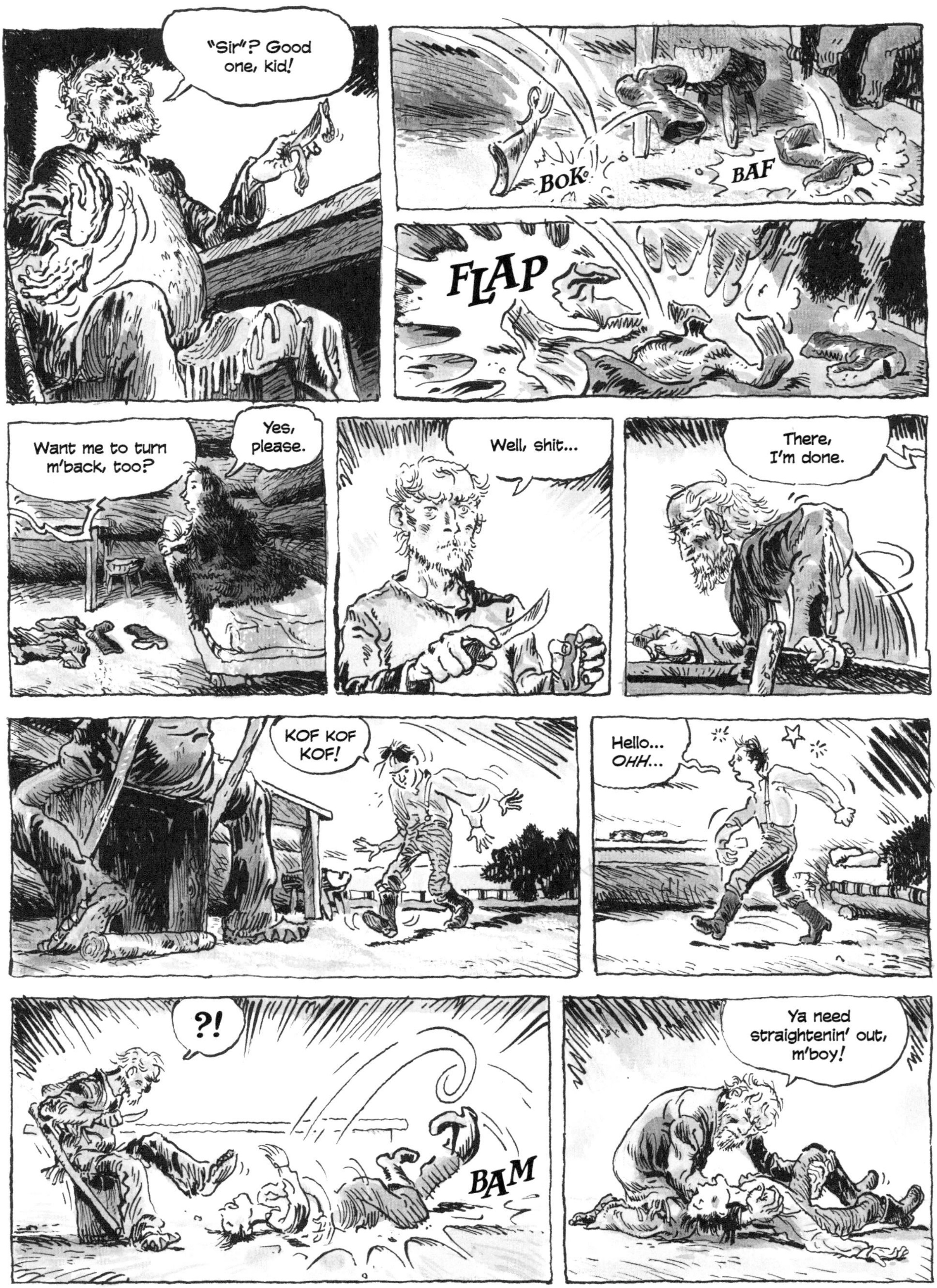

"Sir"? Good one, kid!
BOK
BAF
FLAP
Want me to turn m'back, too?
Yes, please.
Well, shit...
There, I'm done.
KOF KOF KOF!
Hello... OHH...
?!
BAM
Ya need straightenin' out, m'boy!

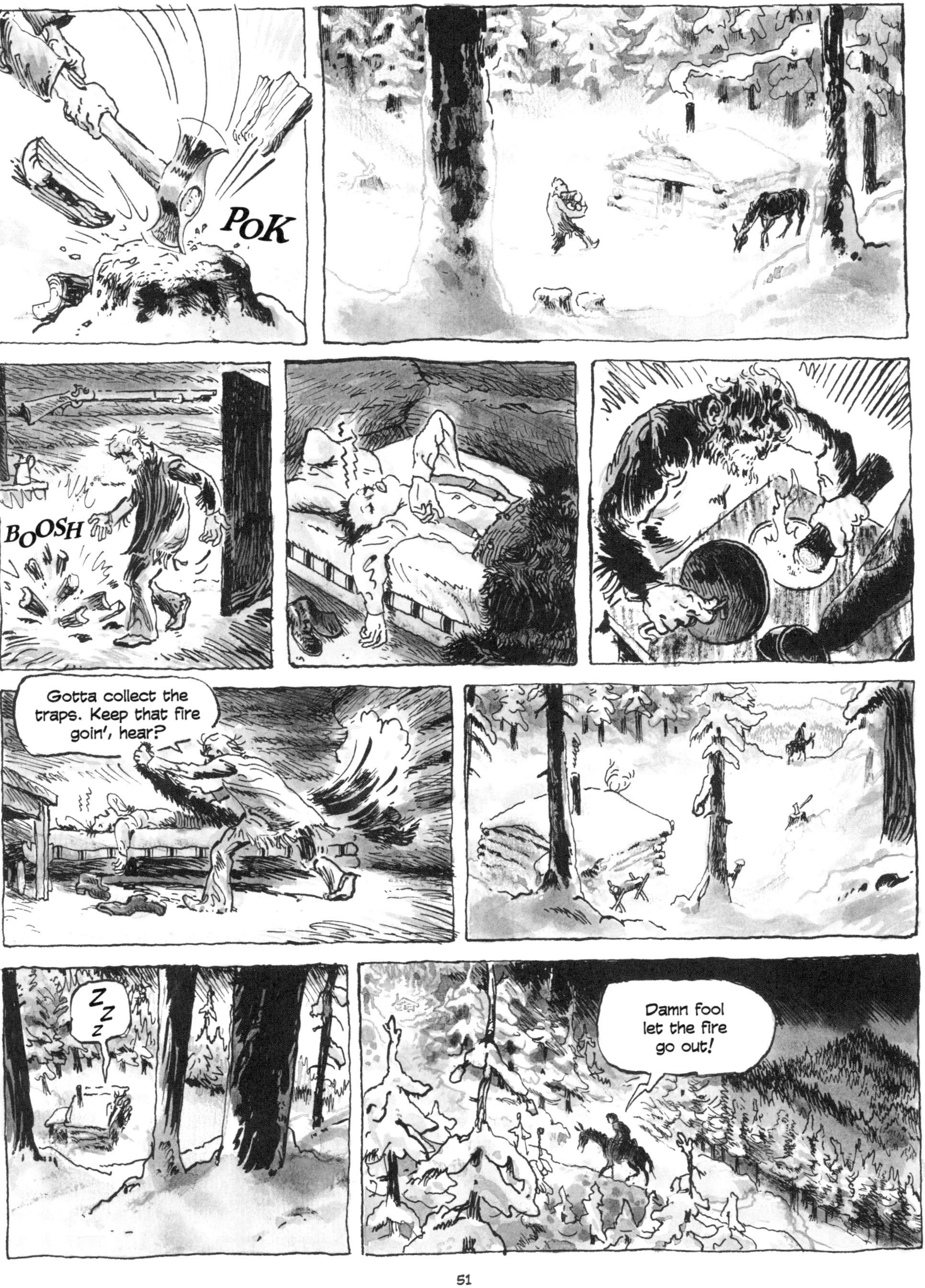
POK
BOOSH
Gotta collect the traps. Keep that fire goin', hear?
ZZZ
Damn fool let the fire go out!

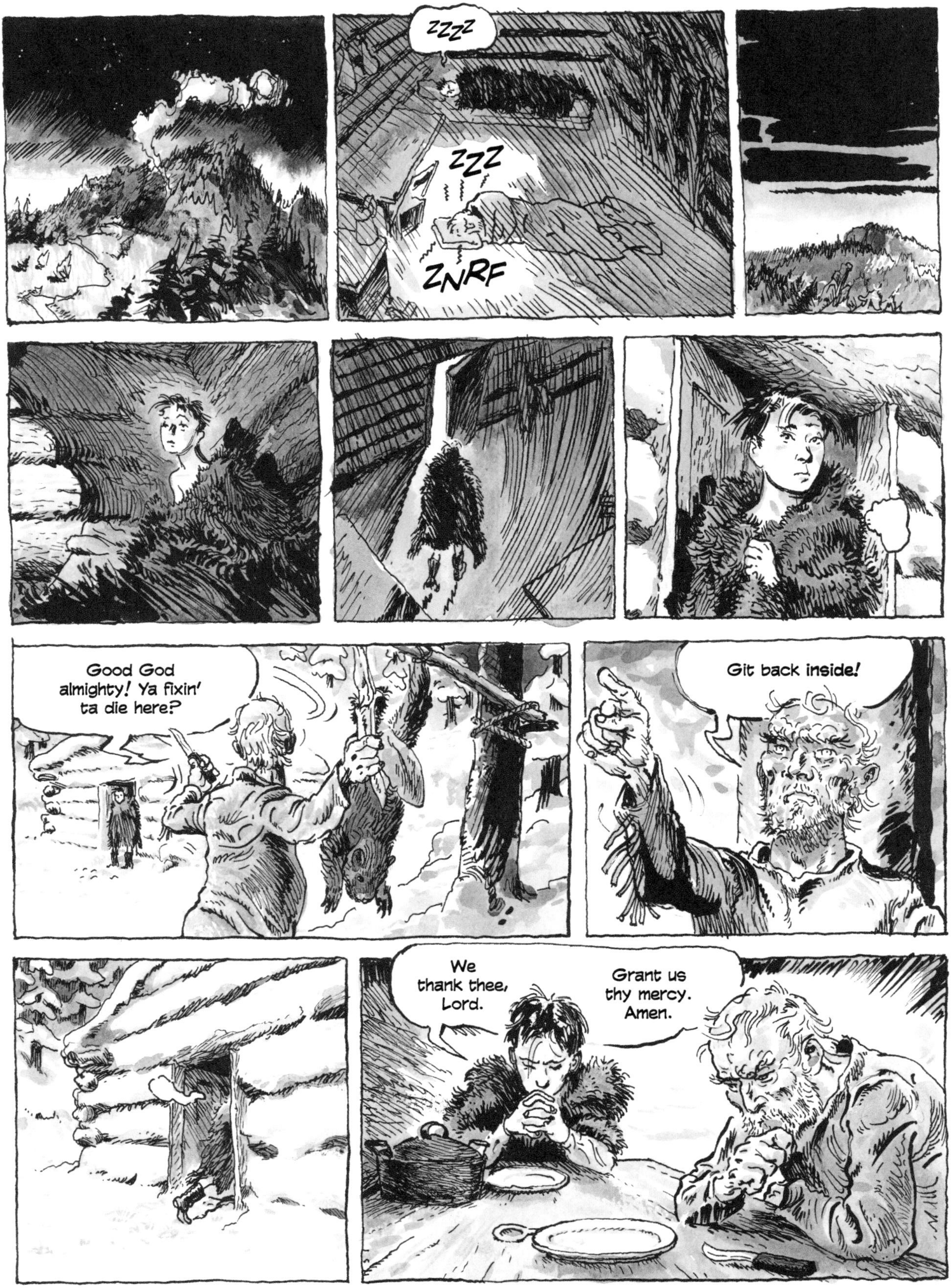
ZZZZ
ZZZ
ZNRF
Good God almighty! Ya fixin' ta die here?
Git back inside!
We thank thee, Lord.
Grant us thy mercy. Amen.

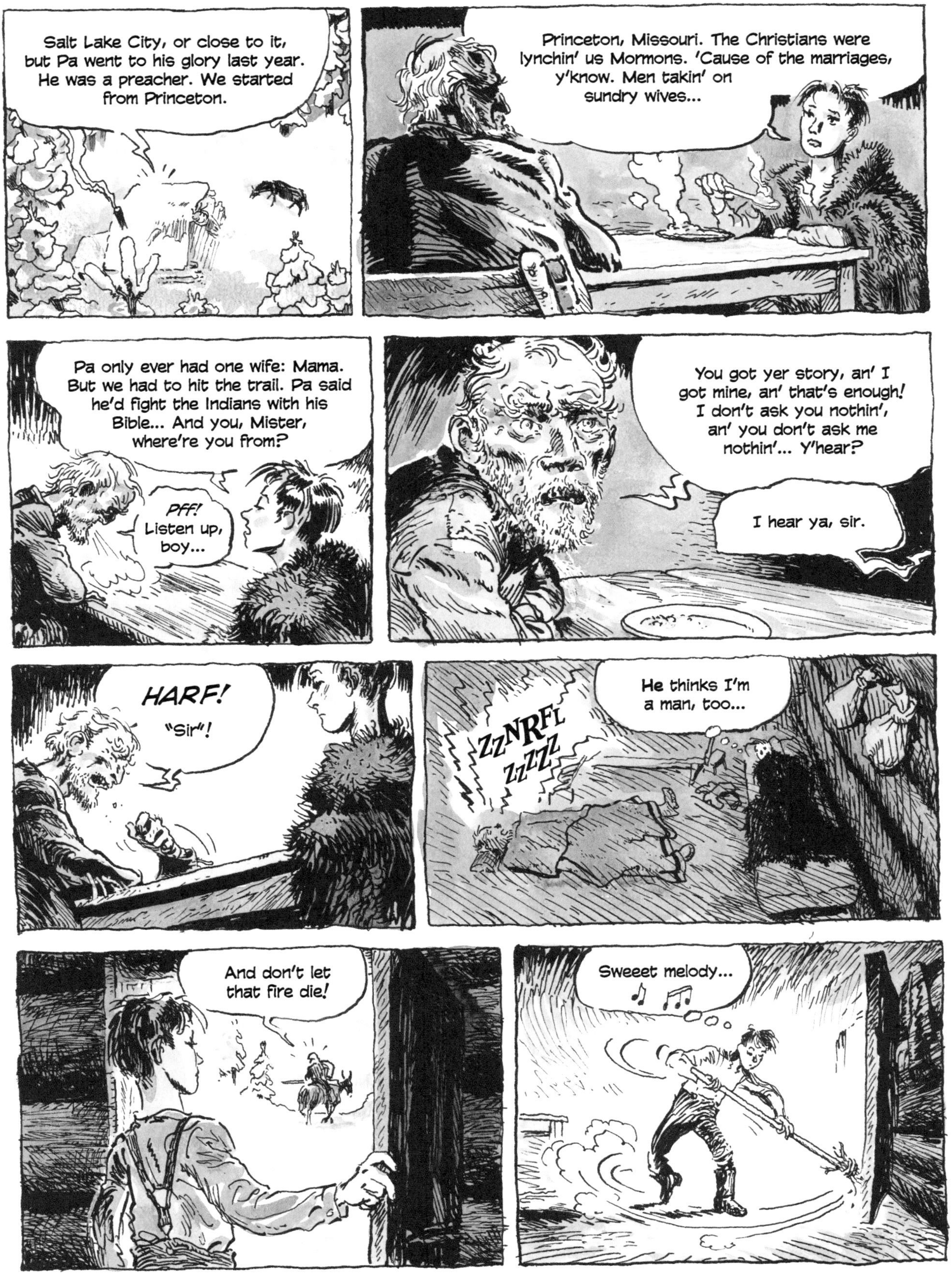

Salt Lake City, or close to it, but Pa went to his glory last year. He was a preacher. We started from Princeton.
Princeton, Missouri. The Christians were lynchin' us Mormons. 'Cause of the marriages, y'know. Men takin' on sundry wives...
Pa only ever had one wife: Mama. But we had to hit the trail. Pa said he'd fight the Indians with his Bible... And you, Mister, where're you from?
Pff! Listen up, boy...
You got yer story, an' I got mine, an' that's enough! I don't ask you nothin', an' you don't ask me nothin'... Y'hear?
I hear ya, sir.
HARF!
"Sir"!
ZZNRFL ZZZZZ
He thinks I'm a man, too...
And don't let that fire die!
Sweeet melody...

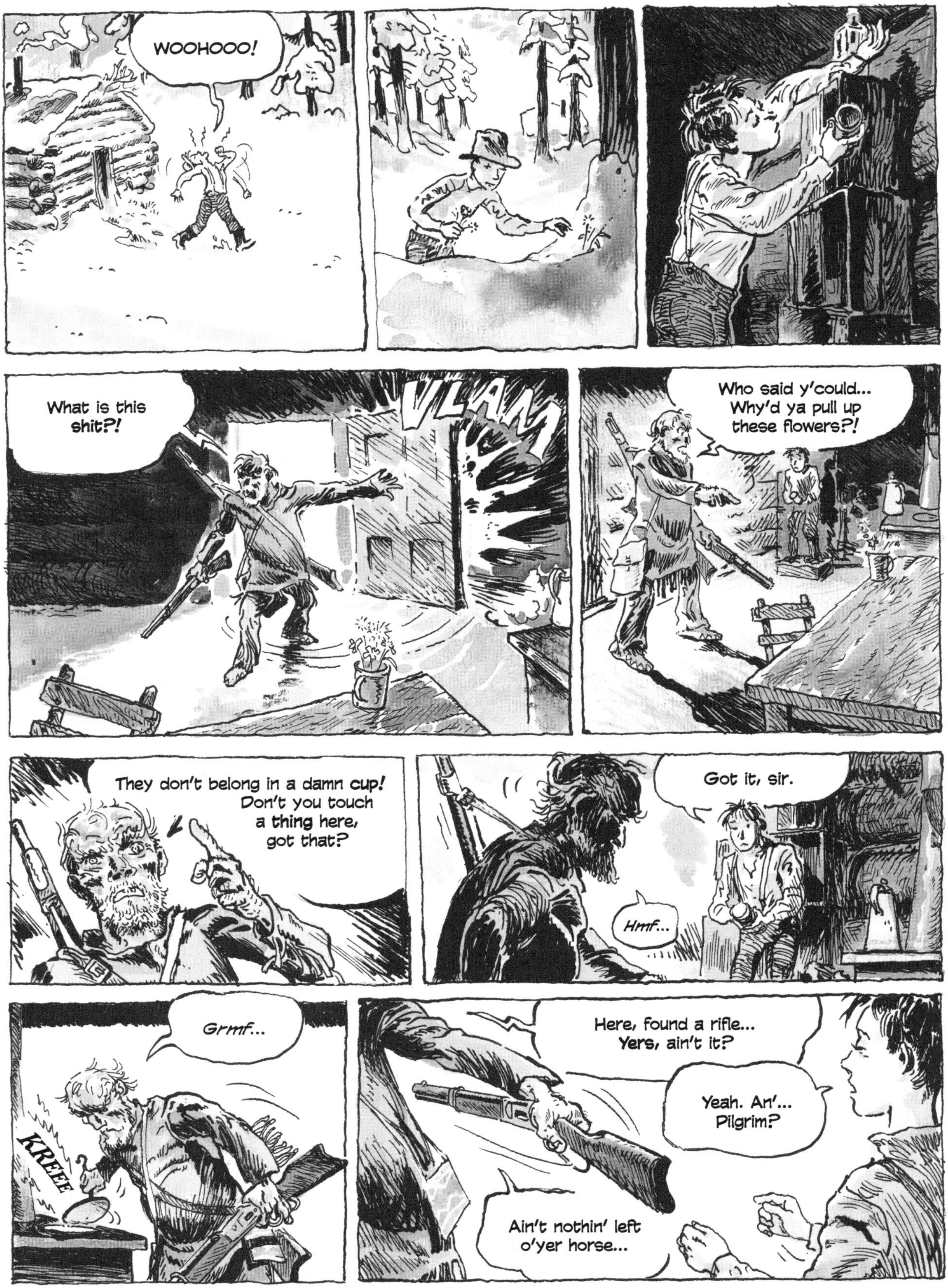
WOOHOOO!
What is this shit?!
VLAM
Who said y'could... Why'd ya pull up these flowers?!
They don't belong in a damn cup! Don't you touch a thing here, got that?
Got it, sir.
Hmf...
Grmf...
KREEE
Here, found a rifle... Yers, ain't it?
Yeah. An'... Pilgrim?
Ain't nothin' left o'yer horse...

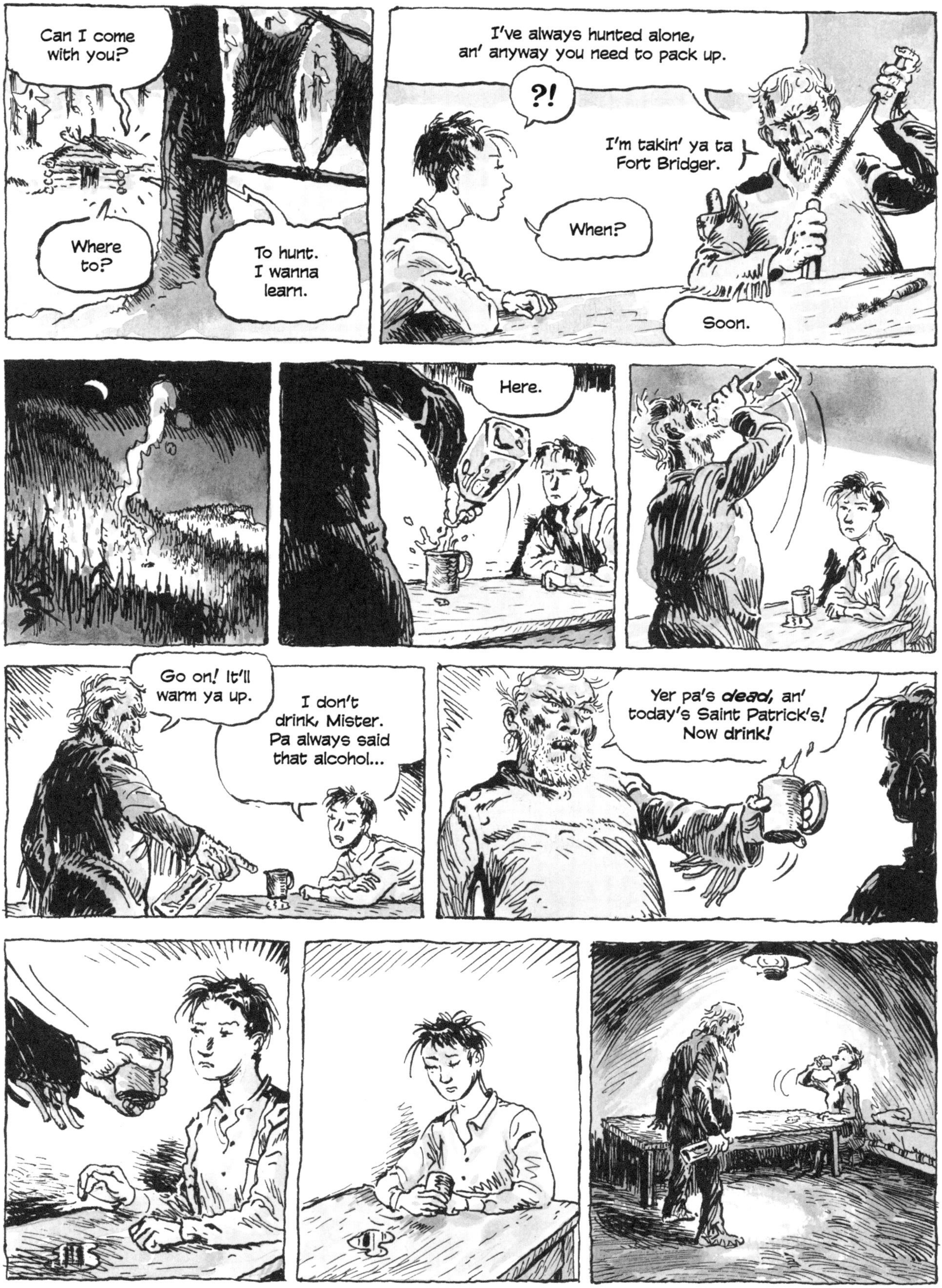

Can I come with you?
Where to?
To hunt. I wanna learn.
I've always hunted alone, an' anyway you need to pack up.
?!
I'm takin' ya ta Fort Bridger.
When?
Soon.
Here.
Go on! It'll warm ya up.
I don't drink, Mister. Pa always said that alcohol...
Yer pa's *dead,* an' today's Saint Patrick's! Now drink!

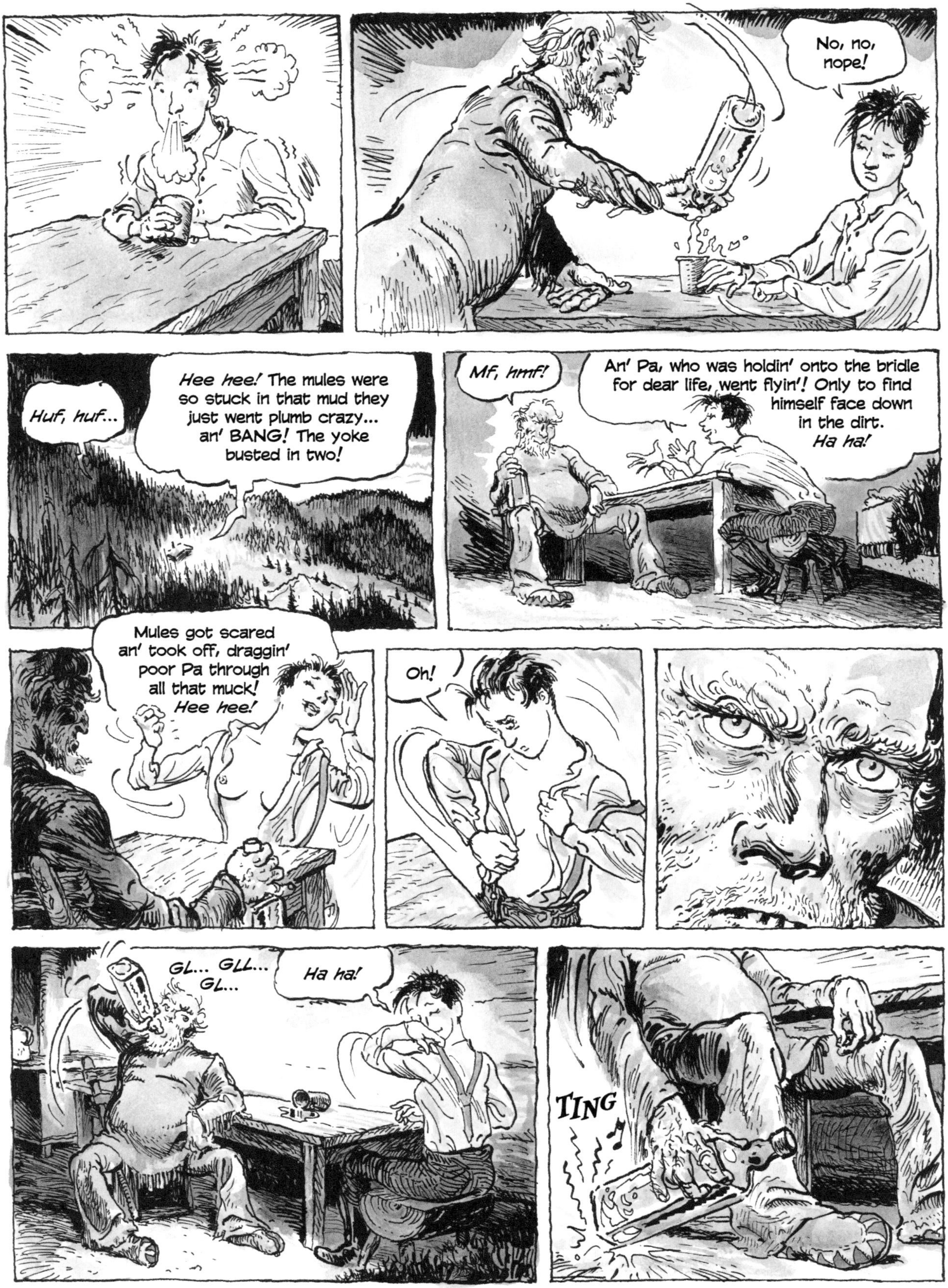
No, no, nope!
Huf, huf...
Hee hee! The mules were so stuck in that mud they just went plumb crazy... an' BANG! The yoke busted in two!
Mf, hmf!
An' Pa, who was holdin' onto the bridle for dear life, went flyin'! Only to find himself face down in the dirt. Ha ha!
Mules got scared an' took off, draggin' poor Pa through all that muck! Hee hee!
Oh!
GL... GLL... GL...
Ha ha!
TING

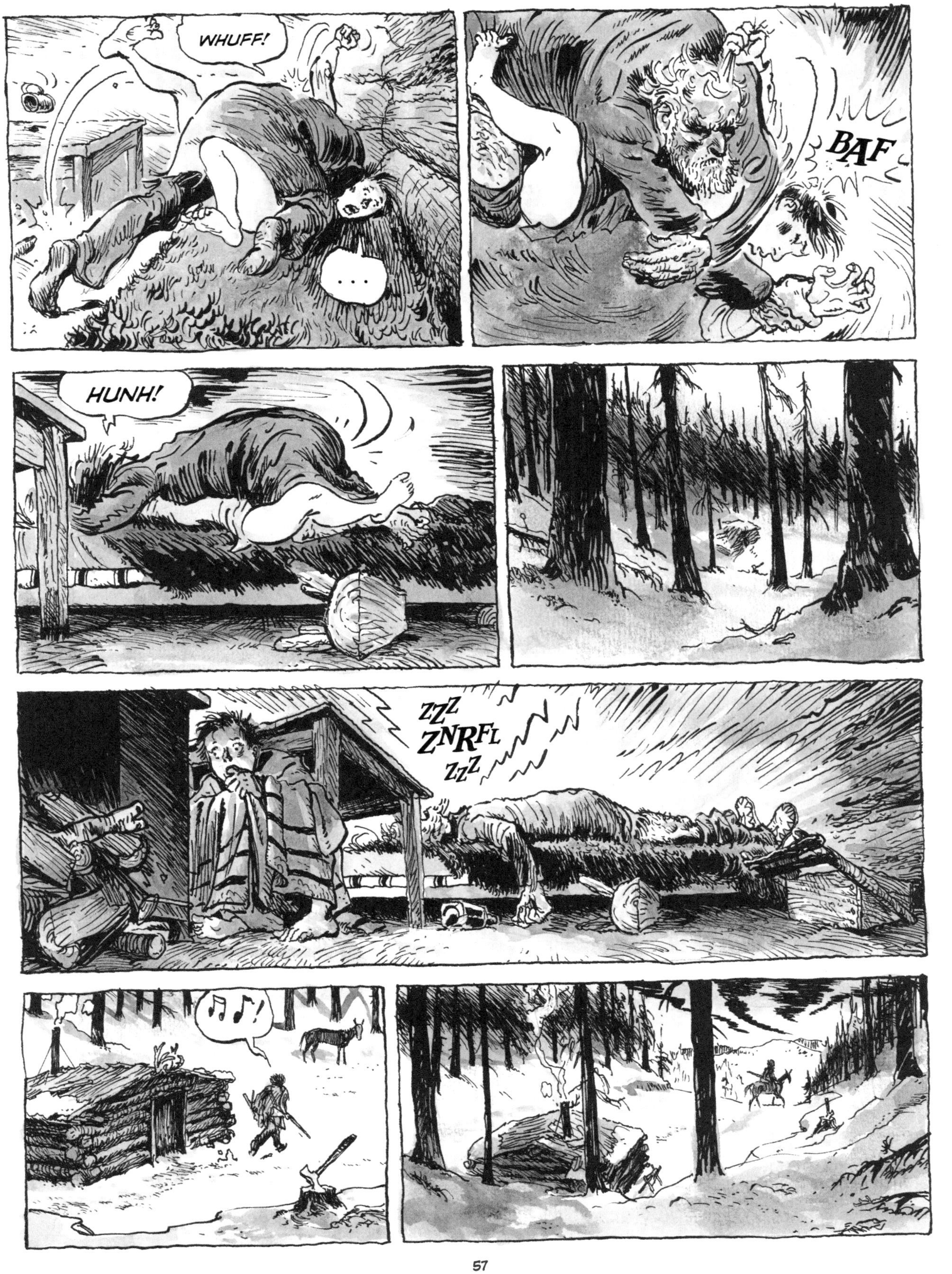
WHUFF!
...
BAF
HUNH!
ZZZ
ZNRFL
ZZZ
♫ ♪!

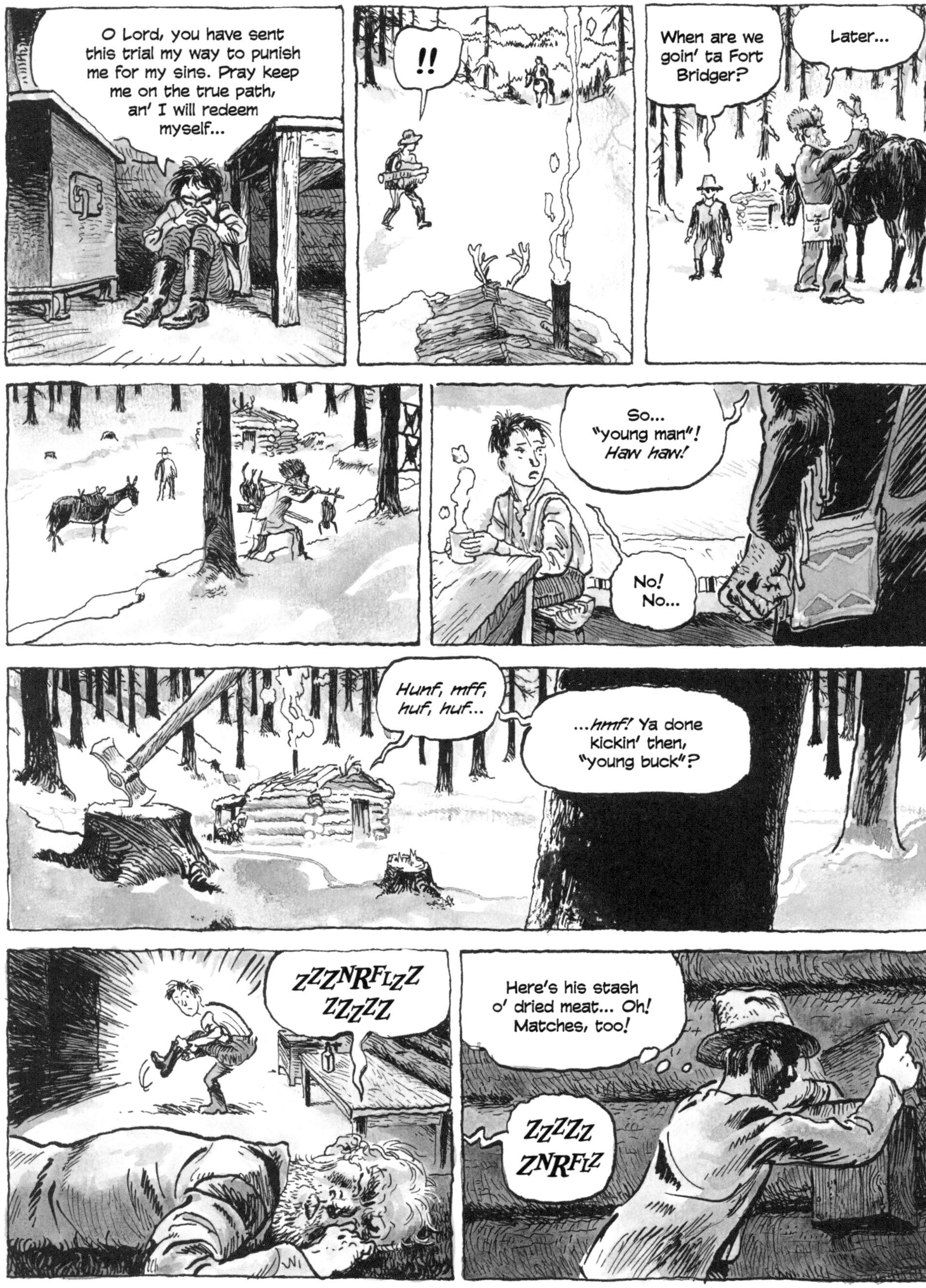
O Lord, you have sent this trial my way to punish me for my sins. Pray keep me on the true path, an' I will redeem myself...
!!
When are we goin' ta Fort Bridger?
Later...
So... "young man"! *Haw haw!*
No! No...
Hunf, mff, huf, huf...
...*hmf!* Ya done kickin' then, "young buck"?
ZZZNRFLZZ ZZZZZ
Here's his stash o' dried meat... Oh! Matches, too!
ZZZZZ ZNRFLZ

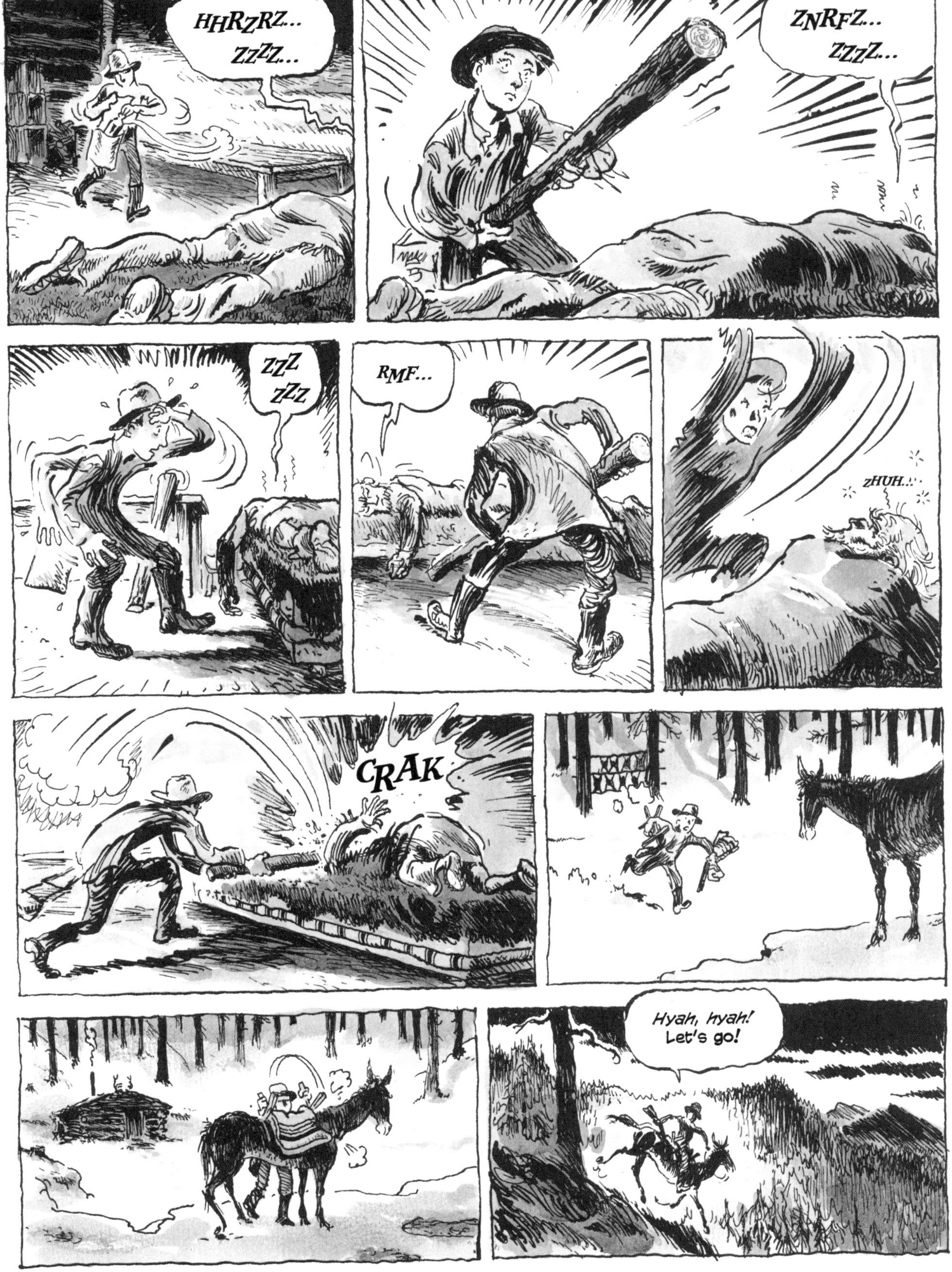
HHRZRZ... ZZZZ...
ZNRFZ... ZZZZ...
ZZZ ZZZ
RMF...
ZHUH..!
CRAK
Hyah, hyah! Let's go!

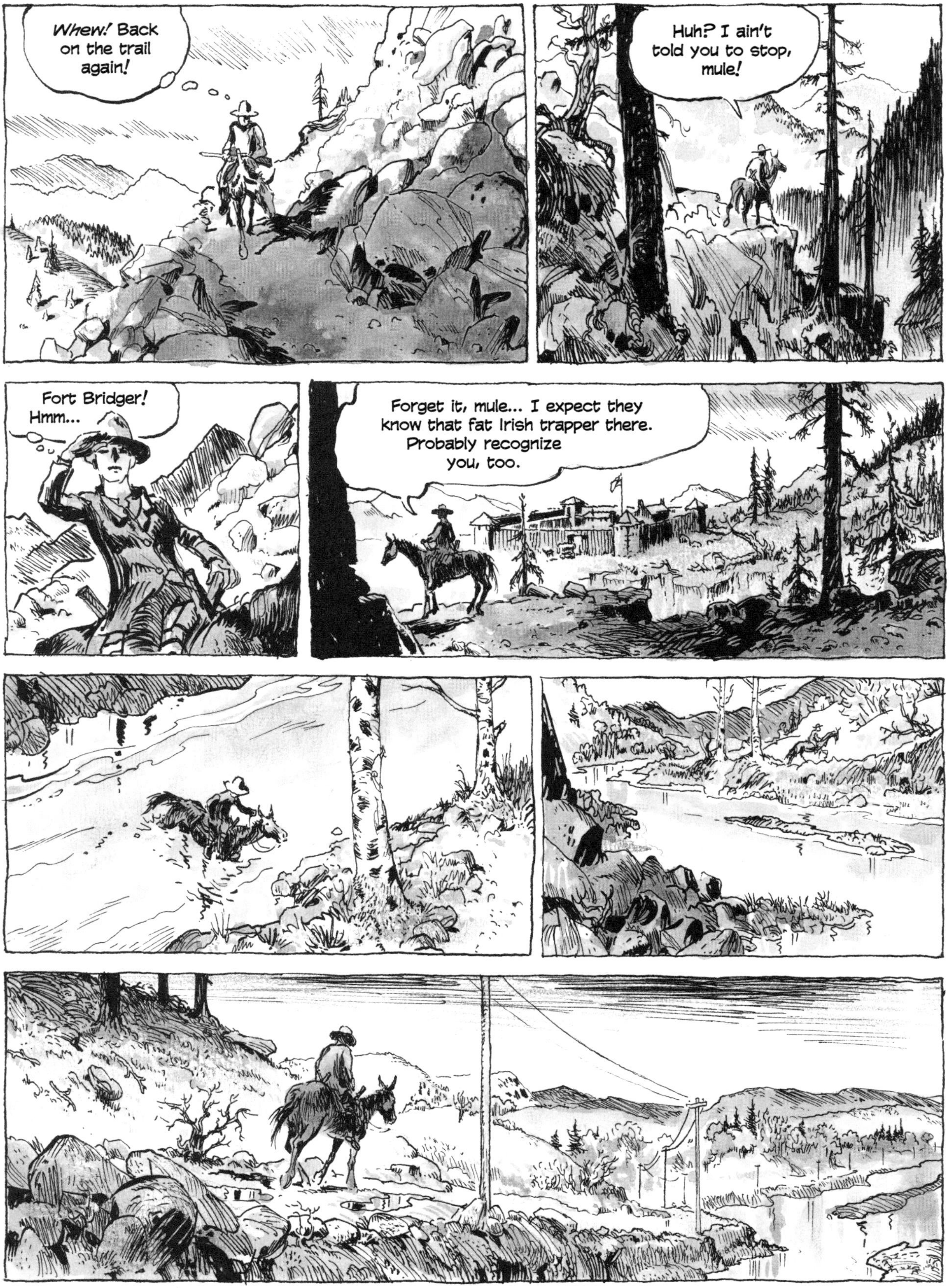
Whew! Back on the trail again!
Huh? I ain't told you to stop, mule!
Fort Bridger! Hmm...
Forget it, mule... I expect they know that fat Irish trapper there. Probably recognize you, too.

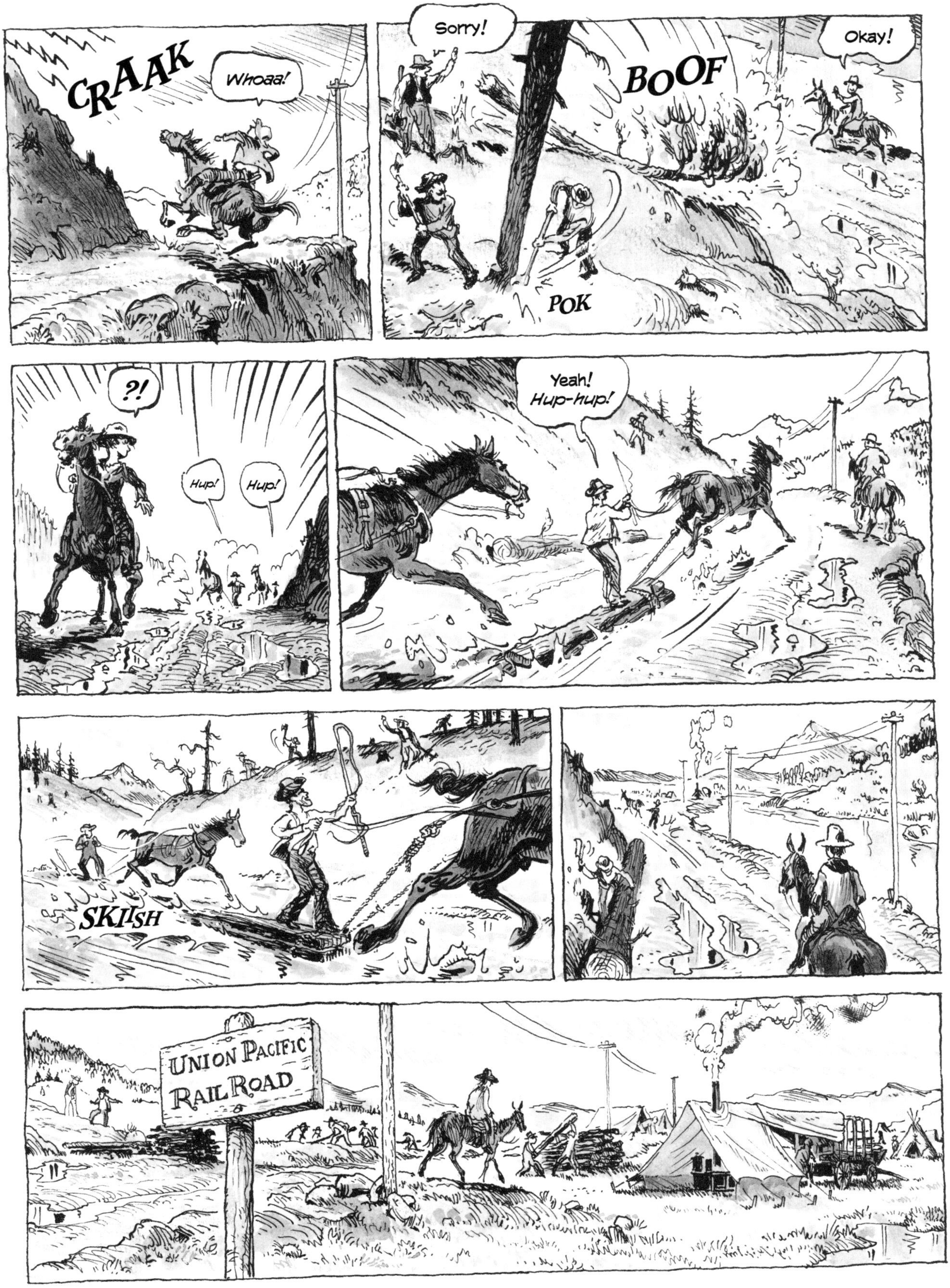
CRAAK
Whoaa!
Sorry!
BOOF
Okay!
POK
?!
Hup!
Hup!
Yeah! Hup-hup!
SKIISH
UNION PACIFIC RAIL ROAD

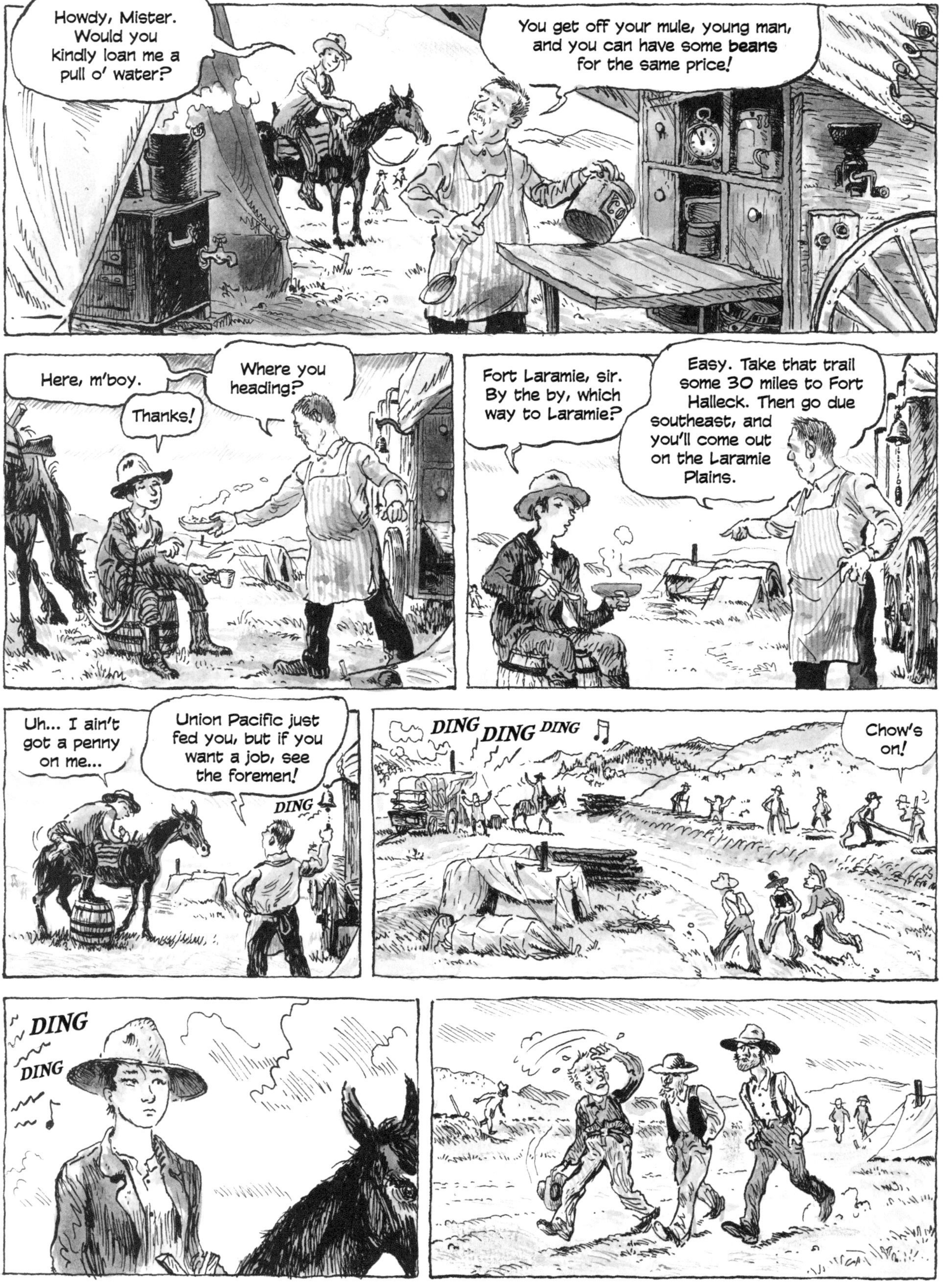
Howdy, Mister. Would you kindly loan me a pull o' water?
You get off your mule, young man, and you can have some **beans** for the same price!
Here, m'boy.
Where you heading?
Thanks!
Fort Laramie, sir. By the by, which way to Laramie?
Easy. Take that trail some 30 miles to Fort Halleck. Then go due southeast, and you'll come out on the Laramie Plains.
Uh... I ain't got a penny on me...
Union Pacific just fed you, but if you want a job, see the foremen!
DING
DING DING DING
Chow's on!
DING
DING

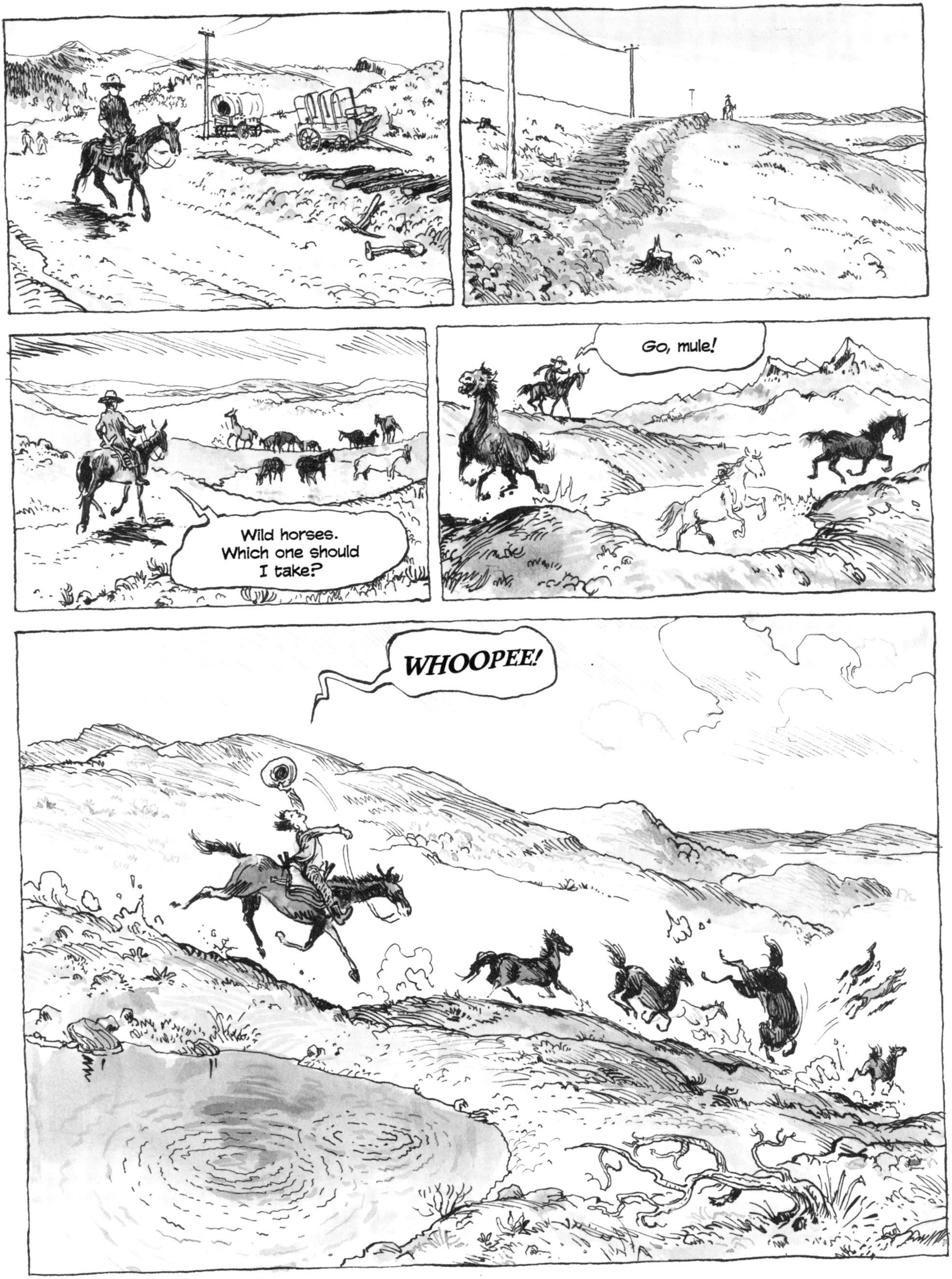
Wild horses. Which one should I take?
Go, mule!
WHOOPEE!

The Women of Laramie

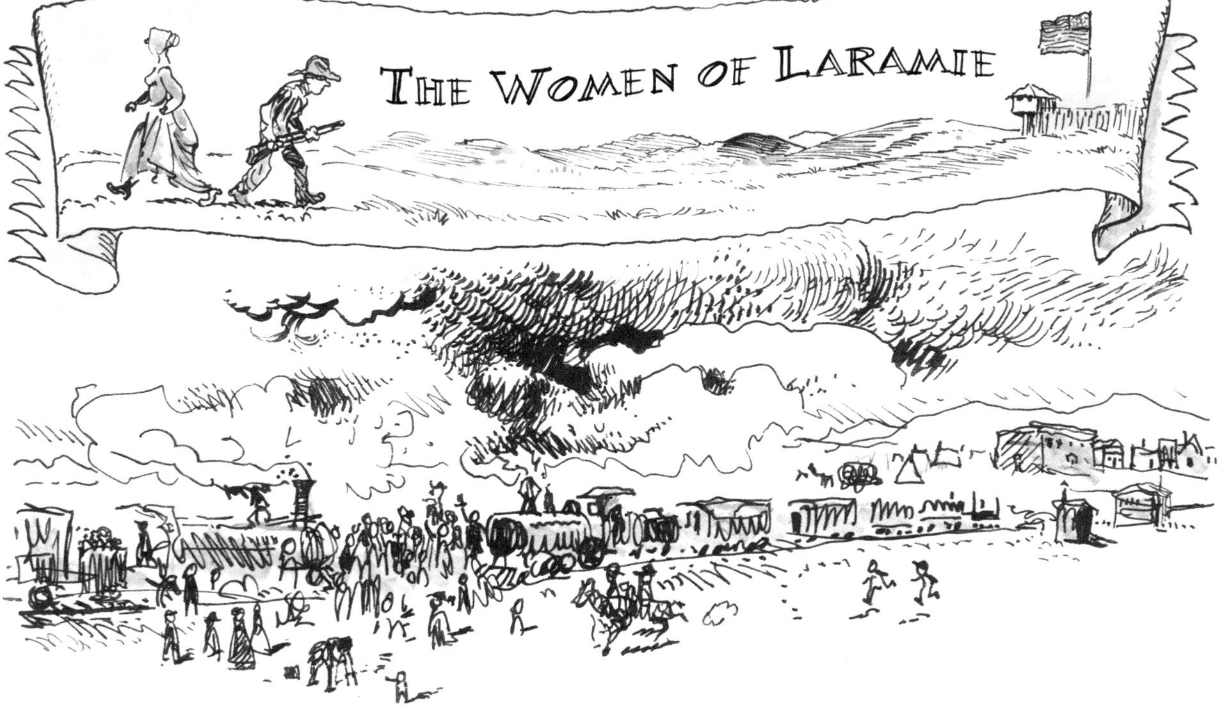

In 1868, both the **Union Pacific Railroad** and the **Central Pacific Railroad** were close to completing the track begun six years earlier, which would finally link Omaha, Nebraska, all the way to Sacramento, California. In the coming months the two lines would converge by the Great Salt Lake.

Martha Jane had no idea yet how important this would be: how this great advance would open up the Territories to those without the means or fortitude to travel the trail. New towns were soon born all along the line, with homesteaders moving in to each one, pushing the frontier ever farther to the **West...**

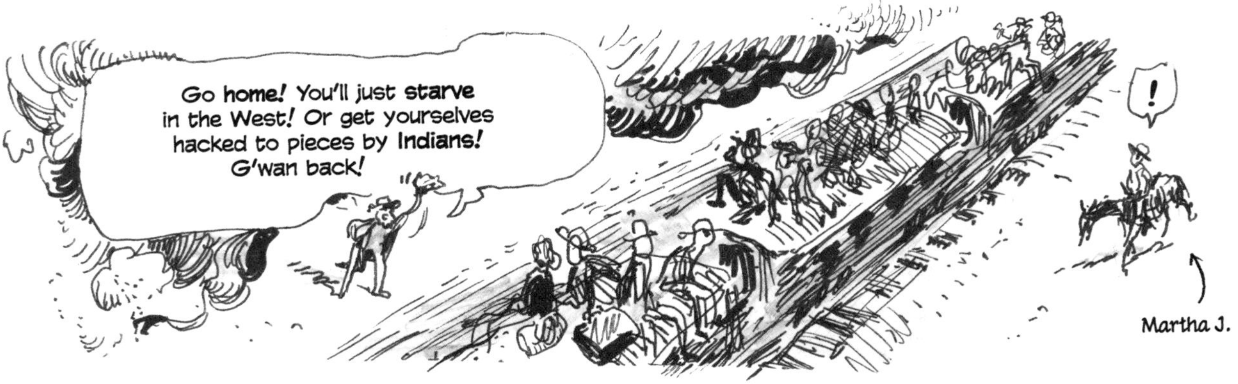
Go **home!** You'll just **starve** in the West! Or get yourselves hacked to pieces by **Indians!** G'wan back!
!
Martha J.

Hunters, tradesmen, and miners risked all to venture farther into Indian territories. THE SIOUX, CHEYENNE, ARAPAHO, AND BLACKFOOT TRIBES felt betrayed by the Government, who'd promised that settlers would only pass **through** Native hunting grounds. By 1862 this inexorable push west to the Rockies would be fraught with ongoing skirmishes, bloodshed, and brutal reprisals...

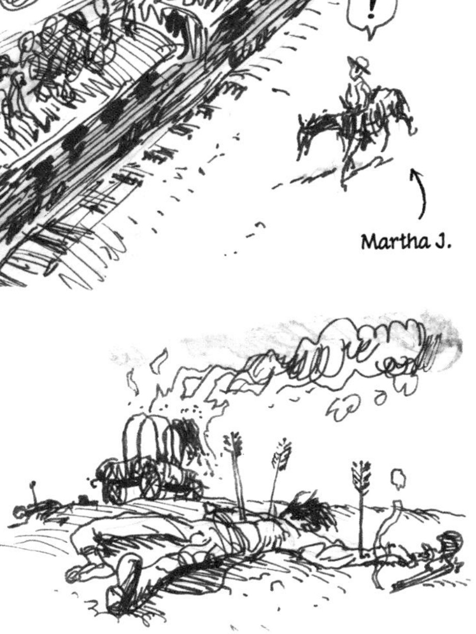

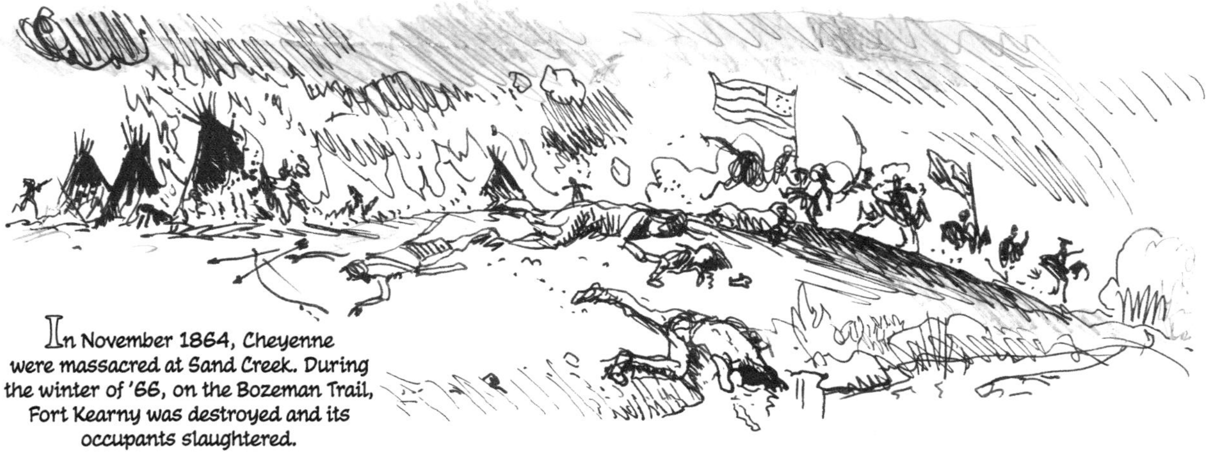

In November 1864, Cheyenne were massacred at Sand Creek. During the winter of '66, on the Bozeman Trail, Fort Kearny was destroyed and its occupants slaughtered.

The April '68 **Treaty of Fort Laramie** was supposed to end hostilities by guaranteeing the removal of forts and the withdrawal of settlers. But Indian Chiefs could not **read** the document, which actually stipulated that tribes be confined in reserves though still allowed to hunt on their ancestral lands.

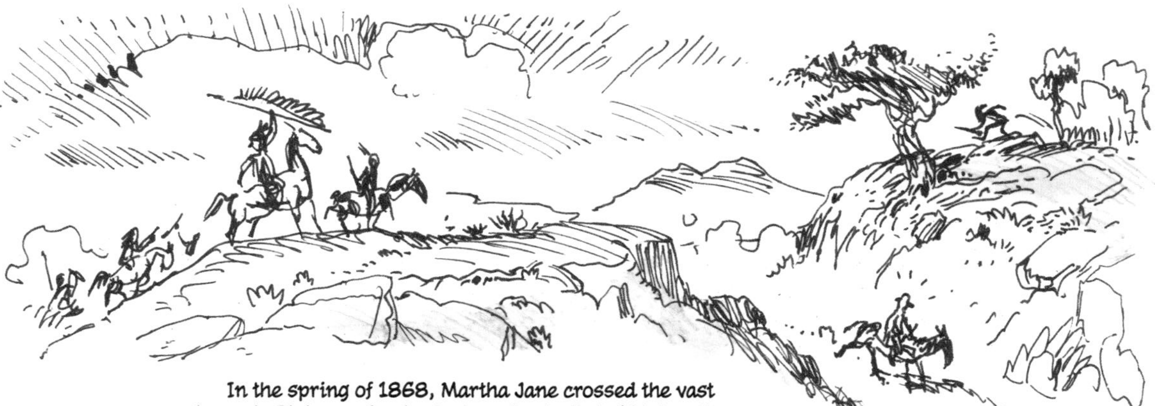

In the spring of 1868, Martha Jane crossed the vast Laramie Plains, going back along the trail she'd taken three years earlier with her father and siblings. We can only **imagine** her riding from place to place, begging for food, sleeping in stables, doing everything possible to hide her femininity.

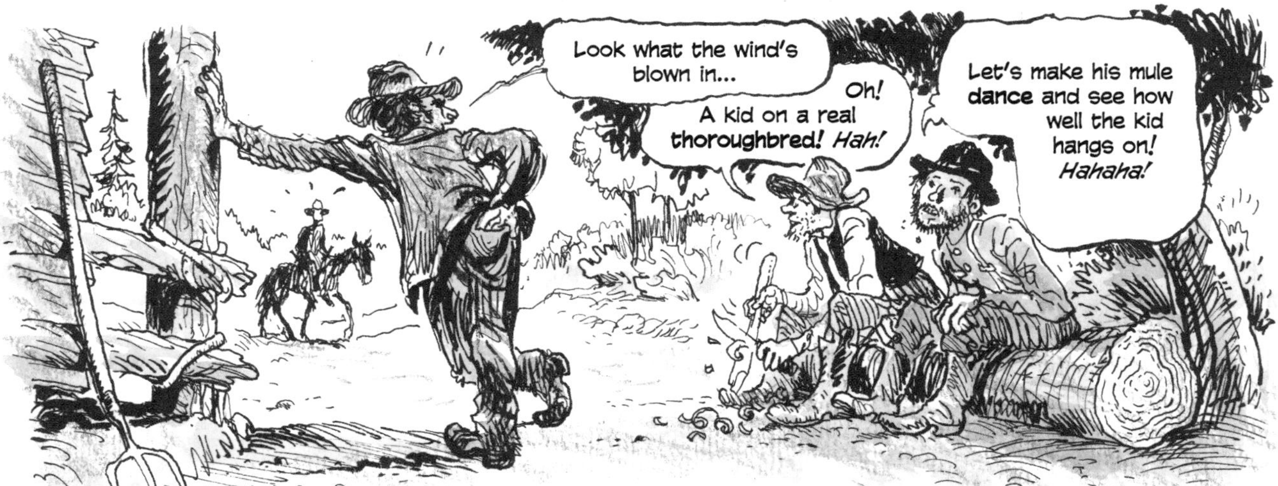
Look what the wind's blown in...
Oh! A kid on a real **thoroughbred!** *Hah!*
Let's make his mule **dance** and see how well the kid hangs on! *Hahaha!*

Martha knew these backcountry outposts were home mostly to brutal ruffians on the run from American justice, men who'd found refuge on the immense frontier lands between the East and the West, where the law did not exist...

...but one day she finally pulled in to FORT LARAMIE, where she found soldiers, of course, but also civilians: homesteaders waiting for spring weather, arms dealers readying for the Plains Indian hunt, natives drunk on cheap alcohol... Martha Jane, hungry and broke, sidled up to a somber group of Mormons.

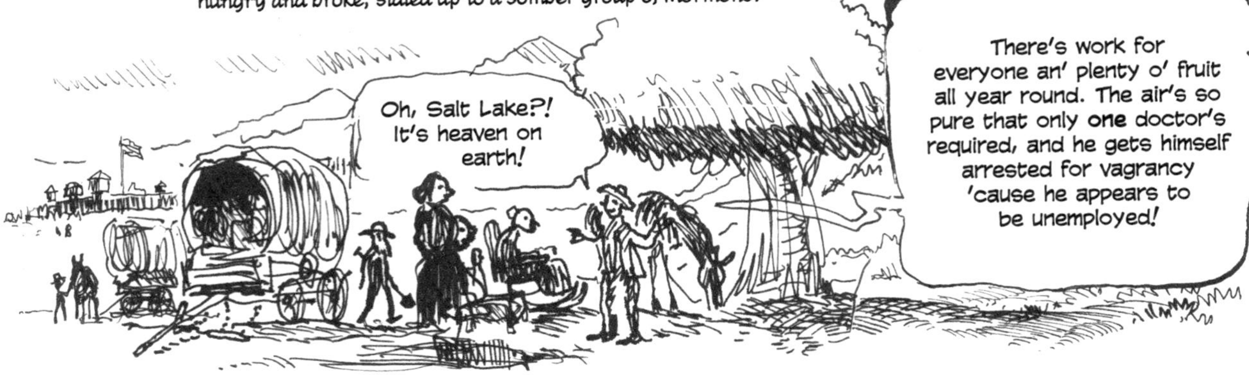
Oh, Salt Lake?! It's heaven on earth!
There's work for everyone an' plenty o' fruit all year round. The air's so pure that only **one** doctor's required, and he gets himself arrested for vagrancy 'cause he appears to be unemployed!

The Mormons, already exhausted by their travel and facing a terrifying trek across the Rocky Mountains, ate up Martha's bluff and bluster about the "kingdom" of the Latter-day Saints... And wasn't Martha Jane herself living proof that people could survive crossing the Rockies?

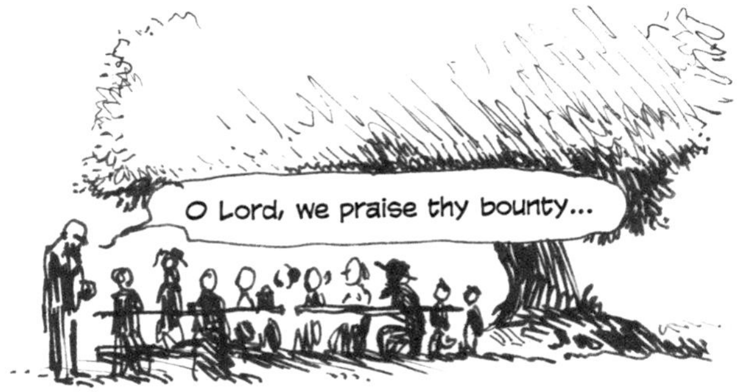
O Lord, we praise thy bounty...

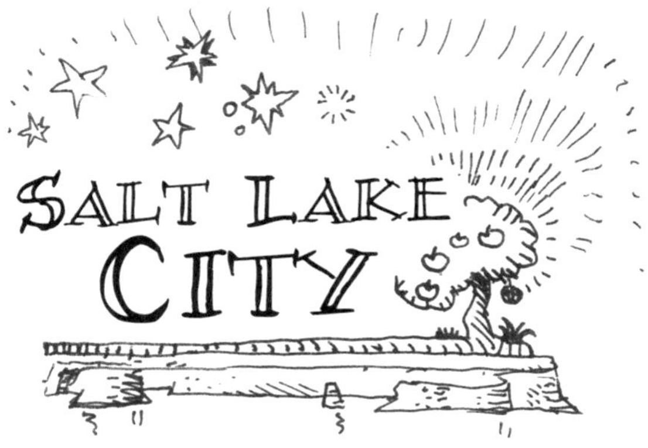
SALT LAKE CITY

And so the Mormons opened their hearts to Martha Jane, generously offering her food and shelter... It didn't last.

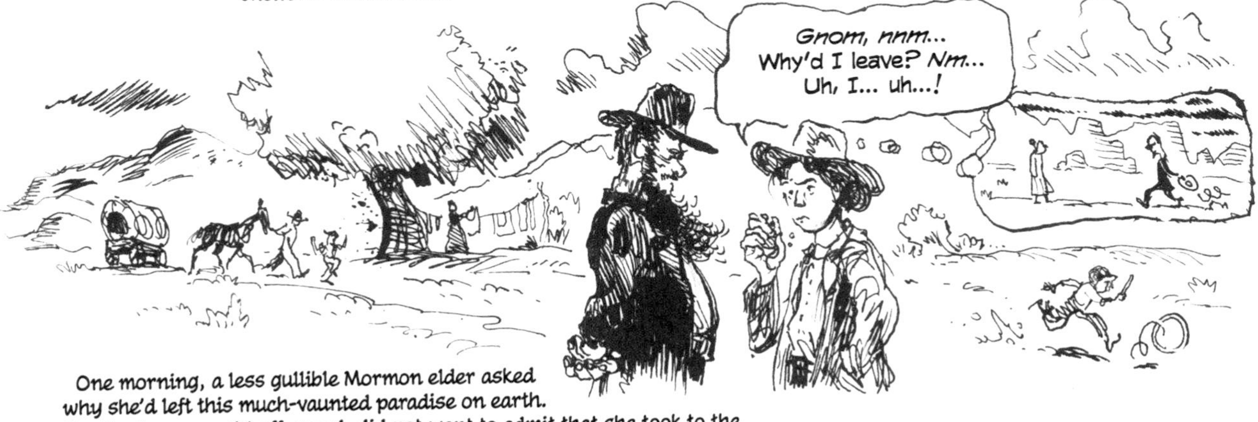
Gnom, nnm... Why'd I leave? *Nm...* Uh, I... uh...!

One morning, a less gullible Mormon elder asked why she'd left this much-vaunted paradise on earth. Martha Jane, caught off-guard, did not want to admit that she took to the road, in part, to escape a "Saint" looking to replenish his stock of wives.

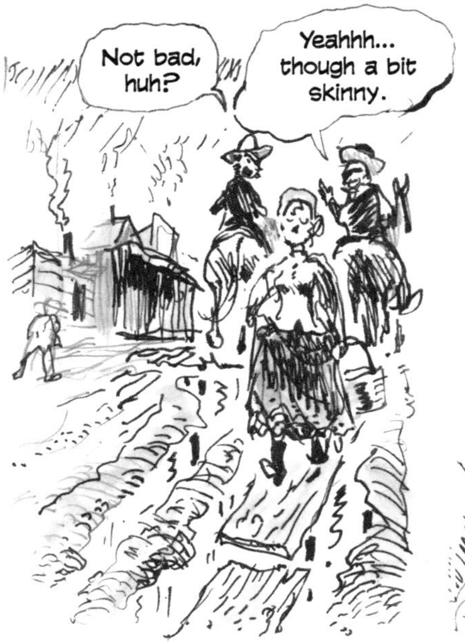
Not bad, huh?
Yeahhh... though a bit skinny.

Giving up on the homesteaders, Martha dared to brave the fort itself. The West's rough living appealed to a mostly male population. Laramie was home to women, too, but they were officers' wives or nannies minding officers' children or women doing officers' laundry, along with cooks and sutlers and whores...

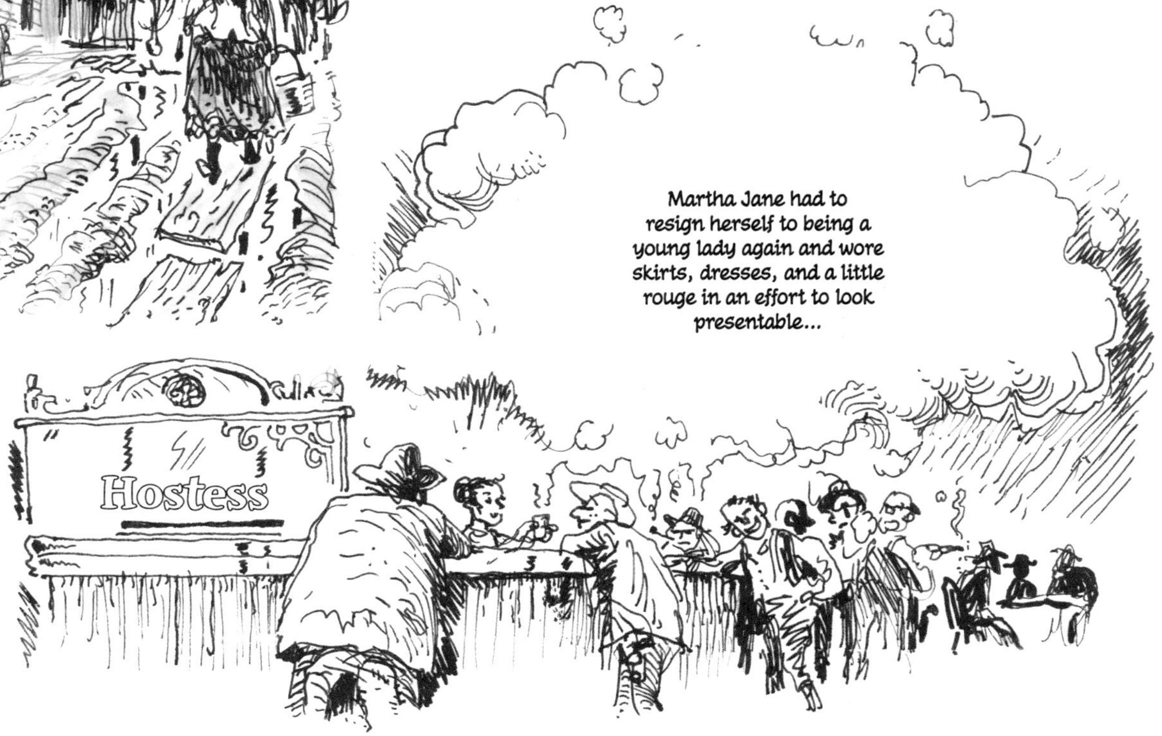
Martha Jane had to resign herself to being a young lady again and wore skirts, dresses, and a little rouge in an effort to look presentable...
Hostess

Working in the fort's kitchen during the day and in the **saloon** at night, she was considered an unusual girl, a shy mix of tall tales and compulsive lies. You should have heard the one she told about crossing the Rockies...

How that entire family of Swedish settlers whose wagon got stuck in a rising river flood was **rescued** by her alone... How **Pilgrim** (her voice a-tremble at the name) had walked day and night till he wore right out, just to save her from the unrelenting snow... How with naught but a knife and frying pan, she forced that hungry pack of wolves surrounding her to run for their lives... How she... How... **HOW!**

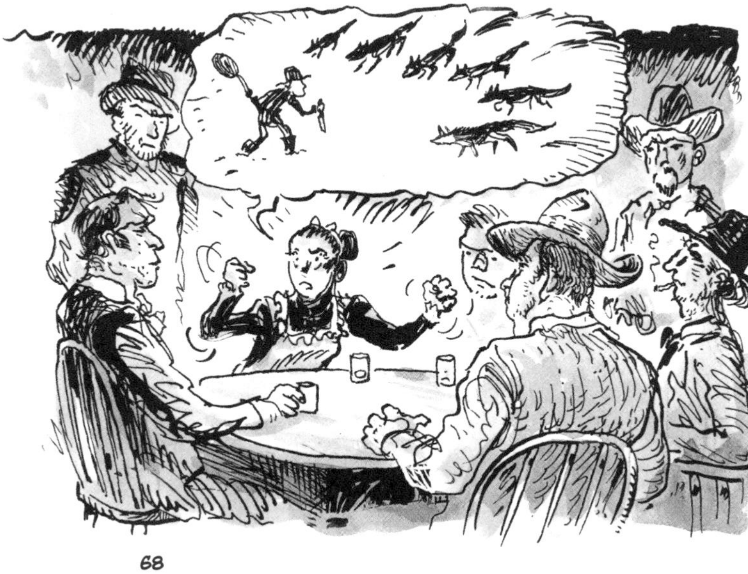

One day, when the freight team arrived at Fort Laramie from Julesburg (the last railway station before the Rockies), Martha Jane recognized the man at the head of the wagons: it was **Abbott,** one of the guides who'd led her family to Virginia City.

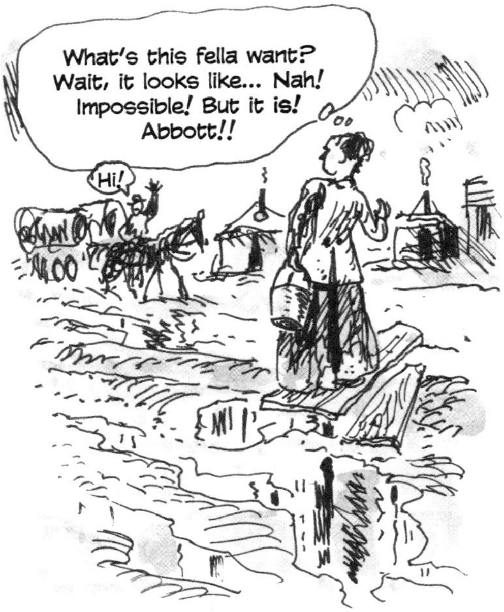
What's this fella want? Wait, it looks like... Nah! Impossible! But it is! Abbott!!
Hi!

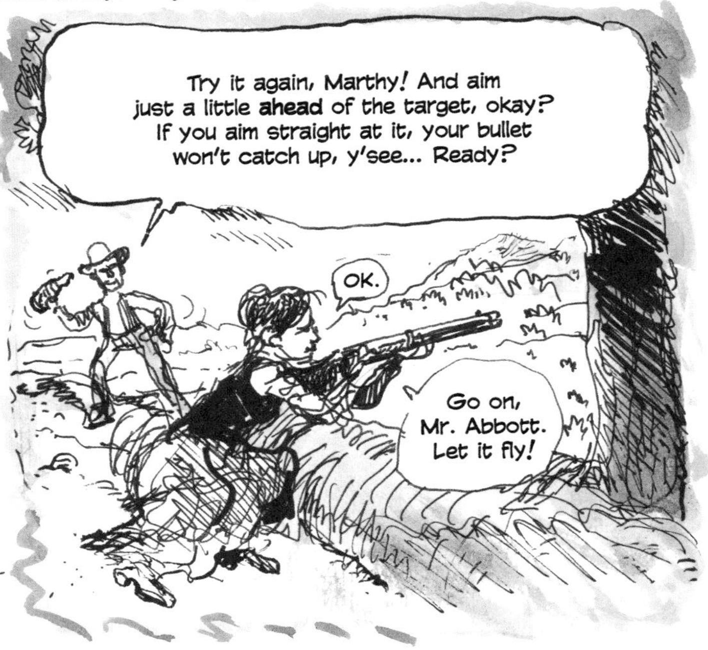
Try it again, Marthy! And aim just a little ahead of the target, okay? If you aim straight at it, your bullet won't catch up, y'see... Ready?
OK.
Go on, Mr. Abbott. Let it fly!

Abbott attached himself to Martha as if he were her big brother. And when he saw she couldn't fend off the advances of drunken soldiers at the saloon, he set out the very next day to find her another job...

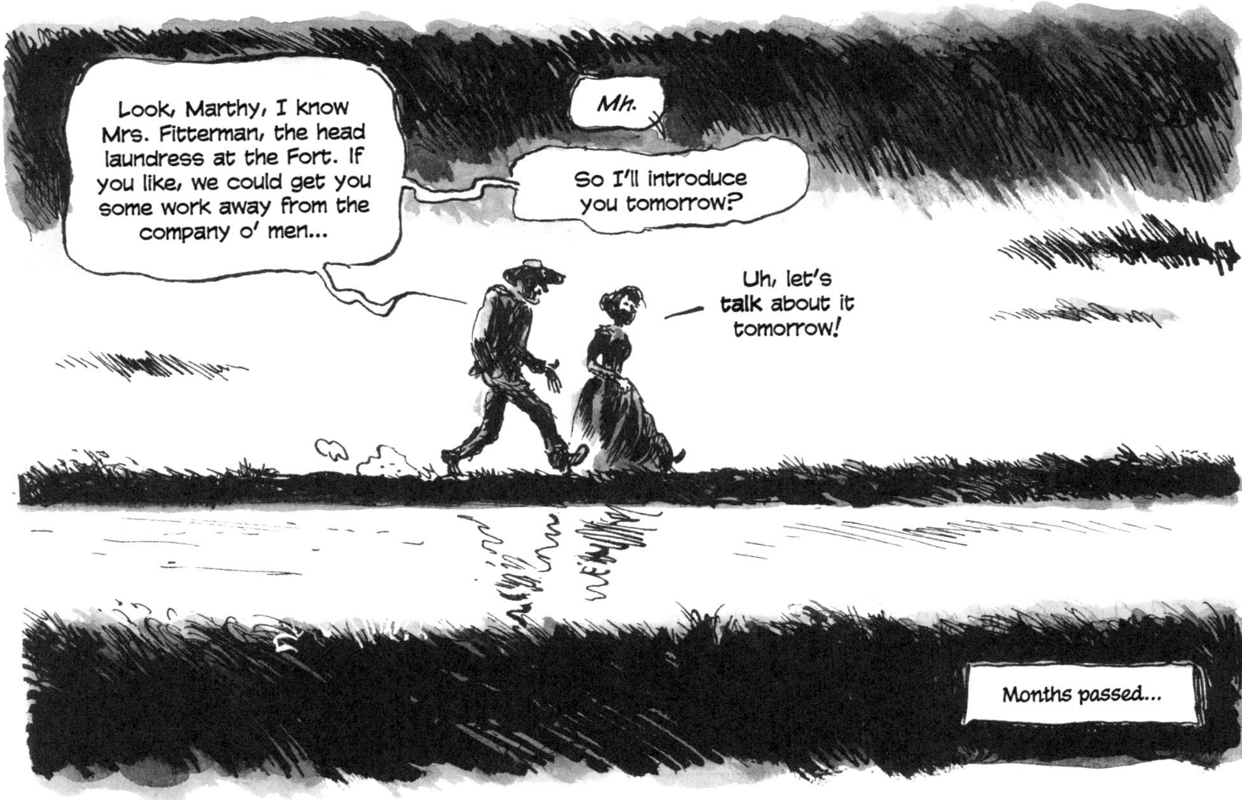
Look, Marthy, I know Mrs. Fitterman, the head laundress at the Fort. If you like, we could get you some work away from the company o' men...
Mh.
So I'll introduce you tomorrow?
Uh, let's talk about it tomorrow!
Months passed...

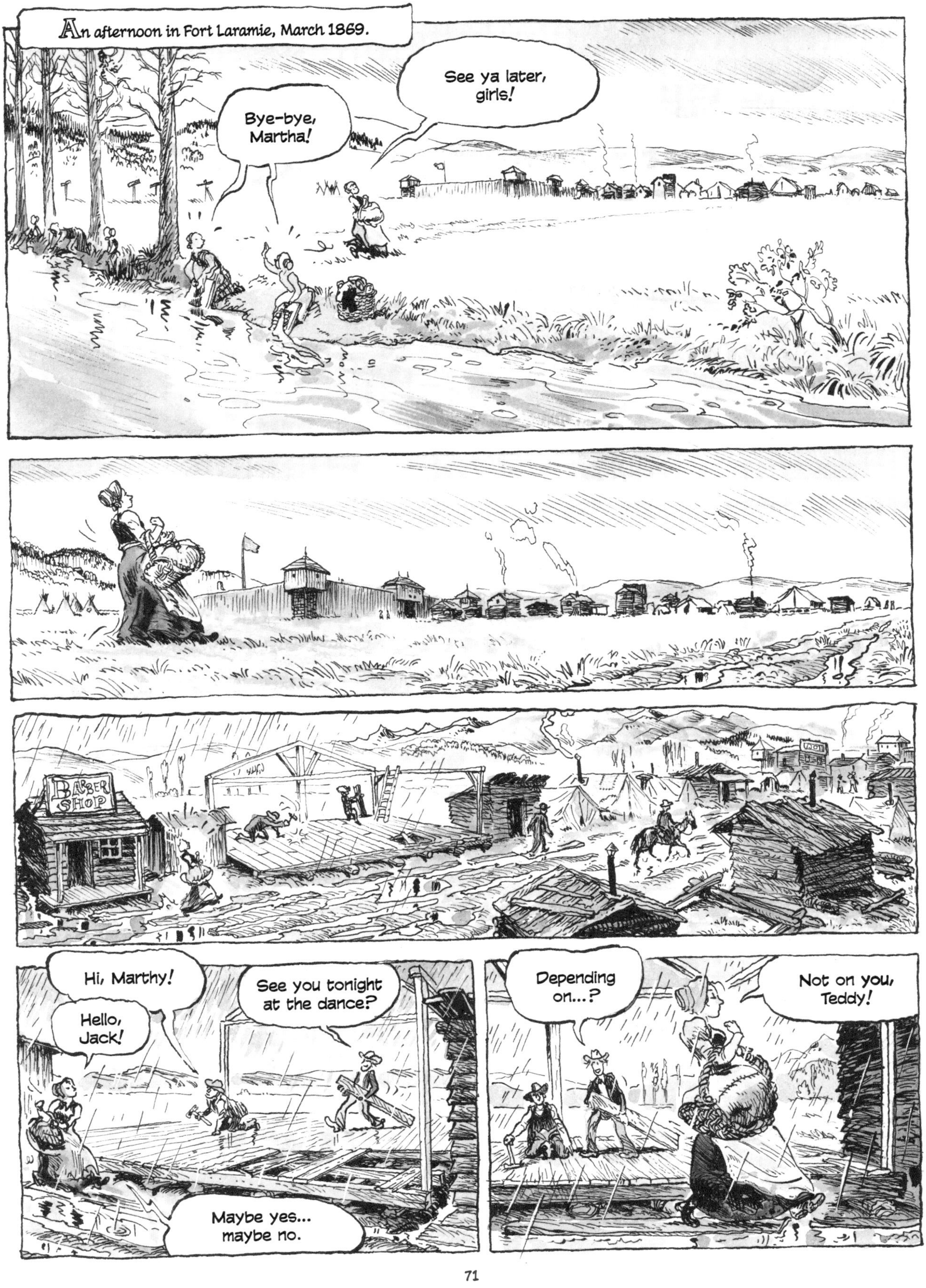
An afternoon in Fort Laramie, March 1869.
Bye-bye, Martha!
See ya later, girls!
!!
BARBER SHOP
Hi, Marthy!
Hello, Jack!
See you tonight at the dance?
Maybe yes... maybe no.
Depending on...?
Not on you, Teddy!

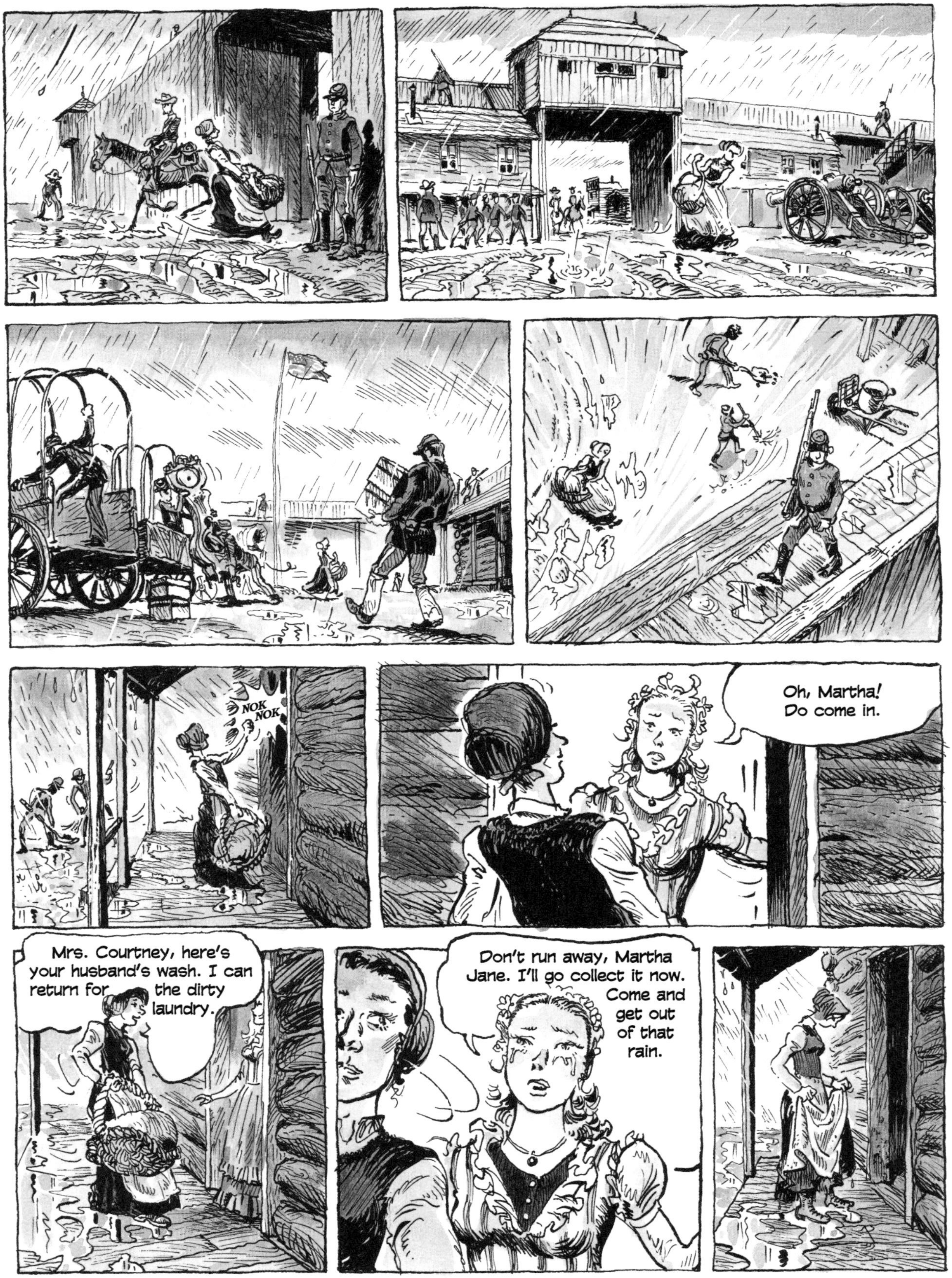
NOK NOK
Oh, Martha! Do come in.
Mrs. Courtney, here's your husband's wash. I can return for the dirty laundry.
Don't run away, Martha Jane. I'll go collect it now. Come and get out of that rain.

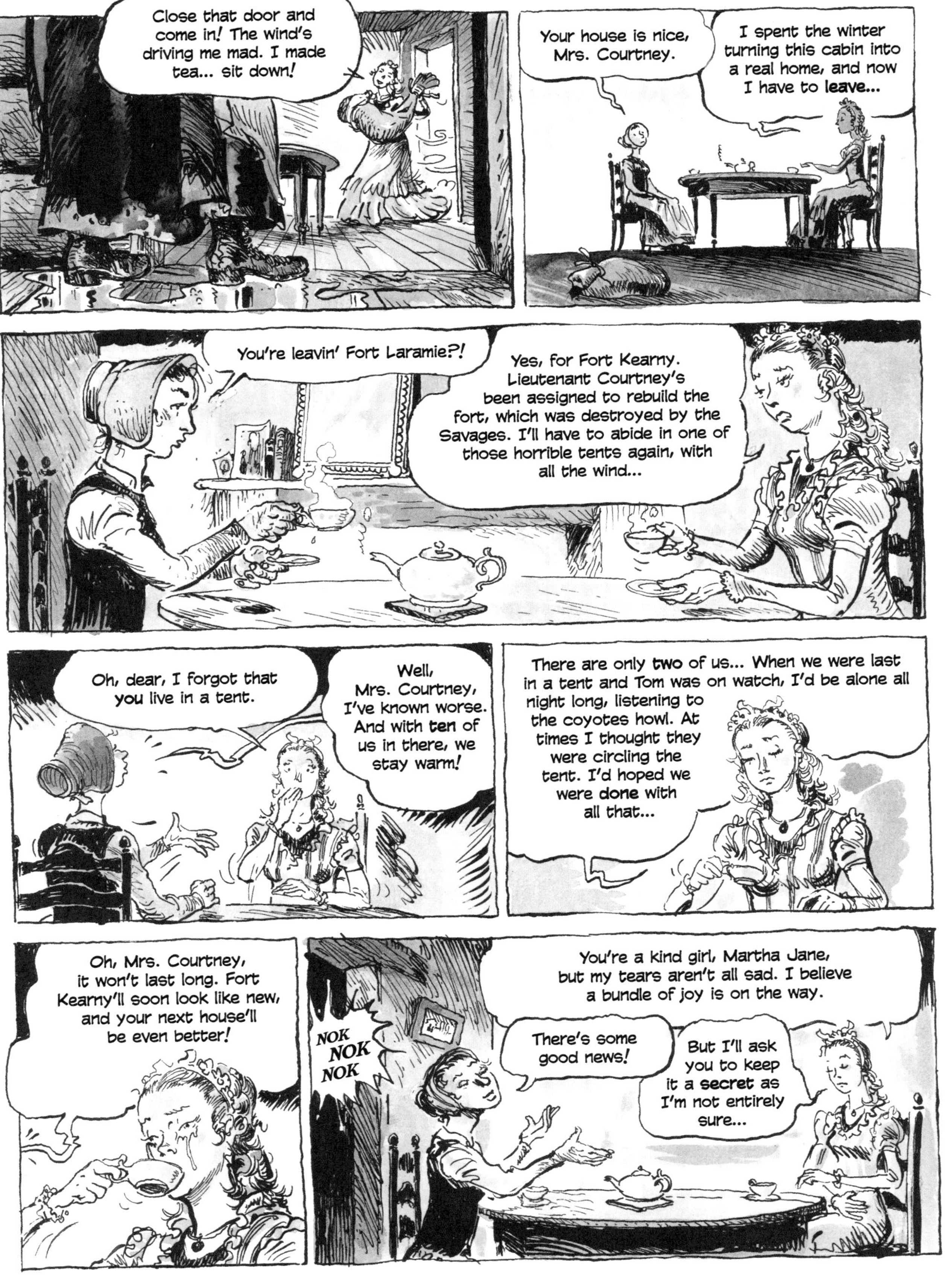
Close that door and come in! The wind's driving me mad. I made tea... sit down!
Your house is nice, Mrs. Courtney.
I spent the winter turning this cabin into a real home, and now I have to leave...
You're leavin' Fort Laramie?!
Yes, for Fort Kearny. Lieutenant Courtney's been assigned to rebuild the fort, which was destroyed by the Savages. I'll have to abide in one of those horrible tents again, with all the wind...
Oh, dear, I forgot that you live in a tent.
Well, Mrs. Courtney, I've known worse. And with ten of us in there, we stay warm!
There are only two of us... When we were last in a tent and Tom was on watch, I'd be alone all night long, listening to the coyotes howl. At times I thought they were circling the tent. I'd hoped we were done with all that...
Oh, Mrs. Courtney, it won't last long. Fort Kearny'll soon look like new, and your next house'll be even better!
You're a kind girl, Martha Jane, but my tears aren't all sad. I believe a bundle of joy is on the way.
NOK NOK NOK
There's some good news!
But I'll ask you to keep it a secret as I'm not entirely sure...

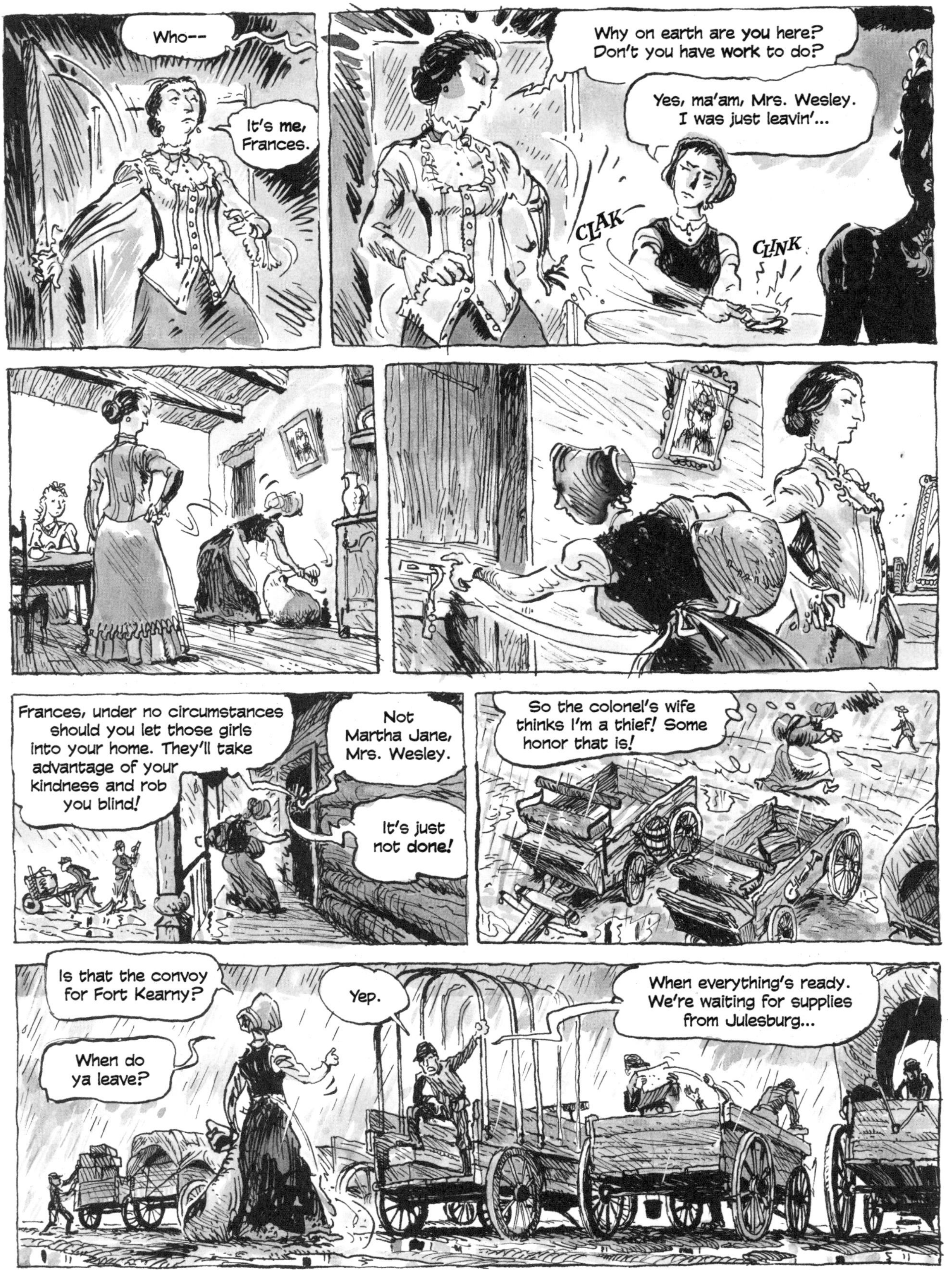
Who--
It's me, Frances.
Why on earth are you here? Don't you have work to do?
Yes, ma'am, Mrs. Wesley. I was just leavin'...
CLAK
CLINK
Frances, under no circumstances should you let those girls into your home. They'll take advantage of your kindness and rob you blind!
Not Martha Jane, Mrs. Wesley.
It's just not done!
So the colonel's wife thinks I'm a thief! Some honor that is!
Is that the convoy for Fort Kearny?
Yep.
When do ya leave?
When everything's ready. We're waiting for supplies from Julesburg...

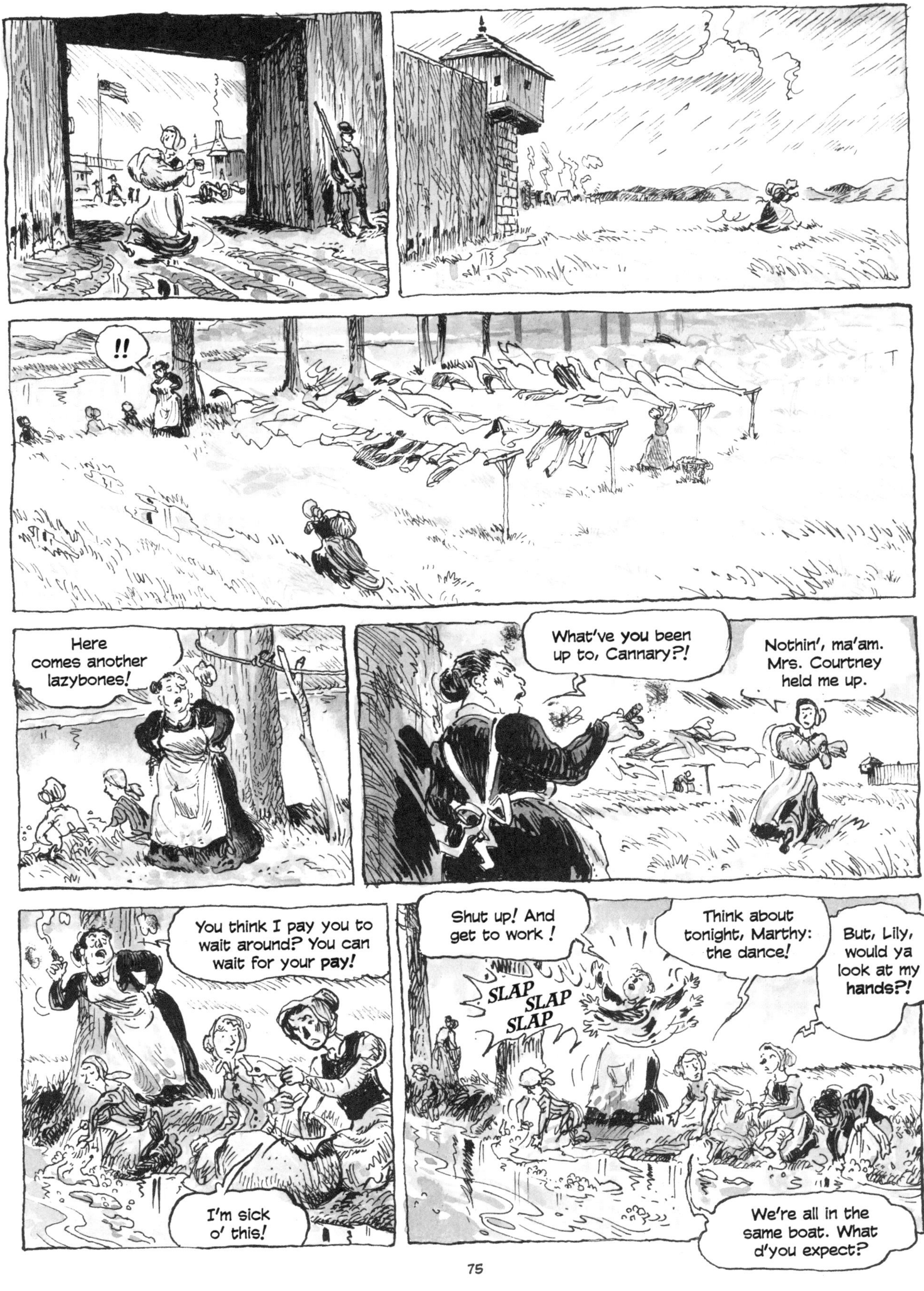
!!
Here comes another lazybones!
What've you been up to, Cannary?!
Nothin', ma'am. Mrs. Courtney held me up.
You think I pay you to wait around? You can wait for your pay!
I'm sick o' this!
Shut up! And get to work!
SLAP SLAP SLAP
Think about tonight, Marthy: the dance!
But, Lily, would ya look at my hands?!
We're all in the same boat. What d'you expect?

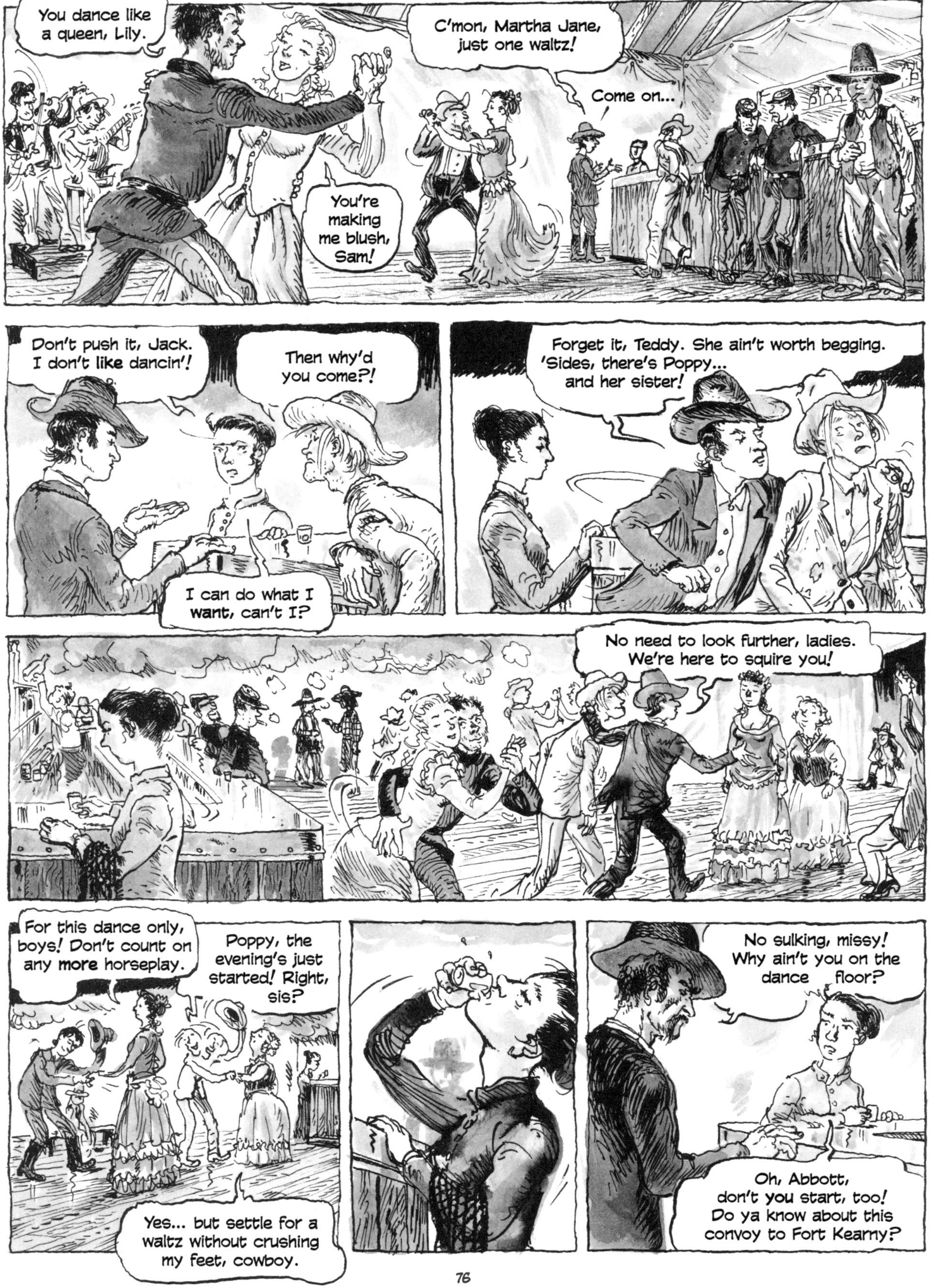

You dance like a queen, Lily.
C'mon, Martha Jane, just one waltz!
Come on...
You're making me blush, Sam!
Don't push it, Jack. I don't **like** dancin'!
Then why'd you come?!
I can do what I **want**, can't I?
Forget it, Teddy. She ain't worth begging. 'Sides, there's Poppy... and her sister!
No need to look further, ladies. We're here to squire you!
For this dance only, boys! Don't count on any **more** horseplay.
Poppy, the evening's just started! Right, sis?
Yes... but settle for a waltz without crushing my feet, cowboy.
No sulking, missy! Why ain't you on the dance floor?
Oh, Abbott, don't **you** start, too! Do ya know about this convoy to Fort Kearny?

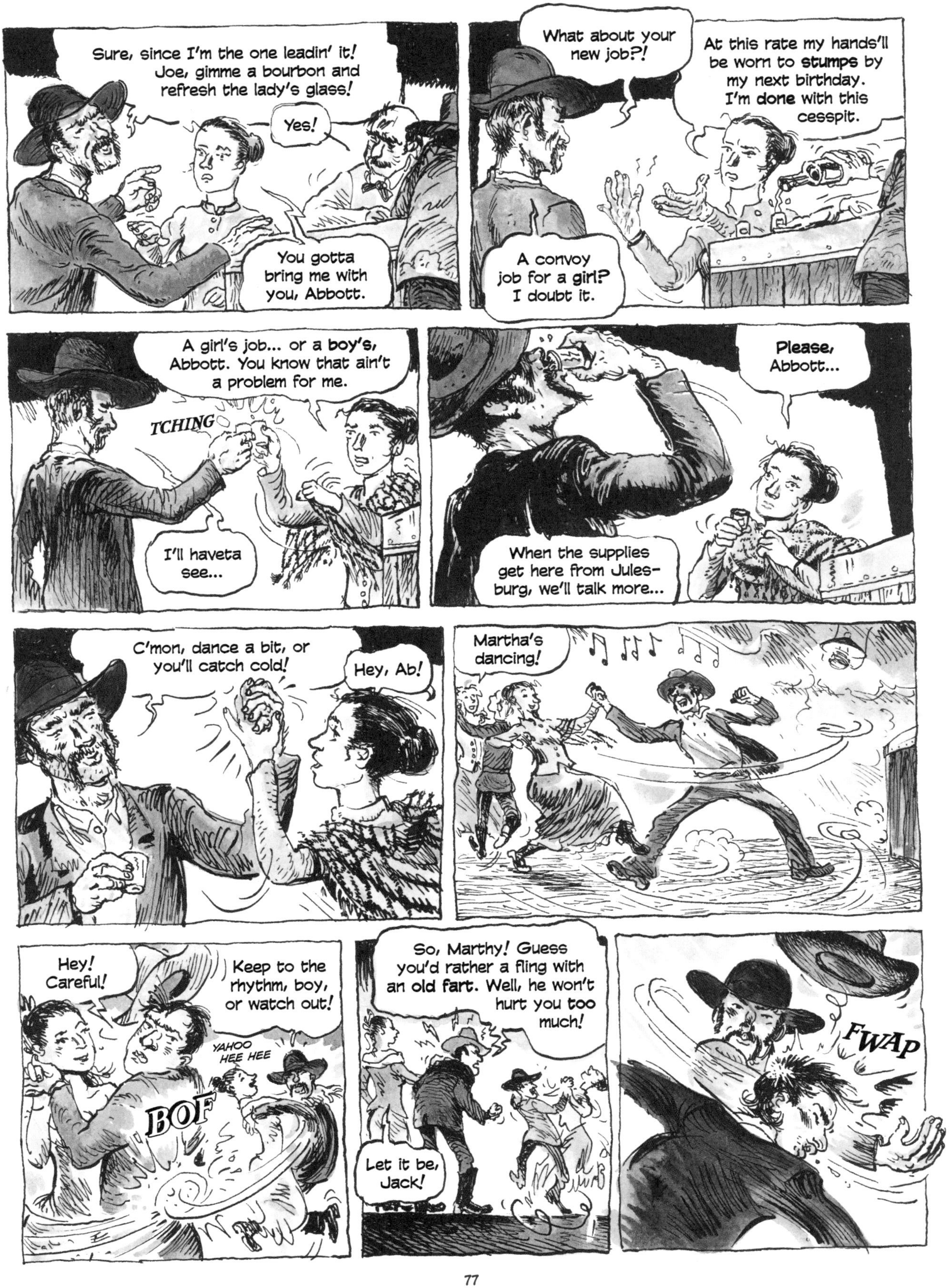
Sure, since I'm the one leadin' it! Joe, gimme a bourbon and refresh the lady's glass!
Yes!
You gotta bring me with you, Abbott.
What about your new job?!
At this rate my hands'll be worn to **stumps** by my next birthday. I'm **done** with this cesspit.
A convoy job for a **girl**? I doubt it.
A girl's job... or a **boy's**, Abbott. You know that ain't a problem for me.
TCHING
I'll haveta see...
Please, Abbott...
When the supplies get here from Julesburg, we'll talk more...
C'mon, dance a bit, or you'll catch cold!
Hey, Ab!
Martha's dancing!
Hey! Careful!
Keep to the rhythm, boy, or watch out!
YAHOO HEE HEE
BOF
So, Marthy! Guess you'd rather a fling with an **old fart**. Well, he won't hurt you **too** much!
Let it be, Jack!
FWAP

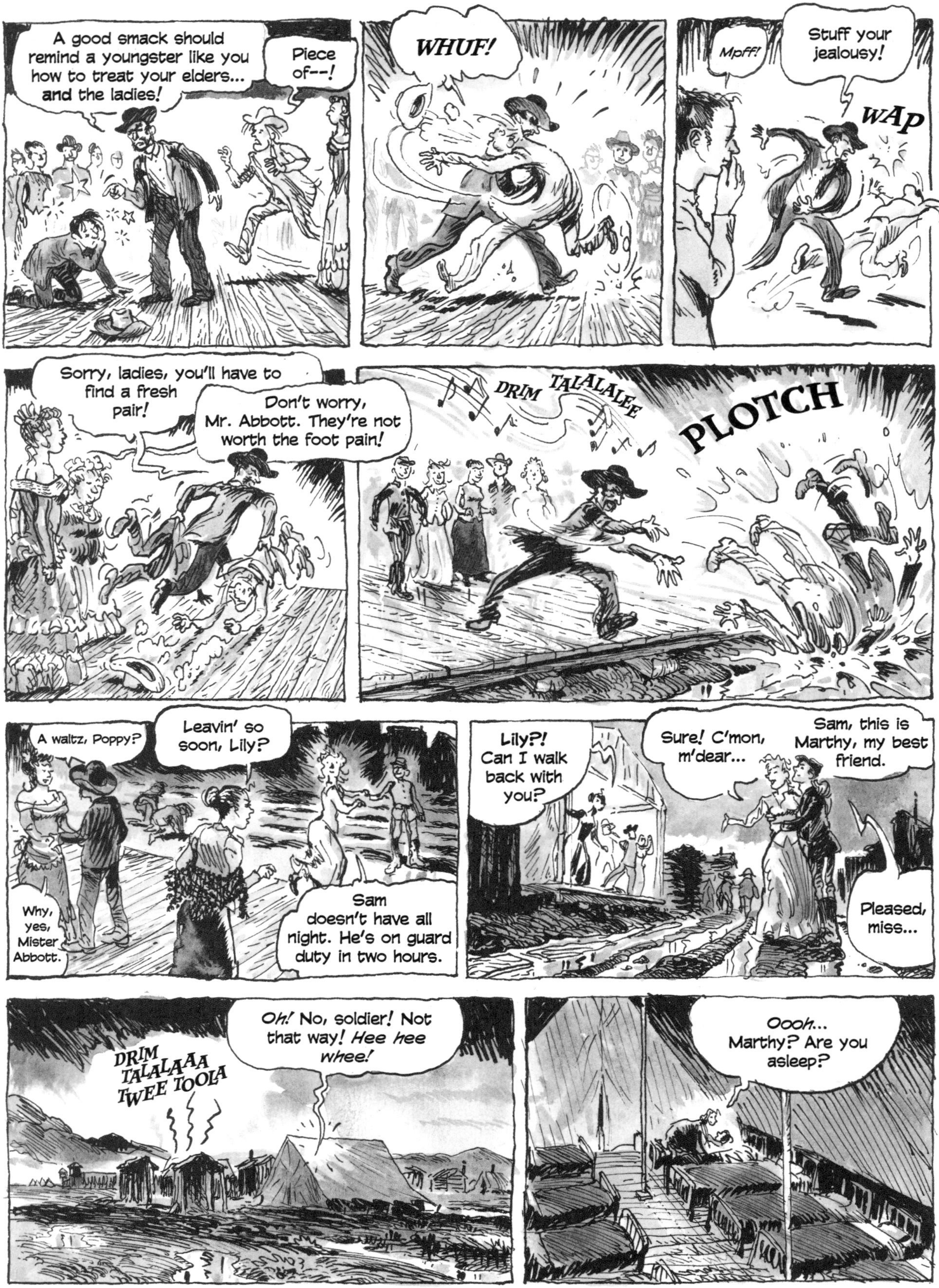
A good smack should remind a youngster like you how to treat your elders... and the ladies!
Piece of--!
WHUF!
Mpff!
Stuff your jealousy!
WAP
Sorry, ladies, you'll have to find a fresh pair!
Don't worry, Mr. Abbott. They're not worth the foot pain!
DRIM TALALALEE
PLOTCH
A waltz, Poppy?
Why, yes, Mister Abbott.
Leavin' so soon, Lily?
Sam doesn't have all night. He's on guard duty in two hours.
Lily?! Can I walk back with you?
Sure! C'mon, m'dear...
Sam, this is Marthy, my best friend.
Pleased, miss...
DRIM TALALAAA TWEE TOOLA
Oh! No, soldier! Not that way! Hee hee whee!
Oooh... Marthy? Are you asleep?

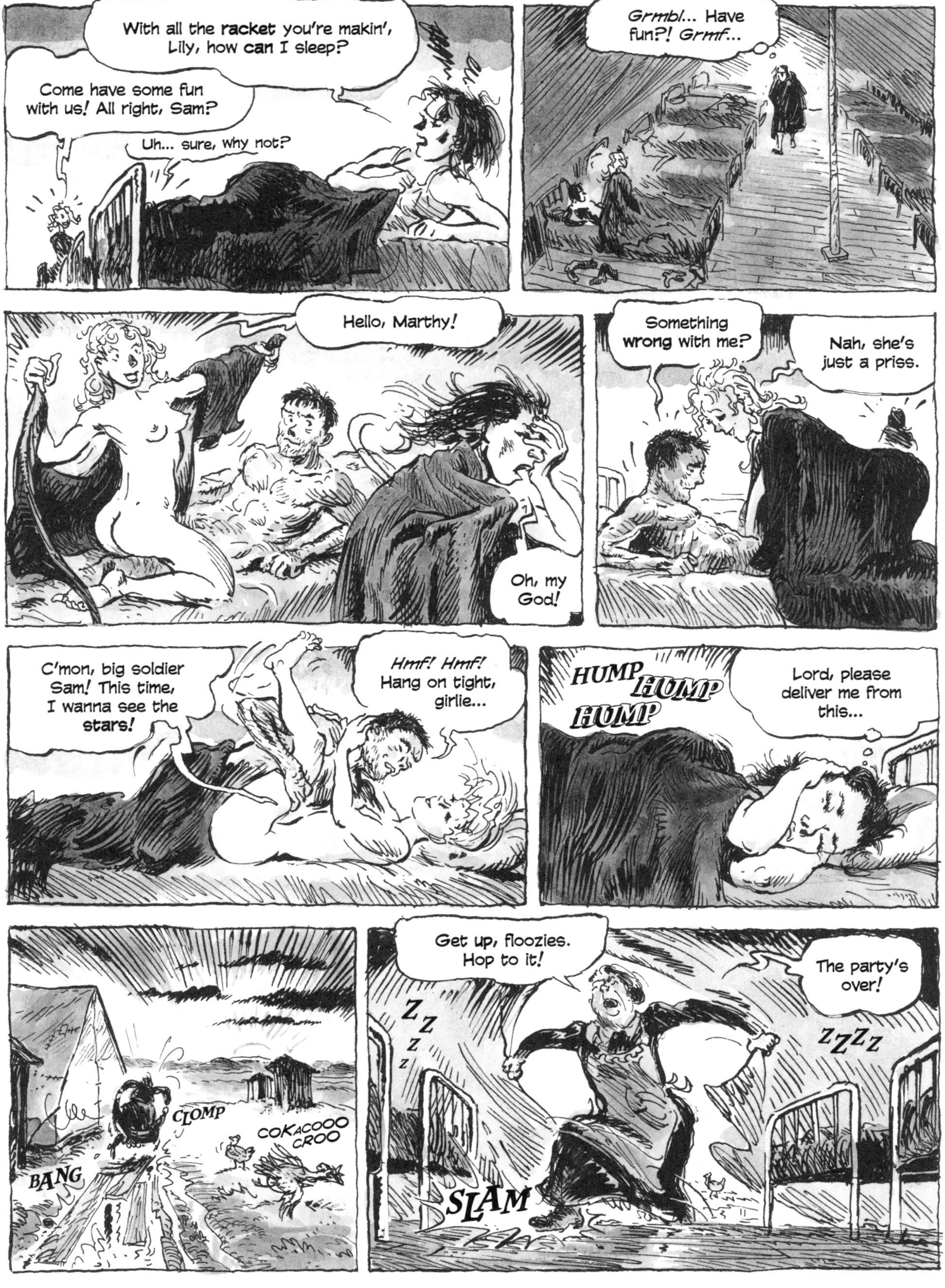
With all the **racket** you're makin', Lily, how **can** I sleep?
Come have some fun with us! All right, Sam?
Uh... sure, why not?
Grmbl... Have fun?! *Grmf*...
Hello, Marthy!
Oh, my God!
Something **wrong** with me?
Nah, she's just a priss.
C'mon, big soldier Sam! This time, I wanna see the **stars**!
Hmf! Hmf! Hang on tight, girlie...
HUMP HUMP HUMP
Lord, please deliver me from this...
CLOMP
COKACOOO CROO
BANG
Get up, floozies. Hop to it!
The party's over!
Z Z Z Z Z
ZZZZ
SLAM

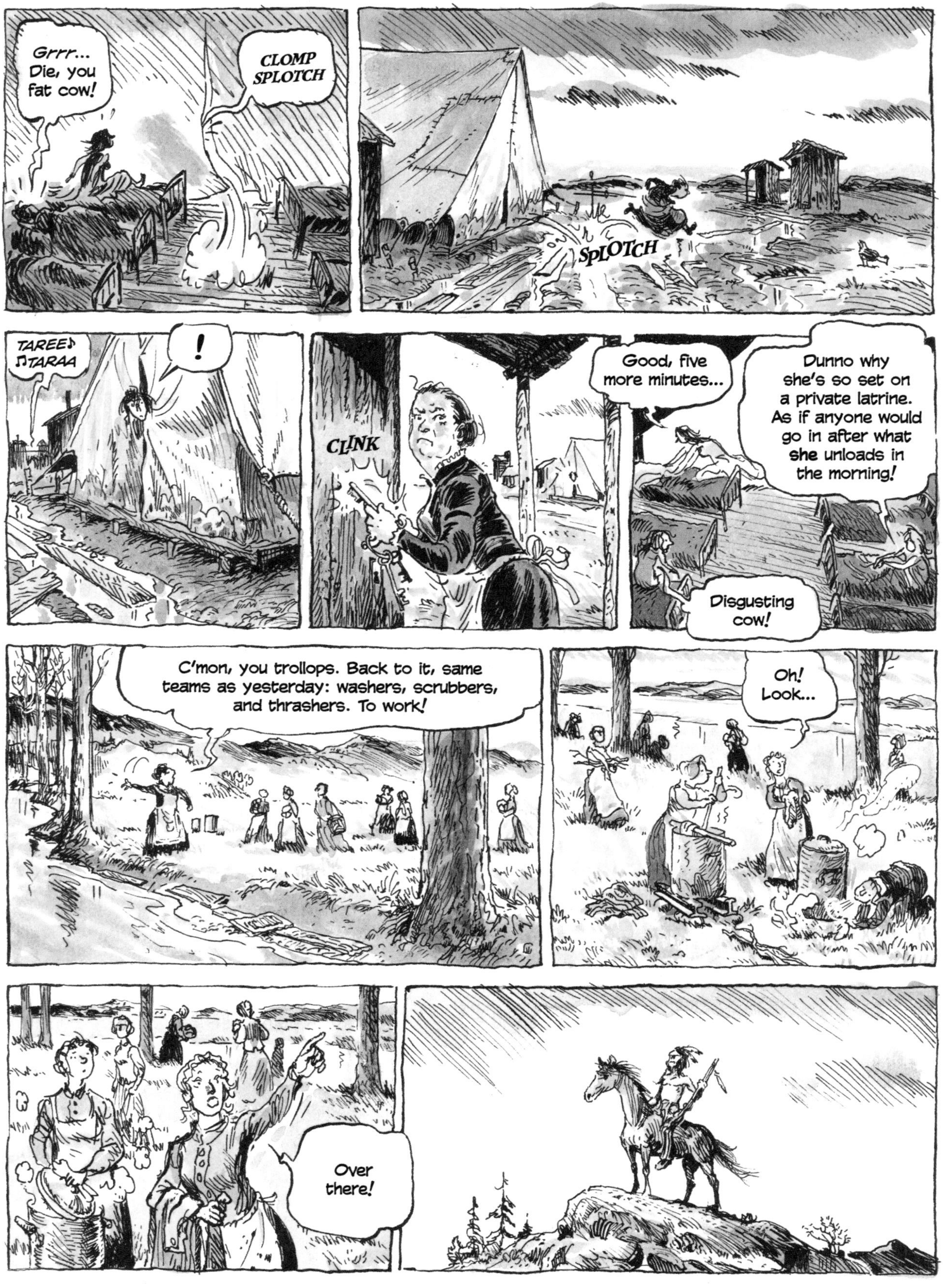

Grrr... Die, you fat cow!
CLOMP SPLOTCH
SPLOTCH
TAREE♪ ♫TARAA
!
CLINK
Good, five more minutes...
Dunno why she's so set on a private latrine. As if anyone would go in after what she unloads in the morning!
Disgusting cow!
C'mon, you trollops. Back to it, same teams as yesterday: washers, scrubbers, and thrashers. To work!
Oh! Look...
Over there!

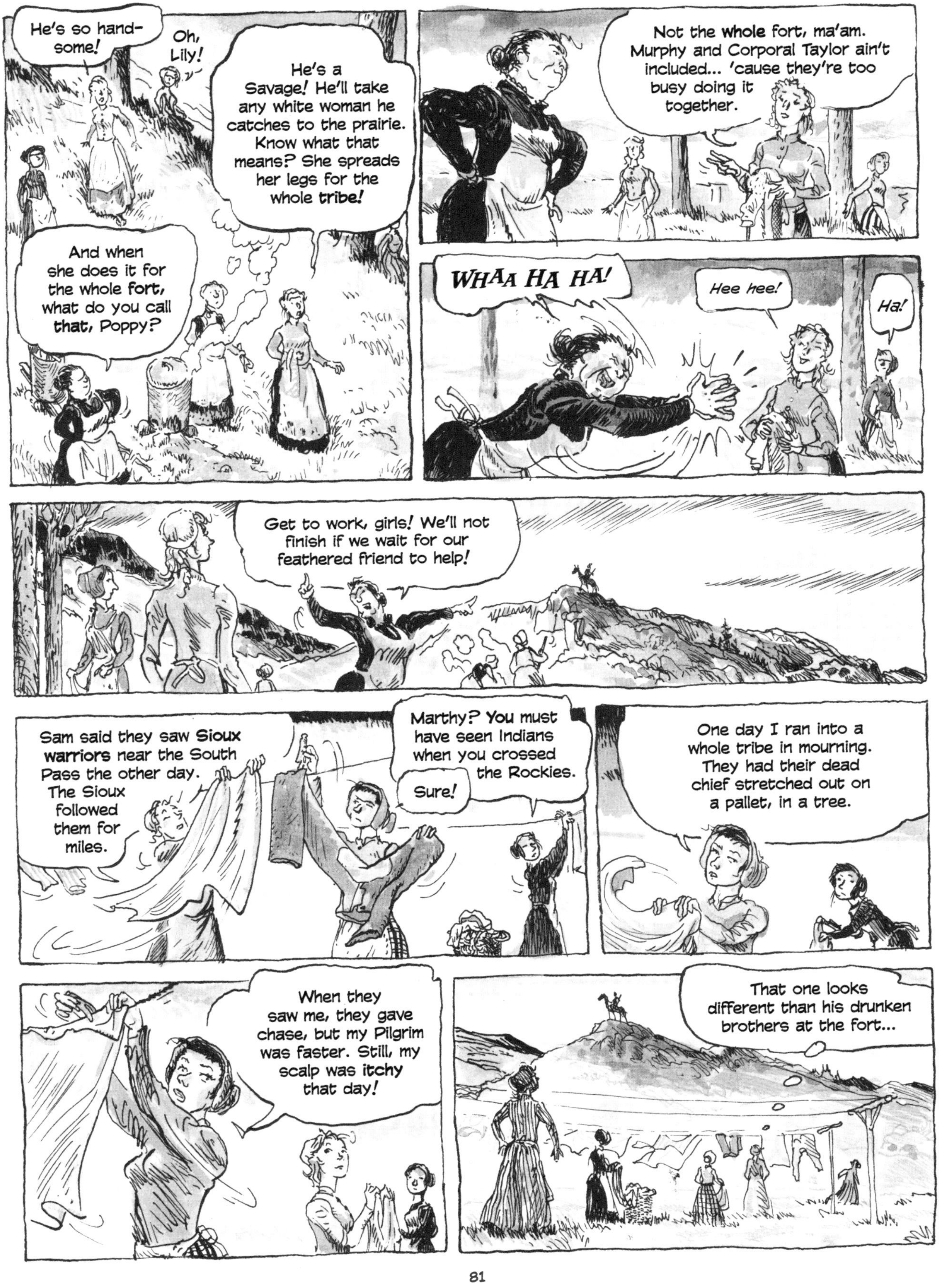
He's so hand-some!
Oh, Lily!
He's a Savage! He'll take any white woman he catches to the prairie. Know what that means? She spreads her legs for the whole tribe!
And when she does it for the whole fort, what do you call that, Poppy?
Not the whole fort, ma'am. Murphy and Corporal Taylor ain't included... 'cause they're too busy doing it together.
WHAA HA HA!
Hee hee!
Ha!
Get to work, girls! We'll not finish if we wait for our feathered friend to help!
Sam said they saw Sioux warriors near the South Pass the other day. The Sioux followed them for miles.
Marthy? You must have seen Indians when you crossed the Rockies.
Sure!
One day I ran into a whole tribe in mourning. They had their dead chief stretched out on a pallet, in a tree.
When they saw me, they gave chase, but my Pilgrim was faster. Still, my scalp was itchy that day!
That one looks different than his drunken brothers at the fort...

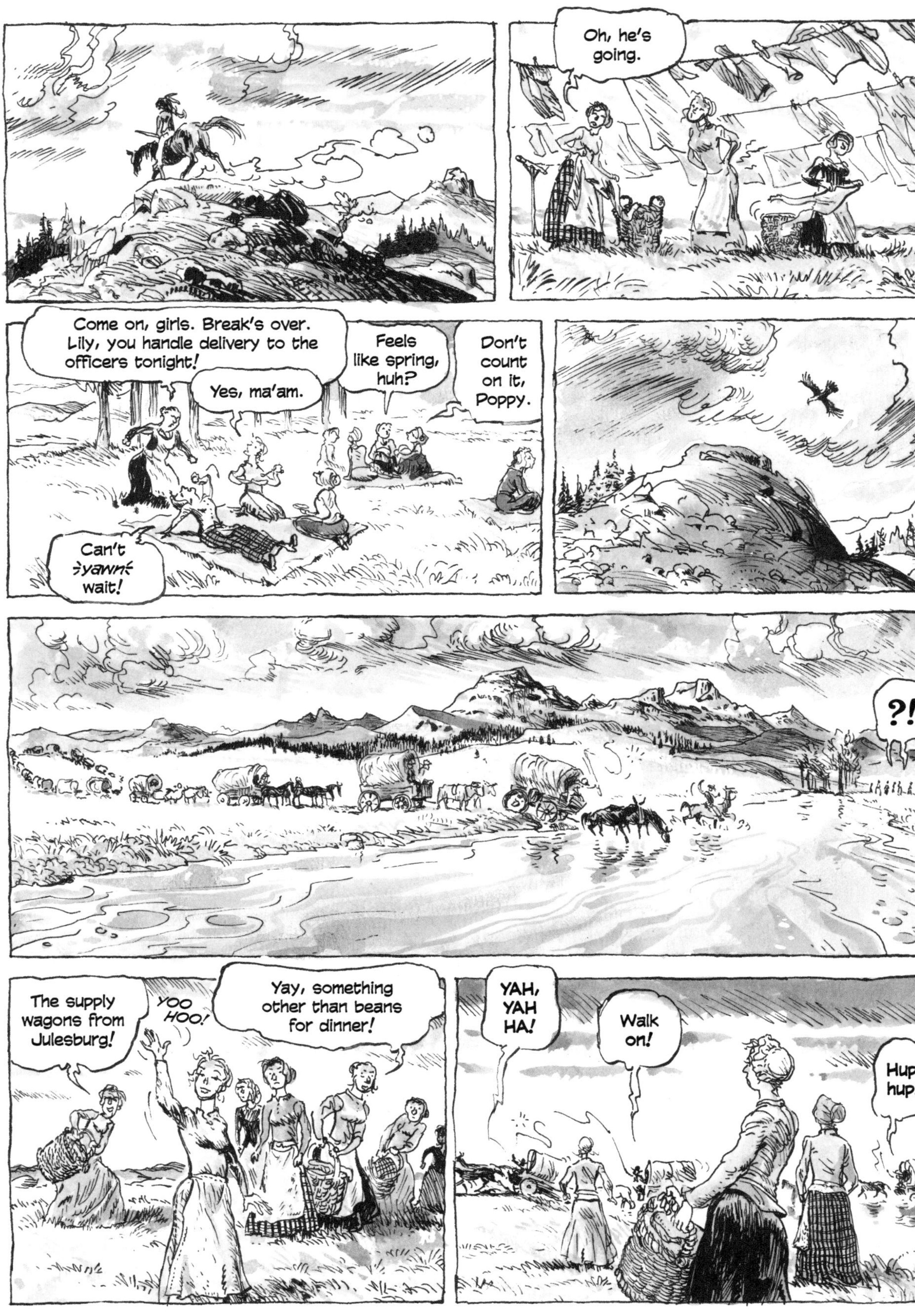

Oh, he's going.
Come on, girls. Break's over. Lily, you handle delivery to the officers tonight!
Yes, ma'am.
Feels like spring, huh?
Don't count on it, Poppy.
Can't ⸗yawn⸗ wait!
?!
The supply wagons from Julesburg!
YOO HOO!
Yay, something other than beans for dinner!
YAH, YAH HA!
Walk on!
Hup, hup!

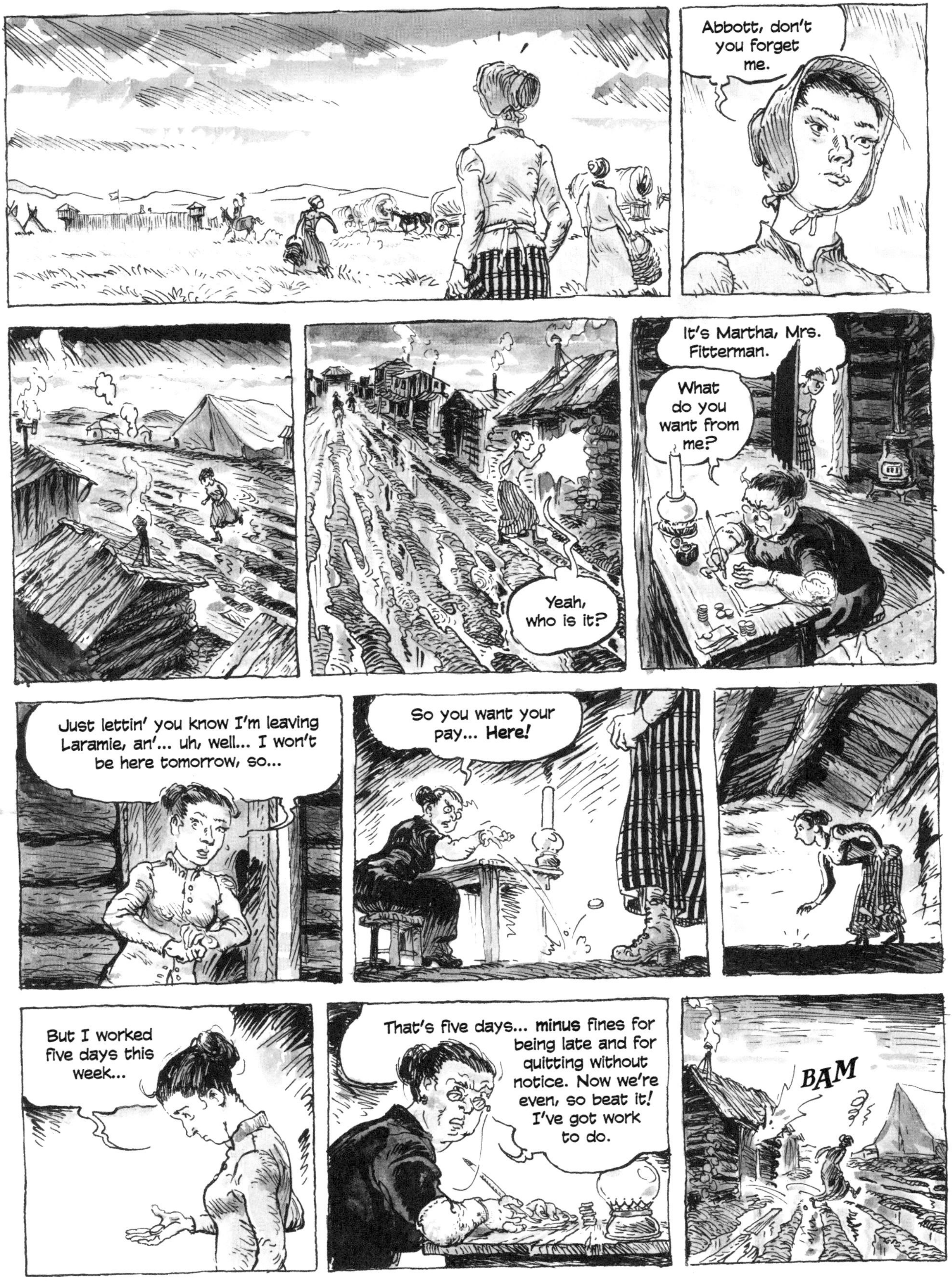

Abbott, don't you forget me.
It's Martha, Mrs. Fitterman.
Yeah, who is it?
What do you want from me?
Just lettin' you know I'm leaving Laramie, an'... uh, well... I won't be here tomorrow, so...
So you want your pay... **Here!**
But I worked five days this week...
That's five days... **minus** fines for being late and for quitting without notice. Now we're even, so beat it! I've got work to do.
BAM

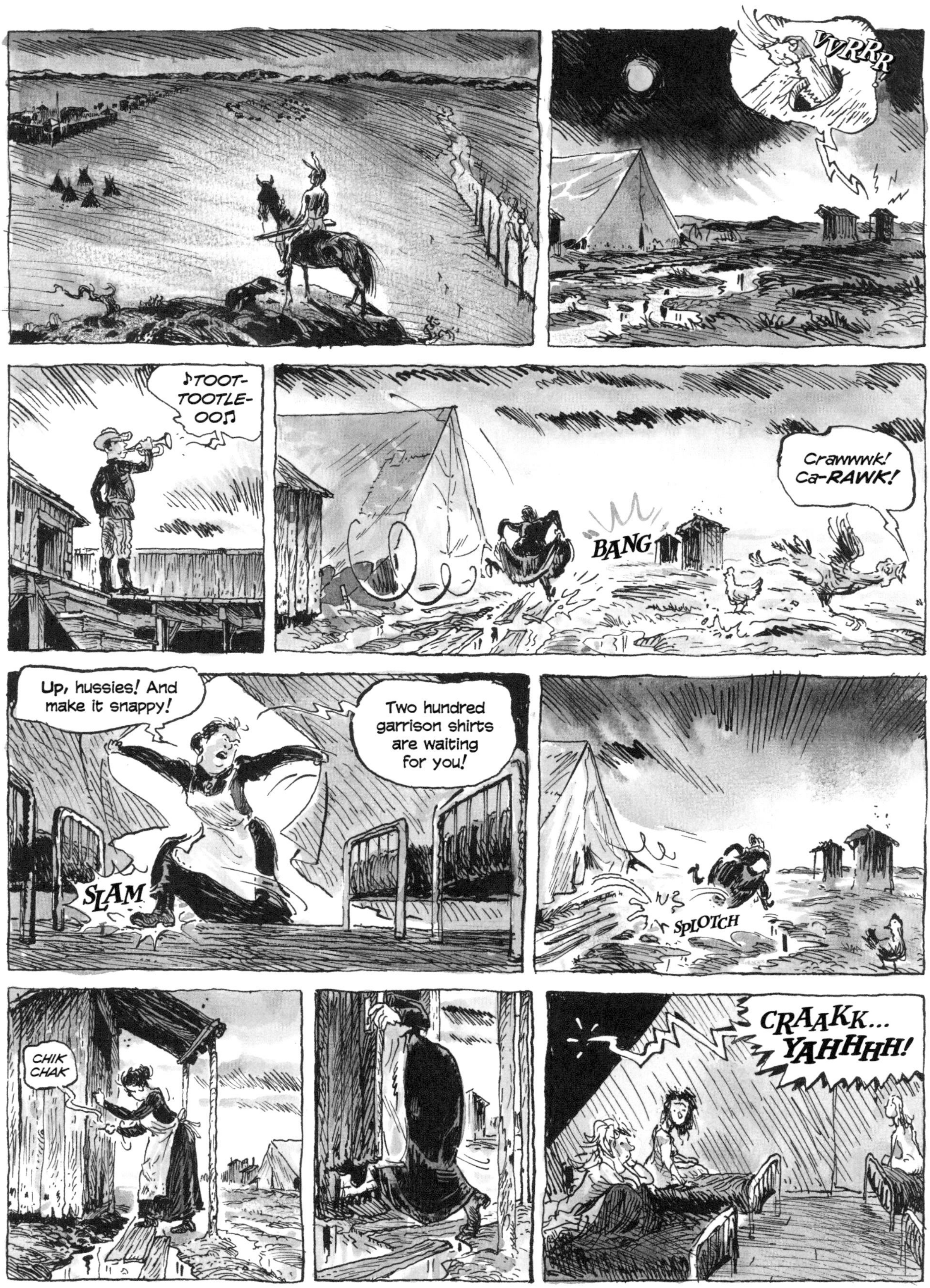
VVRRR
♪TOOT-TOOTLE-OO♫
Crawwwk! Ca-RAWK!
BANG
Up, hussies! And make it snappy!
Two hundred garrison shirts are waiting for you!
SLAM
SPLOTCH
CHIK CHAK
CRAAKK... YAHHHH!

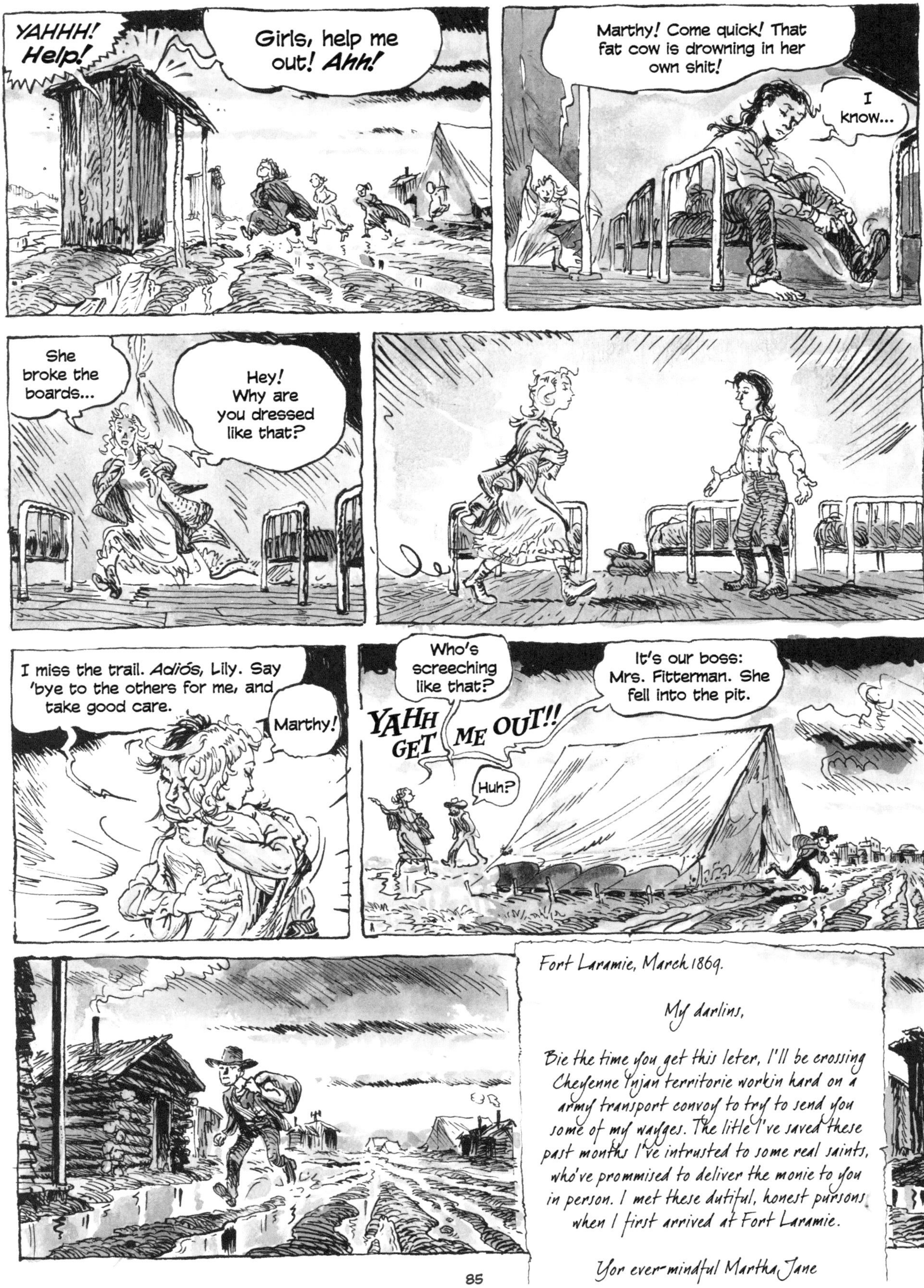
YAHHH! Help!
Girls, help me out! Ahh!
Marthy! Come quick! That fat cow is drowning in her own shit!
I know...
She broke the boards...
Hey! Why are you dressed like that?
I miss the trail. Adiós, Lily. Say 'bye to the others for me, and take good care.
Marthy!
Who's screeching like that?
It's our boss: Mrs. Fitterman. She fell into the pit.
YAHH GET ME OUT!!
Huh?
Fort Laramie, March 1869.
My darlins,
Bie the time you get this leter, I'll be crossing Cheyenne Injan territorie workin hard on a army transport convoy to try to send you some of my wayges. The litle I've saved these past months I've intrusted to some real saints, who've prommised to deliver the monie to you in person. I met these dutiful, honest pursons when I first arrived at Fort Laramie.
Yor ever-mindful Martha Jane

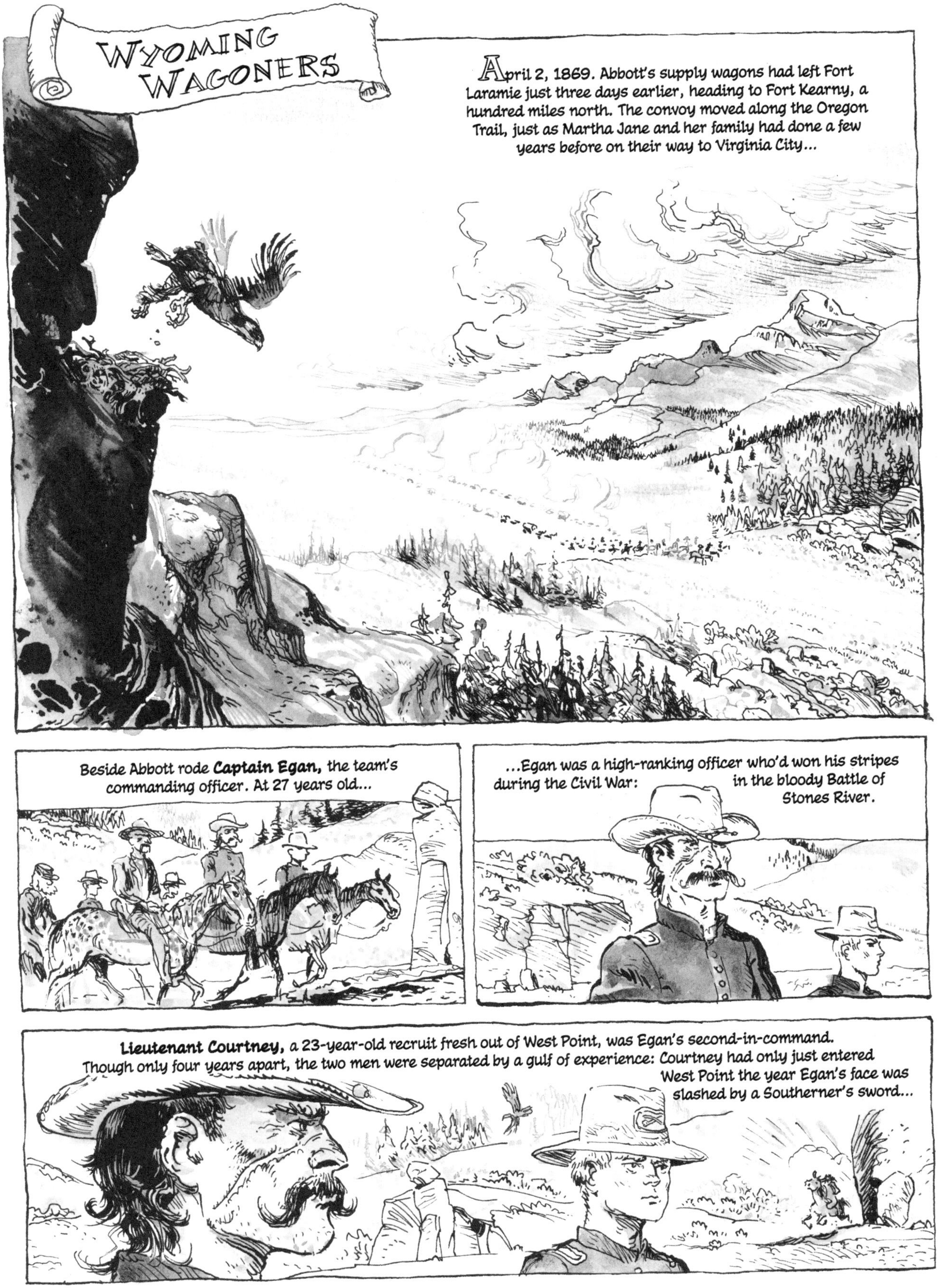
Wyoming Wagoners
April 2, 1869. Abbott's supply wagons had left Fort Laramie just three days earlier, heading to Fort Kearny, a hundred miles north. The convoy moved along the Oregon Trail, just as Martha Jane and her family had done a few years before on their way to Virginia City...
Beside Abbott rode **Captain Egan,** the team's commanding officer. At 27 years old...
...Egan was a high-ranking officer who'd won his stripes during the Civil War:
in the bloody Battle of Stones River.
Lieutenant Courtney, a 23-year-old recruit fresh out of West Point, was Egan's second-in-command. Though only four years apart, the two men were separated by a gulf of experience: Courtney had only just entered West Point the year Egan's face was slashed by a Southerner's sword...

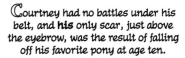

Courtney had no battles under his belt, and **his** only scar, just above the eyebrow, was the result of falling off his favorite pony at age ten.

Arapaho!

So...?

Tawny Owl saw tracks: eight horses, maybe more. Arapaho for sure in these parts, but nothin' ta fear from **them**.

The handful of men behind Egan belonged to the legendary 18th Cavalry Regiment. Their average age was 21, not counting Sgt. Whitaker, who claimed to be 42...

Lt. Courtney's pretty spooked by the scout...

Tawny Owl is his "first" Indian. That's always daunting!

Keep up that palaver, rookies! We'll be talkin' about Indians again soon, by George, **real** ones!

Wah... ahh... **aahhh!**

Walk! Walk! Walk on, ya blasted mules!

WHAK

In the lead: the ambulance wagon, transporting officers' wives...

God almighty, Mrs. Egan, do something!

Wahh! Wanna stop! **Wahhh!**

Shh... ♫Rock-a-bye, baby...♪

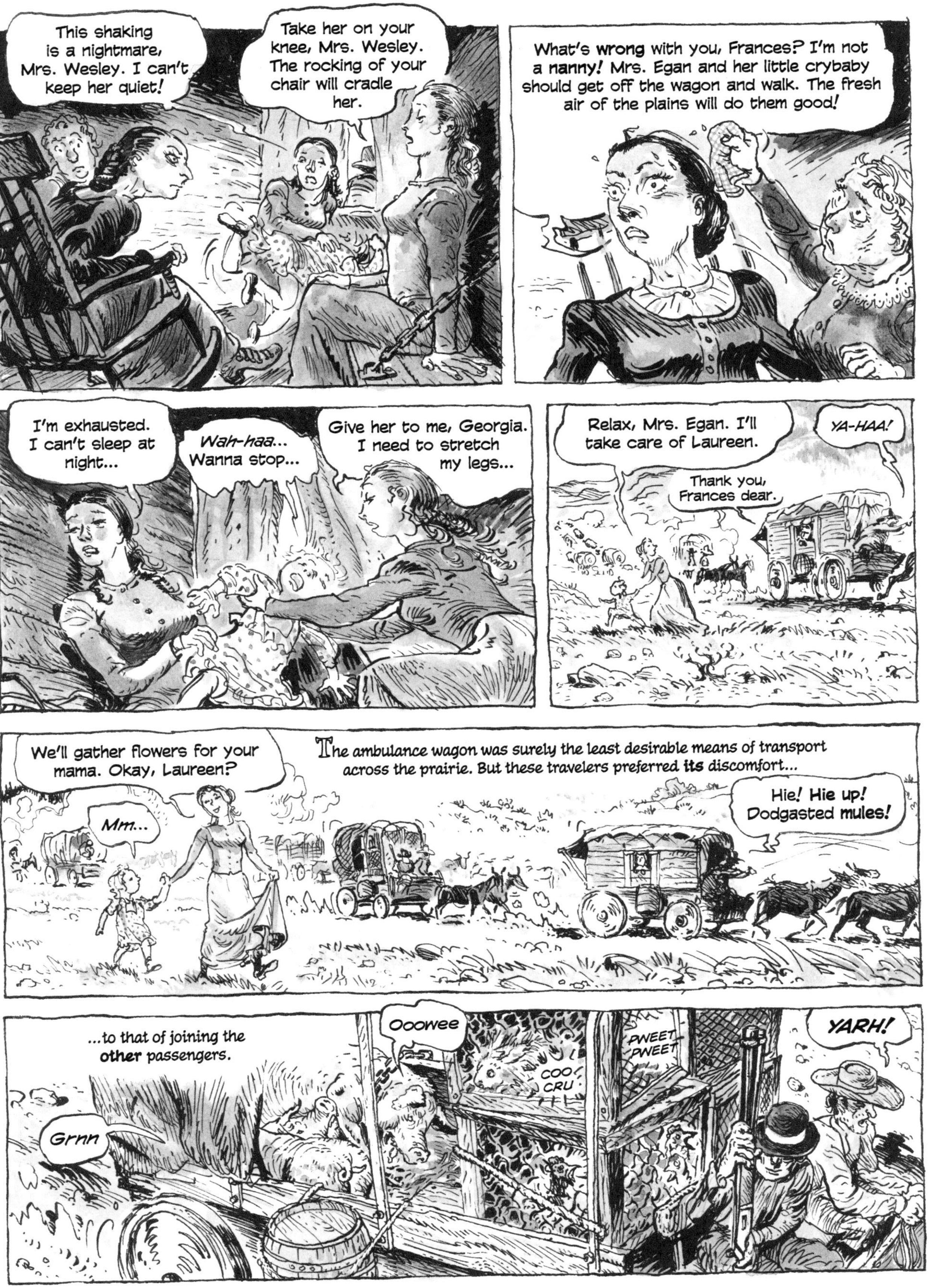
This shaking is a nightmare, Mrs. Wesley. I can't keep her quiet!
Take her on your knee, Mrs. Wesley. The rocking of your chair will cradle her.
What's wrong with you, Frances? I'm not a nanny! Mrs. Egan and her little crybaby should get off the wagon and walk. The fresh air of the plains will do them good!
I'm exhausted. I can't sleep at night...
Wah-haa... Wanna stop...
Give her to me, Georgia. I need to stretch my legs...
Relax, Mrs. Egan. I'll take care of Laureen.
YA-HAA!
Thank you, Frances dear.
We'll gather flowers for your mama. Okay, Laureen?
The ambulance wagon was surely the least desirable means of transport across the prairie. But these travelers preferred its discomfort...
Mm...
Hie! Hie up! Dodgasted mules!
...to that of joining the other passengers.
Ooowee
PWEET PWEET
COO CRU
YARH!
Grnn

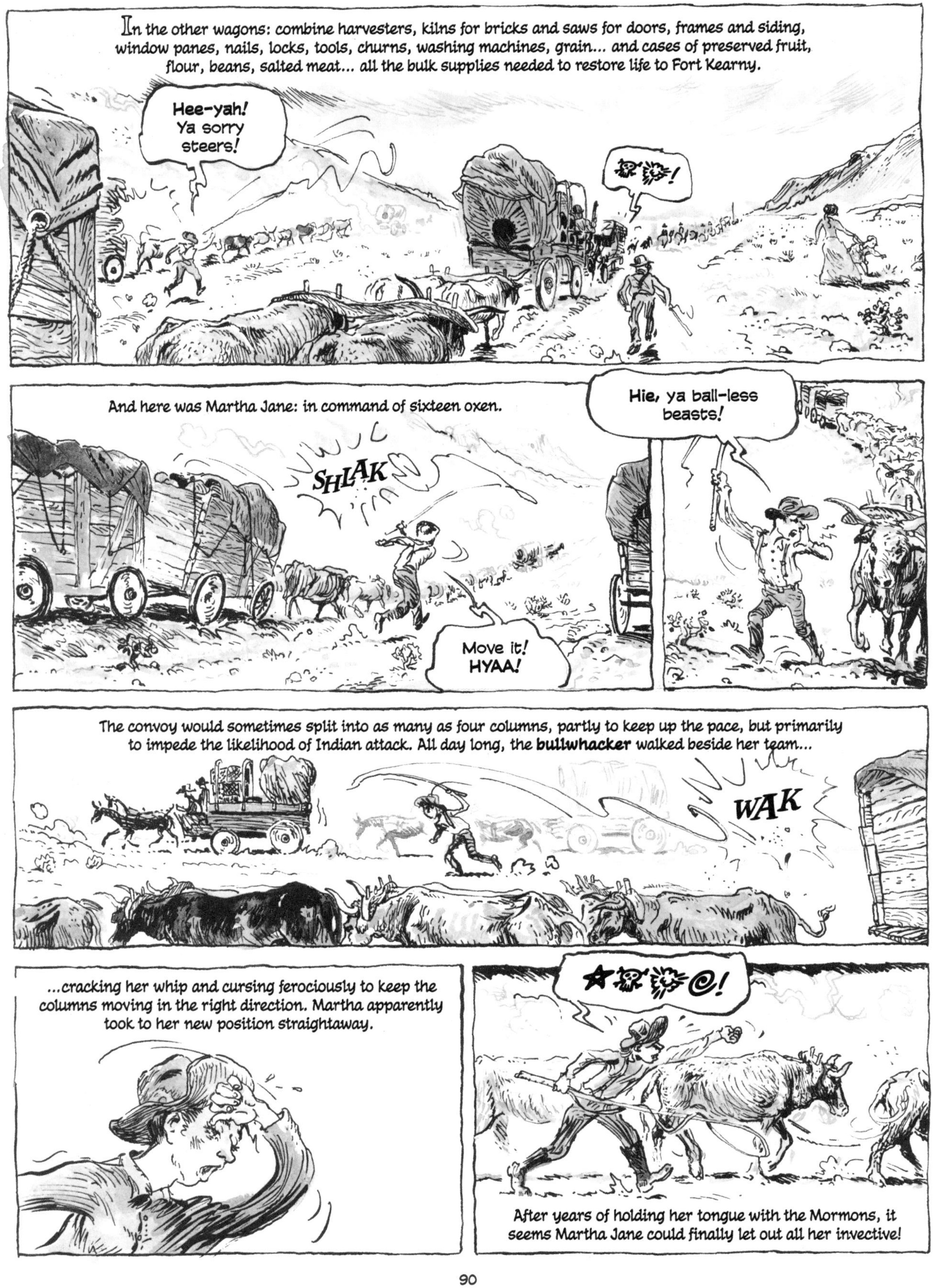
In the other wagons: combine harvesters, kilns for bricks and saws for doors, frames and siding, window panes, nails, locks, tools, churns, washing machines, grain... and cases of preserved fruit, flour, beans, salted meat... all the bulk supplies needed to restore life to Fort Kearny.
Hee-yah! Ya sorry steers!
And here was Martha Jane: in command of sixteen oxen.
SHLAK
Move it! HYAA!
Hie, ya ball-less beasts!
The convoy would sometimes split into as many as four columns, partly to keep up the pace, but primarily to impede the likelihood of Indian attack. All day long, the **bullwhacker** walked beside her team...
WAK
...cracking her whip and cursing ferociously to keep the columns moving in the right direction. Martha apparently took to her new position straightaway.
After years of holding her tongue with the Mormons, it seems Martha Jane could finally let out all her invective!

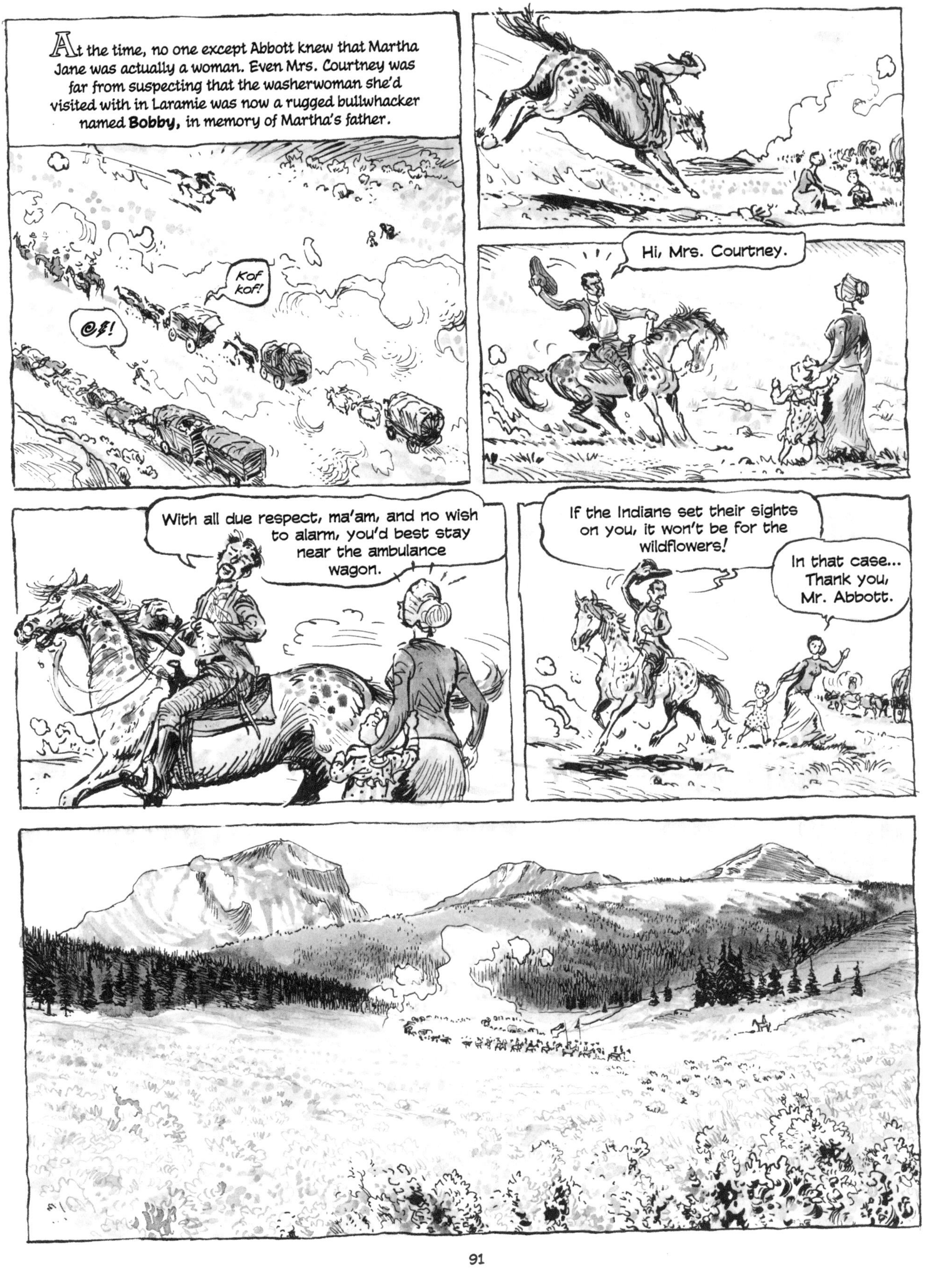
At the time, no one except Abbott knew that Martha Jane was actually a woman. Even Mrs. Courtney was far from suspecting that the washerwoman she'd visited with in Laramie was now a rugged bullwhacker named **Bobby,** in memory of Martha's father.
Kof kof!
@⚡!
Hi, Mrs. Courtney.
With all due respect, ma'am, and no wish to alarm, you'd best stay near the ambulance wagon.
If the Indians set their sights on you, it won't be for the wildflowers!
In that case... Thank you, Mr. Abbott.

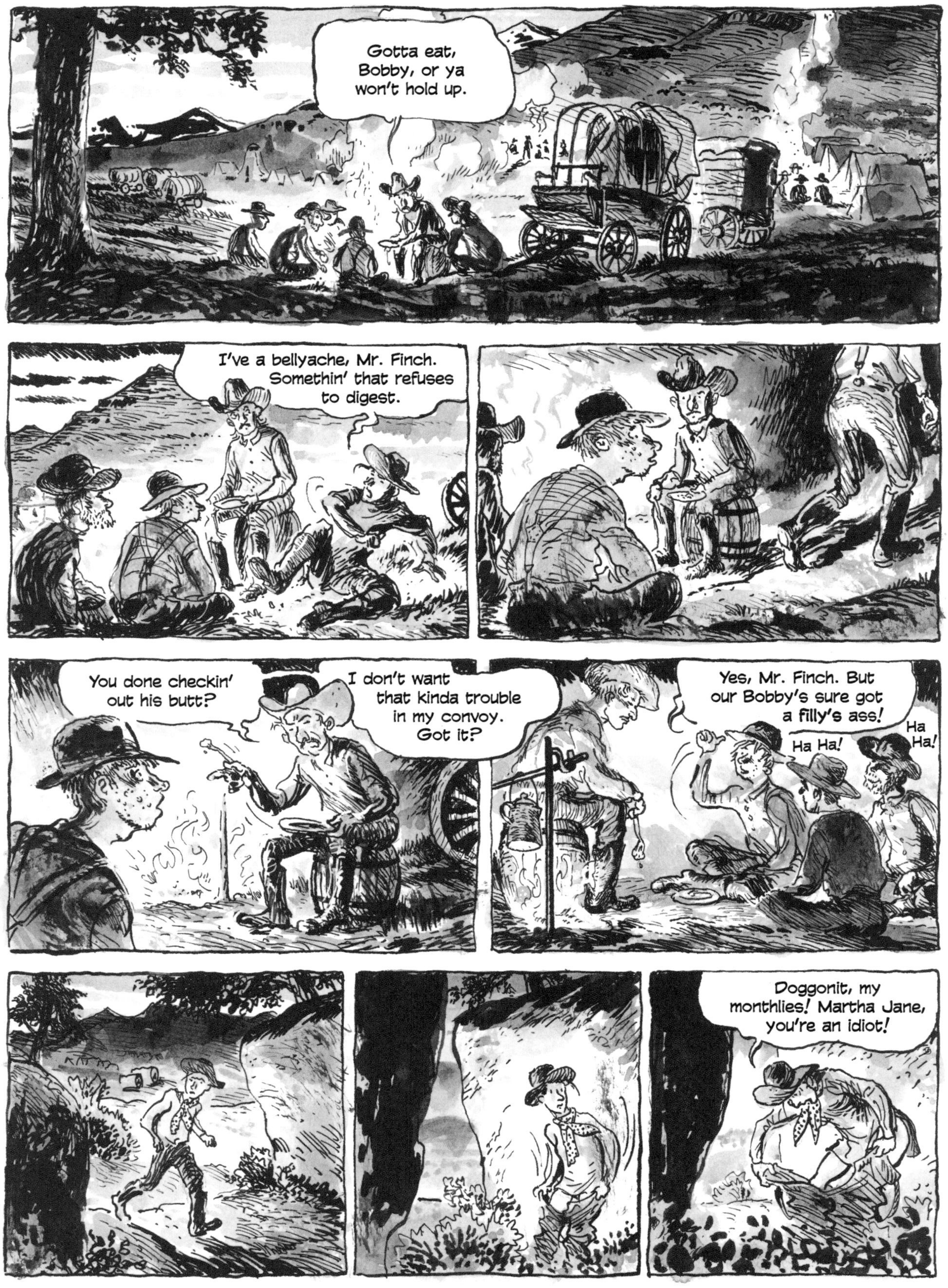

Gotta eat, Bobby, or ya won't hold up.
I've a bellyache, Mr. Finch. Somethin' that refuses to digest.
You done checkin' out his butt?
I don't want that kinda trouble in my convoy. Got it?
Yes, Mr. Finch. But our Bobby's sure got a filly's ass!
Ha Ha!
Ha Ha!
Doggonit, my monthlies! Martha Jane, you're an idiot!

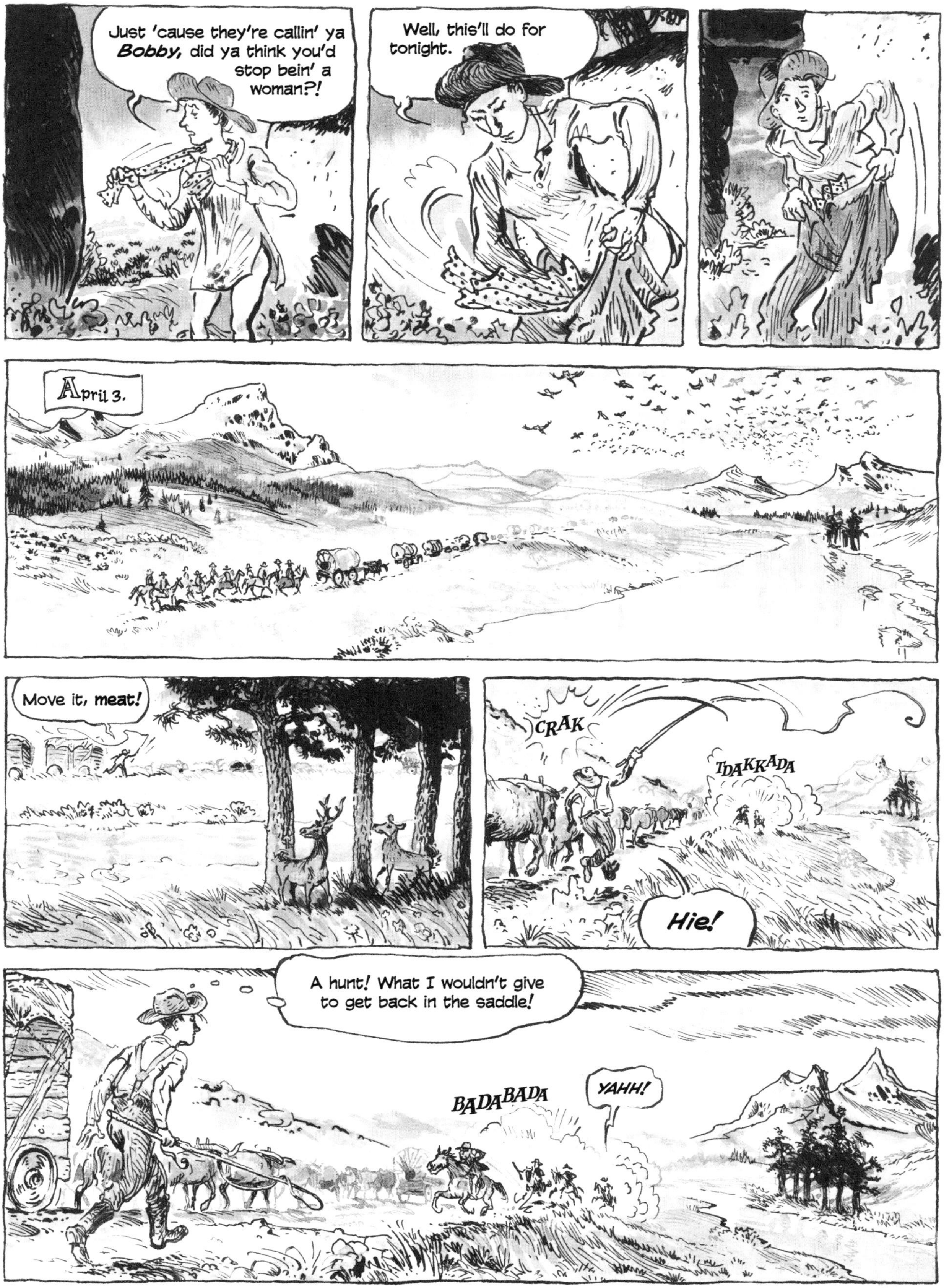

Just 'cause they're callin' ya *Bobby,* did ya think you'd stop bein' a woman?!
Well, this'll do for tonight.
April 3.
Move it, **meat!**
CRAK
TDAKKADA
Hie!
A hunt! What I wouldn't give to get back in the saddle!
BADABADA
YAHH!

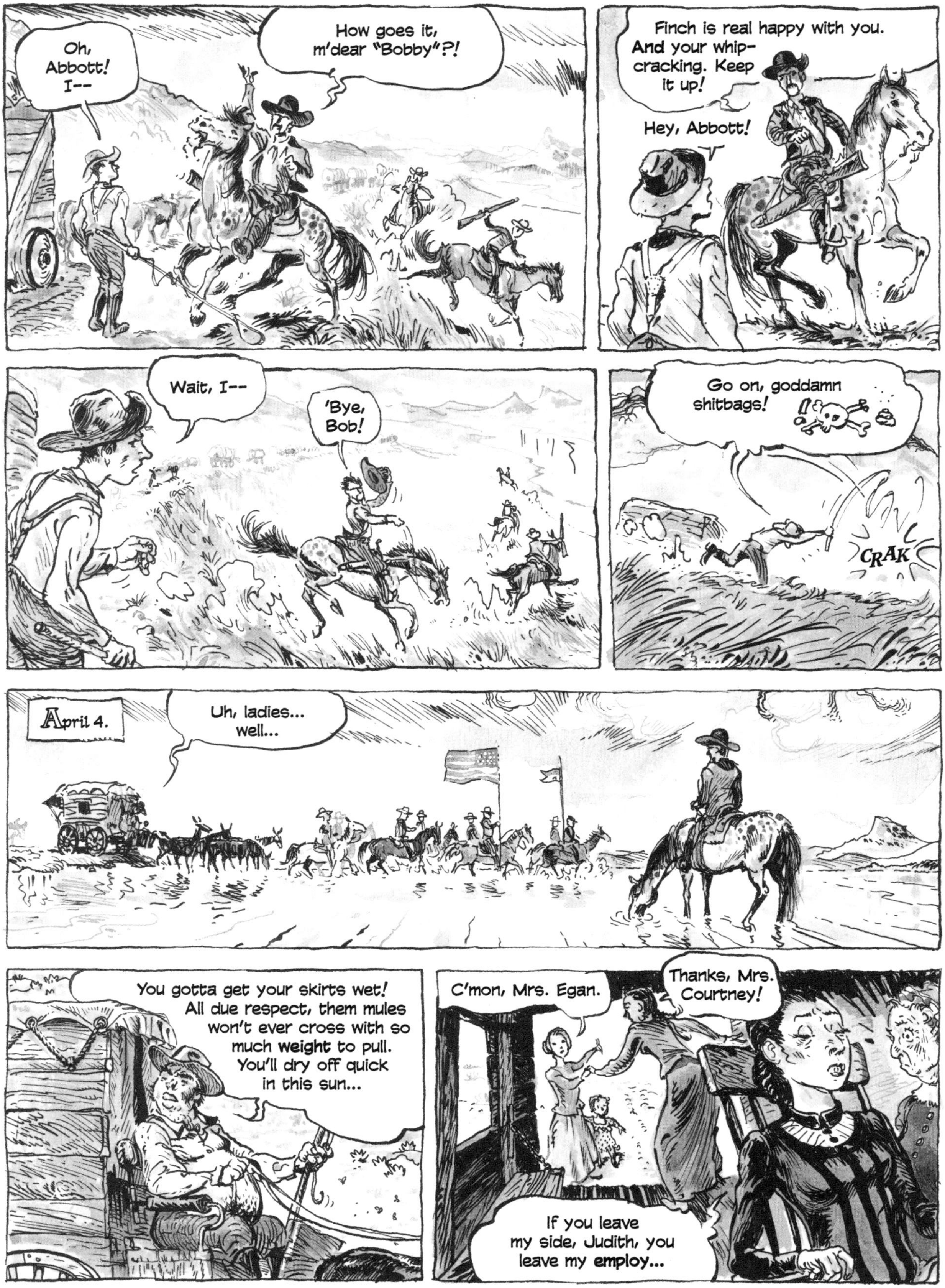
Oh, Abbott! I--
How goes it, m'dear "Bobby"?!
Finch is real happy with you. And your whip-cracking. Keep it up!
Hey, Abbott!
Wait, I--
'Bye, Bob!
Go on, goddamn shitbags!
CRAK
April 4.
Uh, ladies... well...
You gotta get your skirts wet! All due respect, them mules won't ever cross with so much weight to pull. You'll dry off quick in this sun...
C'mon, Mrs. Egan.
Thanks, Mrs. Courtney!
If you leave my side, Judith, you leave my employ...

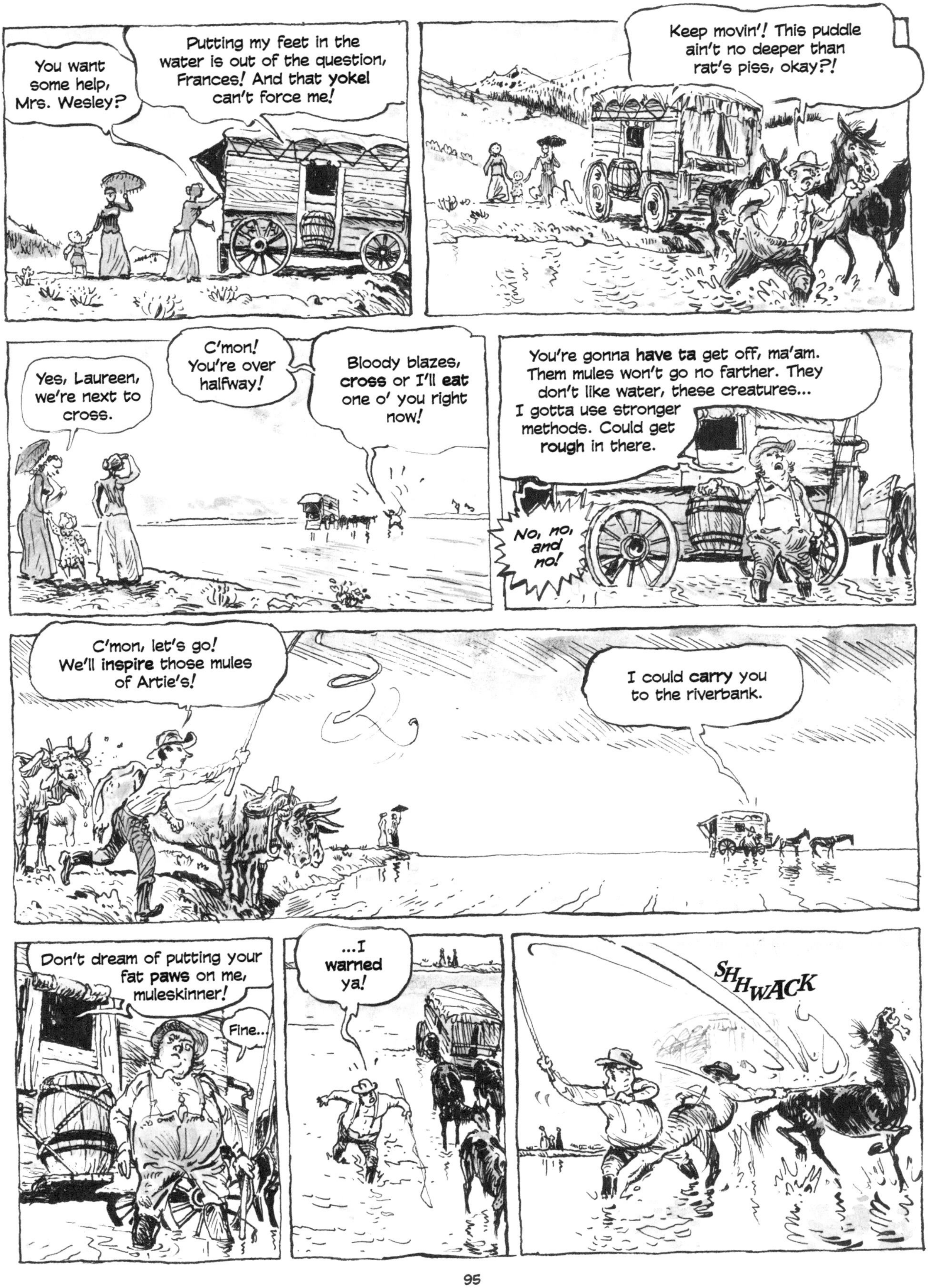
You want some help, Mrs. Wesley?
Putting my feet in the water is out of the question, Frances! And that **yokel** can't force me!
Keep movin'! This puddle ain't no deeper than rat's piss, okay?!
Yes, Laureen, we're next to cross.
C'mon! You're over halfway!
Bloody blazes, **cross** or I'll **eat** one o' you right now!
You're gonna **have ta** get off, ma'am. Them mules won't go no farther. They don't like water, these creatures... I gotta use stronger methods. Could get **rough** in there.
No, no, and no!
C'mon, let's go! We'll **inspire** those mules of Artie's!
I could **carry** you to the riverbank.
Don't dream of putting your fat **paws** on me, muleskinner!
Fine...
...I **warned** ya!
SHHWACK

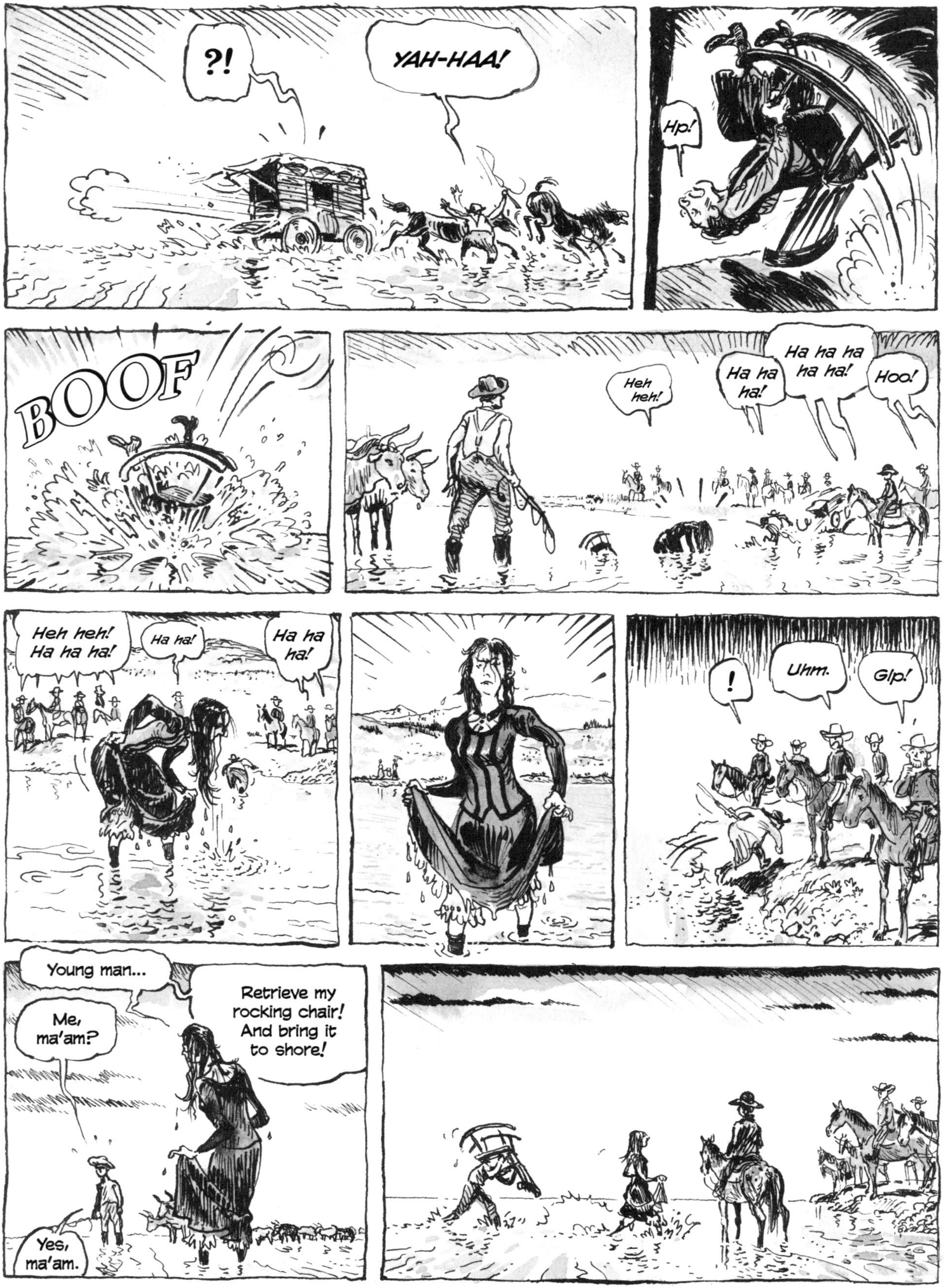
?!
YAH-HAA!
Hp!
BOOF
Heh heh!
Ha ha ha!
Ha ha ha ha ha!
Hoo!
Heh heh! Ha ha ha!
Ha ha!
Ha ha ha!
!
Uhm.
Glp!
Young man...
Me, ma'am?
Retrieve my rocking chair! And bring it to shore!
Yes, ma'am.

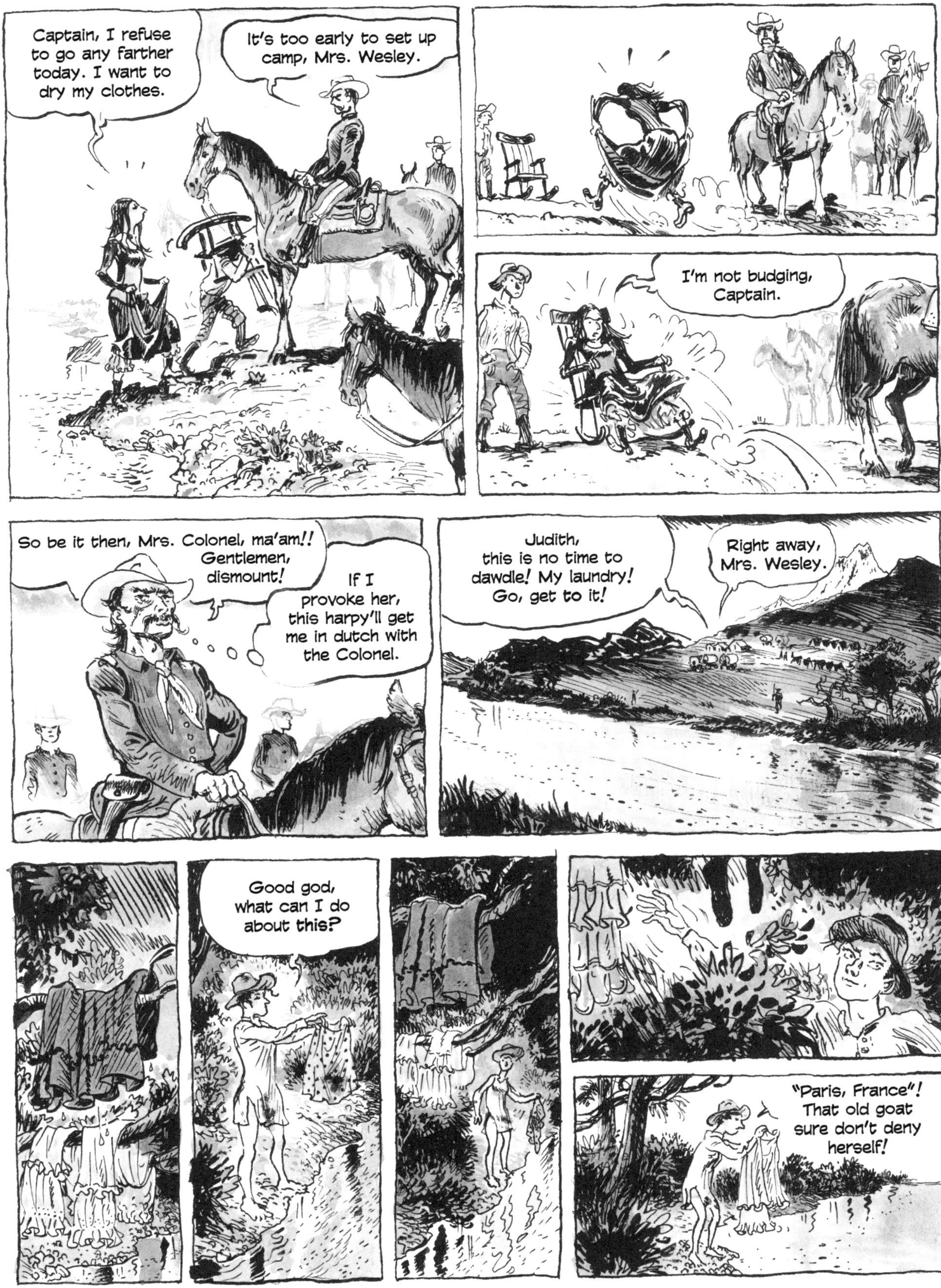
Captain, I refuse to go any farther today. I want to dry my clothes.
It's too early to set up camp, Mrs. Wesley.
I'm not budging, Captain.
So be it then, Mrs. Colonel, ma'am!! Gentlemen, dismount!
If I provoke her, this harpy'll get me in dutch with the Colonel.
Judith, this is no time to dawdle! My laundry! Go, get to it!
Right away, Mrs. Wesley.
Good god, what can I do about this?
"Paris, France"! That old goat sure don't deny herself!

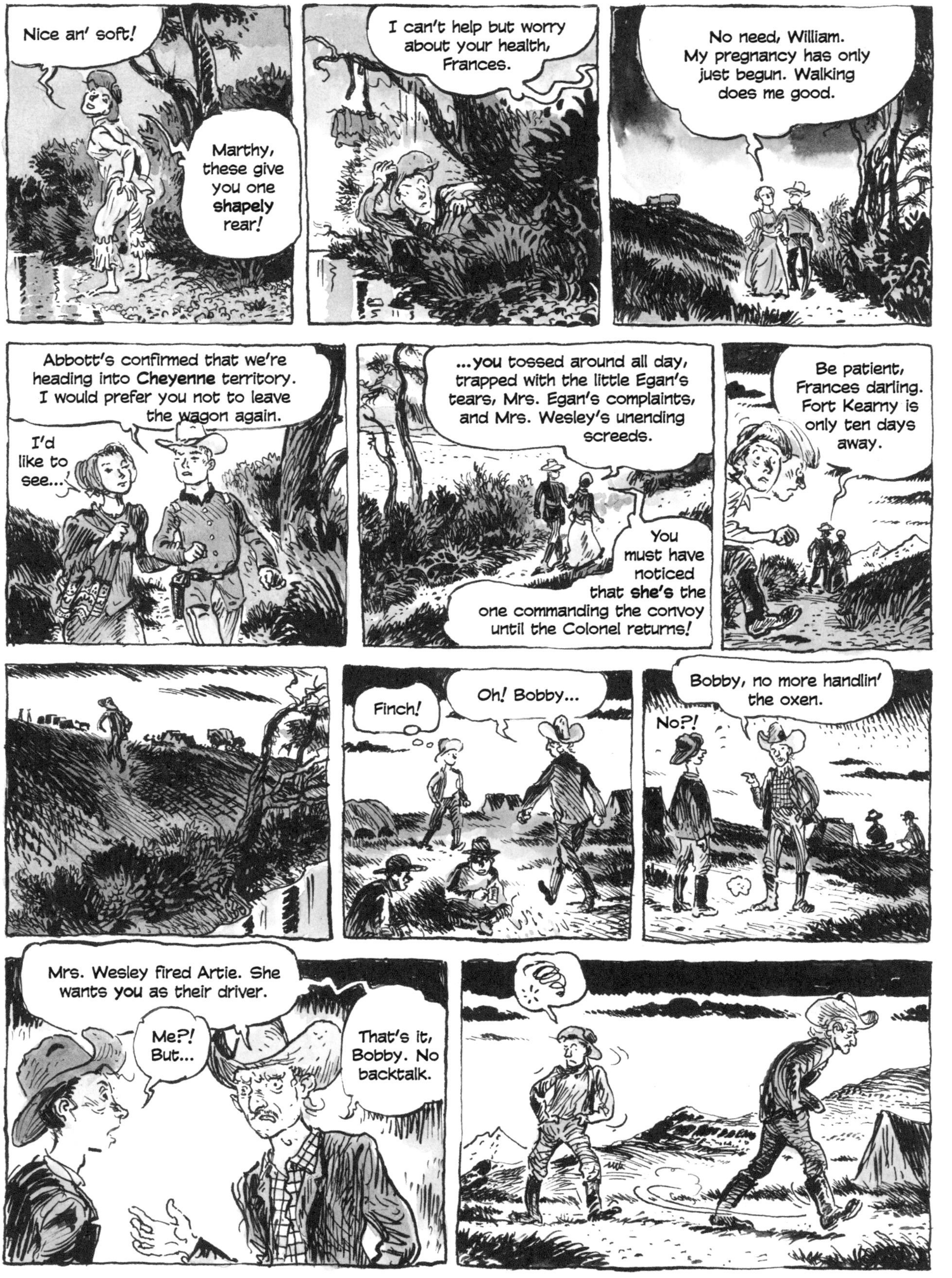

Nice an' soft!
Marthy, these give you one **shapely** rear!
I can't help but worry about your health, Frances.
No need, William. My pregnancy has only just begun. Walking does me good.
Abbott's confirmed that we're heading into **Cheyenne** territory. I would prefer you not to leave the wagon again.
I'd like to see...
...you tossed around all day, trapped with the little Egan's tears, Mrs. Egan's complaints, and Mrs. Wesley's unending screeds.
You must have noticed that **she's** the one commanding the convoy until the Colonel returns!
Be patient, Frances darling. Fort Kearny is only ten days away.
Finch!
Oh! Bobby...
Bobby, no more handlin' the oxen.
No?!
Mrs. Wesley fired Artie. She wants **you** as their driver.
Me?! But...
That's it, Bobby. No backtalk.

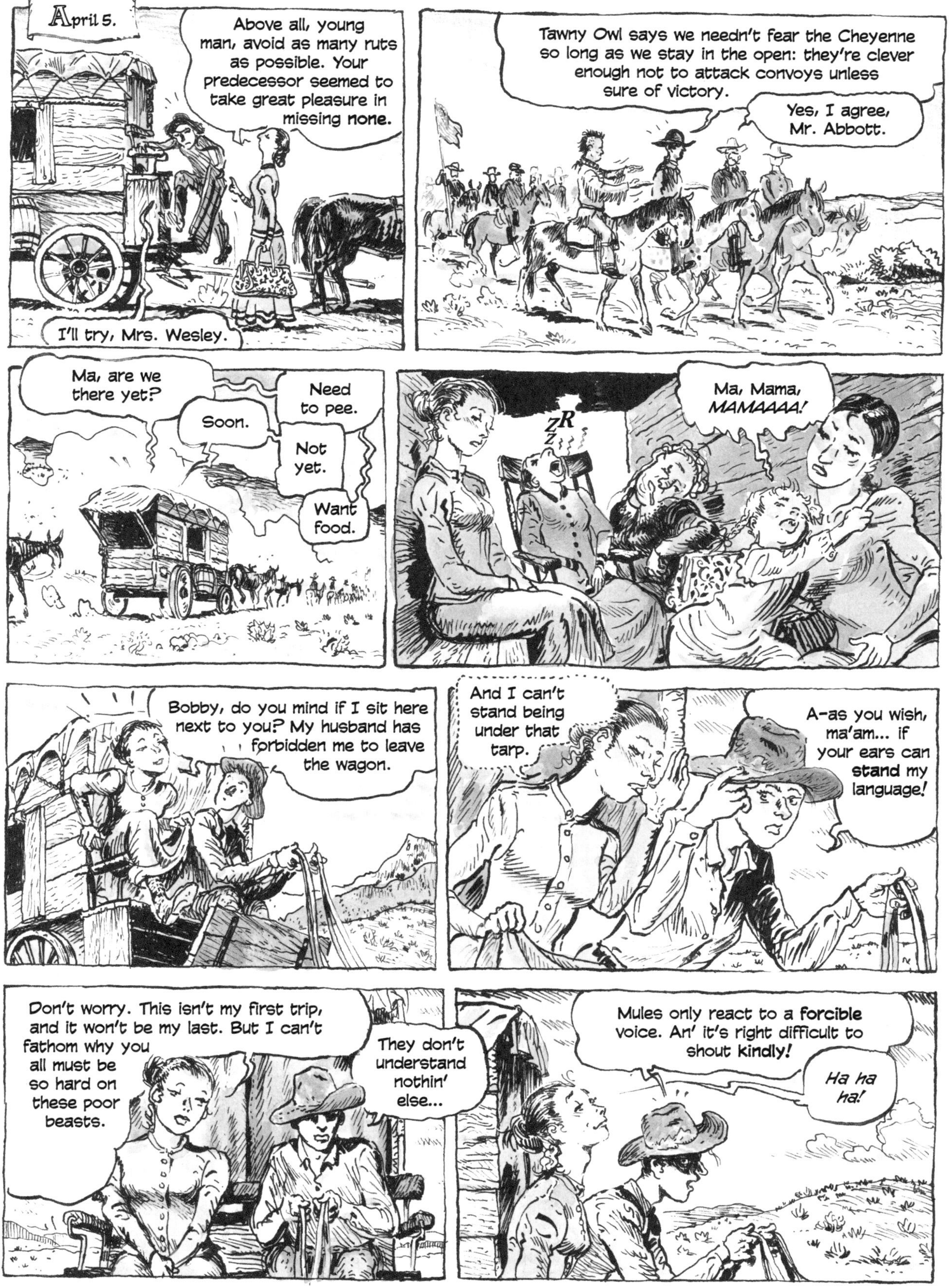
April 5.
Above all, young man, avoid as many ruts as possible. Your predecessor seemed to take great pleasure in missing **none**.
I'll try, Mrs. Wesley.
Tawny Owl says we needn't fear the Cheyenne so long as we stay in the open: they're clever enough not to attack convoys unless sure of victory.
Yes, I agree, Mr. Abbott.
Ma, are we there yet?
Soon.
Need to pee.
Not yet.
Want food.
ZRZ
Ma, Mama, *MAMAAAA!*
Bobby, do you mind if I sit here next to you? My husband has forbidden me to leave the wagon.
And I can't stand being under that tarp.
A-as you wish, ma'am... if your ears can **stand** my language!
Don't worry. This isn't my first trip, and it won't be my last. But I can't fathom why you all must be so hard on these poor beasts.
They don't understand nothin' else...
Mules only react to a **forcible** voice. An' it's right difficult to shout **kindly!**
Ha ha ha!

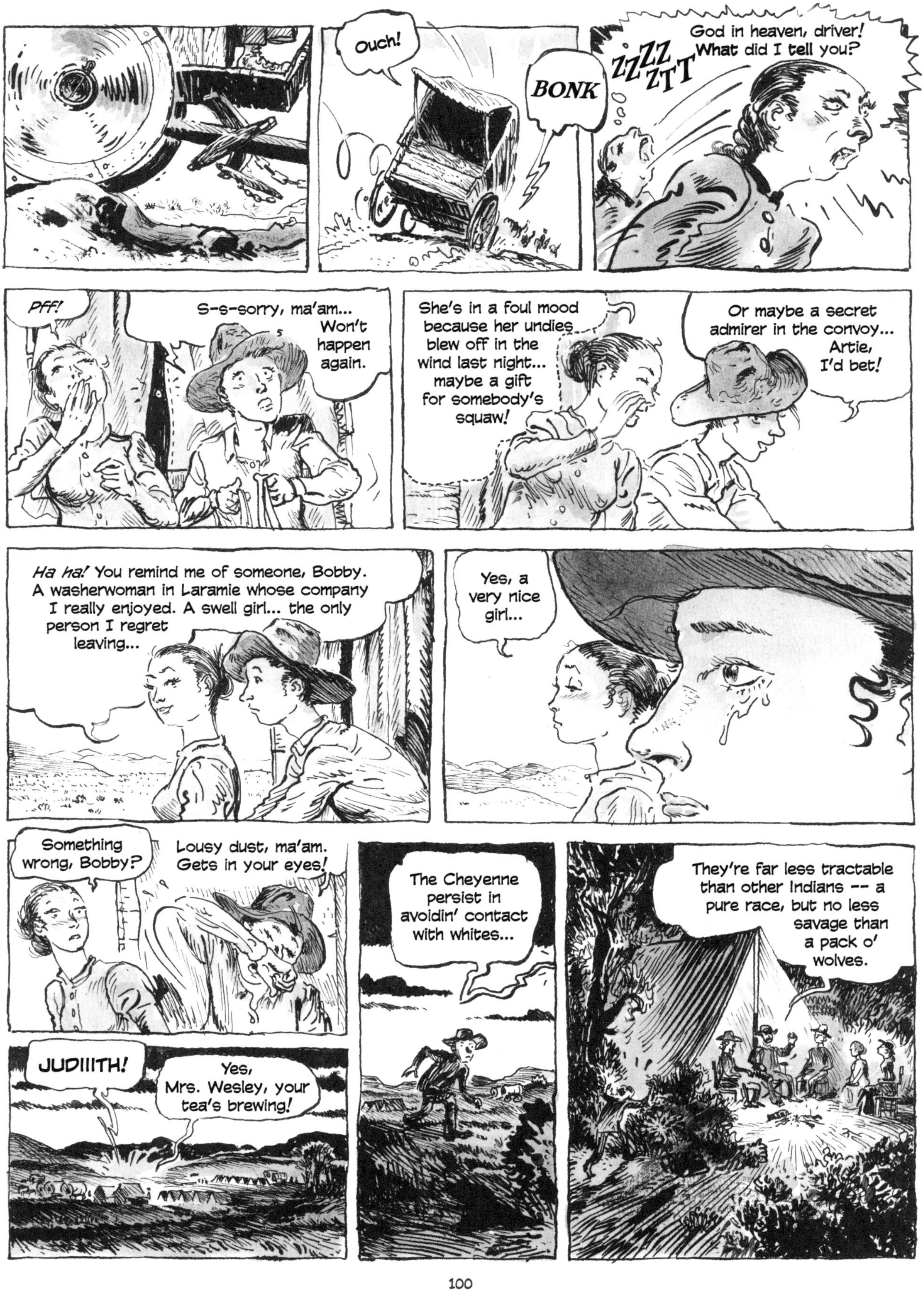
Ouch!
BONK
ZZZZ ZTT
God in heaven, driver! What did I tell you?
Pff!
S-s-sorry, ma'am... Won't happen again.
She's in a foul mood because her undies blew off in the wind last night... maybe a gift for somebody's squaw!
Or maybe a secret admirer in the convoy... Artie, I'd bet!
Ha ha! You remind me of someone, Bobby. A washerwoman in Laramie whose company I really enjoyed. A swell girl... the only person I regret leaving...
Yes, a very nice girl...
Something wrong, Bobby?
Lousy dust, ma'am. Gets in your eyes!
JUDIIITH!
Yes, Mrs. Wesley, your tea's brewing!
The Cheyenne persist in avoidin' contact with whites...
They're far less tractable than other Indians -- a pure race, but no less savage than a pack o' wolves.

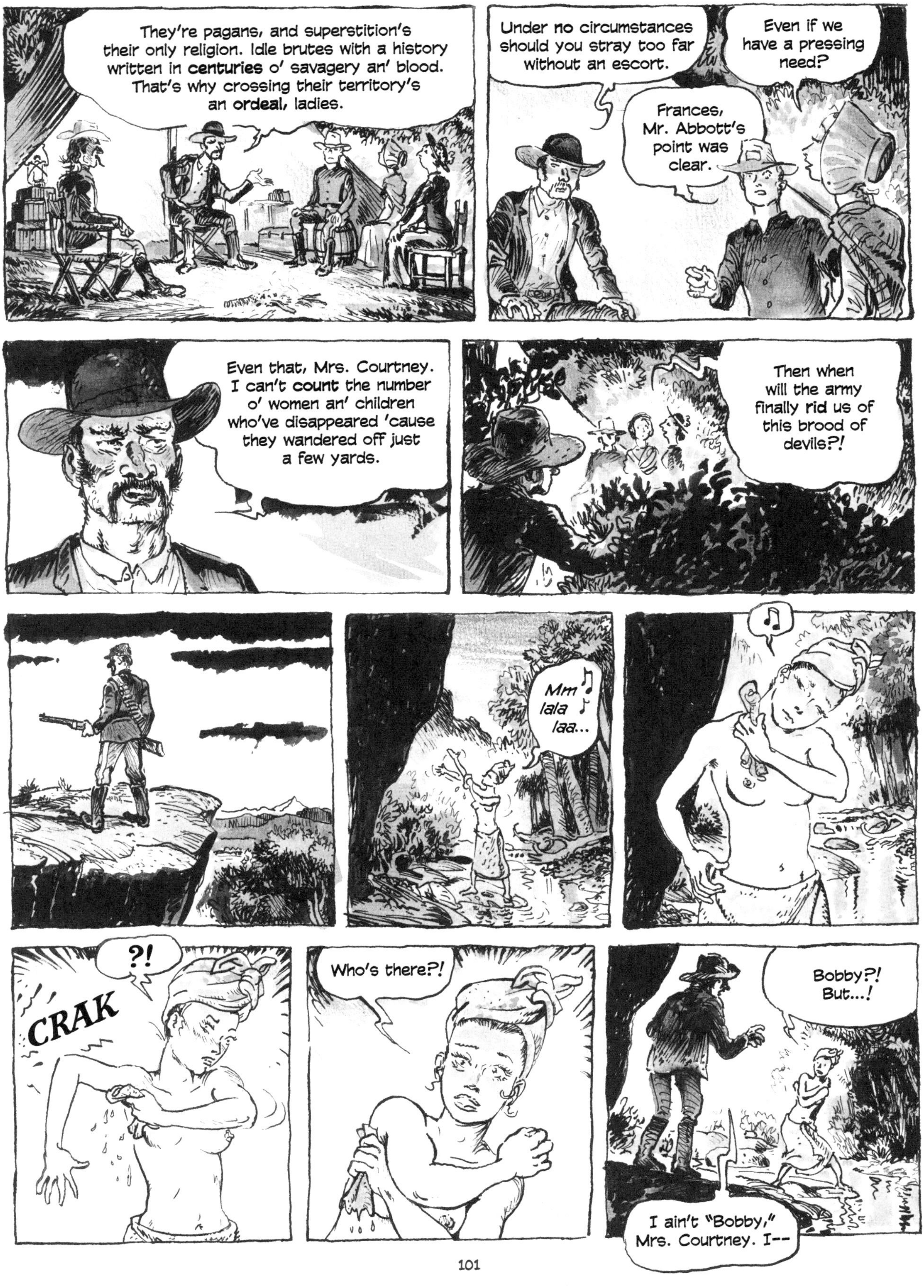

They're pagans, and superstition's their only religion. Idle brutes with a history written in **centuries** o' savagery an' blood. That's why crossing their territory's an **ordeal**, ladies.
Under **no** circumstances should you stray too far without an escort.
Even if we have a pressing need?
Frances, Mr. Abbott's point was clear.
Even that, Mrs. Courtney. I can't **count** the number o' women an' children who've disappeared 'cause they wandered off just a few yards.
Then when will the army finally **rid** us of this brood of devils?!
Mm lala laa... ♪♪
♫
?!
CRAK
Who's there?!
Bobby?! But...!
I ain't "Bobby," Mrs. Courtney. I--

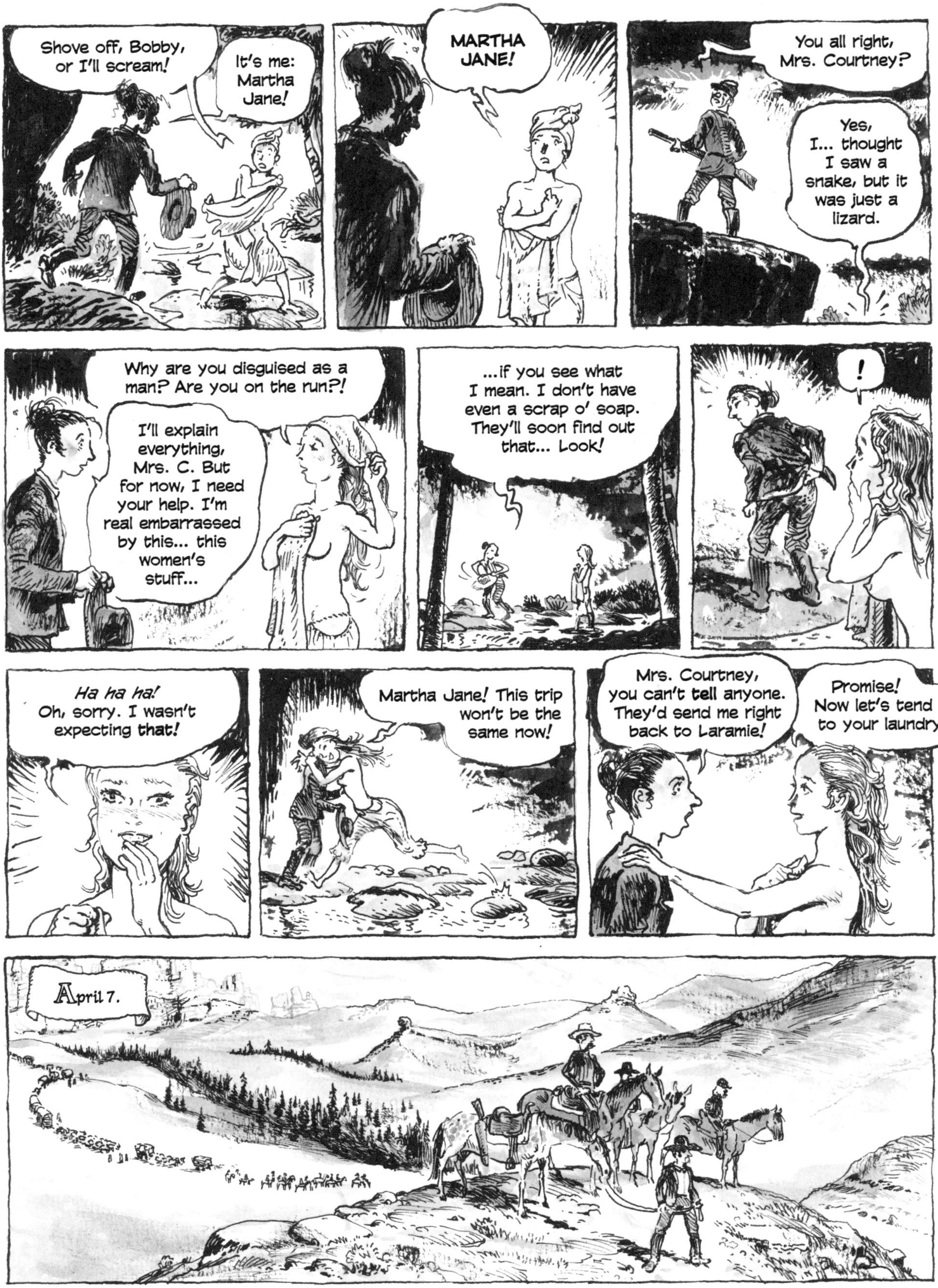
Shove off, Bobby, or I'll scream!
It's me: Martha Jane!
MARTHA JANE!
You all right, Mrs. Courtney?
Yes, I... thought I saw a snake, but it was just a lizard.
Why are you disguised as a man? Are you on the run?!
I'll explain everything, Mrs. C. But for now, I need your help. I'm real embarrassed by this... this women's stuff...
...if you see what I mean. I don't have even a scrap o' soap. They'll soon find out that... Look!
!
Ha ha ha! Oh, sorry. I wasn't expecting **that!**
Martha Jane! This trip won't be the same now!
Mrs. Courtney, you can't **tell** anyone. They'd send me right back to Laramie!
Promise! Now let's tend to your laundry.
April 7.

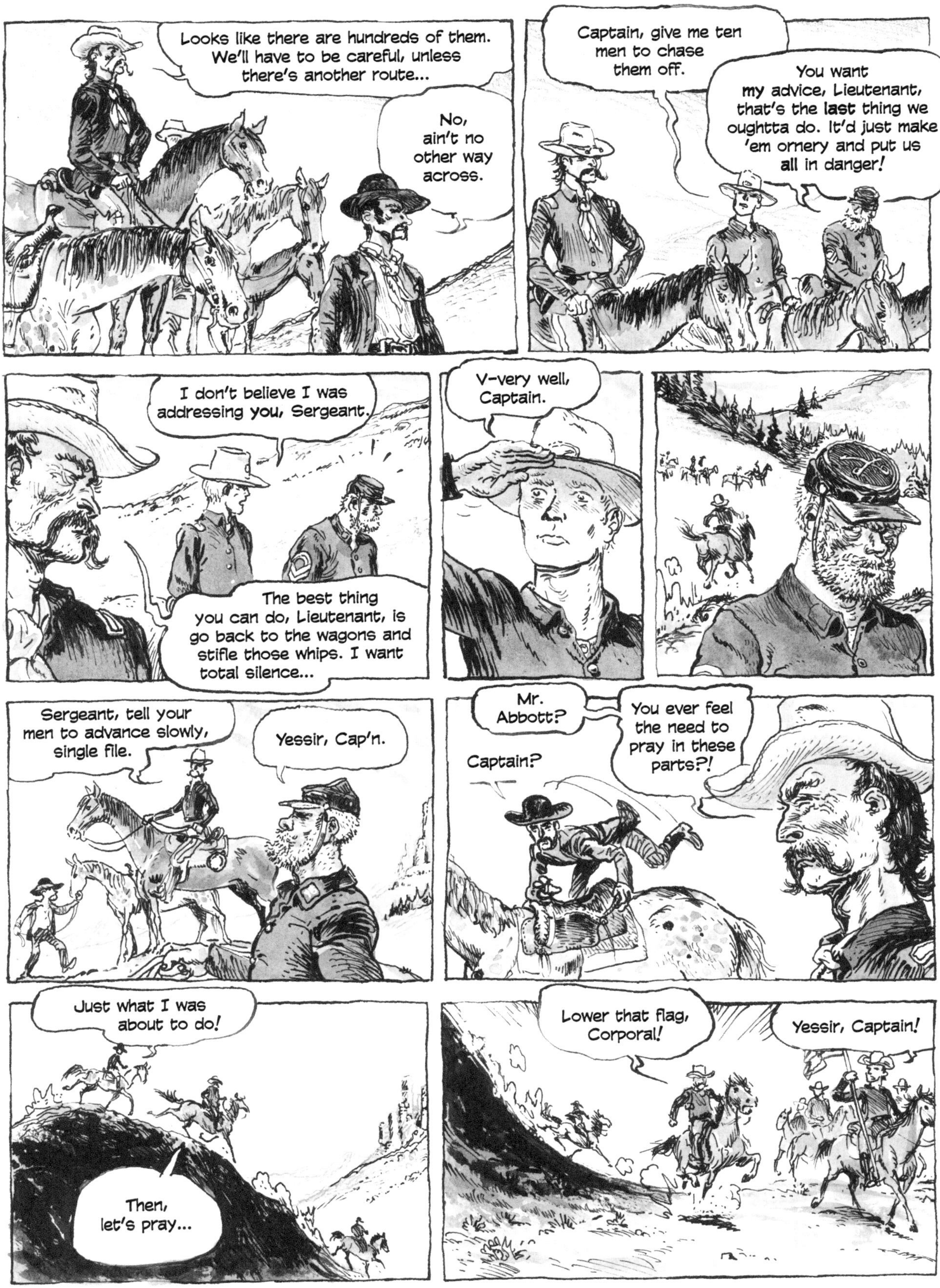
Looks like there are hundreds of them. We'll have to be careful, unless there's another route...
No, ain't no other way across.
Captain, give me ten men to chase them off.
You want my advice, Lieutenant, that's the last thing we oughtta do. It'd just make 'em ornery and put us all in danger!
I don't believe I was addressing you, Sergeant.
The best thing you can do, Lieutenant, is go back to the wagons and stifle those whips. I want total silence...
V-very well, Captain.
Sergeant, tell your men to advance slowly, single file.
Yessir, Cap'n.
Mr. Abbott?
Captain?
You ever feel the need to pray in these parts?!
Just what I was about to do!
Then, let's pray...
Lower that flag, Corporal!
Yessir, Captain!

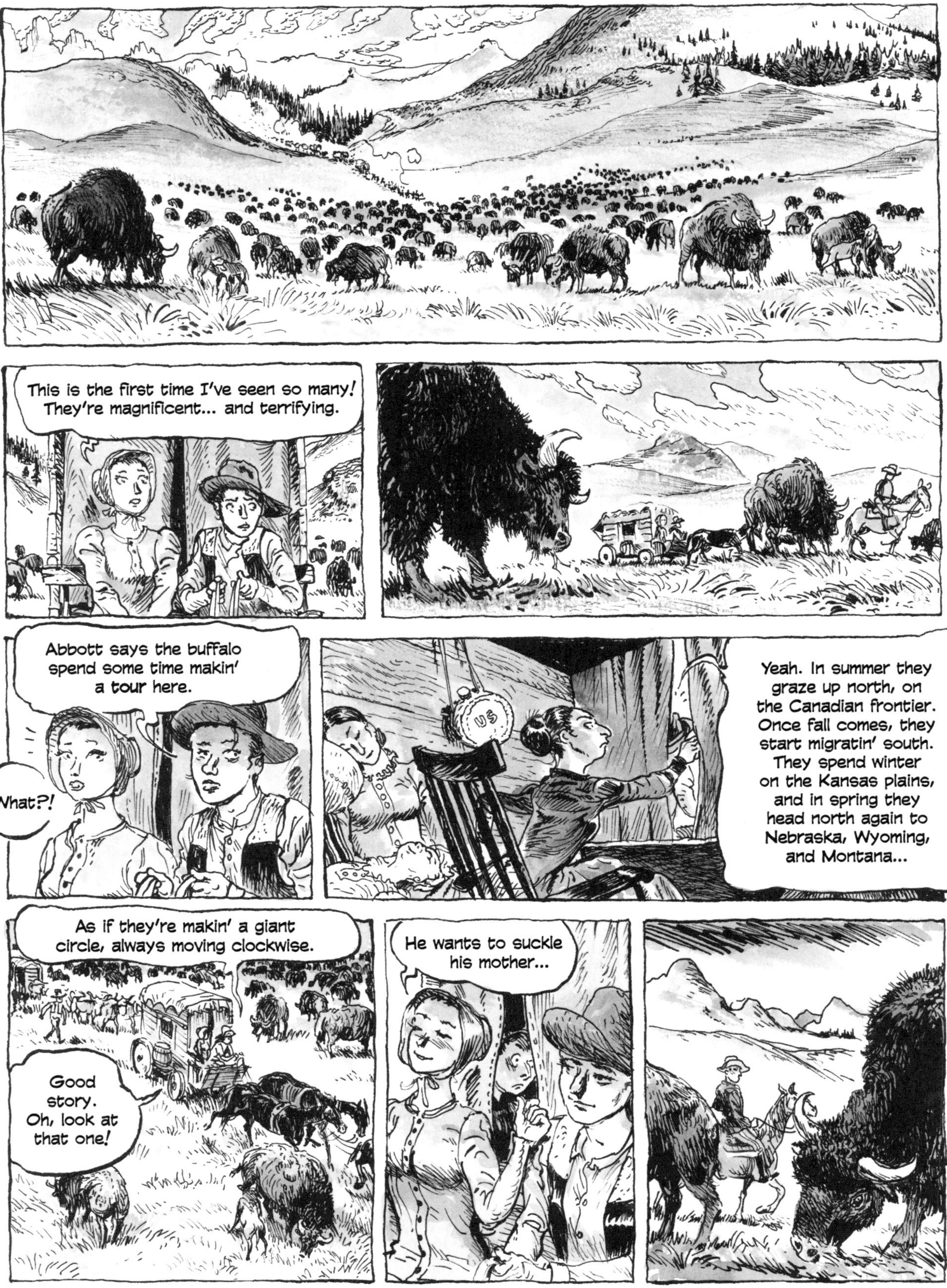
This is the first time I've seen so many! They're magnificent... and terrifying.
Abbott says the buffalo spend some time makin' a tour here.
What?!
Yeah. In summer they graze up north, on the Canadian frontier. Once fall comes, they start migratin' south. They spend winter on the Kansas plains, and in spring they head north again to Nebraska, Wyoming, and Montana...
US
As if they're makin' a giant circle, always moving clockwise.
Good story. Oh, look at that one!
He wants to suckle his mother...

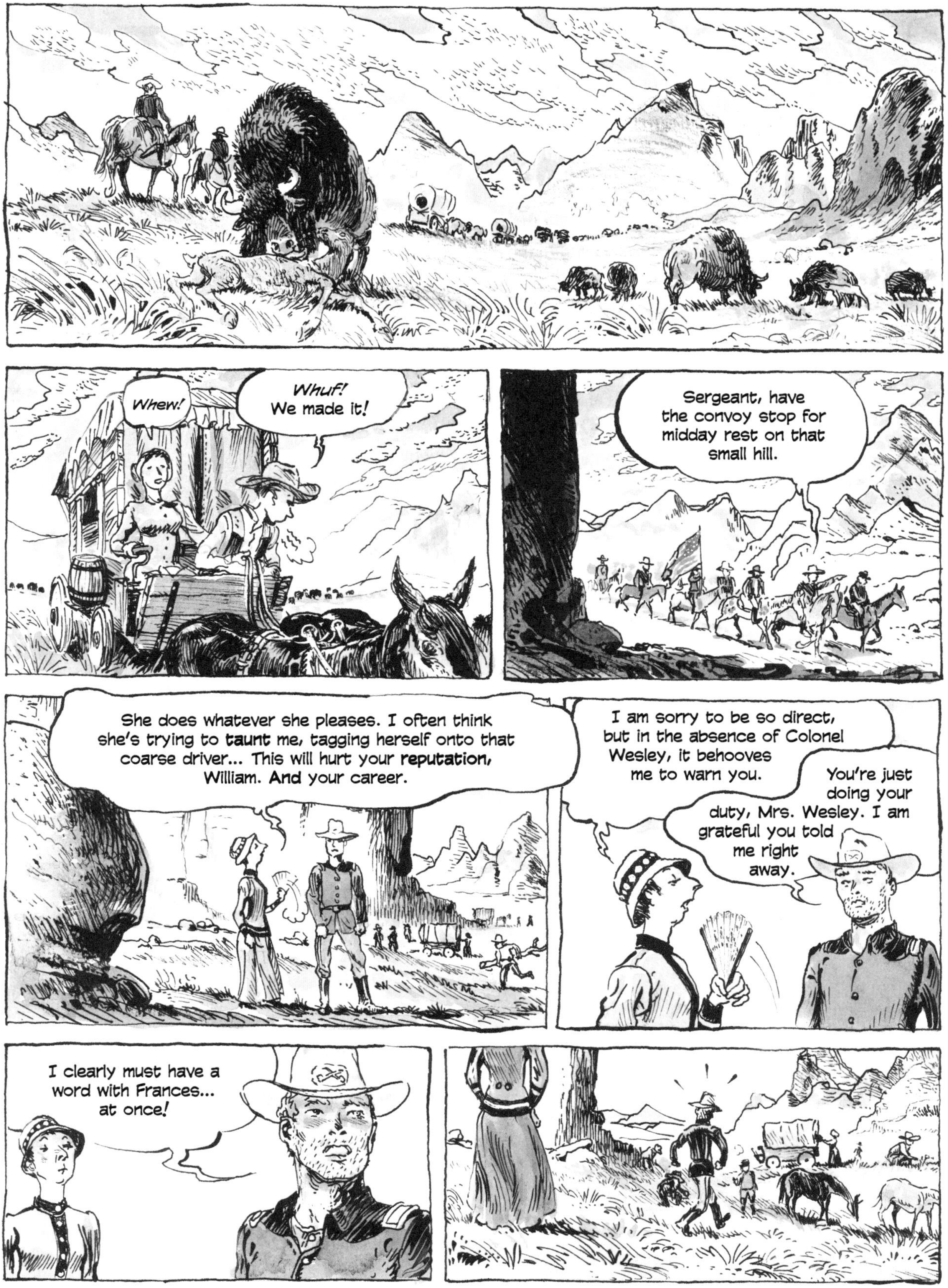
Whew!
Whuf! We made it!
Sergeant, have the convoy stop for midday rest on that small hill.
She does whatever she pleases. I often think she's trying to taunt me, tagging herself onto that coarse driver... This will hurt your reputation, William. And your career.
I am sorry to be so direct, but in the absence of Colonel Wesley, it behooves me to warn you.
You're just doing your duty, Mrs. Wesley. I am grateful you told me right away.
I clearly must have a word with Frances... at once!
!

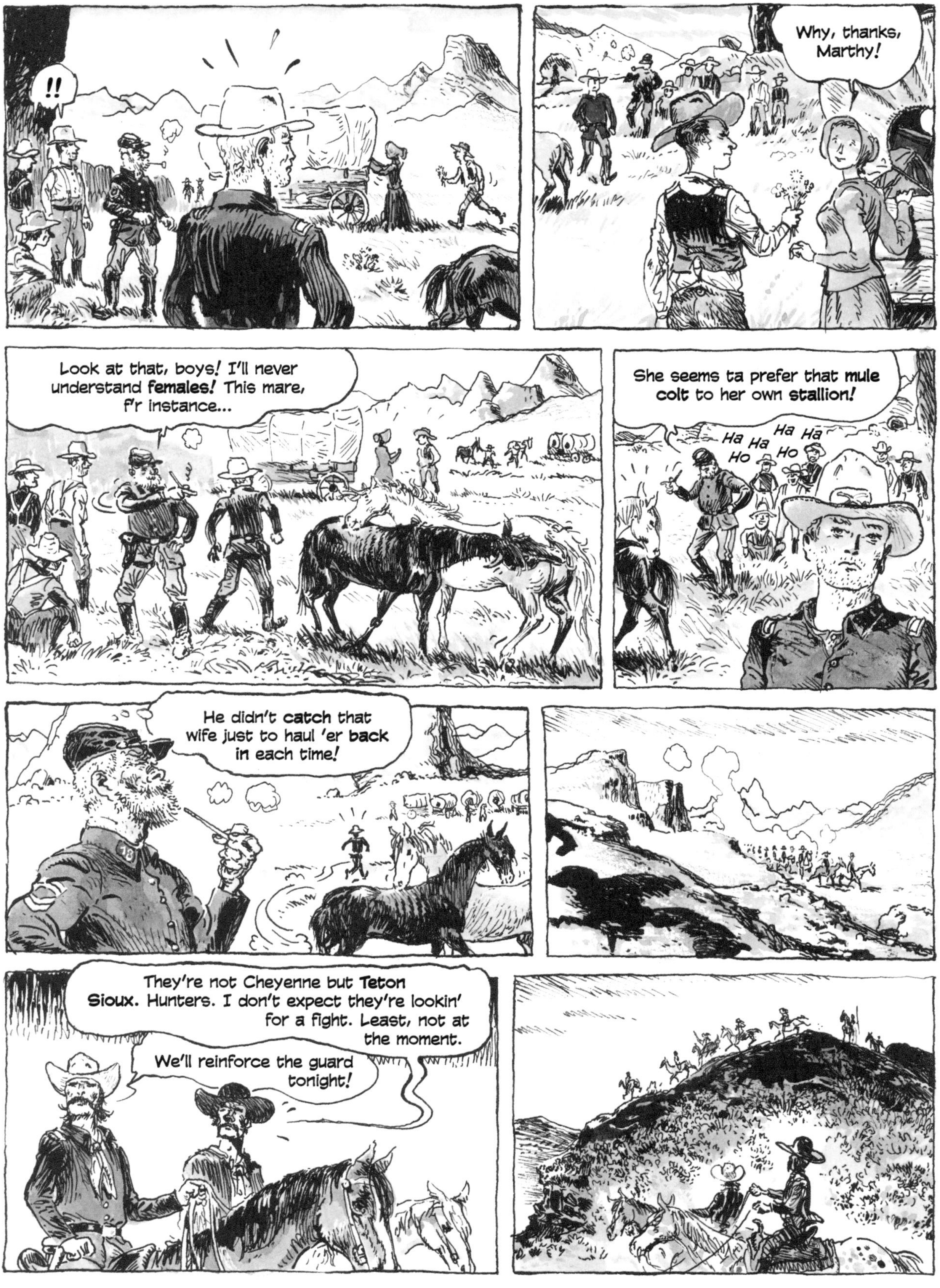
!!
Why, thanks, Marthy!
Look at that, boys! I'll never understand females! This mare, f'r instance...
She seems ta prefer that mule colt to her own stallion!
Ha Ha Ha Ha Ho Ho
He didn't catch that wife just to haul 'er back in each time!
They're not Cheyenne but Teton Sioux. Hunters. I don't expect they're lookin' for a fight. Least, not at the moment.
We'll reinforce the guard tonight!

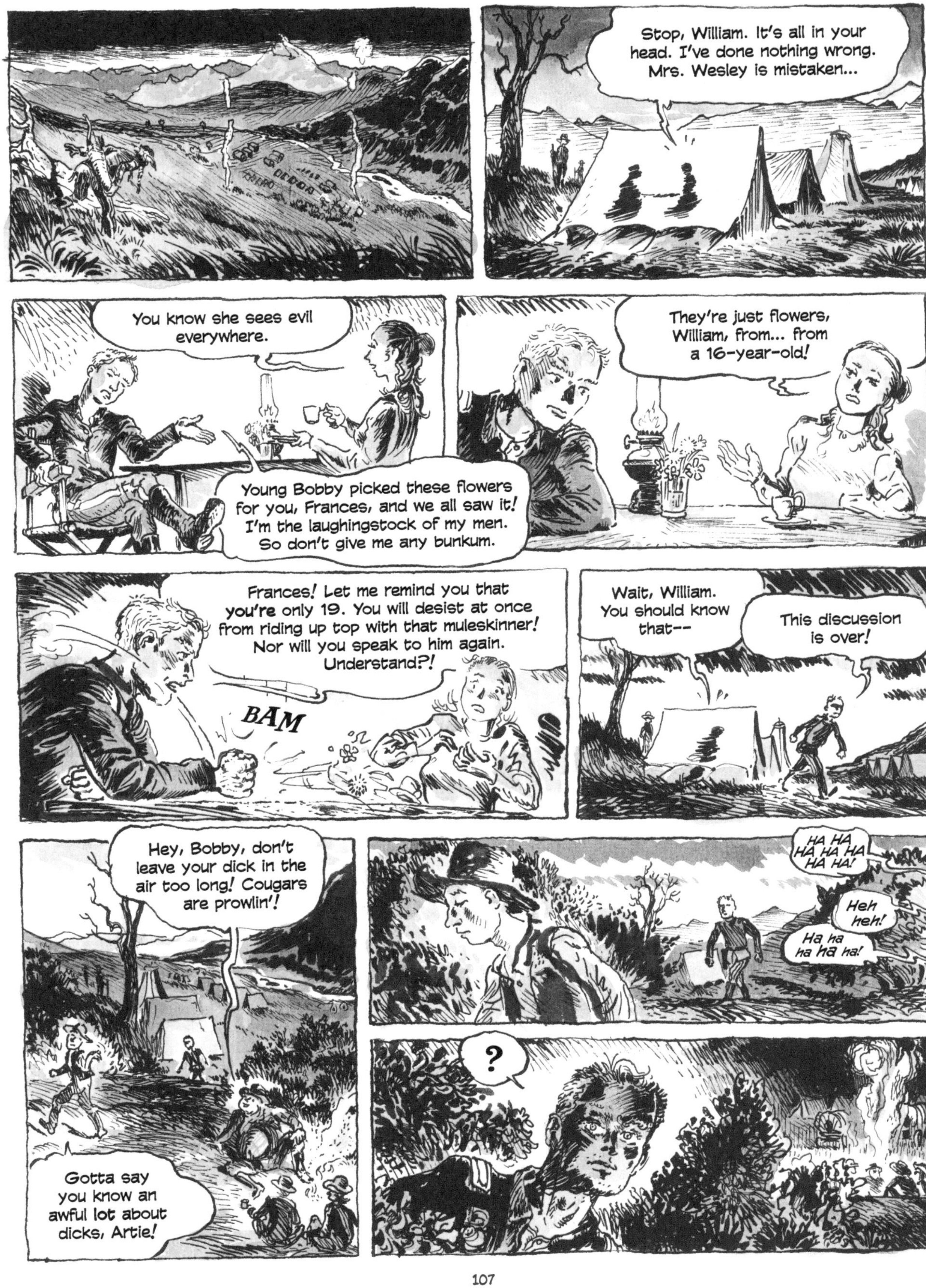
Stop, William. It's all in your head. I've done nothing wrong. Mrs. Wesley is mistaken...
You know she sees evil everywhere.
Young Bobby picked these flowers for you, Frances, and we all saw it! I'm the laughingstock of my men. So don't give me any bunkum.
They're just flowers, William, from... from a 16-year-old!
Frances! Let me remind you that **you're** only 19. You will desist at once from riding up top with that muleskinner! Nor will you speak to him again. Understand?!
BAM
Wait, William. You should know that--
This discussion is over!
Hey, Bobby, don't leave your dick in the air too long! Cougars are prowlin'!
Gotta say you know an awful lot about dicks, Artie!
HA HA HA HA HA HA HA HA!
Heh heh!
Ha ha ha ha ha!
?

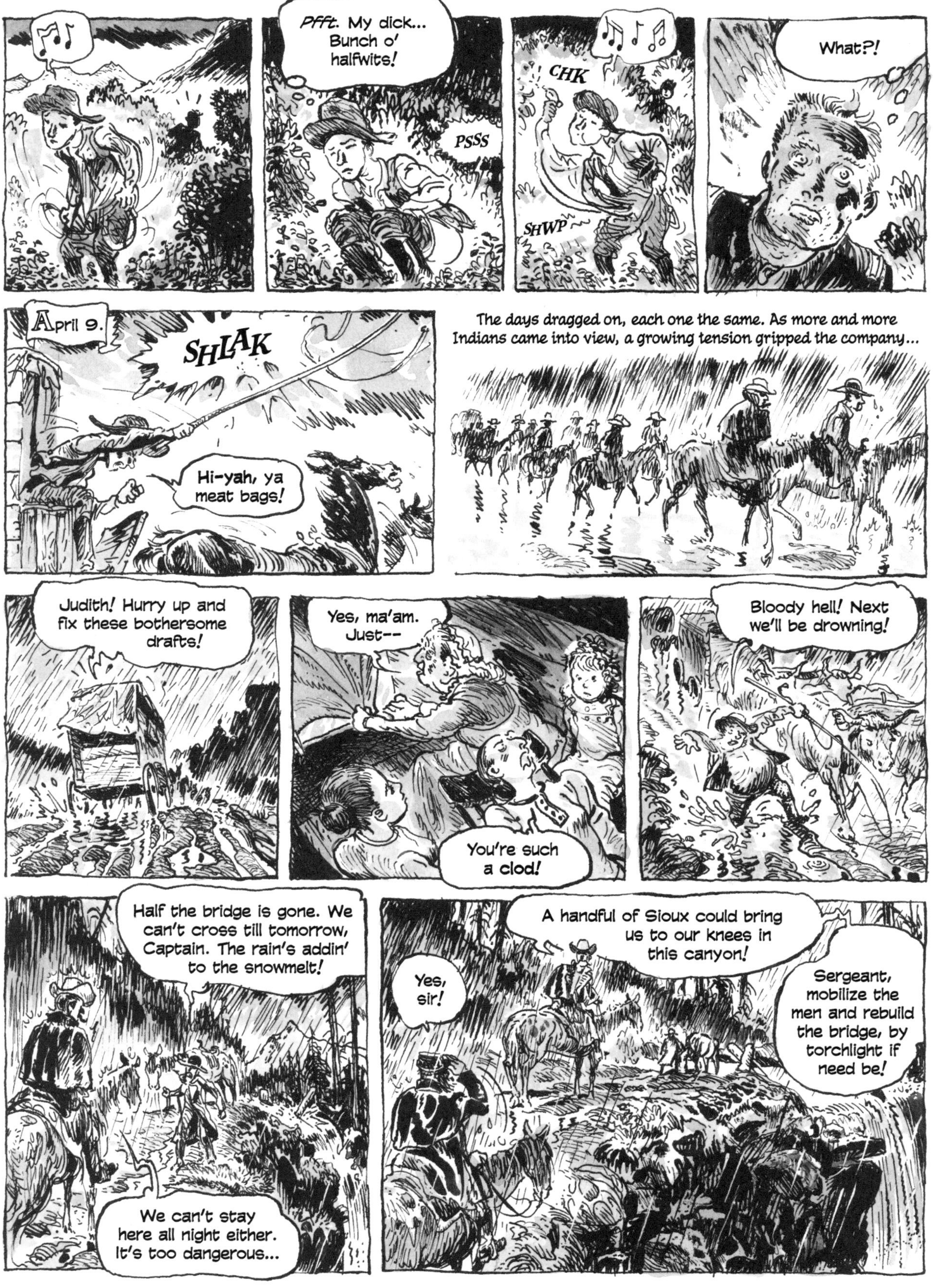
Pfft. My dick... Bunch o' halfwits!
PSSS
CHK
SHWP
What?!
April 9.
SHLAK
Hi-yah, ya meat bags!
The days dragged on, each one the same. As more and more Indians came into view, a growing tension gripped the company...
Judith! Hurry up and fix these bothersome drafts!
Yes, ma'am. Just--
You're such a clod!
Bloody hell! Next we'll be drowning!
Half the bridge is gone. We can't cross till tomorrow, Captain. The rain's addin' to the snowmelt!
We can't stay here all night either. It's too dangerous...
A handful of Sioux could bring us to our knees in this canyon!
Yes, sir!
Sergeant, mobilize the men and rebuild the bridge, by torchlight if need be!

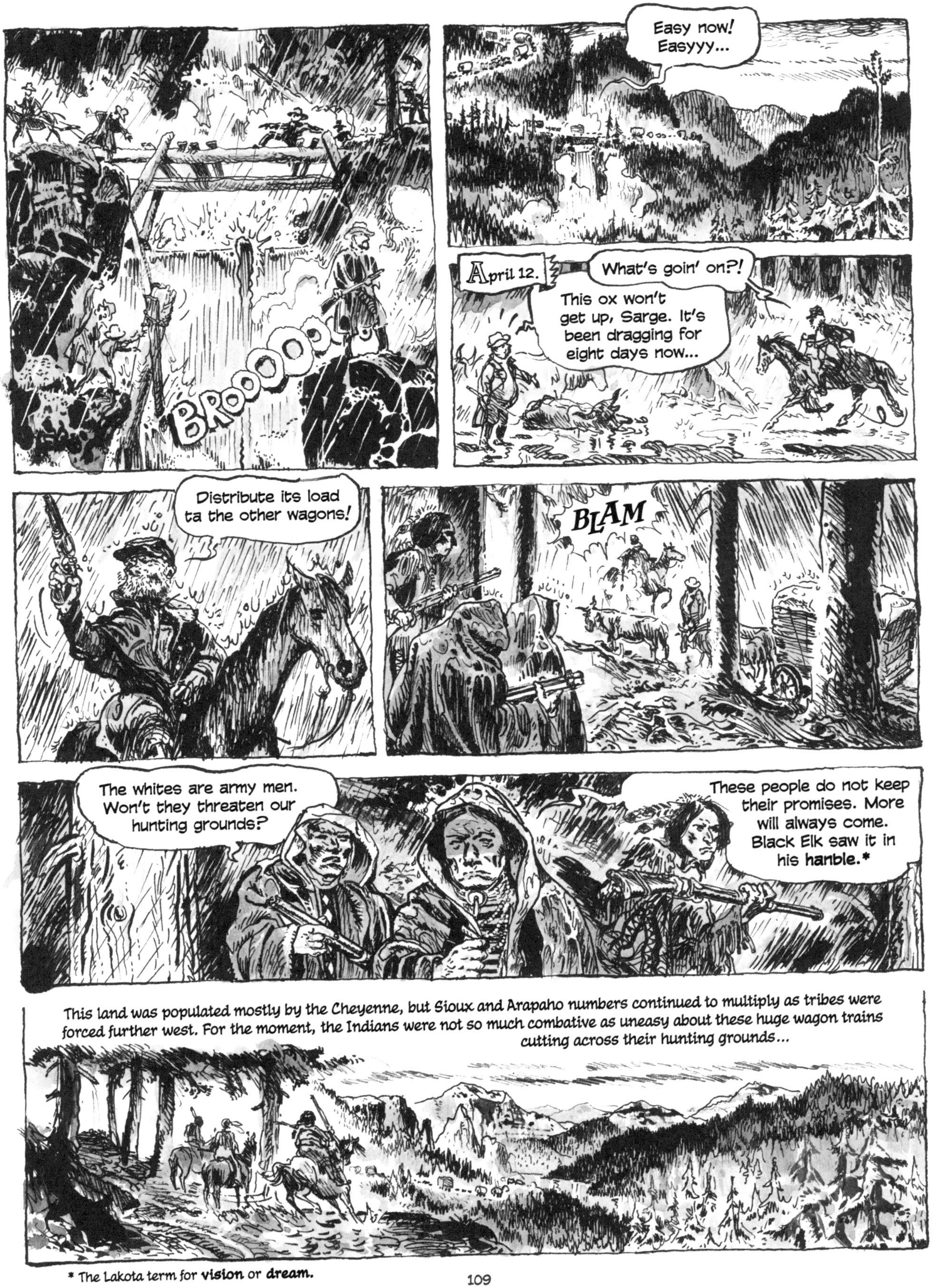
BROOOOO
Easy now! Easyyy...
April 12.
What's goin' on?!
This ox won't get up, Sarge. It's been dragging for eight days now...
Distribute its load ta the other wagons!
BLAM
The whites are army men. Won't they threaten our hunting grounds?
These people do not keep their promises. More will always come. Black Elk saw it in his **hanble.***
This land was populated mostly by the Cheyenne, but Sioux and Arapaho numbers continued to multiply as tribes were forced further west. For the moment, the Indians were not so much combative as uneasy about these huge wagon trains cutting across their hunting grounds...

* The Lakota term for **vision** or **dream.**

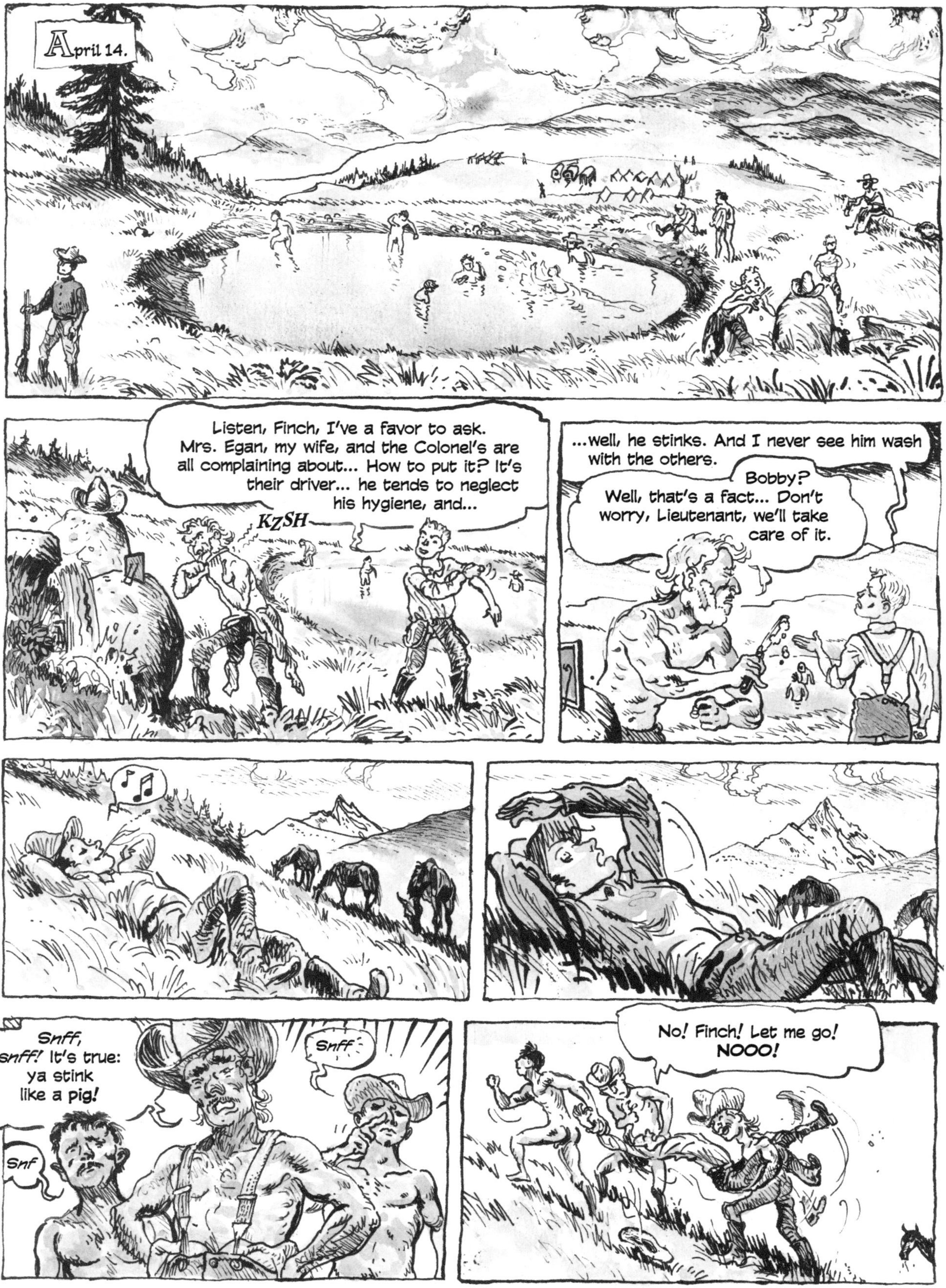
April 14.
Listen, Finch, I've a favor to ask. Mrs. Egan, my wife, and the Colonel's are all complaining about... How to put it? It's their driver... he tends to neglect his hygiene, and...
KZSH
...well, he stinks. And I never see him wash with the others.
Bobby? Well, that's a fact... Don't worry, Lieutenant, we'll take care of it.
Snff, snff! It's true: ya stink like a pig!
Snff
Snf
No! Finch! Let me go! NOOO!

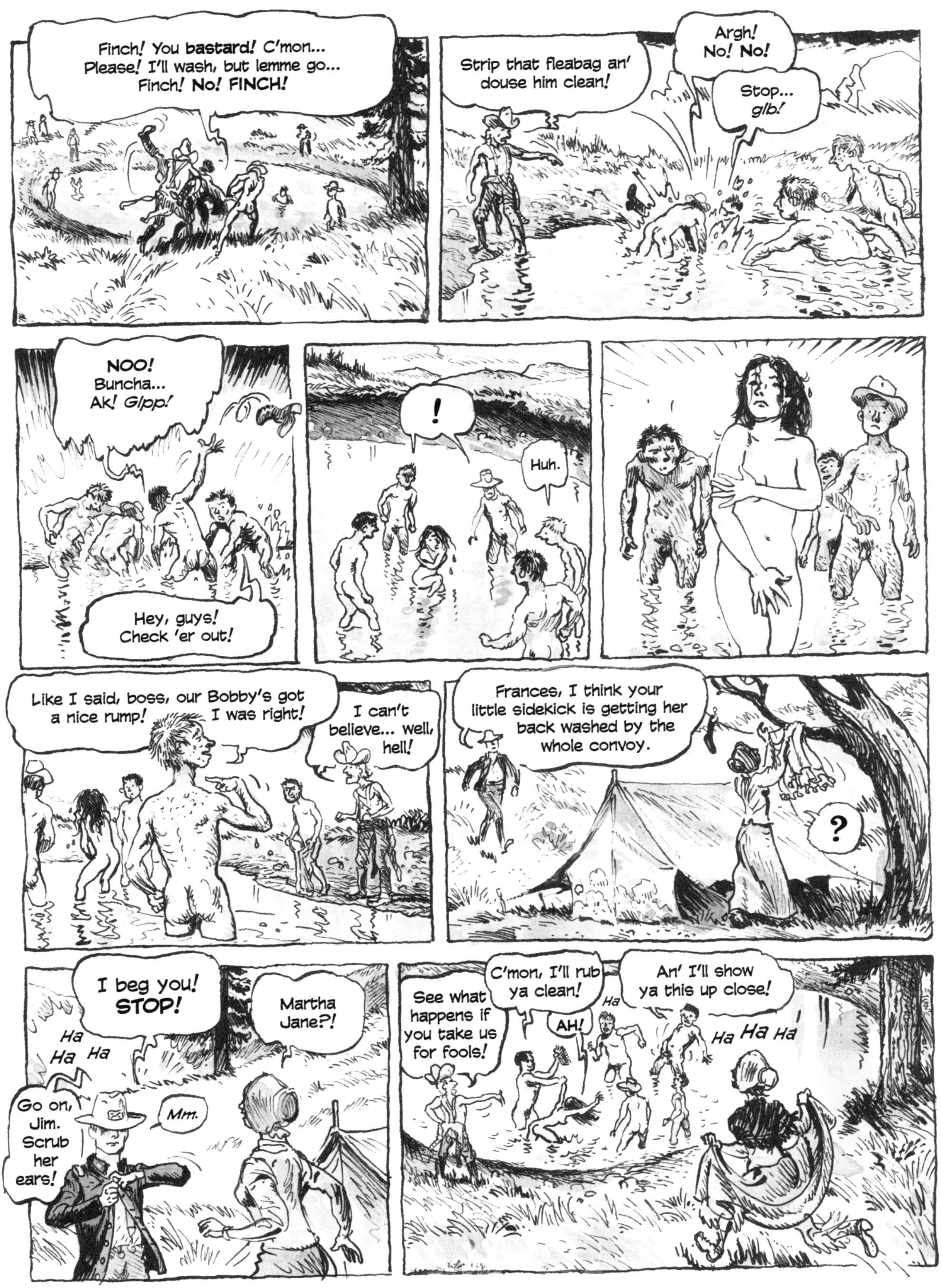

Finch! You bastard! C'mon... Please! I'll wash, but lemme go... Finch! No! FINCH!
Strip that fleabag an' douse him clean!
Argh! No! No!
Stop... glb!
NOO! Buncha... Ak! Glpp!
Hey, guys! Check 'er out!
!
Huh.
Like I said, boss, our Bobby's got a nice rump! I was right!
I can't believe... well, hell!
Frances, I think your little sidekick is getting her back washed by the whole convoy.
?
I beg you! STOP!
Martha Jane?!
Ha Ha Ha
Go on, Jim. Scrub her ears!
Mm.
See what happens if you take us for fools!
C'mon, I'll rub ya clean!
Ha
AH!
An' I'll show ya this up close!
Ha Ha Ha

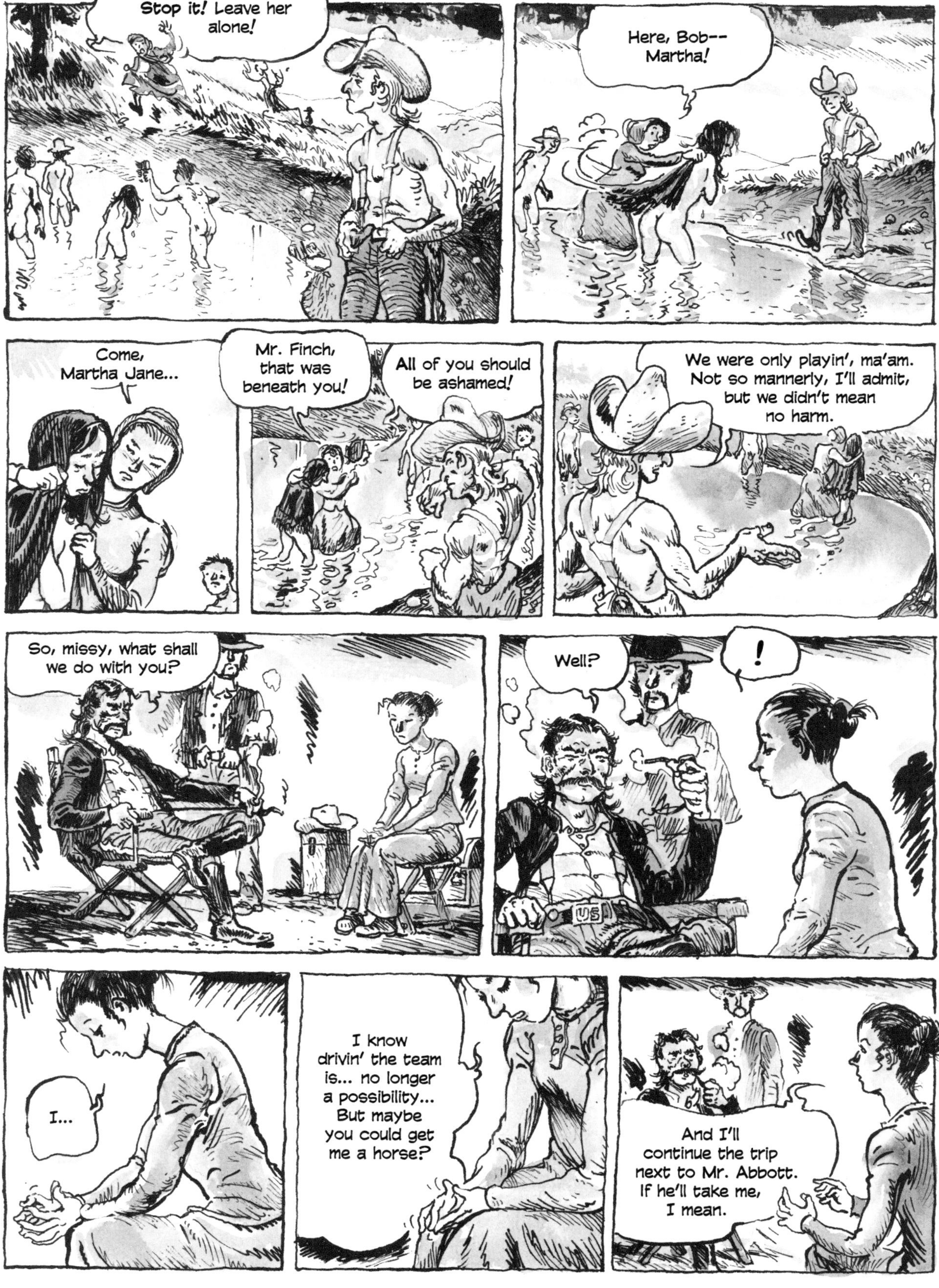
Stop it! Leave her alone!
Here, Bob-- Martha!
Come, Martha Jane...
Mr. Finch, that was beneath you!
All of you should be ashamed!
We were only playin', ma'am. Not so mannerly, I'll admit, but we didn't mean no harm.
So, missy, what shall we do with you?
Well?
!
I...
I know drivin' the team is... no longer a possibility... But maybe you could get me a horse?
And I'll continue the trip next to Mr. Abbott. If he'll take me, I mean.

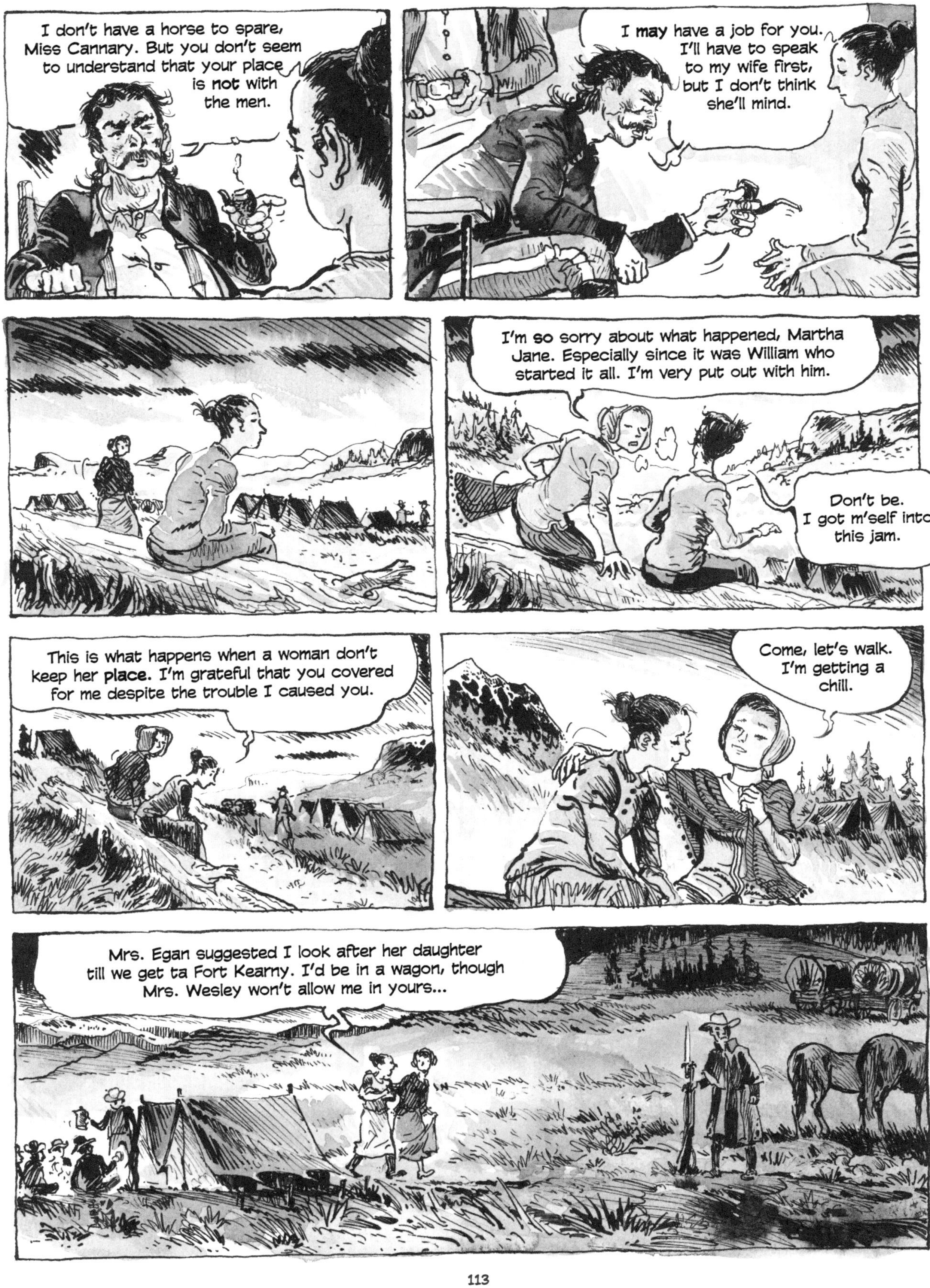
I don't have a horse to spare, Miss Cannary. But you don't seem to understand that your place is not with the men.
I may have a job for you. I'll have to speak to my wife first, but I don't think she'll mind.
I'm so sorry about what happened, Martha Jane. Especially since it was William who started it all. I'm very put out with him.
Don't be. I got m'self into this jam.
This is what happens when a woman don't keep her place. I'm grateful that you covered for me despite the trouble I caused you.
Come, let's walk. I'm getting a chill.
Mrs. Egan suggested I look after her daughter till we get ta Fort Kearny. I'd be in a wagon, though Mrs. Wesley won't allow me in yours...

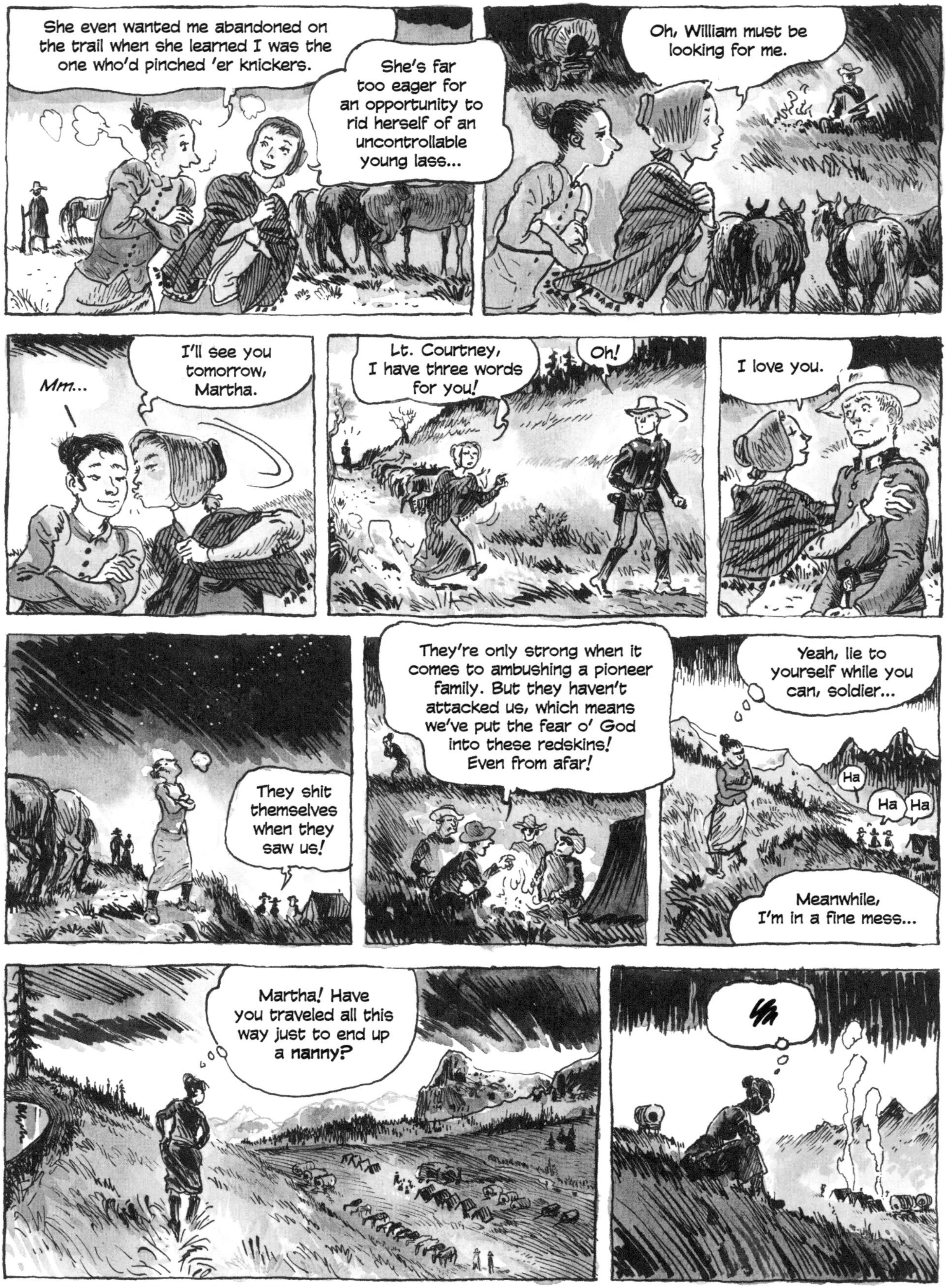

She even wanted me abandoned on the trail when she learned I was the one who'd pinched 'er knickers.
She's far too eager for an opportunity to rid herself of an uncontrollable young lass...
Oh, William must be looking for me.
Mm...
I'll see you tomorrow, Martha.
Lt. Courtney, I have three words for you!
Oh!
I love you.
They shit themselves when they saw us!
They're only strong when it comes to ambushing a pioneer family. But they haven't attacked us, which means we've put the fear o' God into these redskins! Even from afar!
Yeah, lie to yourself while you can, soldier...
Ha
Ha
Ha
Meanwhile, I'm in a fine mess...
Martha! Have you traveled all this way just to end up a nanny?

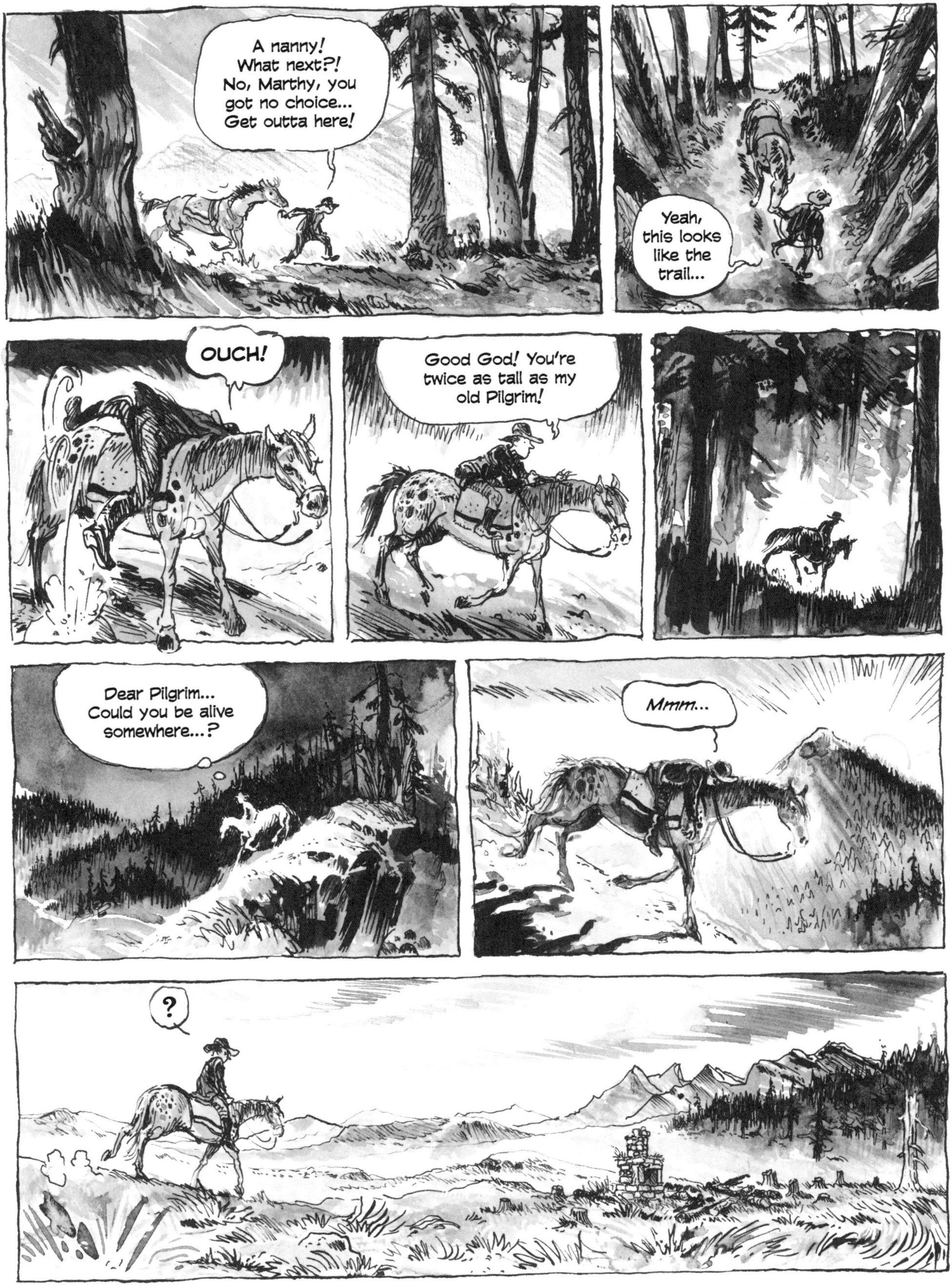
A nanny! What next?! No, Marthy, you got no choice... Get outta here!
Yeah, this looks like the trail...
OUCH!
Good God! You're twice as tall as my old Pilgrim!
Dear Pilgrim... Could you be alive somewhere...?
Mmm...
?

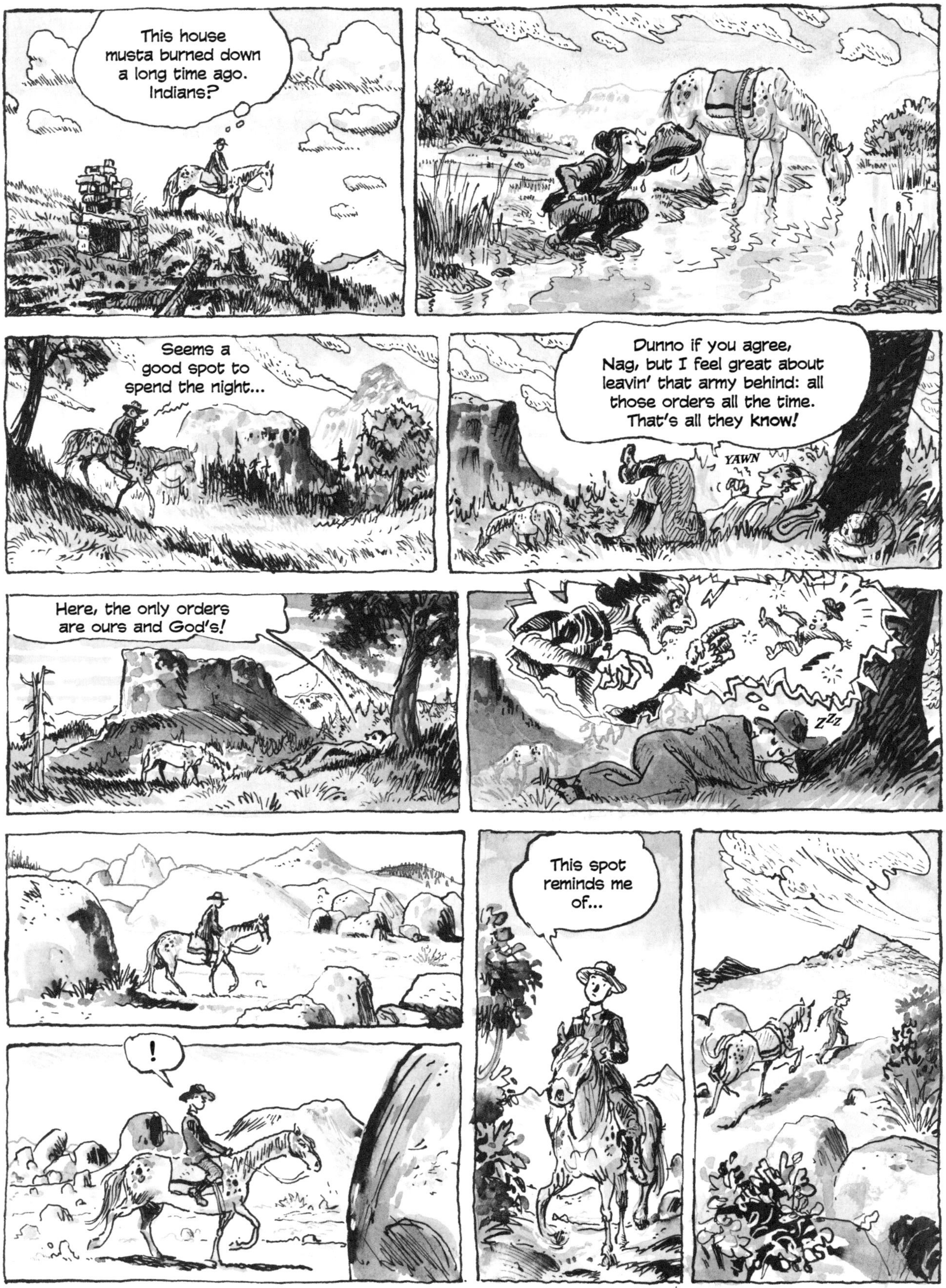

This house musta burned down a long time ago. Indians?
Seems a good spot to spend the night...
Dunno if you agree, Nag, but I feel great about leavin' that army behind: all those orders all the time. That's all they know!
YAWN
Here, the only orders are ours and God's!
ZZZ
This spot reminds me of...
!

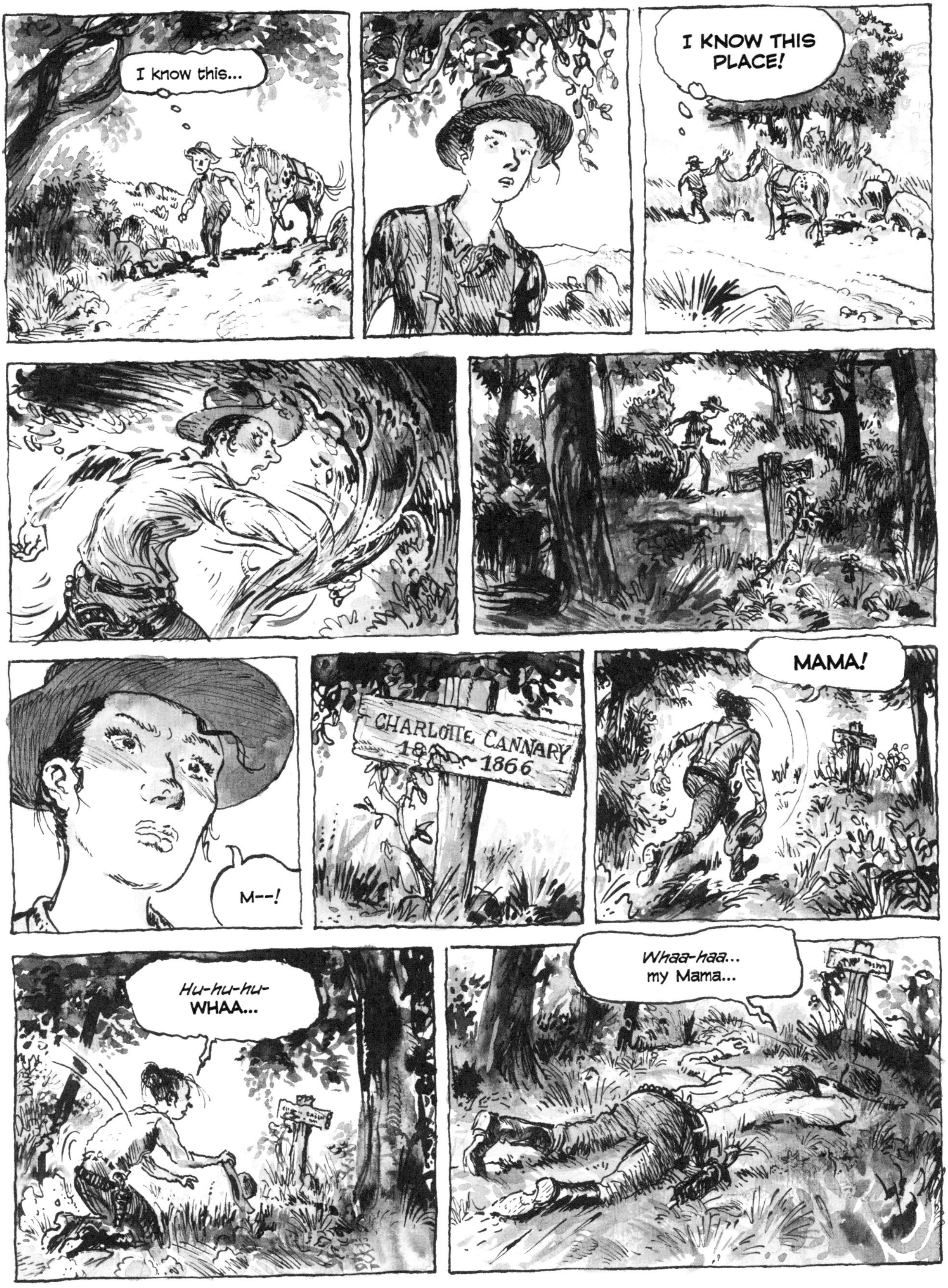
I know this...
I KNOW THIS PLACE!
M--!
CHARLOTTE CANNARY
18 1866
MAMA!
Hu-hu-hu-
WHAA...
Whaa-haa...
my Mama...

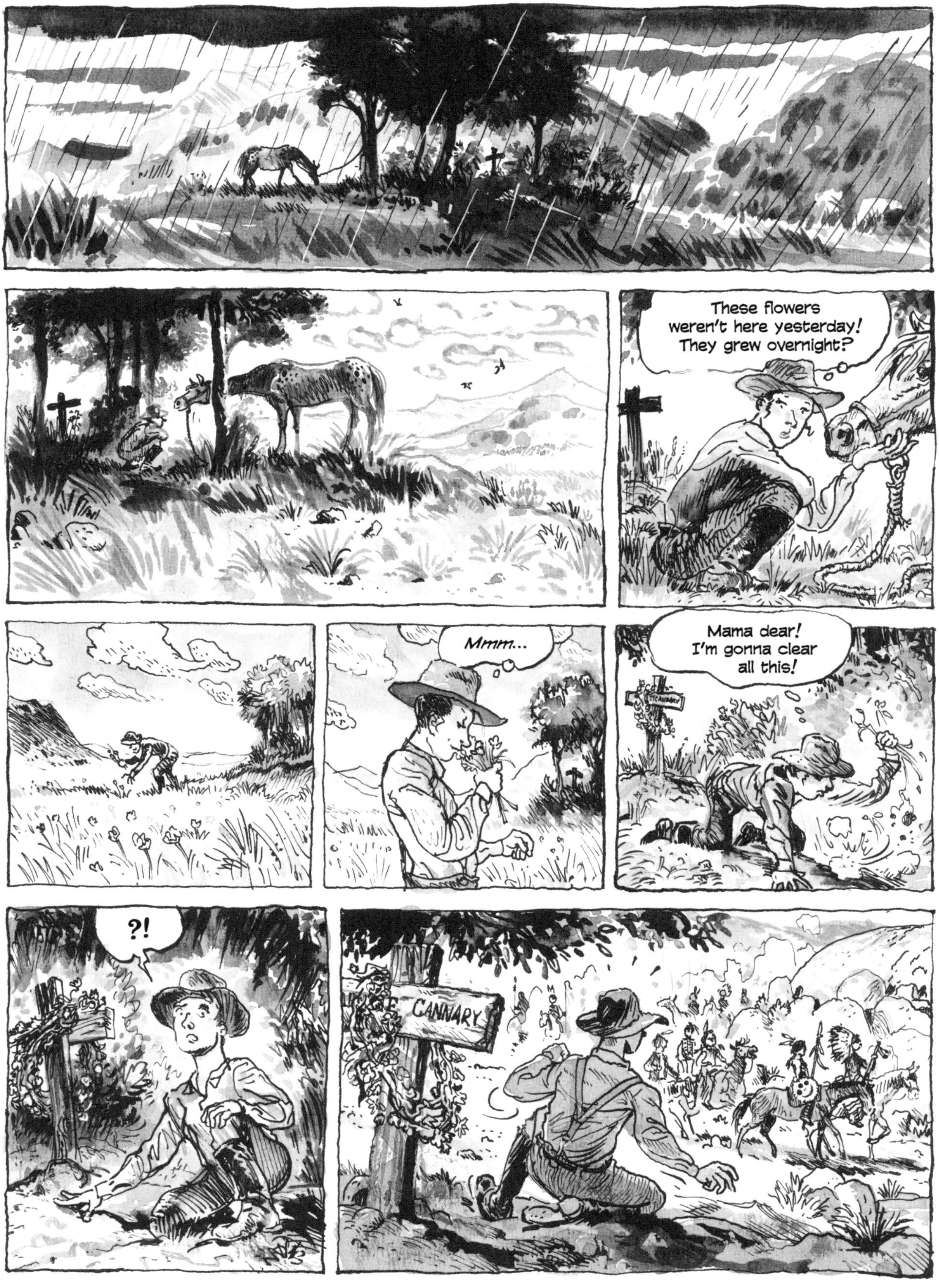
These flowers weren't here yesterday! They grew overnight?
Mmm...
Mama dear! I'm gonna clear all this!
?!
CANNARY

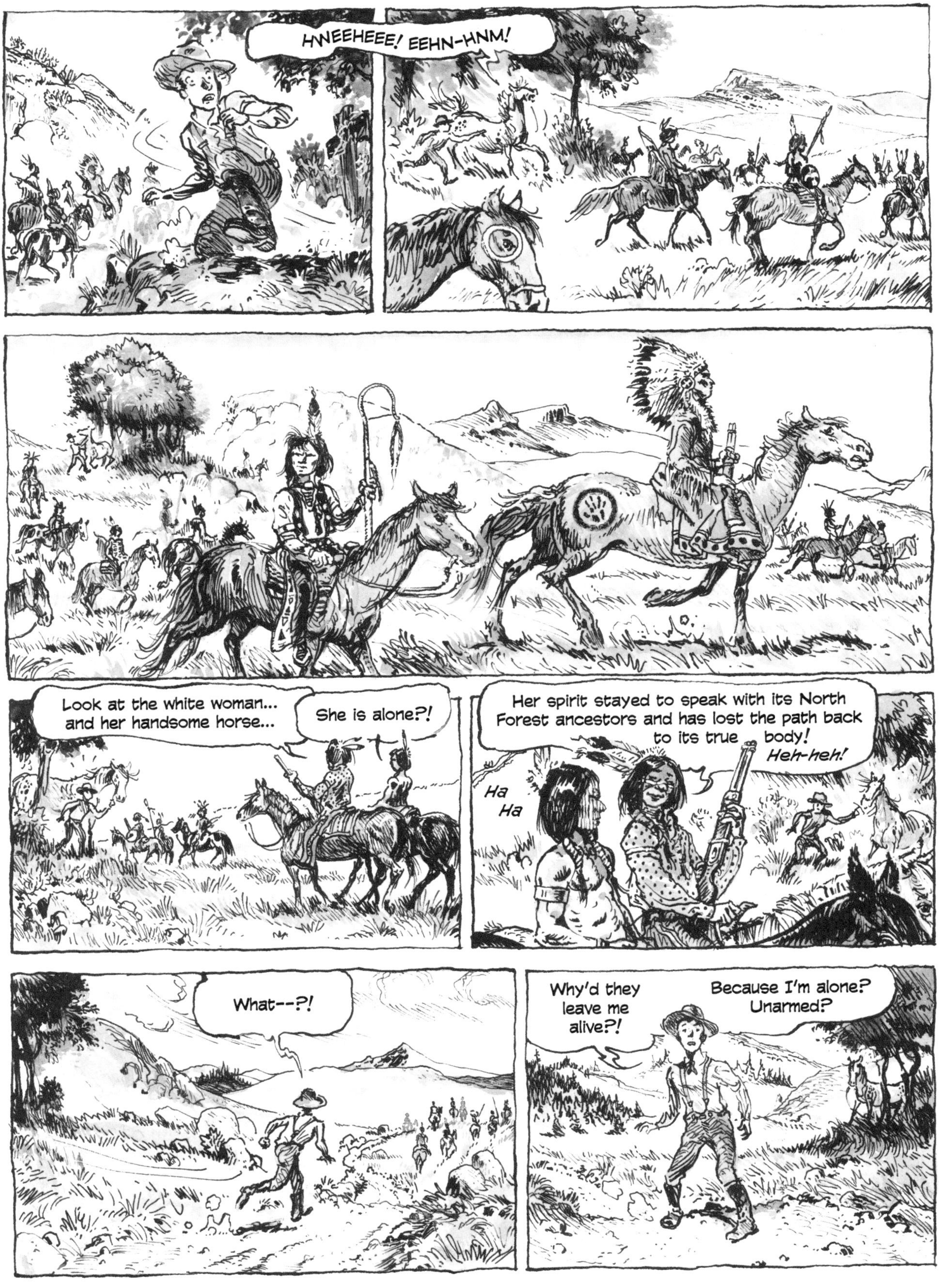
HWEEHEEE! EEHN-HNM!
Look at the white woman...
and her handsome horse...
She is alone?!
Her spirit stayed to speak with its North Forest ancestors and has lost the path back to its true body!
Heh-heh!
Ha
Ha
What--?!
Why'd they leave me alive?!
Because I'm alone? Unarmed?

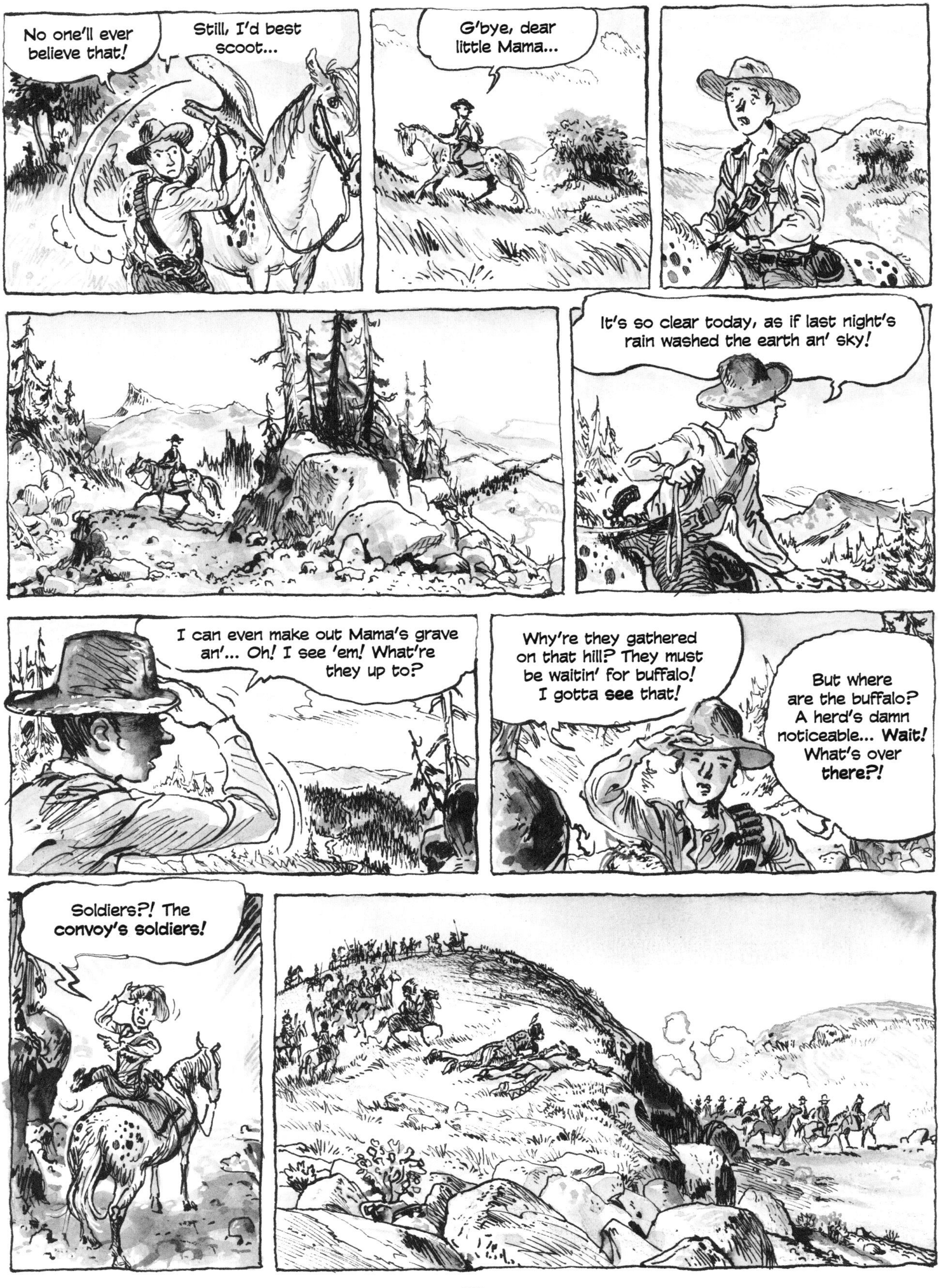

No one'll ever believe that!
Still, I'd best scoot...
G'bye, dear little Mama...
It's so clear today, as if last night's rain washed the earth an' sky!
I can even make out Mama's grave an'... Oh! I see 'em! What're they up to?
Why're they gathered on that hill? They must be waitin' for buffalo! I gotta see that!
But where are the buffalo? A herd's damn noticeable... **Wait!** What's over **there?!**
Soldiers?! The **convoy's soldiers!**

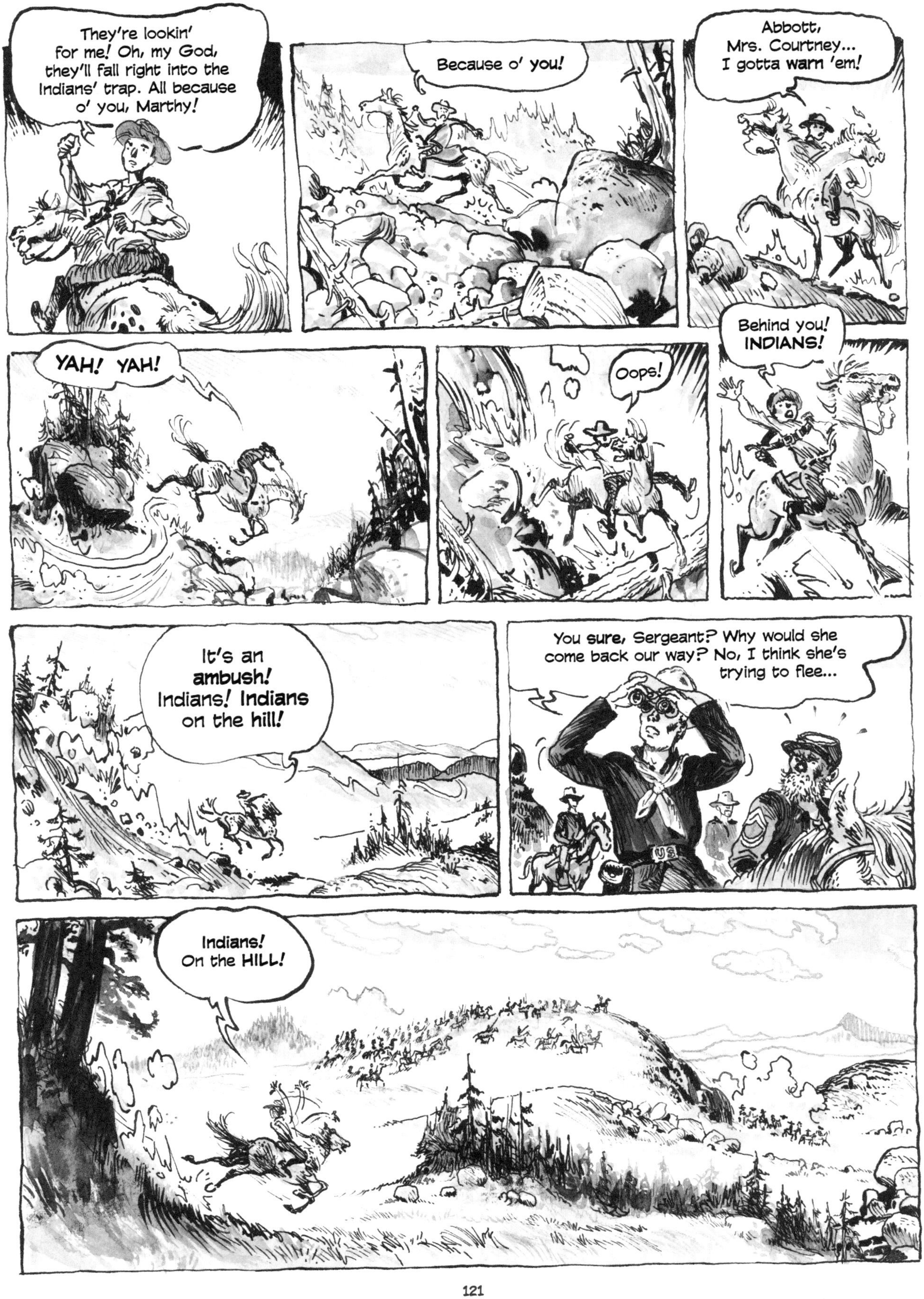
They're lookin' for me! Oh, my God, they'll fall right into the Indians' trap. All because o' you, Marthy!
Because o' you!
Abbott, Mrs. Courtney... I gotta warn 'em!
YAH! YAH!
Oops!
Behind you! INDIANS!
It's an ambush! Indians! Indians on the hill!
You sure, Sergeant? Why would she come back our way? No, I think she's trying to flee...
Indians! On the HILL!

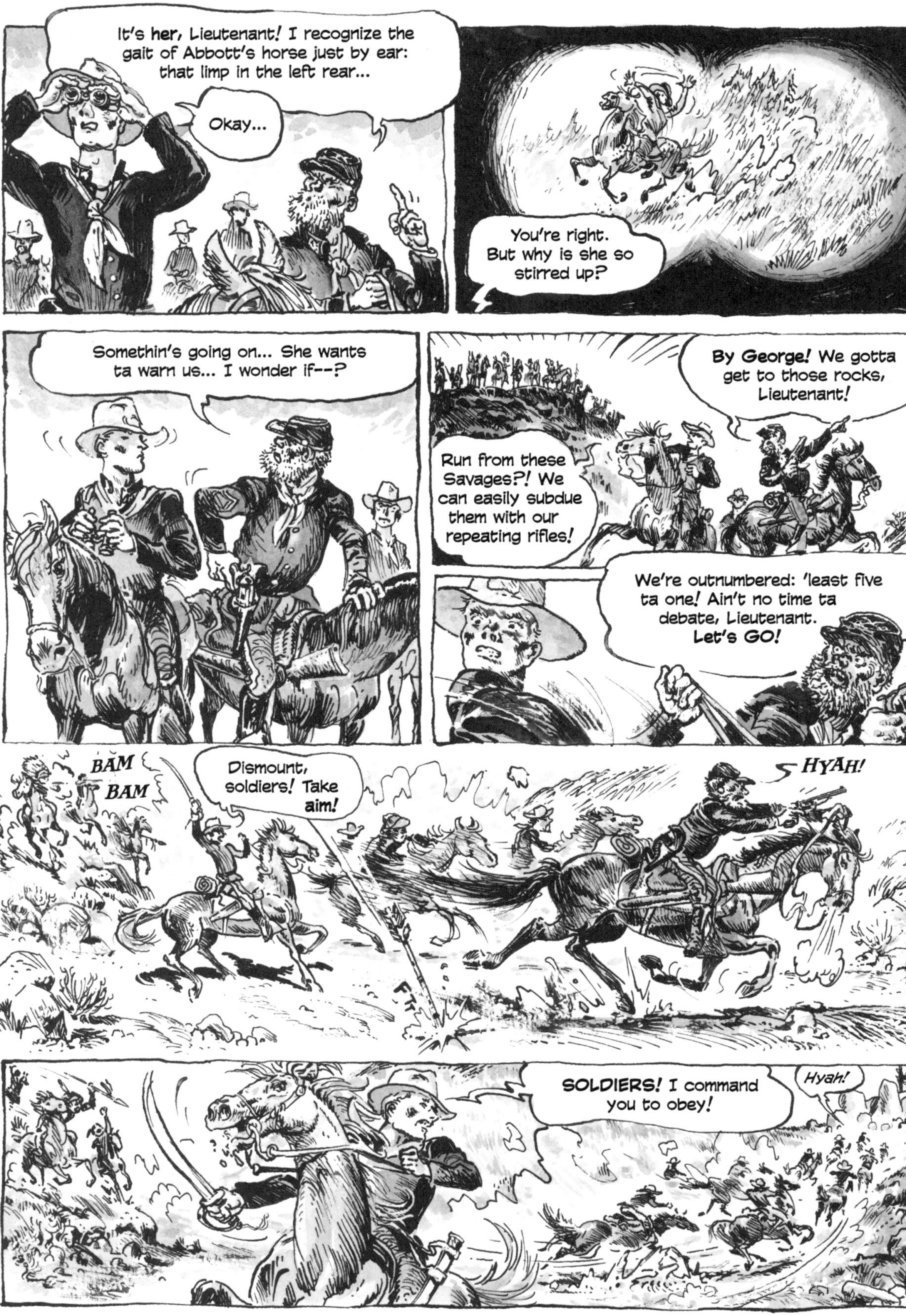
It's her, Lieutenant! I recognize the gait of Abbott's horse just by ear: that limp in the left rear...
Okay...
You're right. But why is she so stirred up?
Somethin's going on... She wants ta warn us... I wonder if--?
By George! We gotta get to those rocks, Lieutenant!
Run from these Savages?! We can easily subdue them with our repeating rifles!
We're outnumbered: 'least five ta one! Ain't no time ta debate, Lieutenant. Let's GO!
BAM
BAM
Dismount, soldiers! Take aim!
HYAH!
SOLDIERS! I command you to obey!
Hyah!

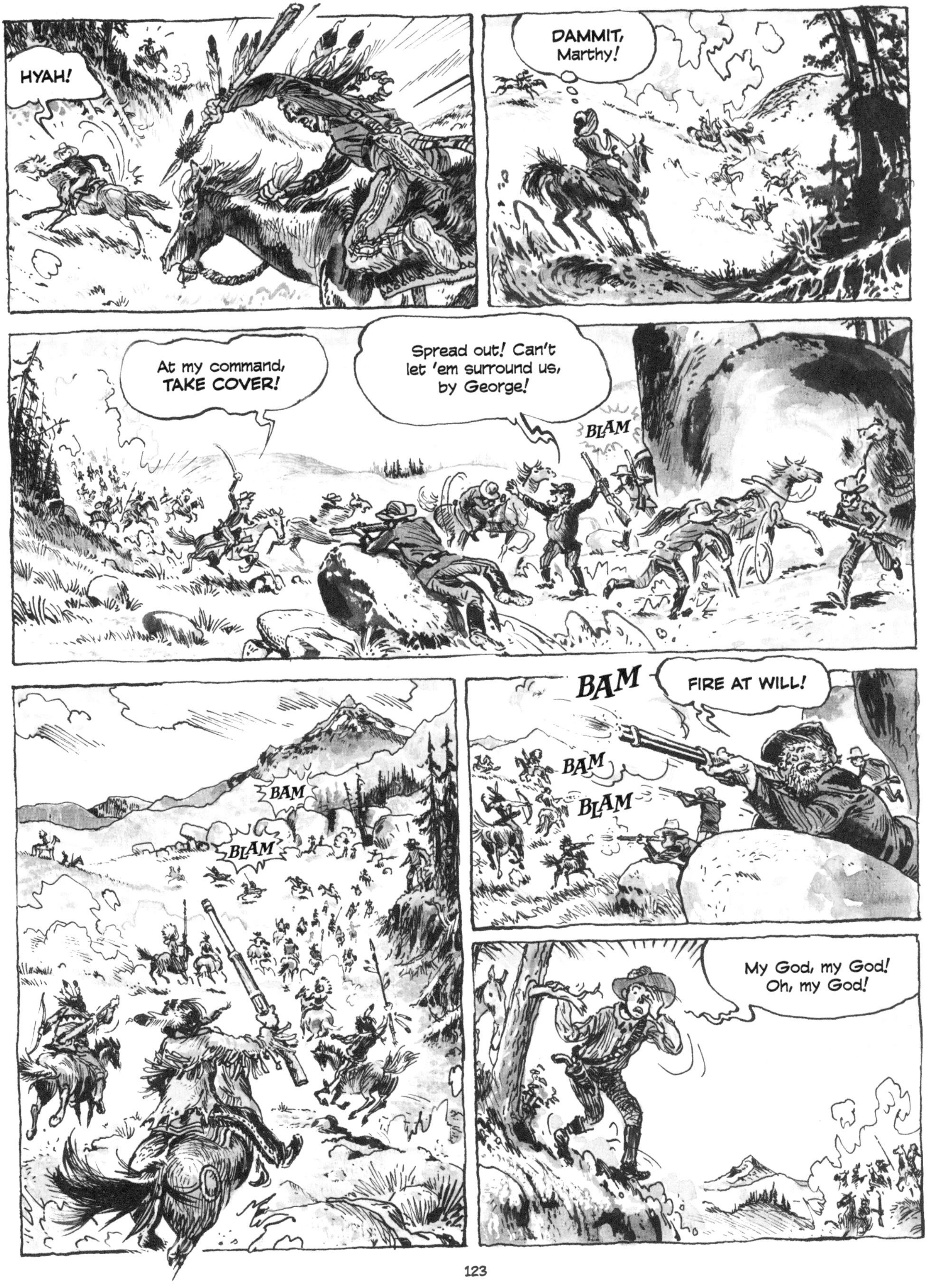
HYAH!
DAMMIT, Marthy!
At my command, TAKE COVER!
Spread out! Can't let 'em surround us, by George!
BLAM
BAM
BLAM
BAM
FIRE AT WILL!
BAM
BLAM
My God, my God! Oh, my God!

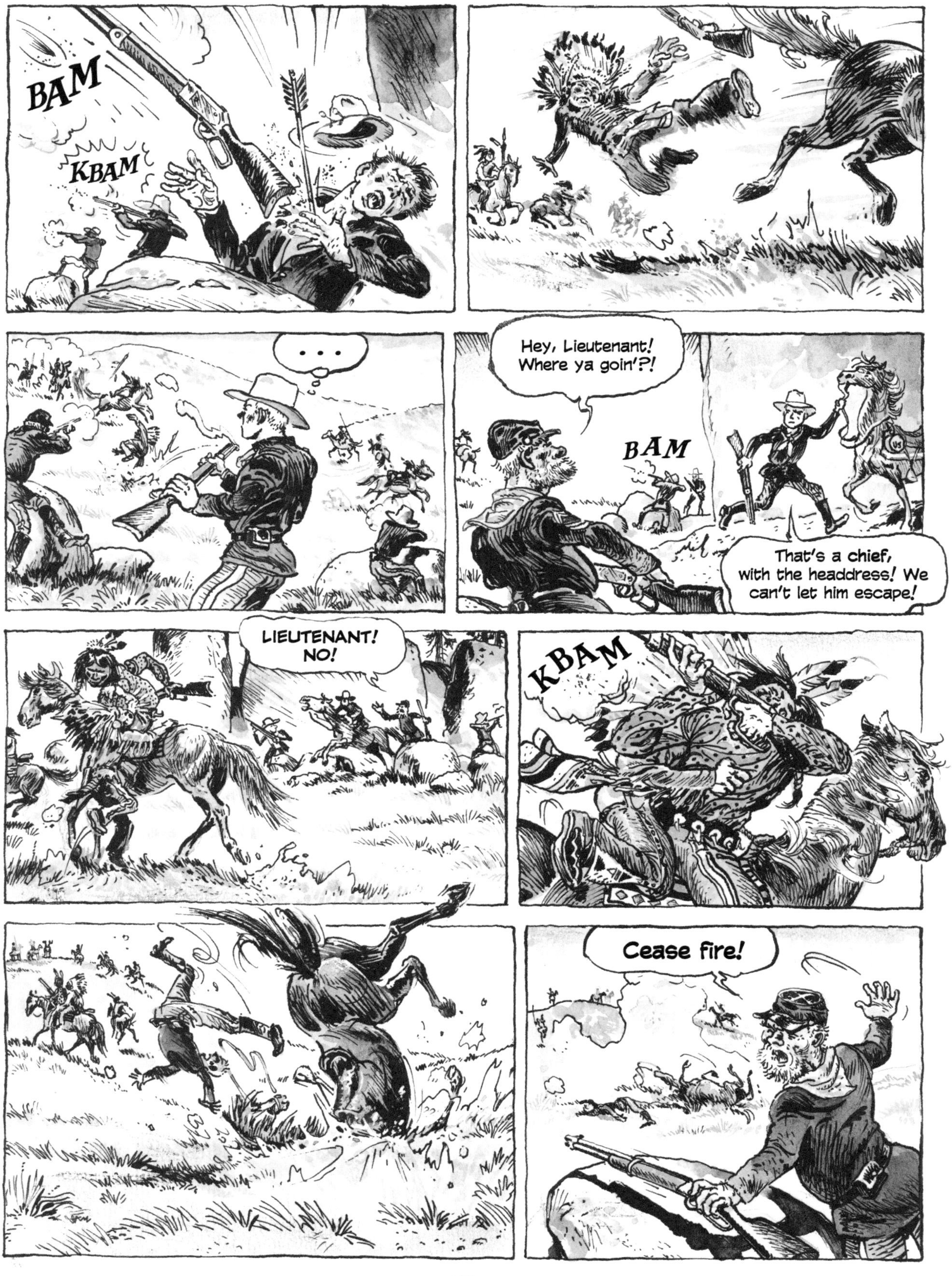
BAM
KBAM
...
Hey, Lieutenant! Where ya goin'?!
BAM
That's a chief, with the headdress! We can't let him escape!
LIEUTENANT! NO!
KBAM
Cease fire!

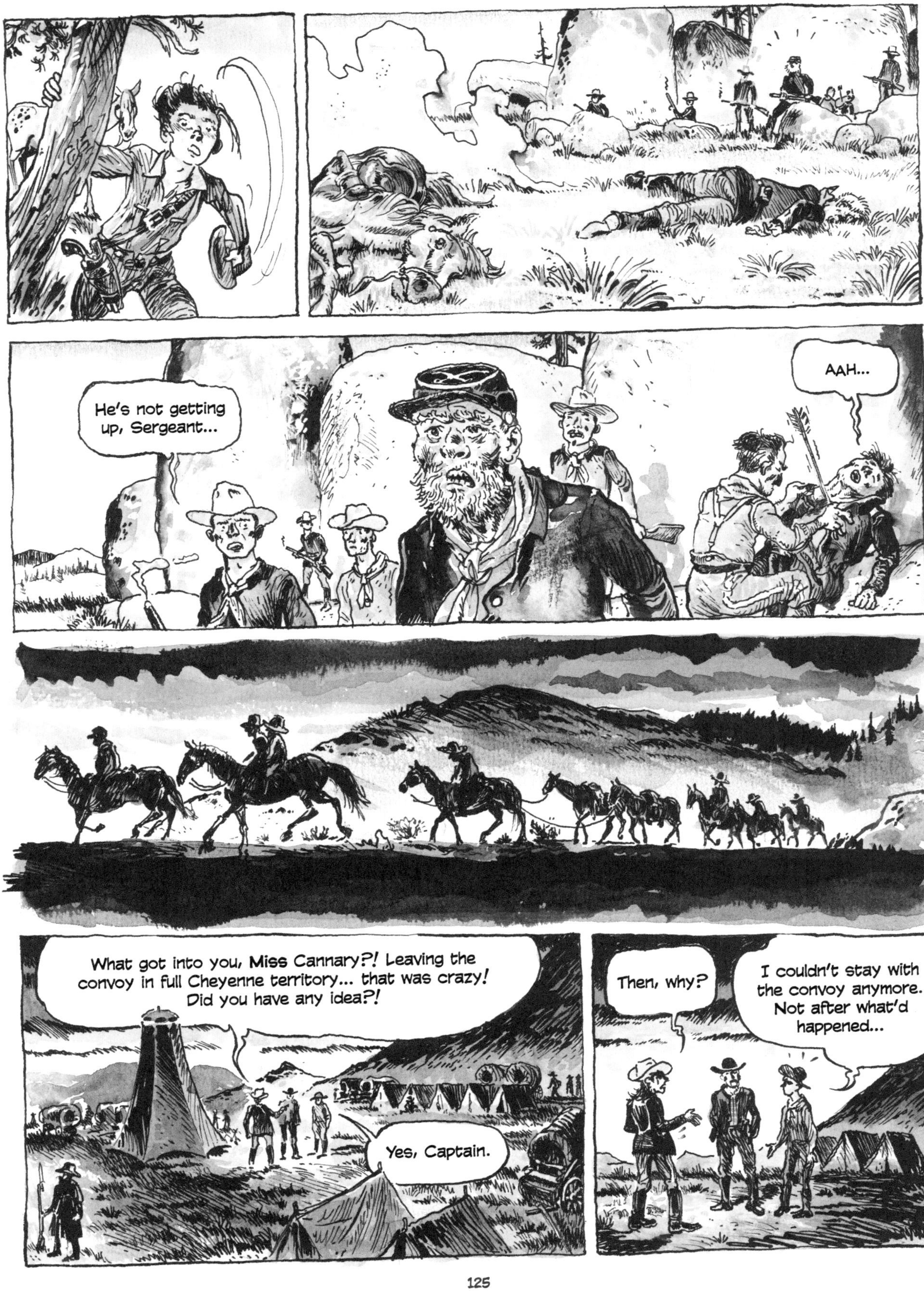
He's not getting up, Sergeant...
AAH...
What got into you, Miss Cannary?! Leaving the convoy in full Cheyenne territory... that was crazy! Did you have any idea?!
Yes, Captain.
Then, why?
I couldn't stay with the convoy anymore. Not after what'd happened...

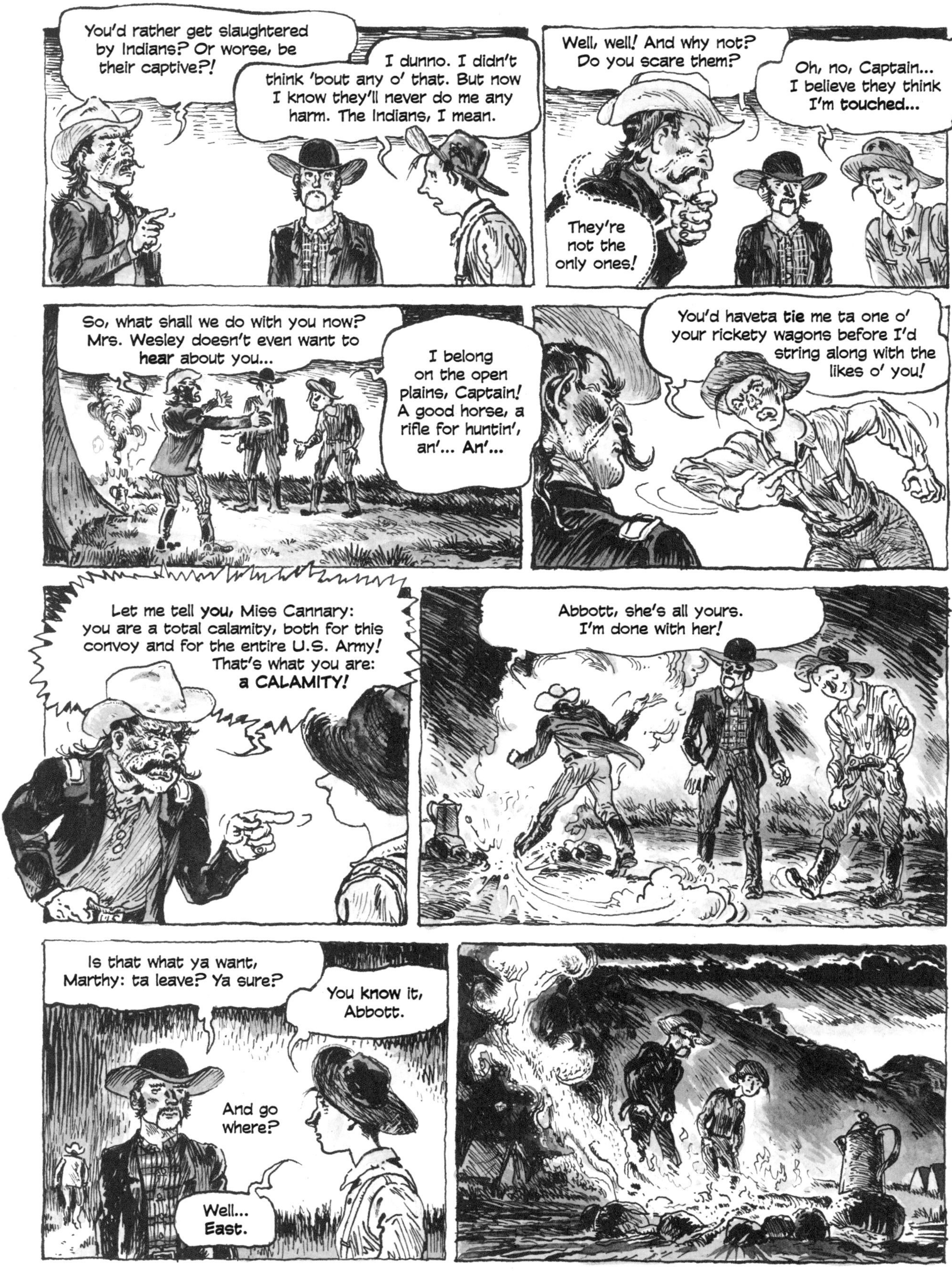
You'd rather get slaughtered by Indians? Or worse, be their captive?!
I dunno. I didn't think 'bout any o' that. But now I know they'll never do me any harm. The Indians, I mean.
Well, well! And why not? Do you scare them?
Oh, no, Captain... I believe they think I'm touched...
They're not the only ones!
So, what shall we do with you now? Mrs. Wesley doesn't even want to hear about you...
I belong on the open plains, Captain! A good horse, a rifle for huntin', an'... An'...
You'd haveta tie me ta one o' your rickety wagons before I'd string along with the likes o' you!
Let me tell you, Miss Cannary: you are a total calamity, both for this convoy and for the entire U.S. Army! That's what you are: a CALAMITY!
Abbott, she's all yours. I'm done with her!
Is that what ya want, Marthy: ta leave? Ya sure?
You know it, Abbott.
And go where?
Well... East.

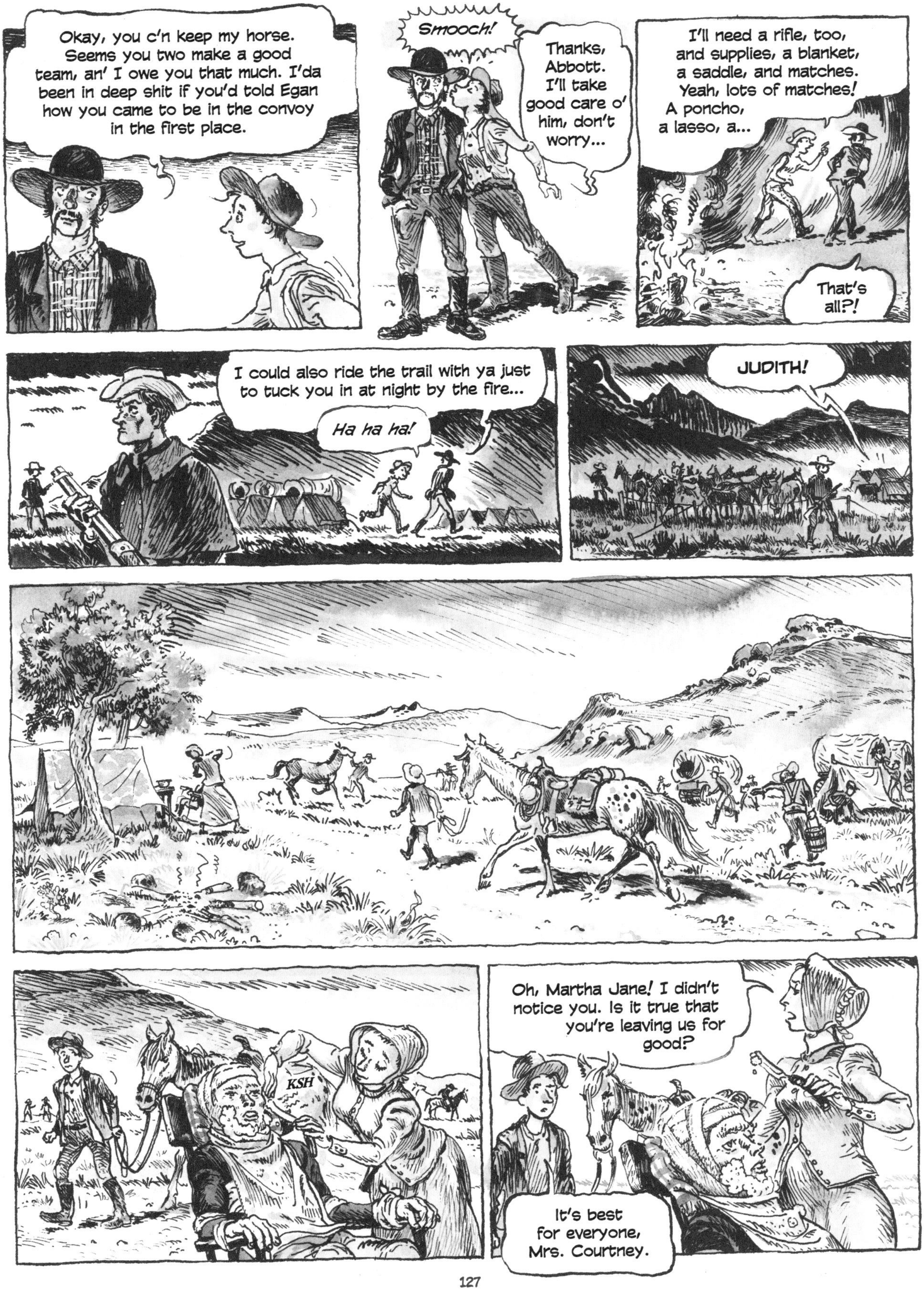
Okay, you c'n keep my horse. Seems you two make a good team, an' I owe you that much. I'da been in deep shit if you'd told Egan how you came to be in the convoy in the first place.
Smooch!
Thanks, Abbott. I'll take good care o' him, don't worry...
I'll need a rifle, too, and supplies, a blanket, a saddle, and matches. Yeah, lots of matches! A poncho, a lasso, a...
That's all?!
I could also ride the trail with ya just to tuck you in at night by the fire...
Ha ha ha!
JUDITH!
KSH
Oh, Martha Jane! I didn't notice you. Is it true that you're leaving us for good?
It's best for everyone, Mrs. Courtney.

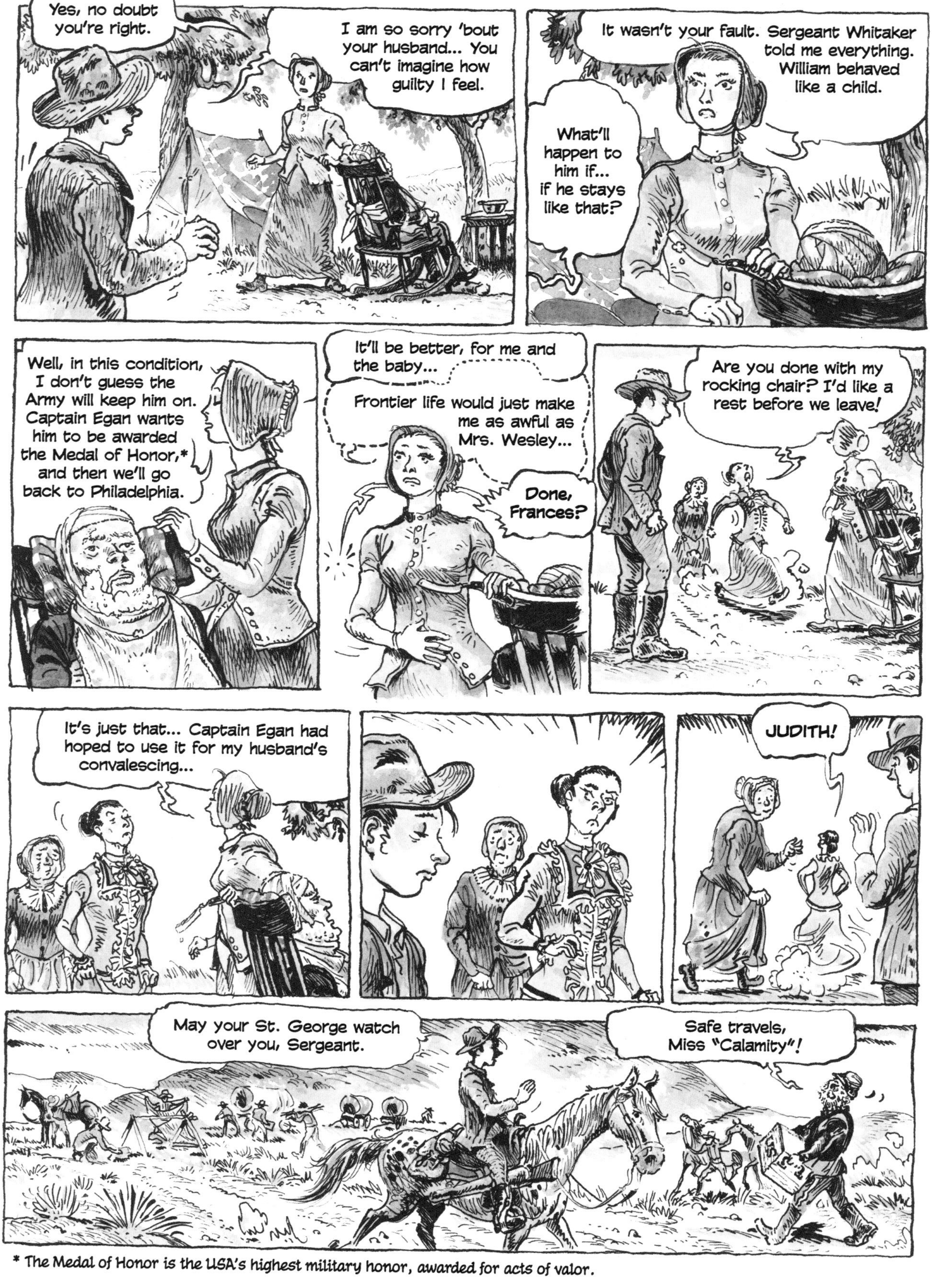
Yes, no doubt you're right.
I am so sorry 'bout your husband... You can't imagine how guilty I feel.
It wasn't your fault. Sergeant Whitaker told me everything. William behaved like a child.
What'll happen to him if... if he stays like that?
Well, in this condition, I don't guess the Army will keep him on. Captain Egan wants him to be awarded the Medal of Honor,* and then we'll go back to Philadelphia.
It'll be better, for me and the baby...
Frontier life would just make me as awful as Mrs. Wesley...
Done, Frances?
Are you done with my rocking chair? I'd like a rest before we leave!
It's just that... Captain Egan had hoped to use it for my husband's convalescing...
JUDITH!
May your St. George watch over you, Sergeant.
Safe travels, Miss "Calamity"!

* The Medal of Honor is the USA's highest military honor, awarded for acts of valor.

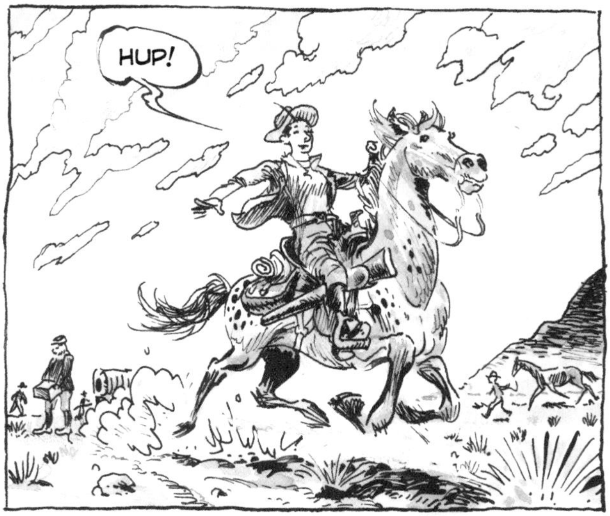
HUP!

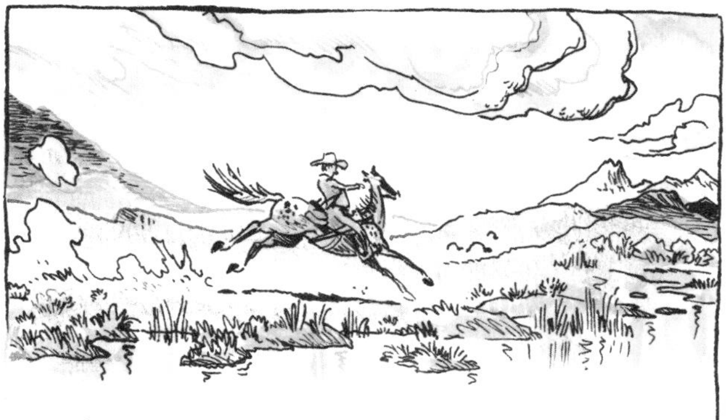

Goose Creek, located somewhere between Montana and Wyoming, was the area that Martha Jane now left behind. This was a time when these two territories were not yet States, and their common border was nebulous...

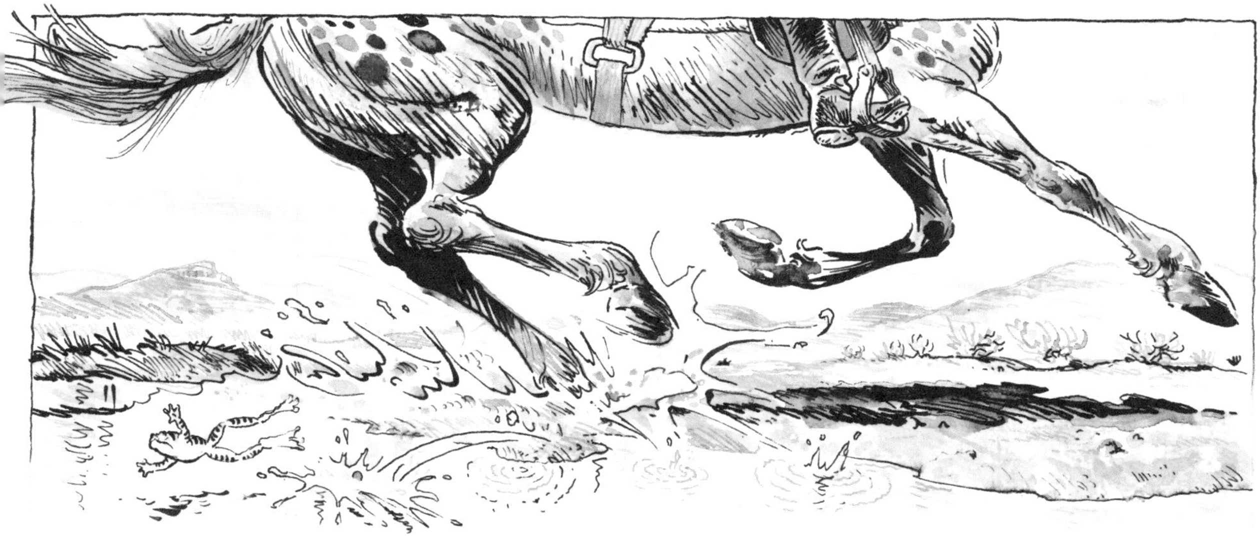

In *Letters to Her Daughter*, Martha Jane said that Captain Egan had given her the nickname "Calamity" at Goose Creek, where she inadvertently became famous in the course of a skirmish with the Indians. The story she told isn't precisely the same as our own, since nothing is ever entirely certain when it comes to Martha Jane Cannary. In her case there is often such a huge gap between legend and reality that any scenario is possible...

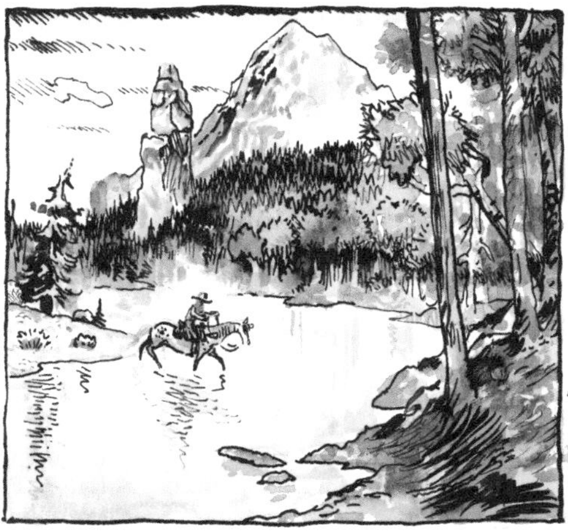

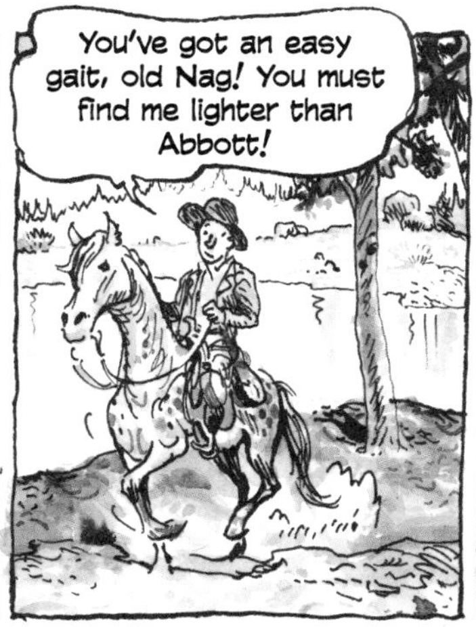
You've got an easy gait, old Nag! You must find me lighter than Abbott!

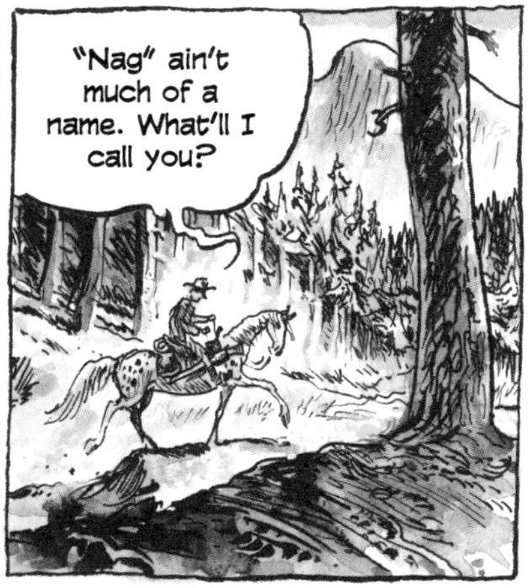
"Nag" ain't much of a name. What'll I call you?

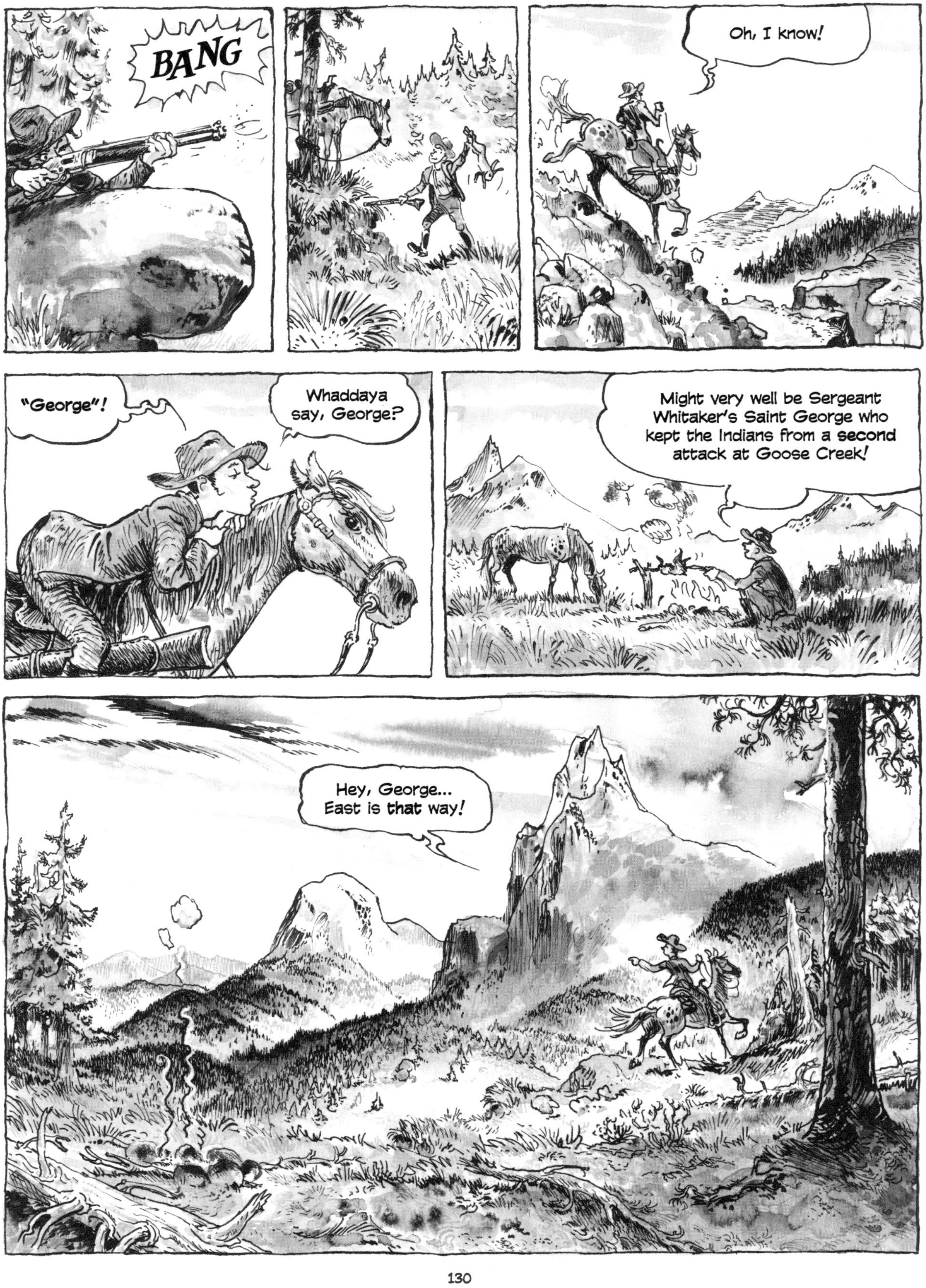
BANG
Oh, I know!
"George"!
Whaddaya say, George?
Might very well be Sergeant Whitaker's Saint George who kept the Indians from a second attack at Goose Creek!
Hey, George... East is that way!

Martha Jane Cannary

(1870~1876)

This is a strange place, like a scar slashed through the prairie: a landscape out of Dante, gouged by water, wind, and ice. The Sioux called this area **Mako Sitcha,** translated by the settlers from the East as...

THE BADLANDS

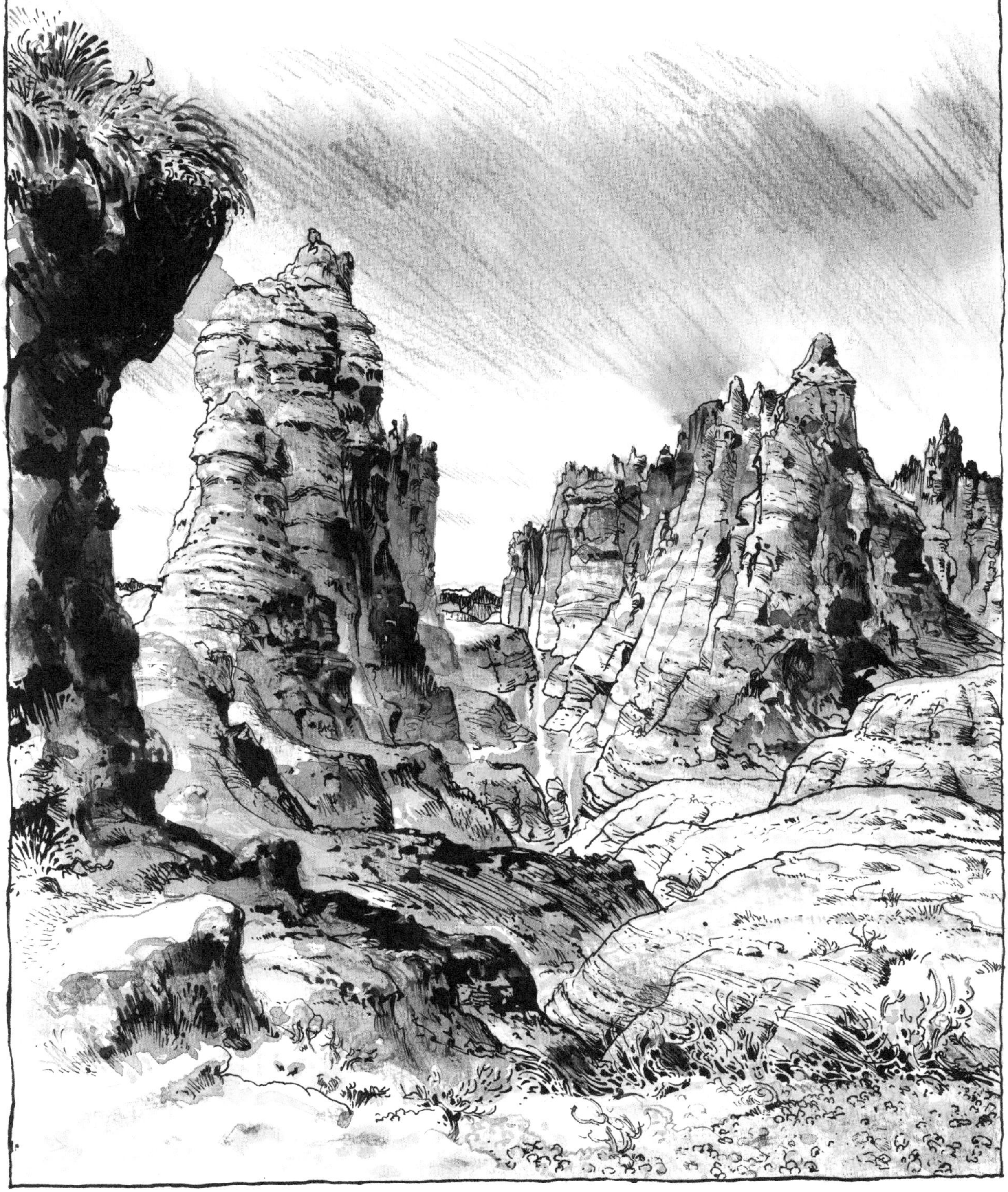

There is nothing to live on, here: no wood to warm yourself, no grass for the livestock. For the Plains Indians, this was the realm of wandering spirits. At the base of this desert valley flows a current, one so small that no map has ever charted it.

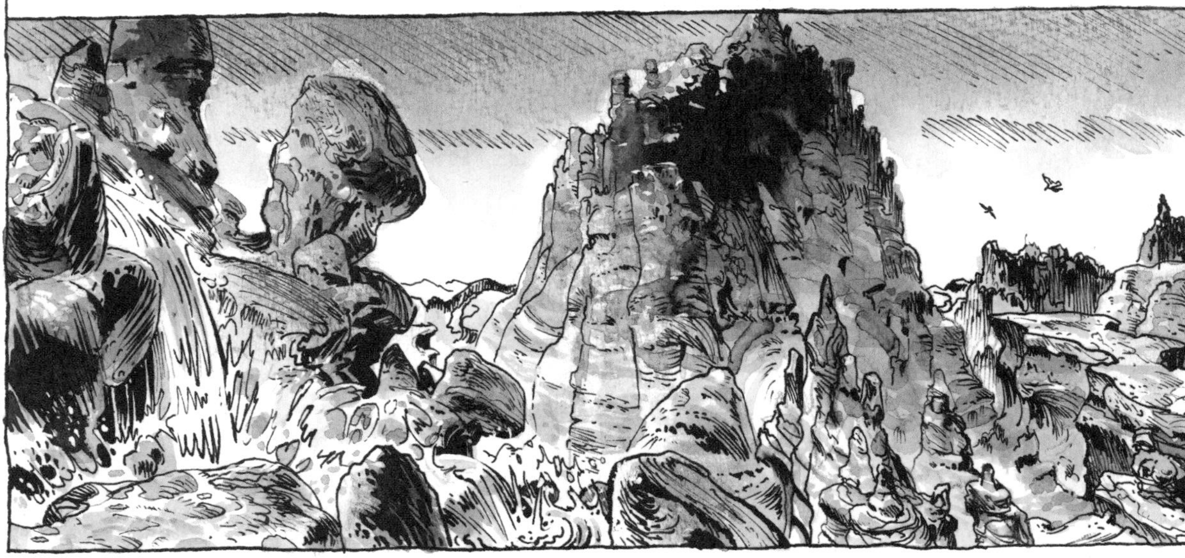

It runs to the north and west, following a tortuous path before breaking out of the Badlands. Once the current reaches sandier terrain, its waters begin to swell, making its way across the plains to pour into the Cheyenne River.

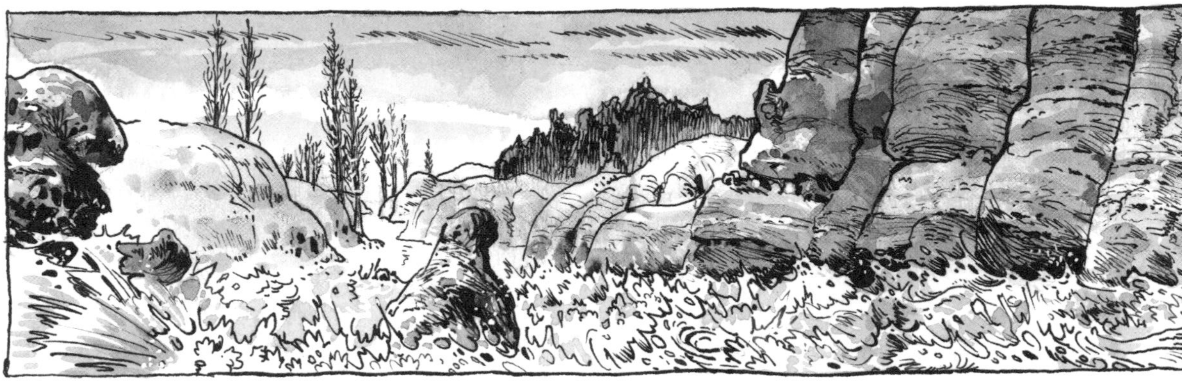

But we won't move beyond the dunes for now, since these narrow ravines mark the territory's most fertile land.

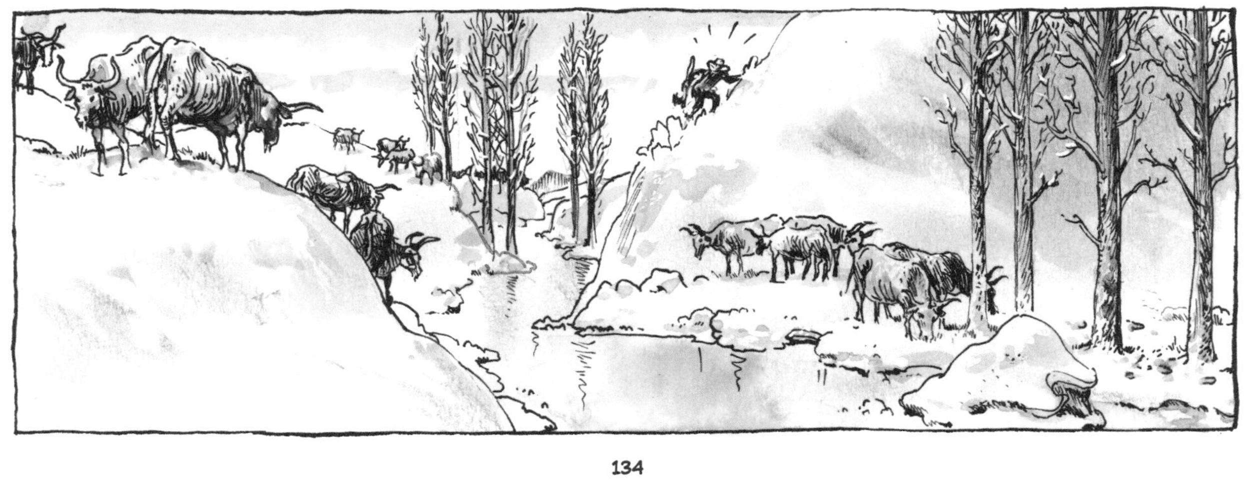

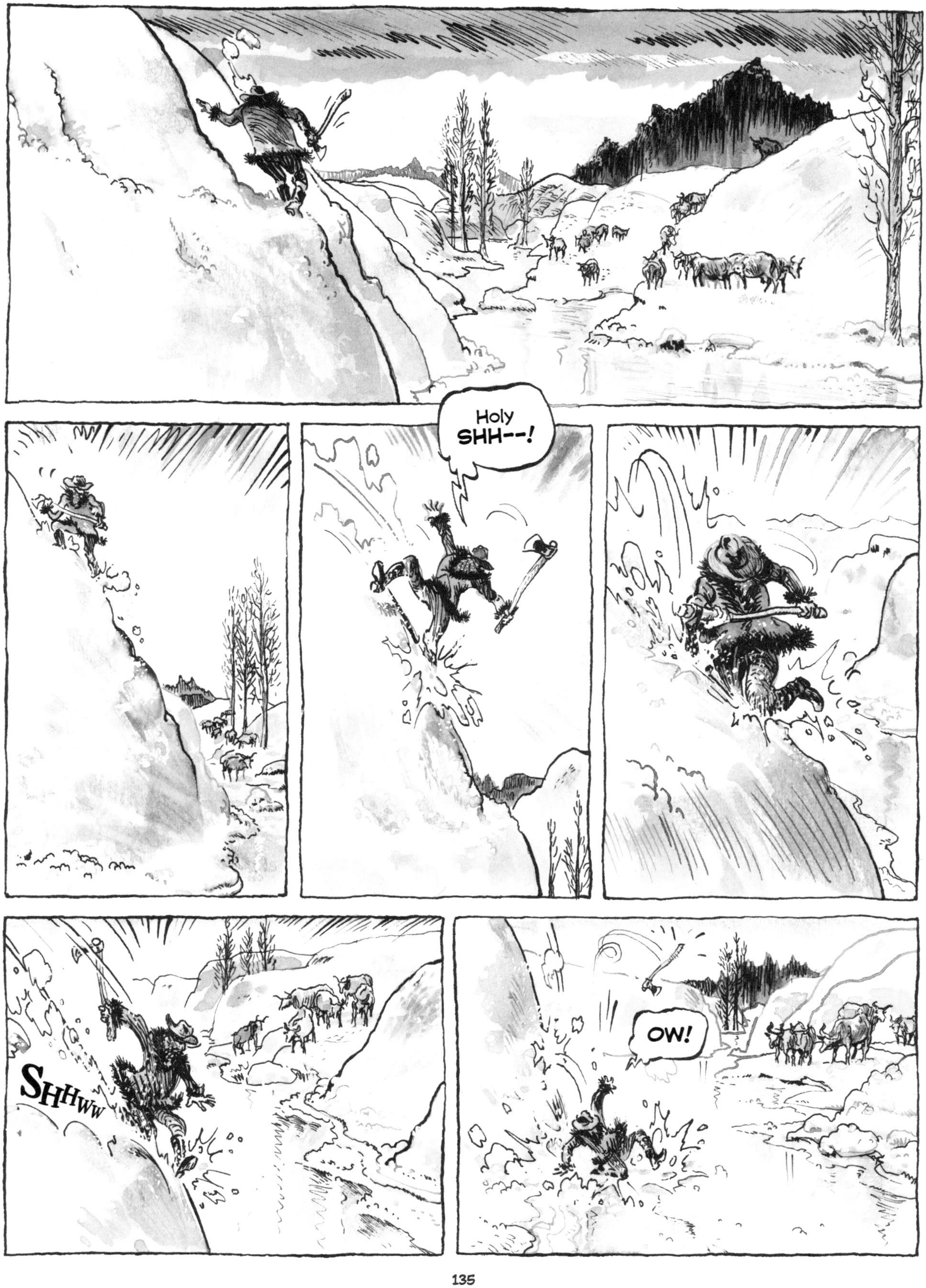
Holy SHH--!
SHHWW
OW!

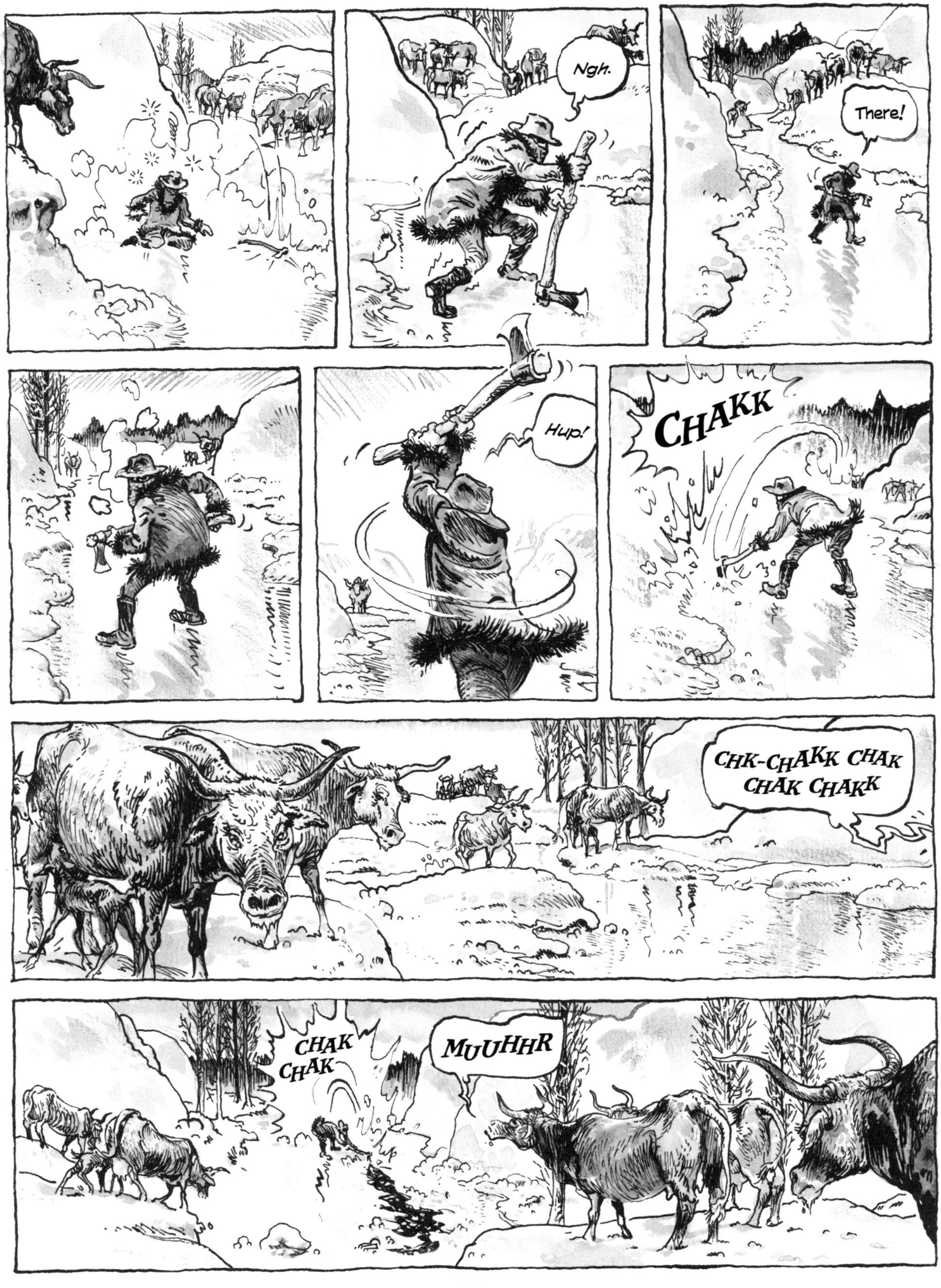
Ngh.
There!
Hup!
CHAKK
CHK-CHAKK CHAK
CHAK CHAKK
CHAK
CHAK
MUUHHR

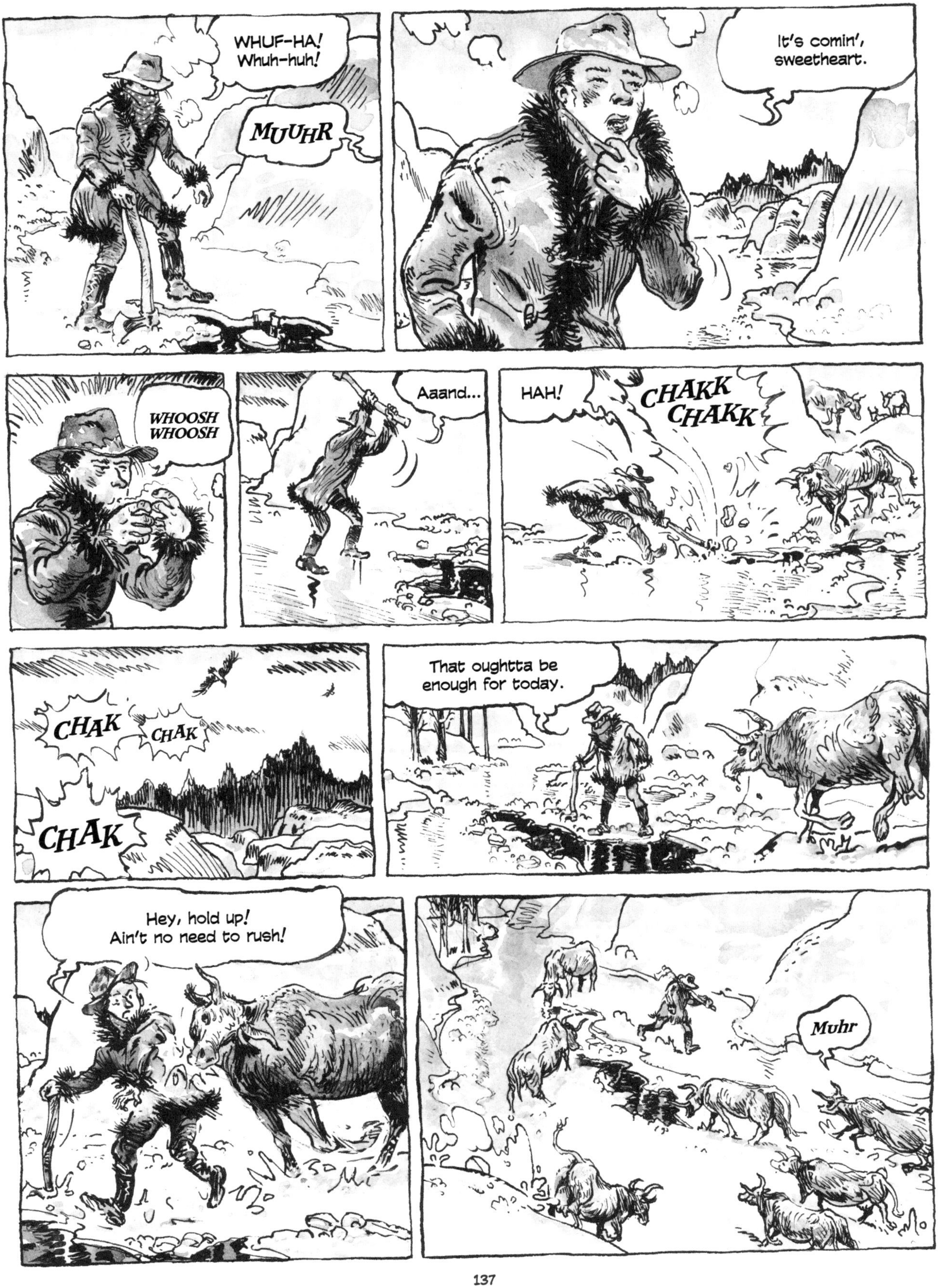
WHUF-HA! Whuh-huh!
MUUHR
It's comin', sweetheart.
WHOOSH WHOOSH
Aaand...
HAH!
CHAKK CHAKK
CHAK
CHAK
CHAK
That oughtta be enough for today.
Hey, hold up! Ain't no need to rush!
Muhr

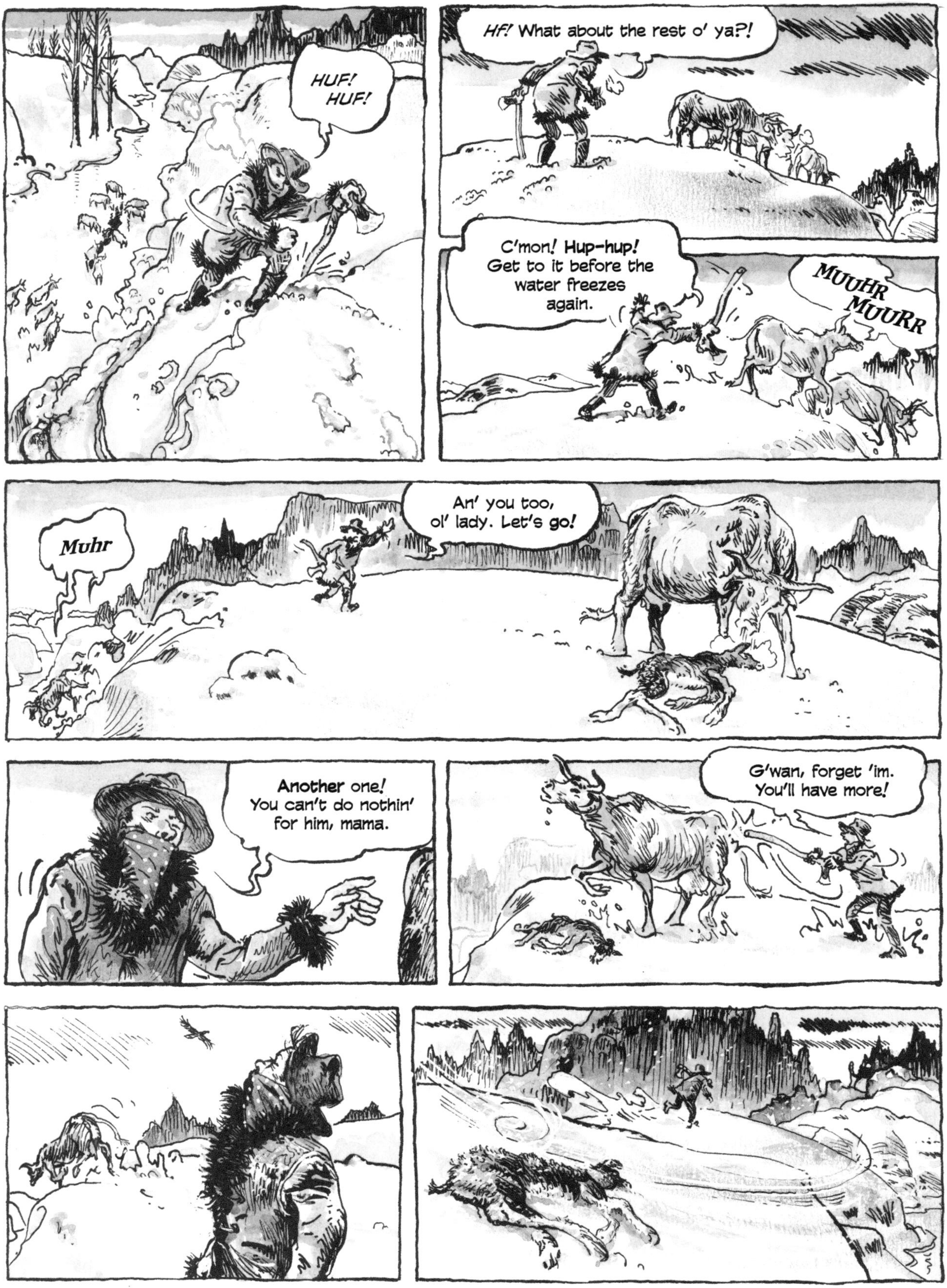
HUF! HUF!
Hf! What about the rest o' ya?!
C'mon! Hup-hup! Get to it before the water freezes again.
MUUHR MUURR
Muhr
An' you too, ol' lady. Let's go!
Another one! You can't do nothin' for him, mama.
G'wan, forget 'im. You'll have more!

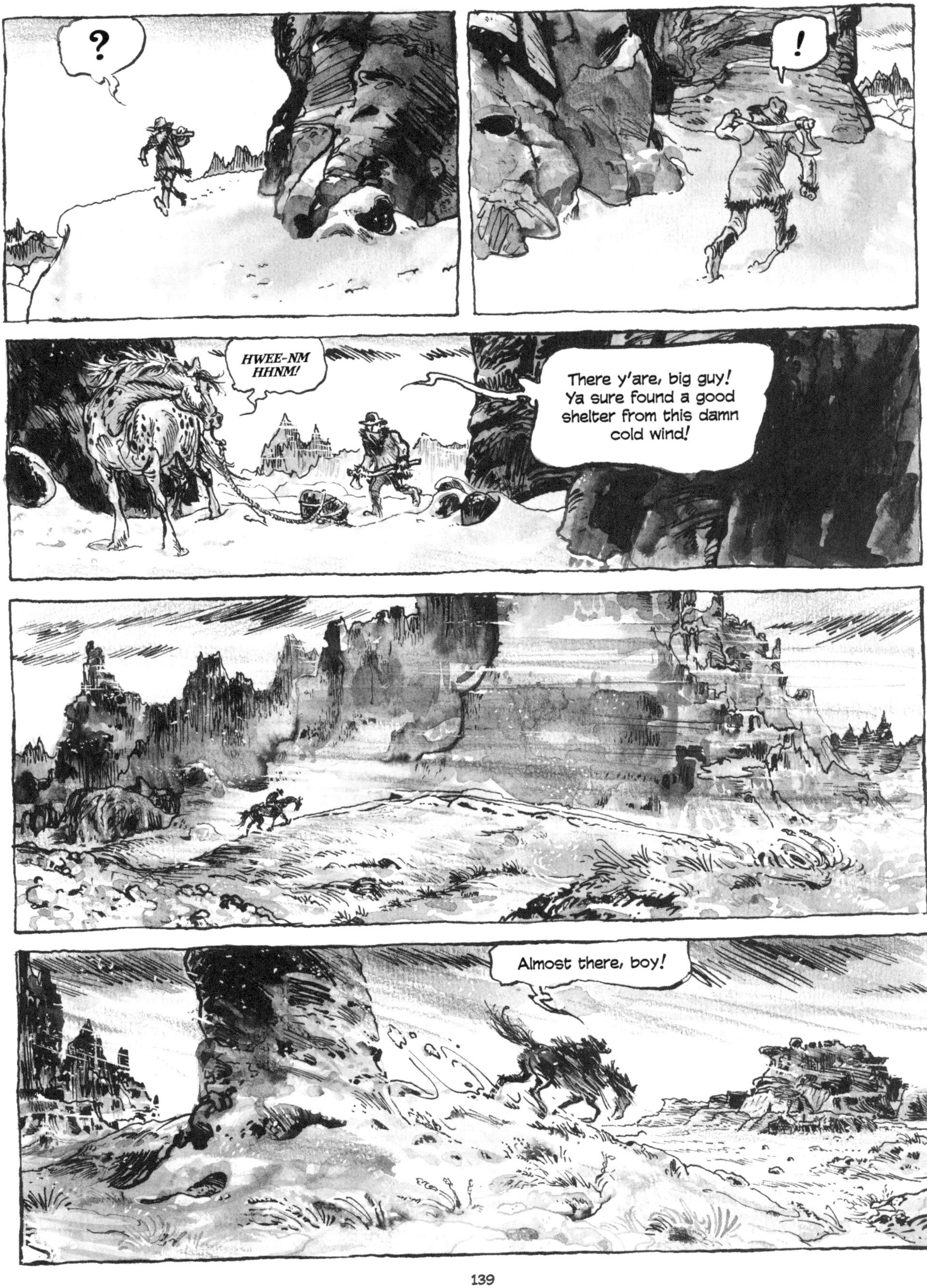
?
!
HWEE-NM HHNM!
There y'are, big guy! Ya sure found a good shelter from this damn cold wind!
Almost there, boy!

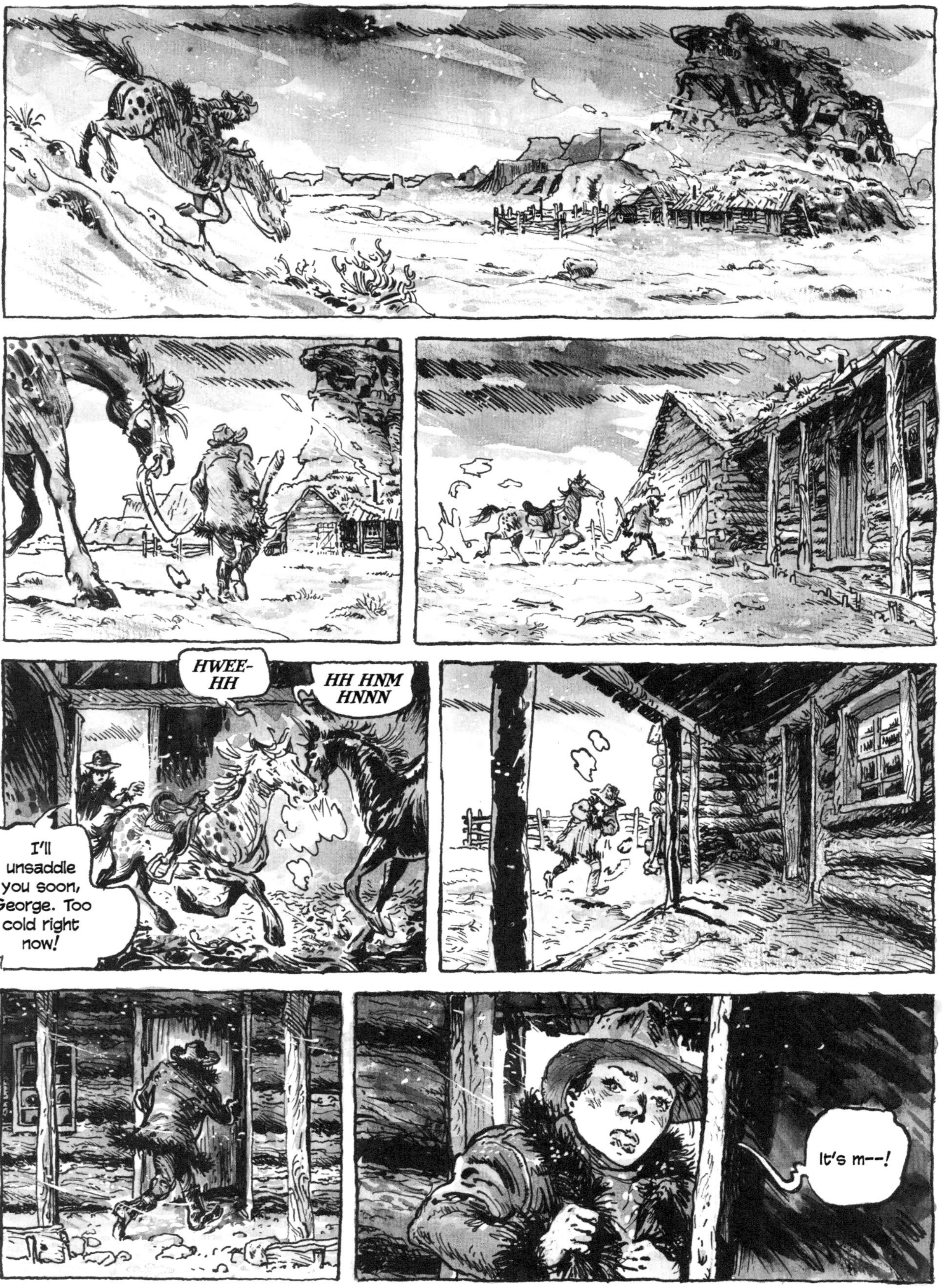
HWEE-HH
HH HNM HNNN
I'll unsaddle you soon, George. Too cold right now!
It's m--!

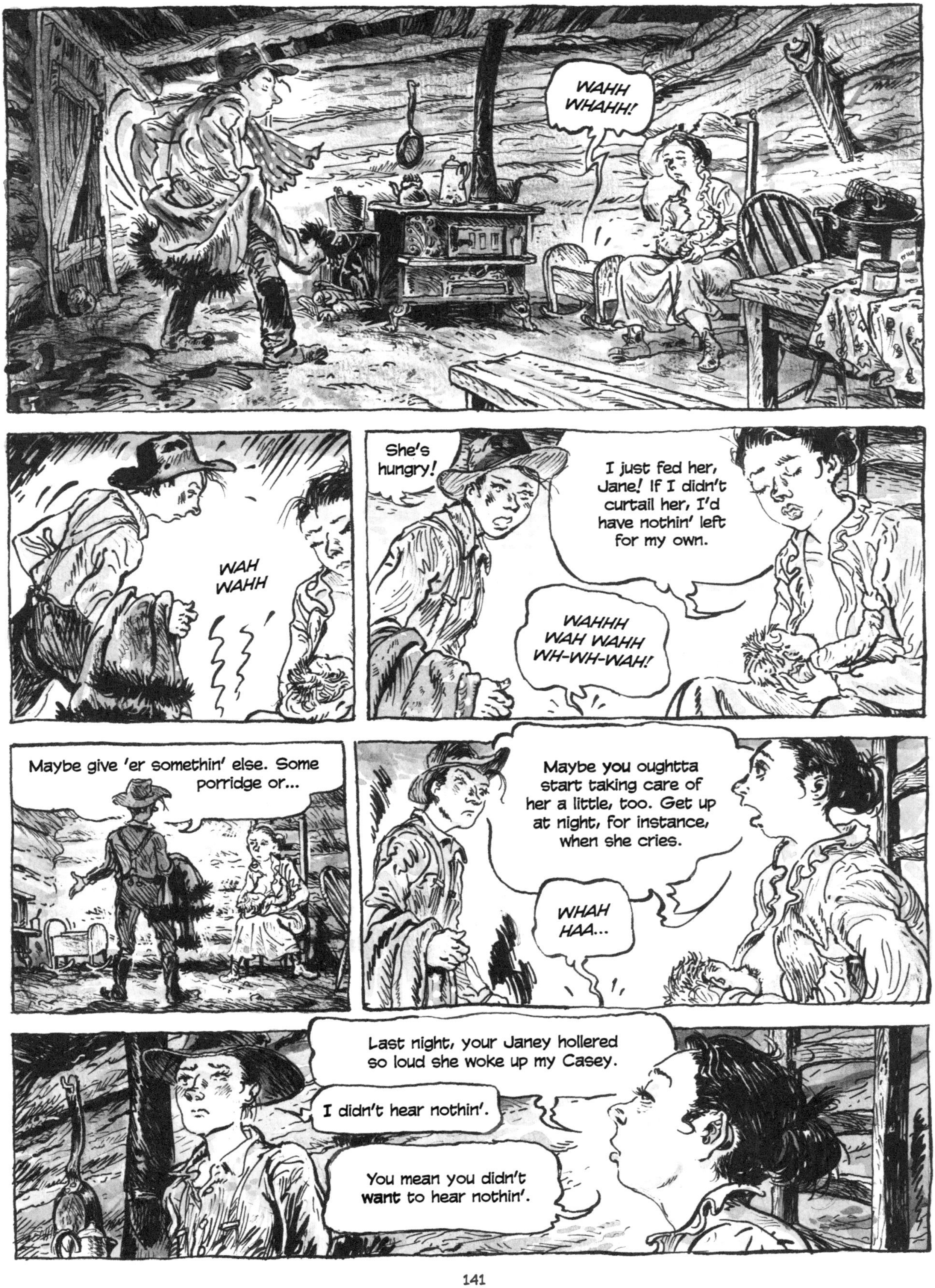
WAHH WHAHH!
WAH WAHH
She's hungry!
I just fed her, Jane! If I didn't curtail her, I'd have nothin' left for my own.
WAHHH WAH WAHH WH-WH-WAH!
Maybe give 'er somethin' else. Some porridge or...
Maybe you oughtta start taking care of her a little, too. Get up at night, for instance, when she cries.
WHAH HAA...
Last night, your Janey hollered so loud she woke up my Casey.
I didn't hear nothin'.
You mean you didn't want to hear nothin'.

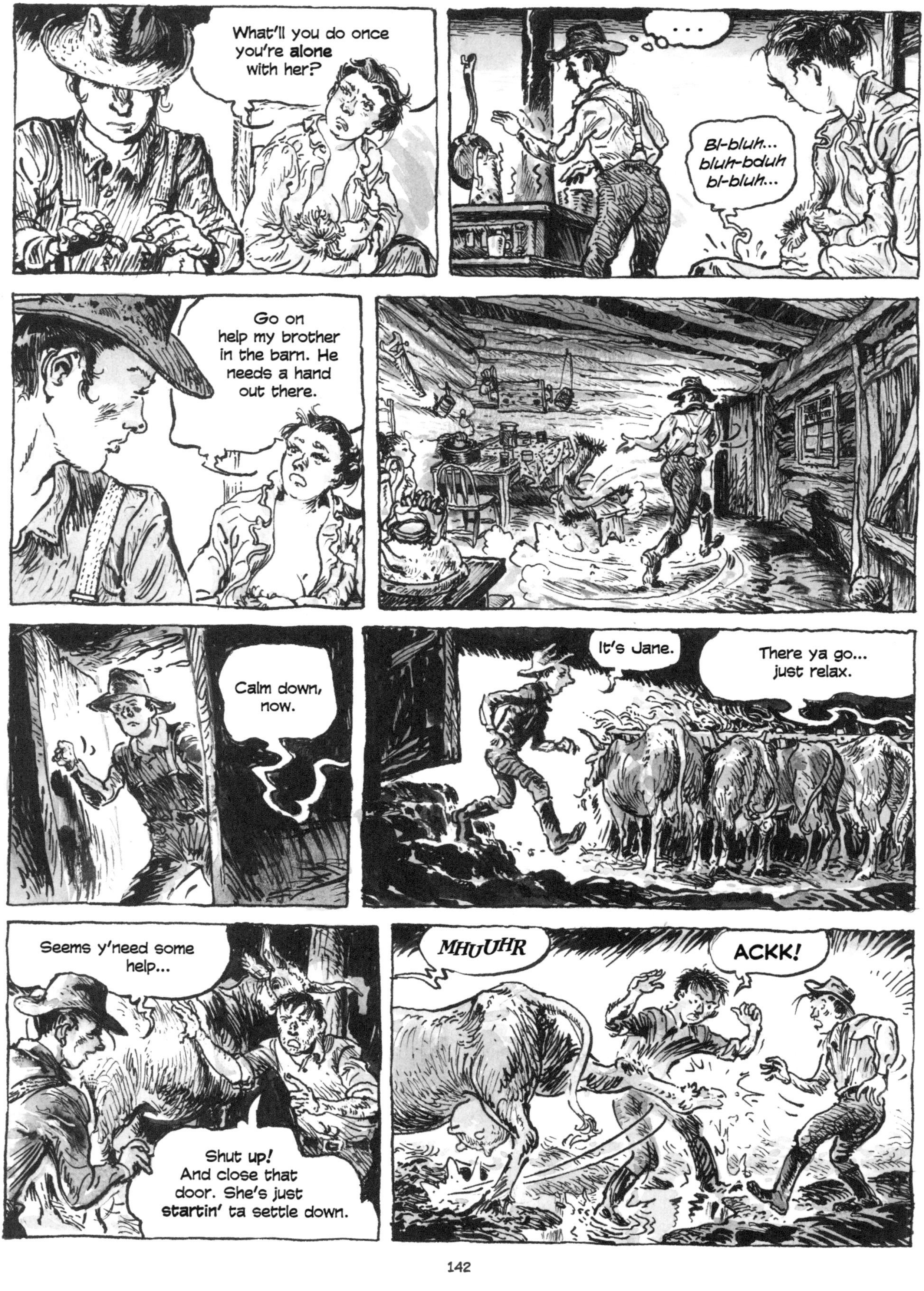
What'll you do once you're **alone** with her?
. . .
Bl-bluh... bluh-bduh bl-bluh...
Go on help my brother in the barn. He needs a hand out there.
Calm down, now.
It's Jane.
There ya go... just relax.
Seems y'need some help...
Shut up! And close that door. She's just **startin'** ta settle down.
MHUUHR
ACKK!

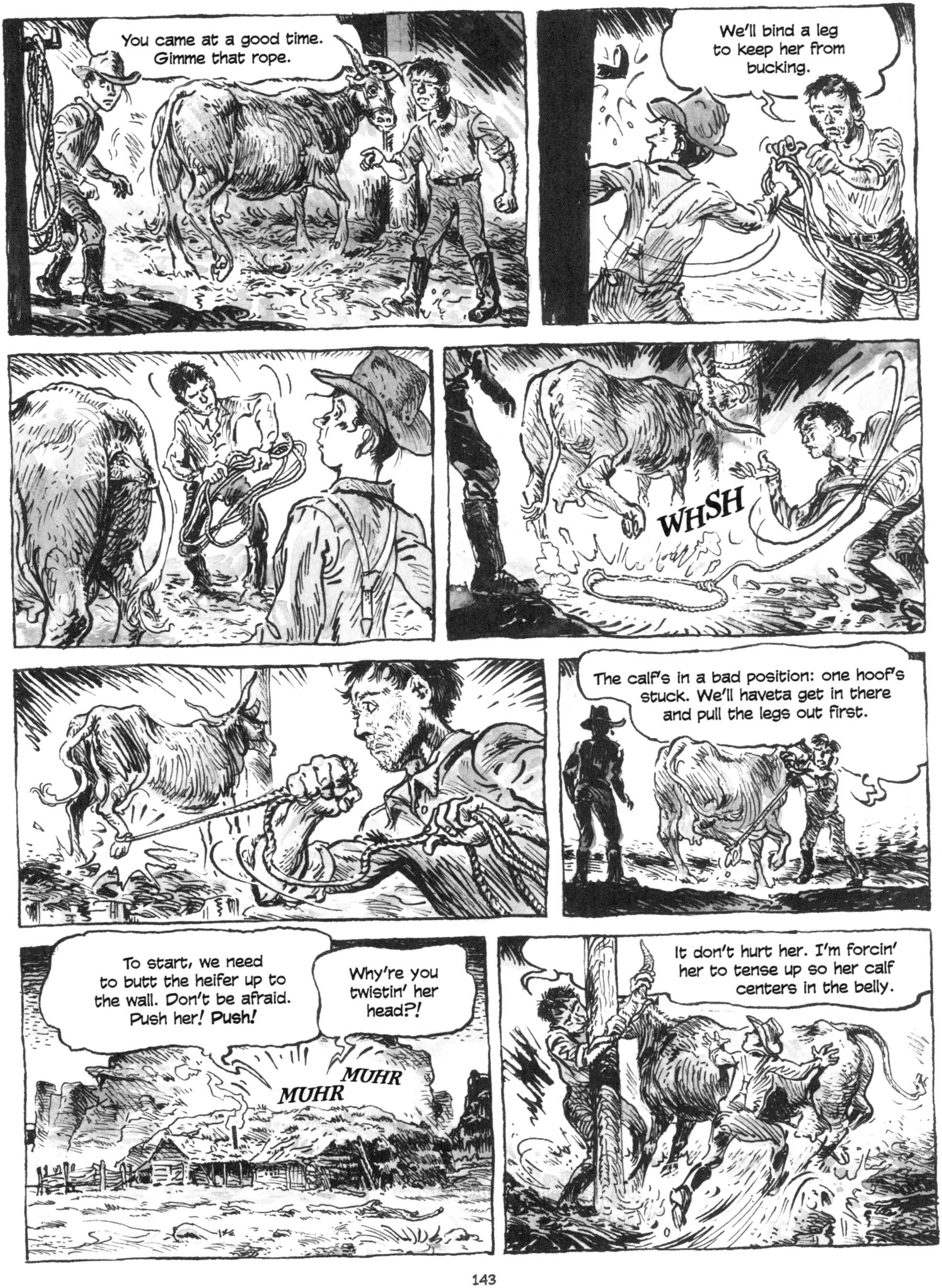
You came at a good time. Gimme that rope.
We'll bind a leg to keep her from bucking.
WHSH
The calf's in a bad position: one hoof's stuck. We'll haveta get in there and pull the legs out first.
To start, we need to butt the heifer up to the wall. Don't be afraid. Push her! Push!
Why're you twistin' her head?!
MUHR
MUHR
It don't hurt her. I'm forcin' her to tense up so her calf centers in the belly.

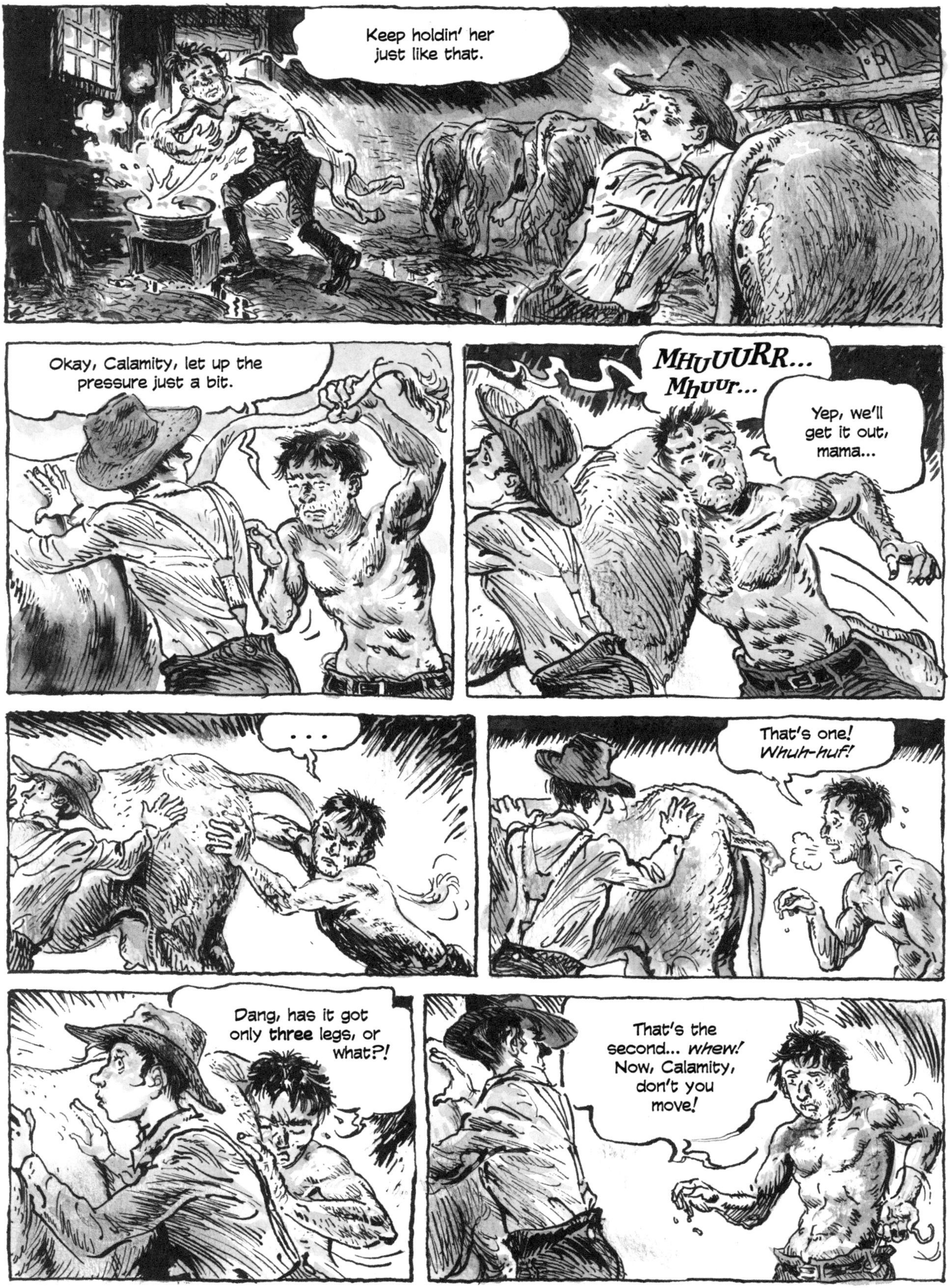

Keep holdin' her just like that.
Okay, Calamity, let up the pressure just a bit.
MHUUURR... Mhuur...
Yep, we'll get it out, mama...
. . .
That's one! *Whuh-huf!*
Dang, has it got only **three** legs, or what?!
That's the second... *whew!* Now, Calamity, don't you move!

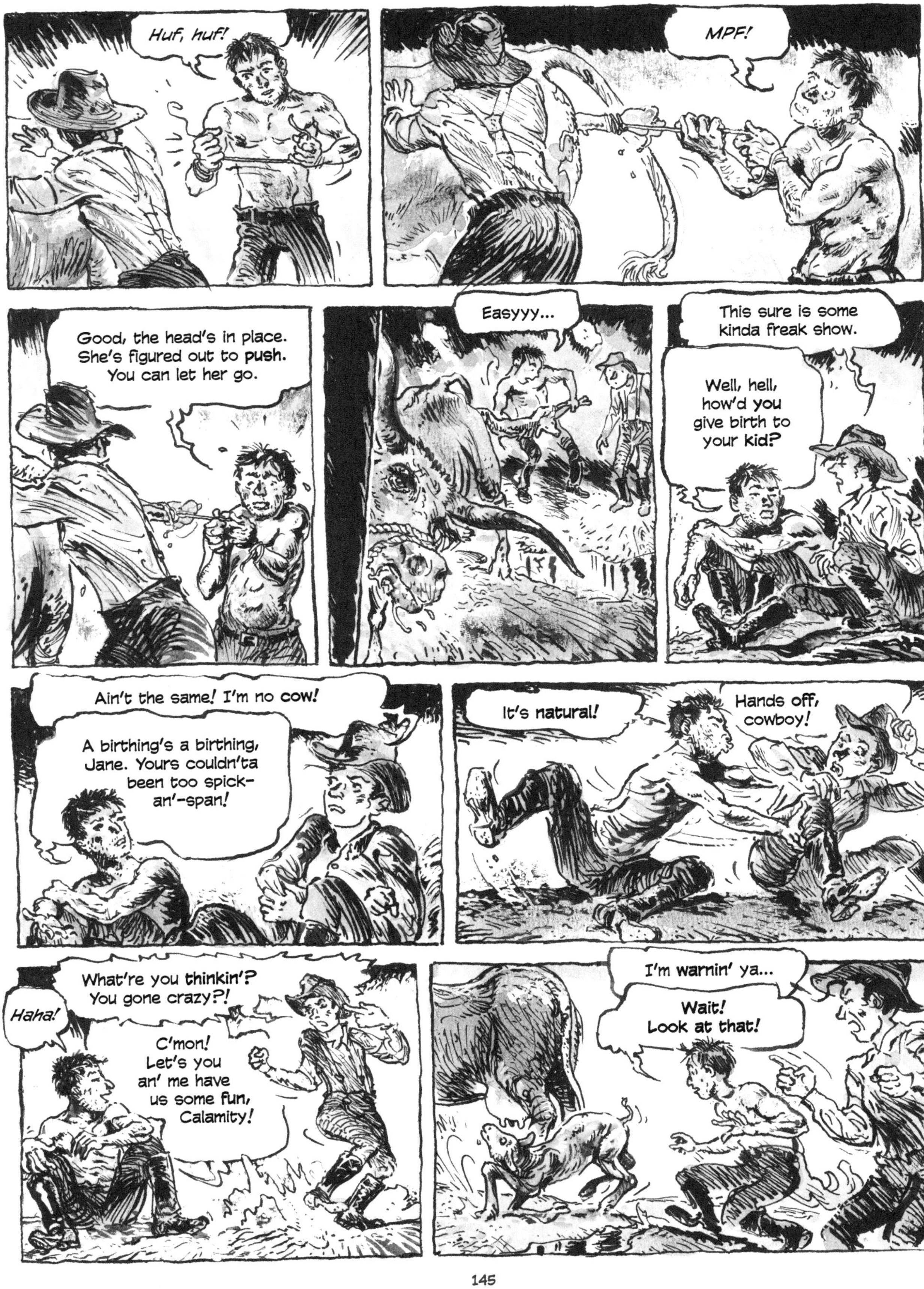
Huf, huf!
MPF!
Good, the head's in place. She's figured out to push. You can let her go.
Easyyy...
This sure is some kinda freak show.
Well, hell, how'd you give birth to your kid?
Ain't the same! I'm no cow!
A birthing's a birthing, Jane. Yours couldn'ta been too spick-an'-span!
It's natural!
Hands off, cowboy!
Haha!
What're you thinkin'? You gone crazy?!
C'mon! Let's you an' me have us some fun, Calamity!
I'm warnin' ya...
Wait! Look at that!

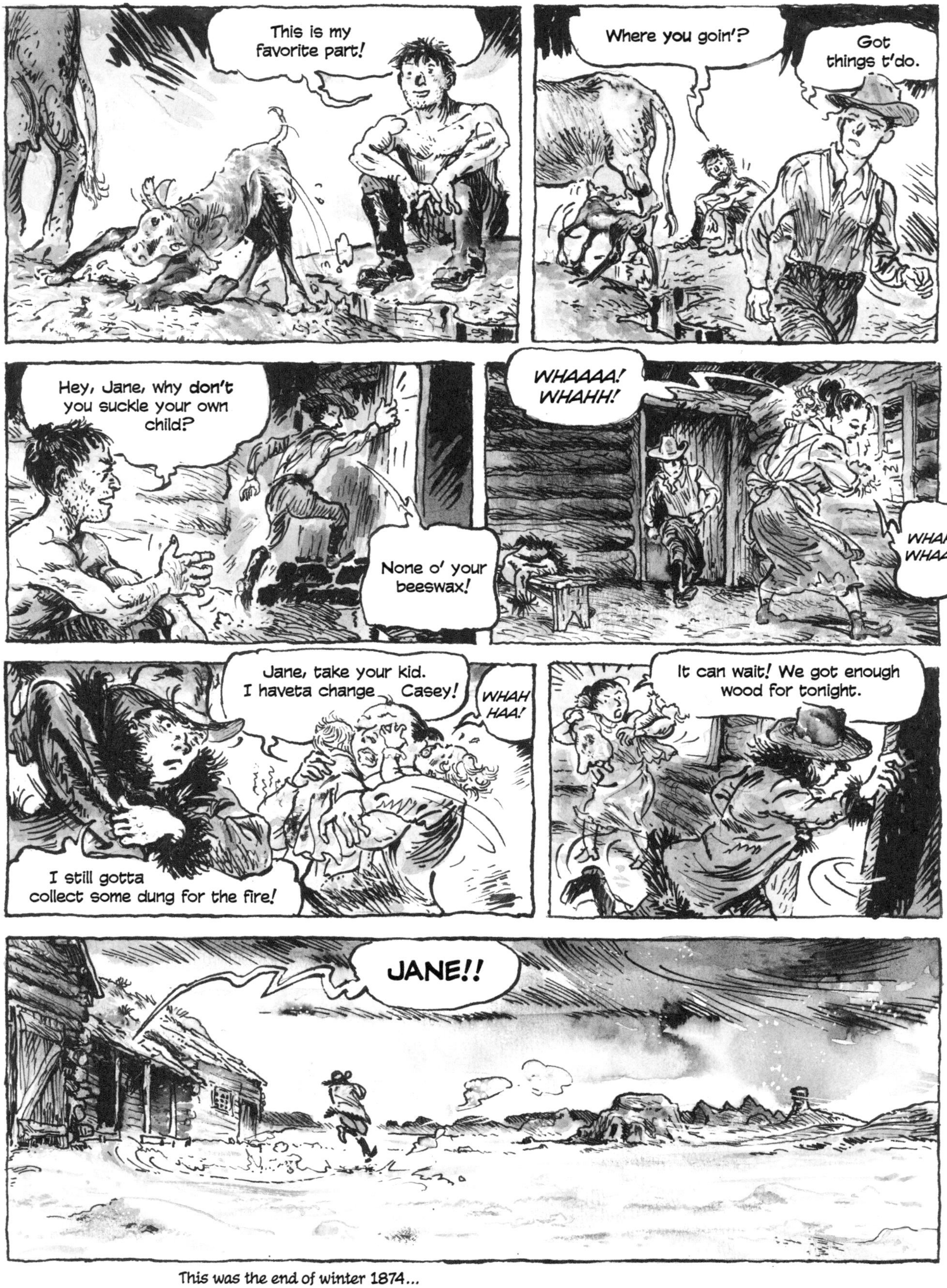
This is my favorite part!
Where you goin'?
Got things t'do.
Hey, Jane, why don't you suckle your own child?
None o' your beeswax!
WHAAAA! WHAHH!
WHAH WHAA!
Jane, take your kid. I haveta change Casey!
WHAH HAA!
I still gotta collect some dung for the fire!
It can wait! We got enough wood for tonight.
JANE!!

This was the end of winter 1874...

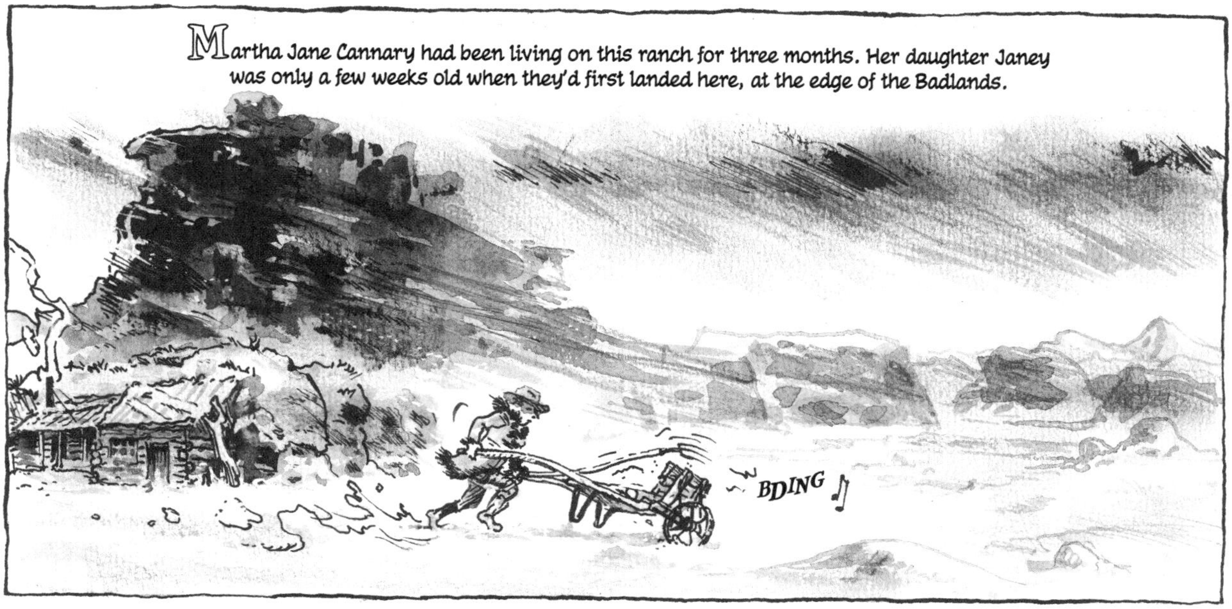
Martha Jane Cannary had been living on this ranch for three months. Her daughter Janey was only a few weeks old when they'd first landed here, at the edge of the Badlands.
BDING

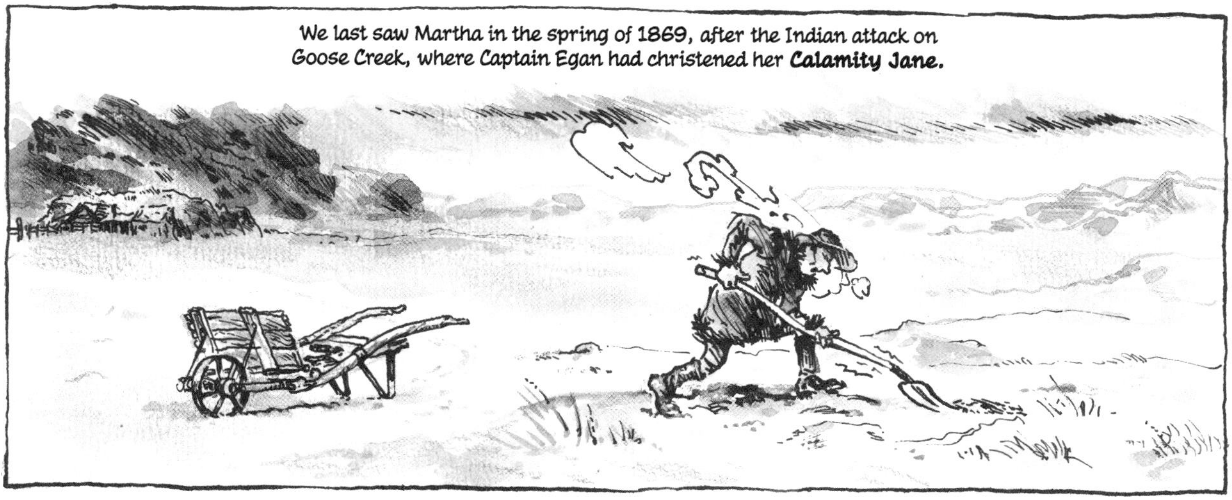
We last saw Martha in the spring of 1869, after the Indian attack on Goose Creek, where Captain Egan had christened her **Calamity Jane.**

It was during the next five years that this young woman could be seen riding the trails through the Western Territories: from Laramie to Abilene, from Cheyenne to Sioux City...

Calamity earned her living doing a thousand small jobs in these towns. She idled in saloons and played poker. She drank to excess and chewed bad tobacco, which yellowed her teeth and left her with foul breath.

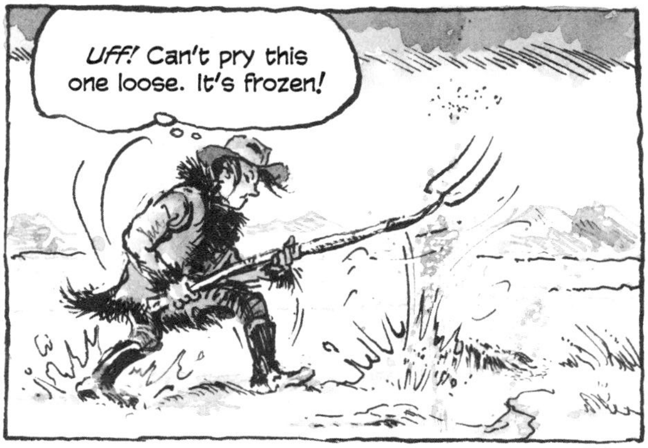
Uff! Can't pry this one loose. It's frozen!

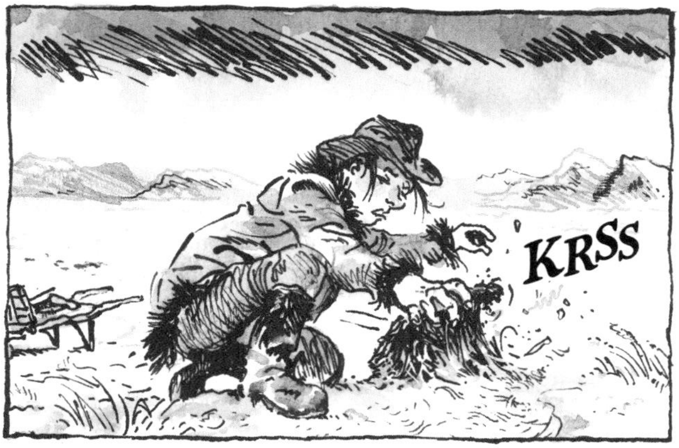
KRSS

From Prairie Queen one day to unwelcome reprobate the next, Calamity Jane embraced her role as an oddball character.

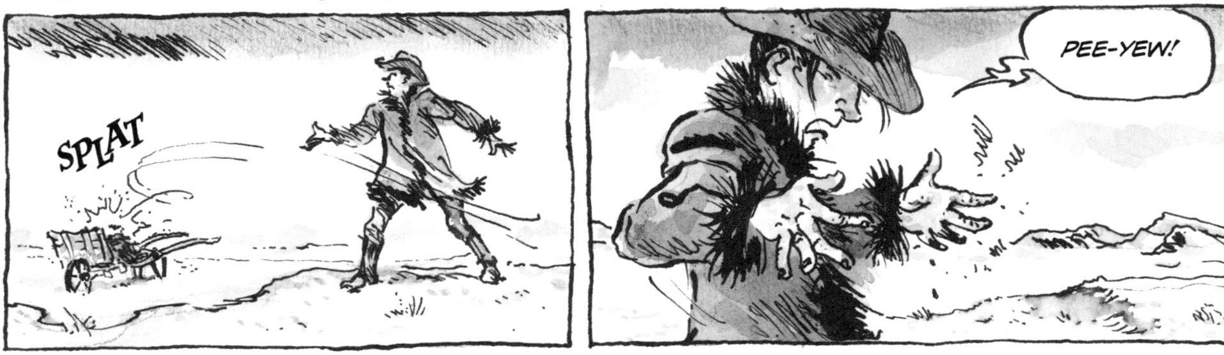
SPLAT
PEE-YEW!

There was little thought to the brothers and sisters she'd left behind in Salt Lake City. Maybe she gradually put them out of her mind, as she had more than enough of her own troubles. Maybe the occasional prayer for them was all she could allow herself.

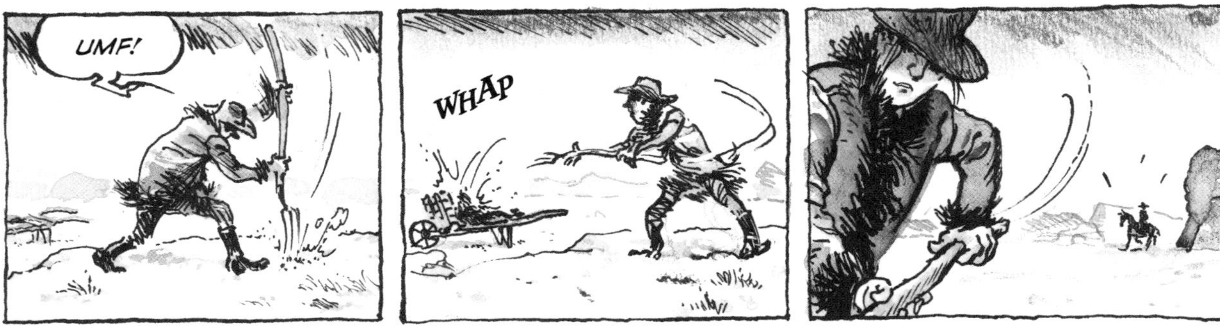
UMF!
WHAP

And then there was Janey's birth, in September 1873. For a time Calamity was forced to give up her aimless drifting...

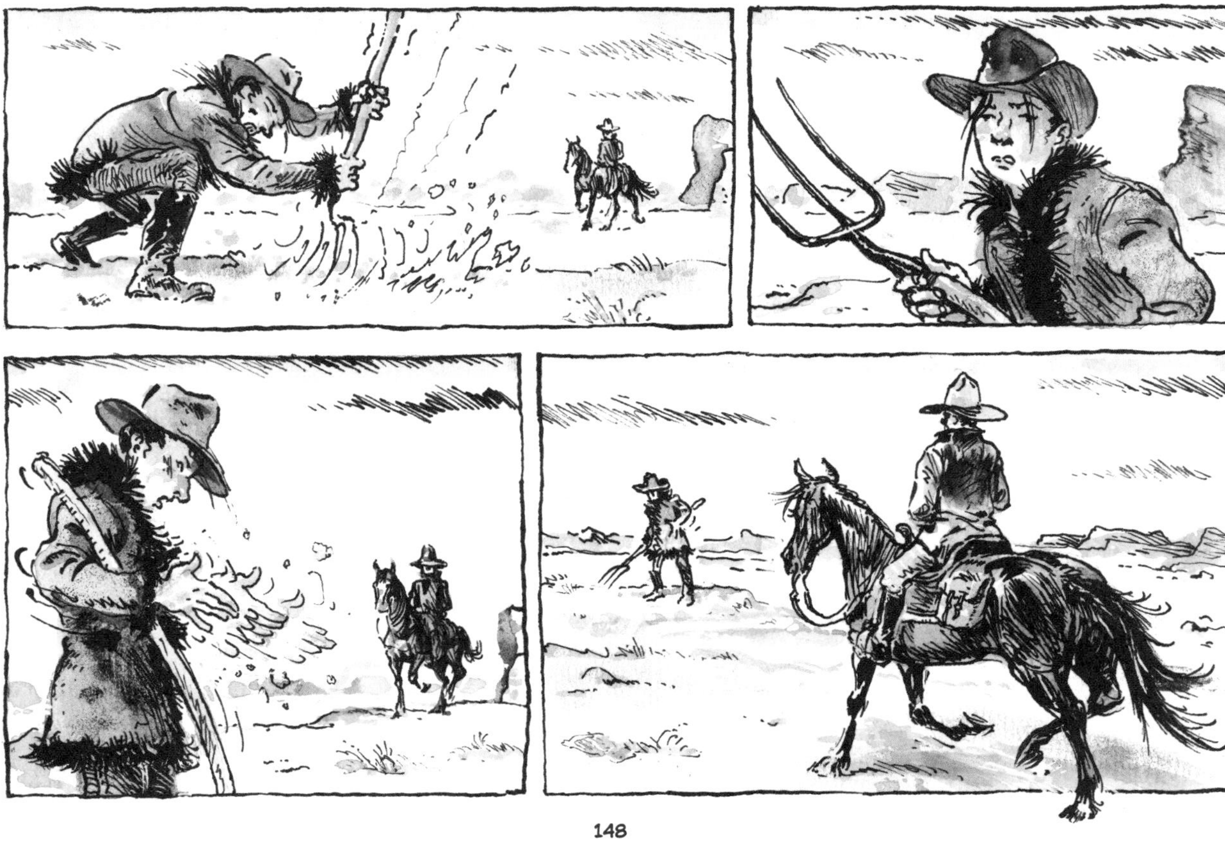

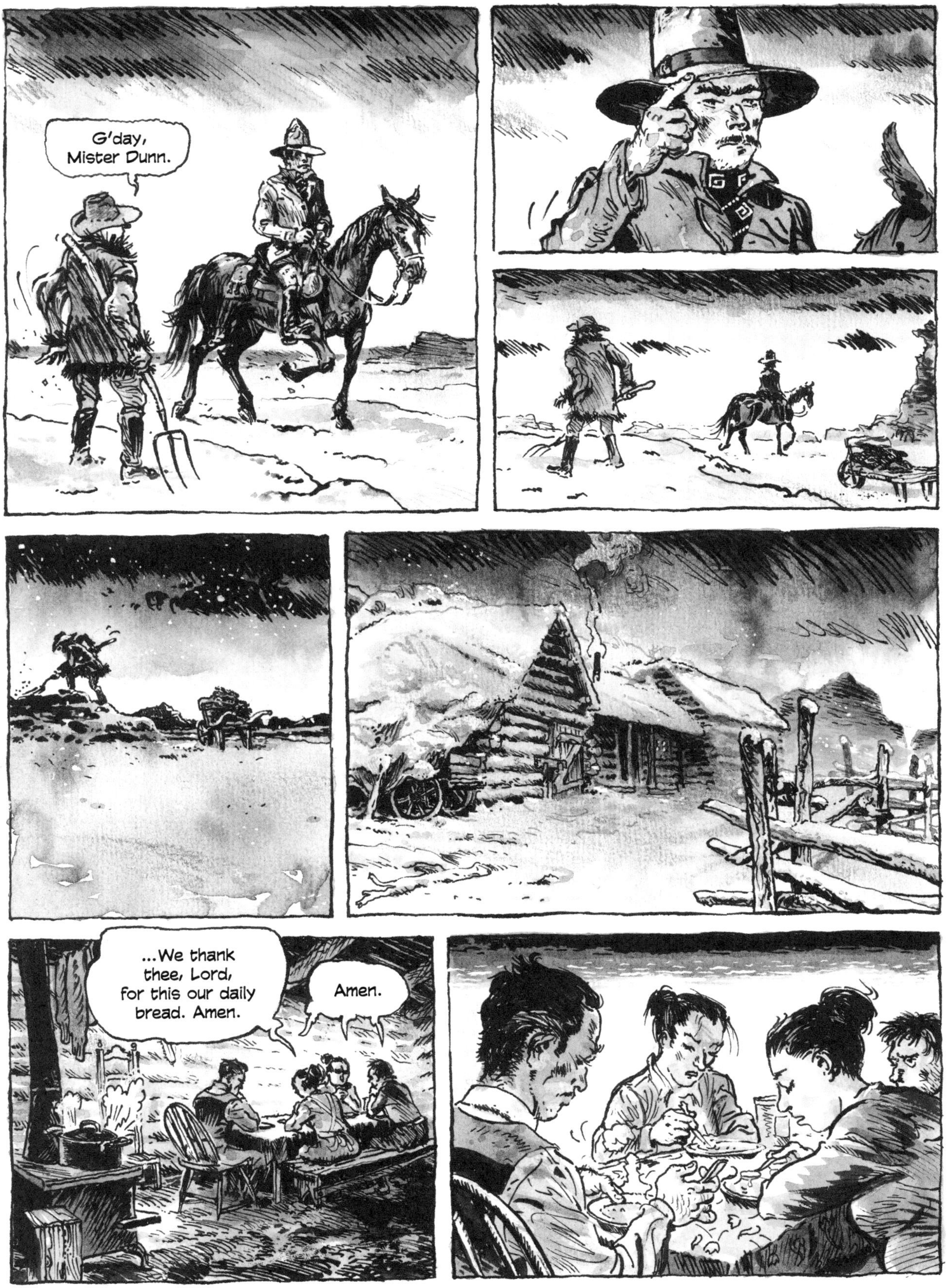
G'day, Mister Dunn.
...We thank thee, Lord, for this our daily bread. Amen.
Amen.

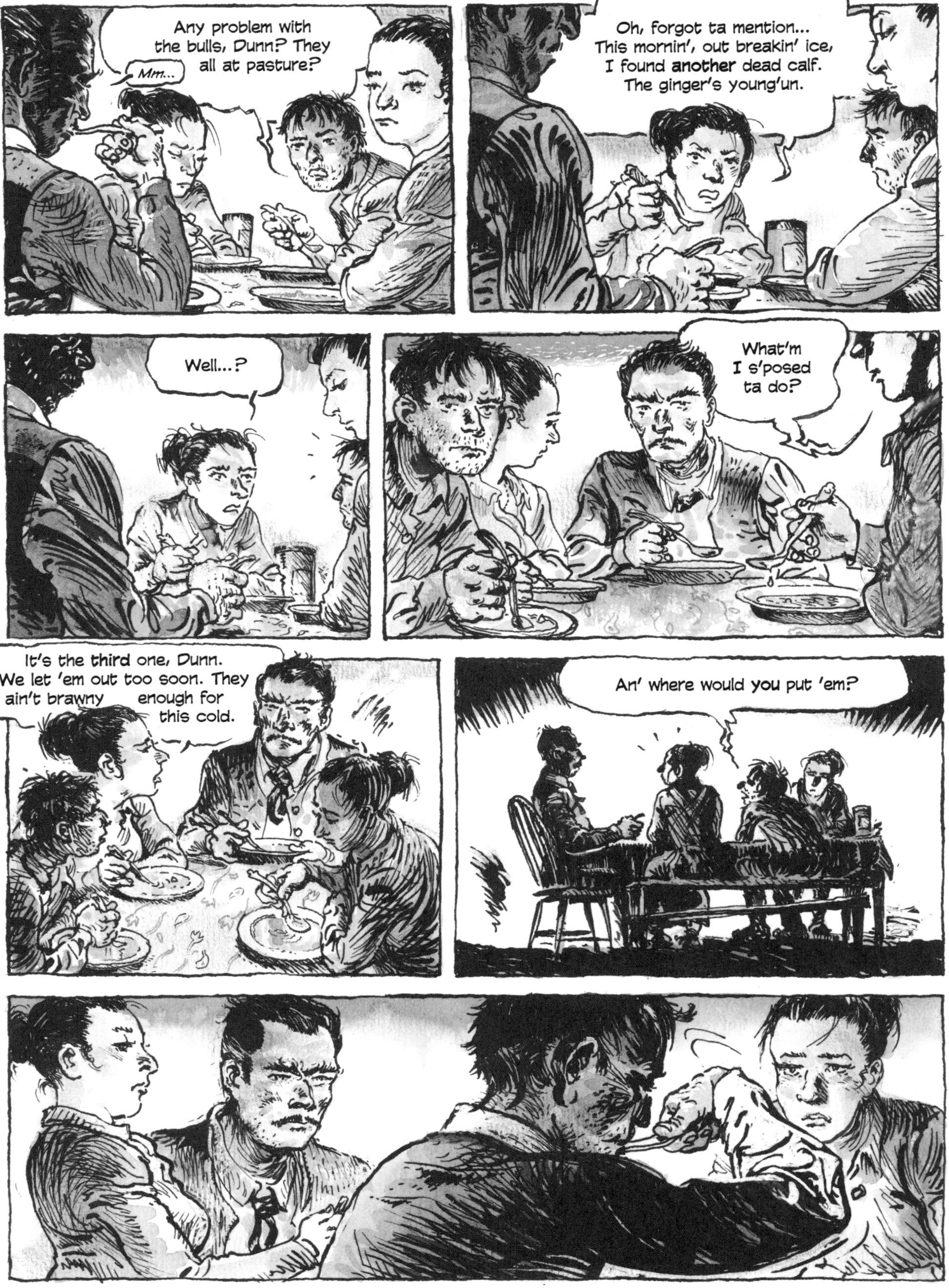
Any problem with the bulls, Dunn? They all at pasture?
Mm...
Oh, forgot ta mention... This mornin', out breakin' ice, I found **another** dead calf. The ginger's young'un.
Well...?
What'm I s'posed ta do?
It's the **third** one, Dunn. We let 'em out too soon. They ain't brawny enough for this cold.
An' where would you put 'em?

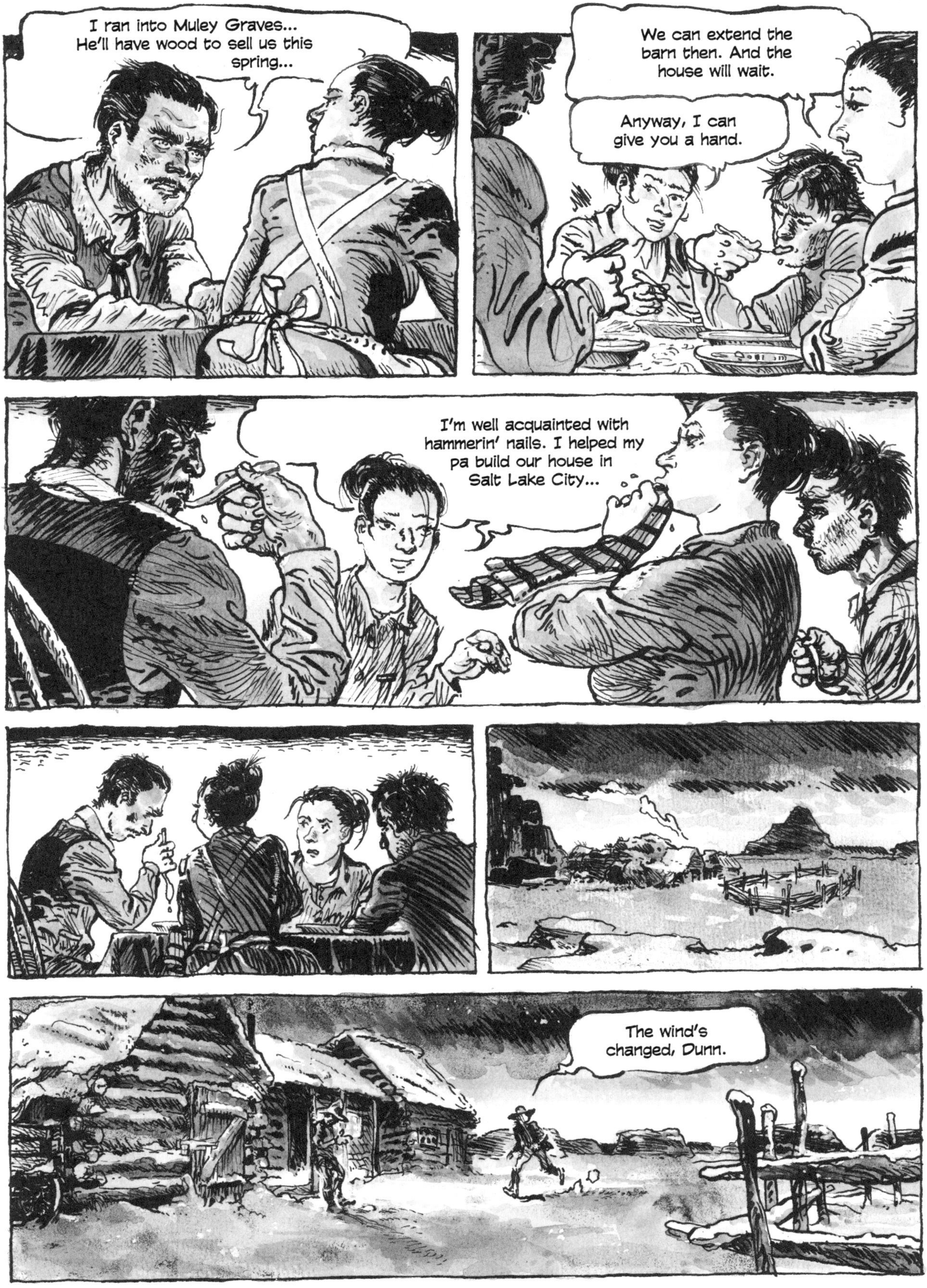
I ran into Muley Graves... He'll have wood to sell us this spring...
We can extend the barn then. And the house will wait.
Anyway, I can give you a hand.
I'm well acquainted with hammerin' nails. I helped my pa build our house in Salt Lake City...
The wind's changed, Dunn.

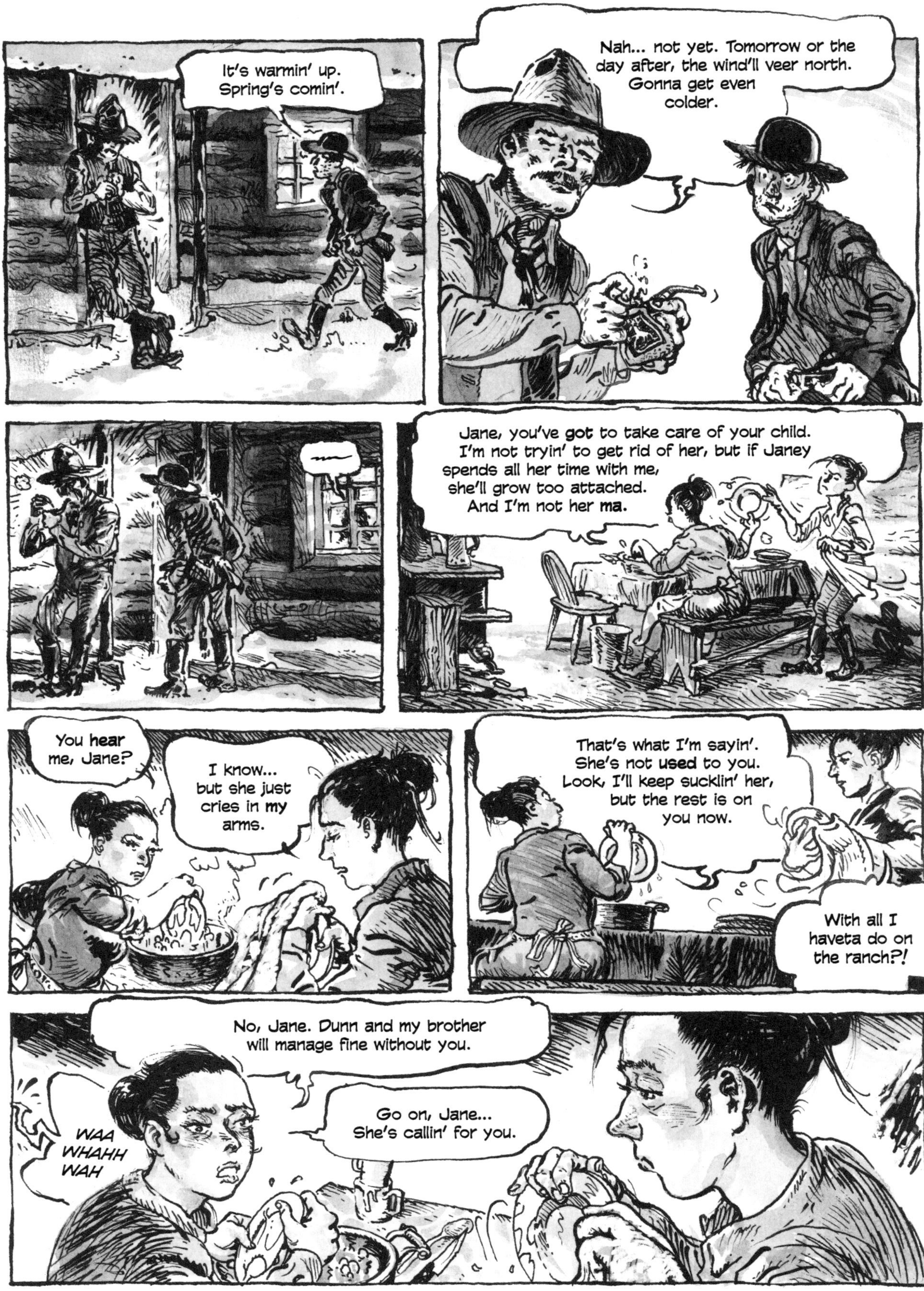
It's warmin' up. Spring's comin'.
Nah... not yet. Tomorrow or the day after, the wind'll veer north. Gonna get even colder.
—
Jane, you've **got** to take care of your child. I'm not tryin' to get rid of her, but if Janey spends all her time with me, she'll grow too attached. And I'm not her **ma.**
You **hear** me, Jane?
I know... but she just cries in **my** arms.
That's what I'm sayin'. She's not **used** to you. Look, I'll keep sucklin' her, but the rest is on you now.
With all I haveta do on the ranch?!
No, Jane. Dunn and my brother will manage fine without you.
WAA WHAHH WAH
Go on, Jane... She's callin' for you.

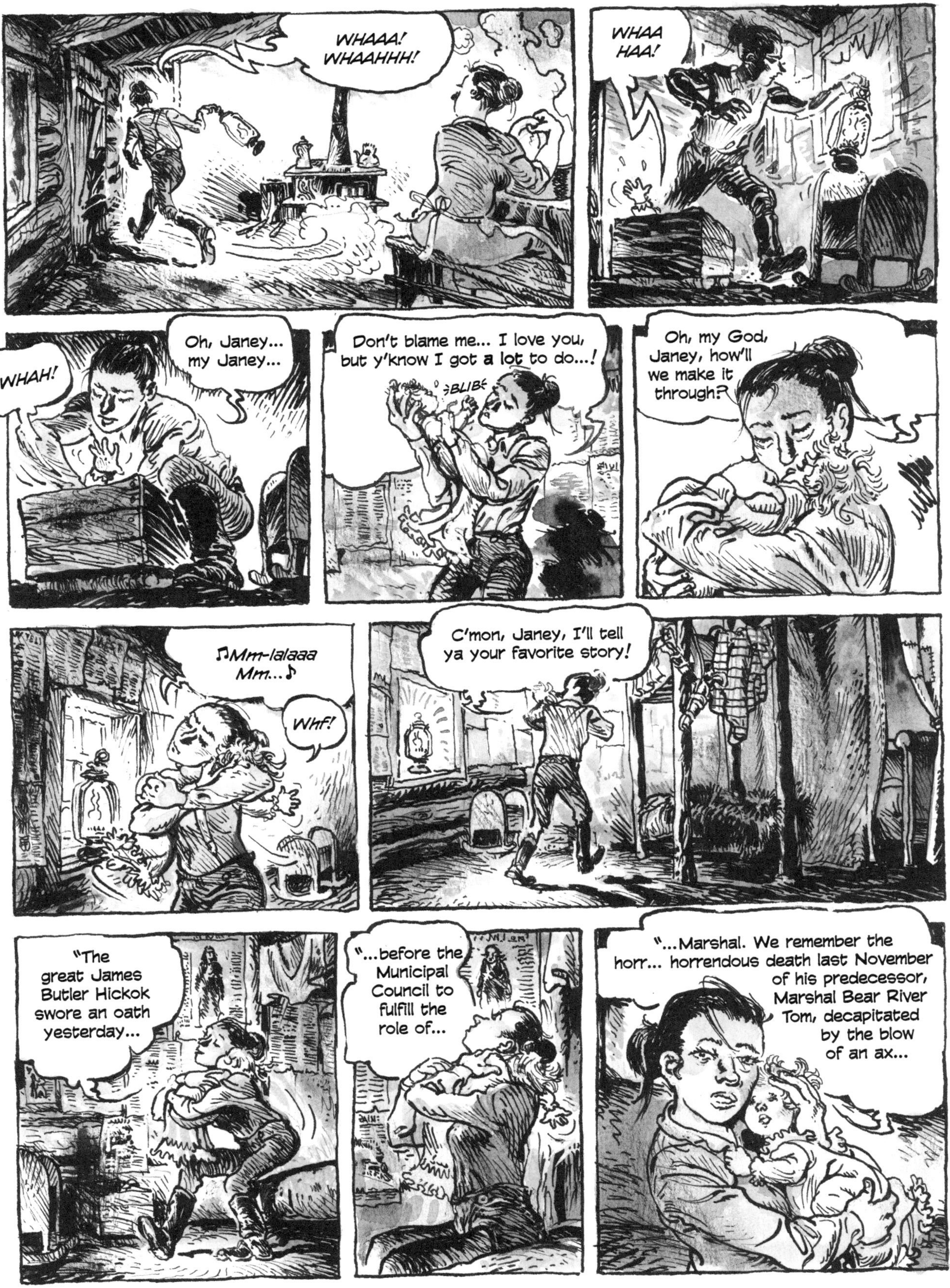
WHAAA! WHAAHHH!
WHAA HAA!
WHAH!
Oh, Janey... my Janey...
Don't blame me... I love you, but y'know I got a lot to do...!
BLIB
Oh, my God, Janey, how'll we make it through?
♫Mm-lalaaa Mm...♪
Whf!
C'mon, Janey, I'll tell ya your favorite story!
"The great James Butler Hickok swore an oath yesterday...
"...before the Municipal Council to fulfill the role of...
"...Marshal. We remember the horr... horrendous death last November of his predecessor, Marshal Bear River Tom, decapitated by the blow of an ax...

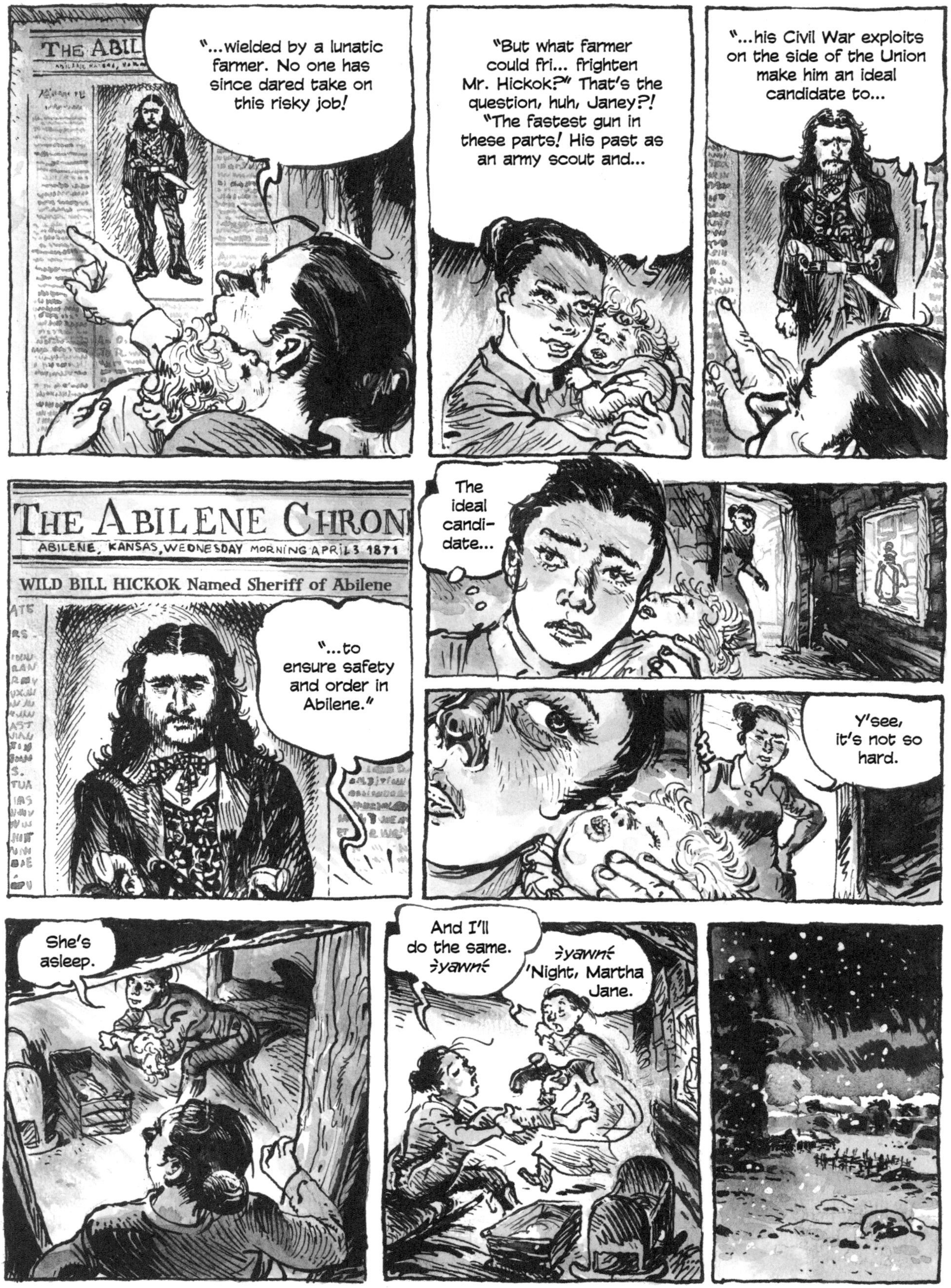

THE ABIL
"...wielded by a lunatic farmer. No one has since dared take on this risky job!
"But what farmer could fri... frighten Mr. Hickok?" That's the question, huh, Janey?! "The fastest gun in these parts! His past as an army scout and...
"...his Civil War exploits on the side of the Union make him an ideal candidate to...
THE ABILENE CHRON
ABILENE, KANSAS, WEDNESDAY MORNING APRIL 3 1871
WILD BILL HICKOK Named Sheriff of Abilene
"...to ensure safety and order in Abilene."
The ideal candi-date...
Y'see, it's not so hard.
She's asleep.
And I'll do the same. ≻yawn≺
≻yawn≺ 'Night, Martha Jane.

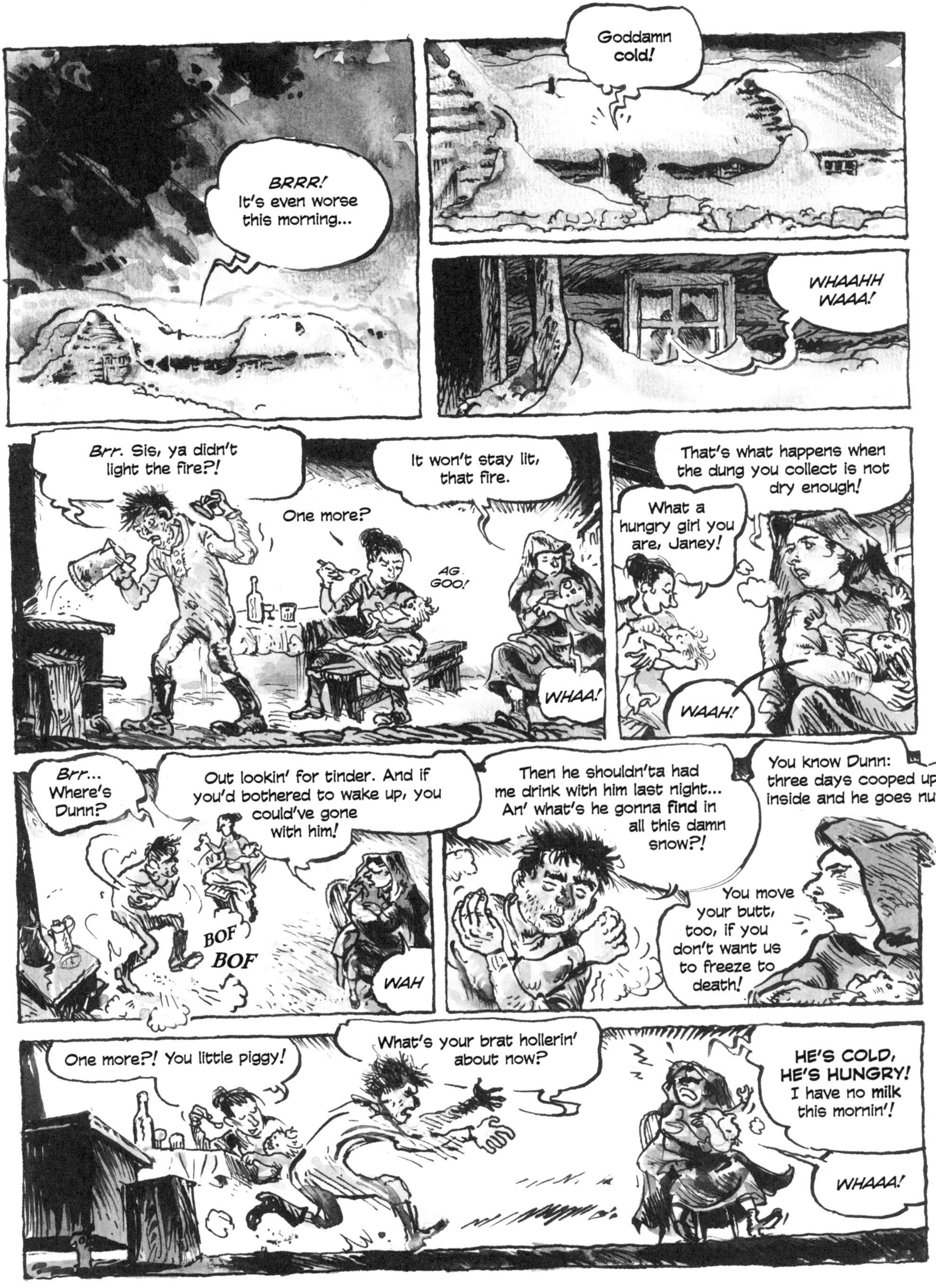
BRRR! It's even worse this morning...
Goddamn cold!
WHAAHH WAAA!
Brr. Sis, ya didn't light the fire?!
One more?
AG GOO!
It won't stay lit, that fire.
WHAA!
That's what happens when the dung you collect is not dry enough!
What a hungry girl you are, Janey!
WAAH!
Brr... Where's Dunn?
Out lookin' for tinder. And if you'd bothered to wake up, you could've gone with him!
BOF
BOF
WAH
Then he shouldn'ta had me drink with him last night... An' what's he gonna find in all this damn snow?!
You know Dunn: three days cooped up inside and he goes nuts!
You move your butt, too, if you don't want us to freeze to death!
One more?! You little piggy!
What's your brat hollerin' about now?
HE'S COLD, HE'S HUNGRY! I have no milk this mornin'!
WHAAA!

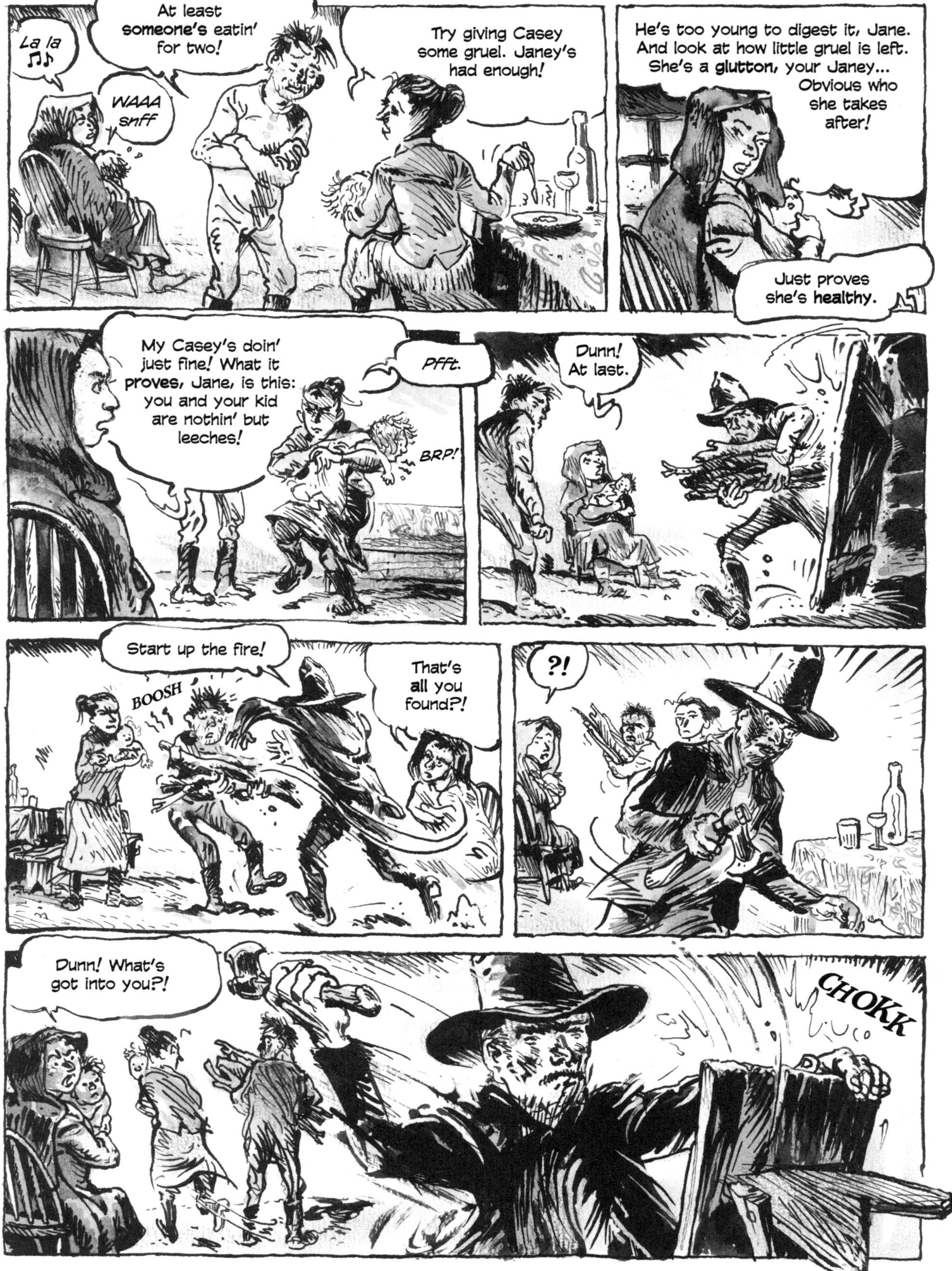
La la ♫♪
At least someone's eatin' for two!
WAAA snff
Try giving Casey some gruel. Janey's had enough!
He's too young to digest it, Jane. And look at how little gruel is left. She's a glutton, your Janey...
Obvious who she takes after!
Just proves she's healthy.
My Casey's doin' just fine! What it proves, Jane, is this: you and your kid are nothin' but leeches!
Pfft.
BRP!
Dunn! At last.
Start up the fire!
BOOSH
That's all you found?!
?!
Dunn! What's got into you?!
CHOKK

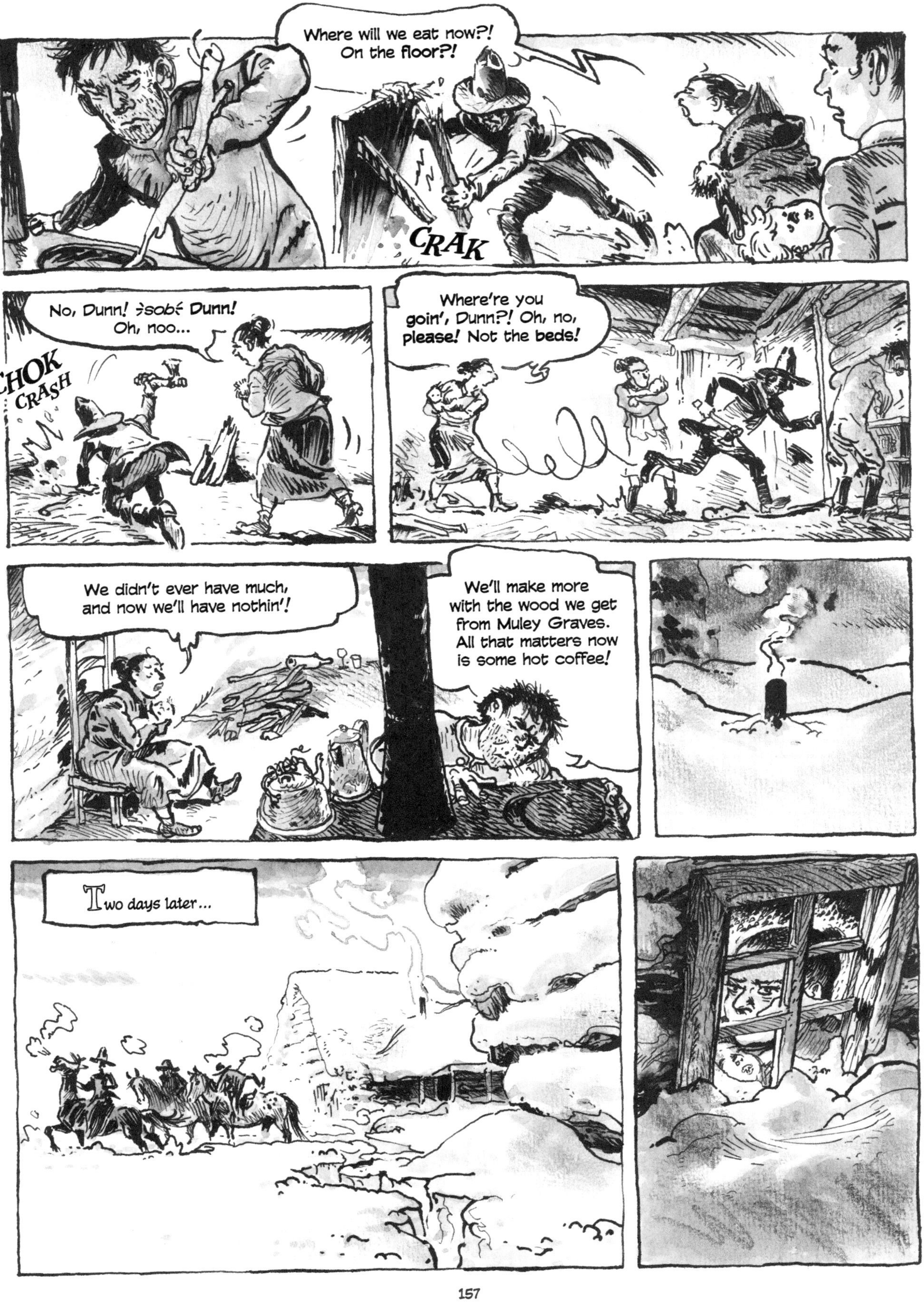
Where will we eat now?! On the floor?!
CRAK
No, Dunn! ⋺sob⋲ Dunn! Oh, noo...
CHOK
CRASH
Where're you goin', Dunn?! Oh, no, please! Not the beds!
We didn't ever have much, and now we'll have nothin'!
We'll make more with the wood we get from Muley Graves. All that matters now is some hot coffee!
Two days later...

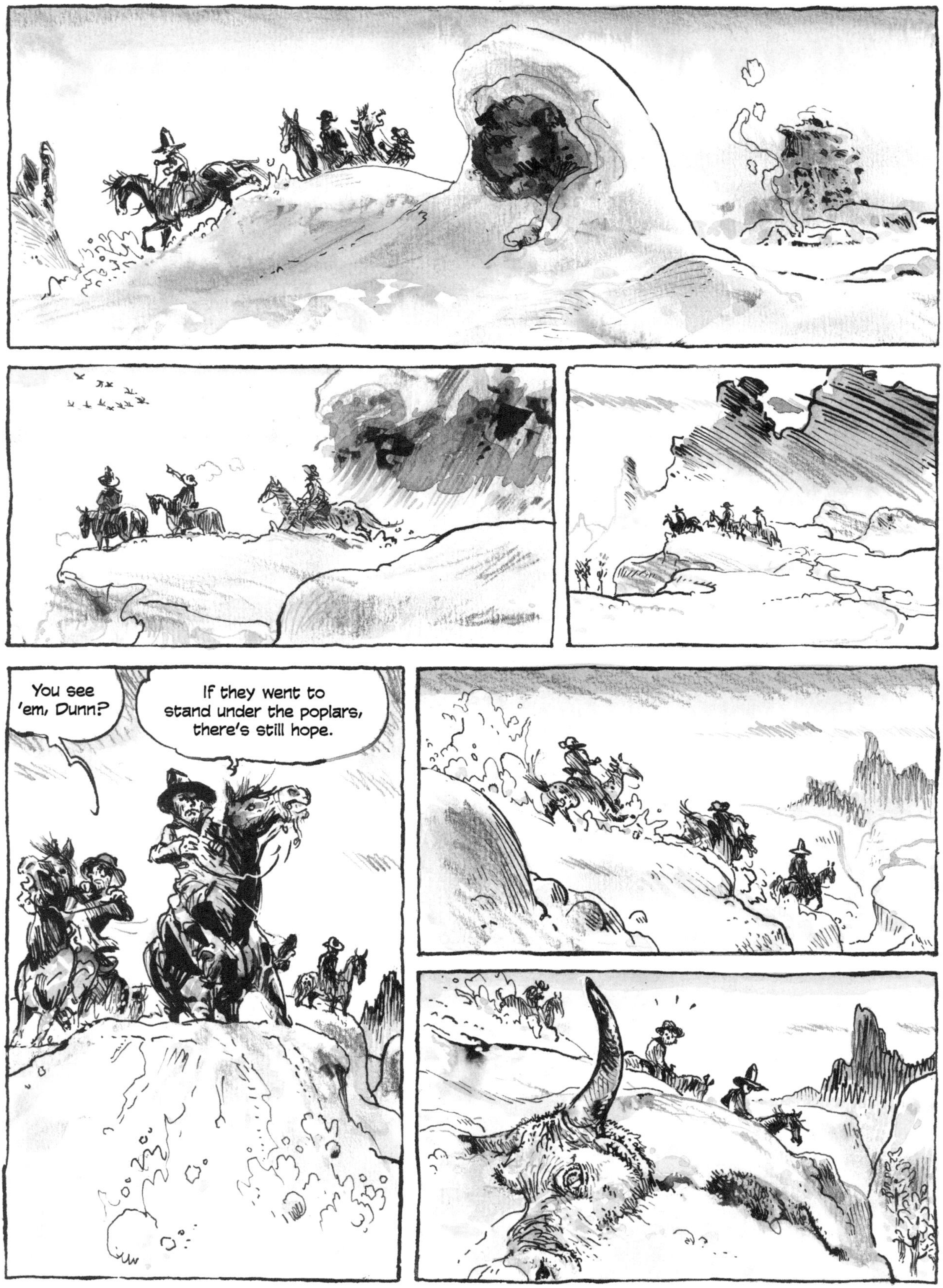
You see 'em, Dunn?
If they went to stand under the poplars, there's still hope.

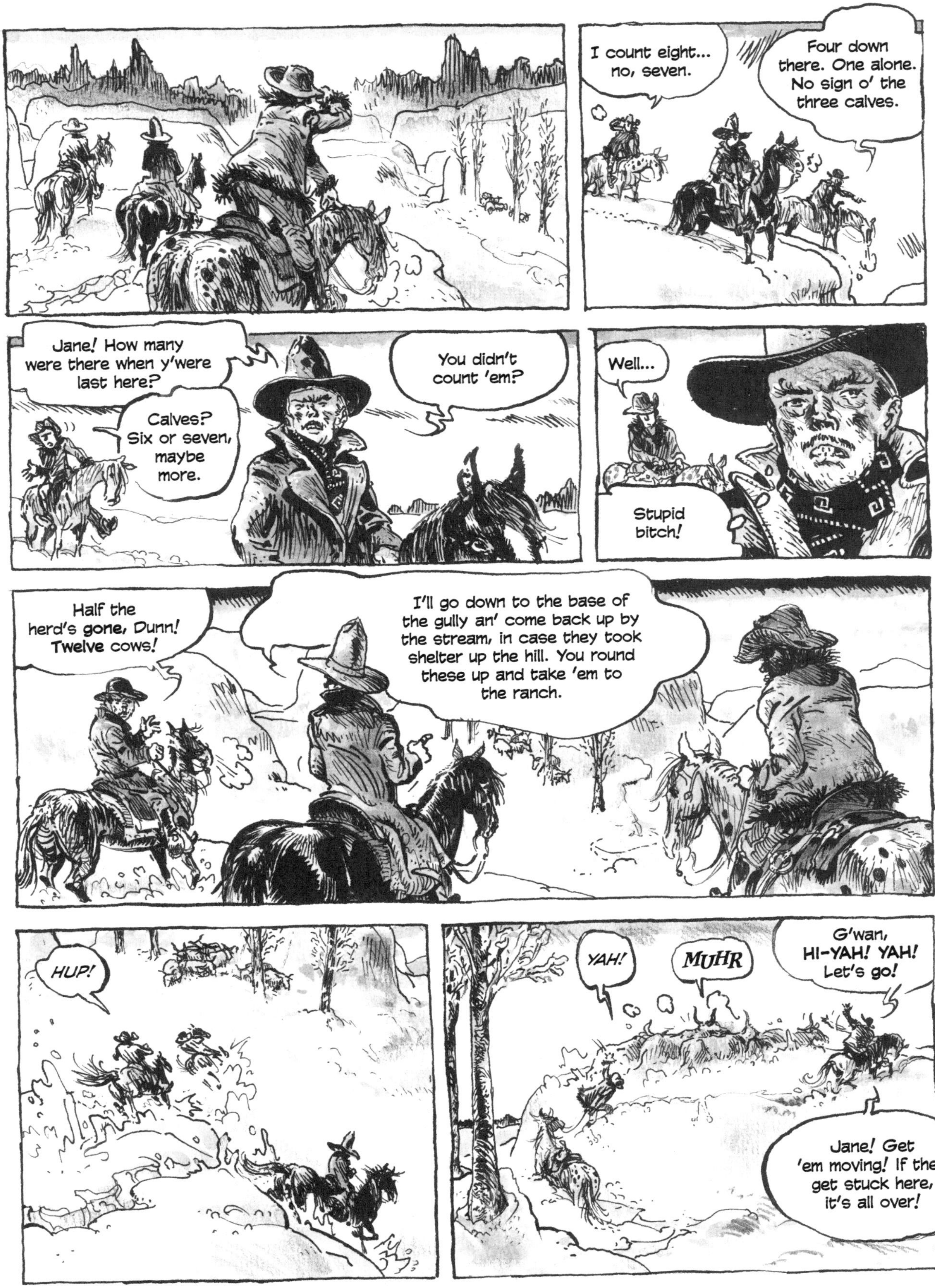

I count eight... no, seven.
Four down there. One alone. No sign o' the three calves.
Jane! How many were there when y'were last here?
Calves? Six or seven, maybe more.
You didn't count 'em?
Well...
Stupid bitch!
Half the herd's **gone**, Dunn! **Twelve** cows!
I'll go down to the base of the gully an' come back up by the stream, in case they took shelter up the hill. You round these up and take 'em to the ranch.
HUP!
YAH!
MUHR
G'wan, **HI-YAH! YAH!** Let's go!
Jane! Get 'em moving! If they get stuck here, it's all over!

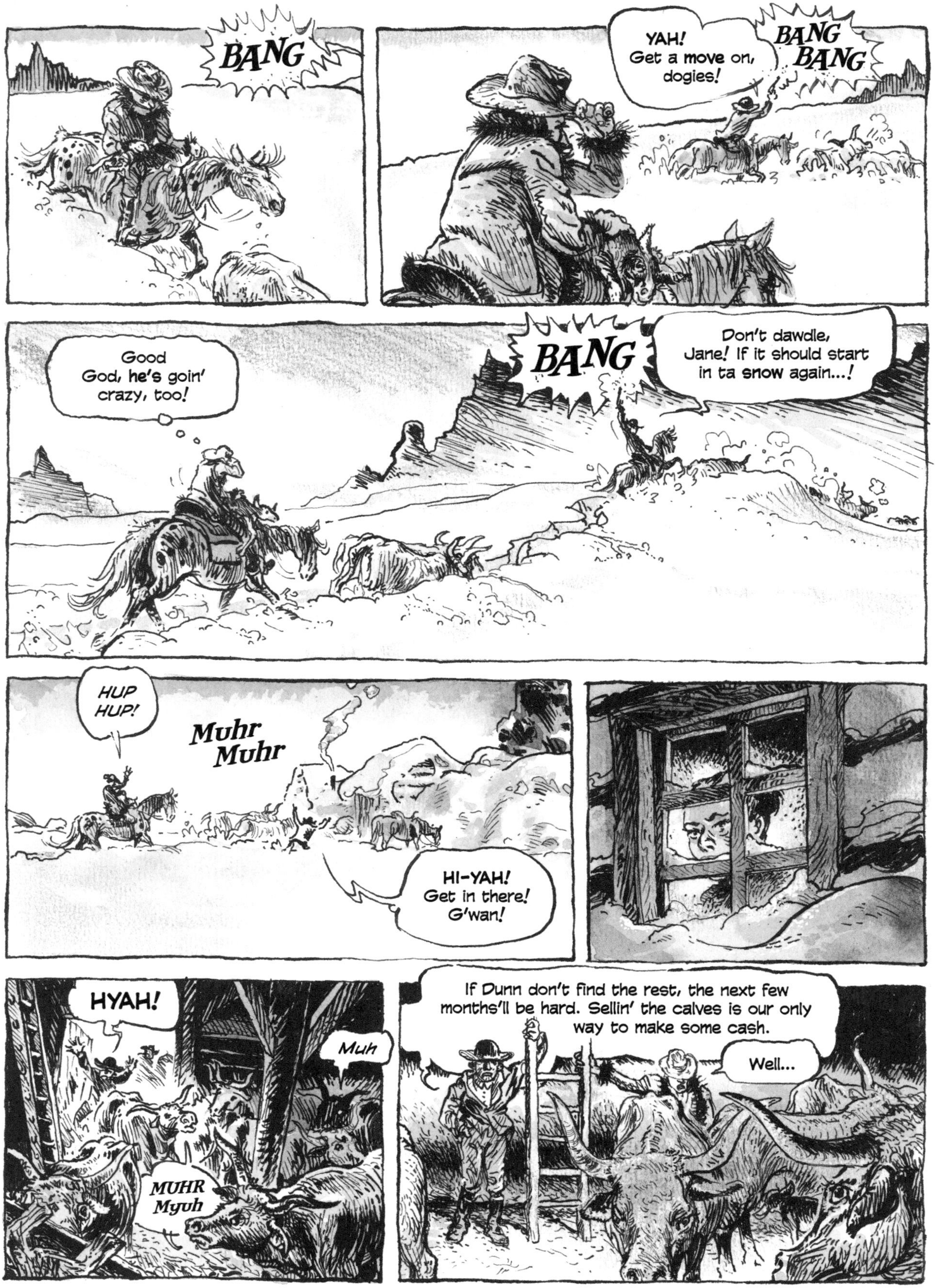

BANG
YAH! Get a move on, dogies!
BANG BANG
Good God, he's goin' crazy, too!
BANG
Don't dawdle, Jane! If it should start in ta snow again...!
HUP HUP!
Muhr Muhr
HI-YAH! Get in there! G'wan!
HYAH!
Muh
MUHR Myuh
If Dunn don't find the rest, the next few months'll be hard. Sellin' the calves is our only way to make some cash.
Well...

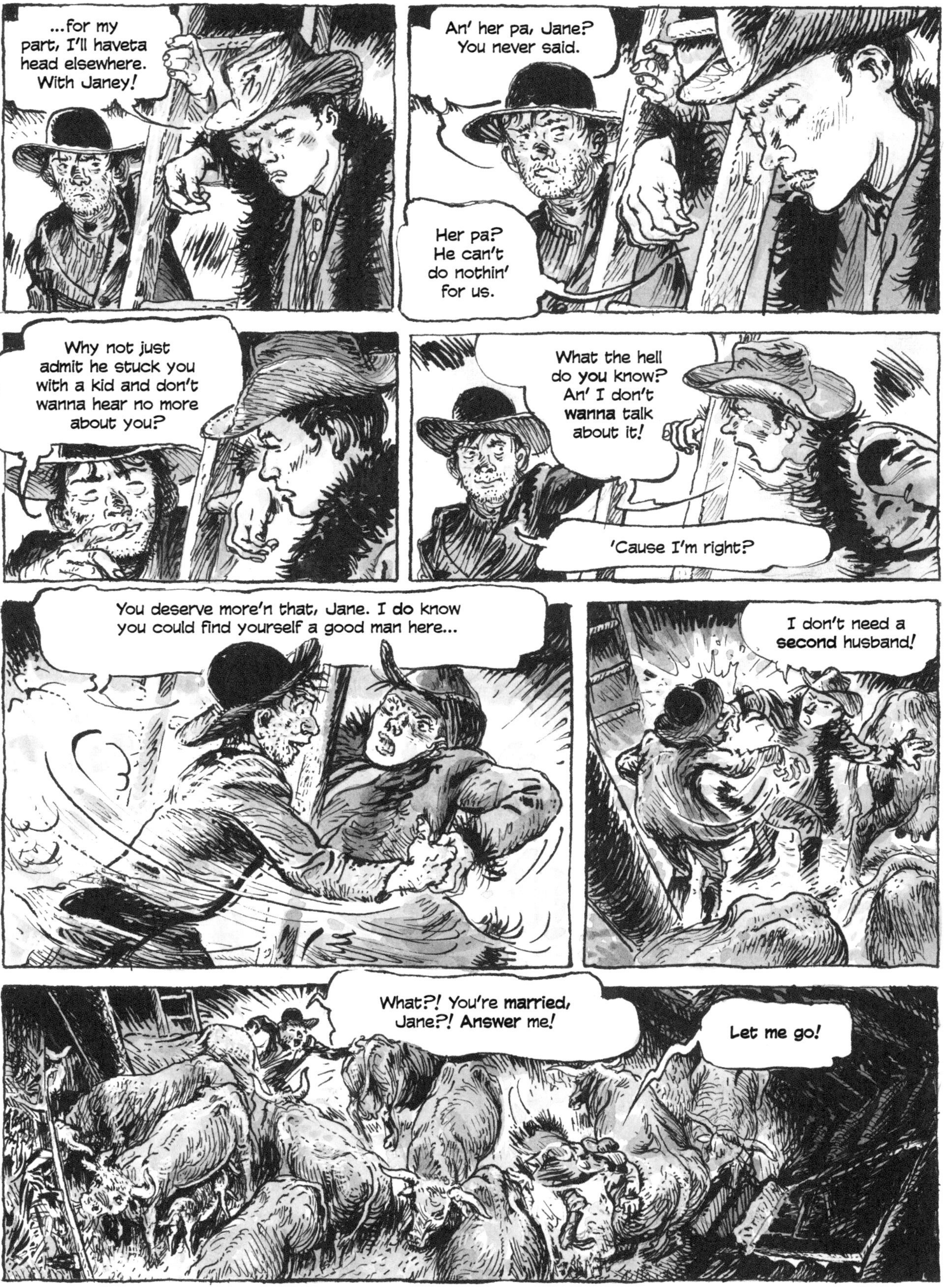
...for my part, I'll haveta head elsewhere. With Janey!
An' her pa, Jane? You never said.
Her pa? He can't do nothin' for us.
Why not just admit he stuck you with a kid and don't wanna hear no more about you?
What the hell do you know? An' I don't wanna talk about it!
'Cause I'm right?
You deserve more'n that, Jane. I do know you could find yourself a good man here...
I don't need a second husband!
What?! You're married, Jane?! Answer me!
Let me go!

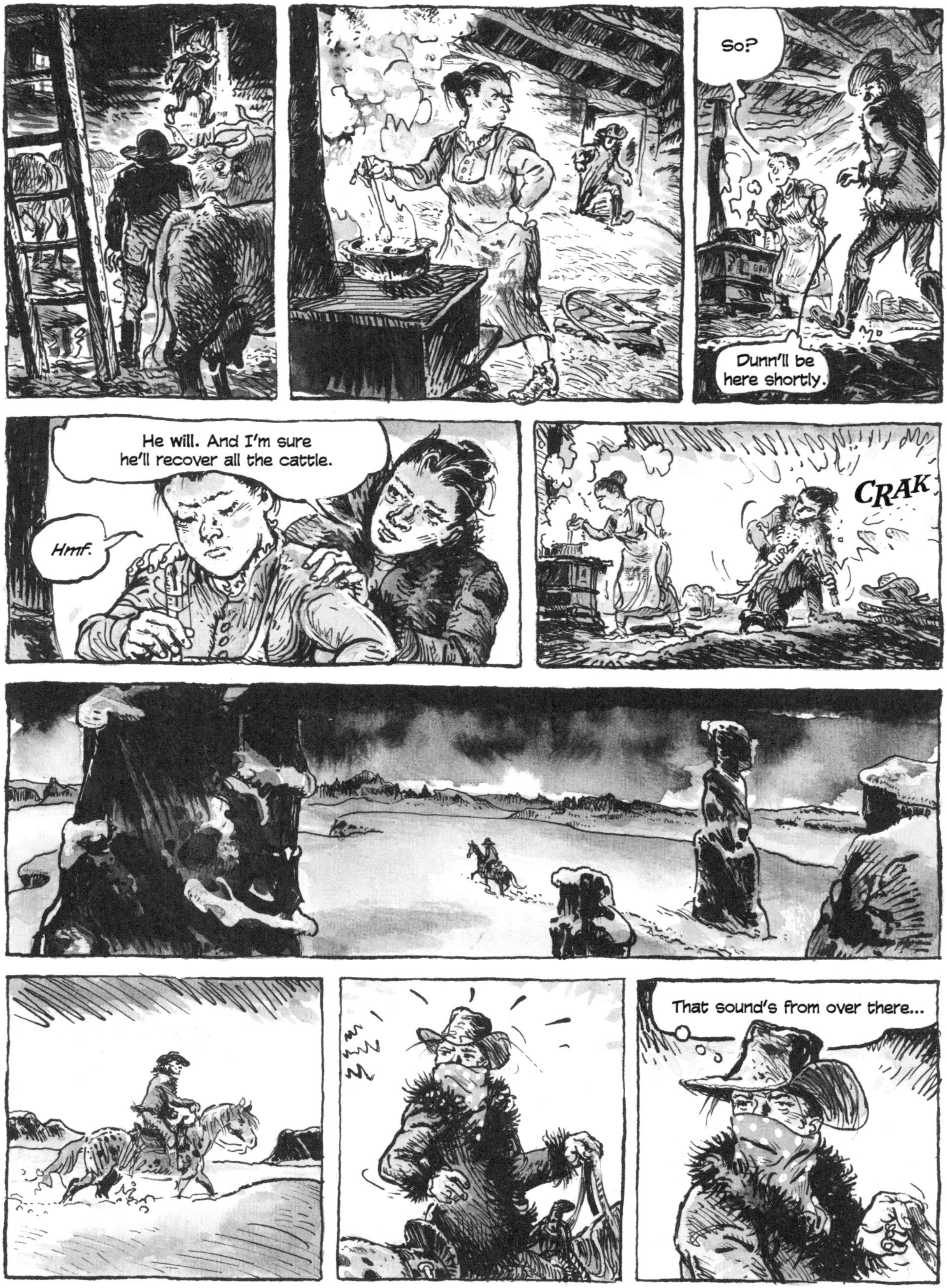
So?
Dunn'll be here shortly.
He will. And I'm sure he'll recover all the cattle.
Hmf.
CRAK
That sound's from over there...

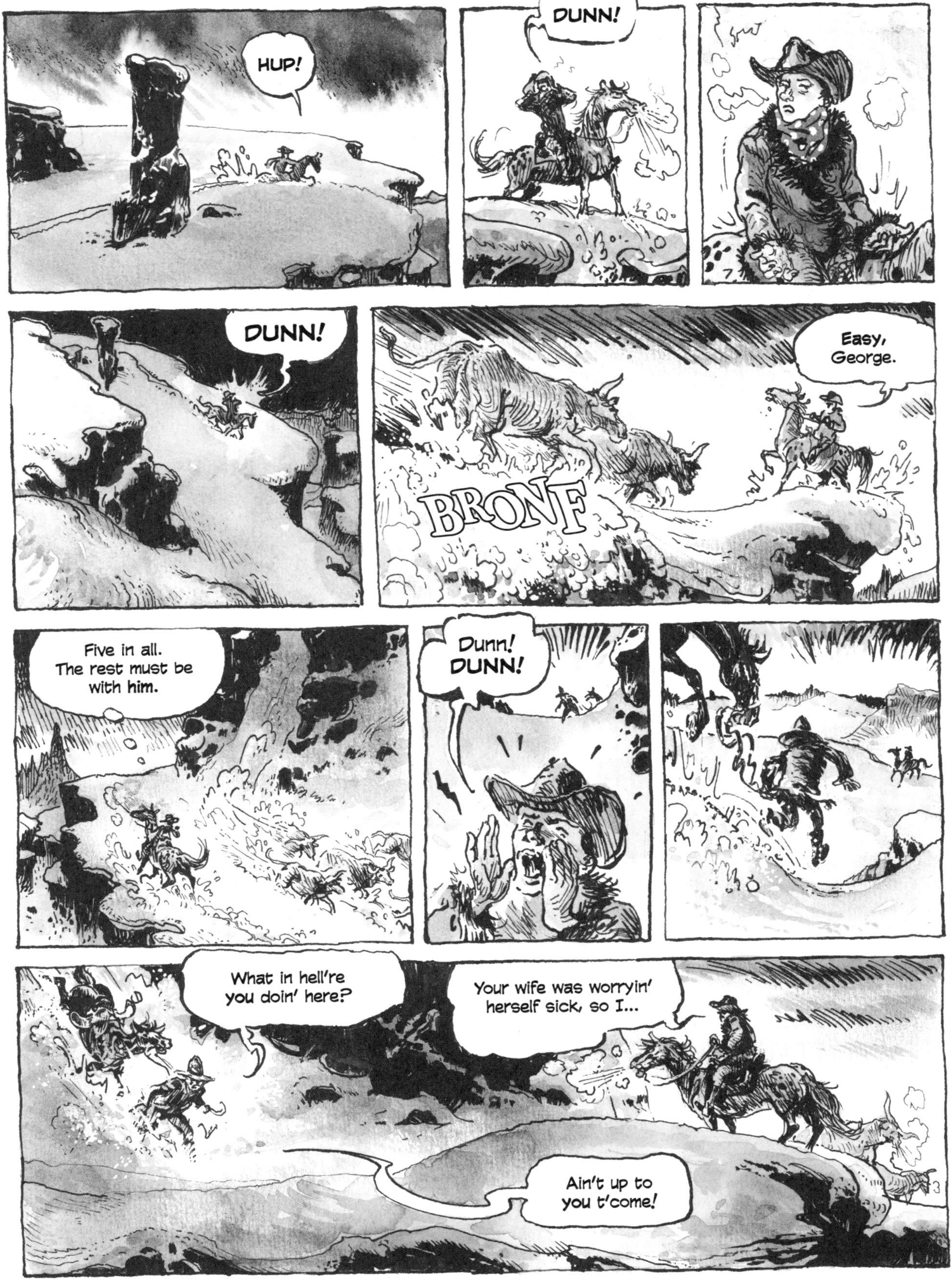
HUP!
DUNN!
DUNN!
Easy, George.
BRONF
Five in all. The rest must be with him.
Dunn! DUNN!
What in hell're you doin' here?
Your wife was worryin' herself sick, so I...
Ain't up to you t'come!

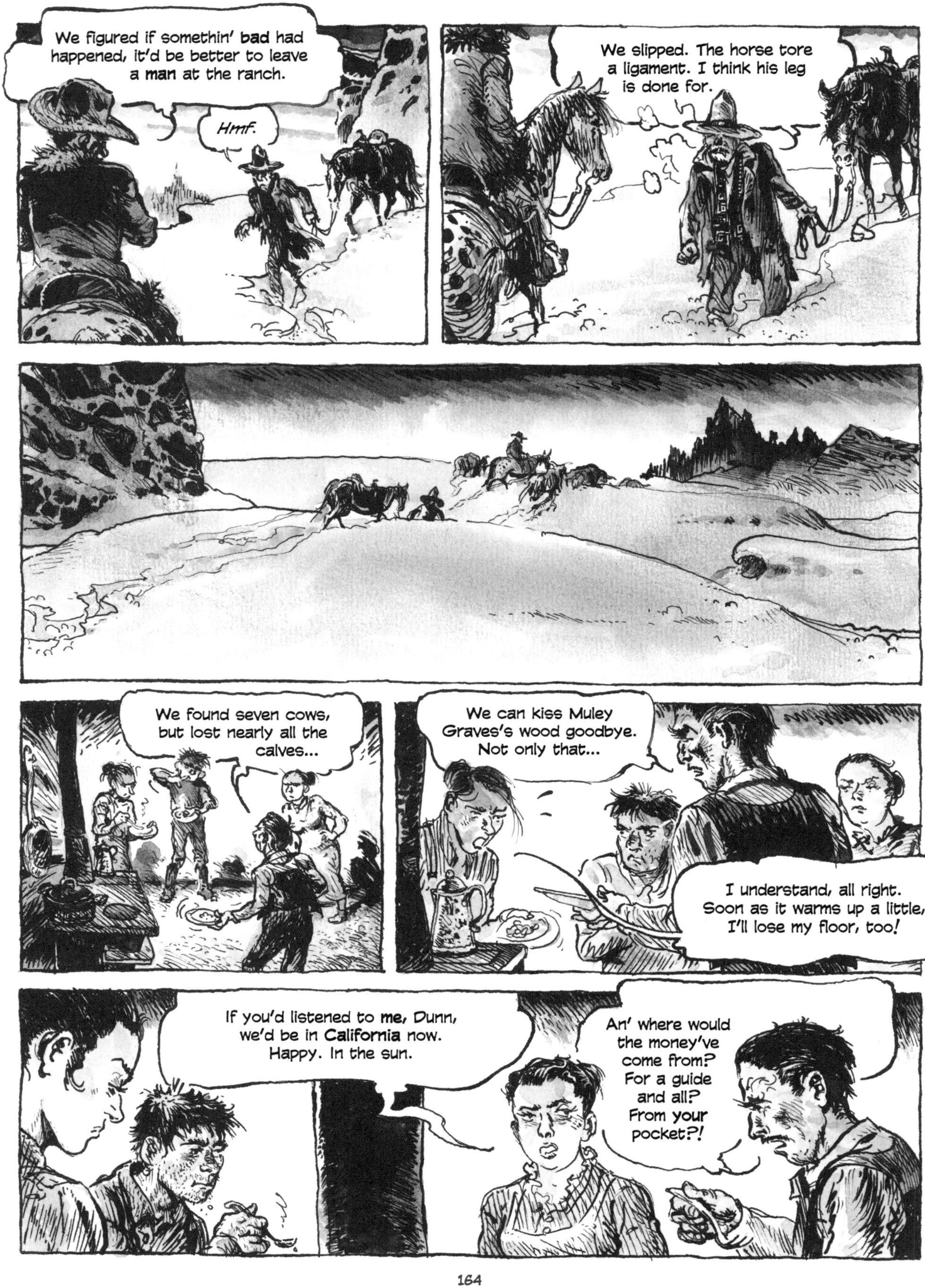

We figured if somethin' **bad** had happened, it'd be better to leave a **man** at the ranch.
Hmf.
We slipped. The horse tore a ligament. I think his leg is done for.
We found seven cows, but lost nearly all the calves...
We can kiss Muley Graves's wood goodbye. Not only that...
I understand, all right. Soon as it warms up a little, I'll lose my floor, too!
If you'd listened to **me**, Dunn, we'd be in **California** now. Happy. In the sun.
An' where would the money've come from? For a guide and all? From **your** pocket?!

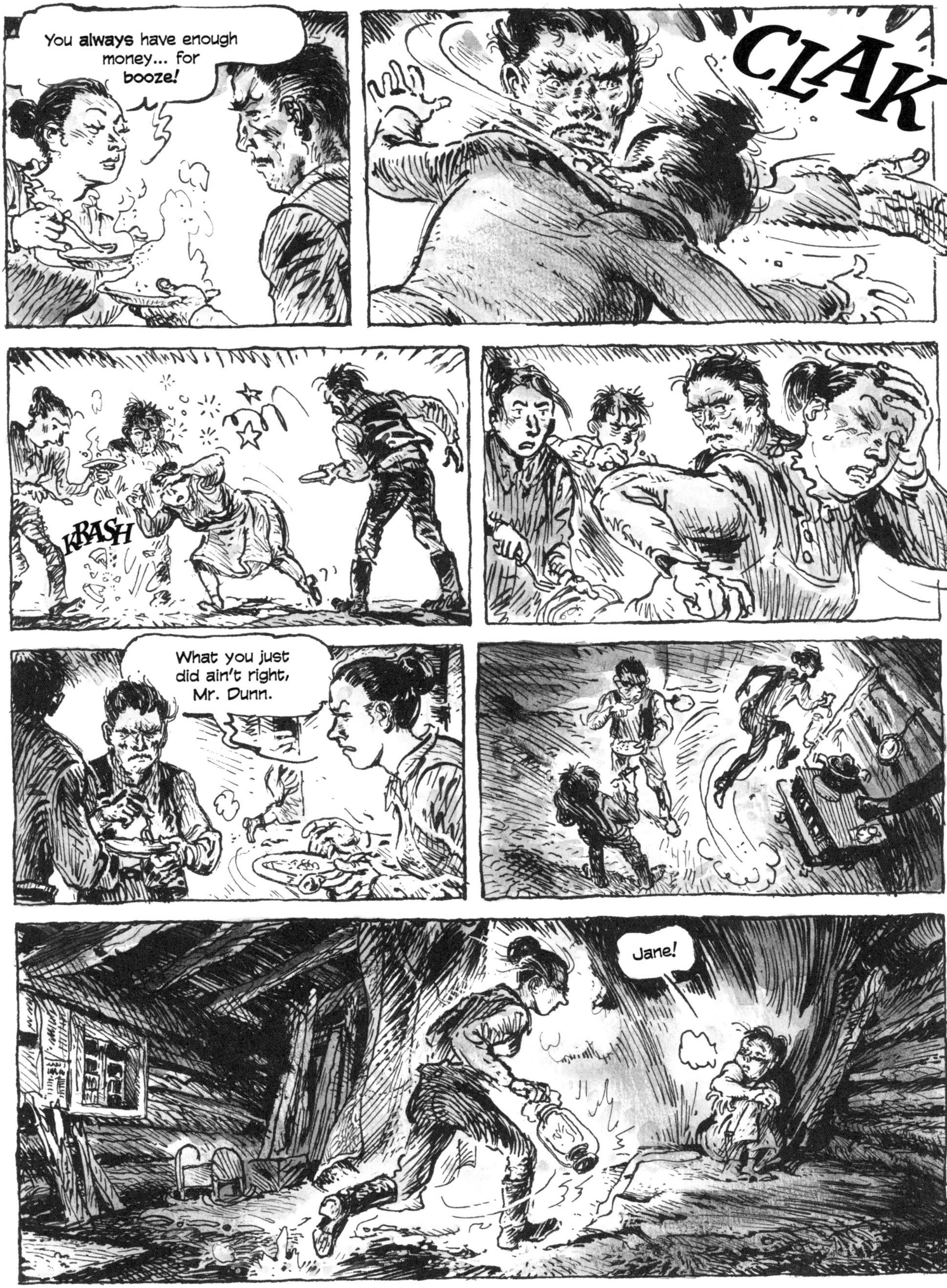
You always have enough money... for booze!
CLAK
KRASH
What you just did ain't right, Mr. Dunn.
Jane!

Don't leave, Jane... Don't leave me all alone. *Snf!*

Marry my brother. You know he fancies you. I'm sure he'll accept your Janey if you give him his own child right away.

He knows I can't marry...

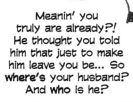

Meanin' you truly are already?! He thought you told him that just to make him leave you be... So **where's** your husband? And **who** is he?

Well...

Snff!

KRATCH

It's him.

?

Him?!

How's that even possible? Spell it out, Jane!

Okay, then... The first time I saw him was in **Abilene**. He'd just become Marshal. But I didn't know a damn thing about a damn thing. I hadn't even **heard** o' Wild Bill Hickok...

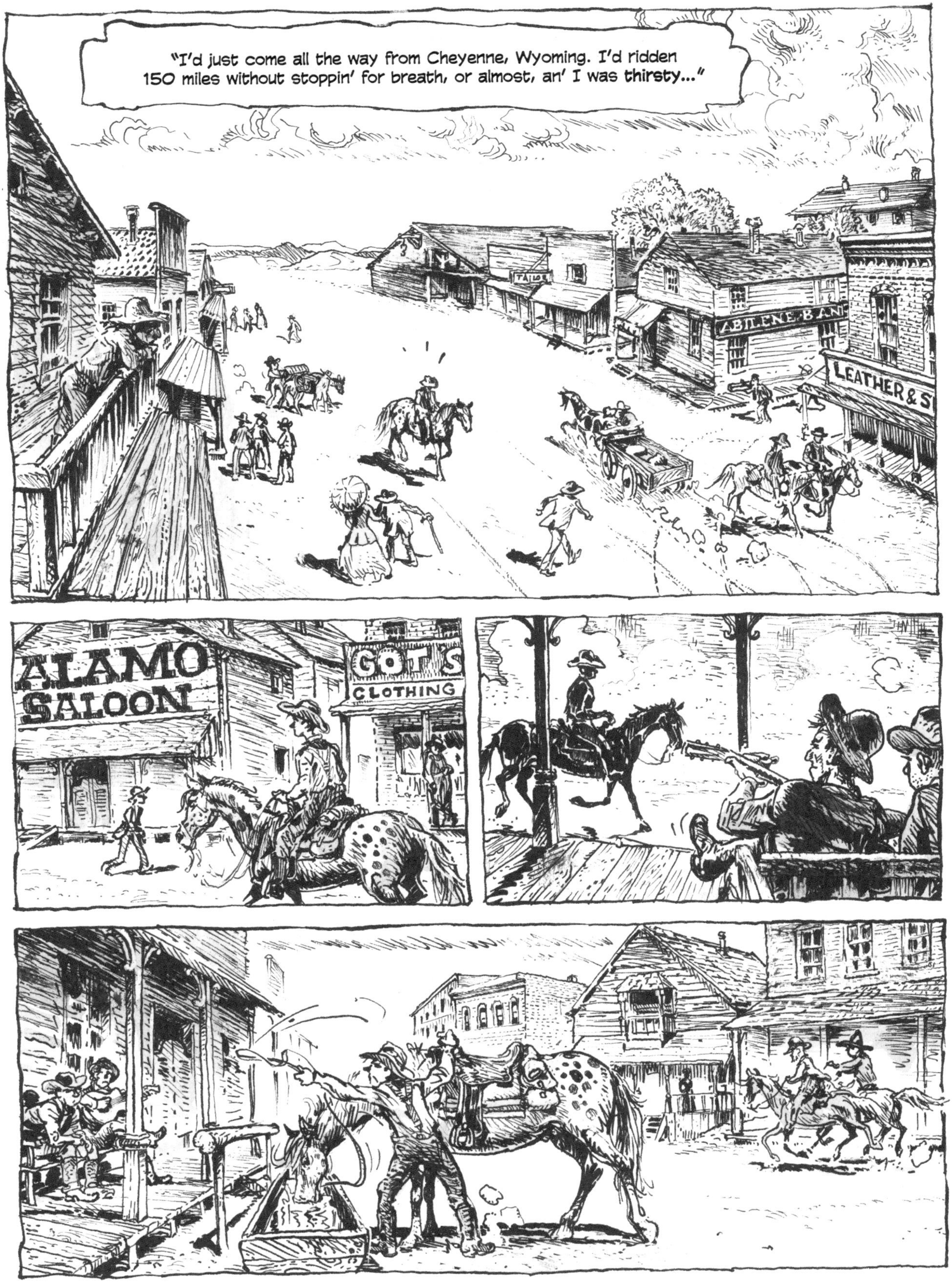
"I'd just come all the way from Cheyenne, Wyoming. I'd ridden 150 miles without stoppin' for breath, or almost, an' I was **thirsty...**"
ABILENE BAN
LEATHER & S
ALAMO SALOON
GOT'S
CLOTHING

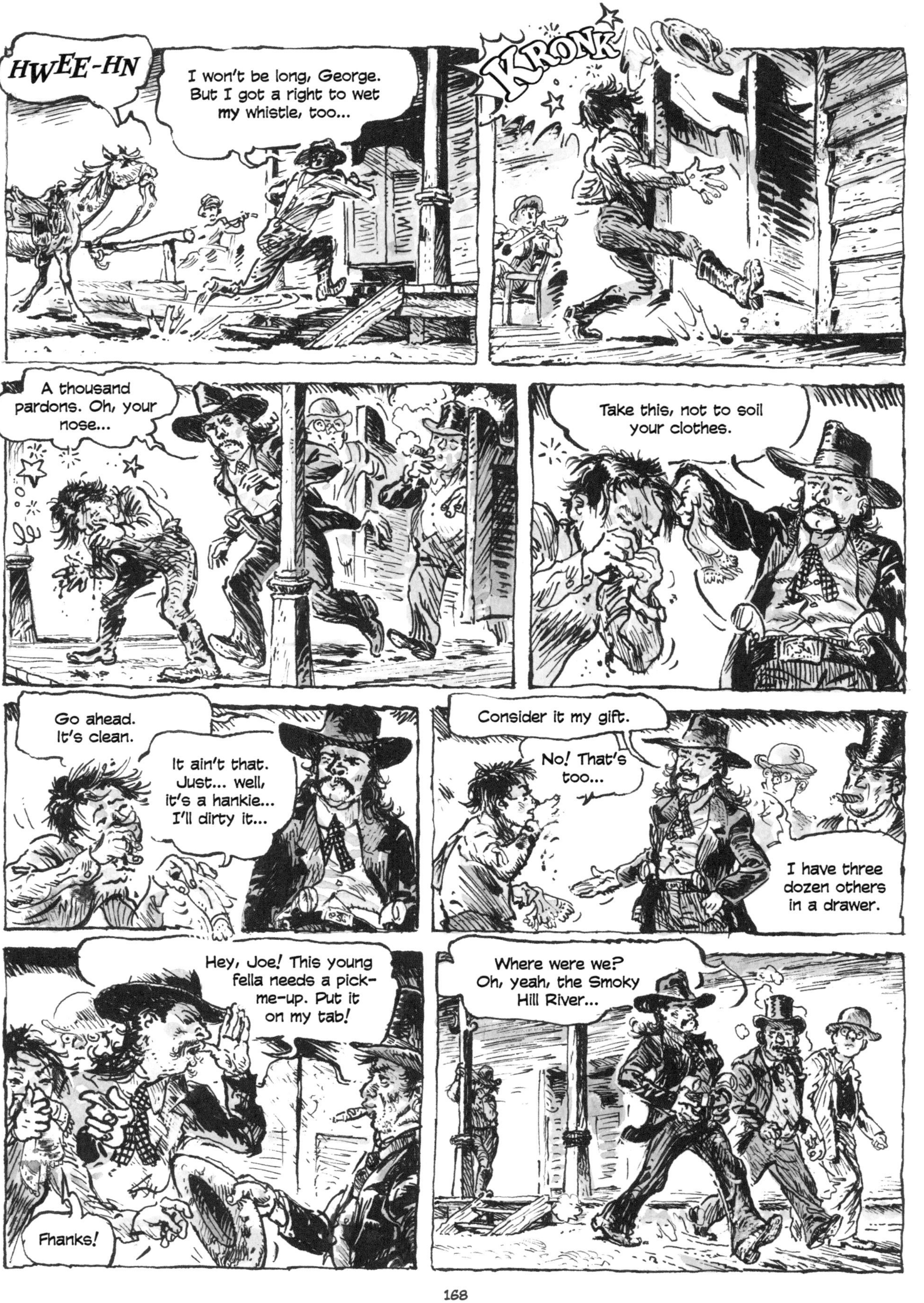
HWEE-HN
I won't be long, George. But I got a right to wet my whistle, too...
KRONK
A thousand pardons. Oh, your nose...
Take this, not to soil your clothes.
Go ahead. It's clean.
It ain't that. Just... well, it's a hankie... I'll dirty it...
Consider it my gift.
No! That's too...
I have three dozen others in a drawer.
Hey, Joe! This young fella needs a pick-me-up. Put it on my tab!
Fhanks!
Where were we? Oh, yeah, the Smoky Hill River...

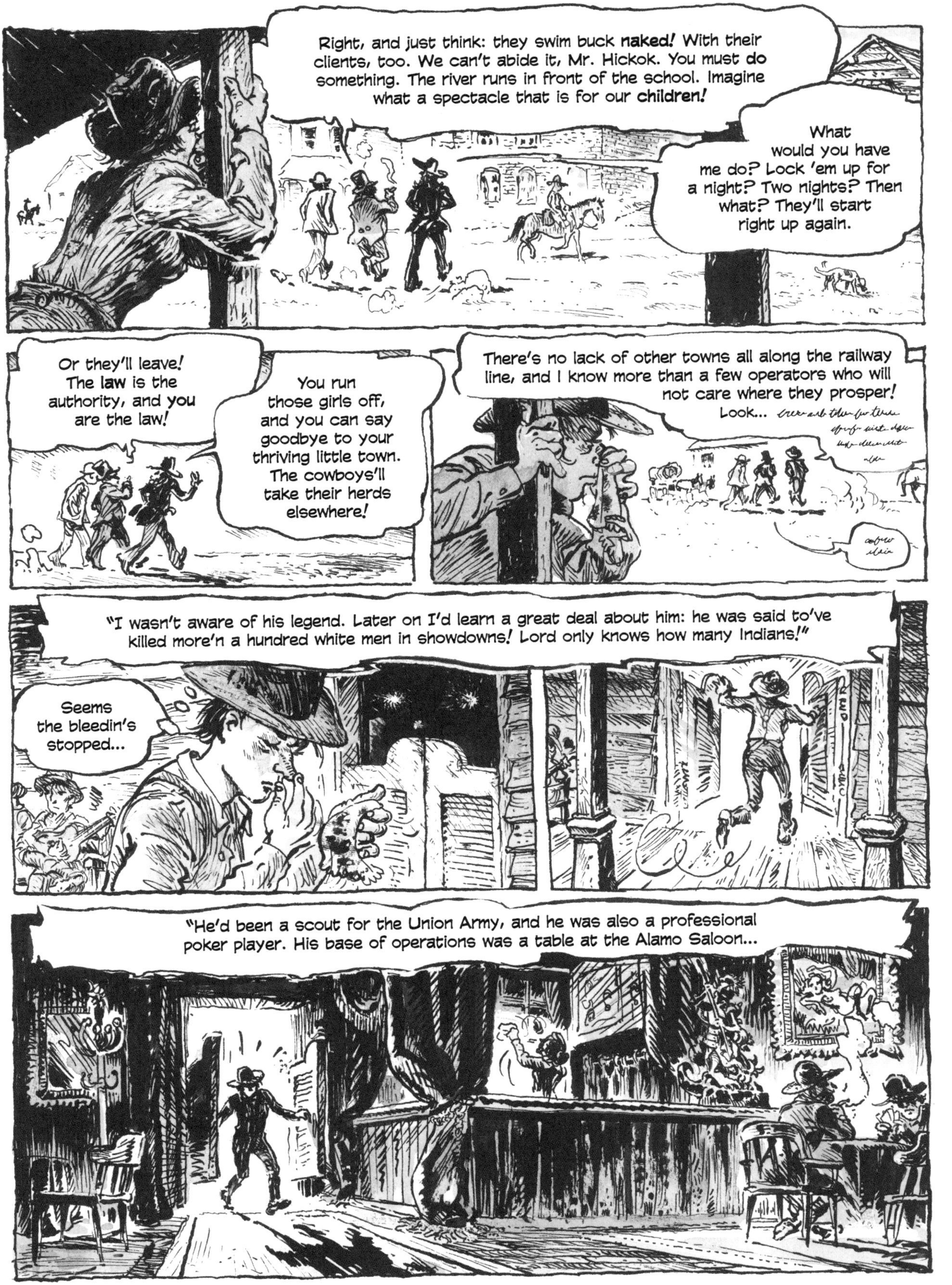

Right, and just think: they swim buck naked! With their clients, too. We can't abide it, Mr. Hickok. You must do something. The river runs in front of the school. Imagine what a spectacle that is for our children!
What would you have me do? Lock 'em up for a night? Two nights? Then what? They'll start right up again.
Or they'll leave! The law is the authority, and you are the law!
You run those girls off, and you can say goodbye to your thriving little town. The cowboys'll take their herds elsewhere!
There's no lack of other towns all along the railway line, and I know more than a few operators who will not care where they prosper! Look...
"I wasn't aware of his legend. Later on I'd learn a great deal about him: he was said to've killed more'n a hundred white men in showdowns! Lord only knows how many Indians!"
Seems the bleedin's stopped...
"He'd been a scout for the Union Army, and he was also a professional poker player. His base of operations was a table at the Alamo Saloon...

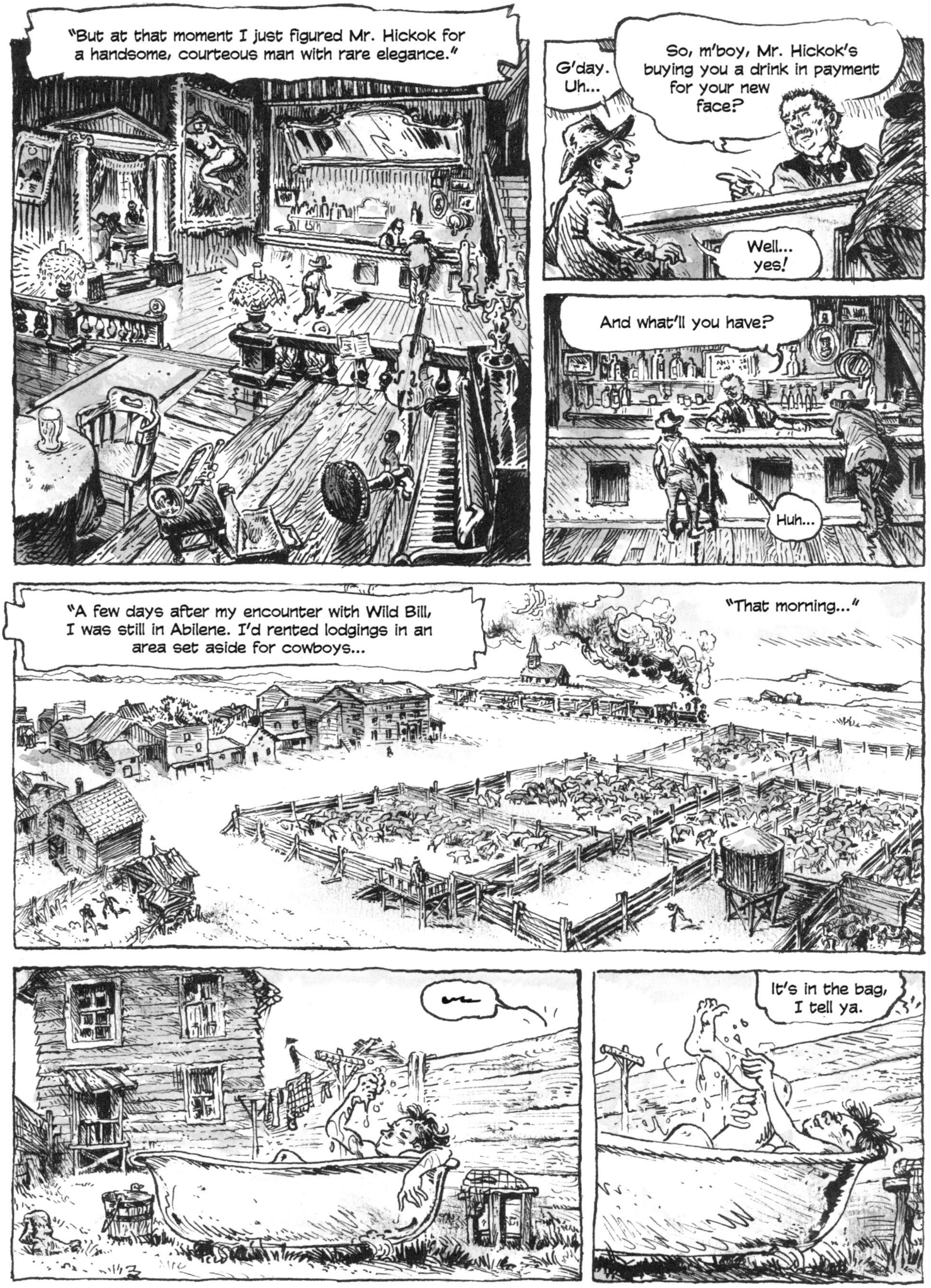
"But at that moment I just figured Mr. Hickok for a handsome, courteous man with rare elegance."
G'day. Uh...
So, m'boy, Mr. Hickok's buying you a drink in payment for your new face?
Well... yes!
And what'll you have?
Huh...
"A few days after my encounter with Wild Bill, I was still in Abilene. I'd rented lodgings in an area set aside for cowboys...
"That morning..."
It's in the bag, I tell ya.

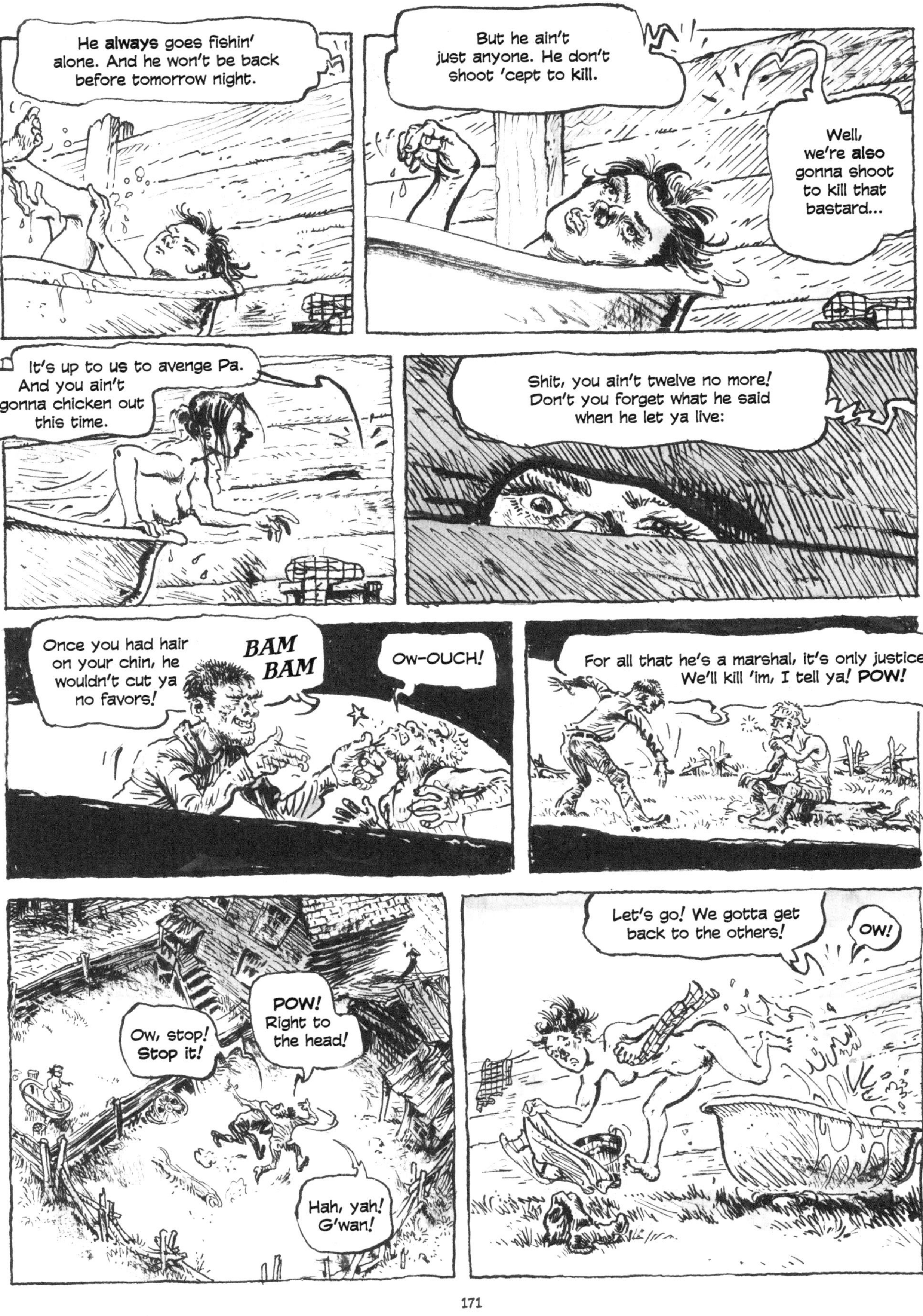
He always goes fishin' alone. And he won't be back before tomorrow night.
But he ain't just anyone. He don't shoot 'cept to kill.
Well, we're also gonna shoot to kill that bastard...
It's up to us to avenge Pa. And you ain't gonna chicken out this time.
Shit, you ain't twelve no more! Don't you forget what he said when he let ya live:
Once you had hair on your chin, he wouldn't cut ya no favors!
BAM BAM
Ow-OUCH!
For all that he's a marshal, it's only justice. We'll kill 'im, I tell ya! POW!
Ow, stop! Stop it!
POW! Right to the head!
Hah, yah! G'wan!
Let's go! We gotta get back to the others!
OW!

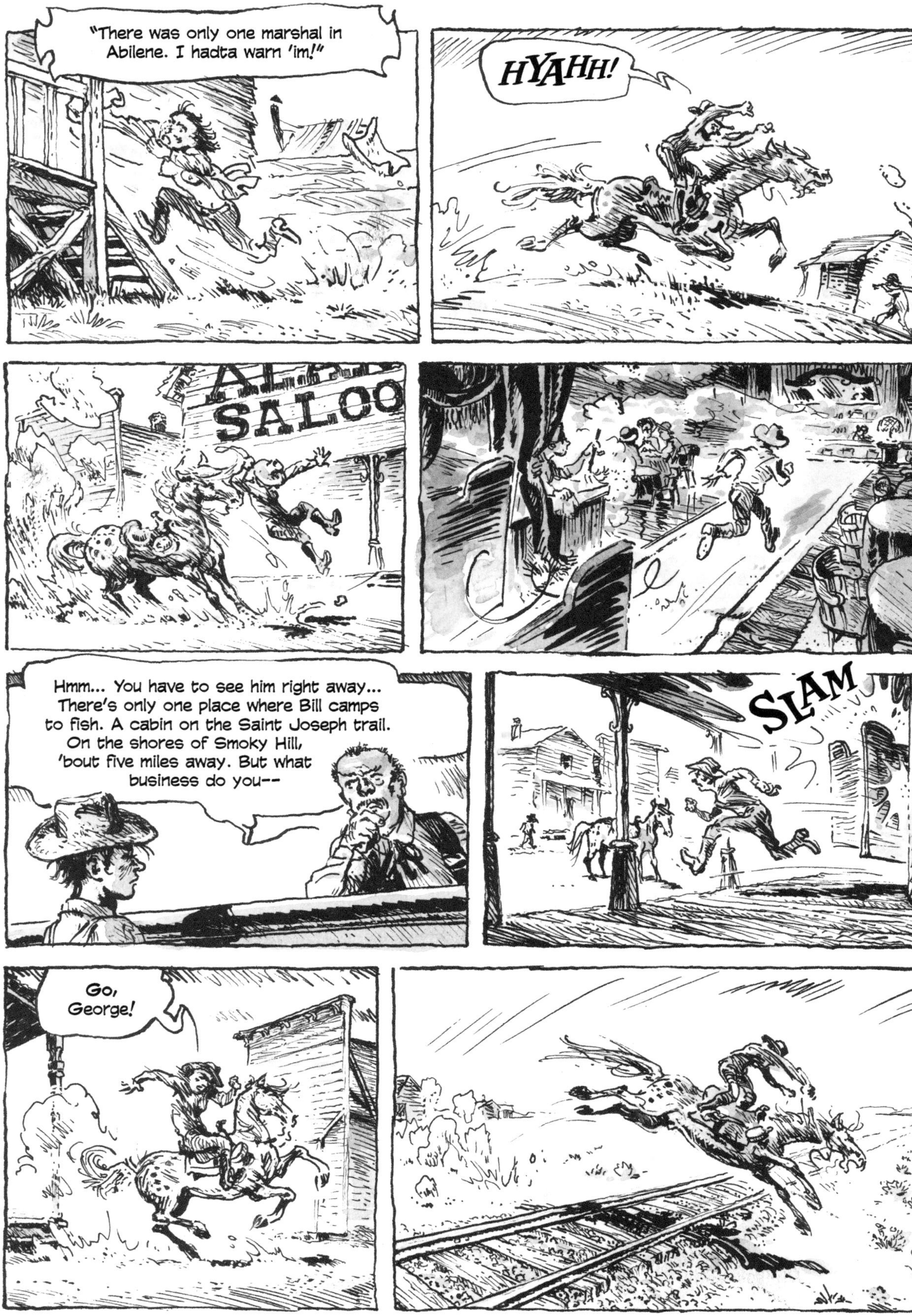
"There was only one marshal in Abilene. I hadta warn 'im!"
HYAHH!
SALOO
Hmm... You have to see him right away... There's only one place where Bill camps to fish. A cabin on the Saint Joseph trail. On the shores of Smoky Hill, 'bout five miles away. But what business do you--
SLAM
Go, George!

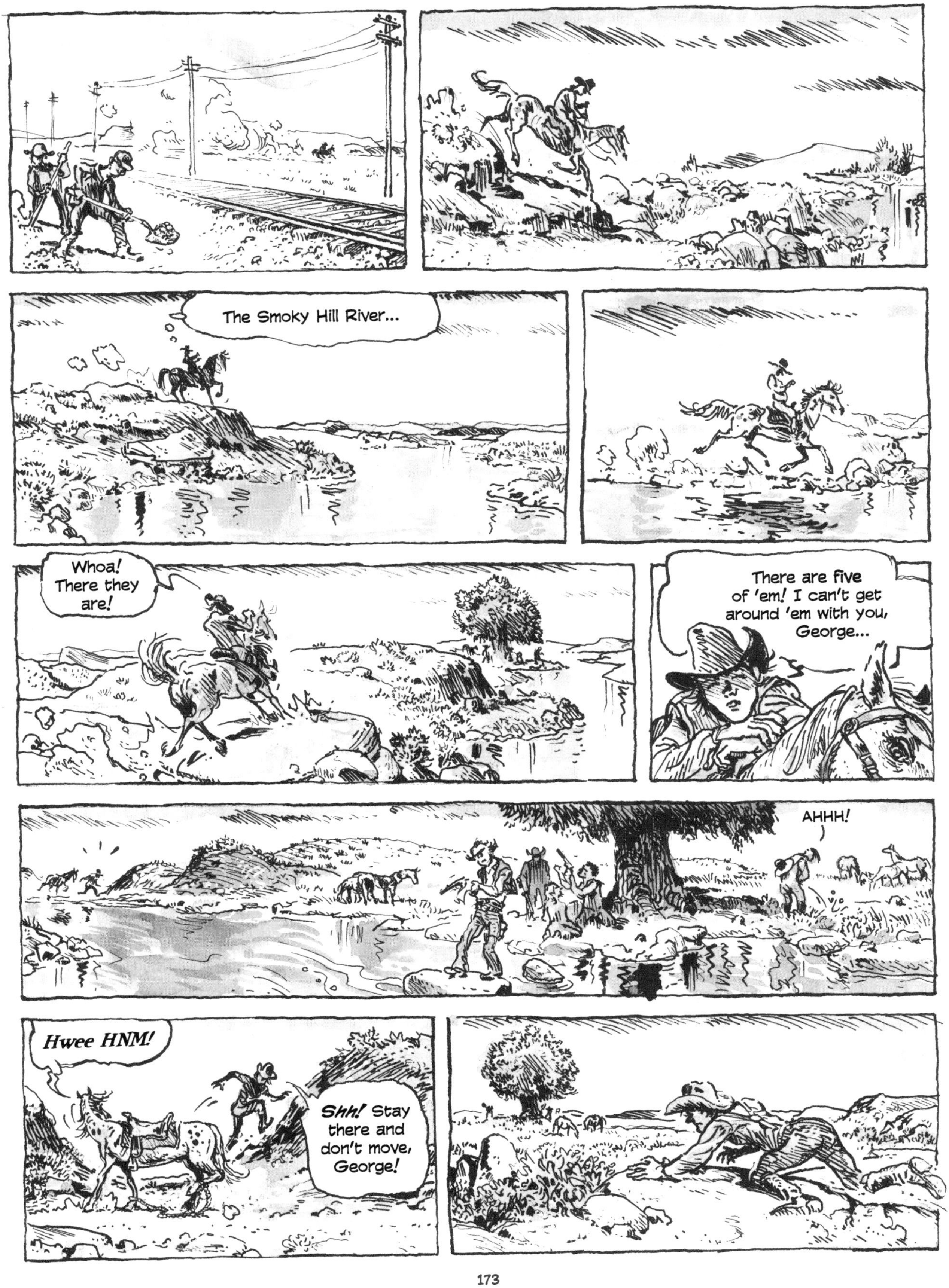
The Smoky Hill River...
Whoa! There they are!
There are five of 'em! I can't get around 'em with you, George...
AHHH!
Hwee HNM!
Shh! Stay there and don't move, George!

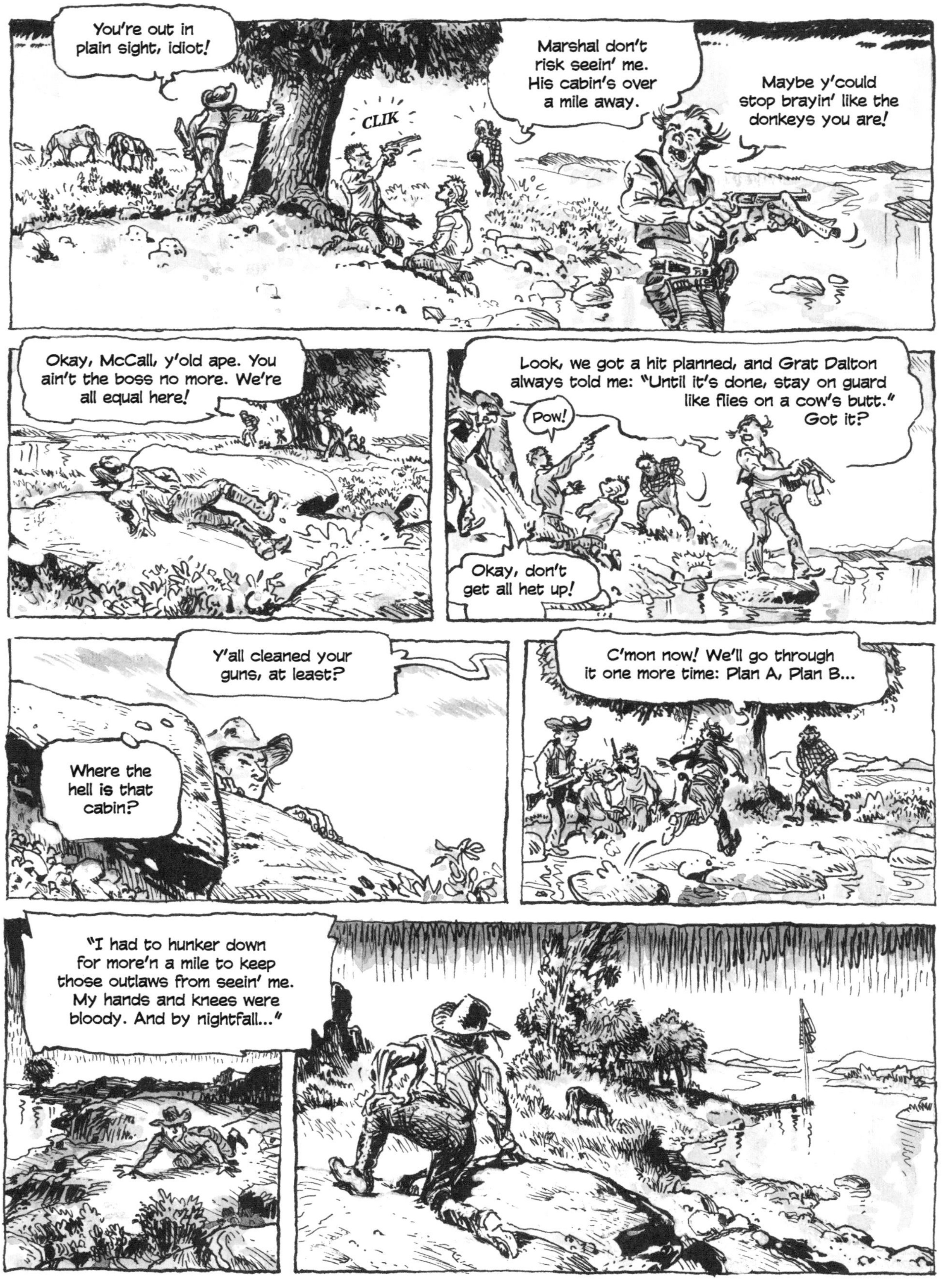
You're out in plain sight, idiot!
CLIK
Marshal don't risk seein' me. His cabin's over a mile away.
Maybe y'could stop brayin' like the donkeys you are!
Okay, McCall, y'old ape. You ain't the boss no more. We're all equal here!
Look, we got a hit planned, and Grat Dalton always told me: "Until it's done, stay on guard like flies on a cow's butt." Got it?
Pow!
Okay, don't get all het up!
Y'all cleaned your guns, at least?
Where the hell is that cabin?
C'mon now! We'll go through it one more time: Plan A, Plan B...
"I had to hunker down for more'n a mile to keep those outlaws from seein' me. My hands and knees were bloody. And by nightfall..."

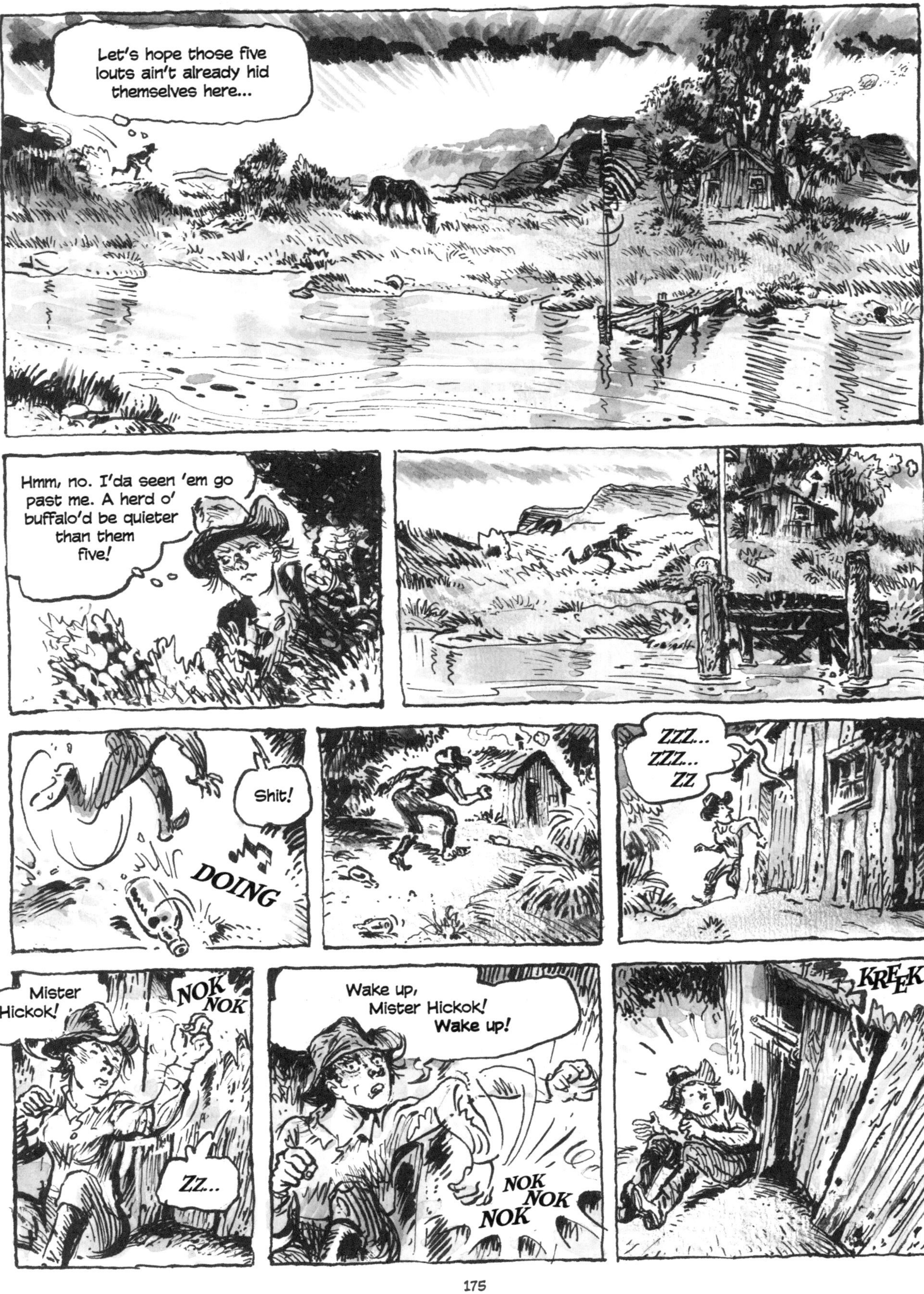
Let's hope those five louts ain't already hid themselves here...
Hmm, no. I'da seen 'em go past me. A herd o' buffalo'd be quieter than them five!
Shit!
DOING
ZZZ... ZZZ... ZZ
Mister Hickok!
NOK NOK
Zz...
Wake up, Mister Hickok! Wake up!
NOK NOK NOK
KREEK

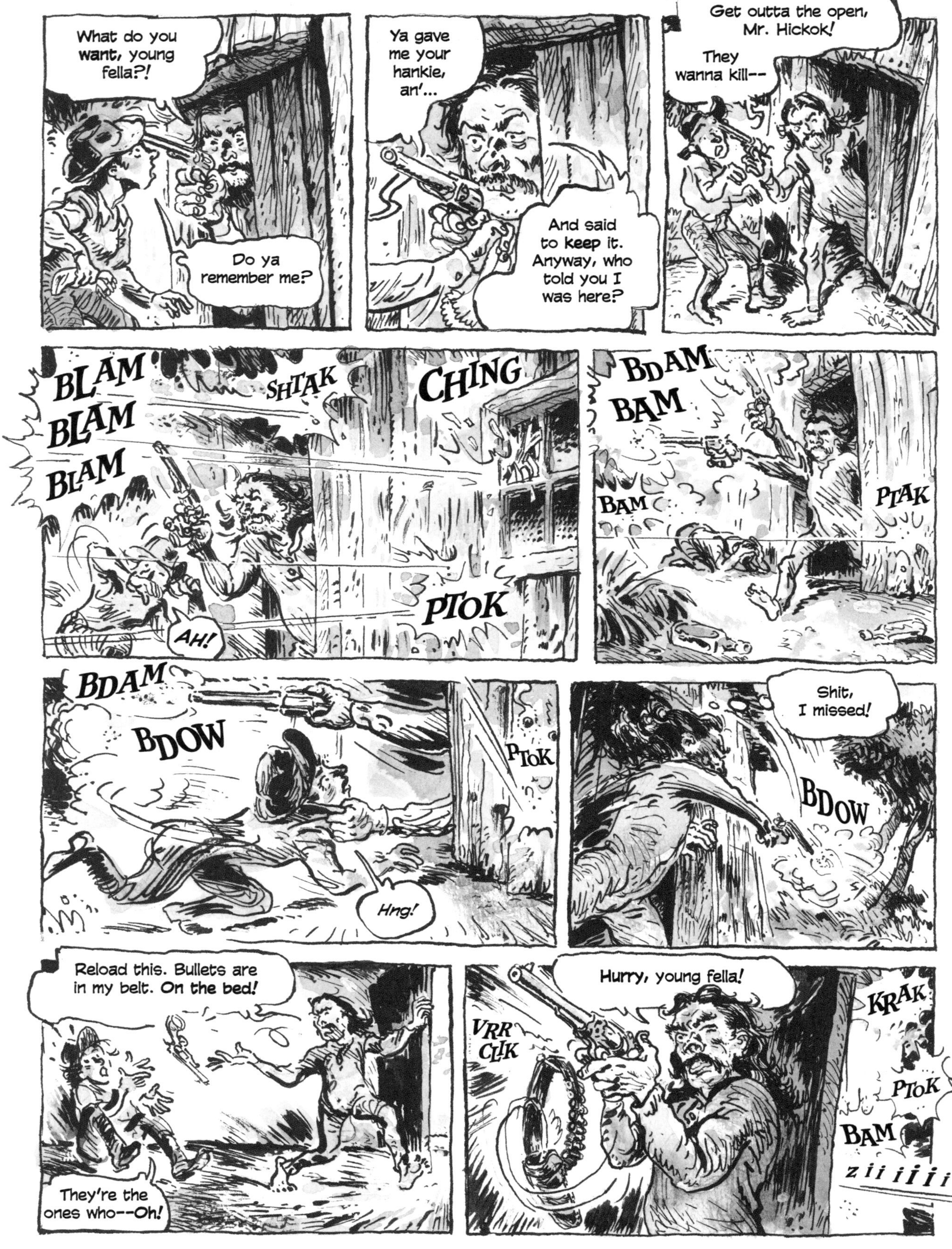

What do you want, young fella?!
Do ya remember me?
Ya gave me your hankie, an'...
And said to keep it. Anyway, who told you I was here?
Get outta the open, Mr. Hickok!
They wanna kill--
BLAM
BLAM
BLAM
SHTAK
CHING
AH!
PTOK
BDAM
BAM
BAM
PTAK
BDAM
BDOW
PTOK
Hng!
Shit, I missed!
BDOW
Reload this. Bullets are in my belt. On the bed!
They're the ones who--Oh!
Hurry, young fella!
VRR CLIK
KRAK
PTOK
BAM
Ziiiiii

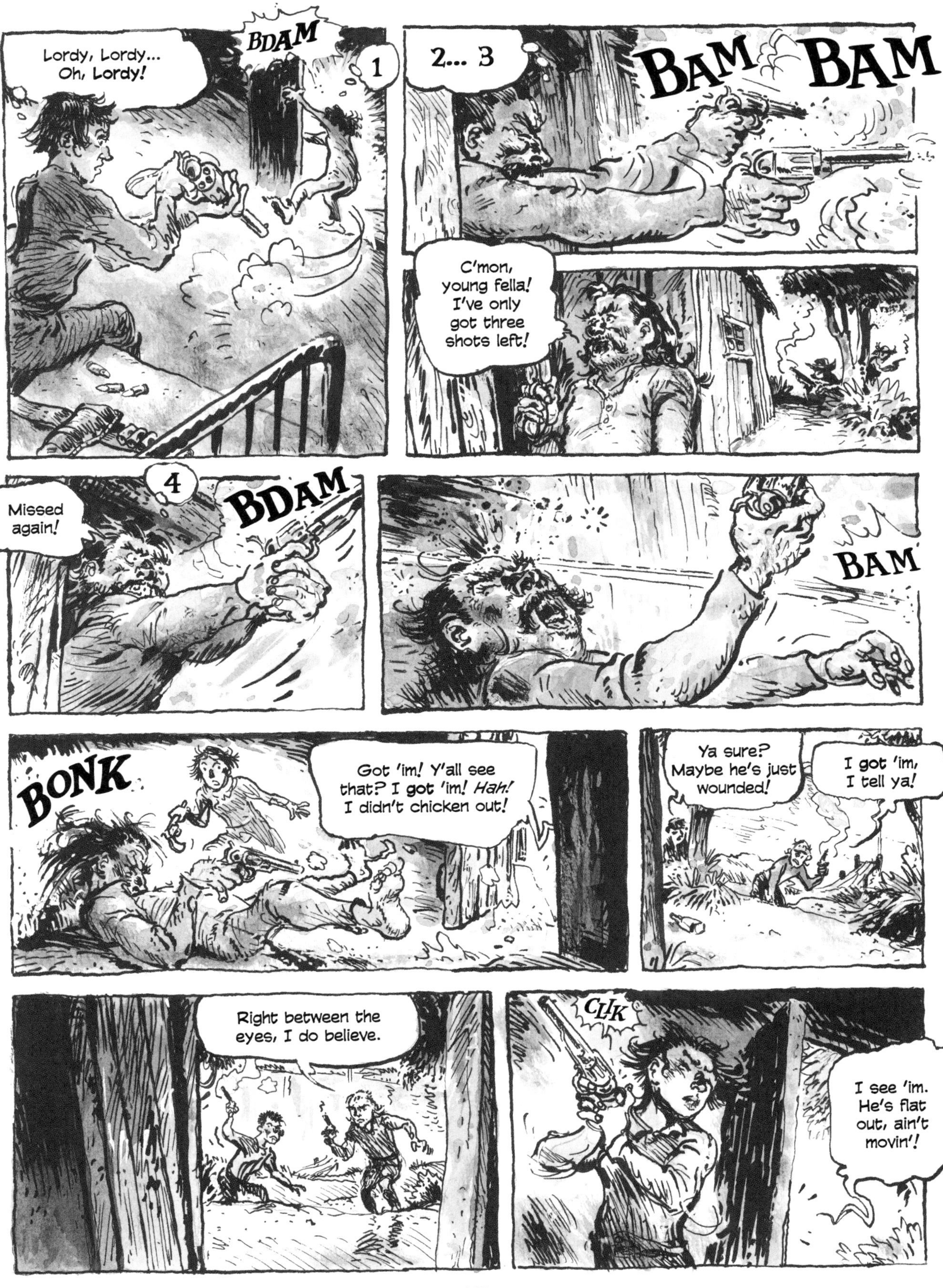
Lordy, Lordy... Oh, Lordy!
BDAM
1
2... 3
BAM
BAM
C'mon, young fella! I've only got three shots left!
Missed again!
4
BDAM
BAM
BONK
Got 'im! Y'all see that? I got 'im! Hah! I didn't chicken out!
Ya sure? Maybe he's just wounded!
I got 'im, I tell ya!
Right between the eyes, I do believe.
CLIK
I see 'im. He's flat out, ain't movin'!

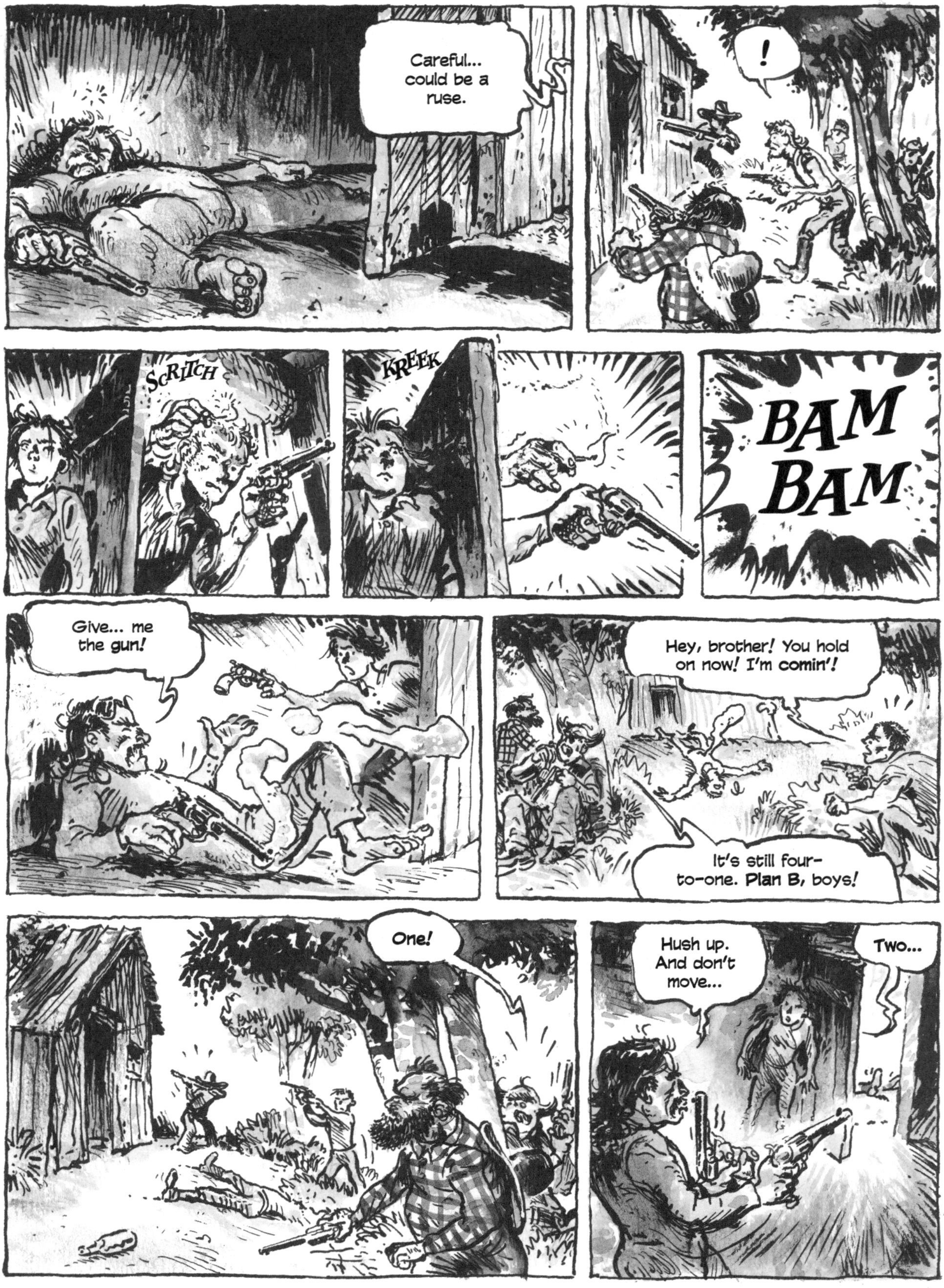
Careful... could be a ruse.
!
SCRITCH
KREEK
BAM BAM
Give... me the gun!
Hey, brother! You hold on now! I'm comin'!
It's still four-to-one. **Plan B**, boys!
One!
Hush up. And don't move...
Two...

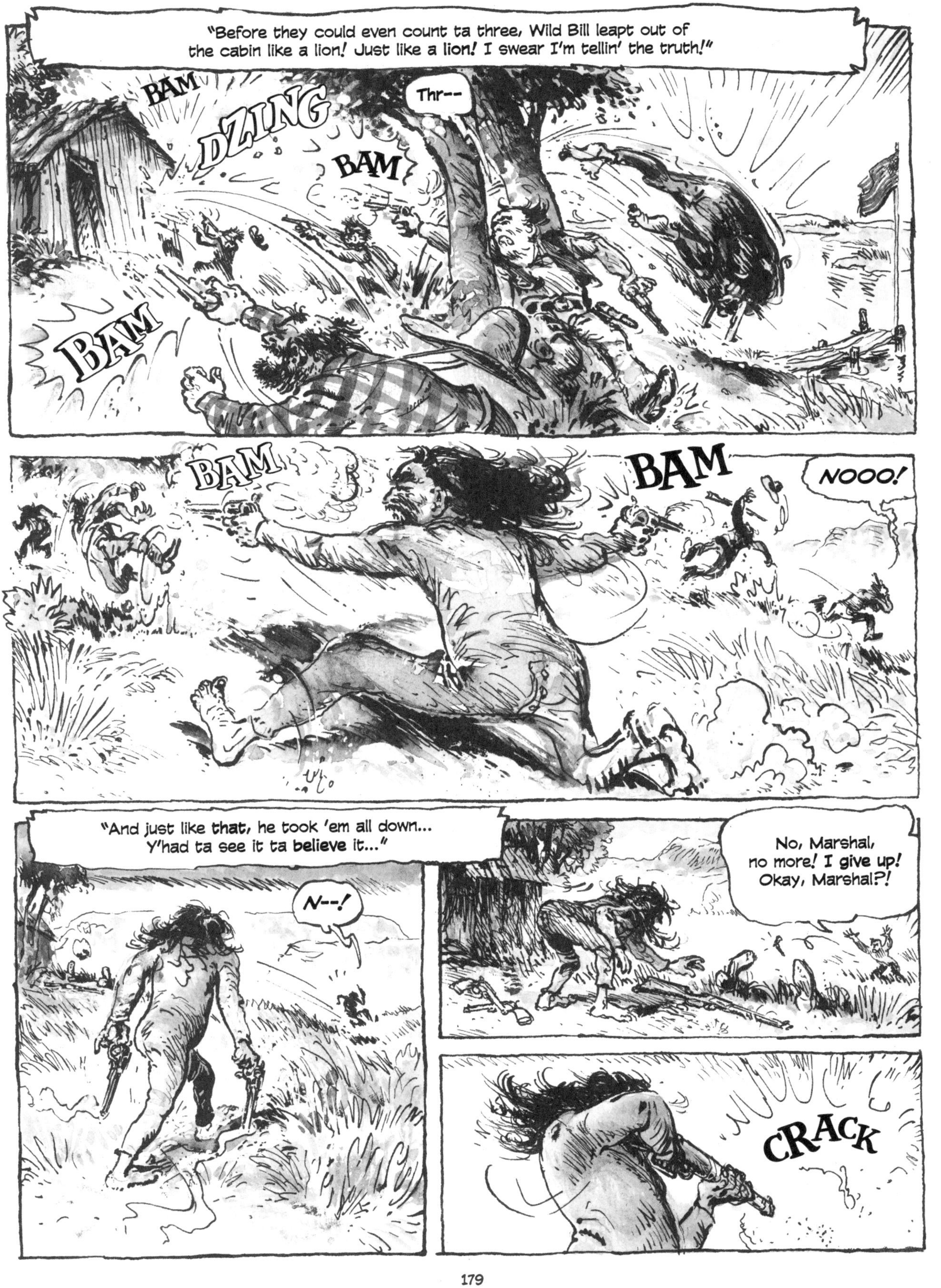
"Before they could even count ta three, Wild Bill leapt out of the cabin like a lion! Just like a lion! I swear I'm tellin' the truth!"
BAM
DZING
Thr--
BAM
BAM
BAM
BAM
NOOO!
"And just like that, he took 'em all down... Y'had ta see it ta believe it..."
N--!
No, Marshal, no more! I give up! Okay, Marshal?!
CRACK

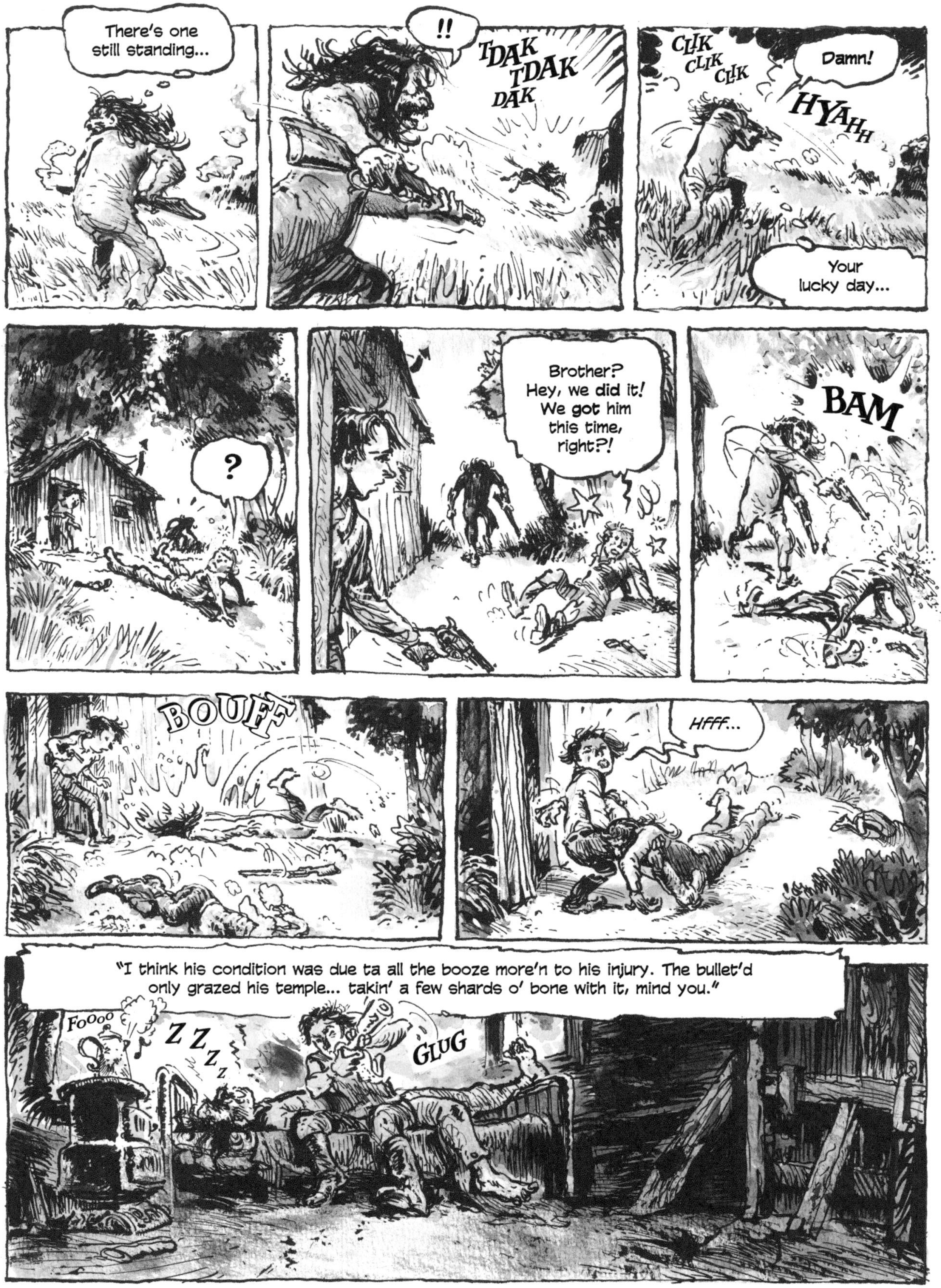

There's one still standing...
!!
TDAK TDAK DAK
CLIK CLIK CLIK
Damn!
HYAHH
Your lucky day...
?
Brother? Hey, we did it! We got him this time, right?!
BAM
BOUFF
Hfff...
"I think his condition was due ta all the booze more'n to his injury. The bullet'd only grazed his temple... takin' a few shards o' bone with it, mind you."
Foooo
Z Z Z Z
GLUG

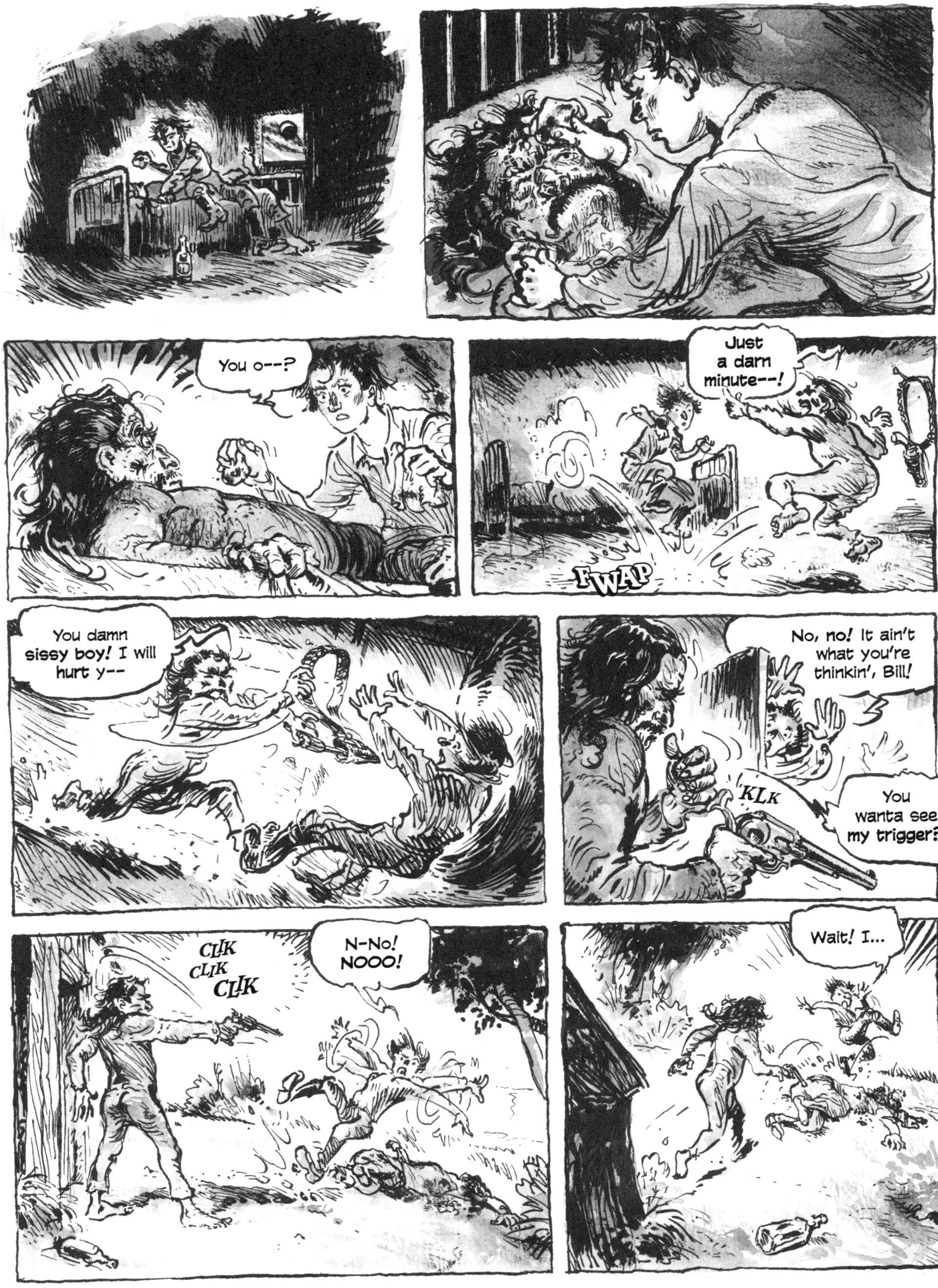
You o--?
Just a darn minute--!
FWAP
You damn sissy boy! I will hurt y--
No, no! It ain't what you're thinkin', Bill!
KLK
You wanta see my trigger?
CLIK CLIK CLIK
N-No! NOOO!
Wait! I...

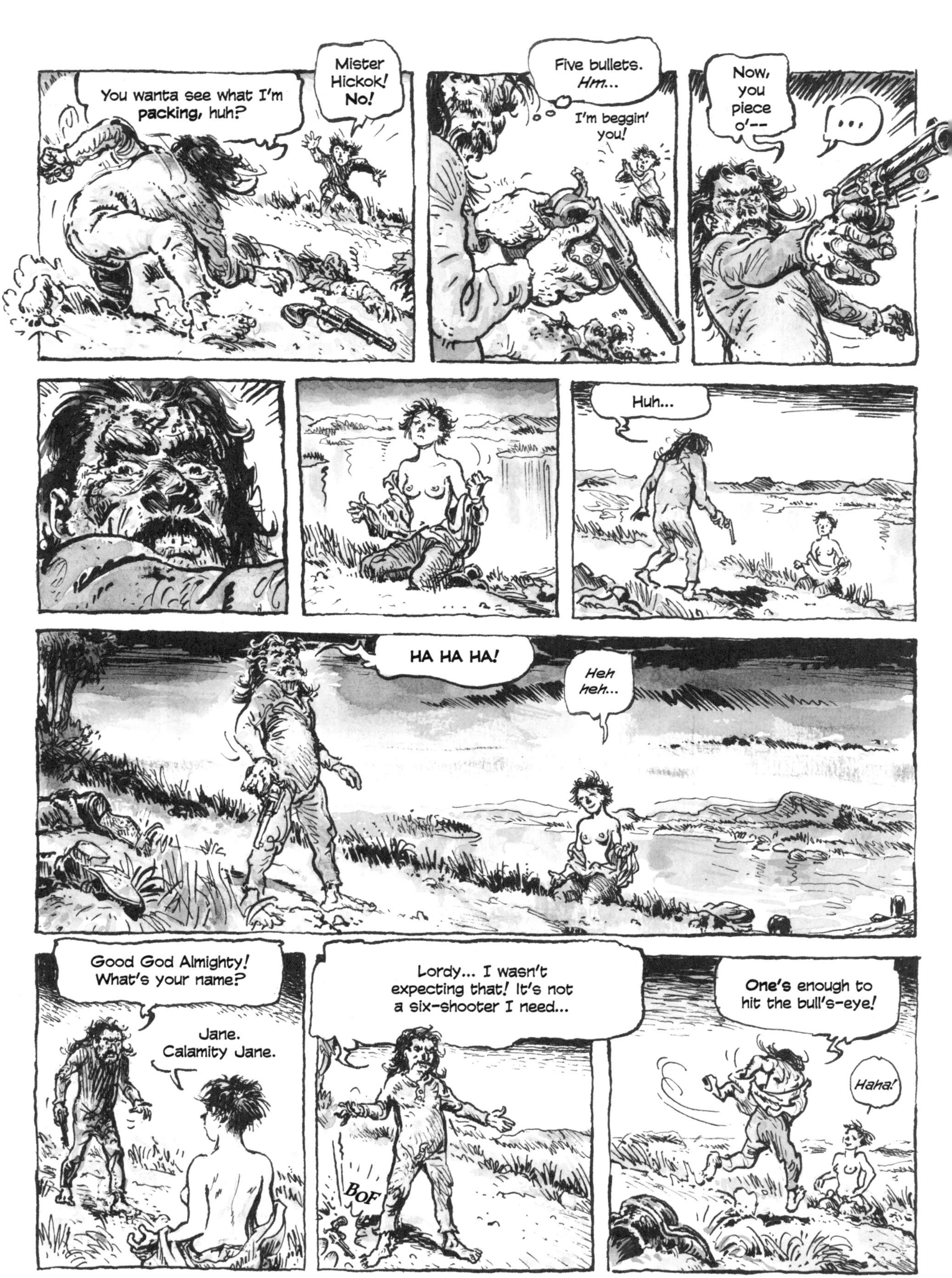
You wanta see what I'm **packing**, huh?
Mister Hickok! **No!**
Five bullets. *Hm...*
I'm beggin' you!
Now, you piece o'--
...
Huh...
HA HA HA!
Heh heh...
Good God Almighty! What's your name?
Jane. Calamity Jane.
Lordy... I wasn't expecting that! It's not a six-shooter I need...
BOF
One's enough to hit the bull's-eye!
Haha!

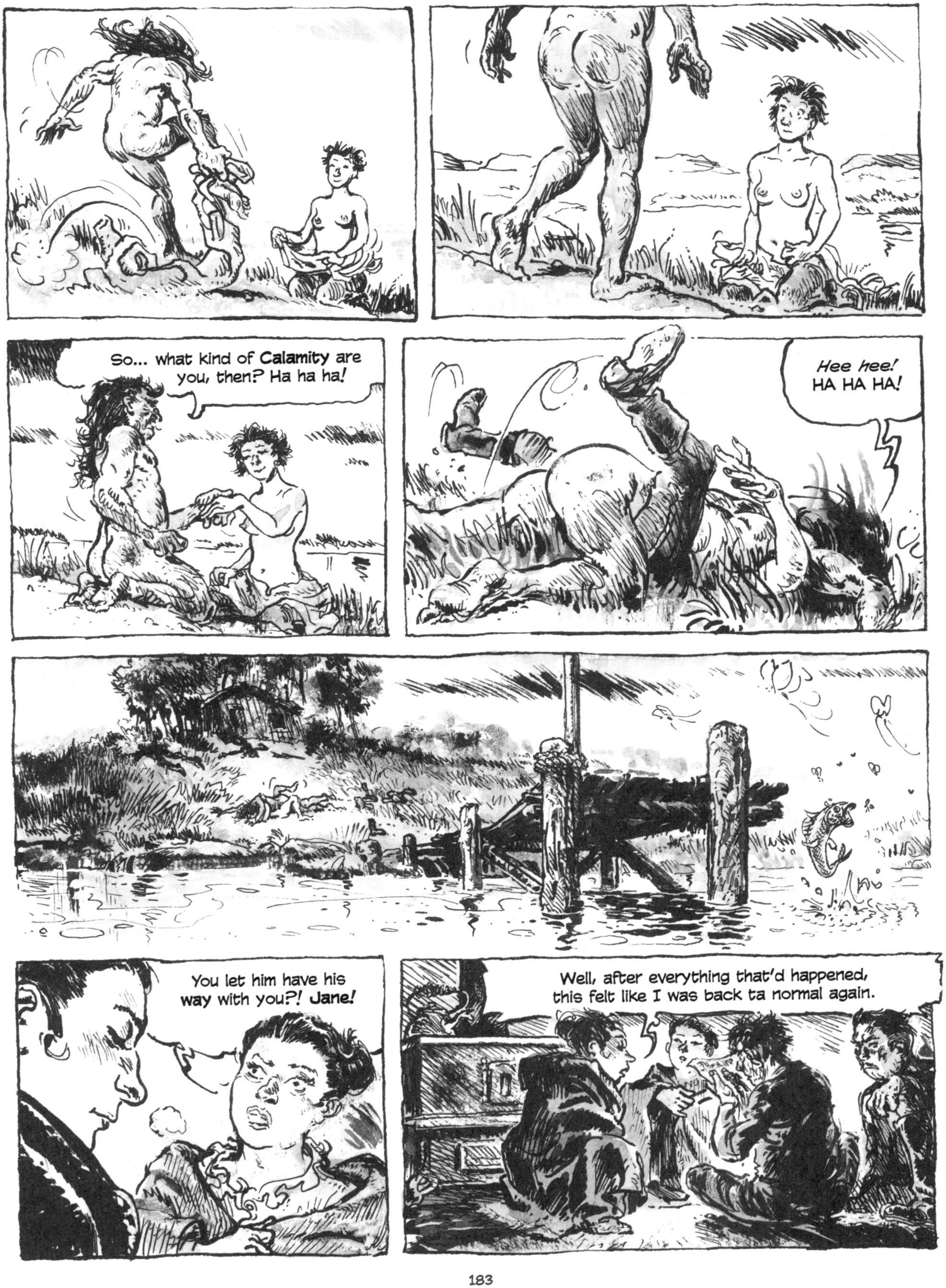
So... what kind of **Calamity** are you, then? Ha ha ha!
Hee hee! HA HA HA!
You let him have his way with you?! **Jane!**
Well, after everything that'd happened, this felt like I was back ta normal again.

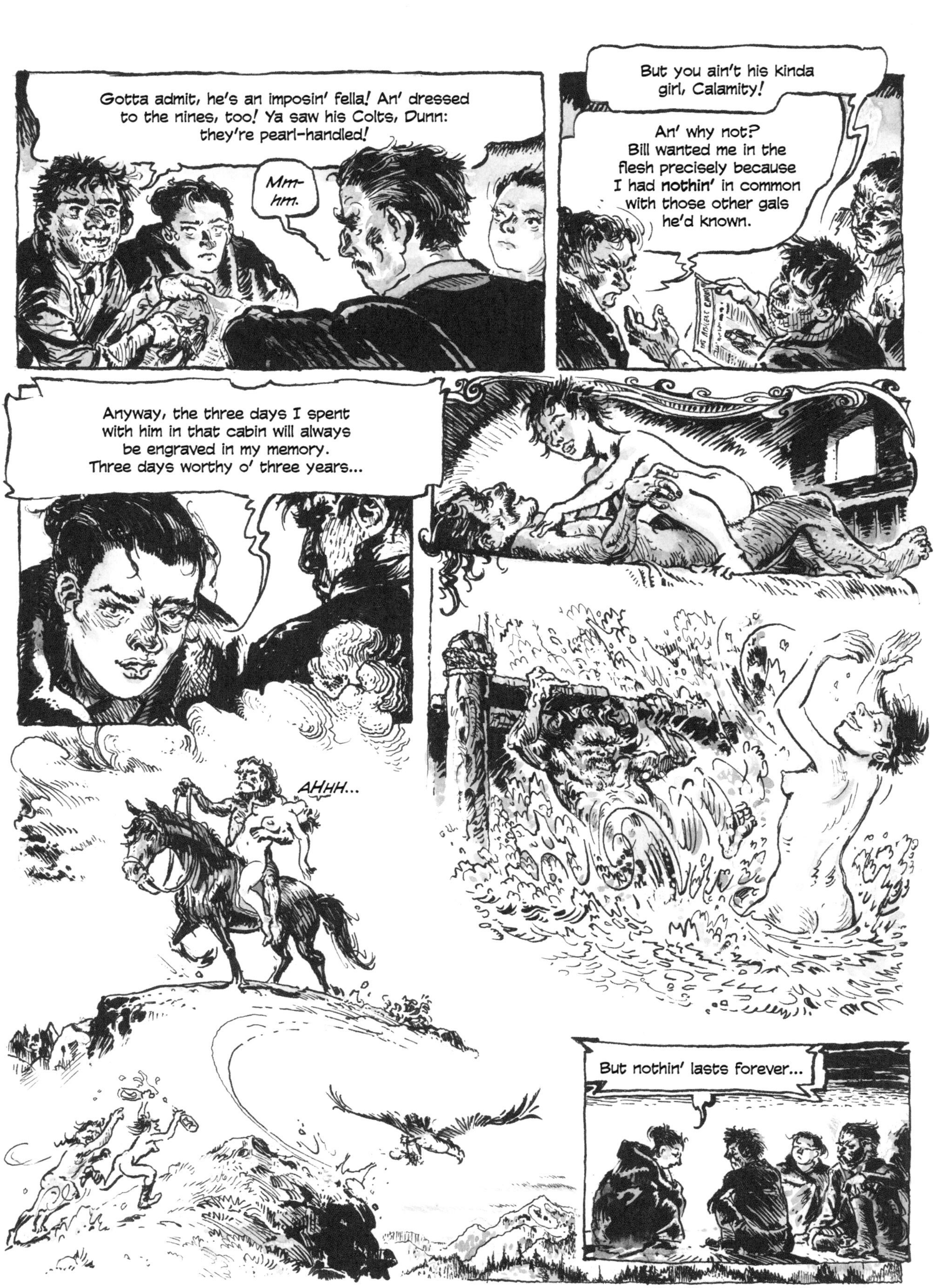

Gotta admit, he's an imposin' fella! An' dressed to the nines, too! Ya saw his Colts, Dunn: they're pearl-handled!
Mm-hm.
But you ain't his kinda girl, Calamity!
An' why not? Bill wanted me in the flesh precisely because I had **nothin'** in common with those other gals he'd known.
Anyway, the three days I spent with him in that cabin will always be engraved in my memory. Three days worthy o' three years...
AHHH...
But nothin' lasts forever...

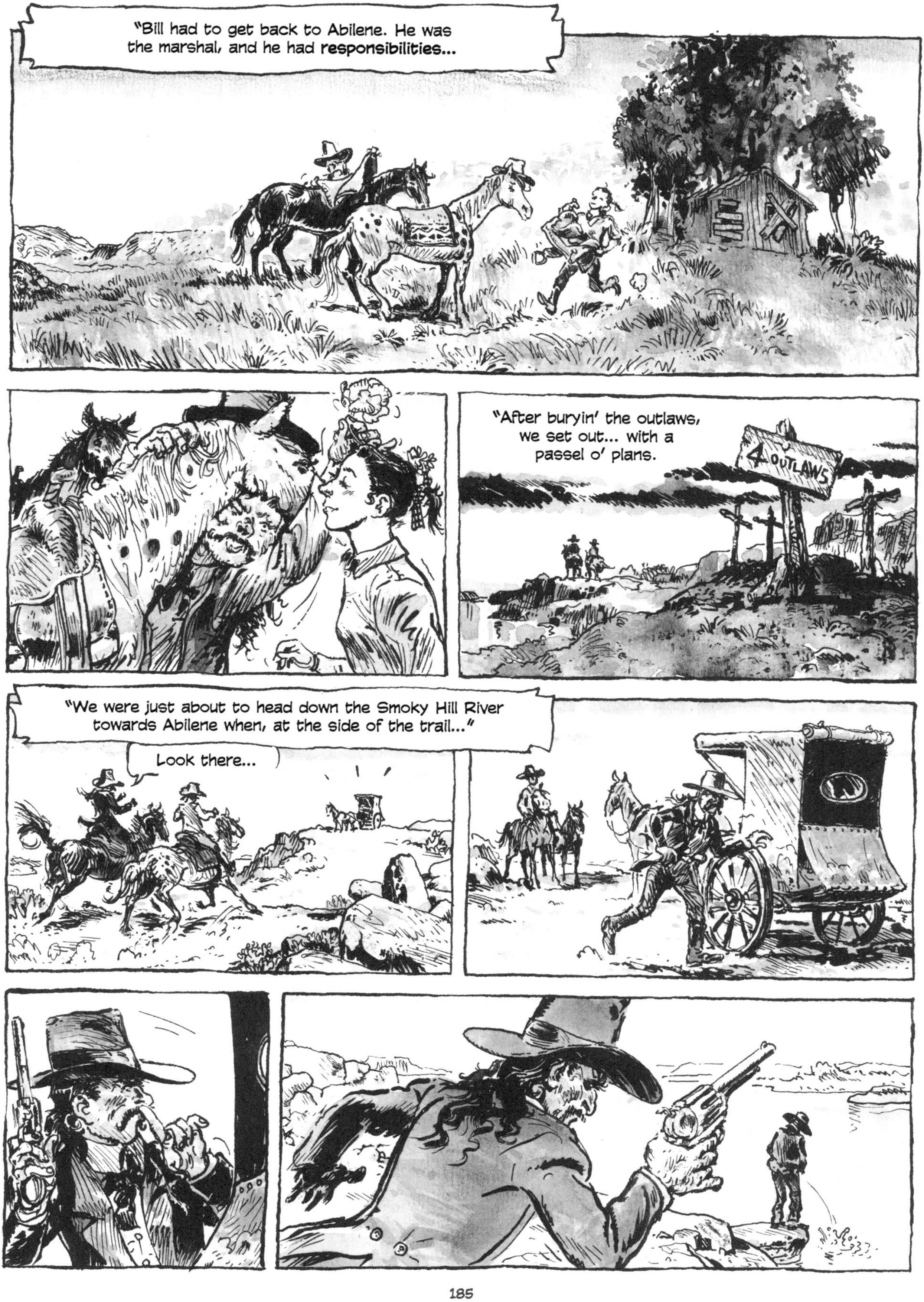
"Bill had to get back to Abilene. He was the marshal, and he had **responsibilities...**
"After buryin' the outlaws, we set out... with a passel o' plans.
4 OUTLAWS
"We were just about to head down the Smoky Hill River towards Abilene when, at the side of the trail..."
Look there...

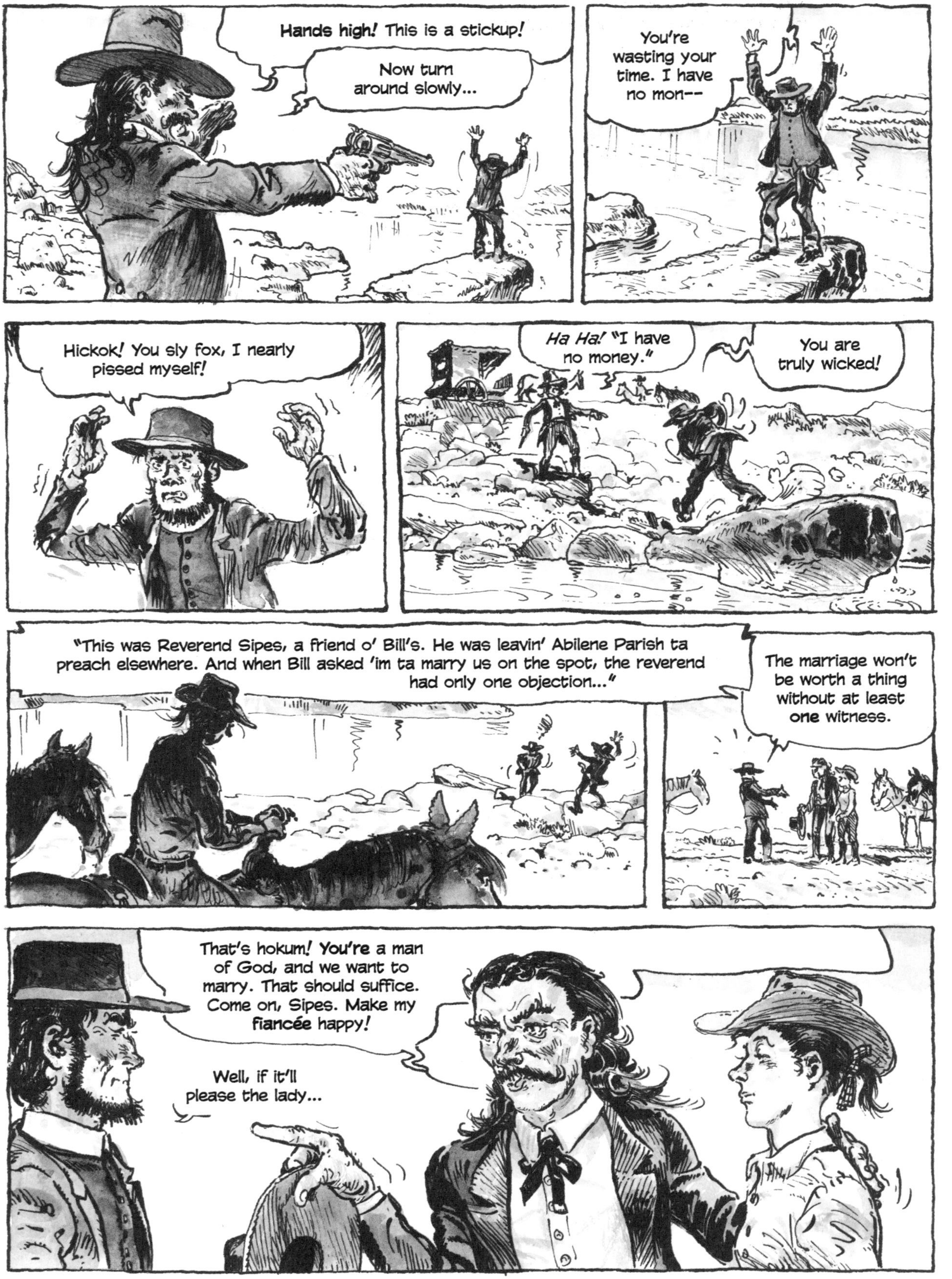
Hands high! This is a stickup!
Now turn around slowly...
You're wasting your time. I have no mon--
Hickok! You sly fox, I nearly pissed myself!
Ha Ha! "I have no money."
You are truly wicked!
"This was Reverend Sipes, a friend o' Bill's. He was leavin' Abilene Parish ta preach elsewhere. And when Bill asked 'im ta marry us on the spot, the reverend had only one objection..."
The marriage won't be worth a thing without at least one witness.
That's hokum! You're a man of God, and we want to marry. That should suffice. Come on, Sipes. Make my fiancée happy!
Well, if it'll please the lady...

"My Bill had the power of persuasion: no one could resist him.

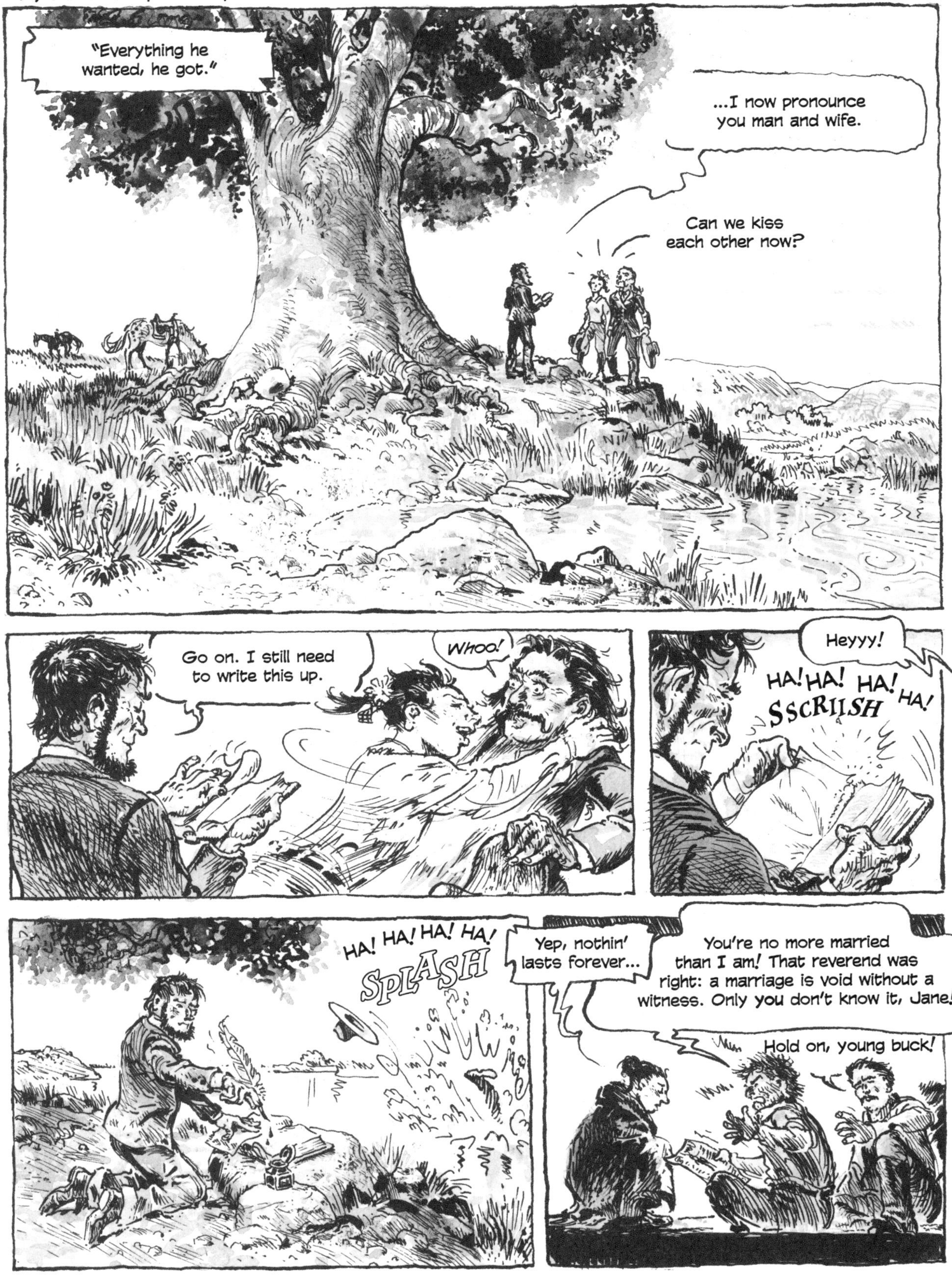
"Everything he wanted, he got."
...I now pronounce you man and wife.
Can we kiss each other now?
Go on. I still need to write this up.
Whoo!
Heyyy!
HA! HA! HA! HA!
SSCRIIISH
HA! HA! HA! HA!
SPLASH
Yep, nothin' lasts forever...
You're no more married than I am! That reverend was right: a marriage is void without a witness. Only you don't know it, Jane!
Hold on, young buck!

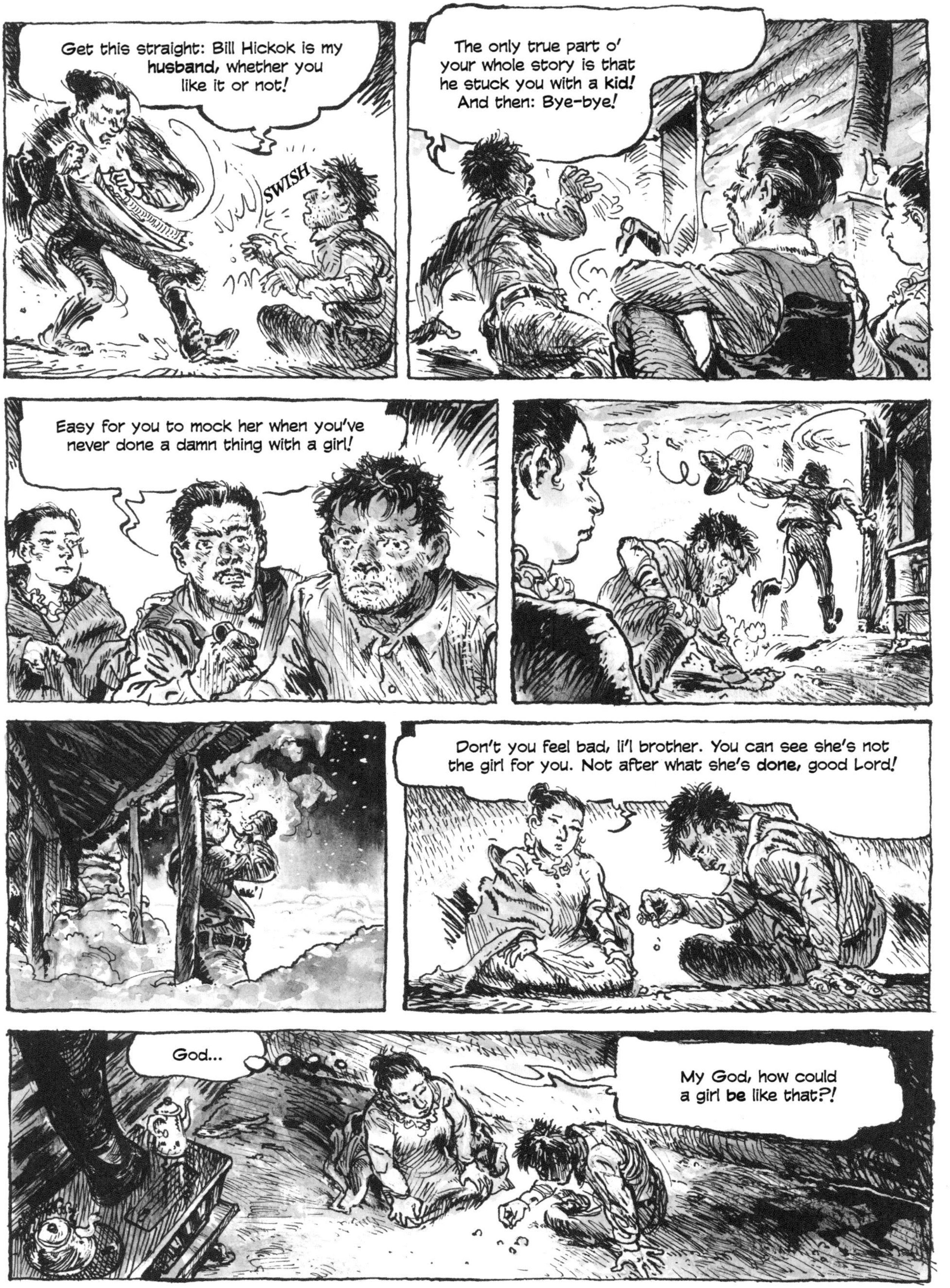
Get this straight: Bill Hickok is my husband, whether you like it or not!
SWISH
The only true part o' your whole story is that he stuck you with a kid! And then: Bye-bye!
Easy for you to mock her when you've never done a damn thing with a girl!
Don't you feel bad, li'l brother. You can see she's not the girl for you. Not after what she's done, good Lord!
God...
My God, how could a girl be like that?!

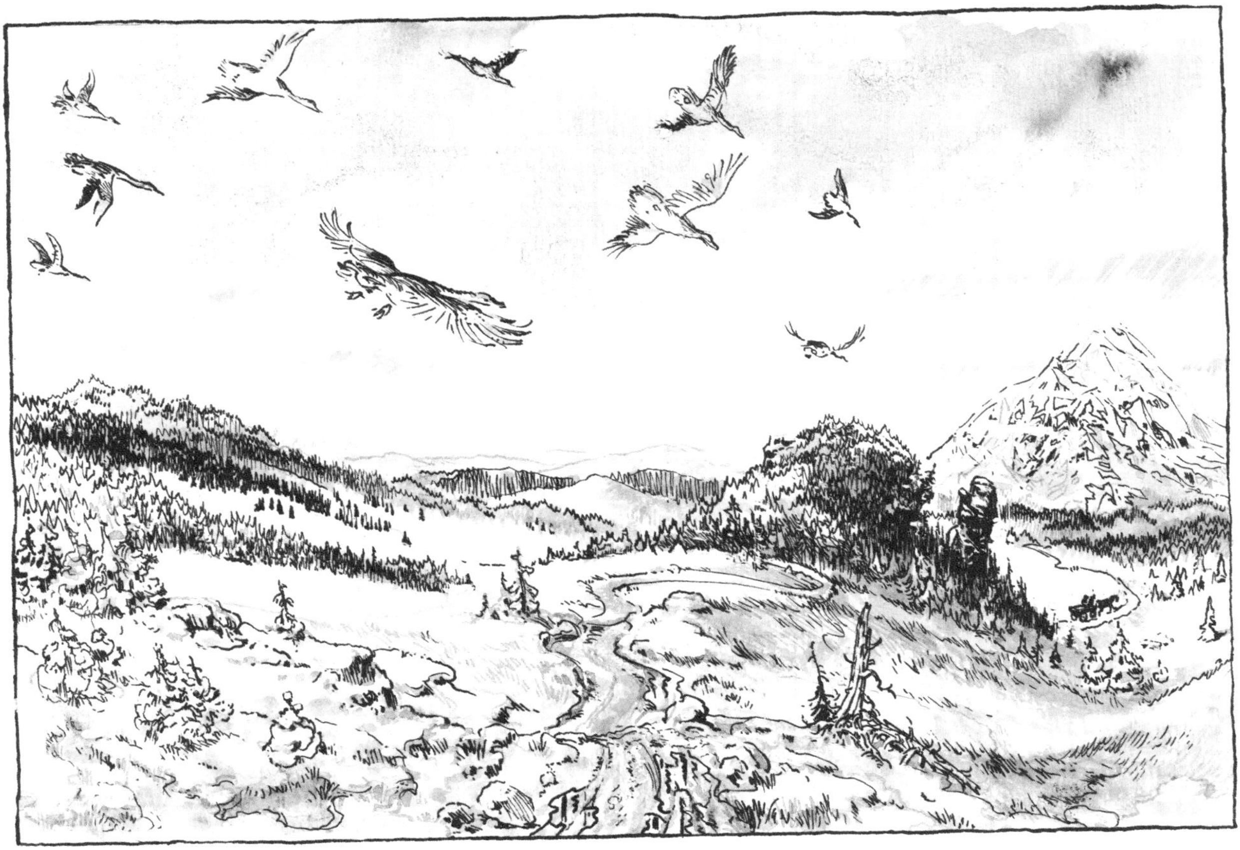

In *Letters to Her Daughter*, Calamity reminisces about her life with Bill Hickok in Abilene and admits that her jealousy soon dominated the relationship. Hickok would not be seen in the light of day with Jane. She was secluded in a hotel room on the outskirts of town...

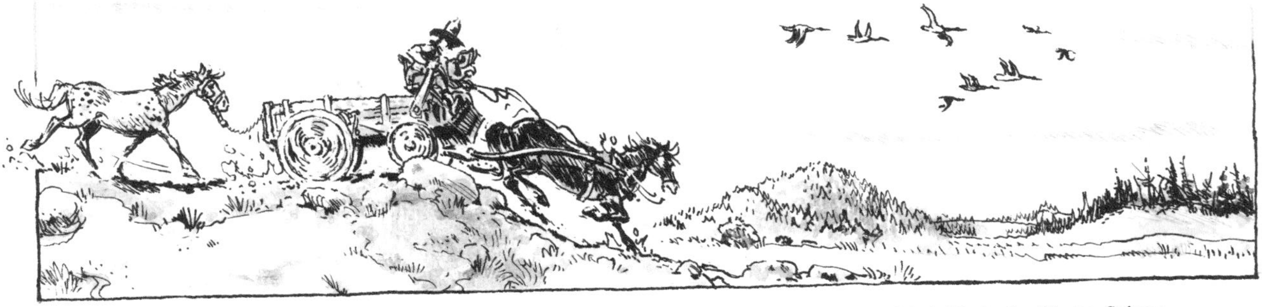

...while Hickok carried on with his life as marshal and professional poker player at his table in the Alamo Saloon. Wild Bill was a consummate ladies' man and racked up countless adventures, notably with the Alamo's dancers.

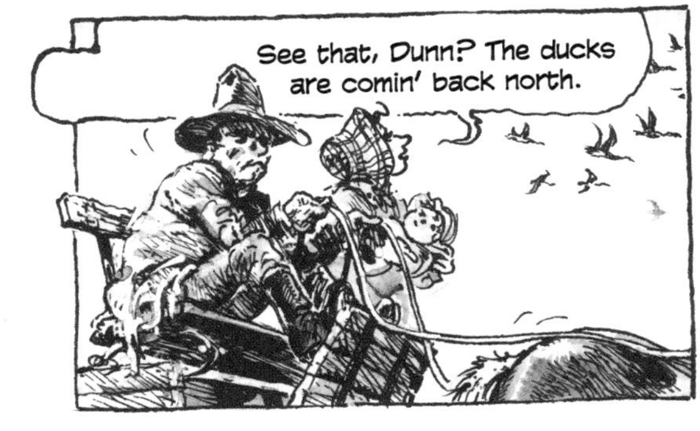
See that, Dunn? The ducks are comin' back north.

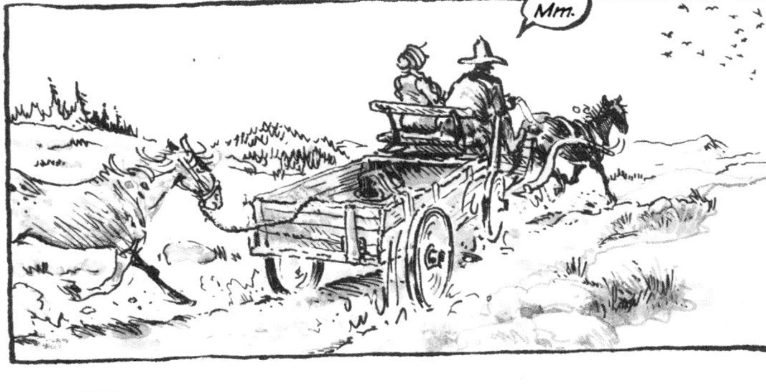
Mm.

Jane mentions a certain "Mamie Werly," who must have been at least three years her senior...

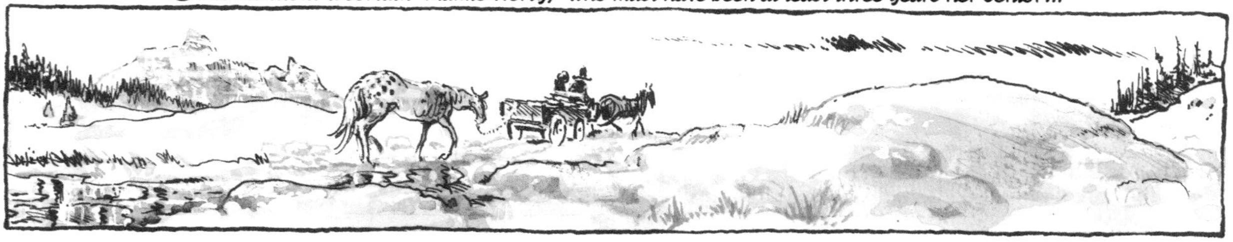

...and who drove Jane crazy with rage! But her biggest rival was undoubtedly **Agnes Lake,** a circus performer who lived back East and with whom Hickok was very much in love. One day he simply abandoned Jane, leaving Abilene to go marry Agnes Lake.

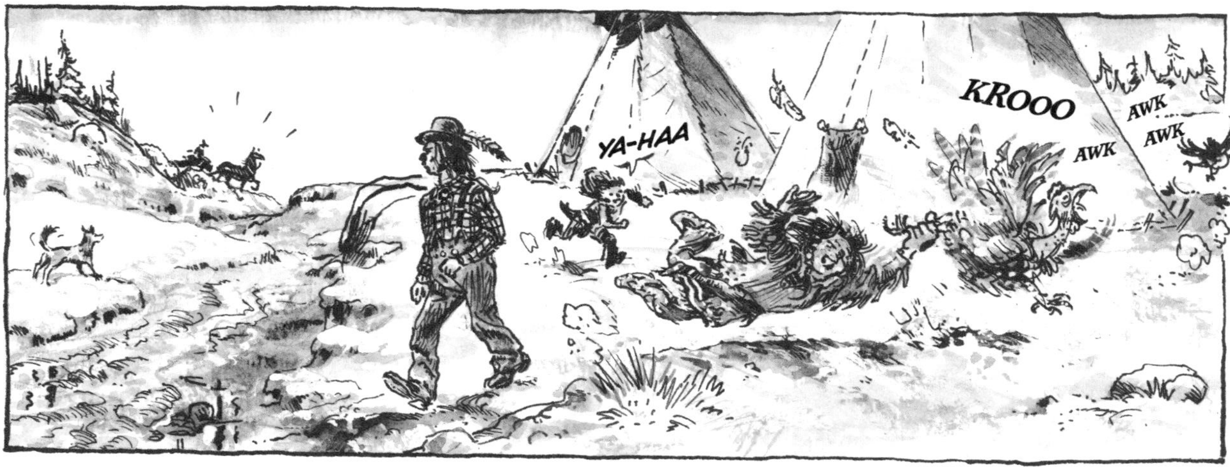
YA-HAA
KROOO
AWK
AWK
AWK

In despair, Jane also left Abilene, and if the dates in her letters are to be believed, she was pregnant with Janey at the time.

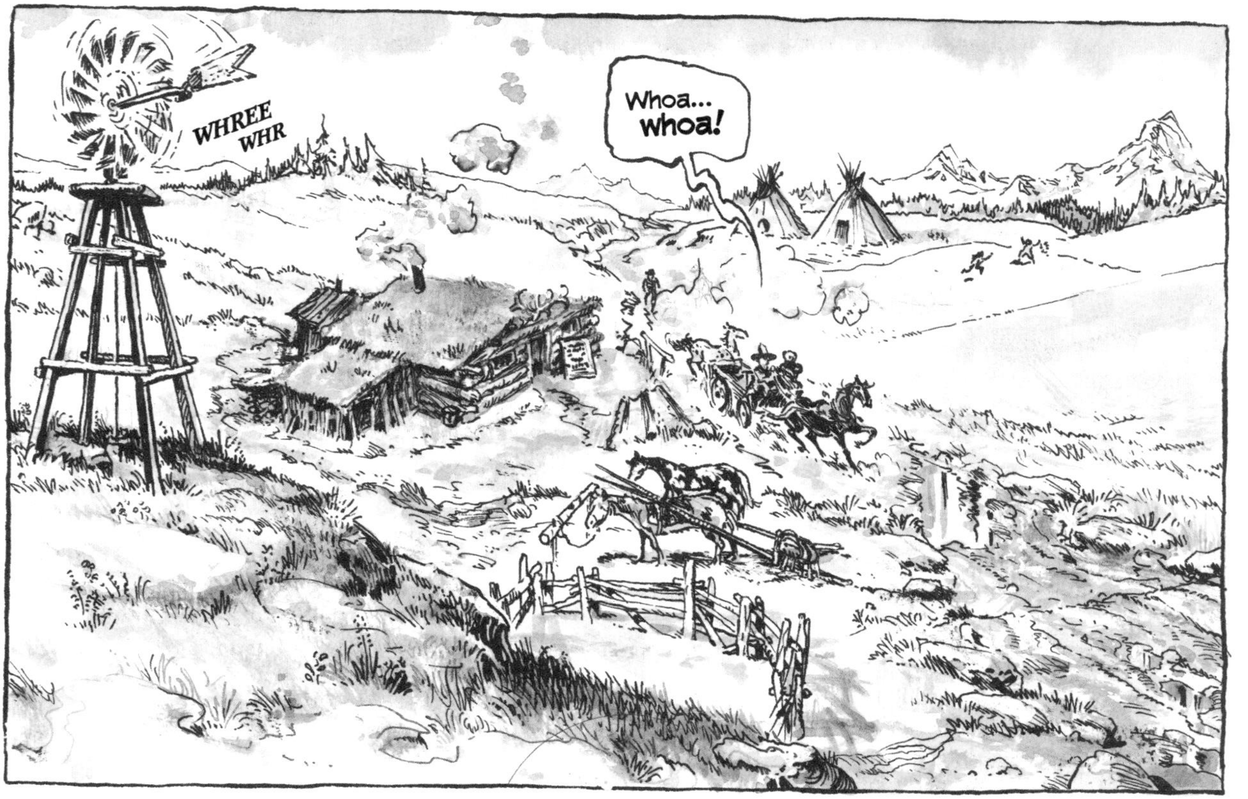
WHREE WHR
Whoa... **whoa!**

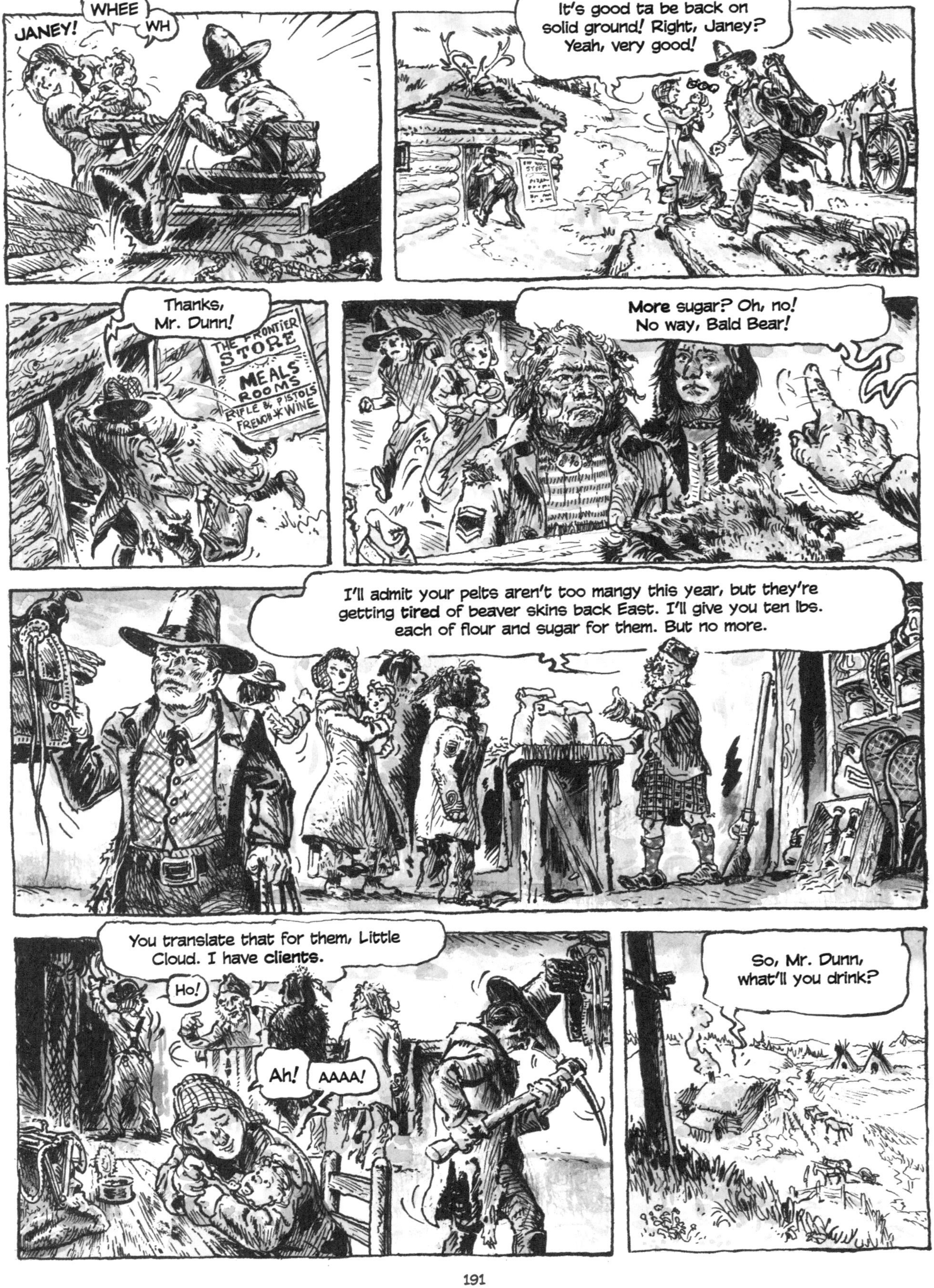
JANEY!
WHEE
WH
It's good ta be back on solid ground! Right, Janey? Yeah, very good!
Thanks, Mr. Dunn!
THE FRONTIER STORE
MEALS ROOMS
RIFLE & PISTOLS
FRENCH ✱ WINE
More sugar? Oh, no! No way, Bald Bear!
I'll admit your pelts aren't too mangy this year, but they're getting tired of beaver skins back East. I'll give you ten lbs. each of flour and sugar for them. But no more.
You translate that for them, Little Cloud. I have clients.
Ho!
Ah!
AAAA!
So, Mr. Dunn, what'll you drink?

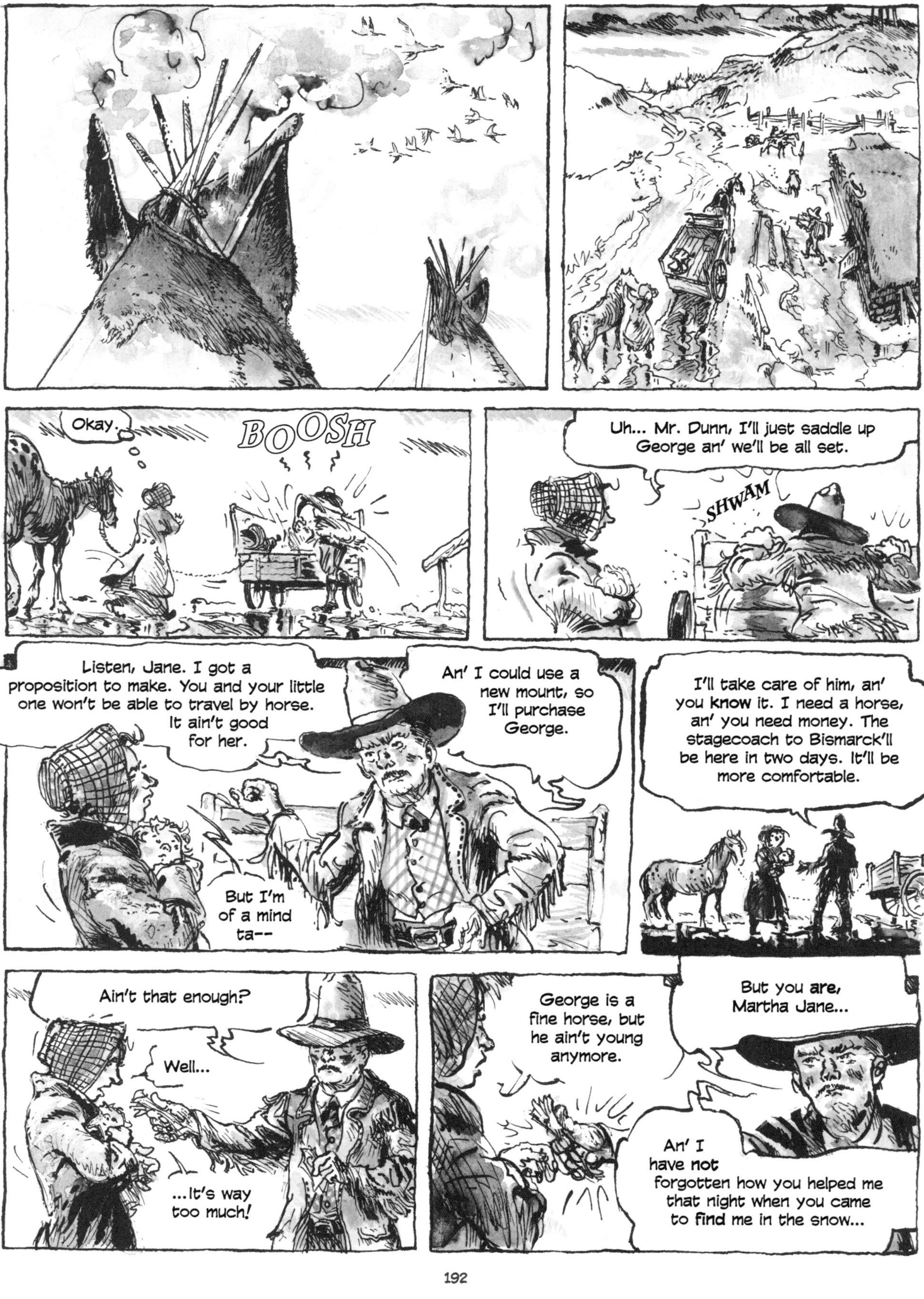
Okay.
BOOSH
Uh... Mr. Dunn, I'll just saddle up George an' we'll be all set.
SHWAM
Listen, Jane. I got a proposition to make. You and your little one won't be able to travel by horse. It ain't good for her.
An' I could use a new mount, so I'll purchase George.
But I'm of a mind ta--
I'll take care of him, an' you **know** it. I need a horse, an' you need money. The stagecoach to Bismarck'll be here in two days. It'll be more comfortable.
Ain't that enough?
Well...
...It's way too much!
George is a fine horse, but he ain't young anymore.
But you **are,** Martha Jane...
An' I have **not** forgotten how you helped me that night when you came to **find** me in the snow...

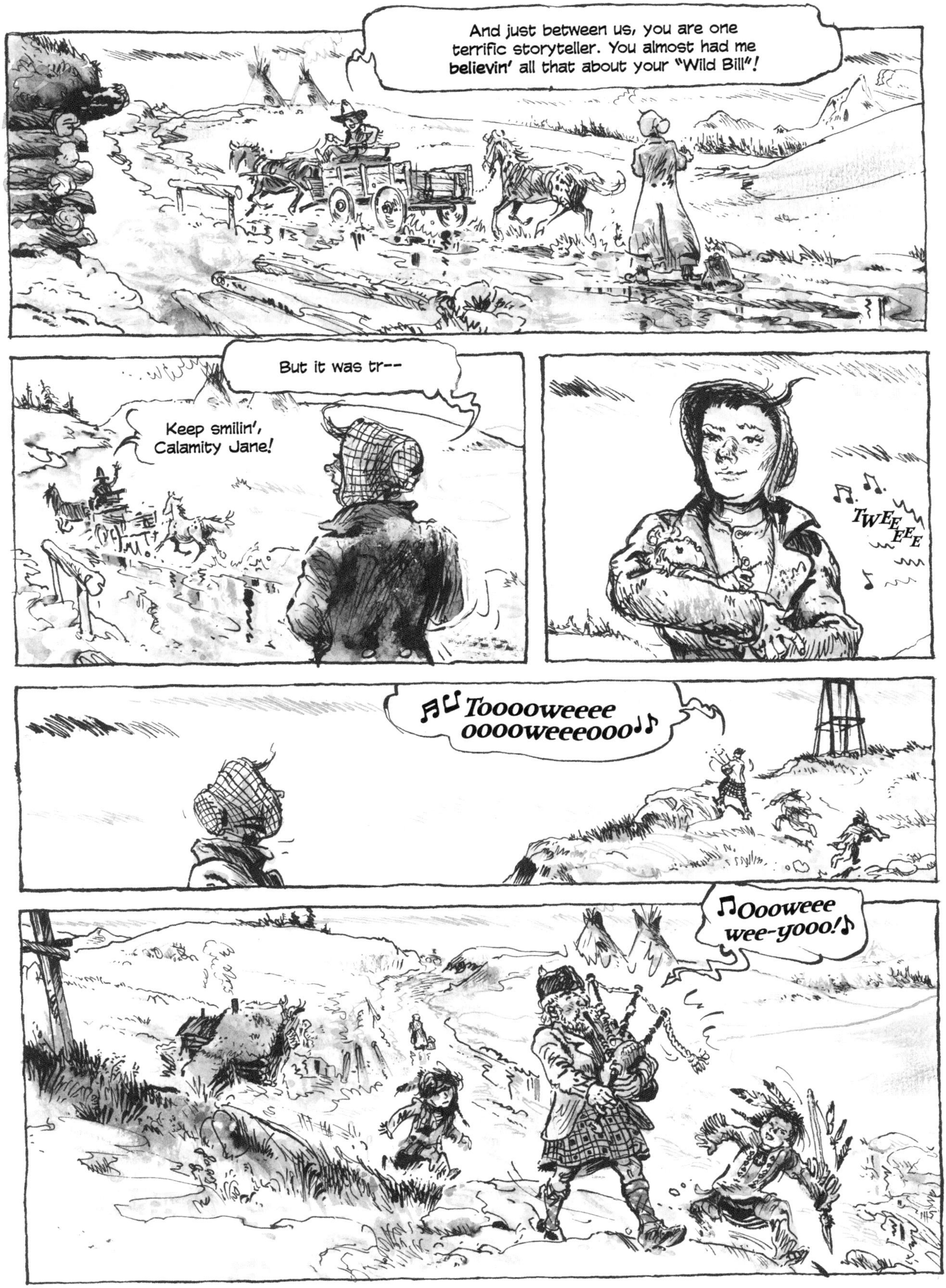
And just between us, you are one terrific storyteller. You almost had me believin' all that about your "Wild Bill"!
But it was tr--
Keep smilin', Calamity Jane!
TWEEEEE
Tooooweeee ooooweeeooo
Oooweee wee-yooo!

The stagecoach carrying Martha Jane and Janey that morning was headed east towards the Missouri River. Martha Jane was leaving the Badlands behind her for good. She would receive no word of Mr. Dunn or his family again.

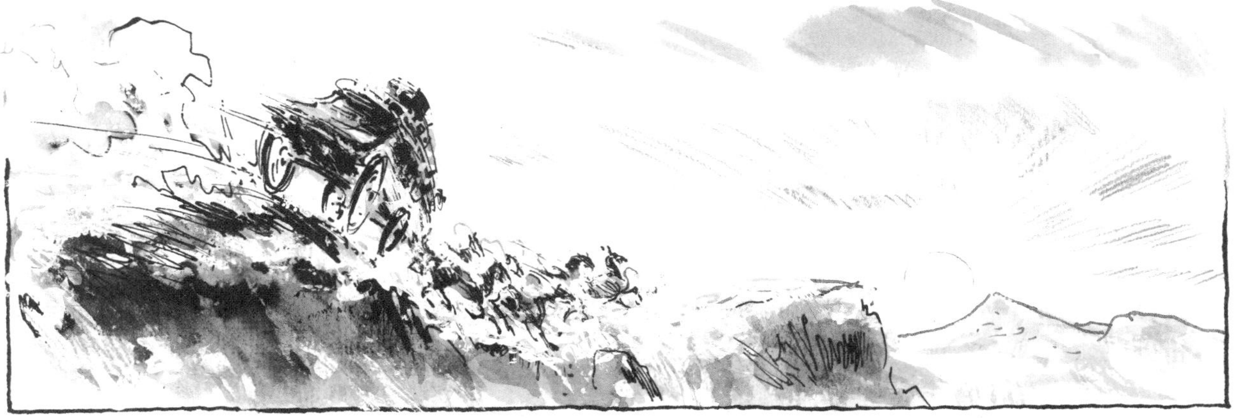

The trail crossed the easternmost region of the Great Plains, extending from the Mississippi to the foothills of the Rockies. Due west, across the Badlands, was still Sioux territory. The 1868 Treaty of Fort Laramie had ceded this area to the Lakota Sioux, and no whites had the right to settle there.

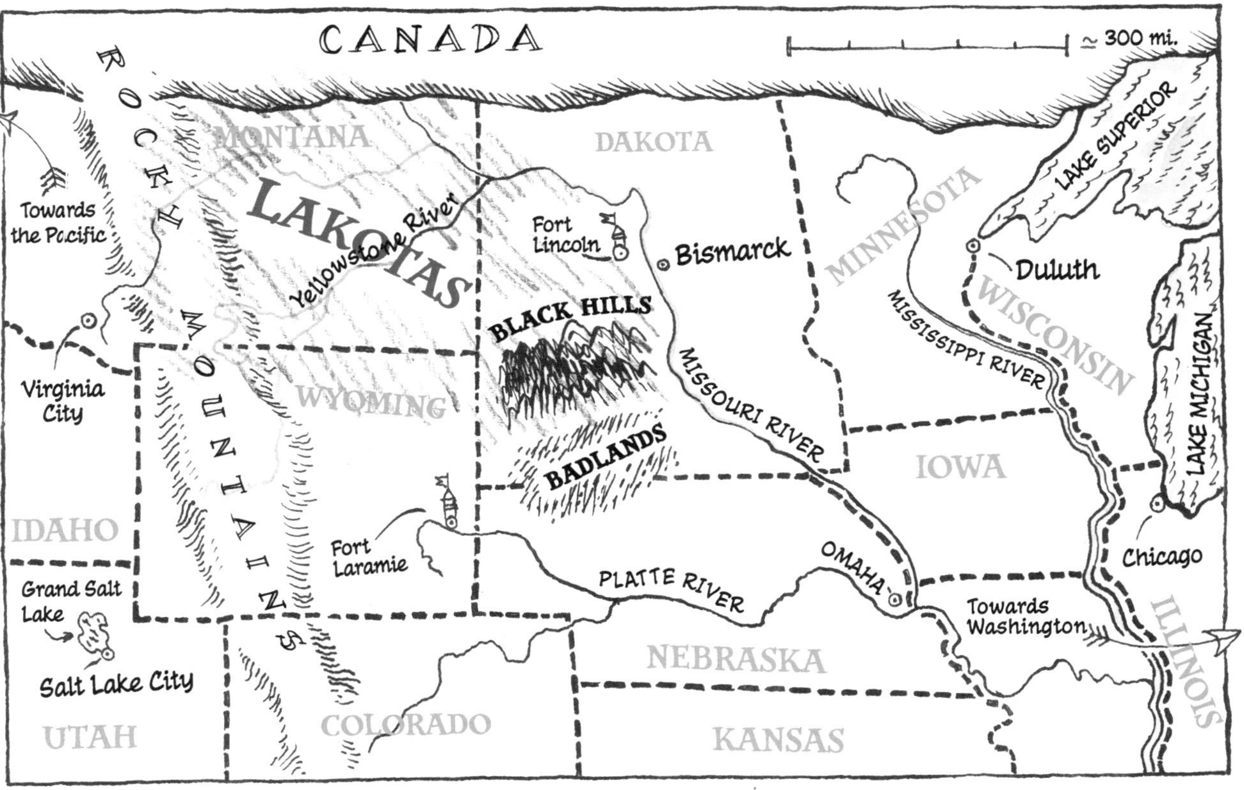
CANADA
≃ 300 mi.
ROCKY MOUNTAINS
MONTANA
DAKOTA
LAKOTAS
Yellowstone River
Towards the Pacific
Fort Lincoln
Bismarck
MINNESOTA
LAKE SUPERIOR
Duluth
WISCONSIN
MISSISSIPPI RIVER
LAKE MICHIGAN
BLACK HILLS
MISSOURI RIVER
Virginia City
WYOMING
BADLANDS
IOWA
IDAHO
Fort Laramie
OMAHA
Chicago
PLATTE RIVER
Grand Salt Lake
Towards Washington
ILLINOIS
NEBRASKA
Salt Lake City
UTAH
COLORADO
KANSAS

But that spring of 1874, a plan was hatched in Washington to steal those Indian lands, though Martha Jane did not yet realize that she would participate in this new depredation.

It had all started the year before when a stock market crash of unprecedented proportions had rattled the national economy. The rail companies had been hit hard and were pressuring the White House to authorize construction of a new railway linking the Great Lakes region to the Pacific Ocean.

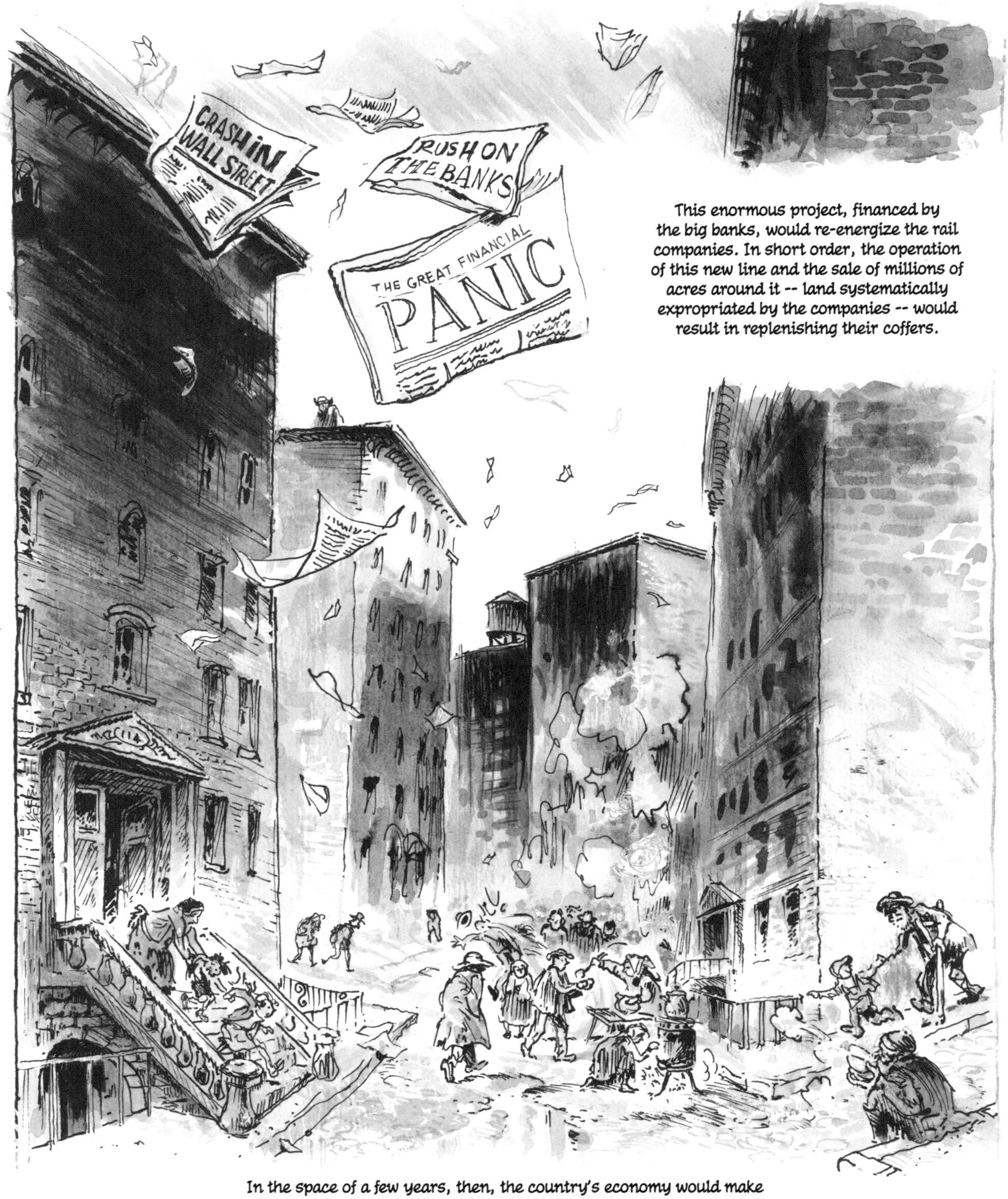
CRASH IN WALL STREET
RUSH ON THE BANKS
THE GREAT FINANCIAL PANIC

This enormous project, financed by the big banks, would re-energize the rail companies. In short order, the operation of this new line and the sale of millions of acres around it -- land systematically expropriated by the companies -- would result in replenishing their coffers.

In the space of a few years, then, the country's economy would make a fresh start and thousands of families would leave their shantytowns in the East to advance the conquest of the West.

But first, the Indians had to be dispatched, since the one problem with this plan was that the railway's projected route would span a good part of the Yellowstone River, at the heart of Lakota territory.

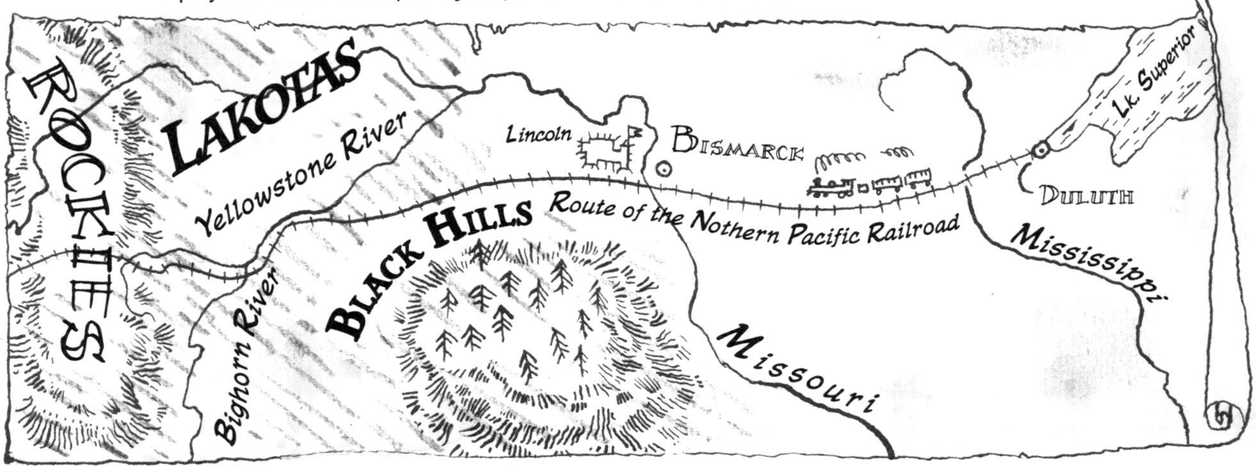

LAKOTAS
ROCKIES
Yellowstone River
Lincoln
BISMARCK
Lk. Superior
DULUTH
BLACK HILLS
Route of the Nothern Pacific Railroad
Mississippi
Bighorn River
Missouri

That President Ulysses Grant eventually ceded to the companies had to do with the unconditional support accorded them by the military. The army had never endorsed the Treaty of Fort Laramie and had long believed that the only good Indian was a dead Indian.

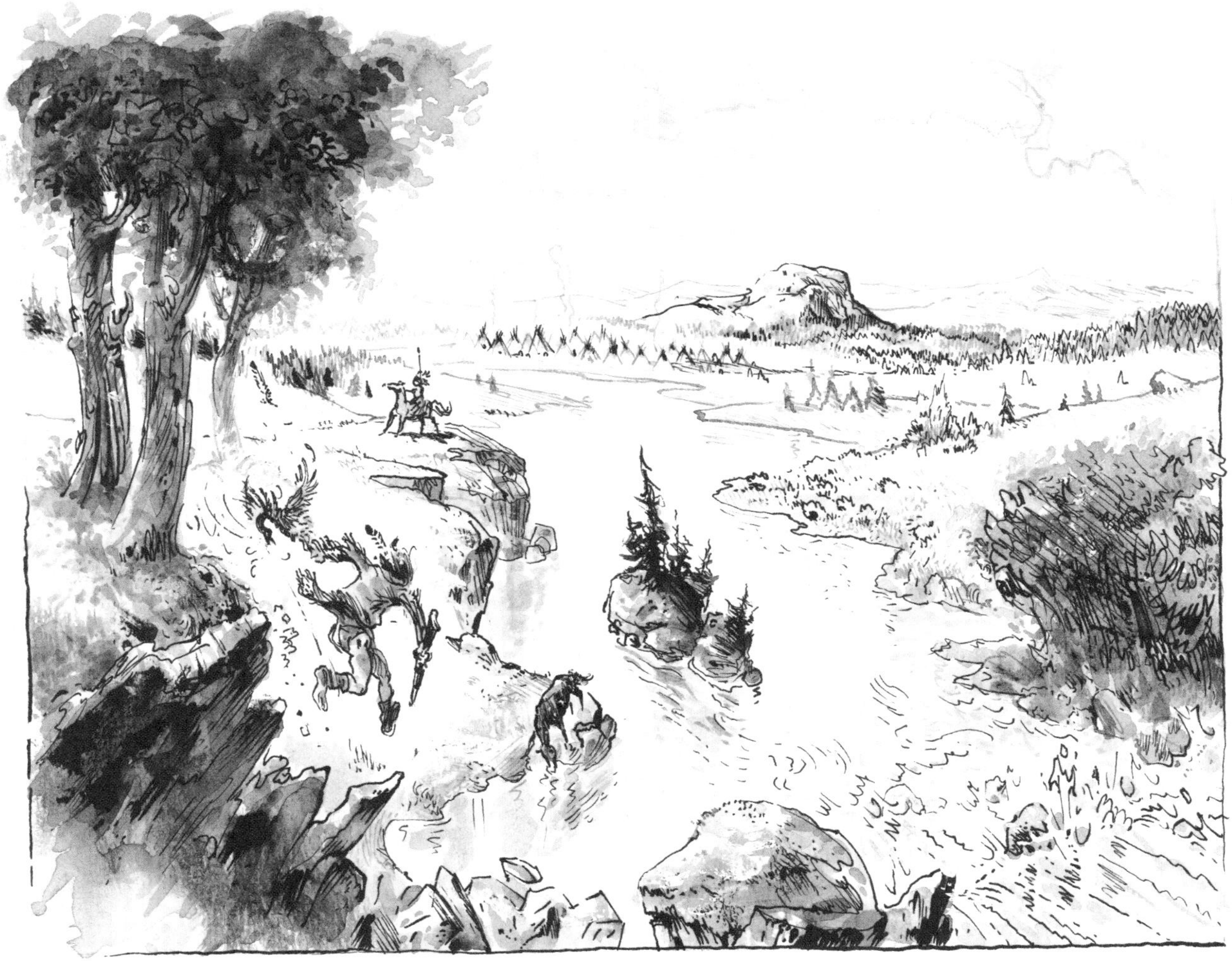

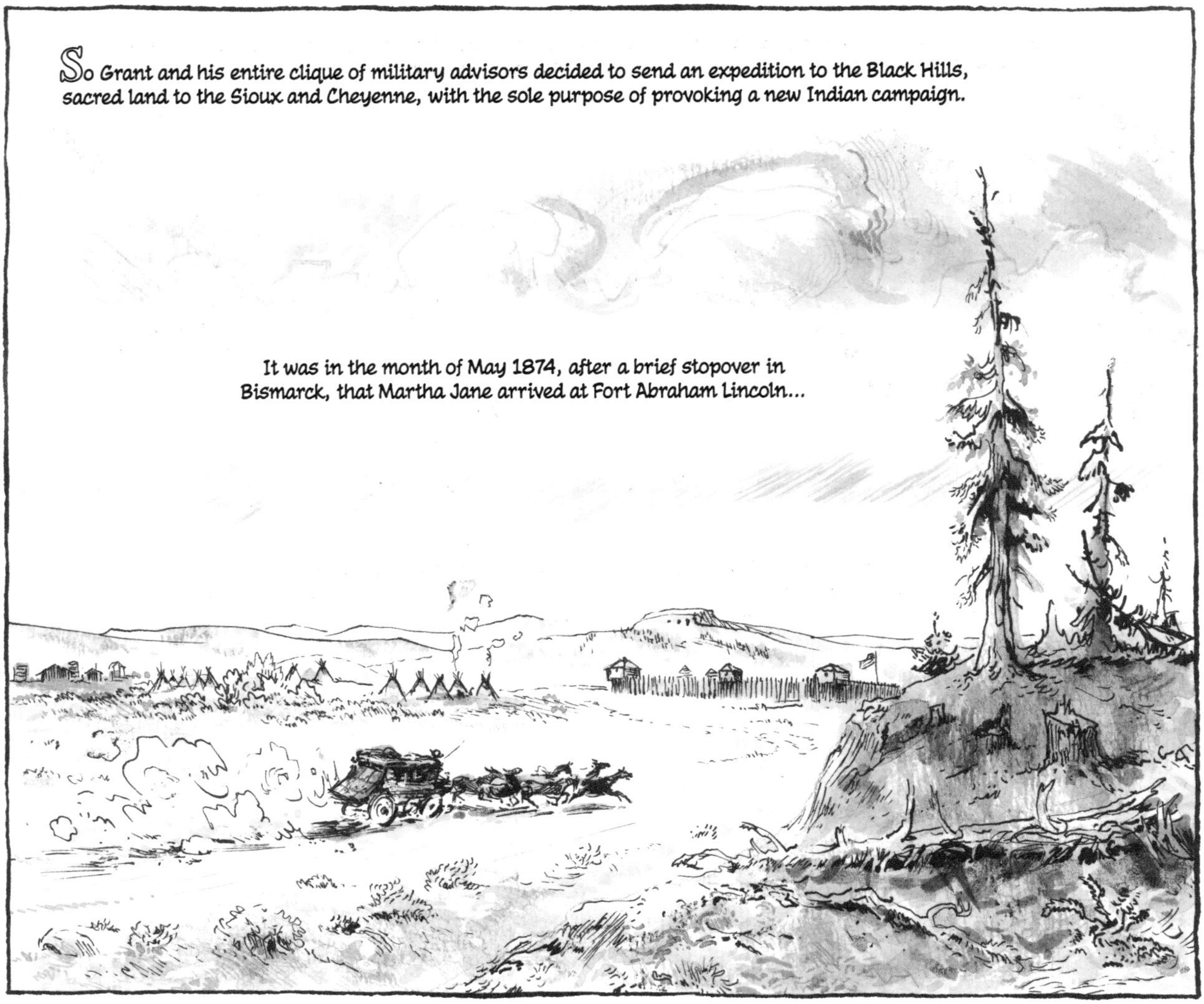
So Grant and his entire clique of military advisors decided to send an expedition to the Black Hills, sacred land to the Sioux and Cheyenne, with the sole purpose of provoking a new Indian campaign.
It was in the month of May 1874, after a brief stopover in Bismarck, that Martha Jane arrived at Fort Abraham Lincoln...

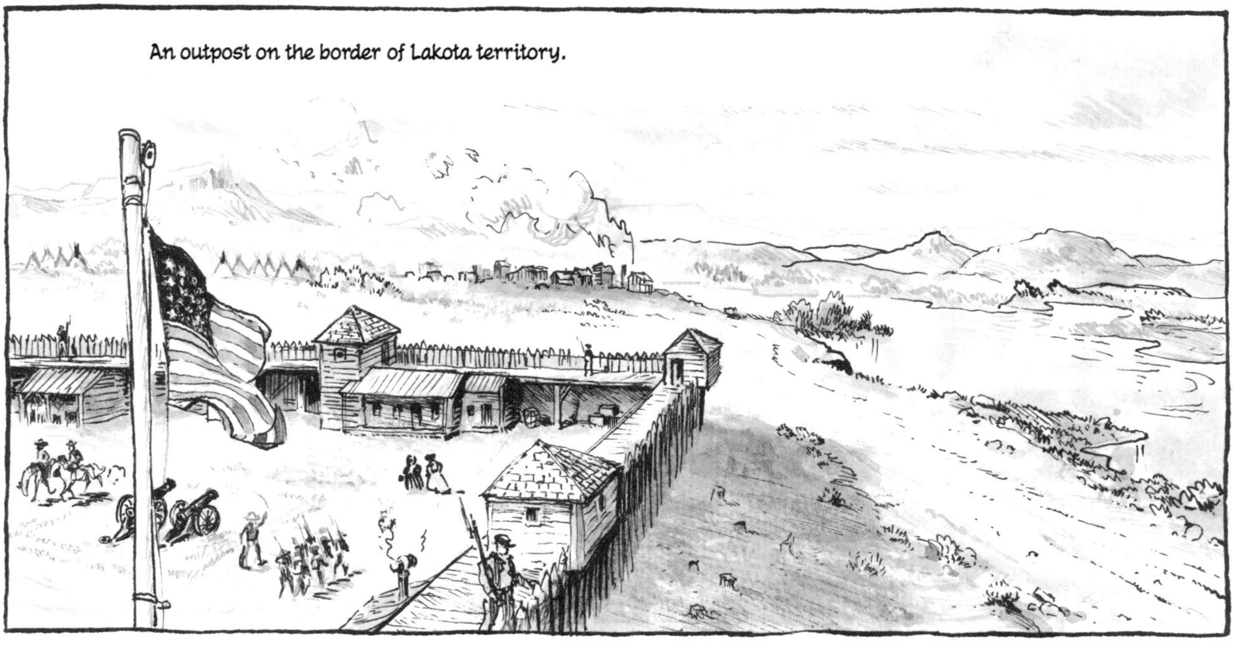
An outpost on the border of Lakota territory.

She landed a job as a waitress in the only saloon in that part of North Dakota.

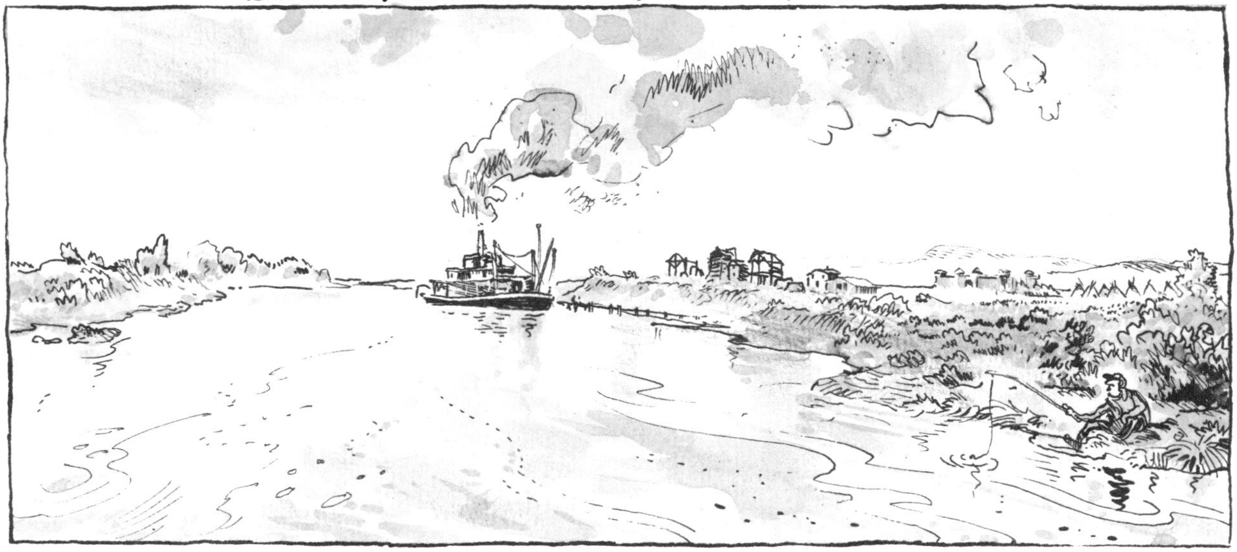

Martha Jane preferred the company of soldiers to that of "self-righteous" townsfolk, which explains her choice to settle yet again near a military post.

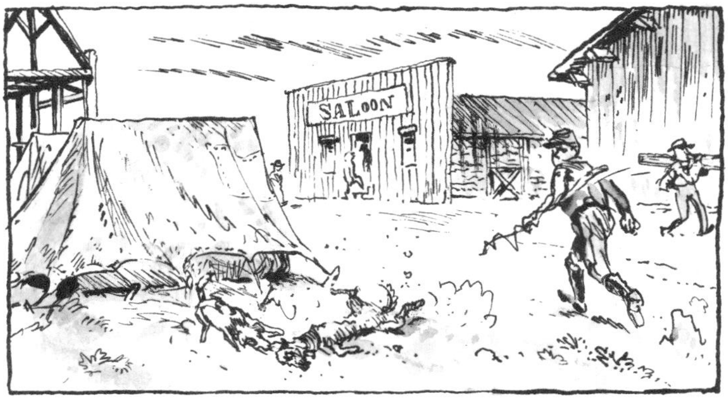
SALOON

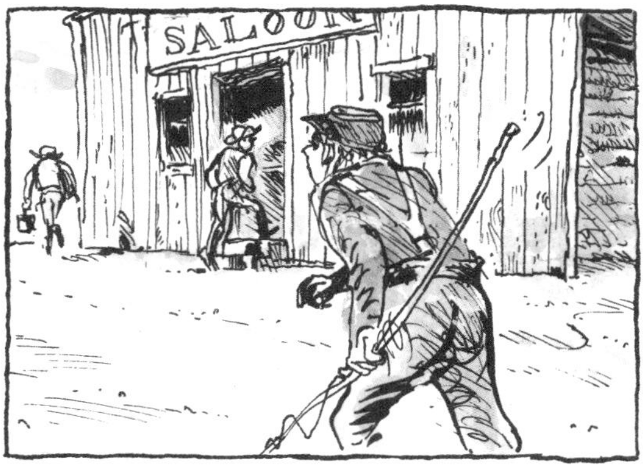
SALOON

There, she learned that the 7th Cavalry Regiment, which had been billeted at the fort for some time, was assigned to the Black Hills expedition. They were just beginning their preparations...

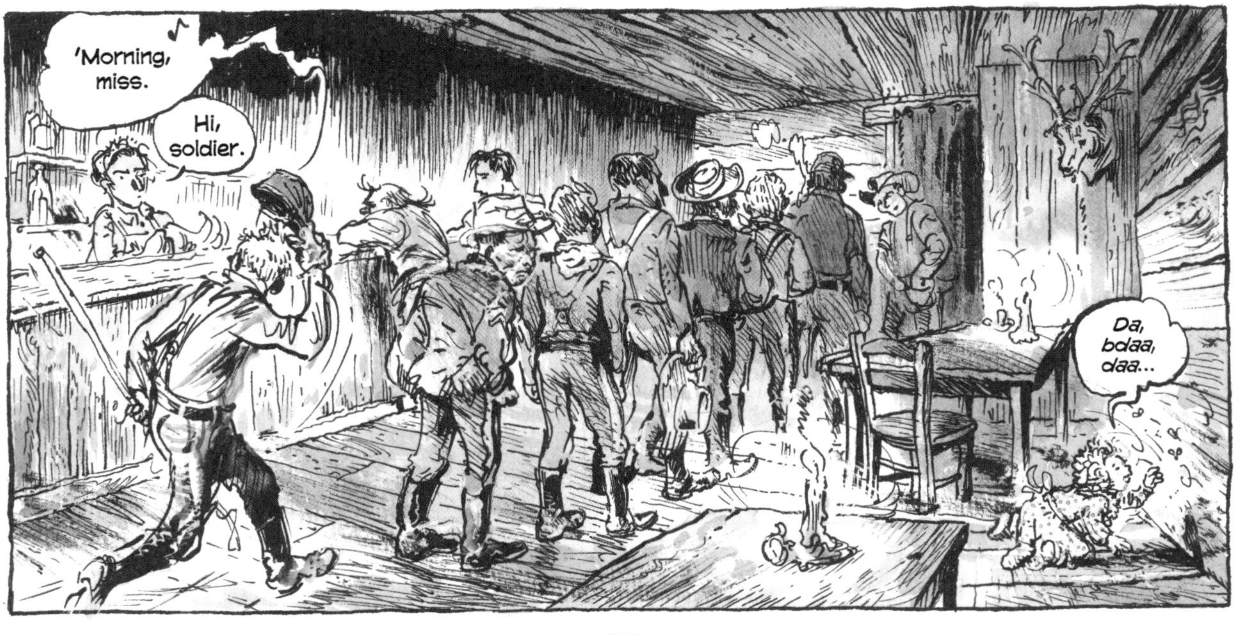
'Morning, miss.
Hi, soldier.
Da, bdaa, daa...

An interminable stretch of drills, drudgery, and especially dawdling to kill the time...

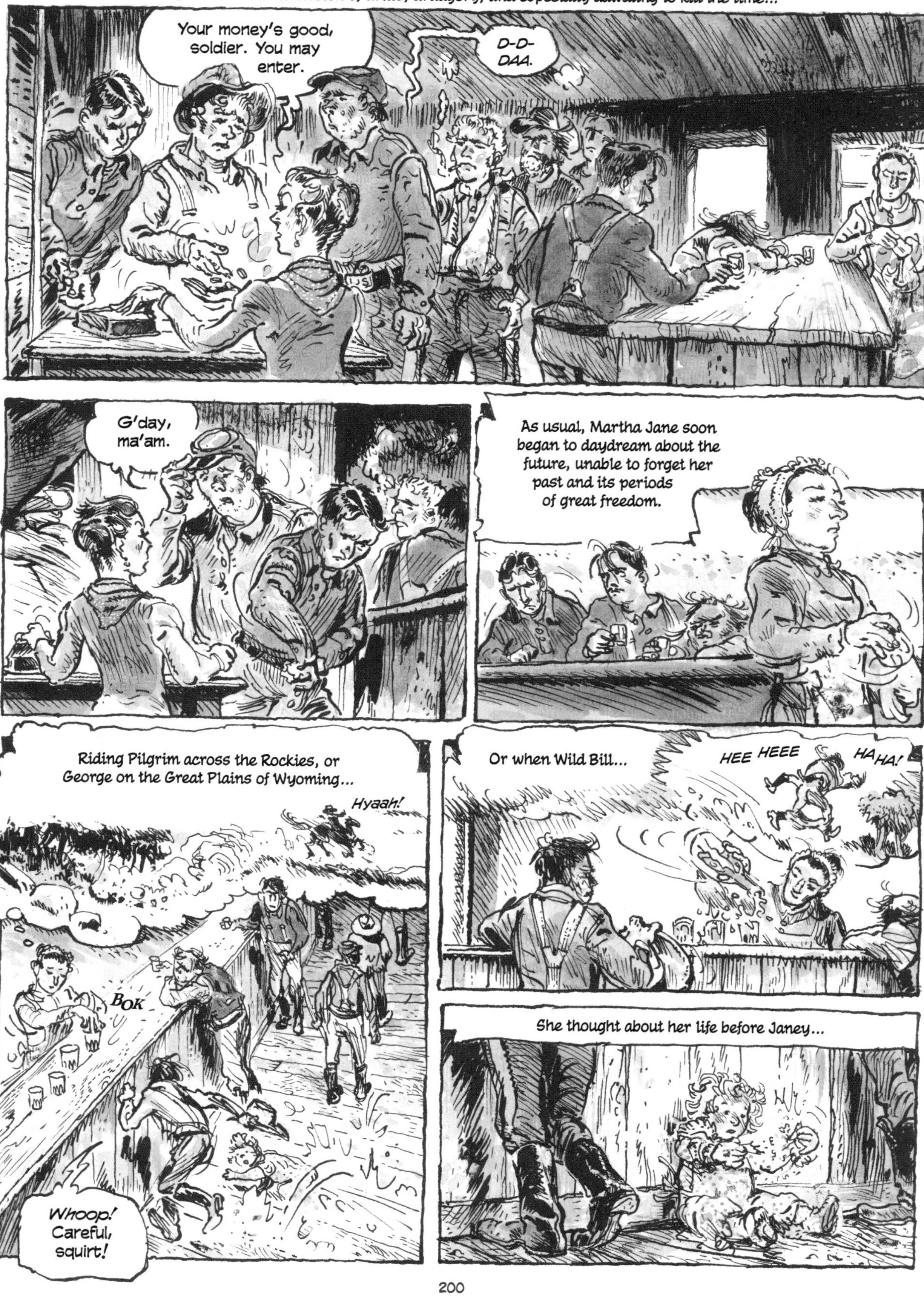
Your money's good, soldier. You may enter.
D-D-DAA.
G'day, ma'am.
As usual, Martha Jane soon began to daydream about the future, unable to forget her past and its periods of great freedom.
Riding Pilgrim across the Rockies, or George on the Great Plains of Wyoming...
Hyaah!
BOK
Whoop! Careful, squirt!
Or when Wild Bill...
HEE HEEE
HA HA!
She thought about her life before Janey...

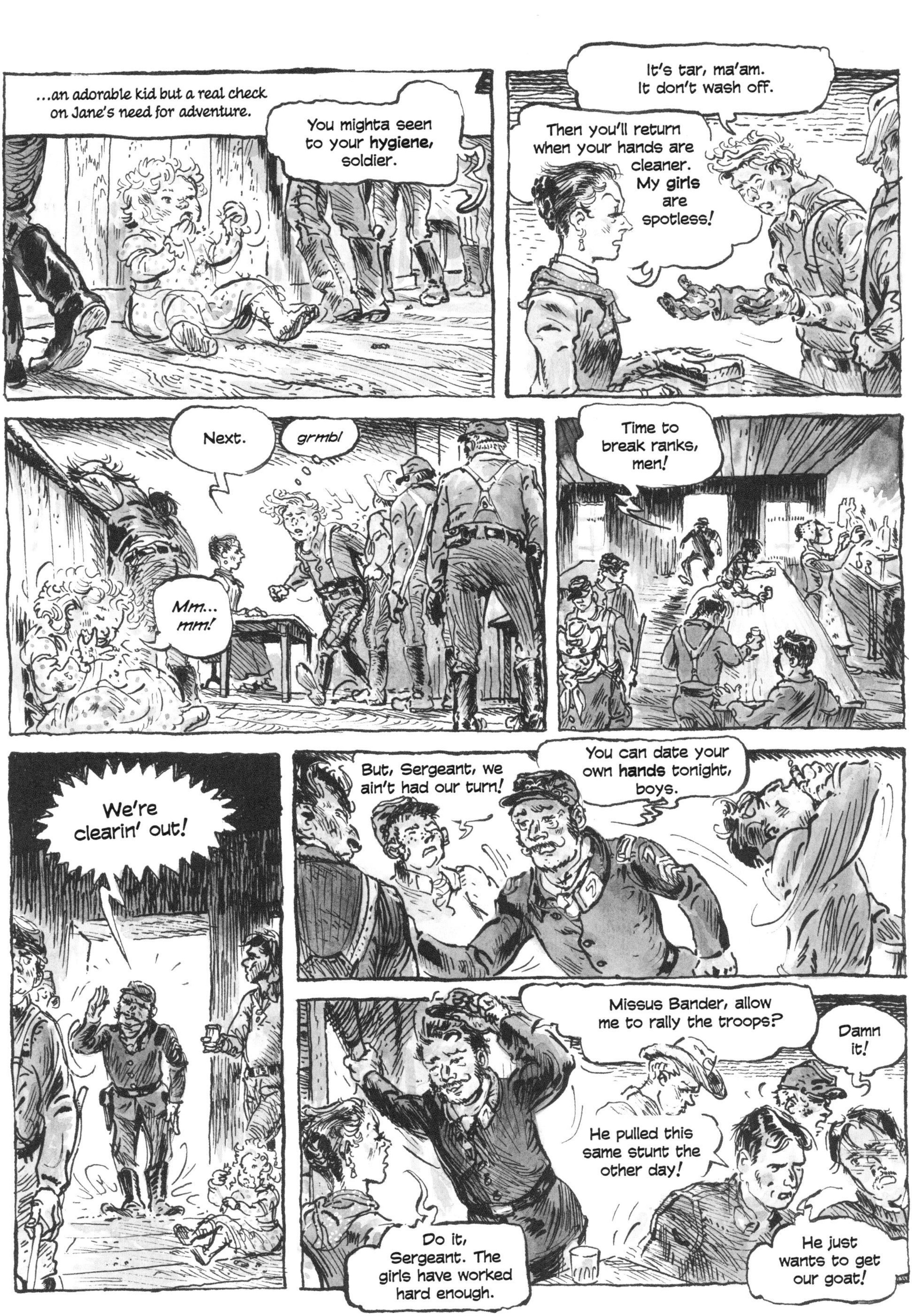
...an adorable kid but a real check on Jane's need for adventure.
You mighta seen to your **hygiene,** soldier.
It's tar, ma'am. It don't wash off.
Then you'll return when your hands are cleaner. My **girls** are spotless!
Next.
grmbl
Mm... mm!
Time to break ranks, men!
We're clearin' out!
But, Sergeant, we ain't had our turn!
You can date your own **hands** tonight, boys.
Missus Bander, allow me to rally the troops?
Damn it!
He pulled this same stunt the other day!
Do it, Sergeant. The girls have worked hard enough.
He just wants to get our goat!

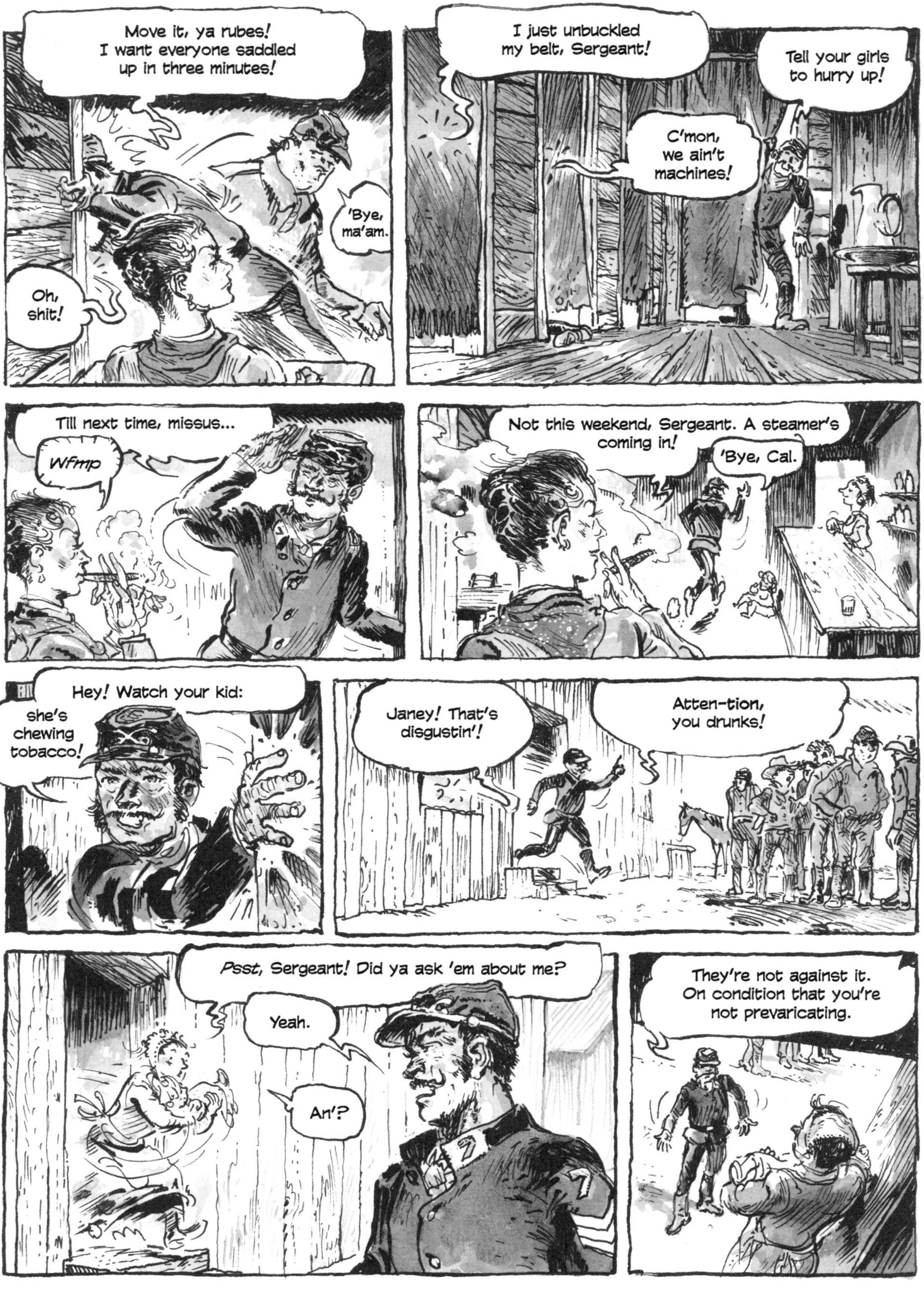

Move it, ya rubes! I want everyone saddled up in three minutes!
'Bye, ma'am.
Oh, shit!
I just unbuckled my belt, Sergeant!
Tell your girls to hurry up!
C'mon, we ain't machines!
Till next time, missus...
Wfmp
Not this weekend, Sergeant. A steamer's coming in!
'Bye, Cal.
Hey! Watch your kid:
she's chewing tobacco!
Janey! That's disgustin'!
Atten-tion, you drunks!
Psst, Sergeant! Did ya ask 'em about me?
Yeah.
An'?
They're not against it. On condition that you're not prevaricating.

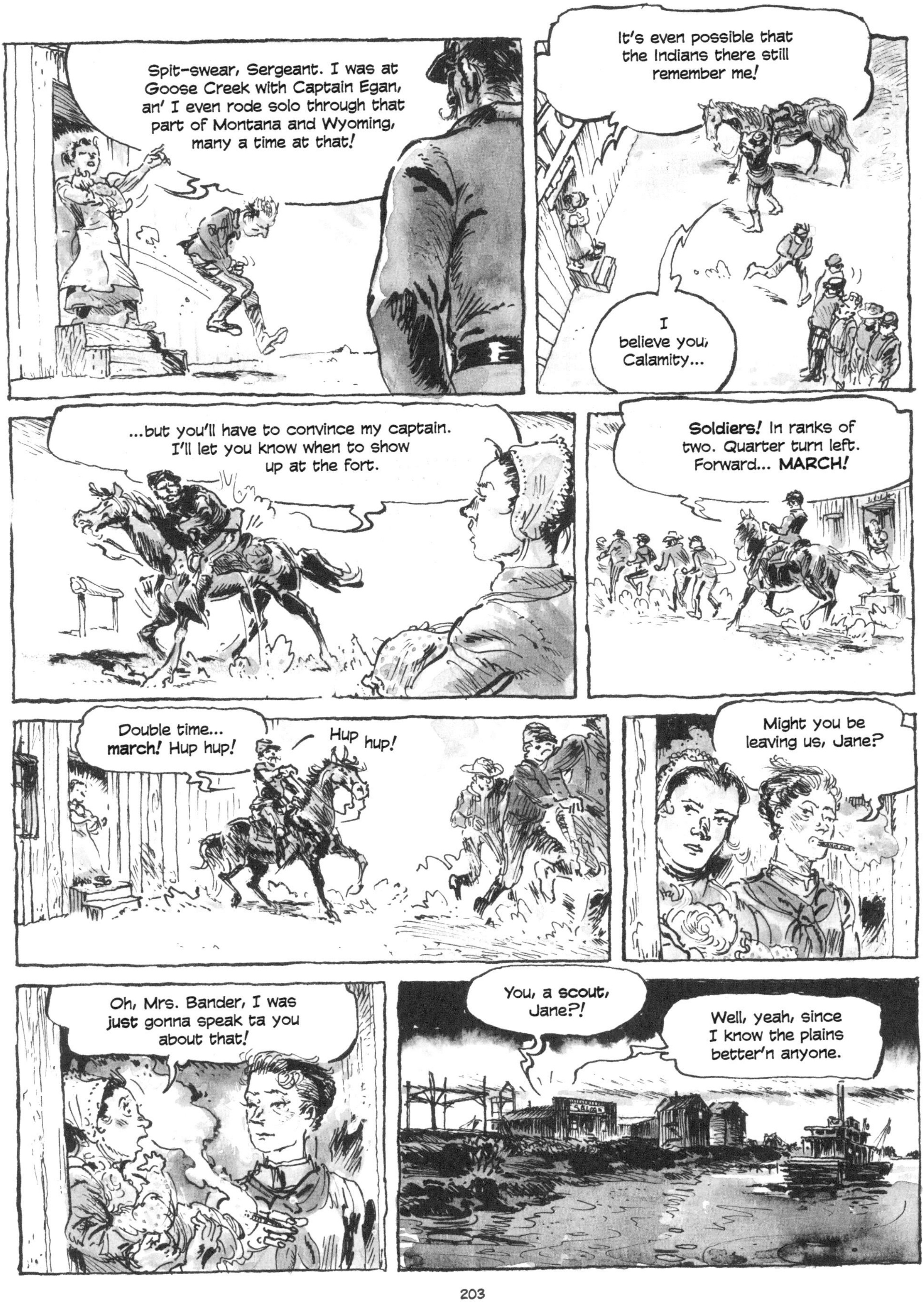
Spit-swear, Sergeant. I was at Goose Creek with Captain Egan, an' I even rode solo through that part of Montana and Wyoming, many a time at that!
It's even possible that the Indians there still remember me!
I believe you, Calamity...
...but you'll have to convince my captain. I'll let you know when to show up at the fort.
Soldiers! In ranks of two. Quarter turn left. Forward... **MARCH!**
Double time... **march!** Hup hup!
Hup hup!
Might you be leaving us, Jane?
Oh, Mrs. Bander, I was **just** gonna speak ta you about that!
You, a **scout,** Jane?!
Well, yeah, since I know the plains better'n anyone.

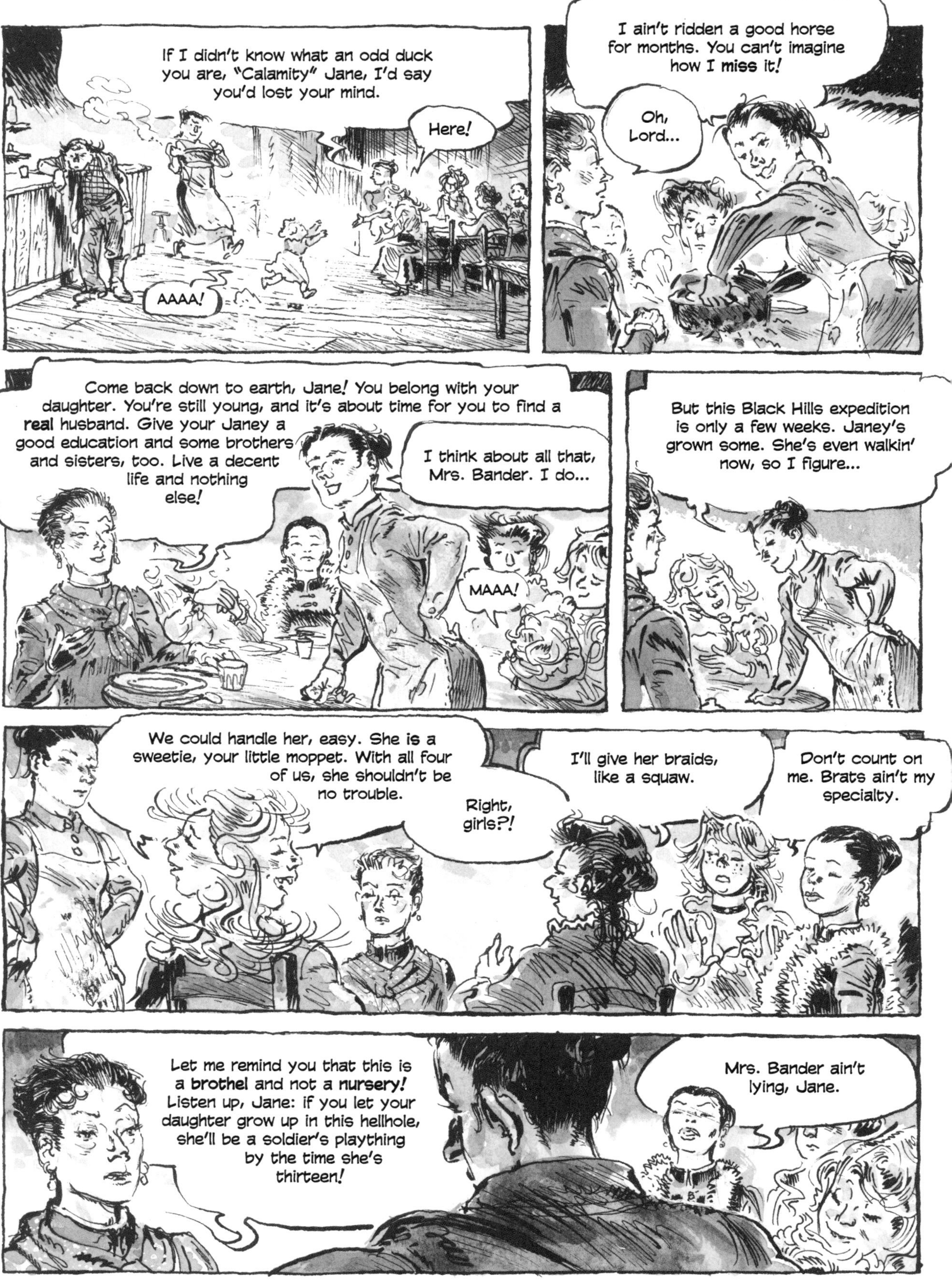

If I didn't know what an odd duck you are, "Calamity" Jane, I'd say you'd lost your mind.
Here!
AAAA!
I ain't ridden a good horse for months. You can't imagine how I miss it!
Oh, Lord...
Come back down to earth, Jane! You belong with your daughter. You're still young, and it's about time for you to find a real husband. Give your Janey a good education and some brothers and sisters, too. Live a decent life and nothing else!
I think about all that, Mrs. Bander. I do...
MAAA!
But this Black Hills expedition is only a few weeks. Janey's grown some. She's even walkin' now, so I figure...
We could handle her, easy. She is a sweetie, your little moppet. With all four of us, she shouldn't be no trouble.
Right, girls?!
I'll give her braids, like a squaw.
Don't count on me. Brats ain't my specialty.
Let me remind you that this is a brothel and not a nursery! Listen up, Jane: if you let your daughter grow up in this hellhole, she'll be a soldier's plaything by the time she's thirteen!
Mrs. Bander ain't lying, Jane.

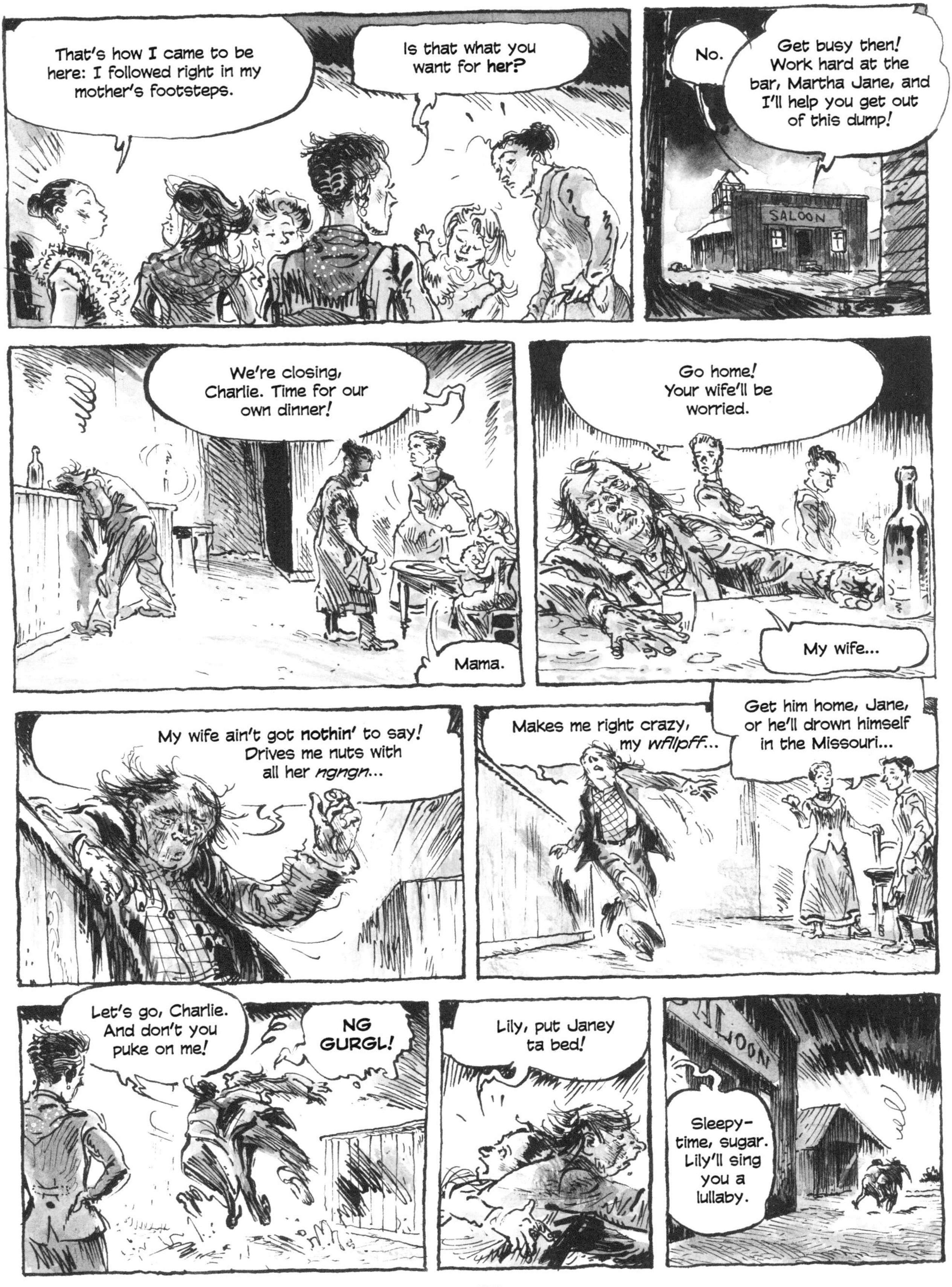
That's how I came to be here: I followed right in my mother's footsteps.
Is that what you want for her?
No.
Get busy then! Work hard at the bar, Martha Jane, and I'll help you get out of this dump!
SALOON
We're closing, Charlie. Time for our own dinner!
Mama.
Go home! Your wife'll be worried.
My wife...
My wife ain't got nothin' to say! Drives me nuts with all her ngngn...
Makes me right crazy, my wfllpff...
Get him home, Jane, or he'll drown himself in the Missouri...
Let's go, Charlie. And don't you puke on me!
NG GURGL!
Lily, put Janey ta bed!
Sleepy-time, sugar. Lily'll sing you a lullaby.

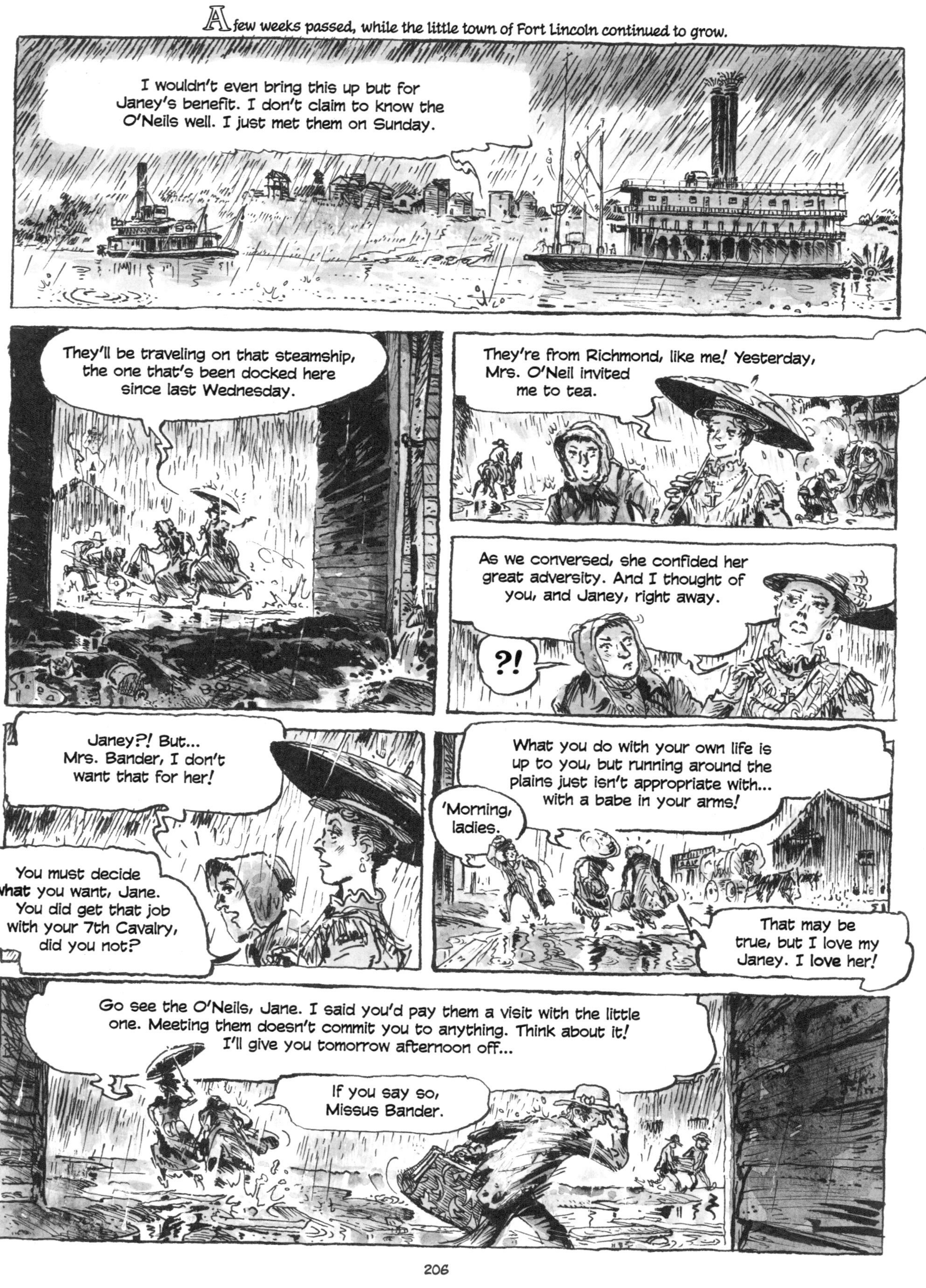
A few weeks passed, while the little town of Fort Lincoln continued to grow.
I wouldn't even bring this up but for Janey's benefit. I don't claim to know the O'Neils well. I just met them on Sunday.
They'll be traveling on that steamship, the one that's been docked here since last Wednesday.
They're from Richmond, like me! Yesterday, Mrs. O'Neil invited me to tea.
As we conversed, she confided her great adversity. And I thought of you, and Janey, right away.
?!
Janey?! But... Mrs. Bander, I don't want that for her!
You must decide **what** you want, Jane. You did get that job with your 7th Cavalry, did you not?
What you do with your own life is up to you, but running around the plains just isn't appropriate with... with a babe in your arms!
'Morning, ladies.
That may be true, but I love my Janey. I **love** her!
Go see the O'Neils, Jane. I said you'd pay them a visit with the little one. Meeting them doesn't commit you to anything. Think about it! I'll give you tomorrow afternoon off...
If you say so, Missus Bander.

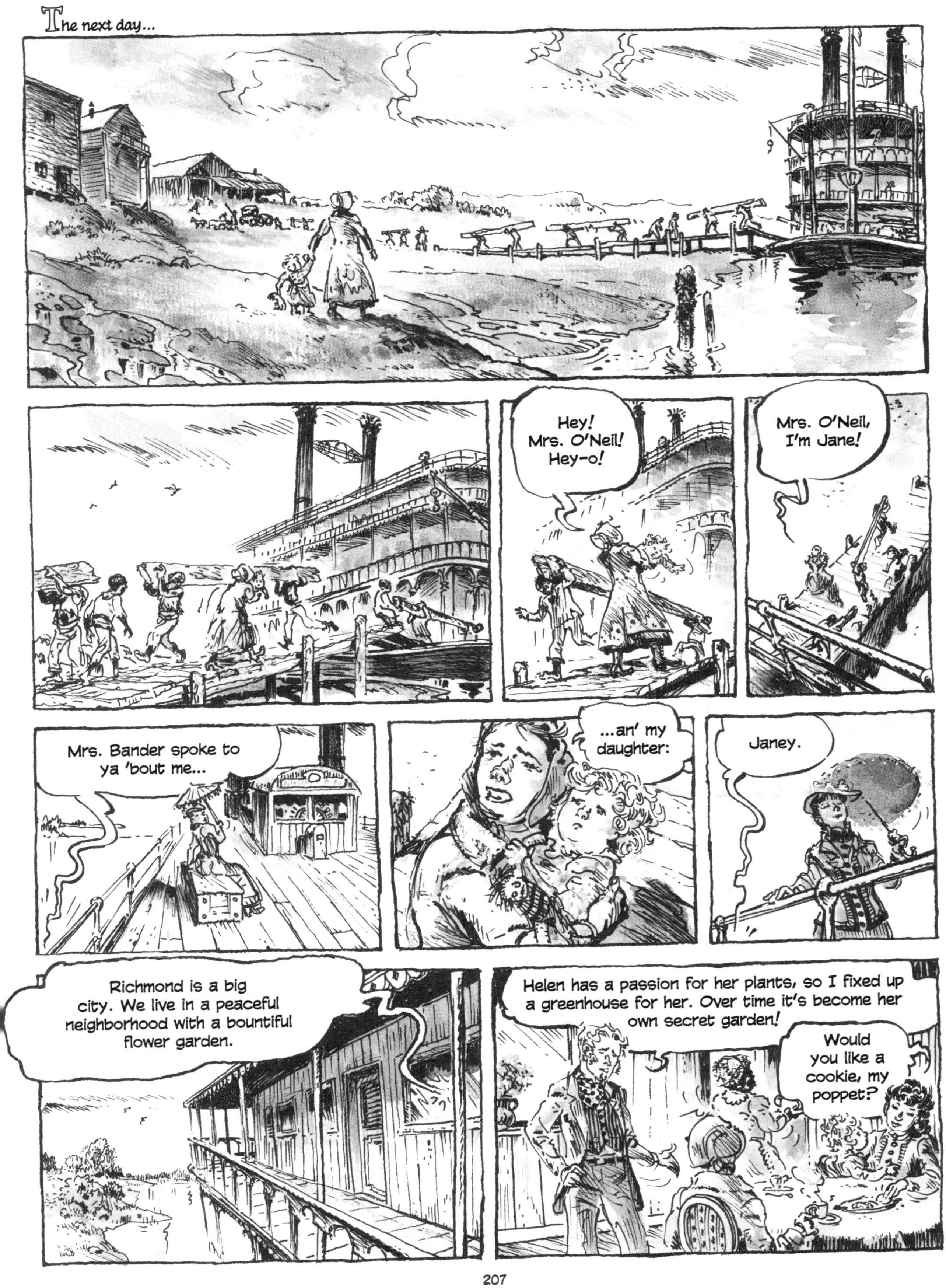
The next day...
Hey! Mrs. O'Neil! Hey-o!
Mrs. O'Neil, I'm Jane!
Mrs. Bander spoke to ya 'bout me...
...an' my daughter:
Janey.
Richmond is a big city. We live in a peaceful neighborhood with a bountiful flower garden.
Helen has a passion for her plants, so I fixed up a greenhouse for her. Over time it's become her own secret garden!
Would you like a cookie, my poppet?

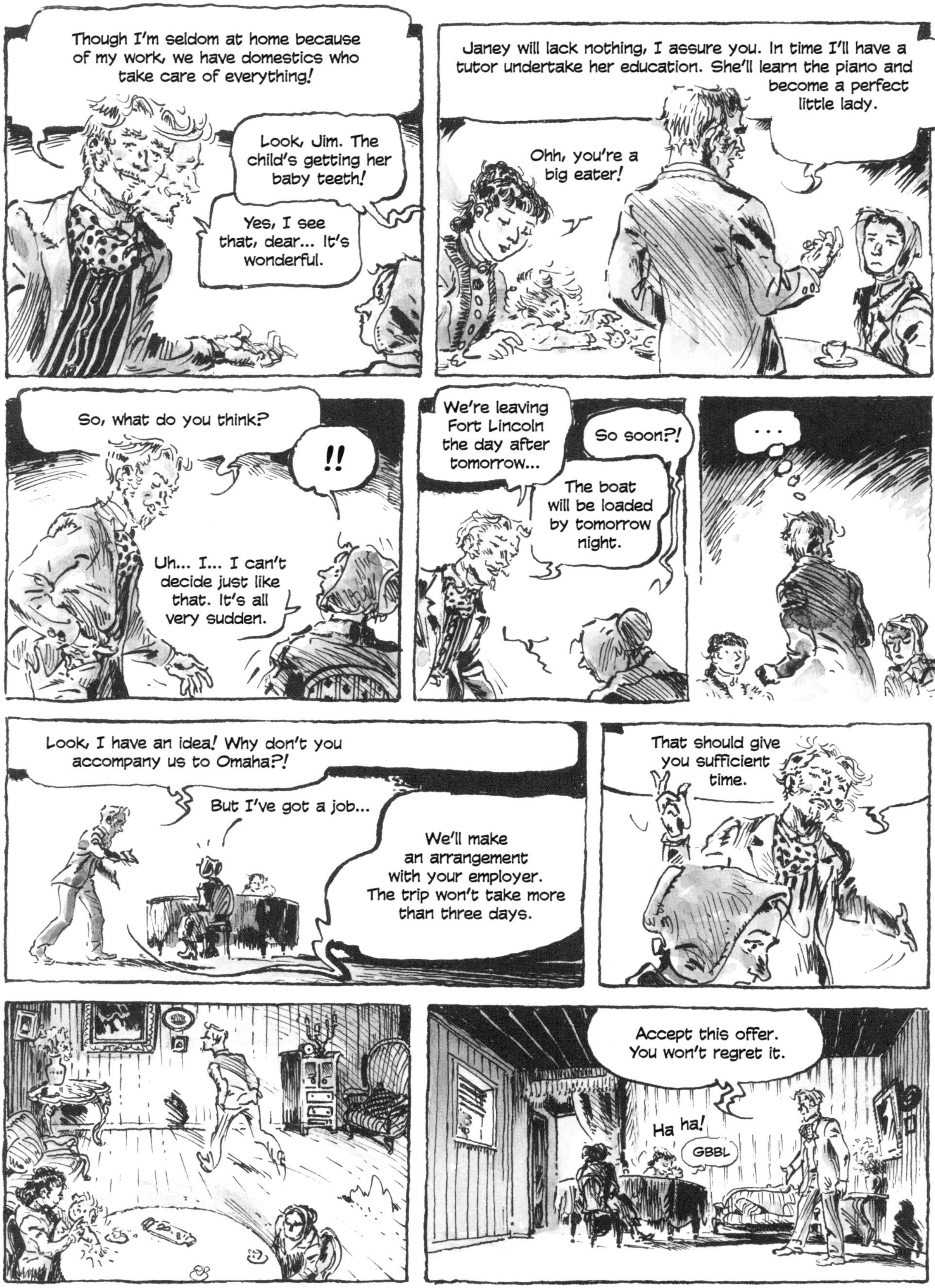
Though I'm seldom at home because of my work, we have domestics who take care of everything!
Look, Jim. The child's getting her baby teeth!
Yes, I see that, dear... It's wonderful.
Janey will lack nothing, I assure you. In time I'll have a tutor undertake her education. She'll learn the piano and become a perfect little lady.
Ohh, you're a big eater!
So, what do you think?
!!
Uh... I... I can't decide just like that. It's all very sudden.
We're leaving Fort Lincoln the day after tomorrow...
So soon?!
The boat will be loaded by tomorrow night.
...
Look, I have an idea! Why don't you accompany us to Omaha?!
But I've got a job...
We'll make an arrangement with your employer. The trip won't take more than three days.
That should give you sufficient time.
Accept this offer. You won't regret it.
Ha ha!
GBBL

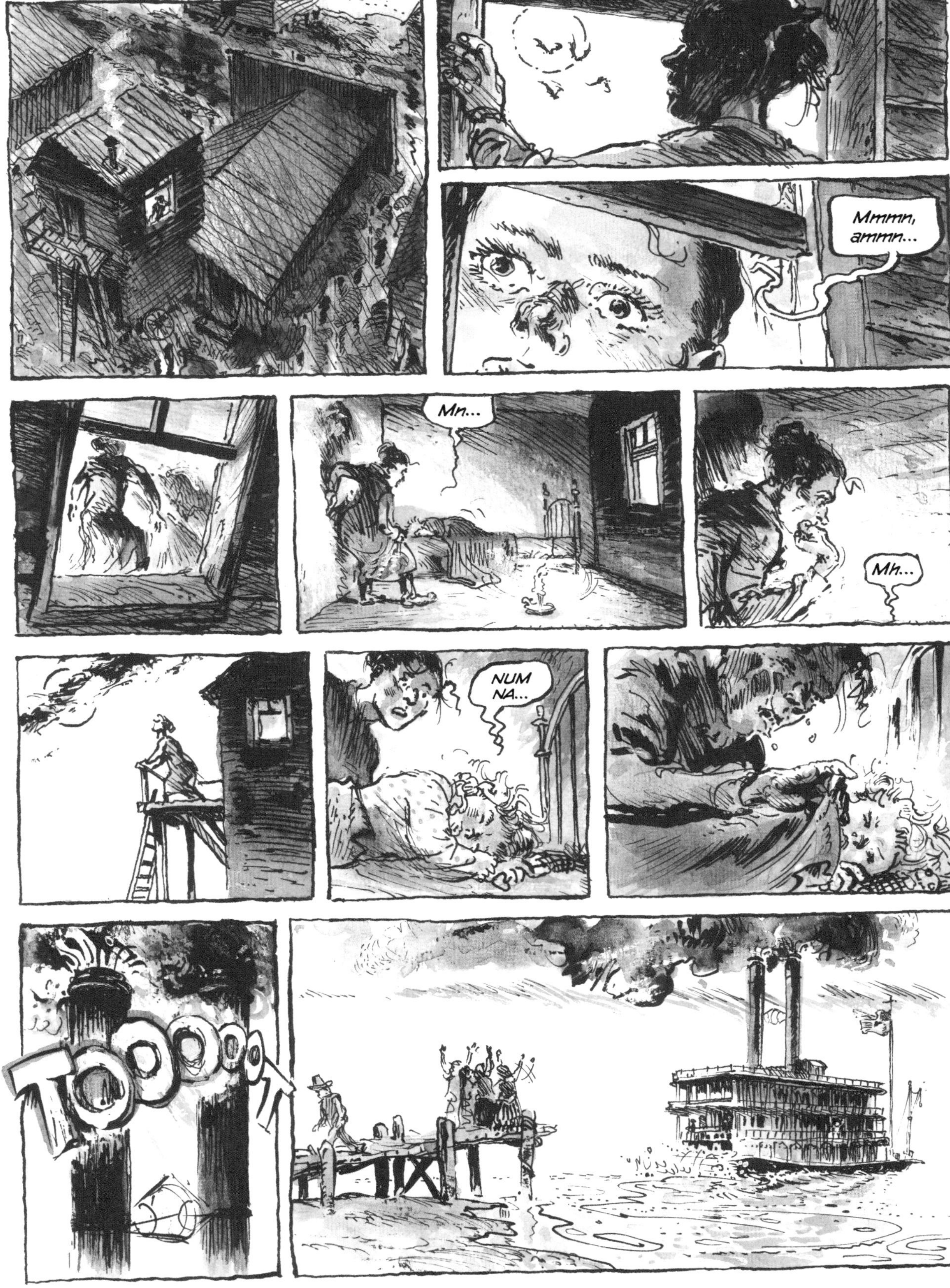
Mmmn, ammn...
Mn...
Mh...
NUM NA...
TOOOOOT

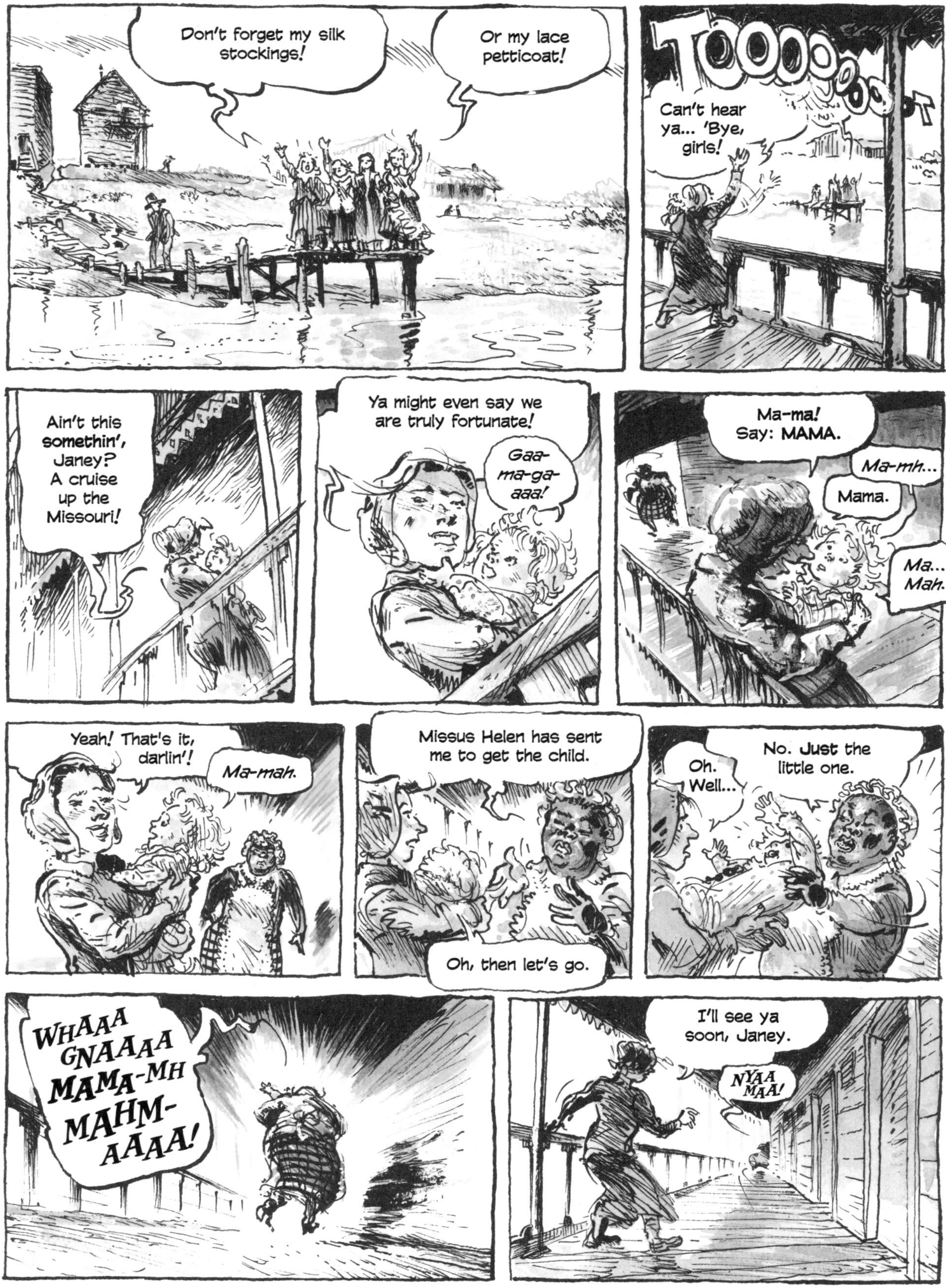

Don't forget my silk stockings!
Or my lace petticoat!
TOOOOOOOOT
Can't hear ya... 'Bye, girls!
Ain't this somethin', Janey? A cruise up the Missouri!
Ya might even say we are truly fortunate!
Gaa-ma-ga-aaa!
Ma-ma! Say: MAMA.
Ma-mh...
Mama.
Ma... Mah.
Yeah! That's it, darlin'!
Ma-mah.
Missus Helen has sent me to get the child.
Oh, then let's go.
Oh. Well...
No. Just the little one.
WHAAA GNAAAA MAMA-MH MAHM-AAAA!
I'll see ya soon, Janey.
NYAA MAA!

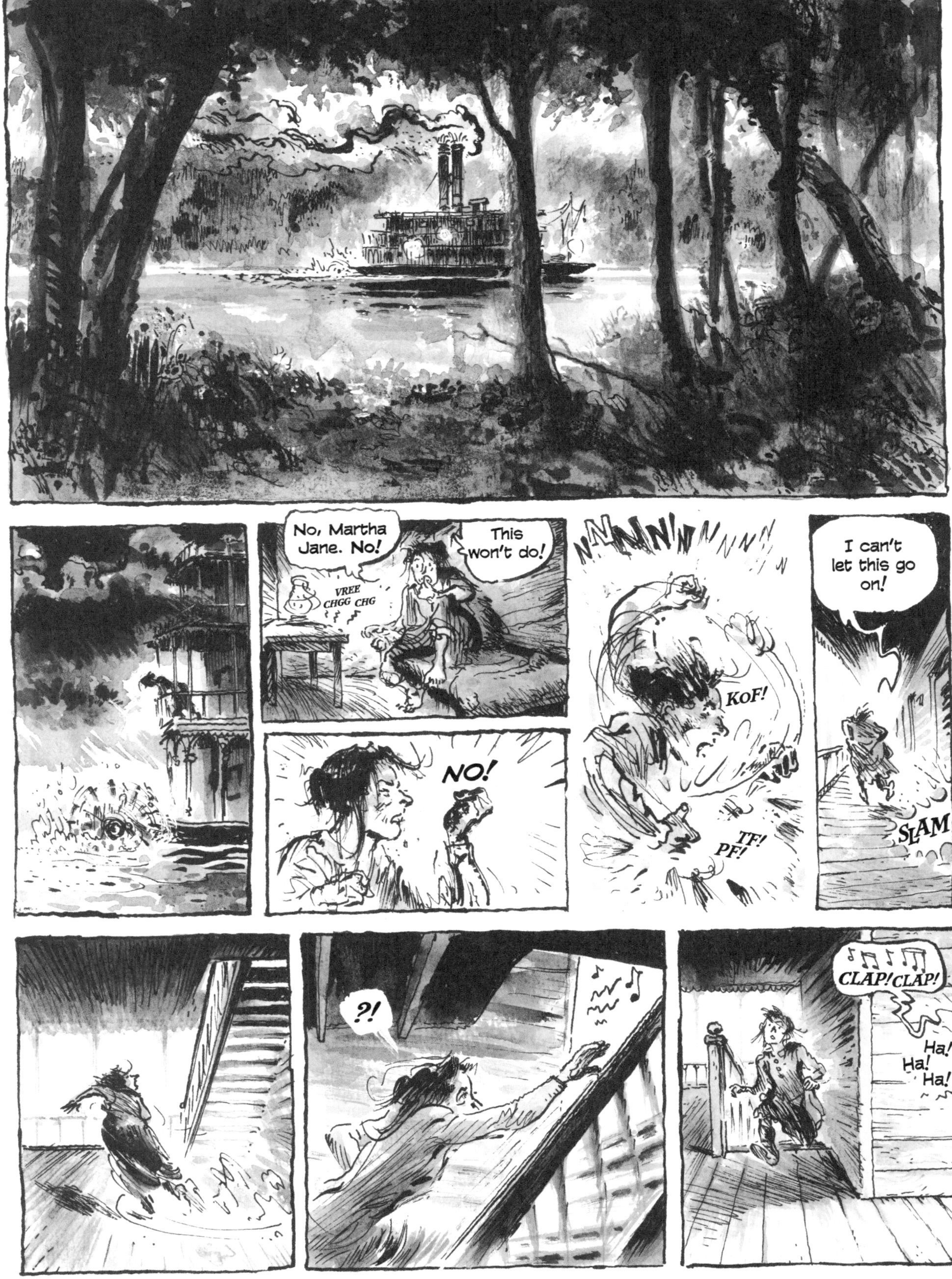

No, Martha Jane. No!
This won't do!
VREE CHGG CHG
NO!
NNNNNNNNN
KoF!
TF! PF!
I can't let this go on!
SLAM
?!
CLAP! CLAP!
Ha! Ha! Ha!

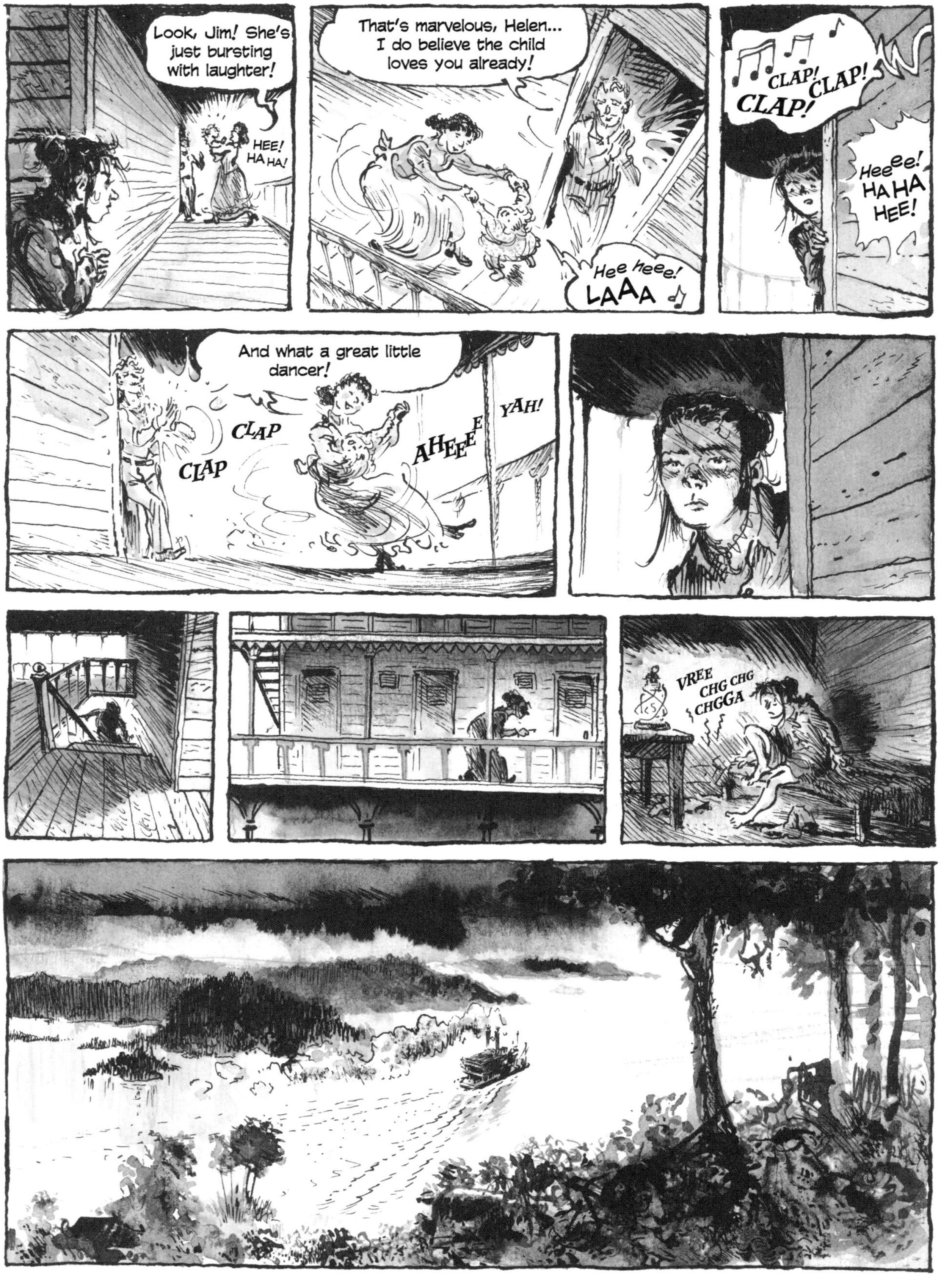
Look, Jim! She's just bursting with laughter!
HEE! HA HA!
That's marvelous, Helen... I do believe the child loves you already!
Hee heee! LAAA
CLAP! CLAP! CLAP!
Heeee! HA HA HEE!
And what a great little dancer!
CLAP
CLAP
AHEEEE
YAH!
VREE CHG CHG CHGGA

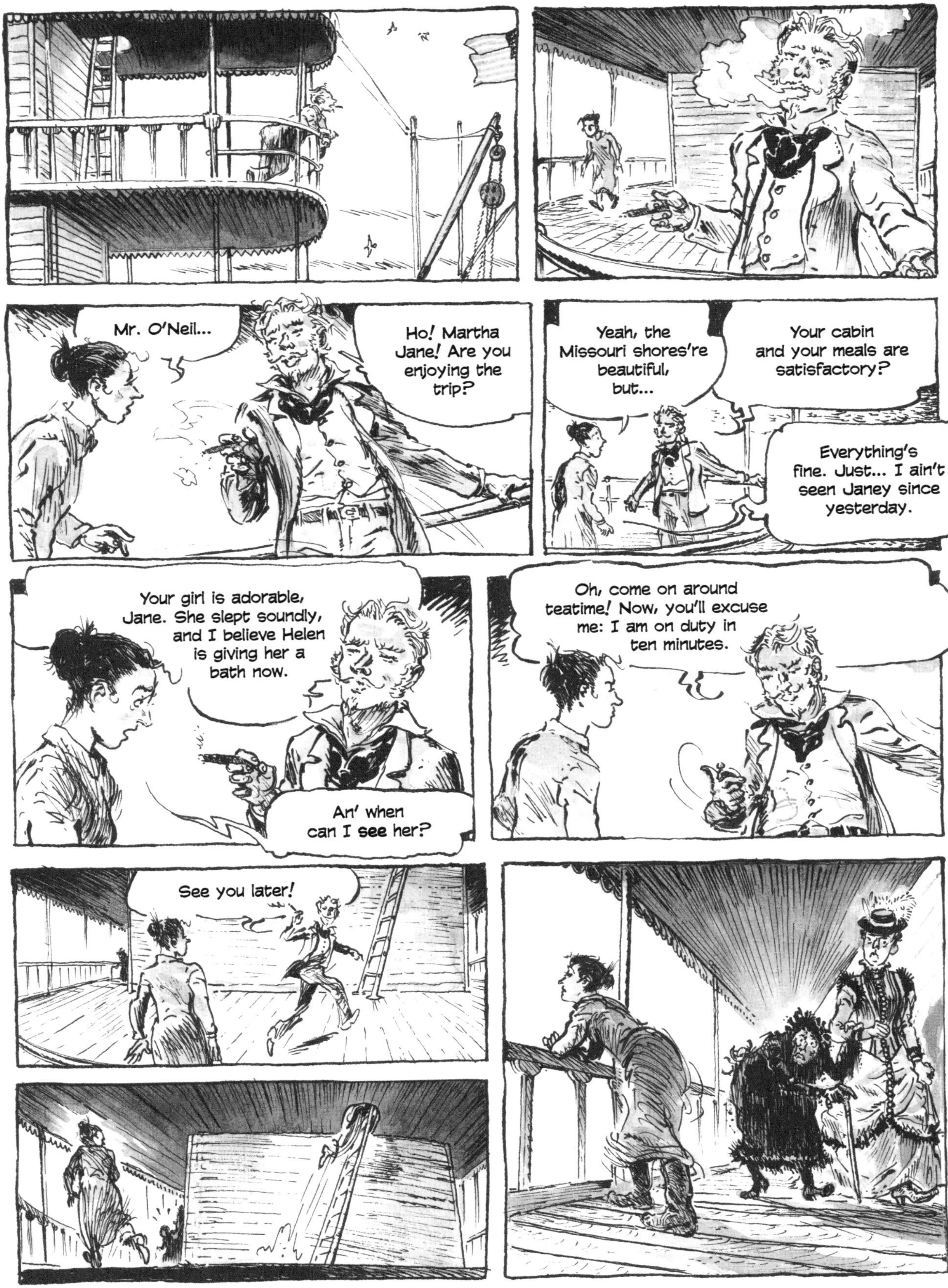
Mr. O'Neil...
Ho! Martha Jane! Are you enjoying the trip?
Yeah, the Missouri shores're beautiful, but...
Your cabin and your meals are satisfactory?
Everything's fine. Just... I ain't seen Janey since yesterday.
Your girl is adorable, Jane. She slept soundly, and I believe Helen is giving her a bath now.
An' when can I see her?
Oh, come on around teatime! Now, you'll excuse me: I am on duty in ten minutes.
See you later!

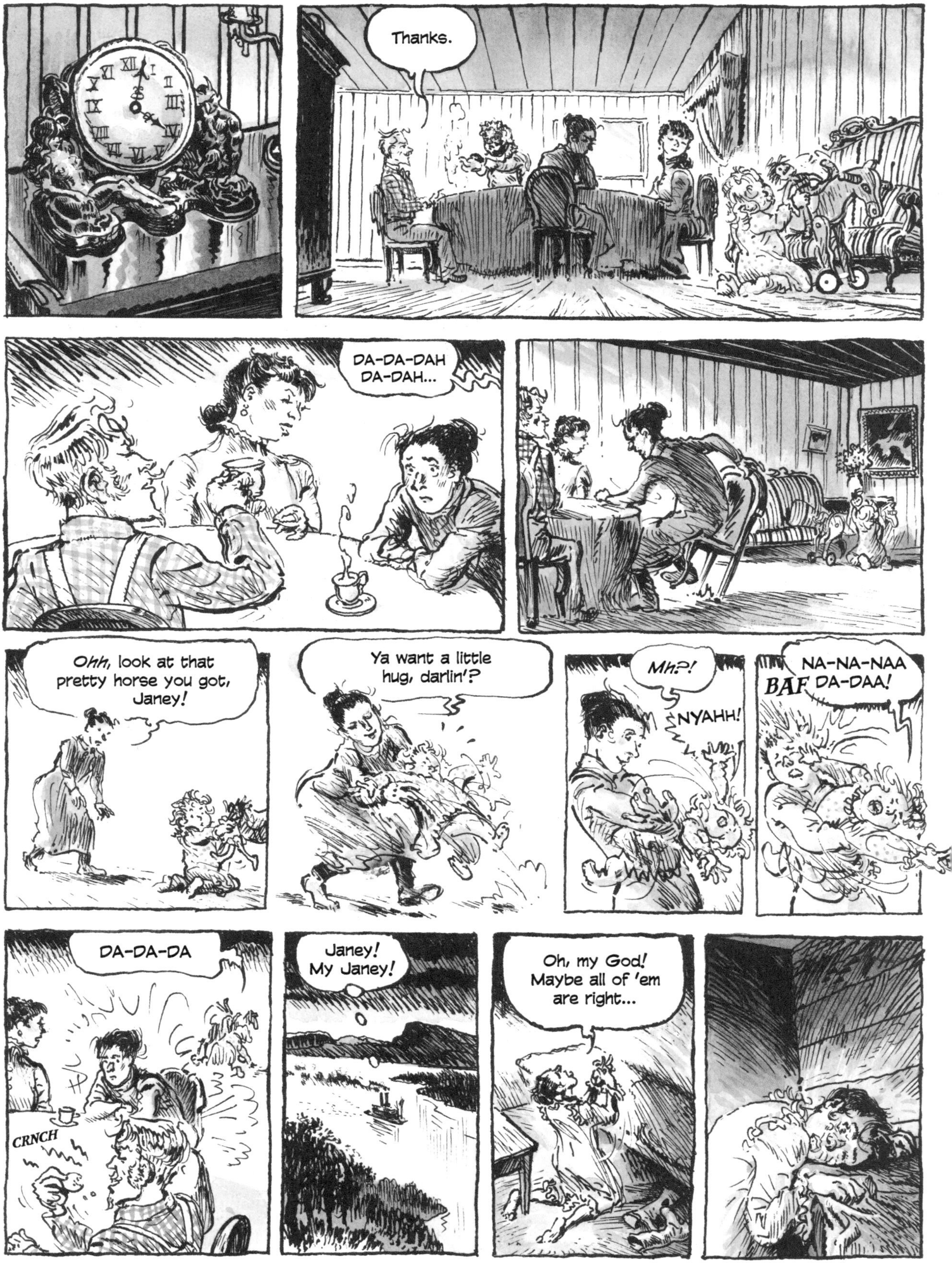
Thanks.
DA-DA-DAH
DA-DAH...
Ohh, look at that pretty horse you got, Janey!
Ya want a little hug, darlin'?
Mh?!
NYAHH!
NA-NA-NAA DA-DAA!
BAF
DA-DA-DA
CRNCH
Janey! My Janey!
Oh, my God! Maybe all of 'em are right...

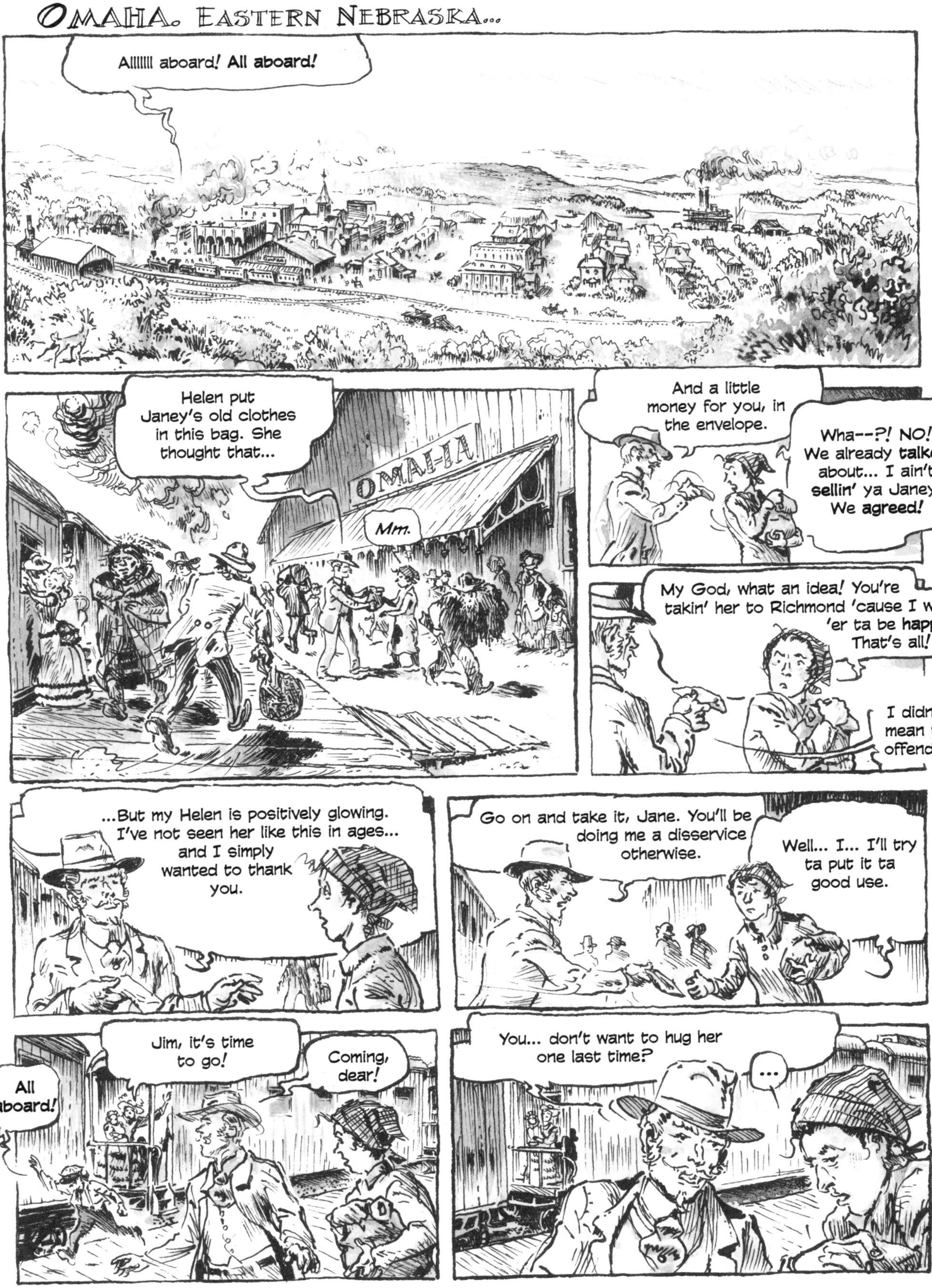

Omaha. Eastern Nebraska...
Allllll aboard! All aboard!
Helen put Janey's old clothes in this bag. She thought that...
Mm.
OMAHA
And a little money for you, in the envelope.
Wha--?! NO! We already talked about... I ain't sellin' ya Janey. We agreed!
My God, what an idea! You're takin' her to Richmond 'cause I want 'er ta be happy! That's all!
I didn't mean to offend...
...But my Helen is positively glowing. I've not seen her like this in ages... and I simply wanted to thank you.
Go on and take it, Jane. You'll be doing me a disservice otherwise.
Well... I... I'll try ta put it ta good use.
All aboard!
Jim, it's time to go!
Coming, dear!
You... don't want to hug her one last time?
...

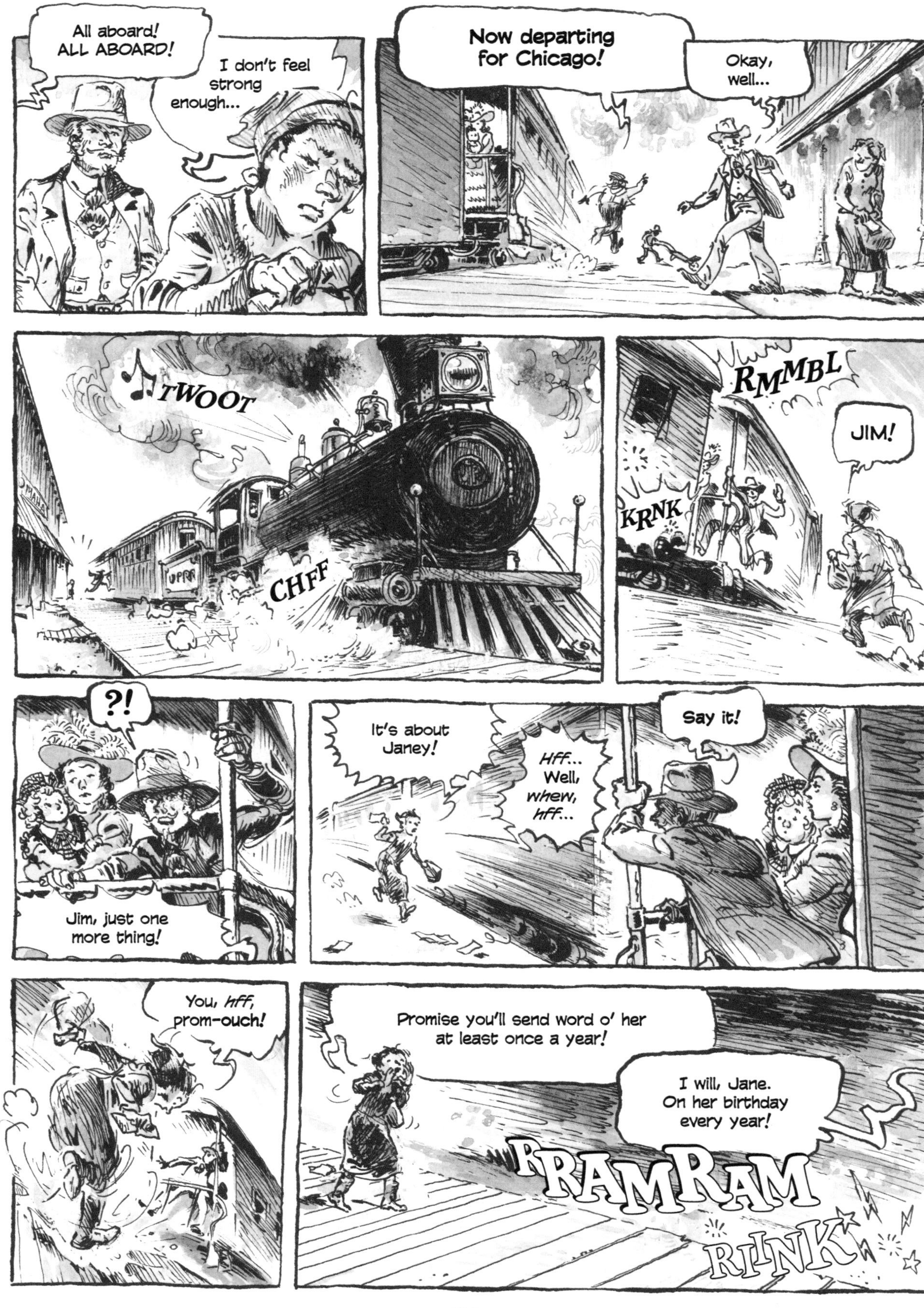
All aboard! ALL ABOARD!
I don't feel strong enough...
Now departing for Chicago!
Okay, well...
TWOOT
CHFF
RMMBL
KRNK
JIM!
?!
Jim, just one more thing!
It's about Janey!
Hff... Well, whew, hff...
Say it!
You, hff, prom-ouch!
Promise you'll send word o' her at least once a year!
I will, Jane. On her birthday every year!
RAMRAM
RIINK

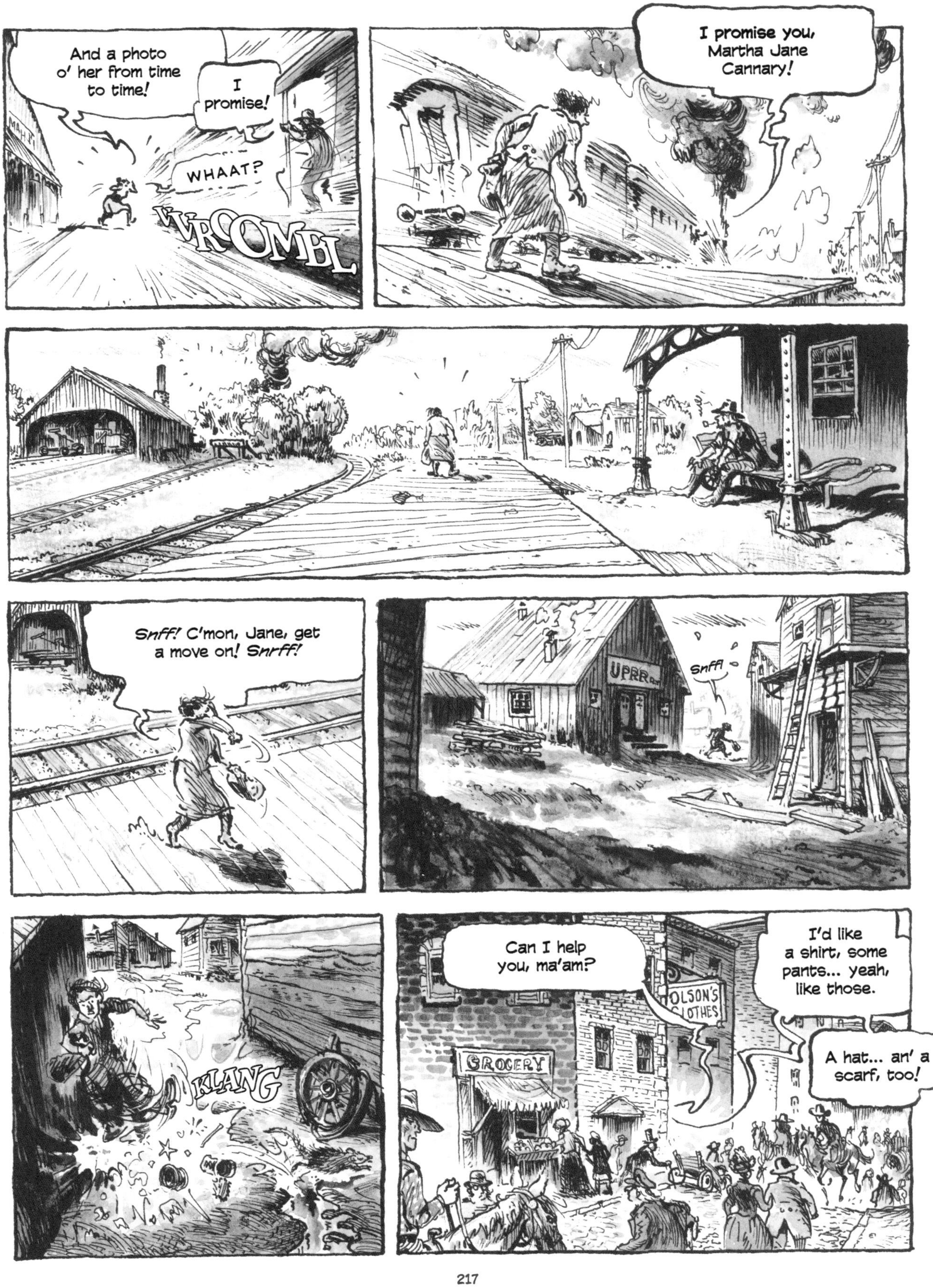
And a photo o' her from time to time!
I promise!
WHAAT?
VVROOMBL
I promise you, Martha Jane Cannary!
UPRR
Snff! C'mon, Jane, get a move on! Snrff!
Snff!
KLANG
Can I help you, ma'am?
OLSON'S CLOTHES
GROCERY
I'd like a shirt, some pants... yeah, like those.
A hat... an' a scarf, too!

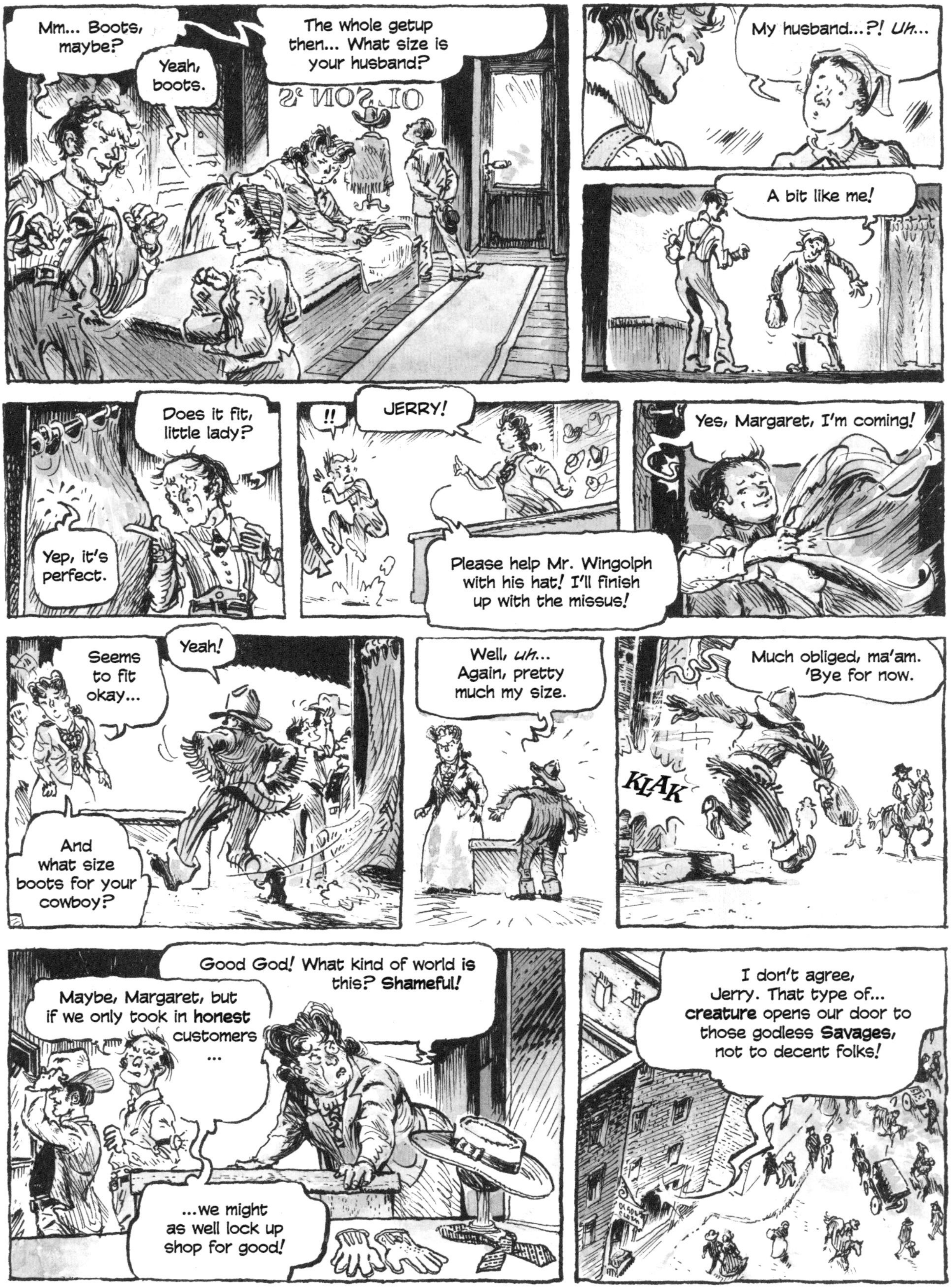

Mm... Boots, maybe?
Yeah, boots.
The whole getup then... What size is your husband?
OLSON'S
My husband...?! *Uh*...
A bit like me!
Does it fit, little lady?
Yep, it's perfect.
!!
JERRY!
Please help Mr. Wingolph with his hat! I'll finish up with the missus!
Yes, Margaret, I'm coming!
Seems to fit okay...
Yeah!
And what size boots for your cowboy?
Well, *uh*... Again, pretty much my size.
Much obliged, ma'am. 'Bye for now.
KLAK
Good God! What kind of world is this? **Shameful!**
Maybe, Margaret, but if we only took in **honest** customers ...
...we might as well lock up shop for good!
I don't agree, Jerry. That type of... **creature** opens our door to those godless **Savages**, not to decent folks!

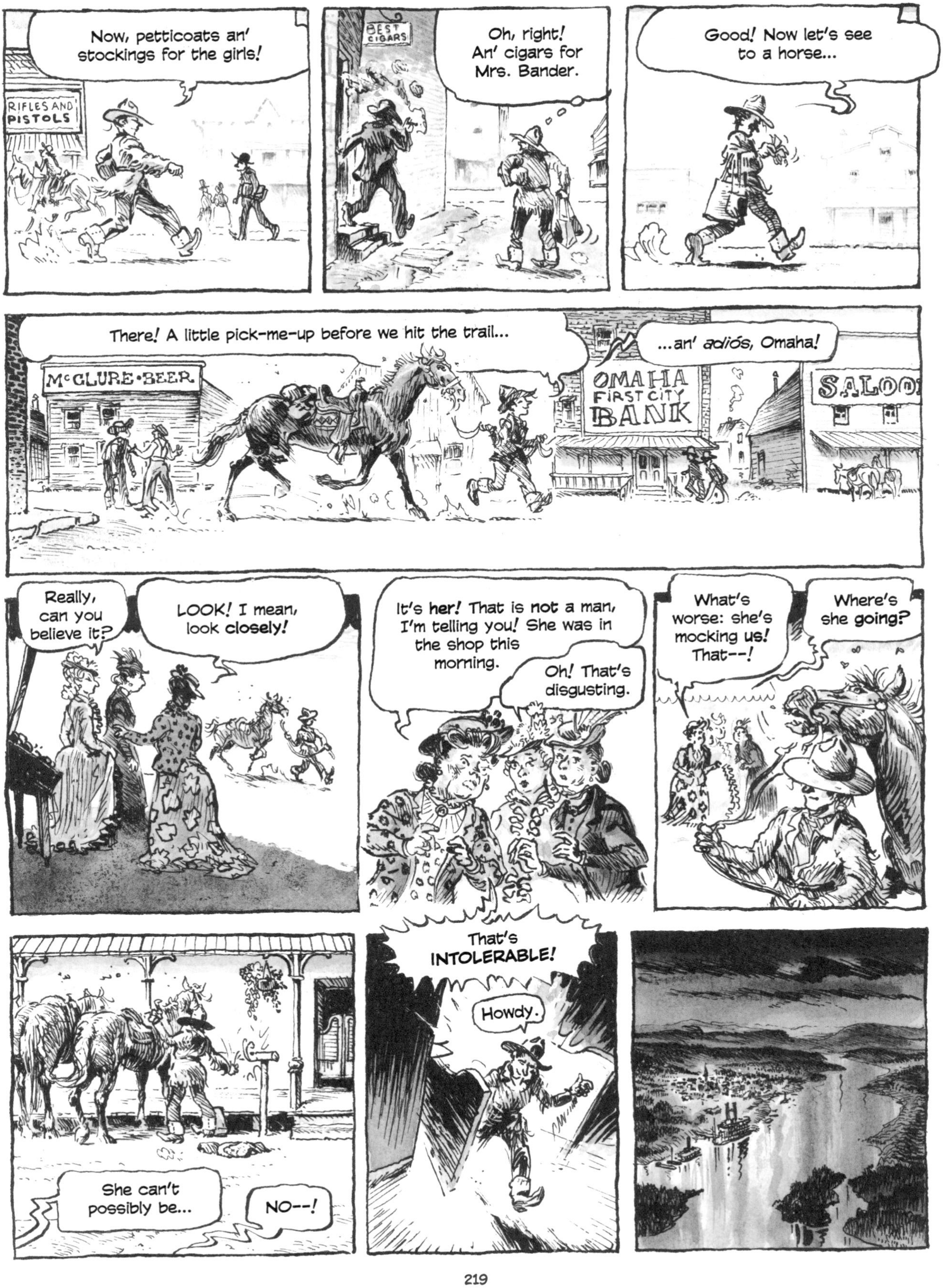
Now, petticoats an' stockings for the girls!
RIFLES AND PISTOLS
BEST CIGARS
Oh, right! An' cigars for Mrs. Bander.
Good! Now let's see to a horse...
There! A little pick-me-up before we hit the trail...
...an' *adiós*, Omaha!
McCLURE·BEER
OMAHA FIRST CITY BANK
SALOO
Really, can you believe it?
LOOK! I mean, look **closely!**
It's **her!** That is **not** a man, I'm telling you! She was in the shop this morning.
Oh! That's disgusting.
What's worse: she's mocking **us!** That--!
Where's she **going?**
She can't possibly be...
NO--!
That's **INTOLERABLE!**
Howdy.

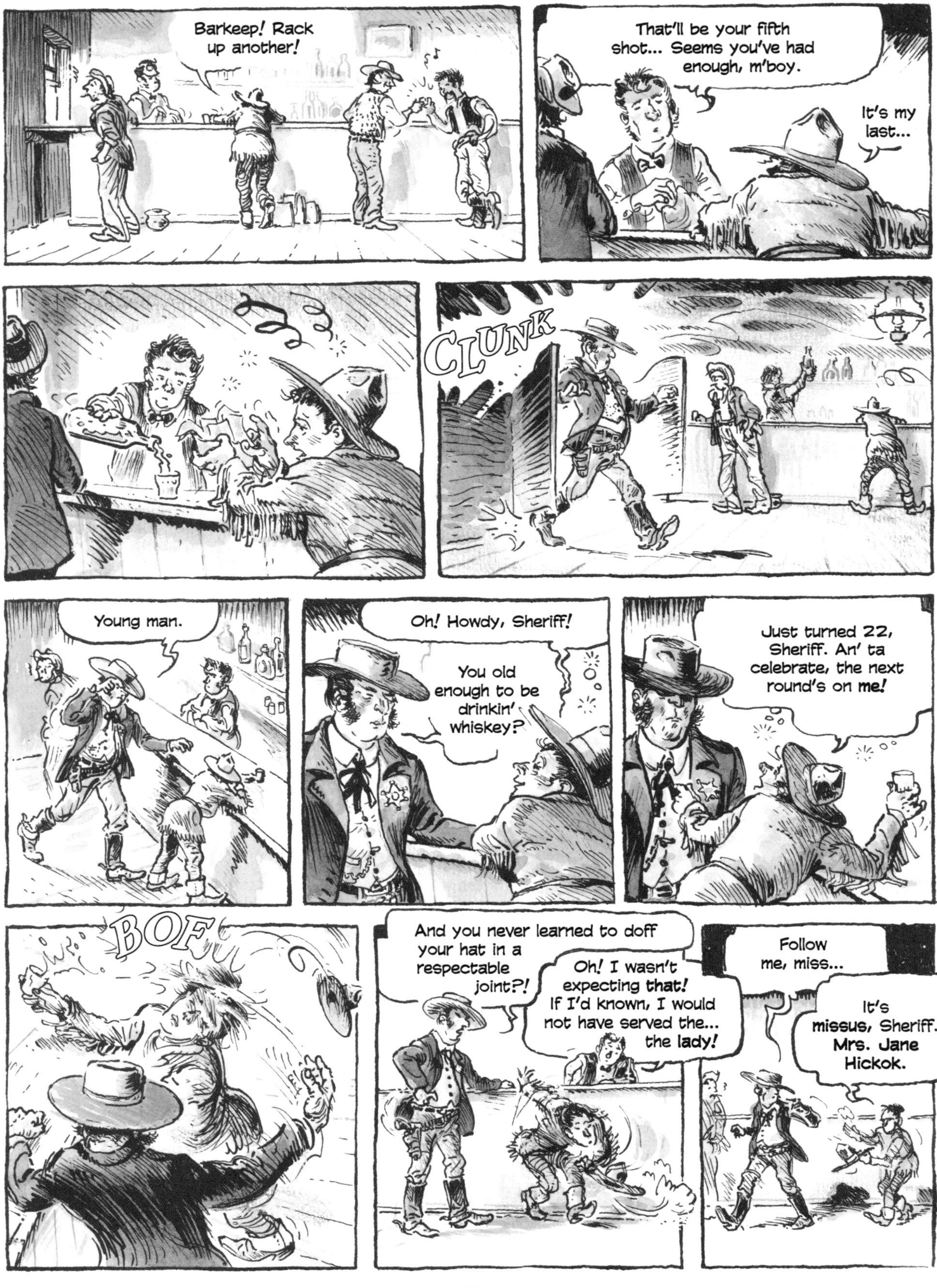
Barkeep! Rack up another!
That'll be your fifth shot... Seems you've had enough, m'boy.
It's my last...
CLUNK
Young man.
Oh! Howdy, Sheriff!
You old enough to be drinkin' whiskey?
Just turned 22, Sheriff. An' ta celebrate, the next round's on **me!**
BOF
And you never learned to doff your hat in a respectable joint?!
Oh! I wasn't expecting **that!** If I'd known, I would not have served the... the **lady!**
Follow me, miss...
It's **missus,** Sheriff. **Mrs. Jane Hickok.**

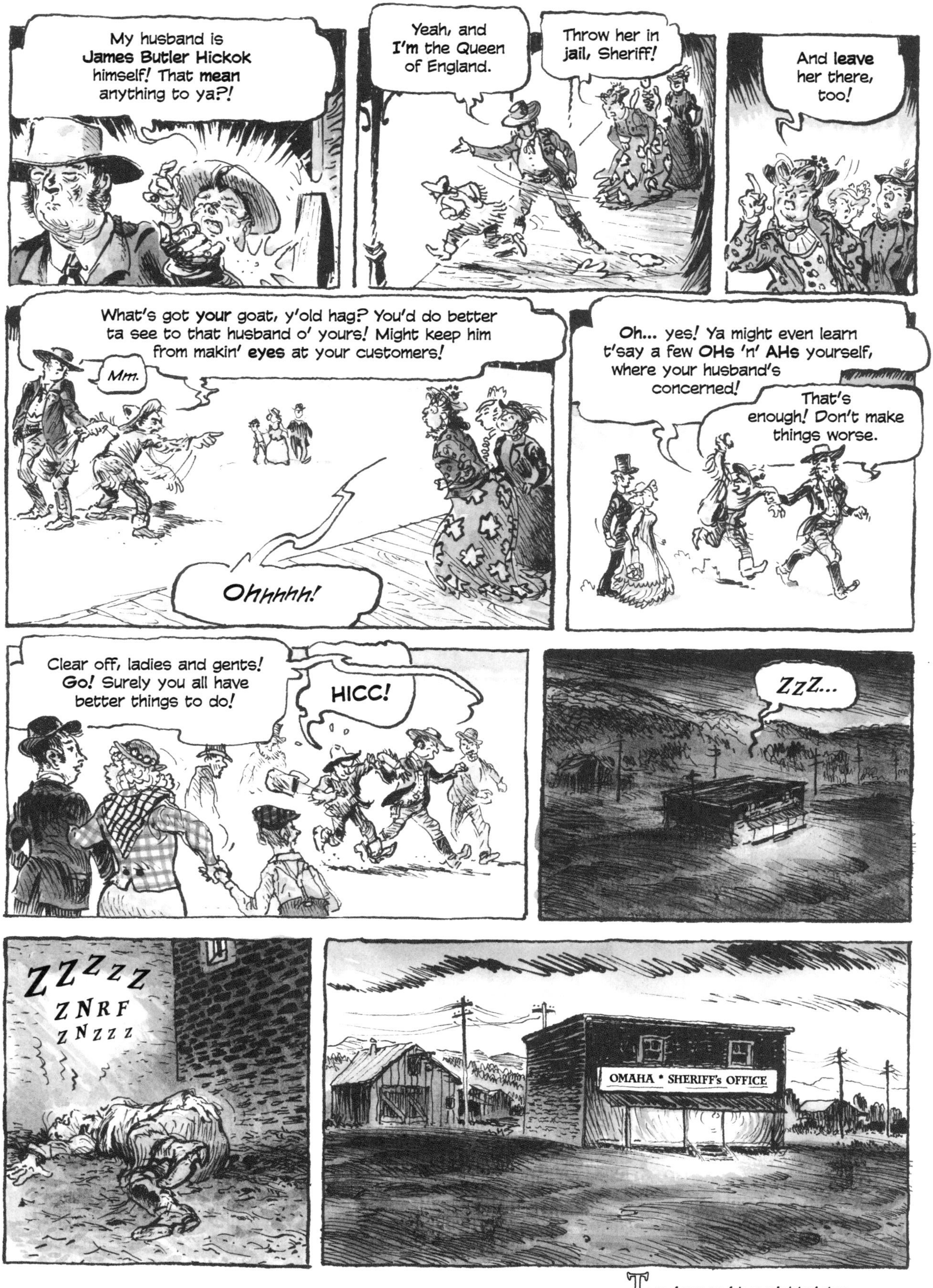

My husband is James Butler Hickok himself! That mean anything to ya?!
Yeah, and I'm the Queen of England.
Throw her in jail, Sheriff!
And leave her there, too!
What's got your goat, y'old hag? You'd do better ta see to that husband o' yours! Might keep him from makin' eyes at your customers!
Mm.
Ohhhhh!
Oh... yes! Ya might even learn t'say a few OHs 'n' AHs yourself, where your husband's concerned!
That's enough! Don't make things worse.
Clear off, ladies and gents! Go! Surely you all have better things to do!
HICC!
ZZZ...
ZZZZZ
ZNRF
ZNZZZ
OMAHA * SHERIFF's OFFICE

Two days and two nights later...

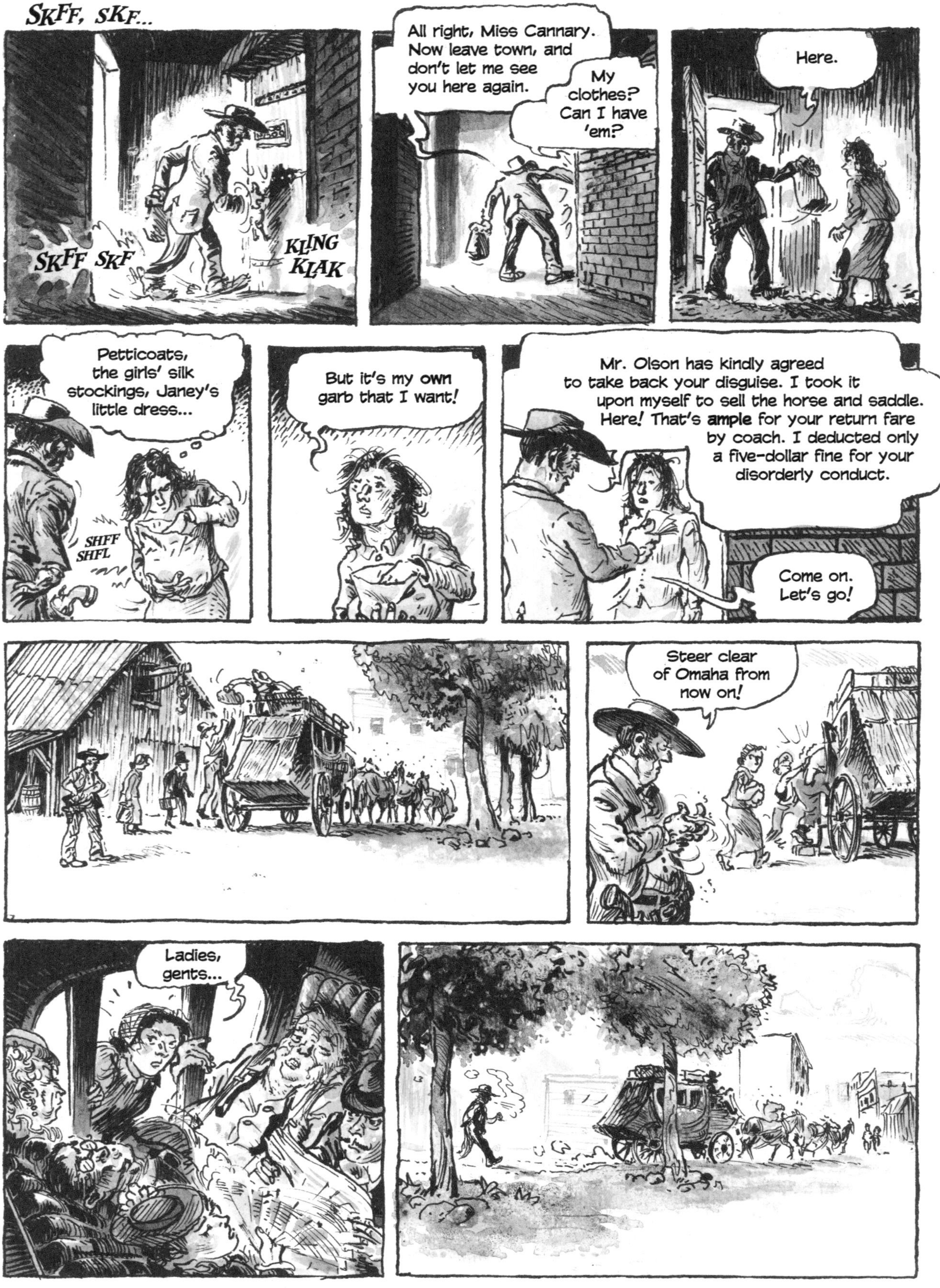
SKFF, SKF...
SKFF SKF
KLING KLAK
All right, Miss Cannary. Now leave town, and don't let me see you here again.
My clothes? Can I have 'em?
Here.
Petticoats, the girls' silk stockings, Janey's little dress...
SHFF SHFL
But it's my own garb that I want!
Mr. Olson has kindly agreed to take back your disguise. I took it upon myself to sell the horse and saddle. Here! That's **ample** for your return fare by coach. I deducted only a five-dollar fine for your disorderly conduct.
Come on. Let's go!
Steer clear of Omaha from now on!
Ladies, gents...

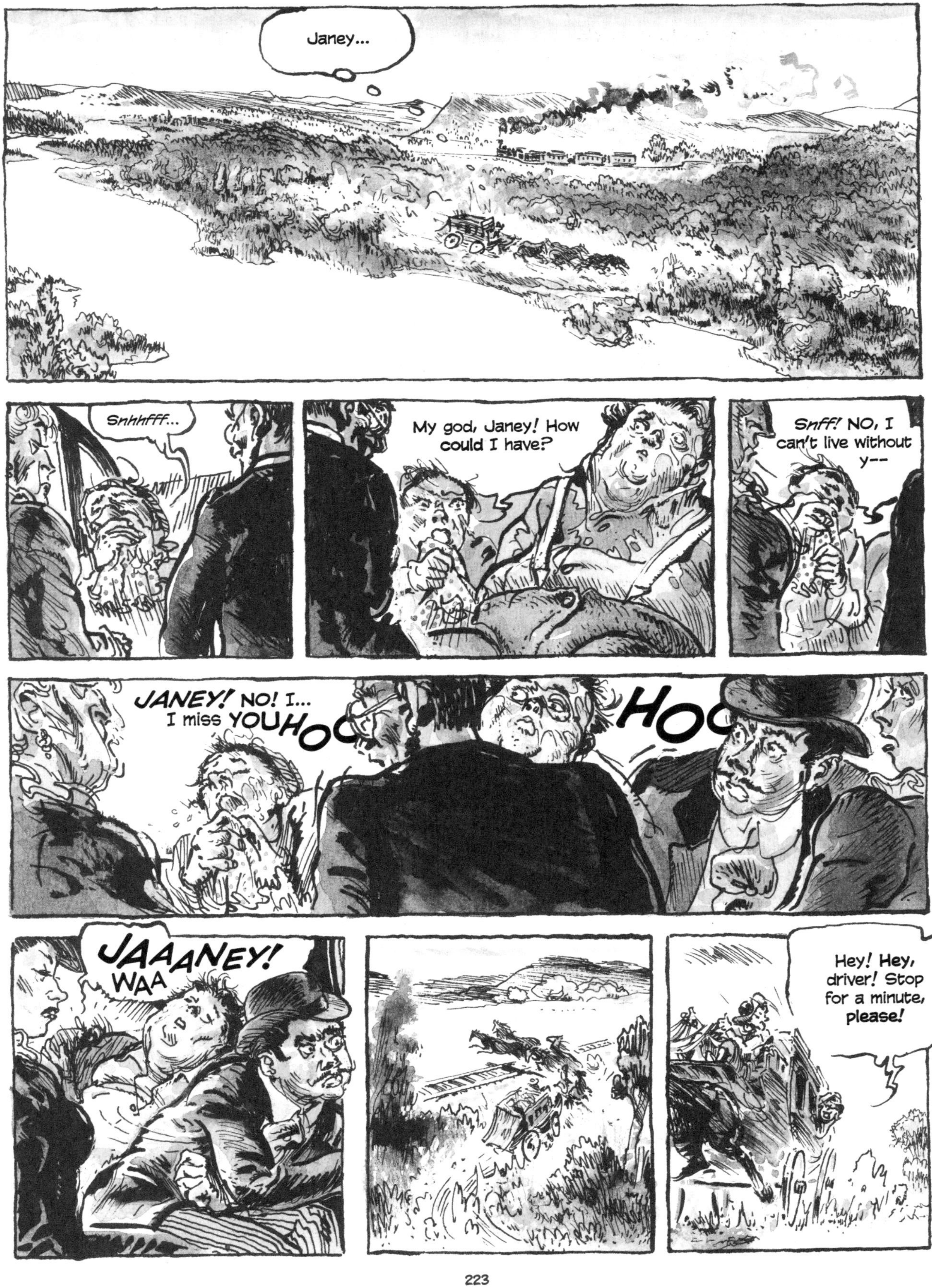
Janey...
Snhhfff...
My god, Janey! How could I have?
Snff! NO, I can't live without y--
JANEY! NO! I... I miss YOUHOO
HOO
JAAANEY! WAA
Hey! Hey, driver! Stop for a minute, please!

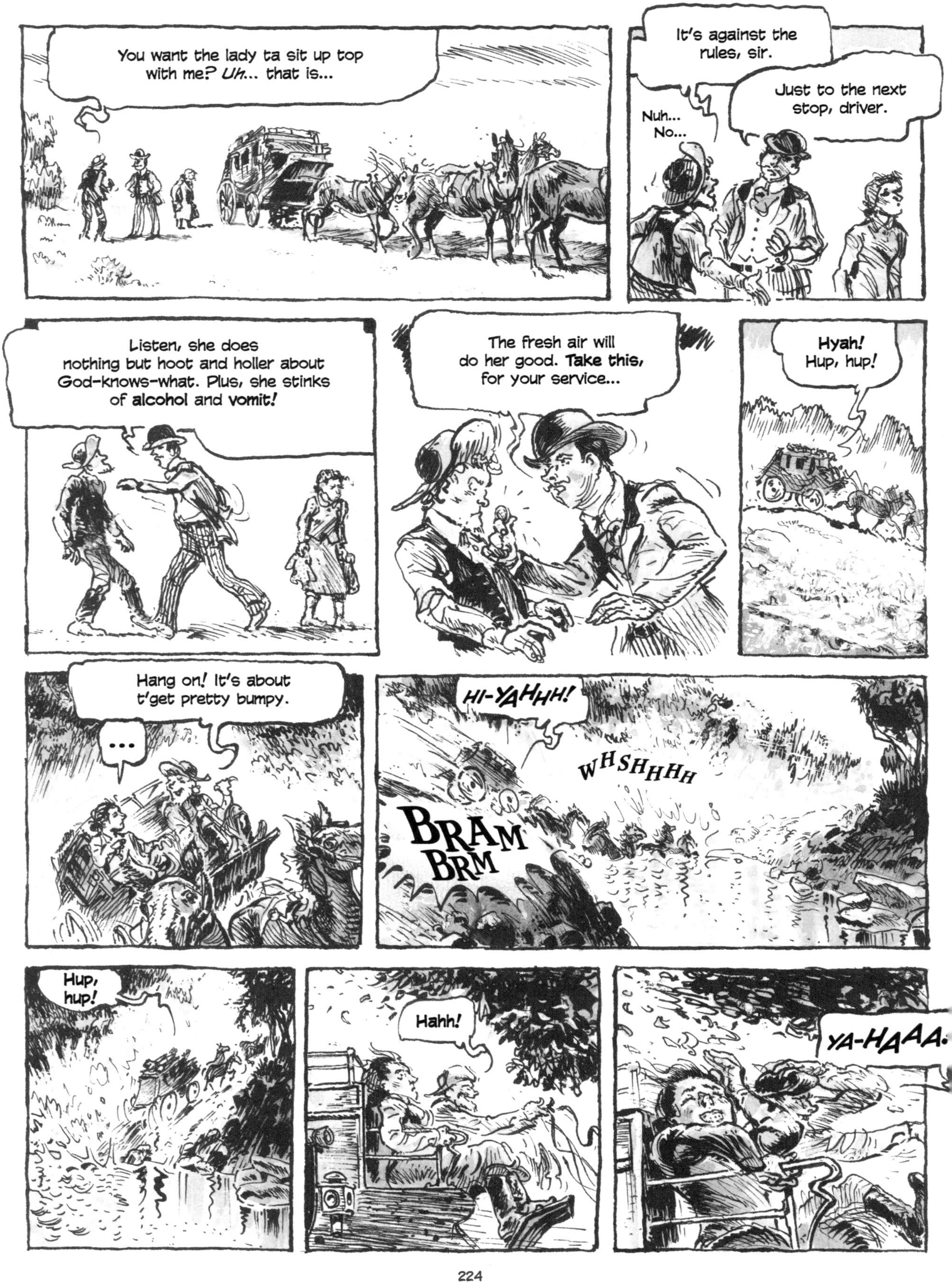
You want the lady ta sit up top with me? *Uh*... that is...
It's against the rules, sir.
Nuh... No...
Just to the next stop, driver.
Listen, she does nothing but hoot and holler about God-knows-what. Plus, she stinks of **alcohol** and **vomit!**
The fresh air will do her good. **Take this,** for your service...
Hyah! Hup, hup!
Hang on! It's about t'get pretty bumpy.
...
HI-YAHHH!
WHSHHHH
BRAM BRM
Hup, hup!
Hahh!
YA-HAAA.

In *Letters to Her Daughter,* Calamity Jane often speaks highly of the O'Neils. Jim wrote to her every year in September, on Janey's birthday. Every now and then the letter would contain a photo of the child, who, according to Calamity, was the spitting image of her father, Hickok.

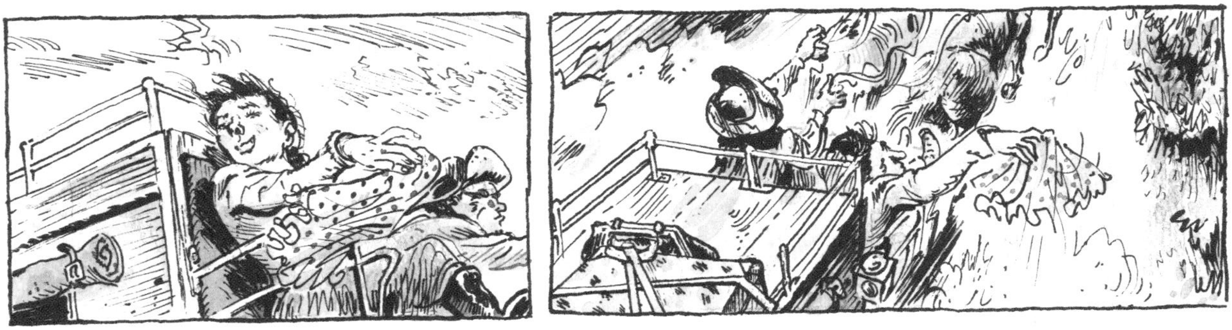

Upon their return to Richmond, the O'Neils wasted no time in having Janey baptized, giving her the name **Jean Irene.** But Helen O'Neil's newfound happiness was not to last. She died before her adopted daughter turned six.

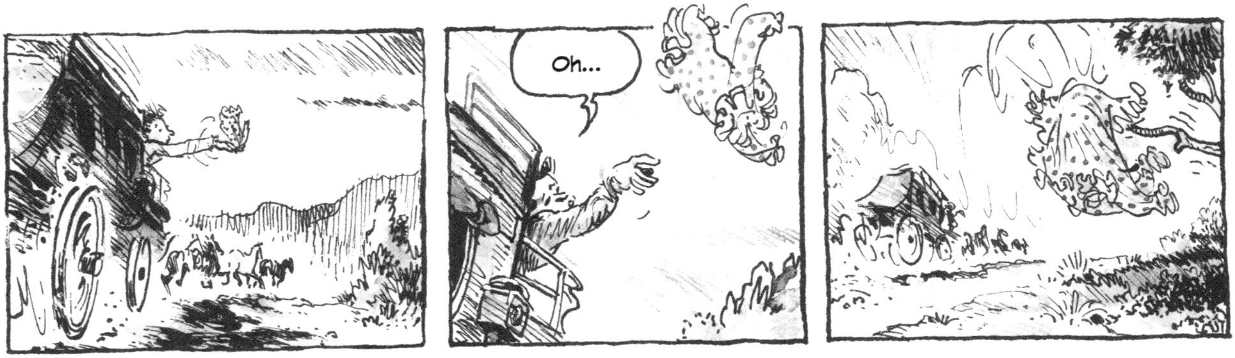
Oh...

From that moment on, Jim O'Neil, a longtime Captain in the U.S. Merchant Marine, brought Jean Irene with him on all his travels, and this is how she came to discover the world... by sea.

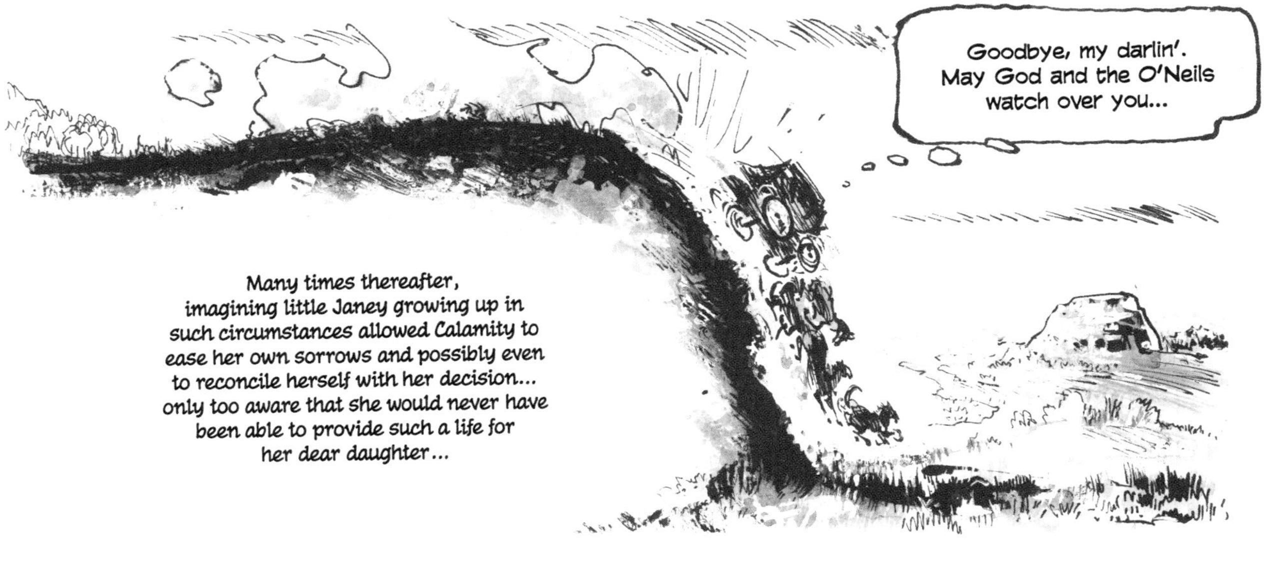
Goodbye, my darlin'. May God and the O'Neils watch over you...
Many times thereafter, imagining little Janey growing up in such circumstances allowed Calamity to ease her own sorrows and possibly even to reconcile herself with her decision... only too aware that she would never have been able to provide such a life for her dear daughter...

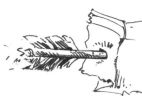

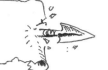

FROM THE BLACK HILLS TO THE LITTLE BIGHORN

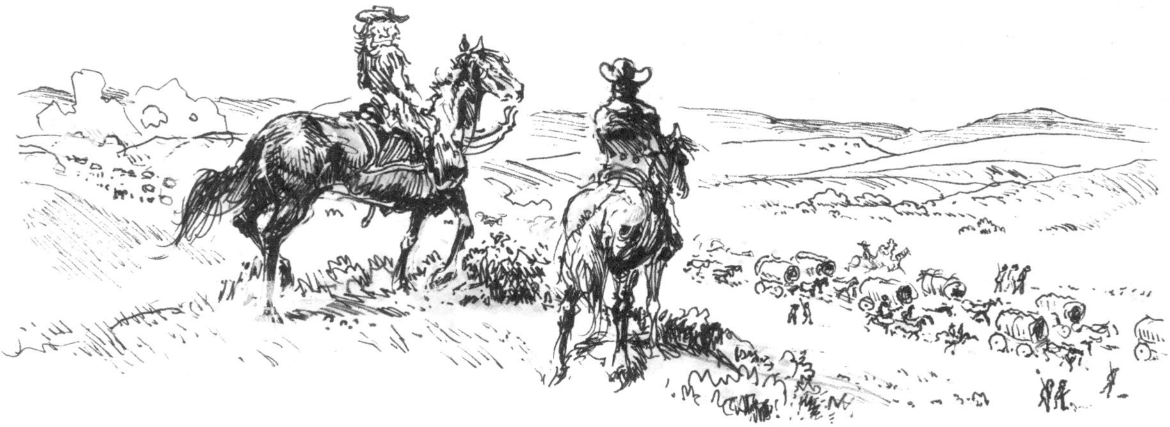

On July 2, 1874, Lieutenant Colonel George A. Custer's 7th Cavalry finally left Fort Abraham Lincoln for the Black Hills. His convoy consisted of a hundred wagons and a thousand soldiers. Also joining the expedition were geologists, engineers, and news dispatchers.

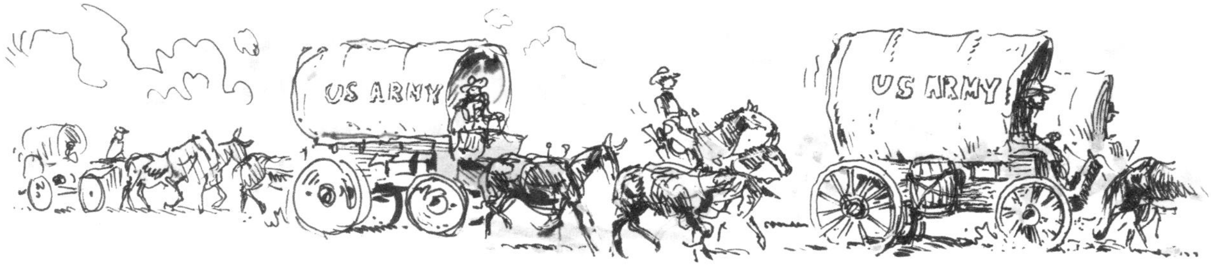
US ARMY
US ARMY

Martha Jane Cannary had always boasted of having been one of Custer's scouts... But her name has yet to be found in the army pay registers! It's more likely that Marthy was a wagon driver again, still quite an extraordinary post for a woman at that time...

...All the more so since she didn't have to hide her identity in the army. From then on, she was accepted as who she was: Calamity Jane, Prairie Queen.

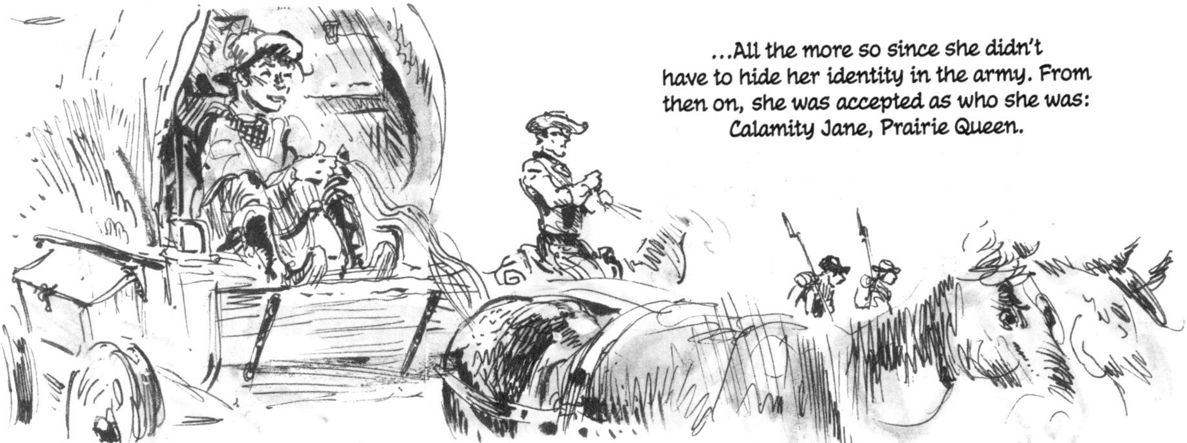

But before following this expedition to the heart of the Black Hills, we must first linger on the larger-than-life character of its commander...

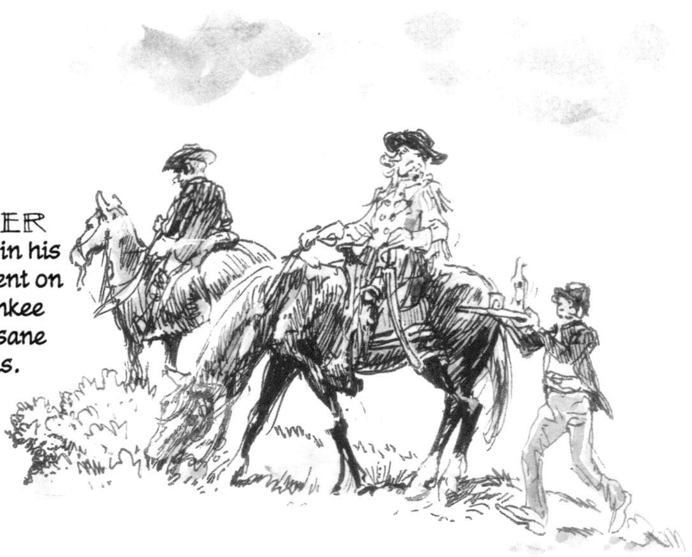

GEORGE ARMSTRONG CUSTER was an officer hungry for fortune and fame. Last in his graduating class at West Point, he nonetheless went on during the Civil War to become the youngest Yankee General in the U.S. Volunteers, thanks to his insane audacity and his keen grasp of public relations.

After the war, Custer reverted to his U.S. Army rank of Captain.

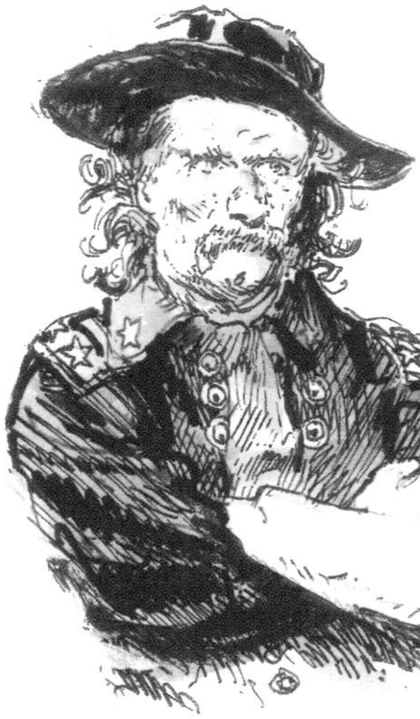

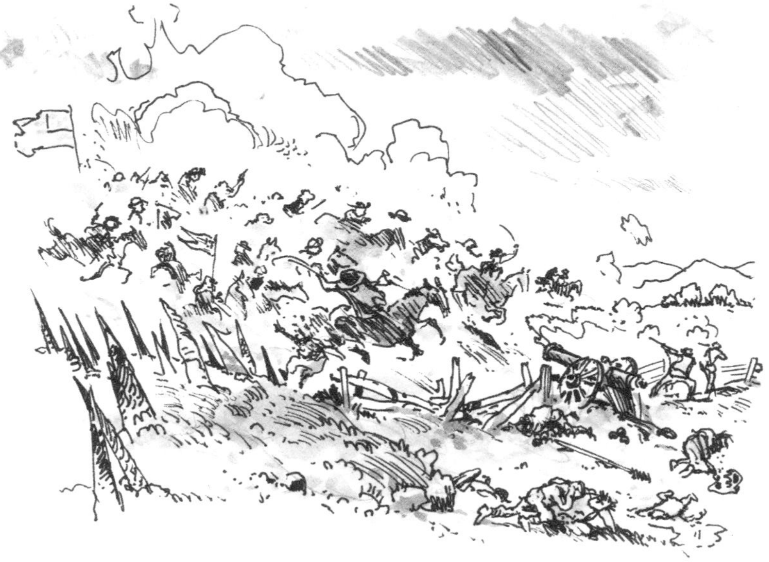

He was soon awarded his stripes as Lieutenant Colonel and given command of the prestigious 7th Cavalry. The 1867 campaign he led against the Cheyenne in Kansas was attended by hordes of journalists and photographers. Custer liked to brag about his exploits and, even more, to pose for the camera.

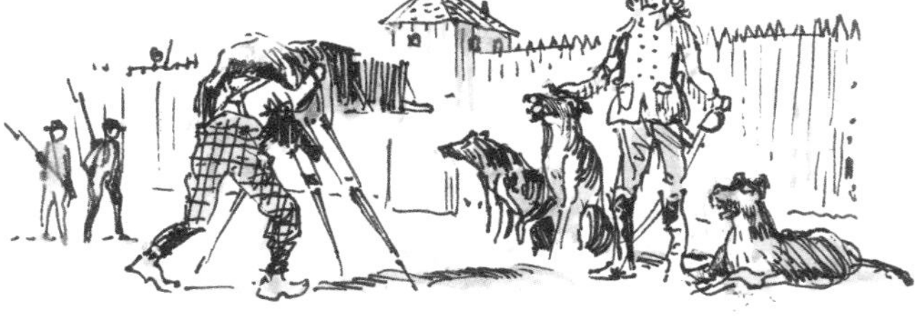

But the Cheyenne most often avoided direct confrontation with the Bluecoats, who were far more numerous and better armed. So, for long periods, the press had nothing on Custer save garrison gossip about his tumultuous relationship with his wife Elizabeth.

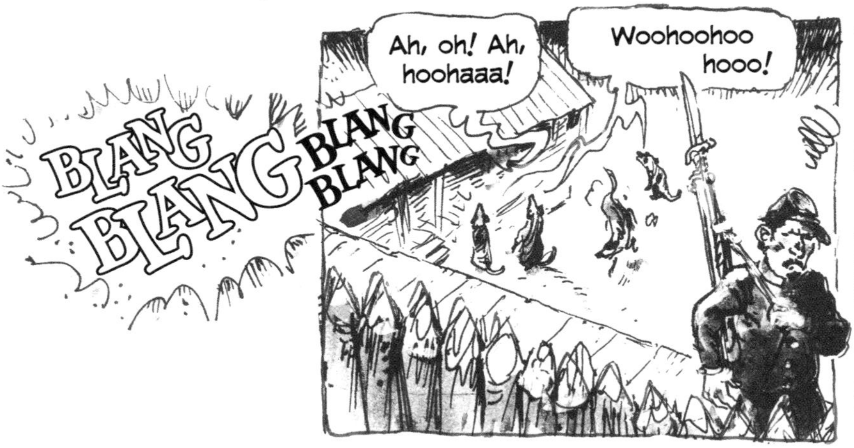

BLANG BLANG
BLANG BLANG
Ah, oh! Ah, hoohaaa!
Woohoohoo hooo!

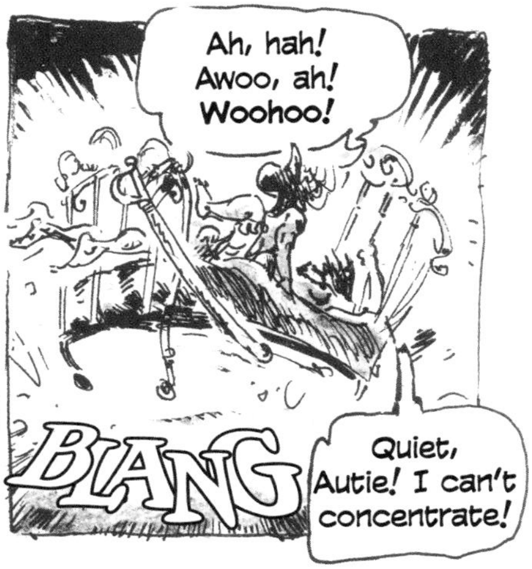

Ah, hah! Awoo, ah! Woohoo!
BLANG
Quiet, Autie! I can't concentrate!

The Custers were a colorful couple, both exaggerated and extreme in their bickering as well as in their passion.

It was in November 1868 that Custer had his first substantial victory.

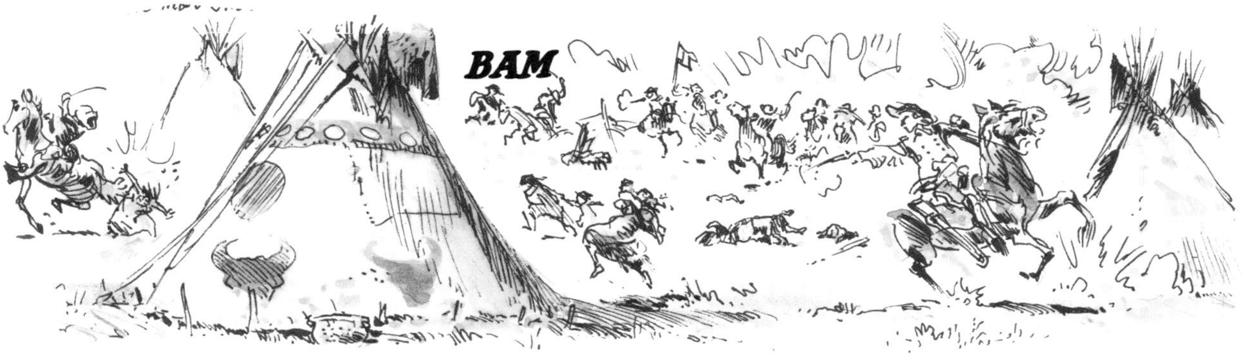

BAM

The deadly charge that he led on the Cheyenne encampment at Washita River culminated in the death of dozens of women and children. The journalists at his beck and call recast this odious massacre as a heroic charge. Custer thus became a symbol to the national populace, who condemned the Indian race as a hindrance to the march of progress.

Even his own men, those who knew him best, judged him harshly: "Egocentric, arrogant, and vain (he insists on being called 'General'), a crazy jughead" * who would lead them to their death on the shores of the Little Bighorn River one fine day in June 1876.

But that battle is still two years off, as we return now to the Black Hills expedition...

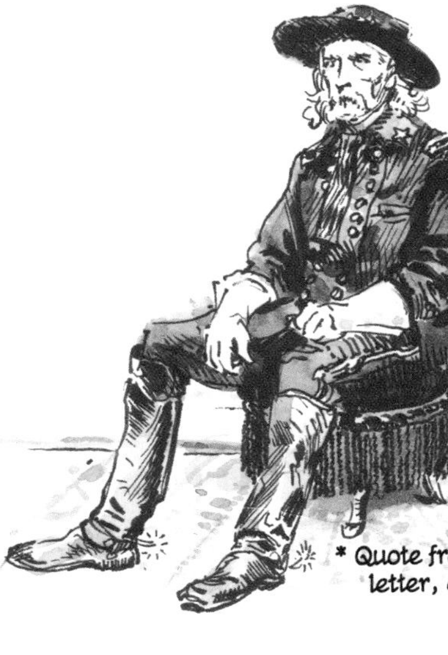

* Quote from a soldier's letter, circa 1876.

The Sioux's name for the Black Hills was **Paha Sapa.** Apart from a handful of foolhardy trappers, no white man had dared venture near. On July 23, 1874, Custer's expedition entered the Land of the Great Spirit, with no reaction from the Indians...

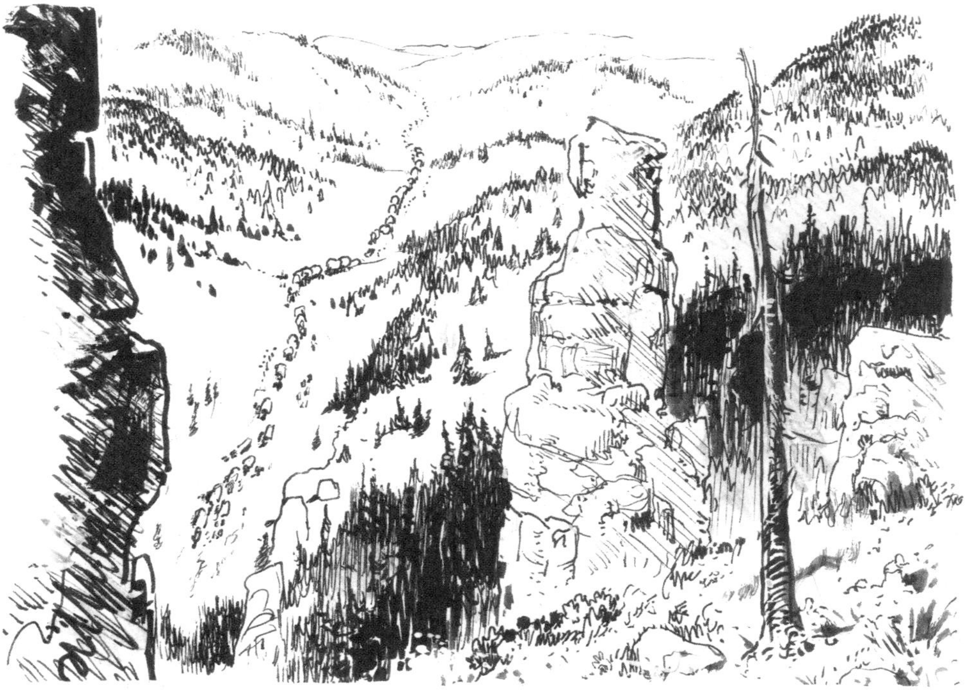

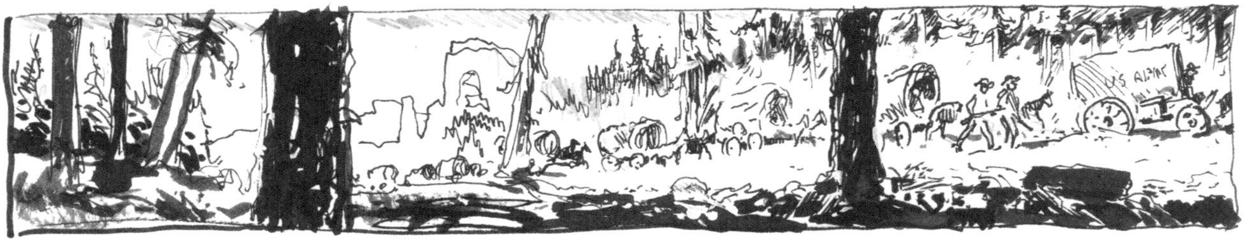

But discretion was hardly the point... Each night an orchestra played **Garryowen,** the soldiers' favorite marching tune. The dark forests were lit up by great bonfires, which also served to roast the deer meat... It was perhaps in this context that Martha Jane heard her name called out by a young soldier...

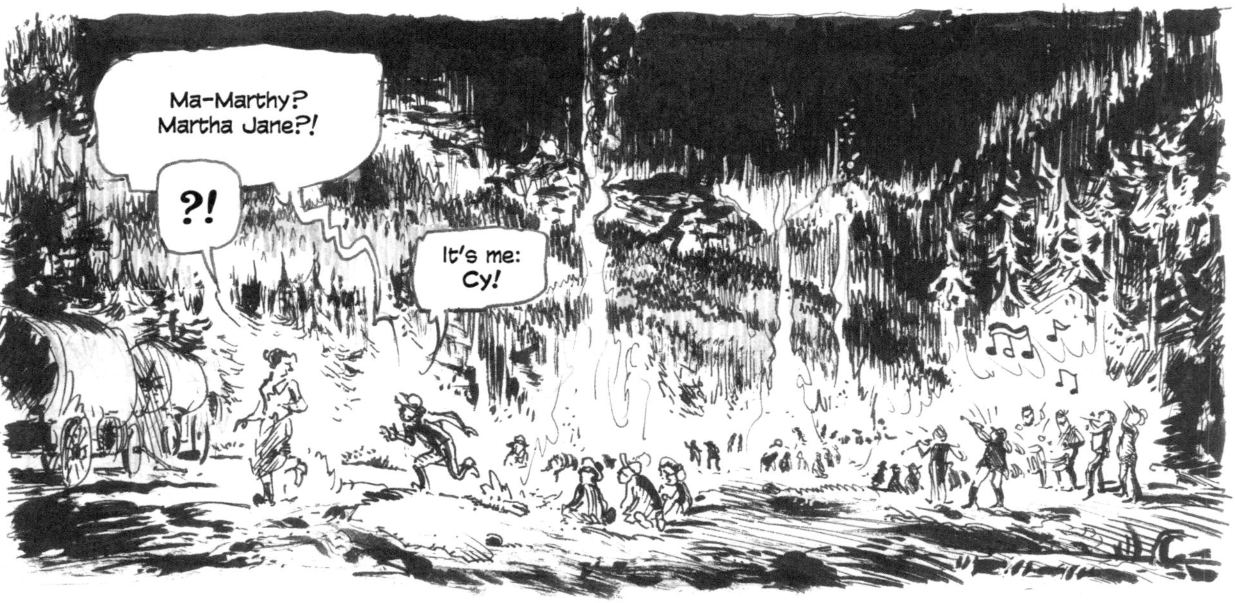
Ma-Marthy? Martha Jane?!
?!
It's me: Cy!

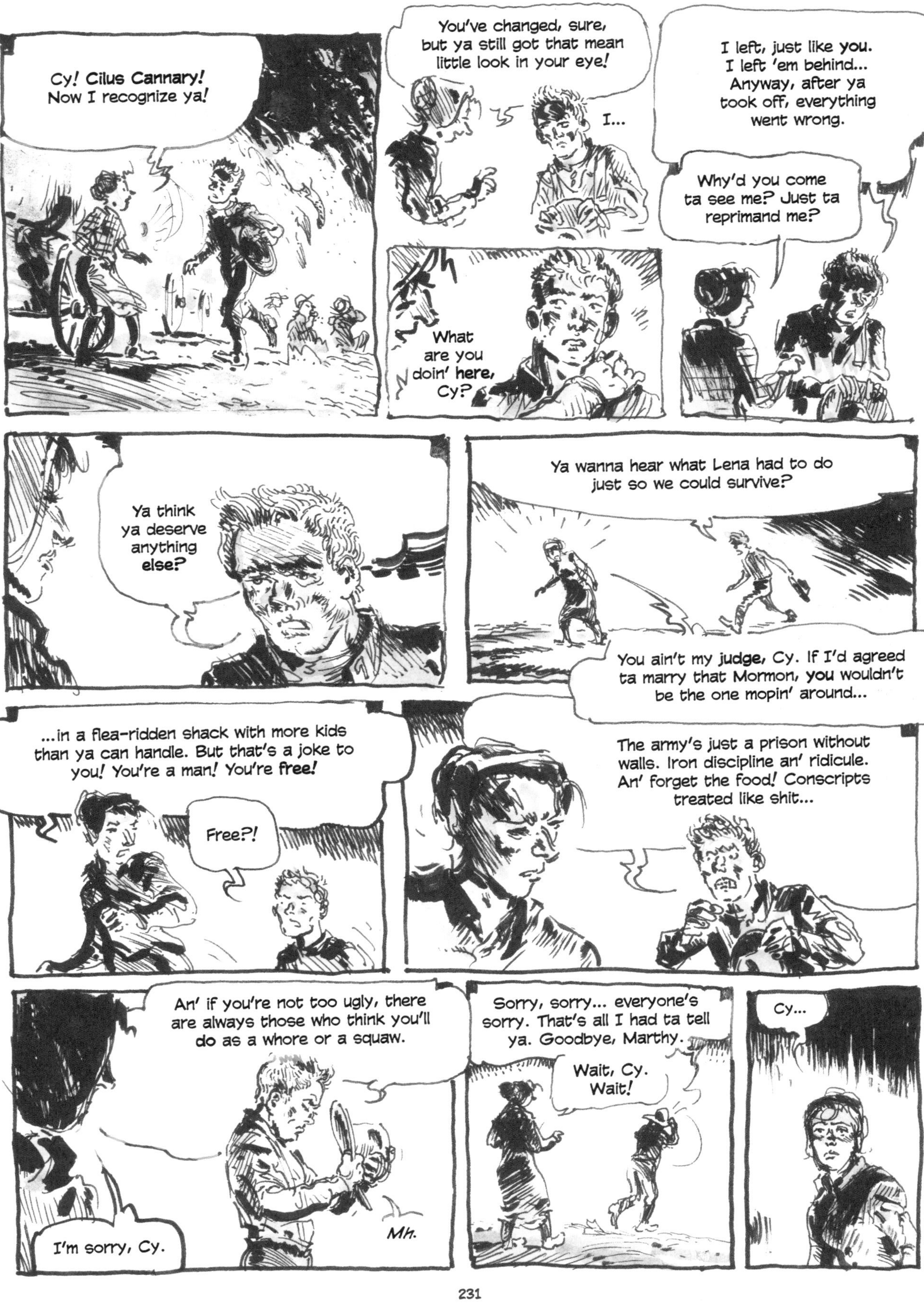

Cy! Cilus Cannary! Now I recognize ya!
You've changed, sure, but ya still got that mean little look in your eye!
I...
I left, just like you. I left 'em behind... Anyway, after ya took off, everything went wrong.
What are you doin' here, Cy?
Why'd you come ta see me? Just ta reprimand me?
Ya think ya deserve anything else?
Ya wanna hear what Lena had to do just so we could survive?
You ain't my judge, Cy. If I'd agreed ta marry that Mormon, you wouldn't be the one mopin' around...
...in a flea-ridden shack with more kids than ya can handle. But that's a joke to you! You're a man! You're free!
Free?!
The army's just a prison without walls. Iron discipline an' ridicule. An' forget the food! Conscripts treated like shit...
An' if you're not too ugly, there are always those who think you'll do as a whore or a squaw.
I'm sorry, Cy.
Mh.
Sorry, sorry... everyone's sorry. That's all I had ta tell ya. Goodbye, Marthy.
Wait, Cy. Wait!
Cy...

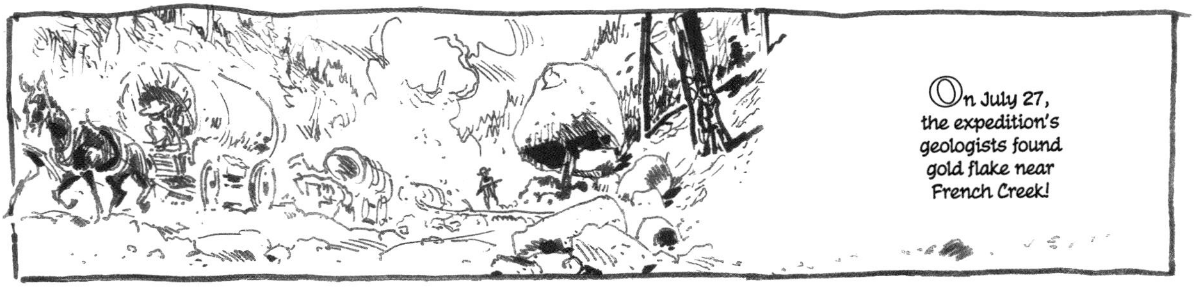
On July 27, the expedition's geologists found gold flake near French Creek!

And more promising gold veins turned up over the next few days.

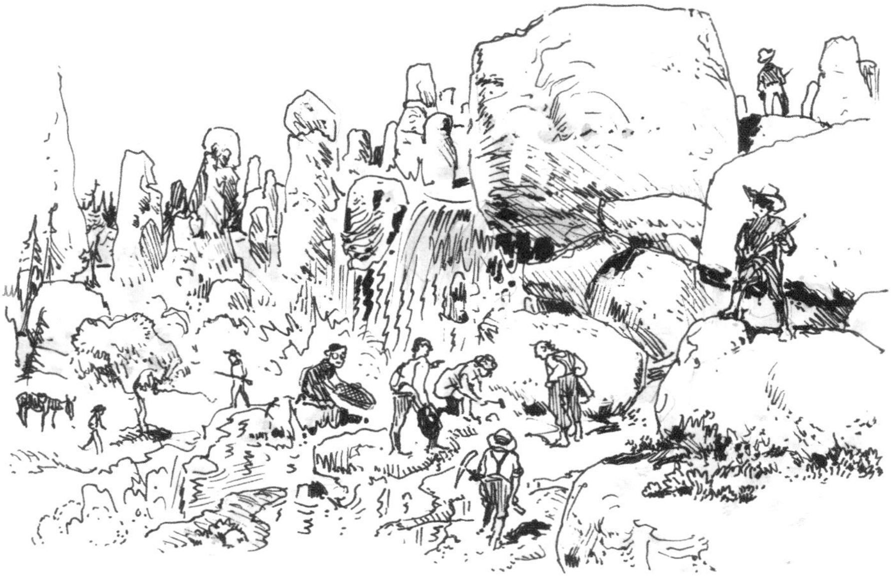

In mid-August Custer decided to withdraw from the Black Hills, without having encountered one single Indian. A strategic location was designated for the construction of a fort intended to protect workers and engineers for the future Northern Pacific Railroad. Upon his return to Fort Abraham Lincoln, Custer discovered that the success of his expedition had already made the headlines. In the following weeks and months, thousands of prospectors overran the Black Hills, and the American government did nothing to discourage them. By the summer of 1875 more than 10,000 people were illegally camped in the sacred mountains...

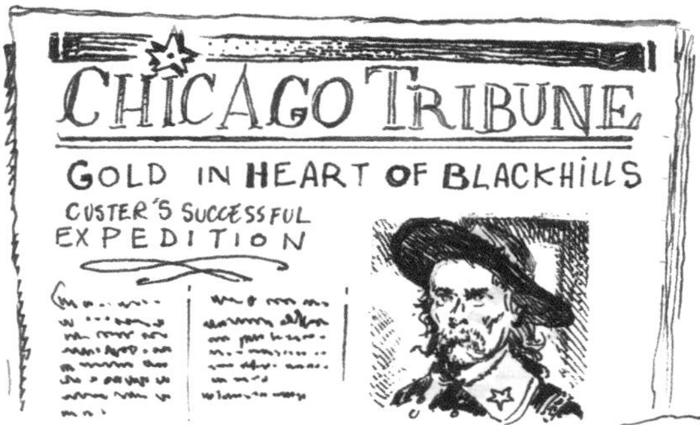
CHICAGO TRIBUNE
GOLD IN HEART OF BLACKHILLS
CUSTER'S SUCCESSFUL EXPEDITION

...and by 1876 that number was 25,000.

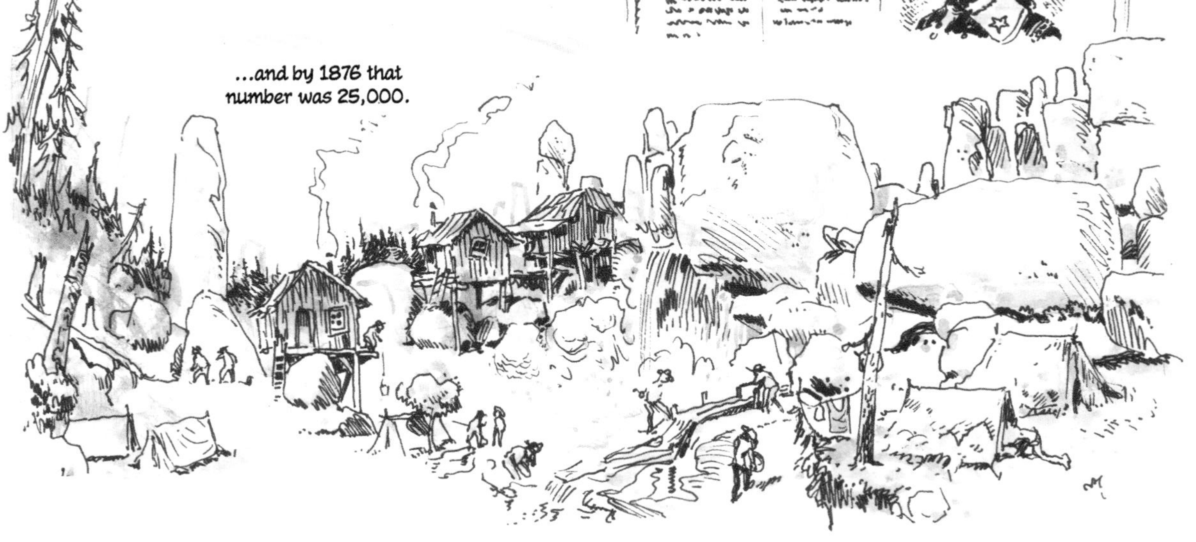

The great chiefs of the Sioux and Cheyenne confronted the Commissioner of Indian Affairs, who informed them of the government's intention to purchase the Black Hills and counseled returning to their reserves.

"As of January 31, 1876, any Indian who has not returned to his reserve will be considered a renegade and will be treated as such by the army."

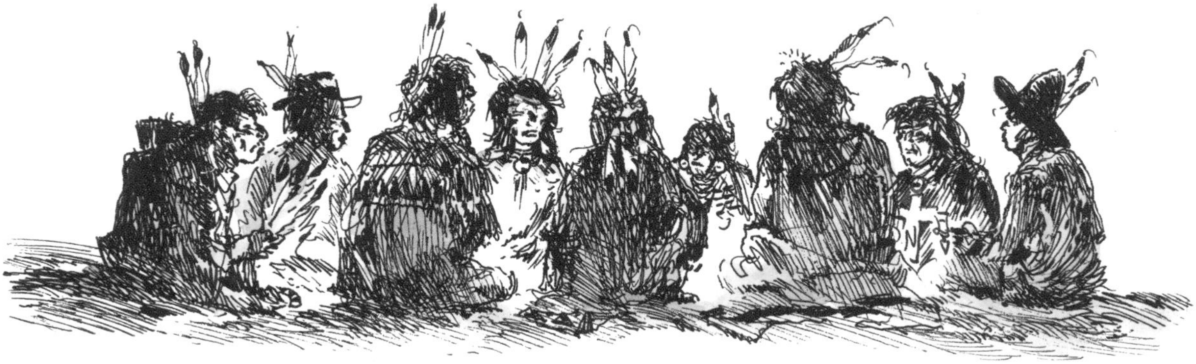

While certain chiefs such as Red Cloud had already resigned themselves to the fate dictated by the whites, others such as Sitting Bull with his Hunkpapa Sioux and Crazy Horse with his Oglala tribe rejected any compromise and went on the warpath...

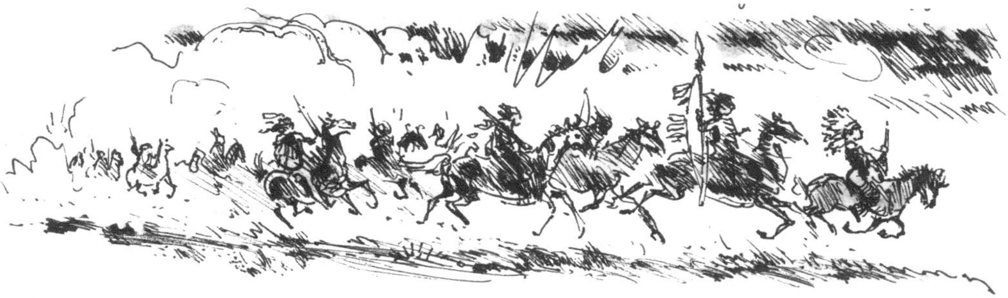

...which is what the military had been hoping for since the 1868 Treaty of Fort Laramie.

After that, events unrolled very quickly. In early June '76, squadrons of Bluecoats descended on the lands occupied by intractable Natives, with a goal to "clean house" once and for all. But on June 17, 1876, a setback for the soldiers took place at Rosebud Creek, where Crazy Horse and his Oglala Indians set a thousand of General Crook's men to flight.

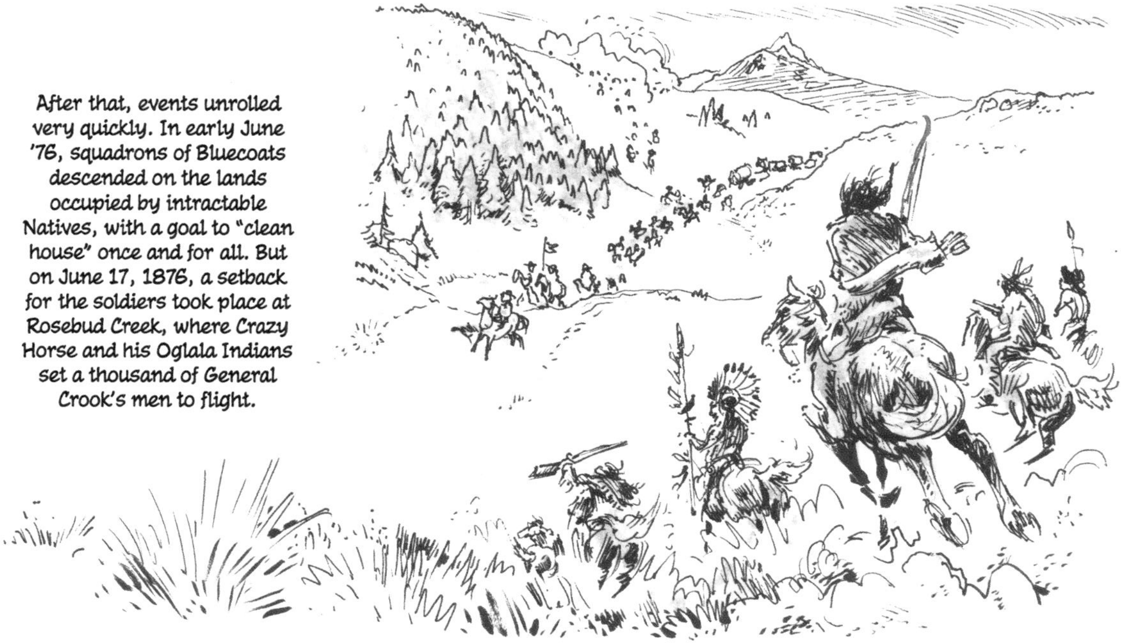

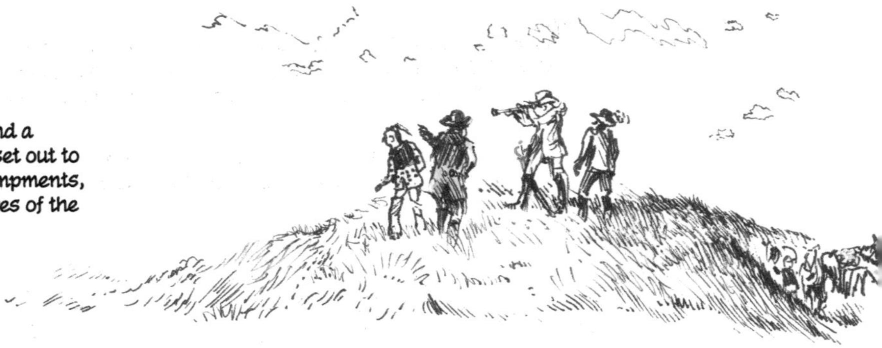

A few days later, Custer and a detachment from the 7th Cavalry set out to find the Sioux and Cheyenne encampments, locating them on the eastern shores of the Little Bighorn River.

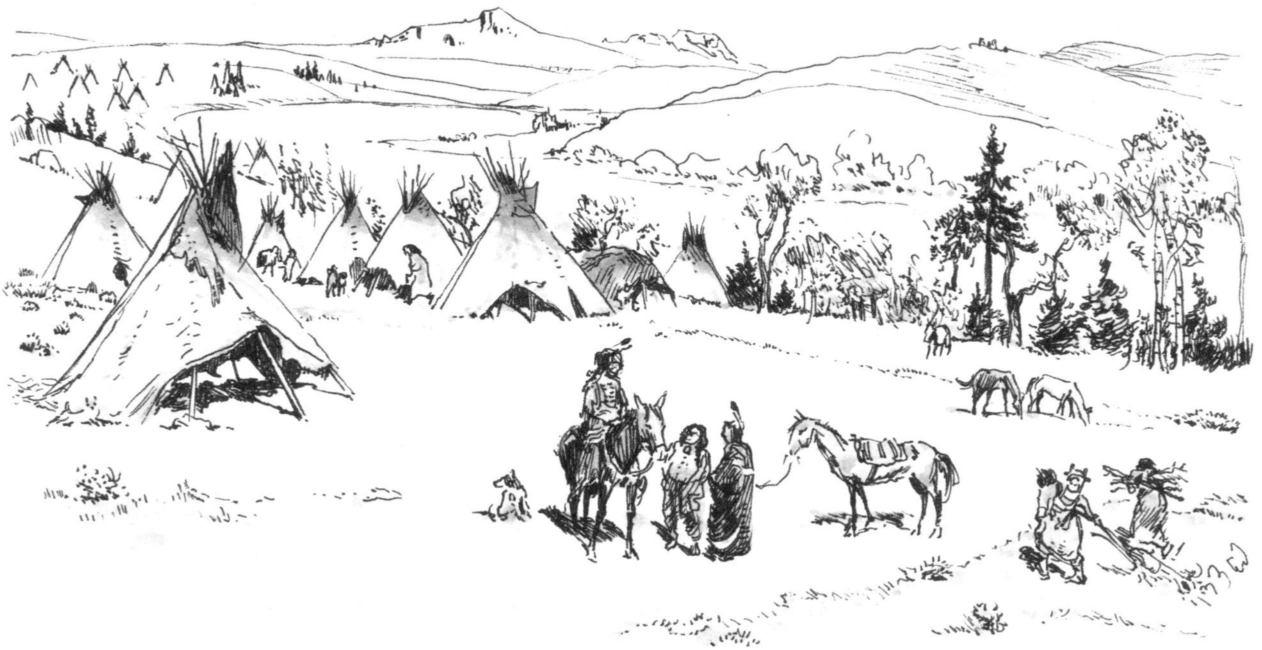

Rather than wait for the bulk of his troops, Custer resolved to attack, in order to secure the glorious victory for himself. He never doubted the outcome of combat: his men were armed with repeating rifles, whereas the Indian warriors wielded only axes and clubs.

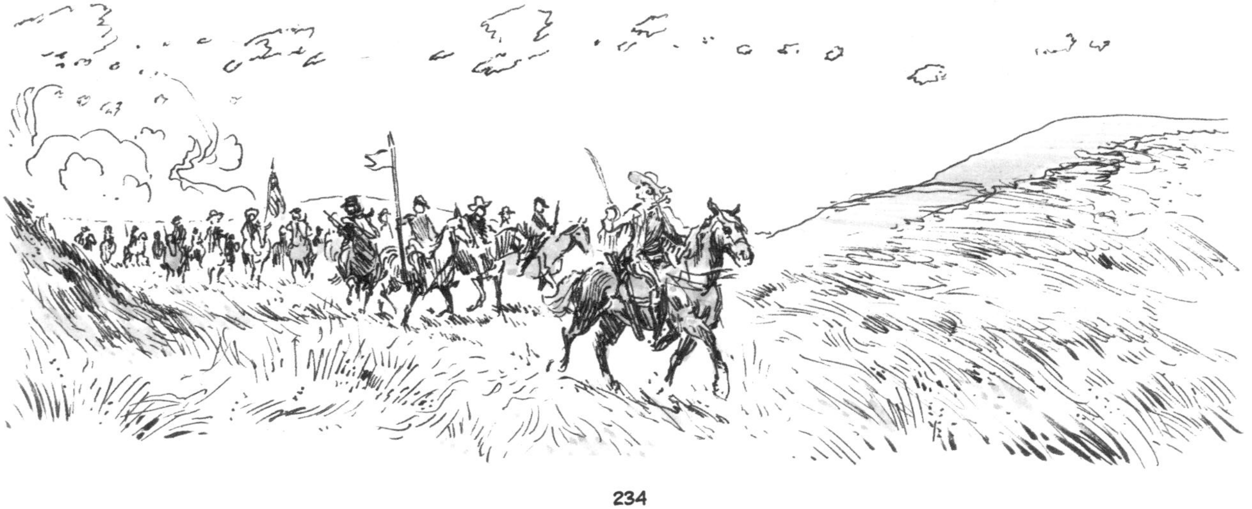

But Custer did not take into account the determination of the Sioux and Cheyenne...

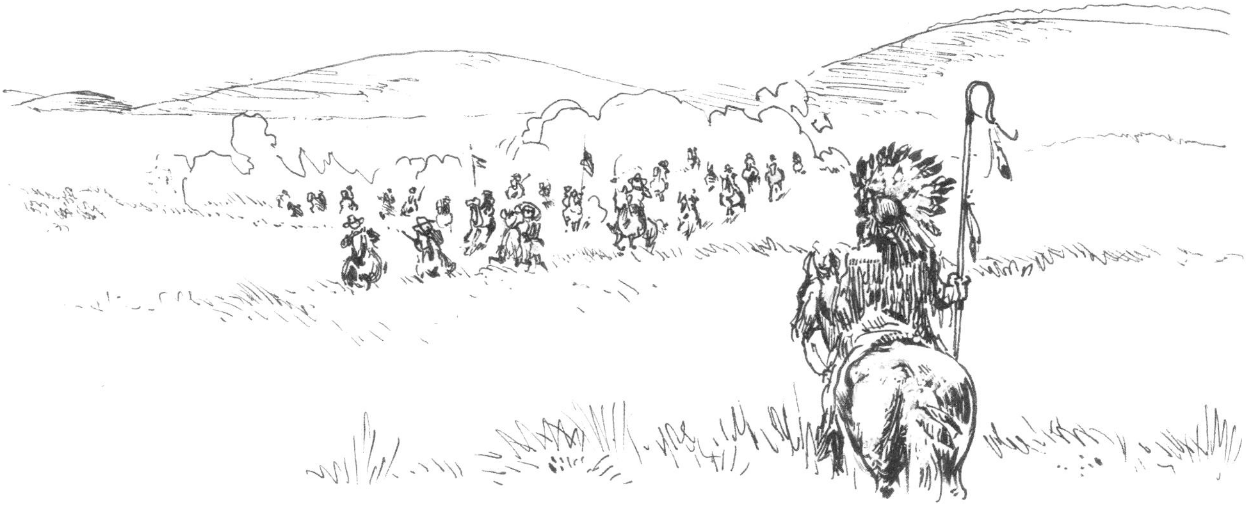

When the young warriors charged into battle, engaging in man-to-man combat, it was the end of Custer and his 265 men. Quickly overwhelmed, they vainly attempted to regroup on a hilltop...

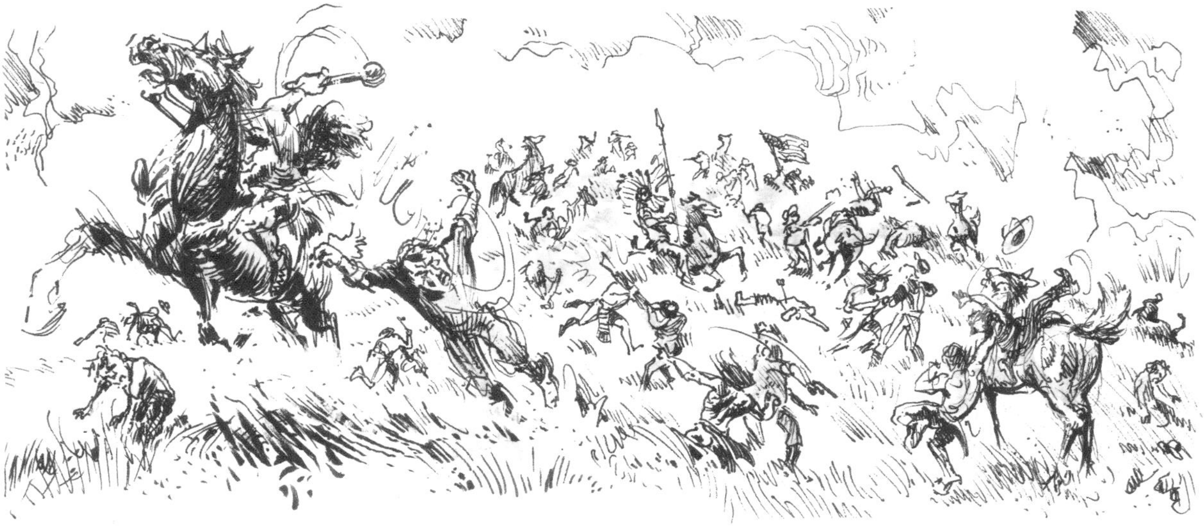

"At the end, it was total chaos. The Indians' horses mowed down the soldiers, trampling them. The adversaries were so close to one another that the soldiers could not take aim. They simply fired at random with no time to reload." *

The Sioux lost 66 men that day, and the Cheyenne only seven or perhaps a few more. The warrior who killed George Armstrong Custer remains unknown to this day.

* From *Cheyenne Memories* by John Stands In Timber, 1967.

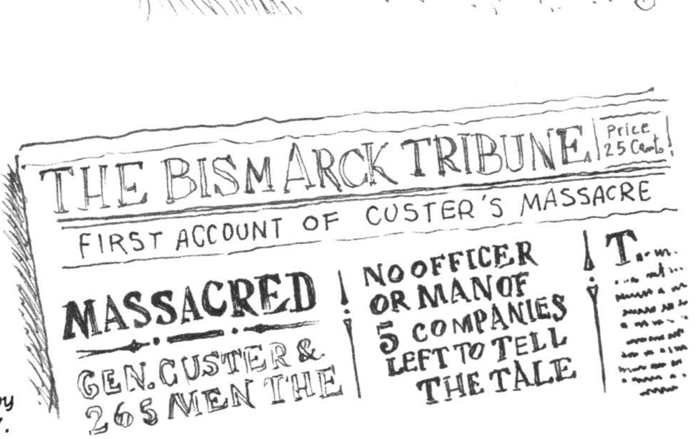
THE BISMARCK TRIBUNE
Price 25 Cents
FIRST ACCOUNT OF CUSTER'S MASSACRE
MASSACRED
GEN. CUSTER & 265 MEN THE
NO OFFICER OR MAN OF 5 COMPANIES LEFT TO TELL THE TALE

As for Calamity Jane, if she did indeed accompany the 7th Cavalry to the Little Bighorn, she had to turn back the night before the battle, due to a bout of pneumonia.

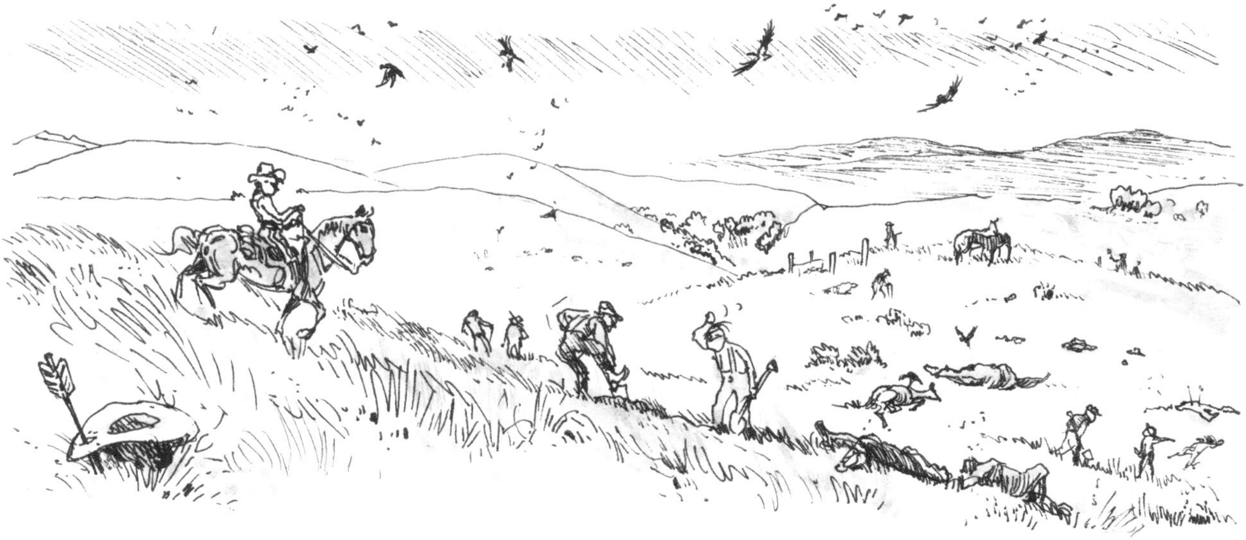

I went to the battlefield after Custer's Last Stand, and I never want to see such a horrifying sight again... The squaws had dismembered the soldiers' corpses, cut off their heads, and torn out their eyes.

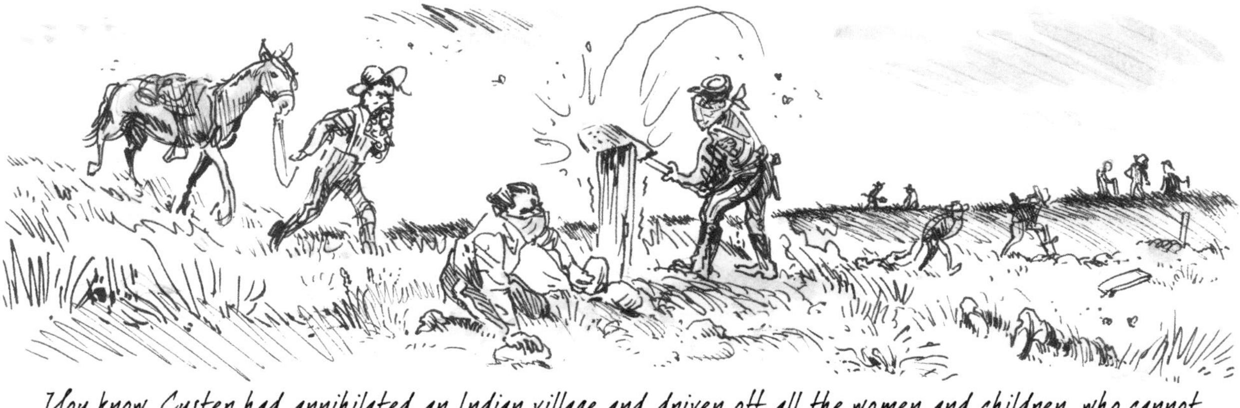

You know, Custer had annihilated an Indian village and driven off all the women and children, who cannot be blamed for taking their vengeance. Your Uncle Cy was in that battle, Janey. I found him in pieces, his head in one spot, his arms and legs elsewhere. I dug a grave, wrapped his remains in a saddle blanket, and buried him.

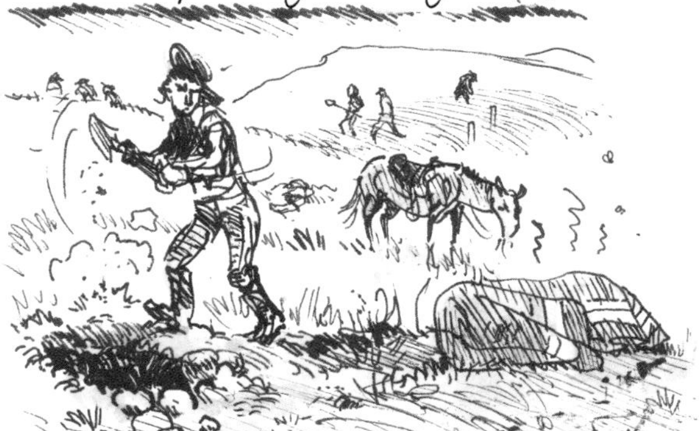

I cannot think of him without crying. *

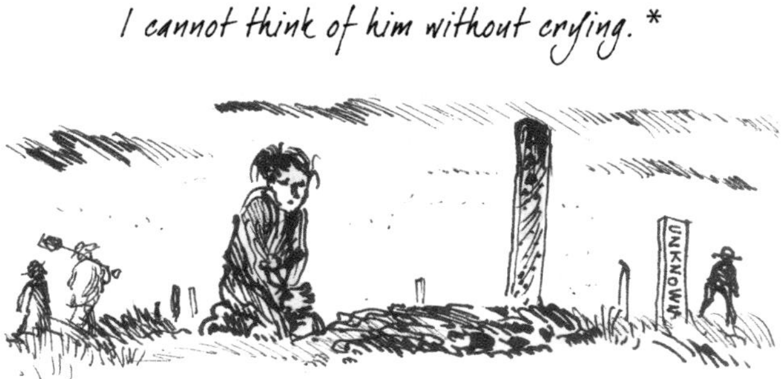
UNKNOWN

* From *Letters to Her Daughter* by Calamity Jane.

News of Custer's death was regarded as a great tragedy, and this sealed the fate of the Plains Indians:

"After the battle, the Indians separated into hunting parties. It was a good summer for most, but they didn't know that it would be their last summer of freedom, that the whites would not rest until all the Indians were hoarded onto reserves." *

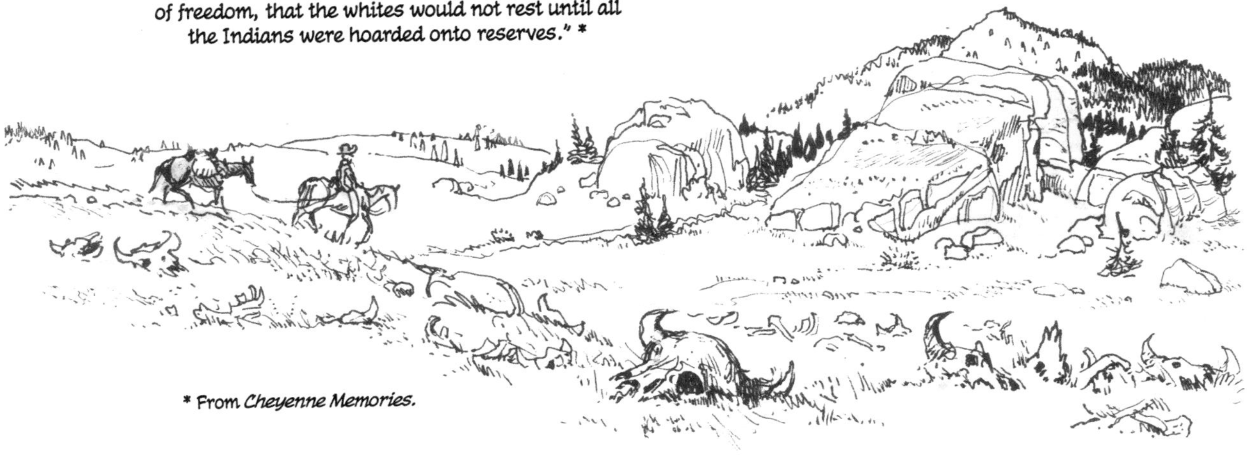

* From *Cheyenne Memories.*

Meanwhile, the number of prospectors' camps in the Black Hills grew daily. Some even became small towns. One has remained renowned because of its reputation as the most lawless and dangerous in all the West:

DEADWOOD.

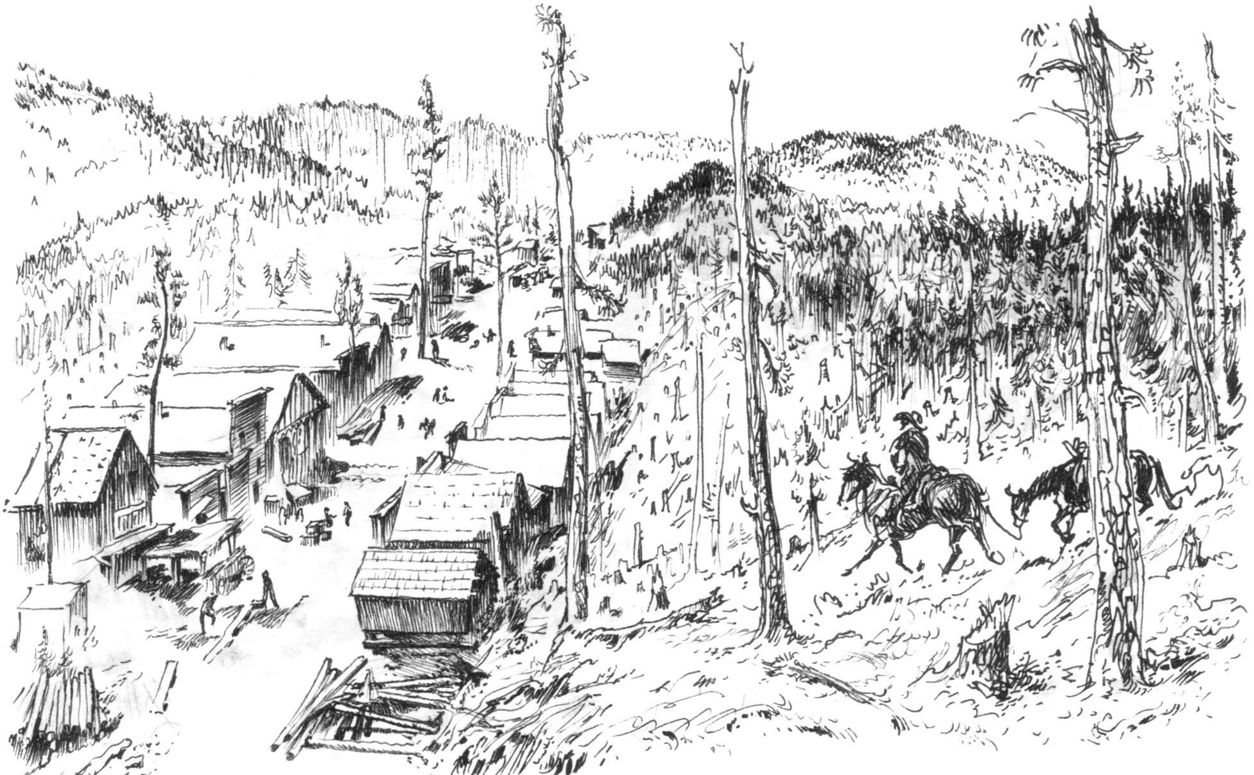

Calamity Jane settled in Deadwood in early July 1876. A certain individual had set up summer quarters there in order to fleece any lucky prospectors. That individual was **Wild Bill Hickok.**

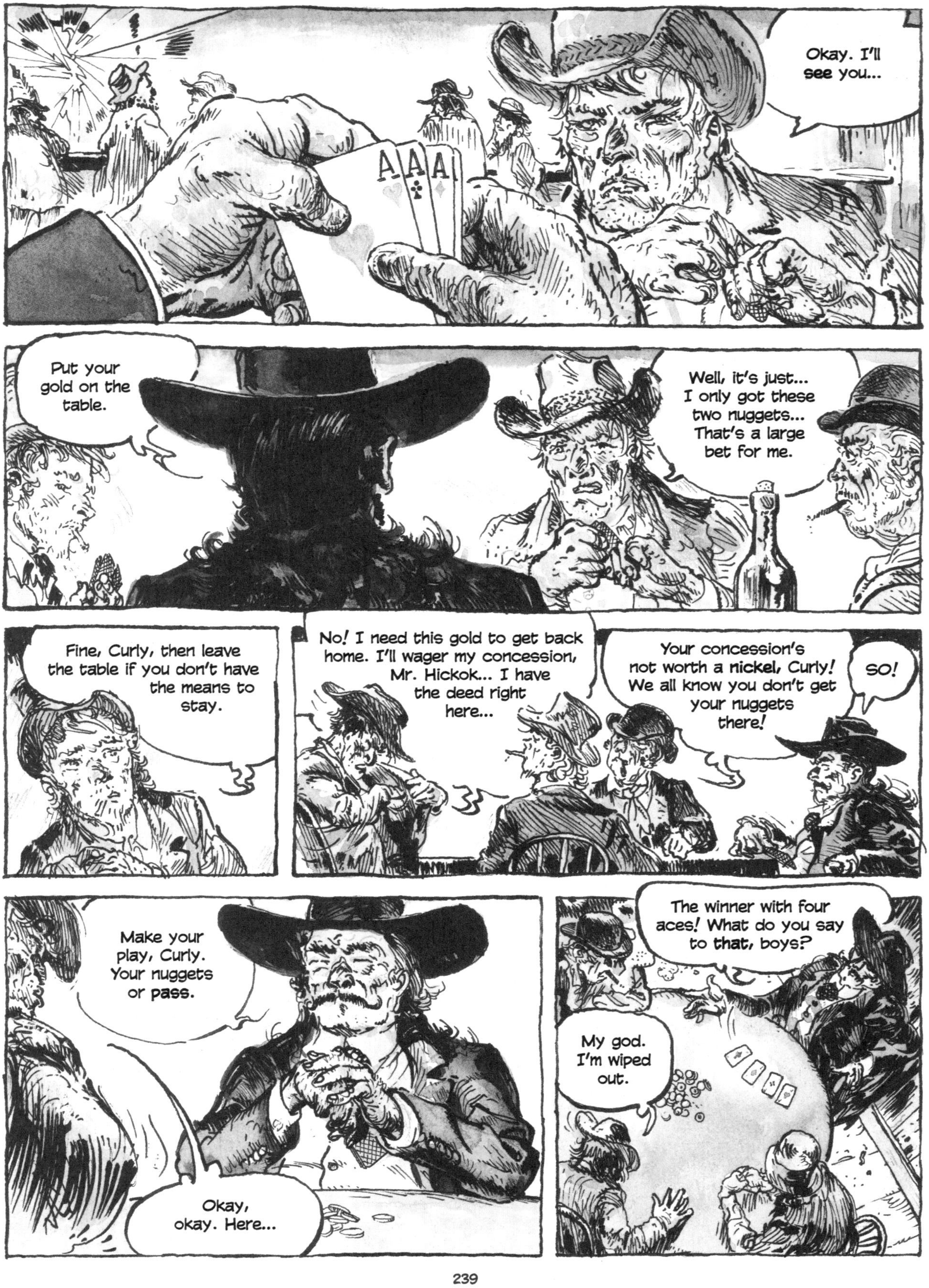

Okay. I'll see you...
Put your gold on the table.
Well, it's just... I only got these two nuggets... That's a large bet for me.
Fine, Curly, then leave the table if you don't have the means to stay.
No! I need this gold to get back home. I'll wager my concession, Mr. Hickok... I have the deed right here...
Your concession's not worth a nickel, Curly! We all know you don't get your nuggets there!
SO!
Make your play, Curly. Your nuggets or pass.
Okay, okay. Here...
The winner with four aces! What do you say to that, boys?
My god. I'm wiped out.

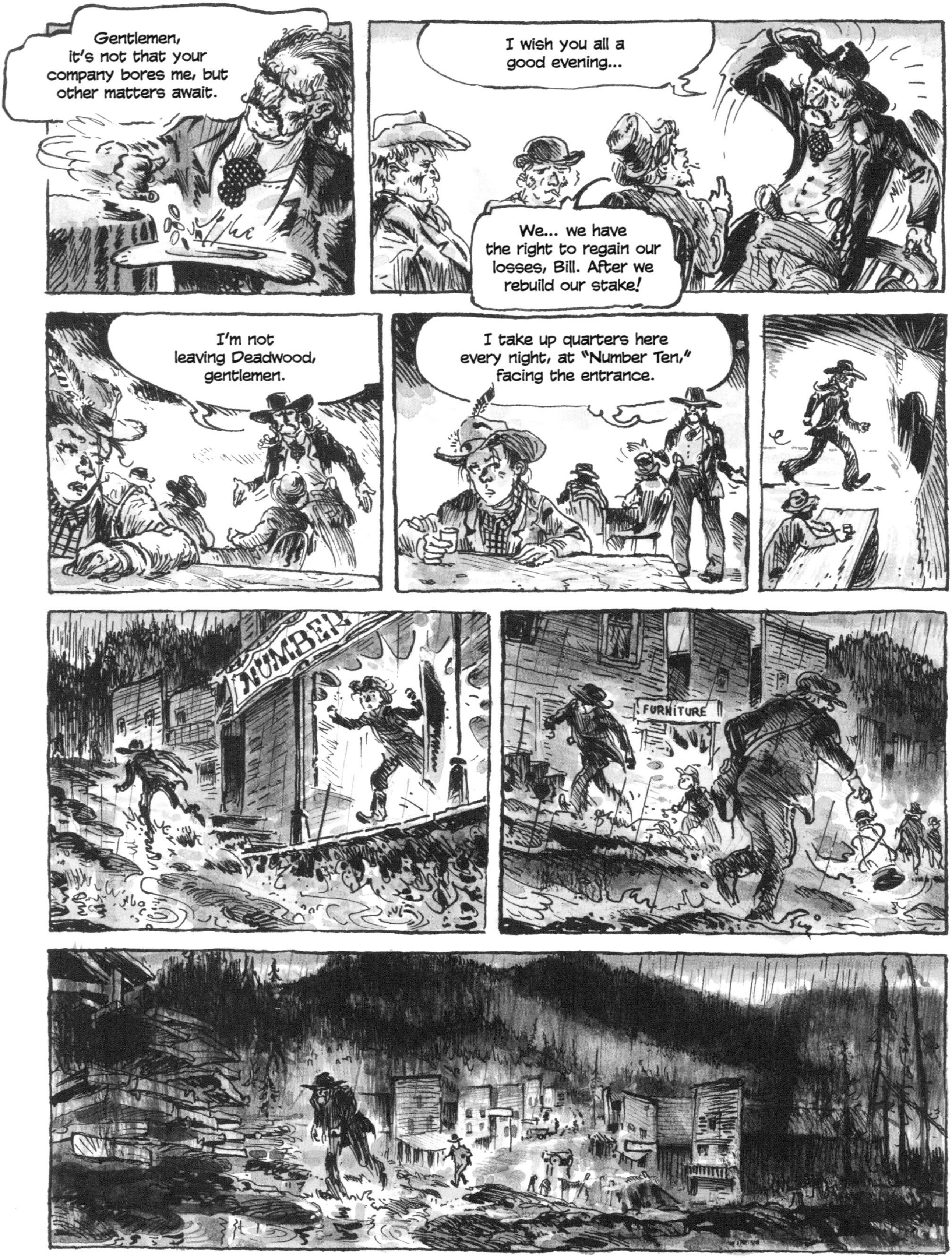
Gentlemen, it's not that your company bores me, but other matters await.
I wish you all a good evening...
We... we have the right to regain our losses, Bill. After we rebuild our stake!
I'm not leaving Deadwood, gentlemen.
I take up quarters here every night, at "Number Ten," facing the entrance.
NUMBER
FURNITURE

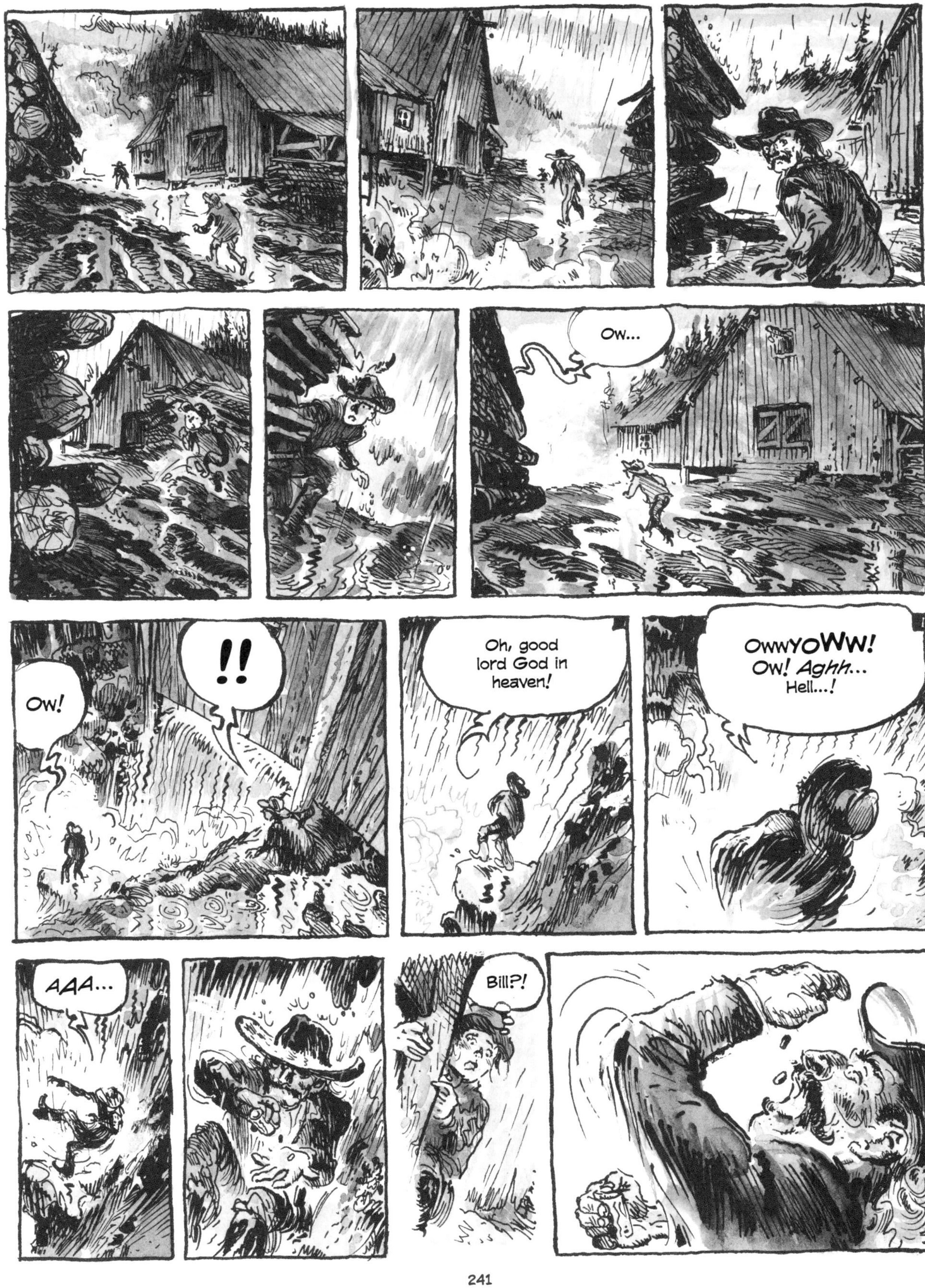
Ow...
Ow!
!!
Oh, good lord God in heaven!
OwwYOWW! Ow! Aghh... Hell...!
AAA...
Bill?!

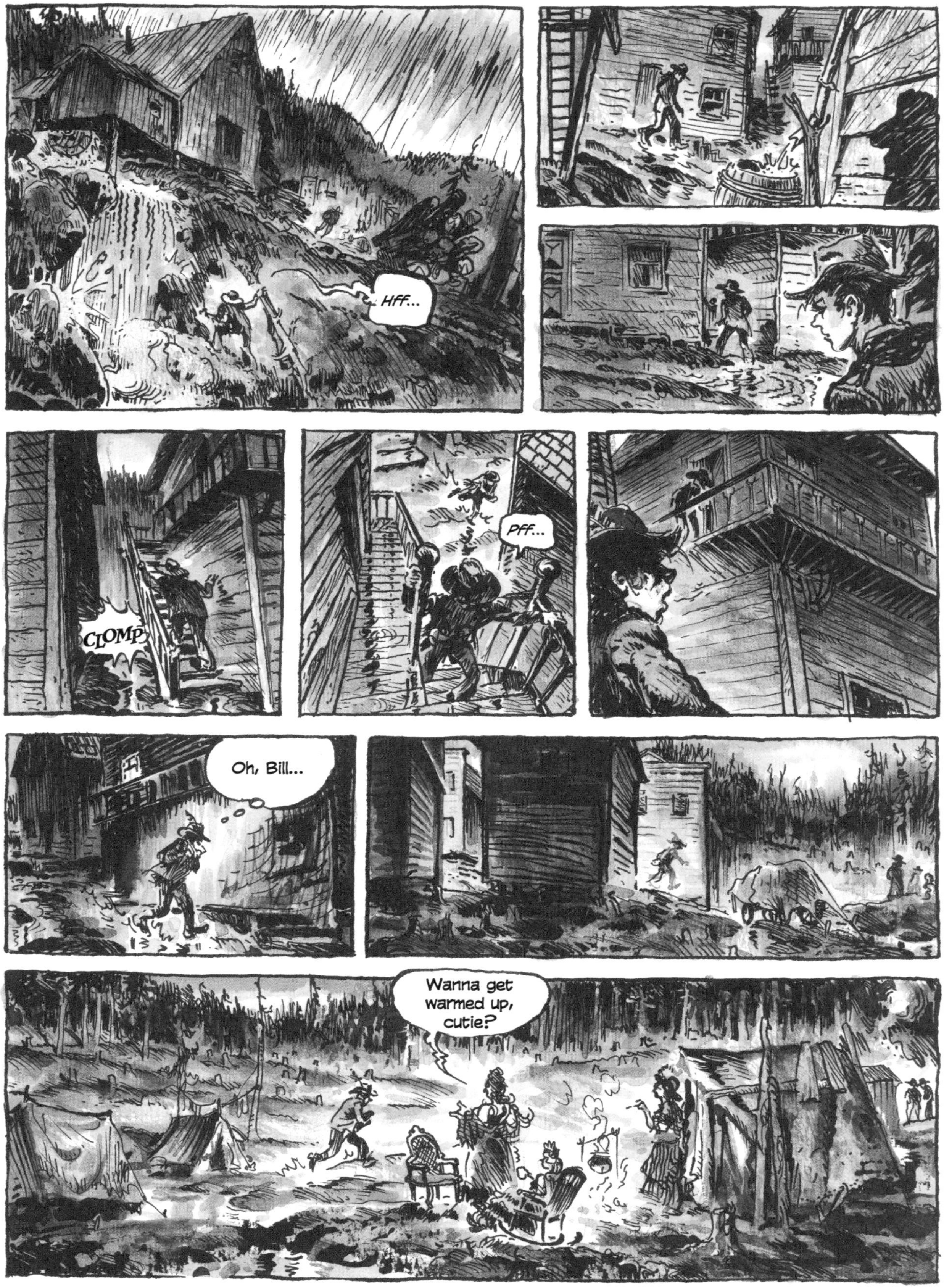
Hff...
CLOMP
Pff...
Oh, Bill...
Wanna get warmed up, cutie?

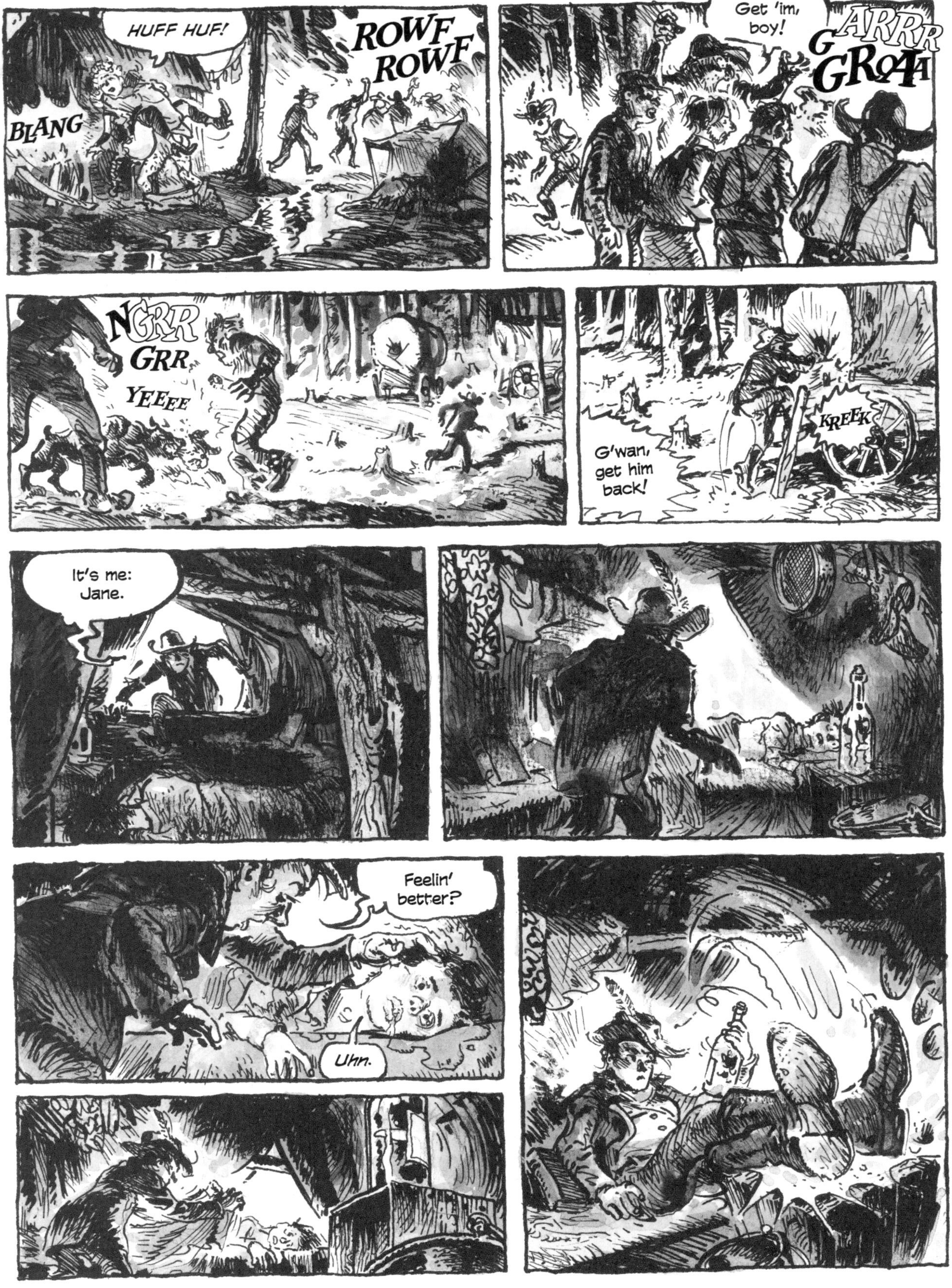
HUFF HUF!
BLANG
ROWF ROWF
Get 'im, boy!
GARRR
GROAA
NGRR
GRR
YEEEE
KREEK
G'wan, get him back!
It's me: Jane.
Feelin' better?
Uhn.

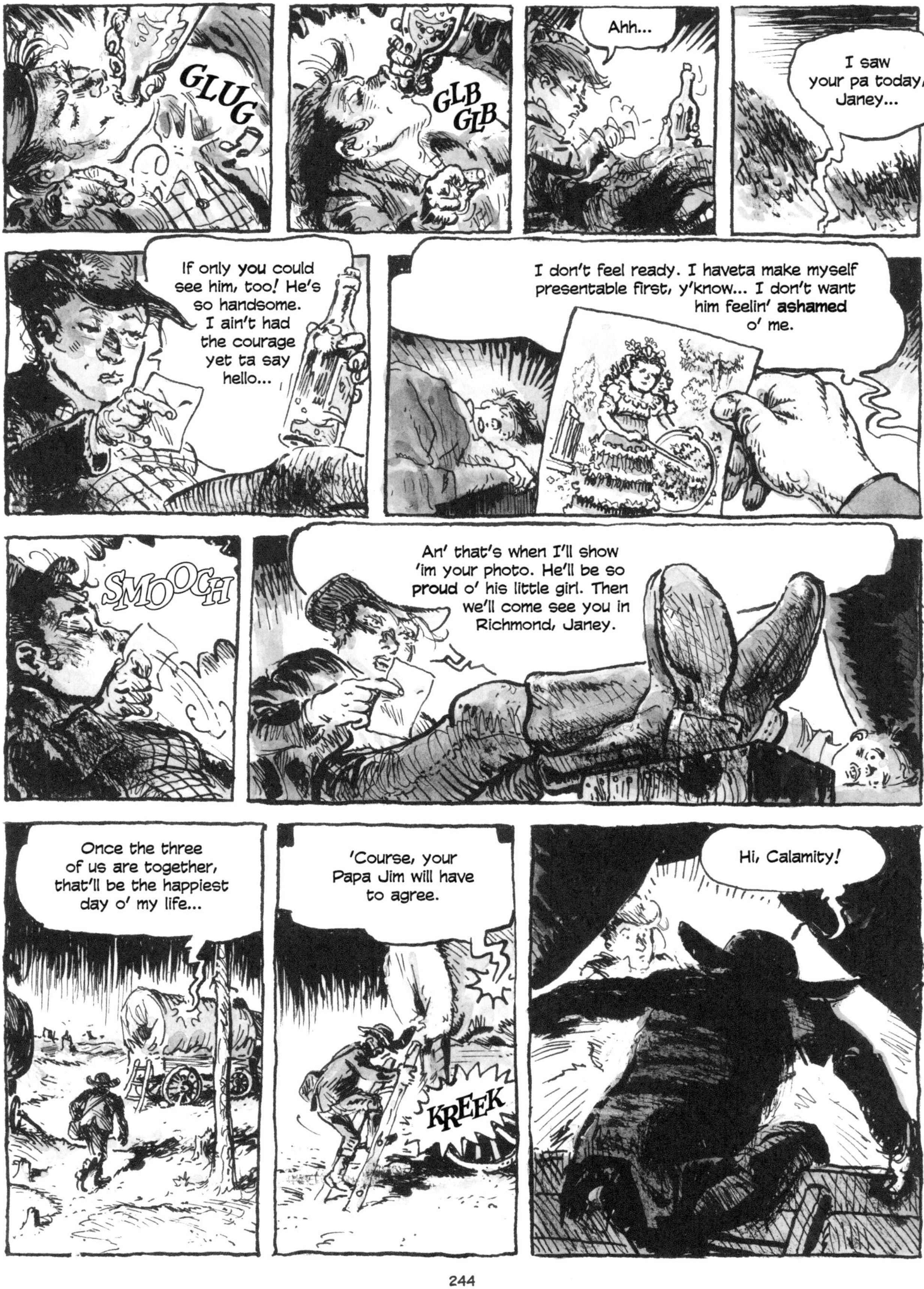
GLUG
GLB GLB
Ahh...
I saw your pa today, Janey...
If only **you** could see him, too! He's so handsome. I ain't had the courage yet ta say hello...
I don't feel ready. I haveta make myself presentable first, y'know... I don't want him feelin' **ashamed** o' me.
SMOOCH
An' that's when I'll show 'im your photo. He'll be so **proud** o' his little girl. Then we'll come see you in Richmond, Janey.
Once the three of us are together, that'll be the happiest day o' my life...
'Course, your Papa Jim will have to agree.
KREEK
Hi, Calamity!

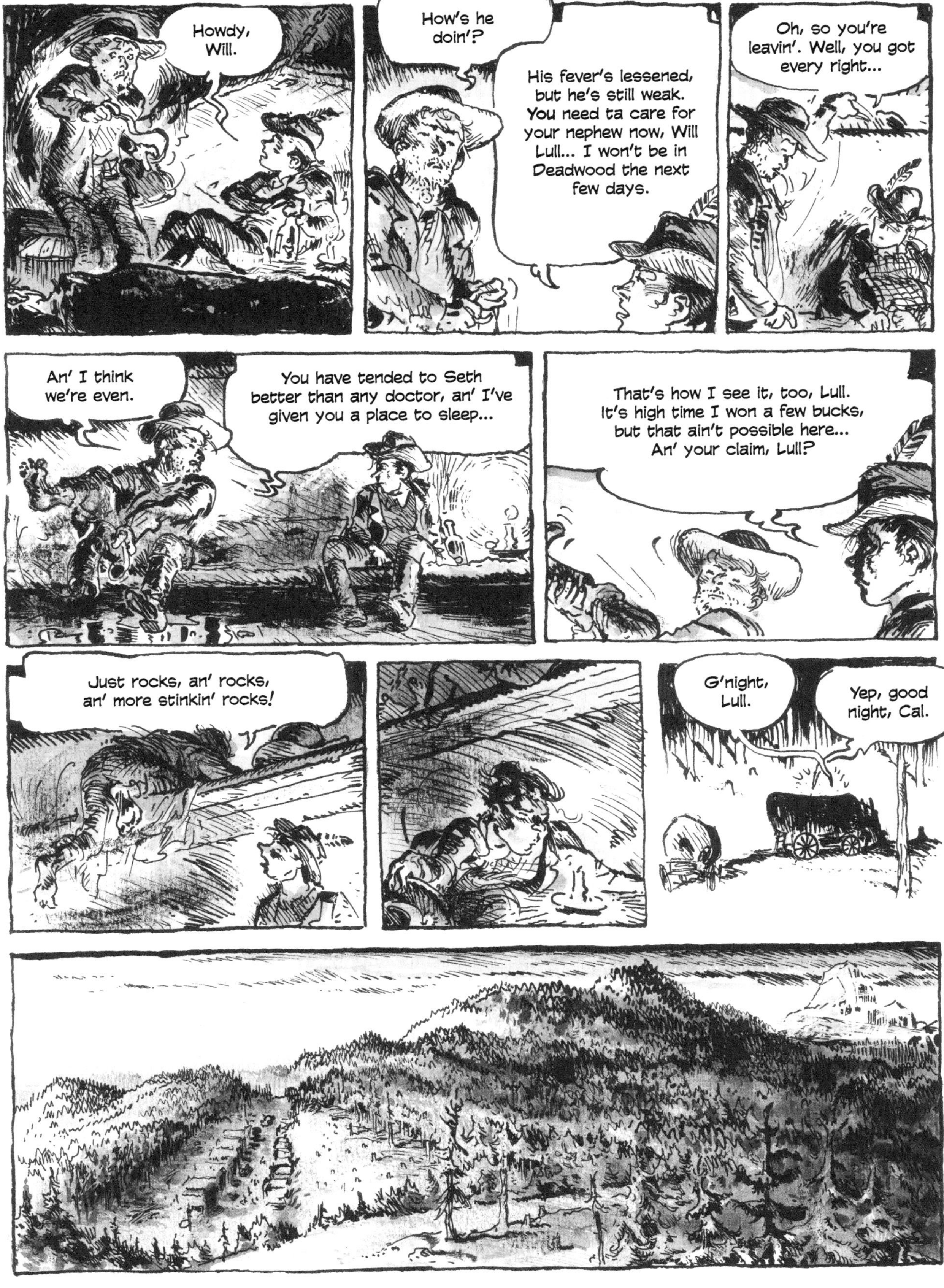

Howdy, Will.
How's he doin'?
His fever's lessened, but he's still weak. You need ta care for your nephew now, Will Lull... I won't be in Deadwood the next few days.
Oh, so you're leavin'. Well, you got every right...
An' I think we're even.
You have tended to Seth better than any doctor, an' I've given you a place to sleep...
That's how I see it, too, Lull. It's high time I won a few bucks, but that ain't possible here... An' your claim, Lull?
Just rocks, an' rocks, an' more stinkin' rocks!
G'night, Lull.
Yep, good night, Cal.

In *Letters to her Daughter,* Martha Jane claims to have been Wild Bill's partner at cards that summer. A fantasy on her part? Hickok was certainly a pro, whereas Jane was not. Not yet...

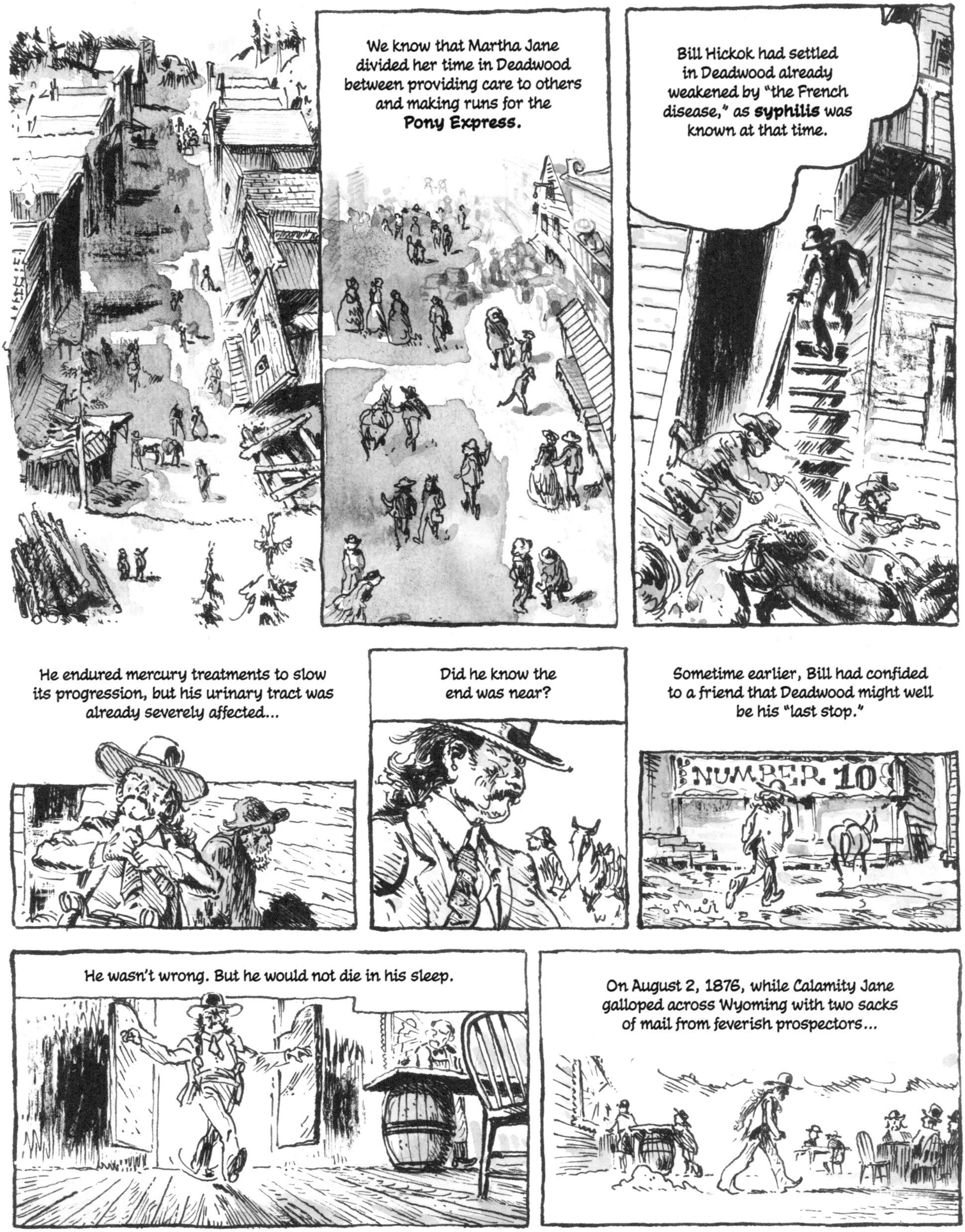

We know that Martha Jane divided her time in Deadwood between providing care to others and making runs for the **Pony Express.**
Bill Hickok had settled in Deadwood already weakened by "the French disease," as **syphilis** was known at that time.
He endured mercury treatments to slow its progression, but his urinary tract was already severely affected...
Did he know the end was near?
Sometime earlier, Bill had confided to a friend that Deadwood might well be his "last stop."
NUMBER 10
He wasn't wrong. But he would not die in his sleep.
On August 2, 1876, while Calamity Jane galloped across Wyoming with two sacks of mail from feverish prospectors...

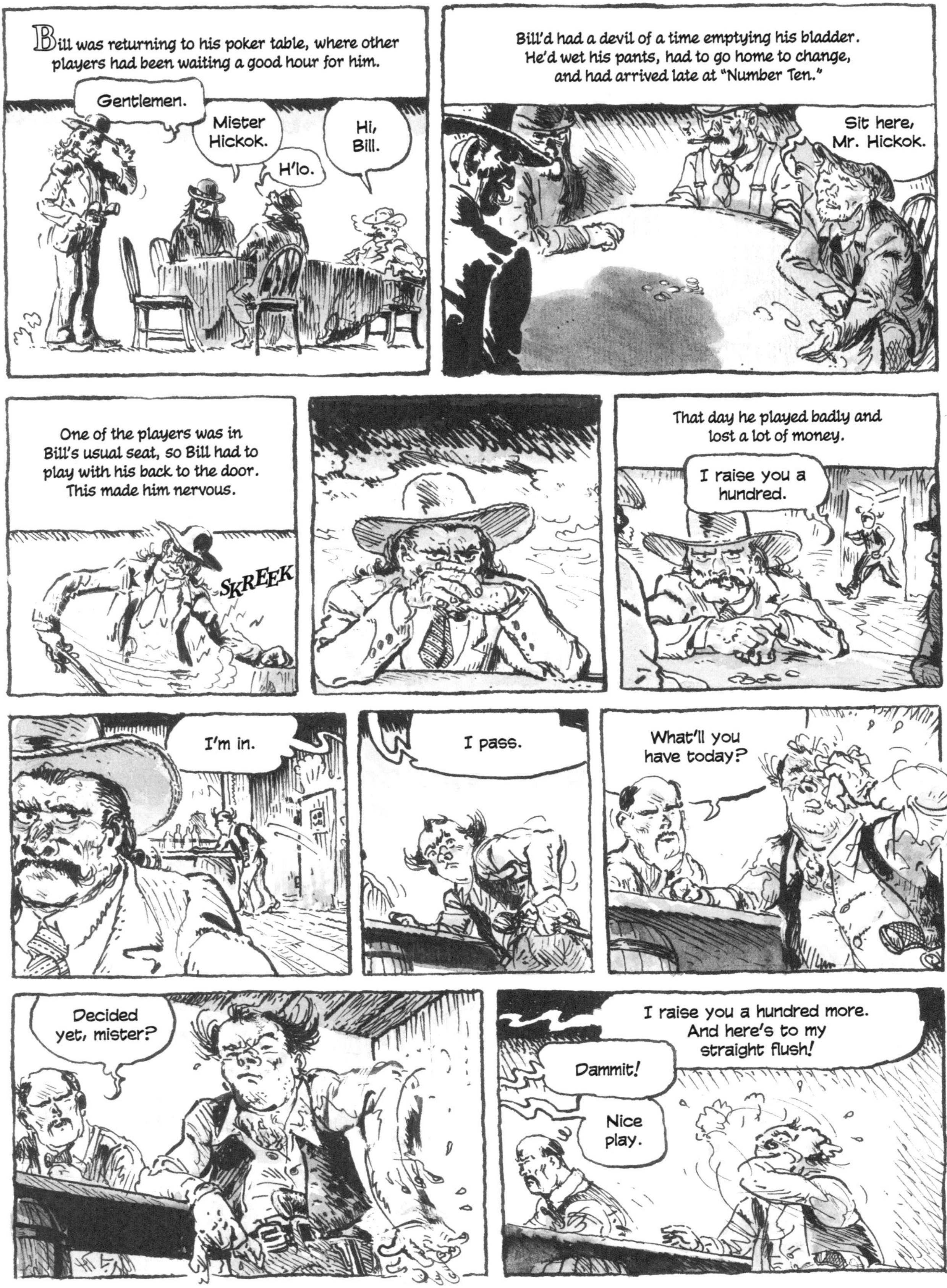

Bill was returning to his poker table, where other players had been waiting a good hour for him.
Gentlemen.
Mister Hickok.
H'lo.
Hi, Bill.
Bill'd had a devil of a time emptying his bladder. He'd wet his pants, had to go home to change, and had arrived late at "Number Ten."
Sit here, Mr. Hickok.
One of the players was in Bill's usual seat, so Bill had to play with his back to the door. This made him nervous.
SKREEK
That day he played badly and lost a lot of money.
I raise you a hundred.
I'm in.
I pass.
What'll you have today?
Decided yet, mister?
I raise you a hundred more. And here's to my straight flush!
Dammit!
Nice play.

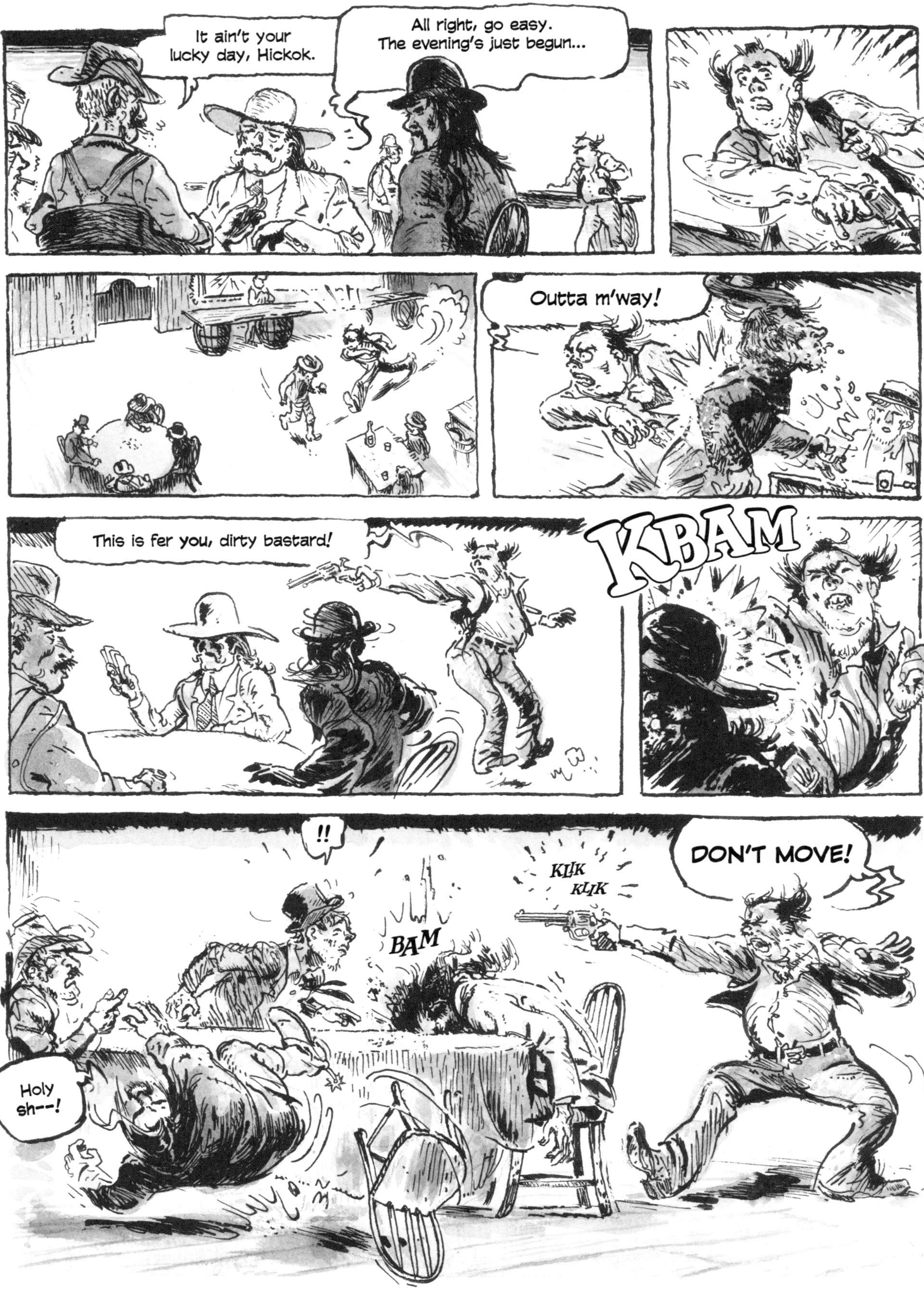

It ain't your lucky day, Hickok.
All right, go easy. The evening's just begun...
Outta m'way!
This is fer you, dirty bastard!
KBAM
!!
BAM
KLIK KLIK
DON'T MOVE!
Holy sh--!

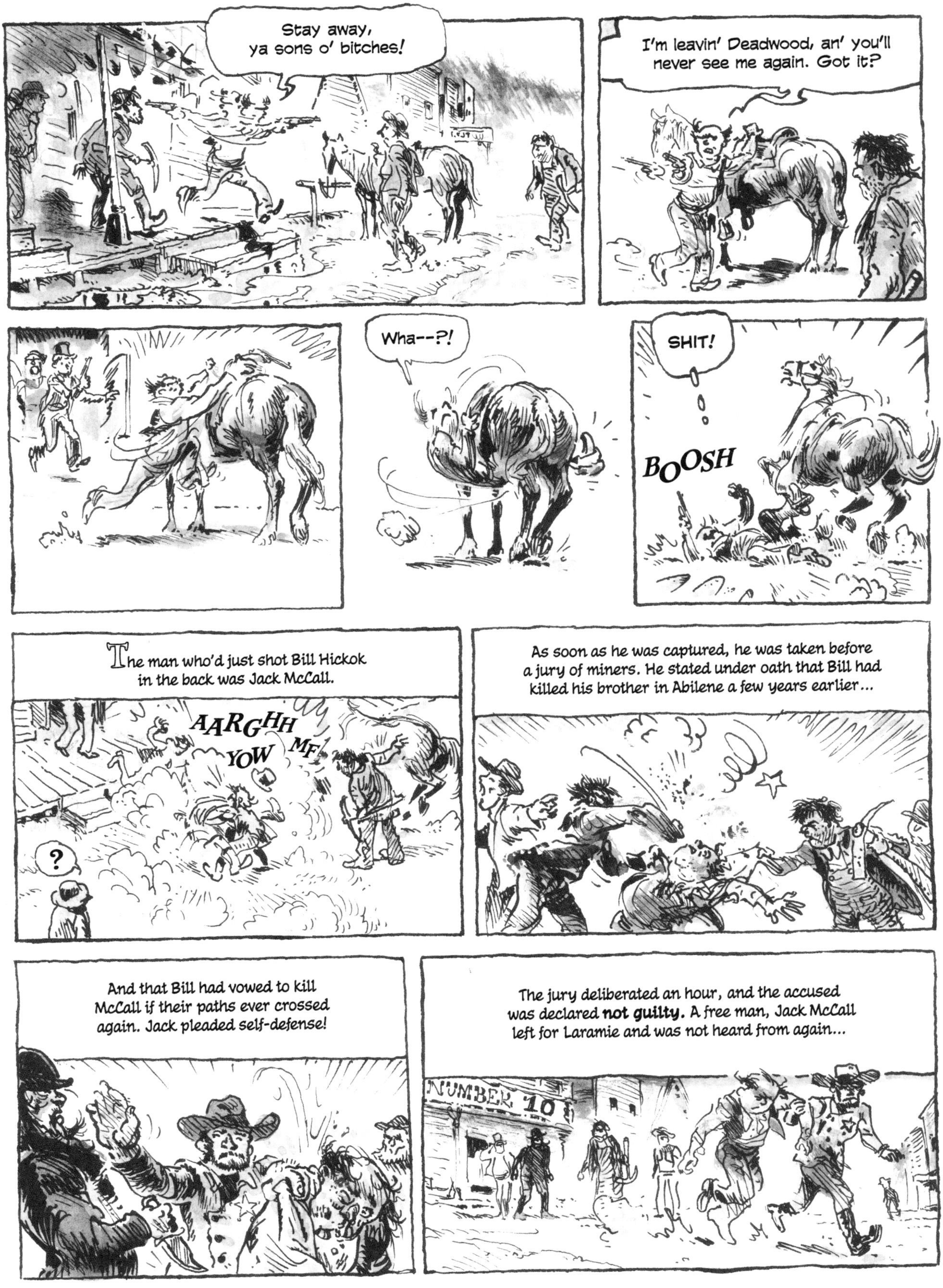

Stay away, ya sons o' bitches!
I'm leavin' Deadwood, an' you'll never see me again. Got it?
Wha--?!
SHIT!
BOOSH
The man who'd just shot Bill Hickok in the back was Jack McCall.
AARGHH
YOW
MF
?
As soon as he was captured, he was taken before a jury of miners. He stated under oath that Bill had killed his brother in Abilene a few years earlier...
And that Bill had vowed to kill McCall if their paths ever crossed again. Jack pleaded self-defense!
The jury deliberated an hour, and the accused was declared **not guilty.** A free man, Jack McCall left for Laramie and was not heard from again...
NUMBER 10

Bill Hickok was buried on Friday, August 8, 1876. Four hundred people attended the funeral of the West's most famous man. Not one shed a tear.

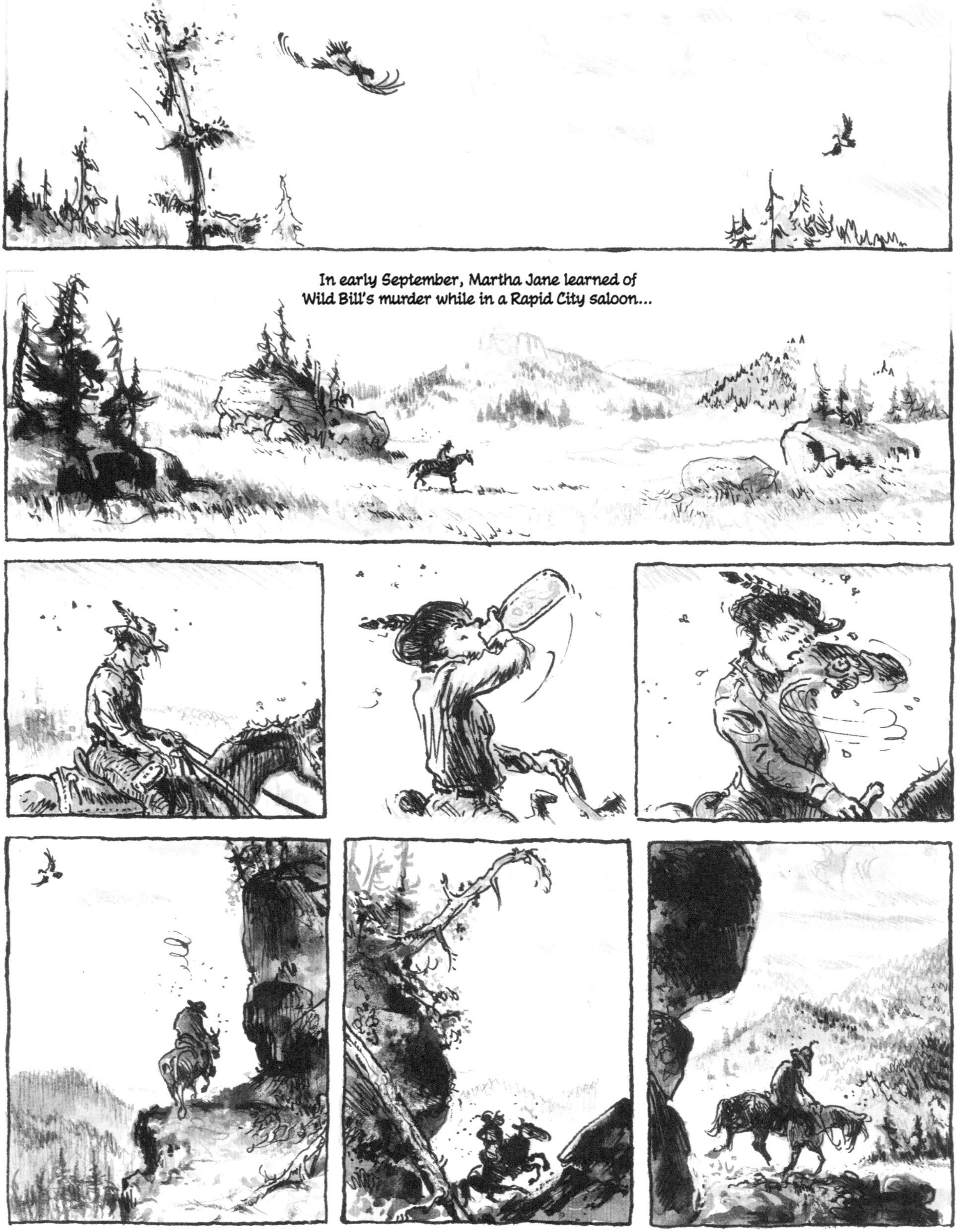
In early September, Martha Jane learned of Wild Bill's murder while in a Rapid City saloon...

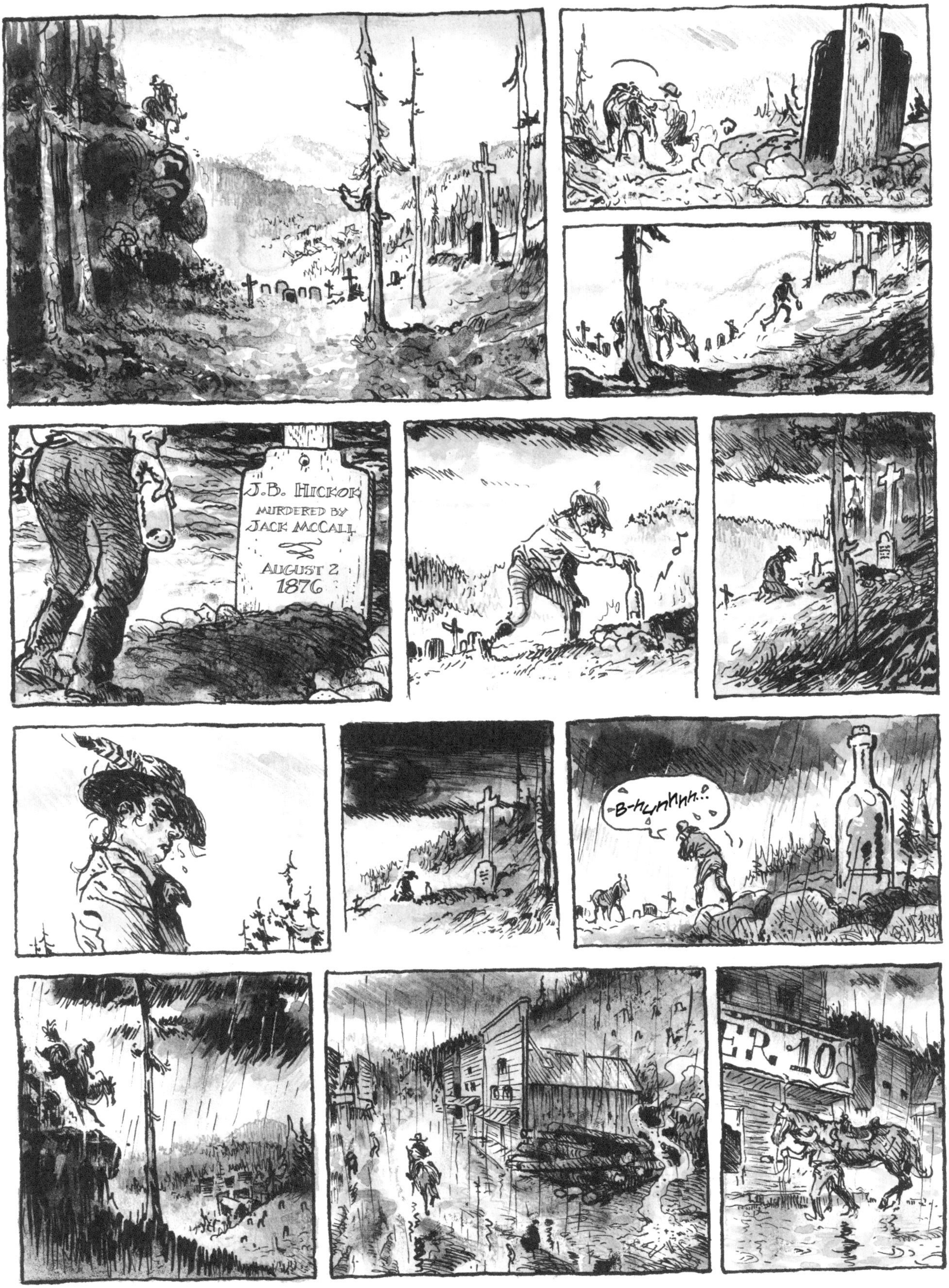
J.B. Hickok
Murdered by
Jack McCall
August 2
1876
B-hnnnnn..!

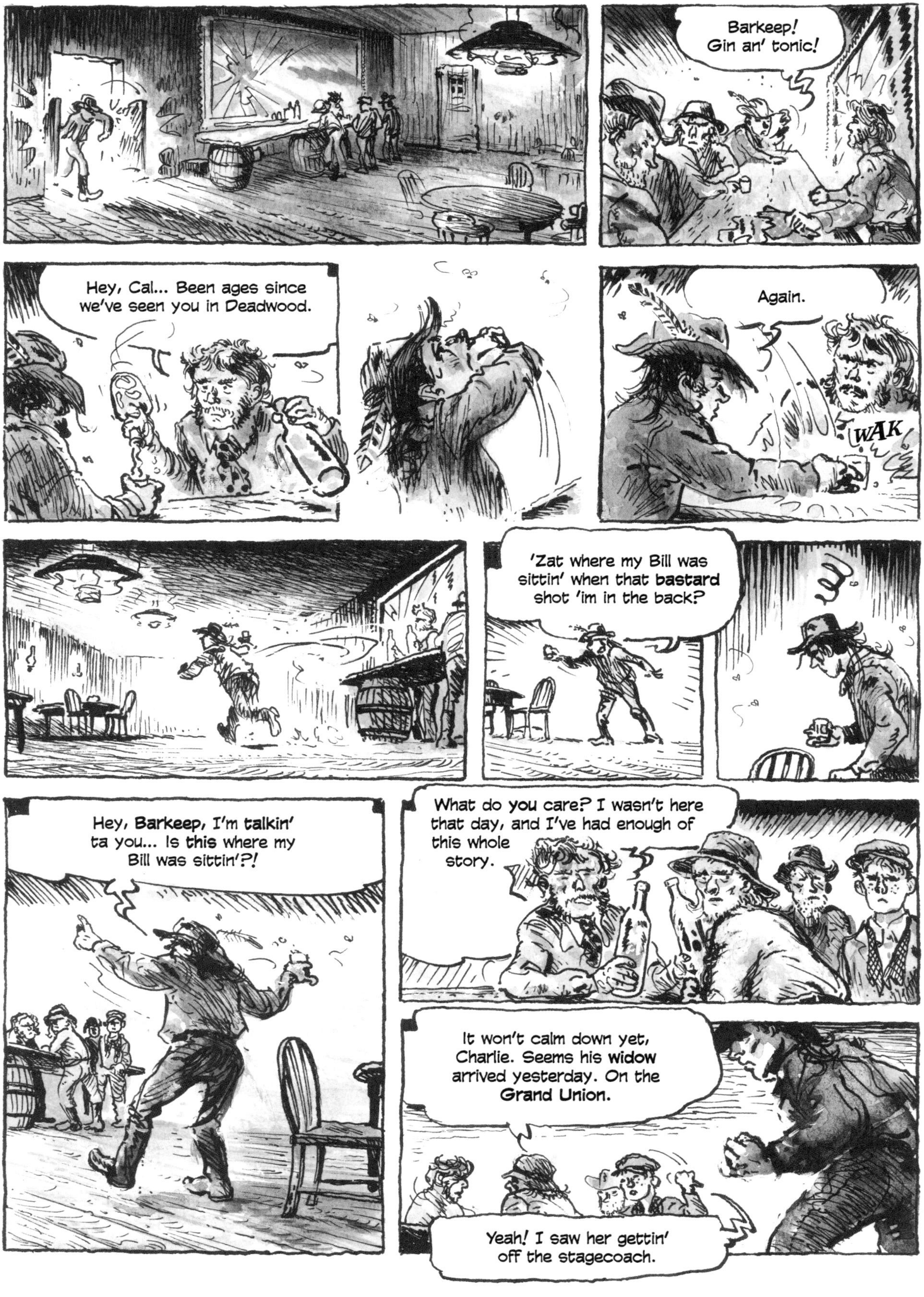
Barkeep! Gin an' tonic!
Hey, Cal... Been ages since we've seen you in Deadwood.
Again.
WAK
'Zat where my Bill was sittin' when that bastard shot 'im in the back?
Hey, Barkeep, I'm talkin' ta you... Is this where my Bill was sittin'?!
What do you care? I wasn't here that day, and I've had enough of this whole story.
It won't calm down yet, Charlie. Seems his widow arrived yesterday. On the Grand Union.
Yeah! I saw her gettin' off the stagecoach.

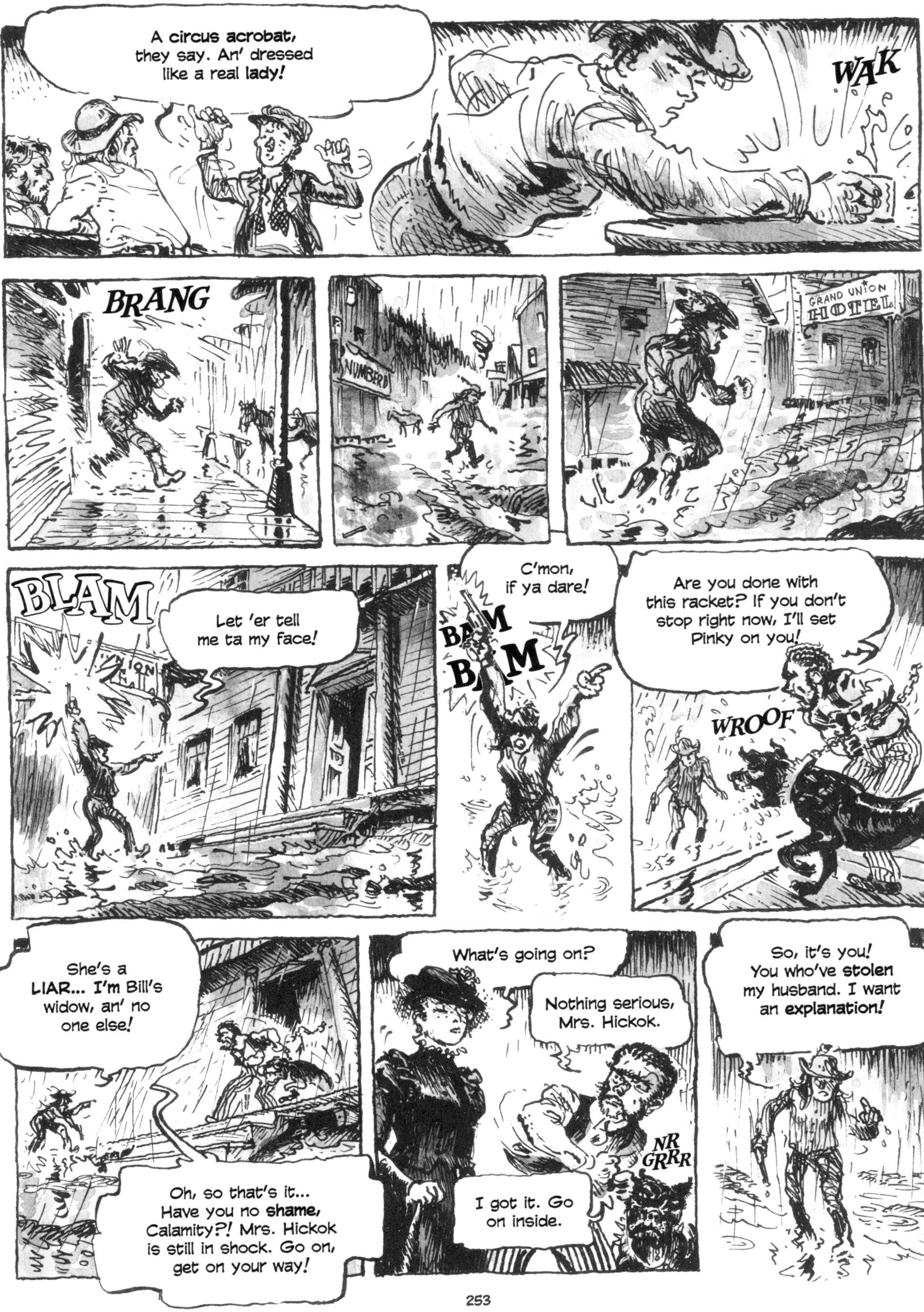
A circus acrobat, they say. An' dressed like a real lady!
WAK
BRANG
GRAND UNION HOTEL
BLAM
Let 'er tell me ta my face!
C'mon, if ya dare!
BAM
BAM
Are you done with this racket? If you don't stop right now, I'll set Pinky on you!
WROOF
She's a LIAR... I'm Bill's widow, an' no one else!
Oh, so that's it... Have you no shame, Calamity?! Mrs. Hickok is still in shock. Go on, get on your way!
What's going on?
Nothing serious, Mrs. Hickok.
NR GRRR
I got it. Go on inside.
So, it's you! You who've stolen my husband. I want an explanation!

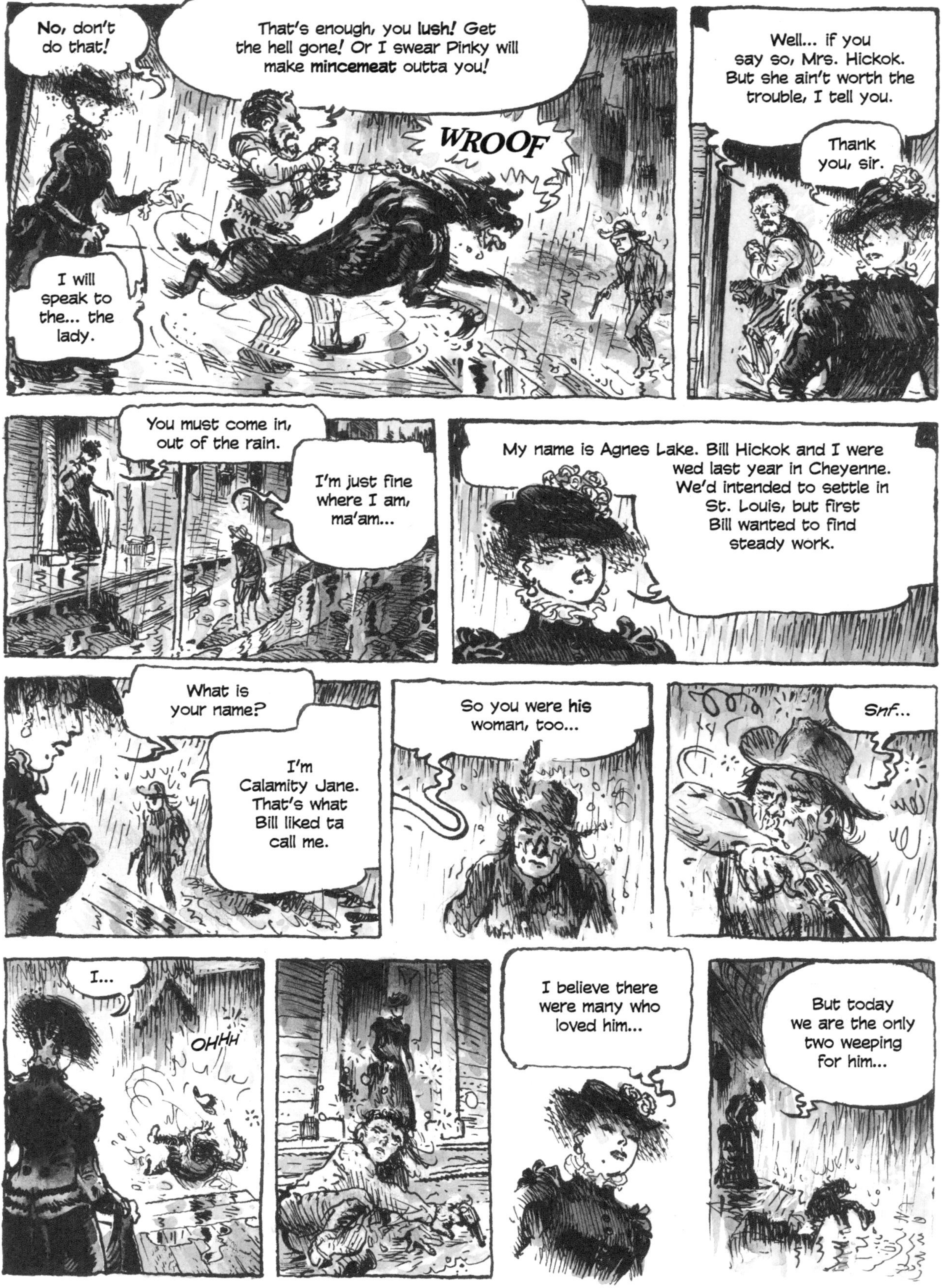
No, don't do that!
That's enough, you lush! Get the hell gone! Or I swear Pinky will make mincemeat outta you!
WROOF
I will speak to the... the lady.
Well... if you say so, Mrs. Hickok. But she ain't worth the trouble, I tell you.
Thank you, sir.
You must come in, out of the rain.
I'm just fine where I am, ma'am...
My name is Agnes Lake. Bill Hickok and I were wed last year in Cheyenne. We'd intended to settle in St. Louis, but first Bill wanted to find steady work.
What is your name?
I'm Calamity Jane. That's what Bill liked ta call me.
So you were his woman, too...
Snf...
I...
OHHH
I believe there were many who loved him...
But today we are the only two weeping for him...

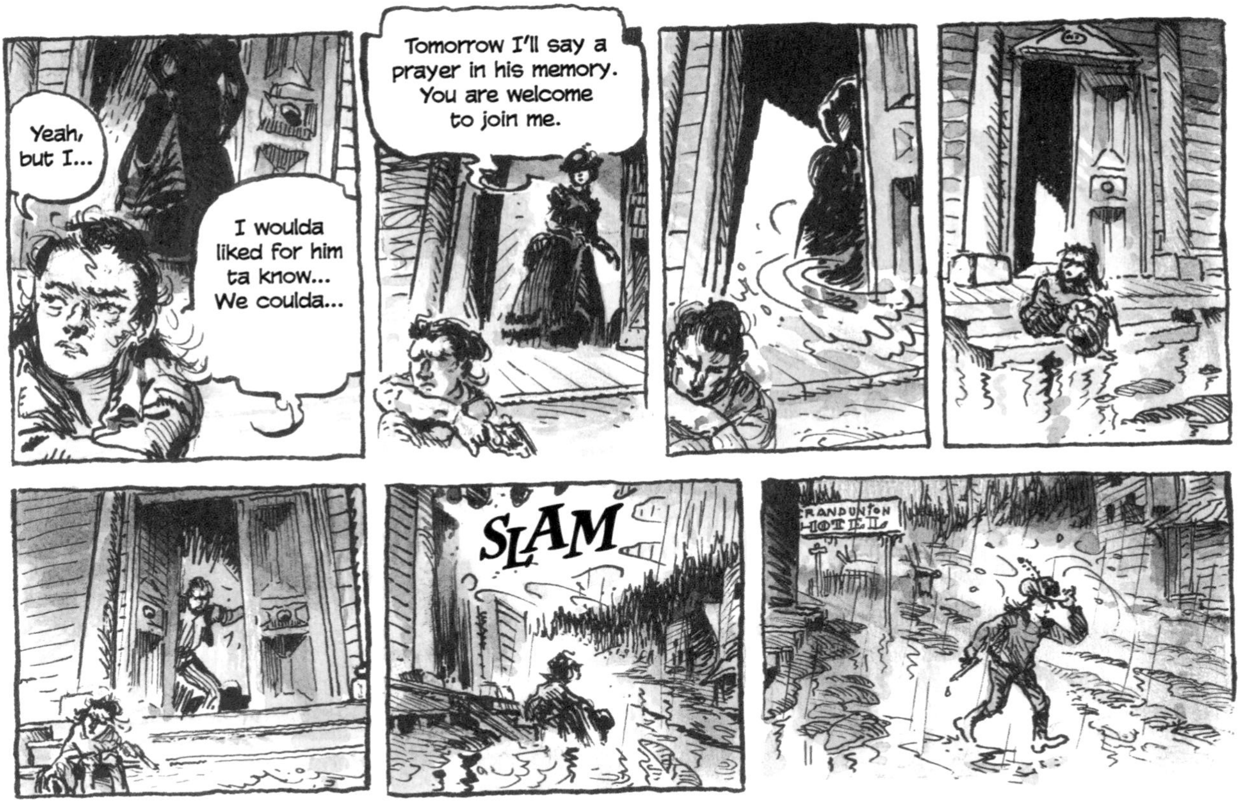
Yeah, but I...
I woulda liked for him ta know... We coulda...
Tomorrow I'll say a prayer in his memory. You are welcome to join me.
SLAM

Martha Jane did not attend the service the following day. That same night, she left for Cheyenne again with the prospectors' mail.

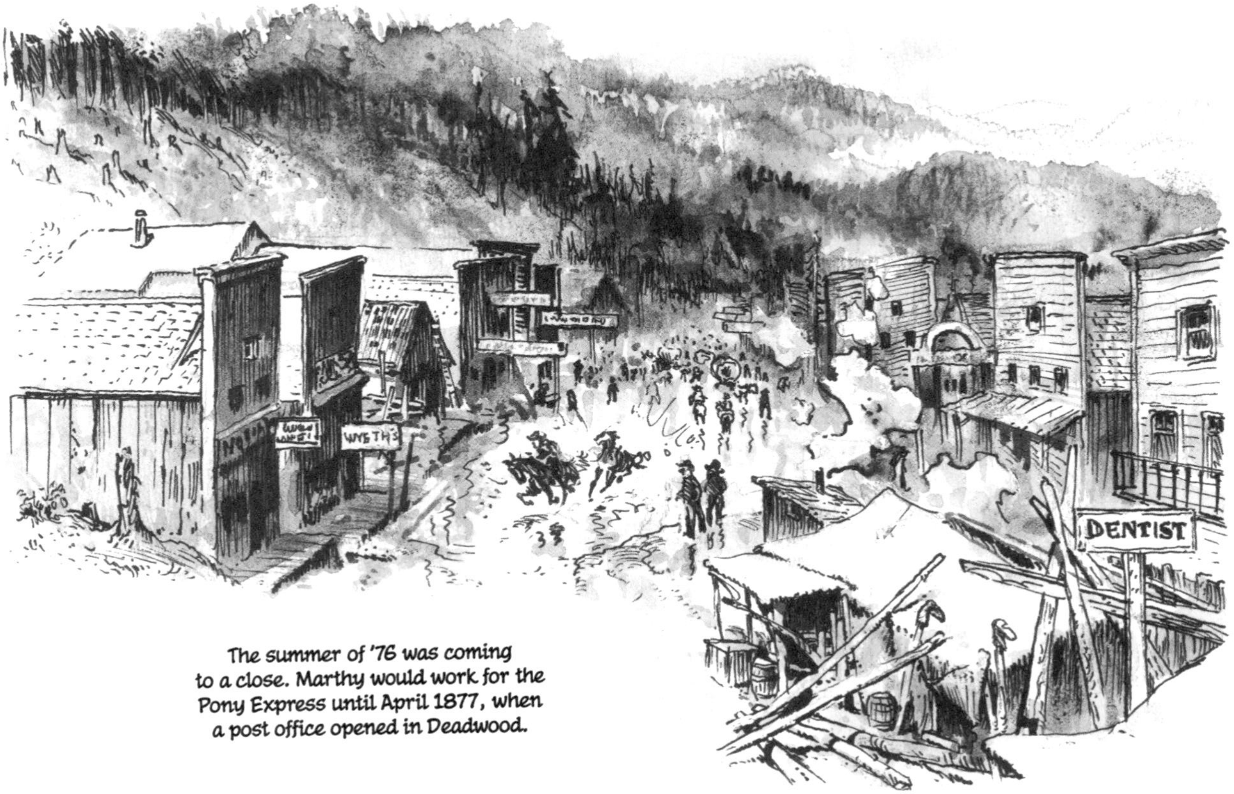
DENTIST
The summer of '76 was coming to a close. Marthy would work for the Pony Express until April 1877, when a post office opened in Deadwood.

Martha Jane Cannary
(1877~1903)

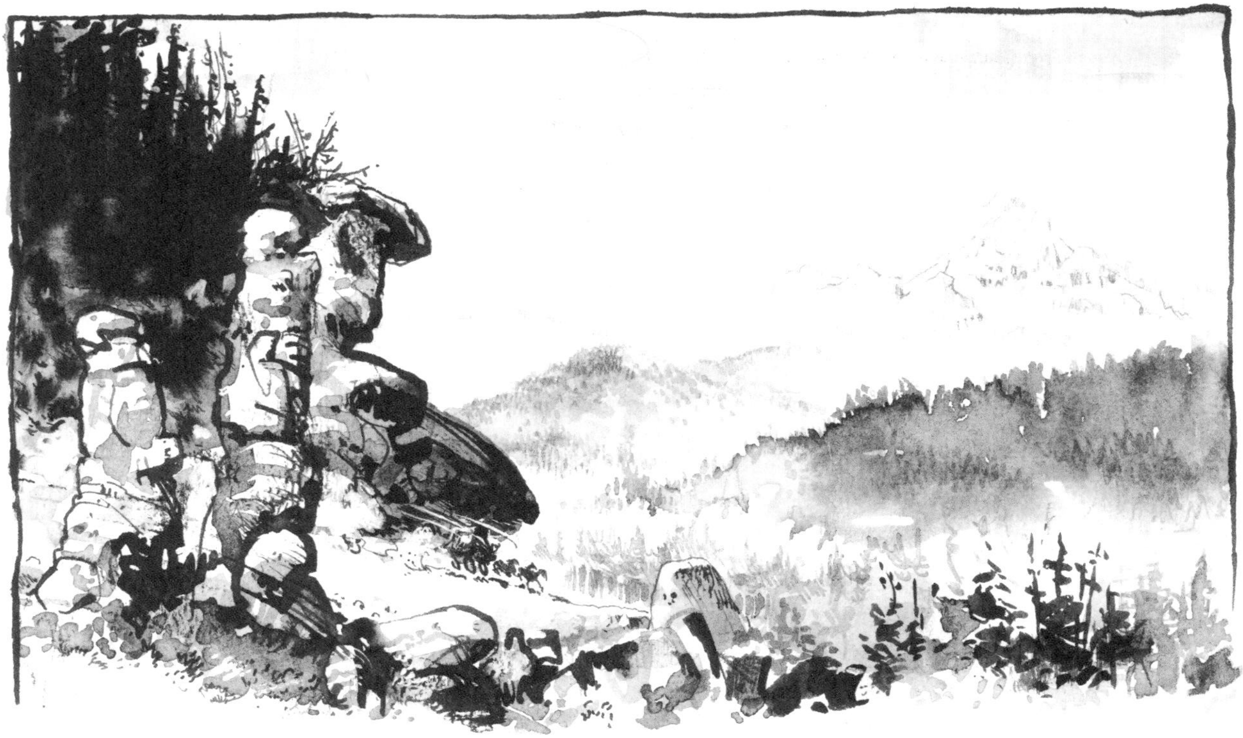

This stagecoach belongs to Wells Fargo. It runs from Cheyenne to Deadwood -- some 250 miles -- in about fifty hours.

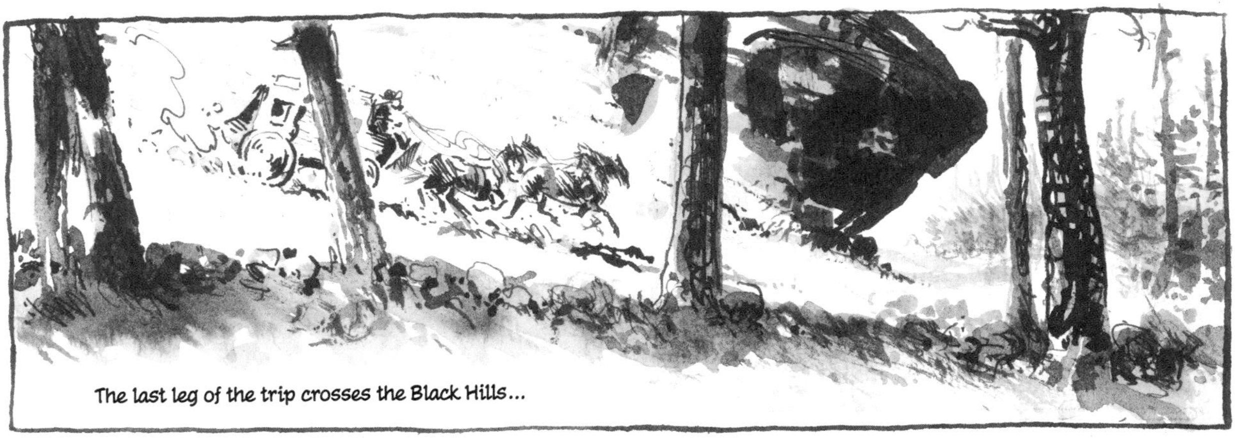

The last leg of the trip crosses the Black Hills...

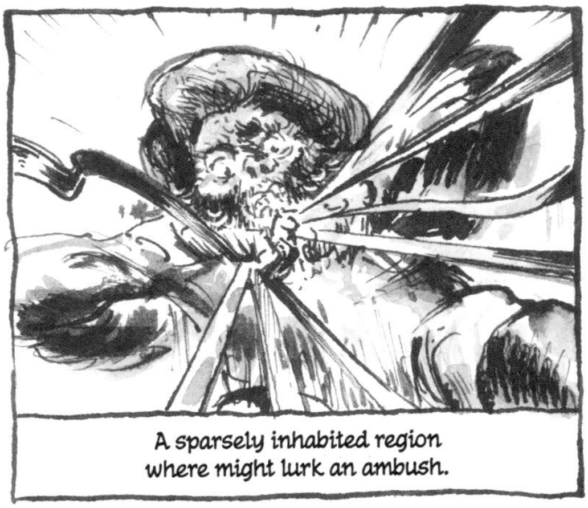

A sparsely inhabited region
where might lurk an ambush.

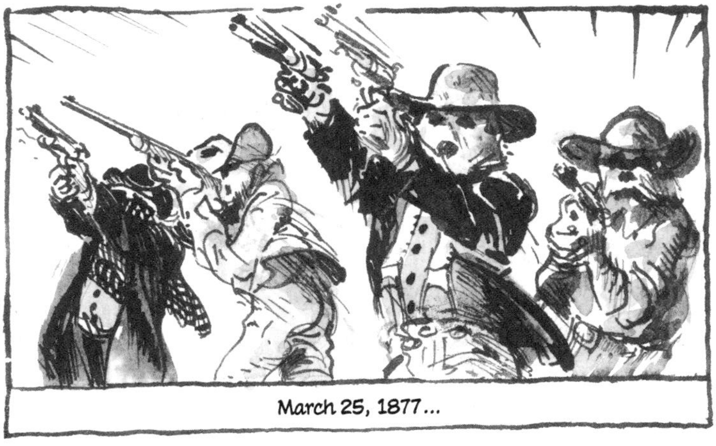

March 25, 1877...

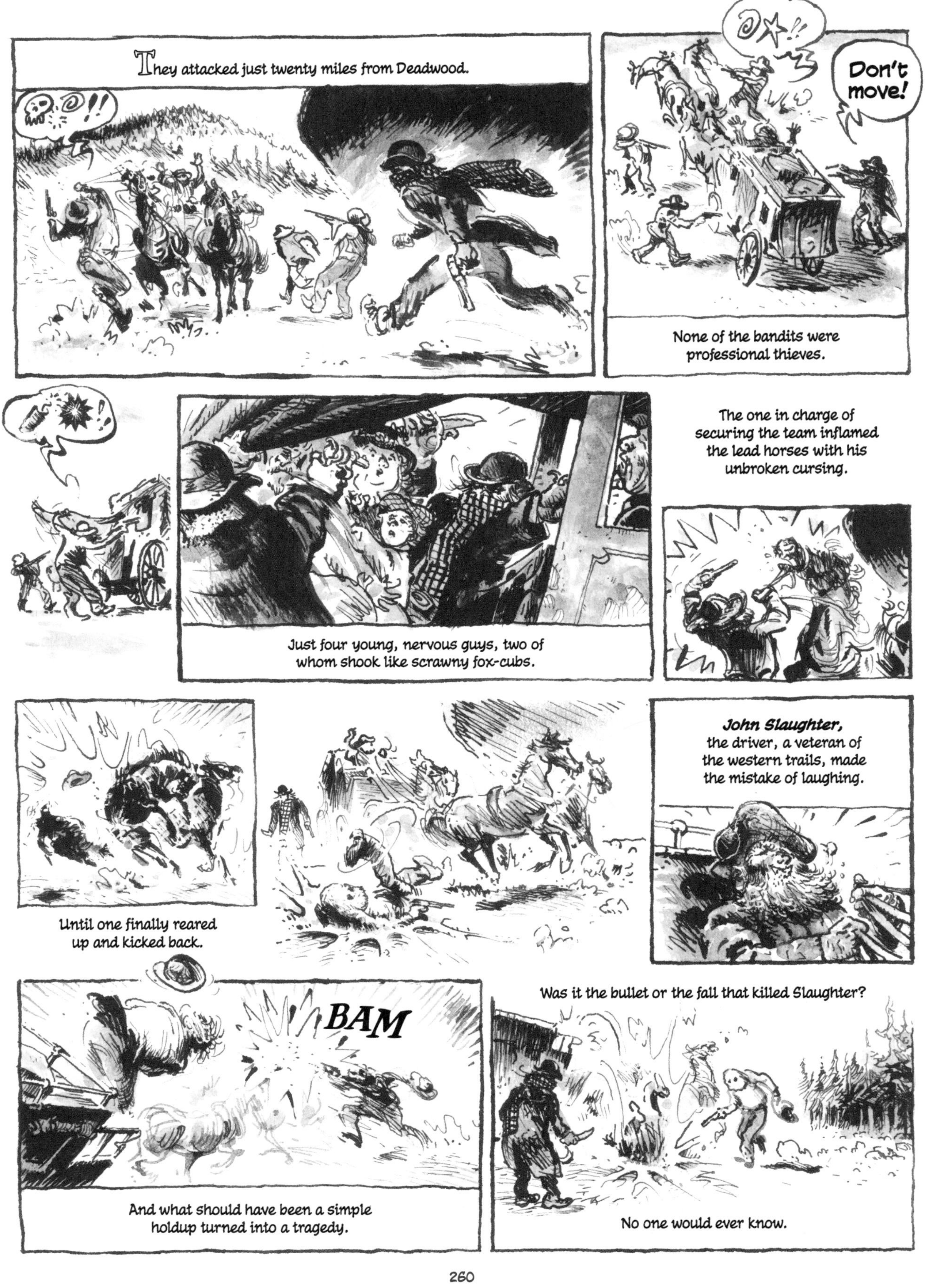
They attacked just twenty miles from Deadwood.
!!
Don't move!
!!
None of the bandits were professional thieves.
!
Just four young, nervous guys, two of whom shook like scrawny fox-cubs.
The one in charge of securing the team inflamed the lead horses with his unbroken cursing.
Until one finally reared up and kicked back.
John Slaughter, the driver, a veteran of the western trails, made the mistake of laughing.
BAM
And what should have been a simple holdup turned into a tragedy.
Was it the bullet or the fall that killed Slaughter?
No one would ever know.

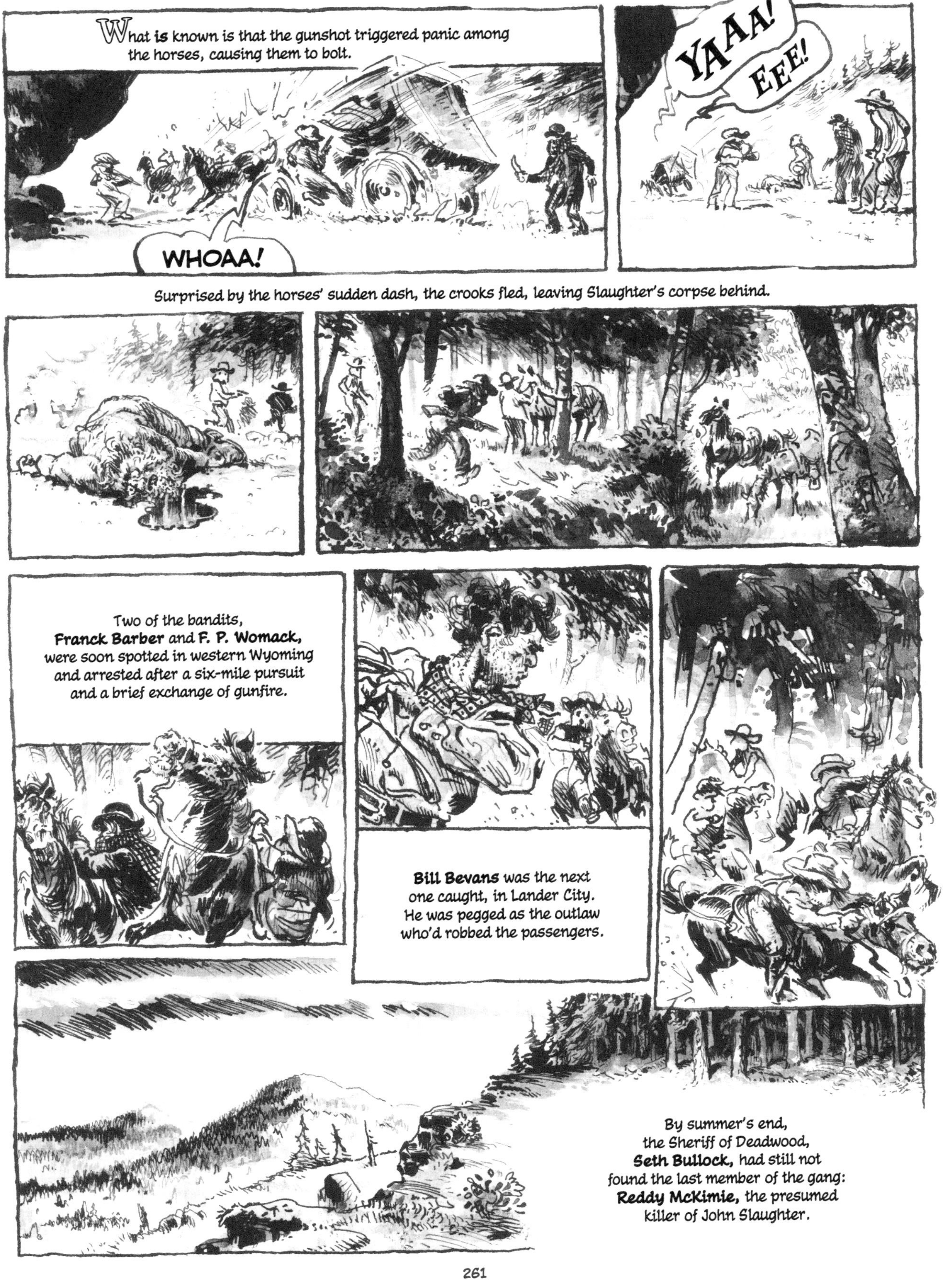
What is known is that the gunshot triggered panic among the horses, causing them to bolt.
WHOAA!
YAAA!
EEE!
Surprised by the horses' sudden dash, the crooks fled, leaving Slaughter's corpse behind.
Two of the bandits, Franck Barber and F. P. Womack, were soon spotted in western Wyoming and arrested after a six-mile pursuit and a brief exchange of gunfire.
Bill Bevans was the next one caught, in Lander City. He was pegged as the outlaw who'd robbed the passengers.
By summer's end, the Sheriff of Deadwood, Seth Bullock, had still not found the last member of the gang: Reddy McKimie, the presumed killer of John Slaughter.

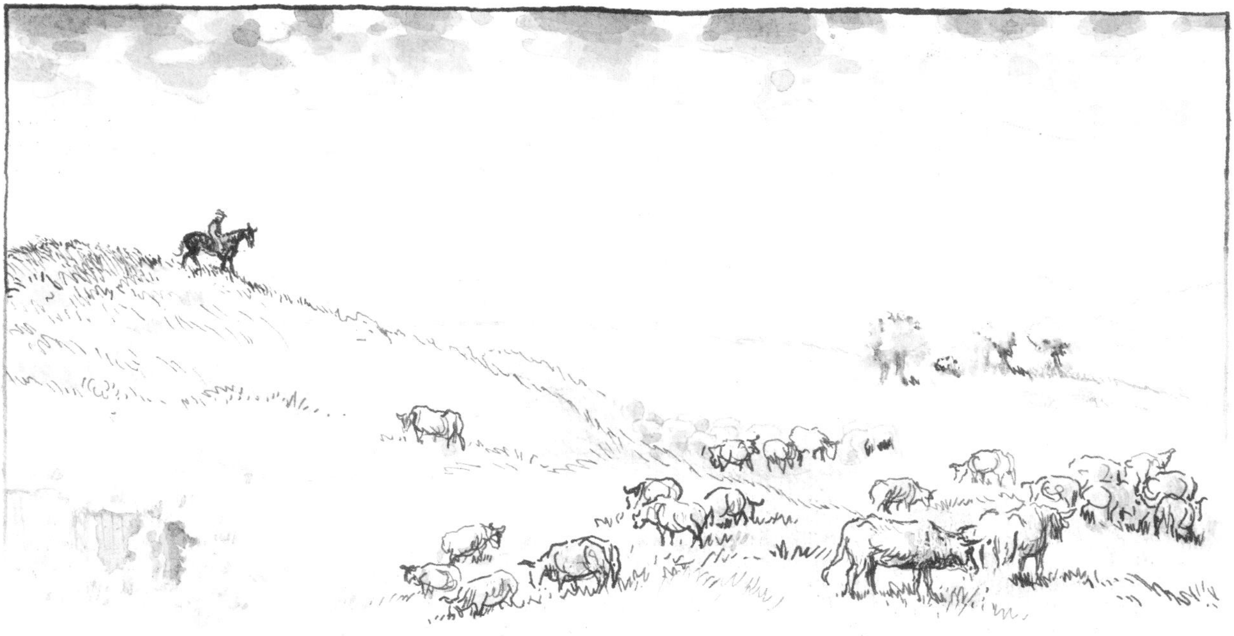

Martha Jane Cannary had spent the entire winter plying the Pony Express. In April 1877, when a U.S. Post Office opened in Deadwood, the company's riders all found themselves out of work.

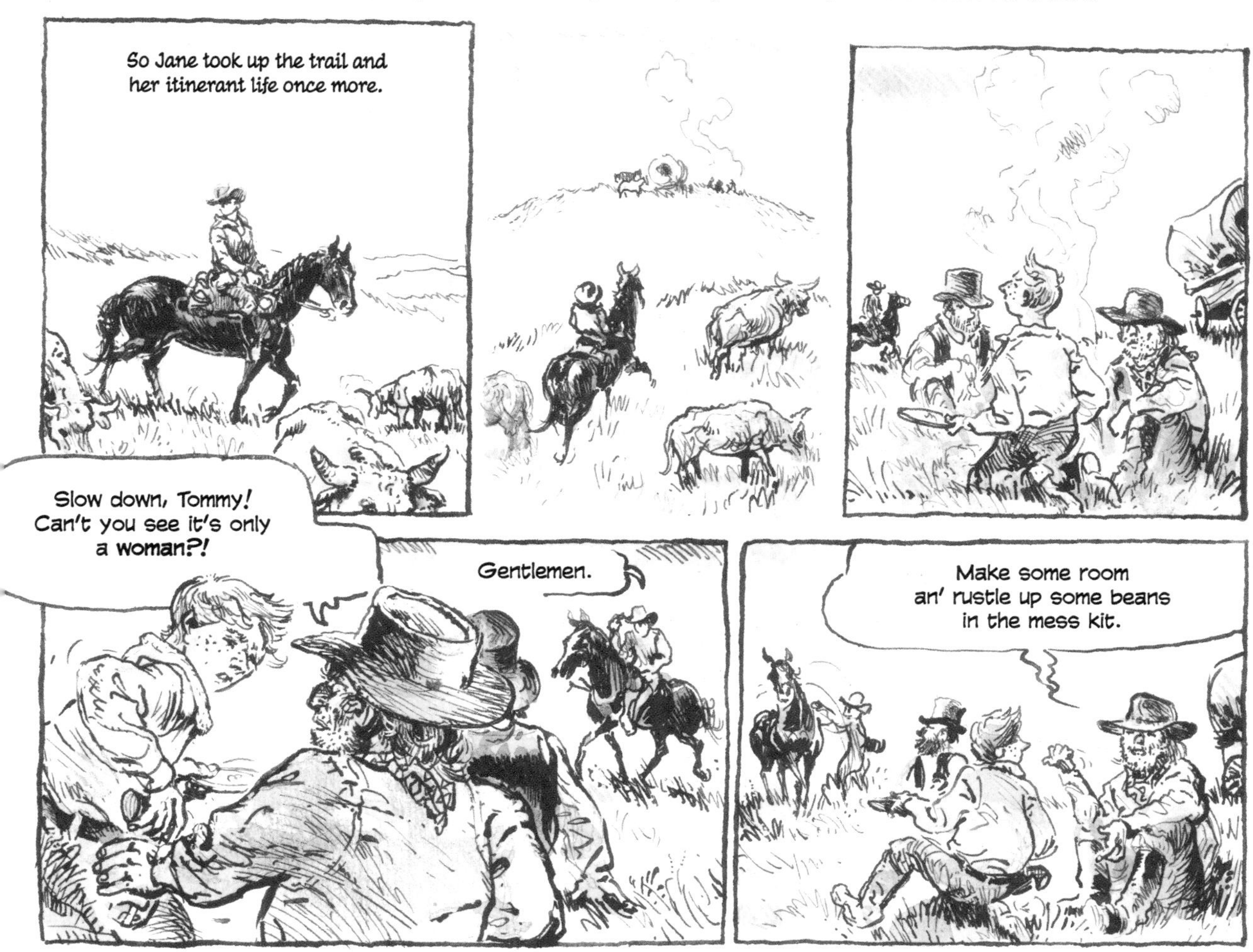
So Jane took up the trail and her itinerant life once more.
Slow down, Tommy! Can't you see it's only a **woman**?!
Gentlemen.
Make some room an' rustle up some beans in the mess kit.

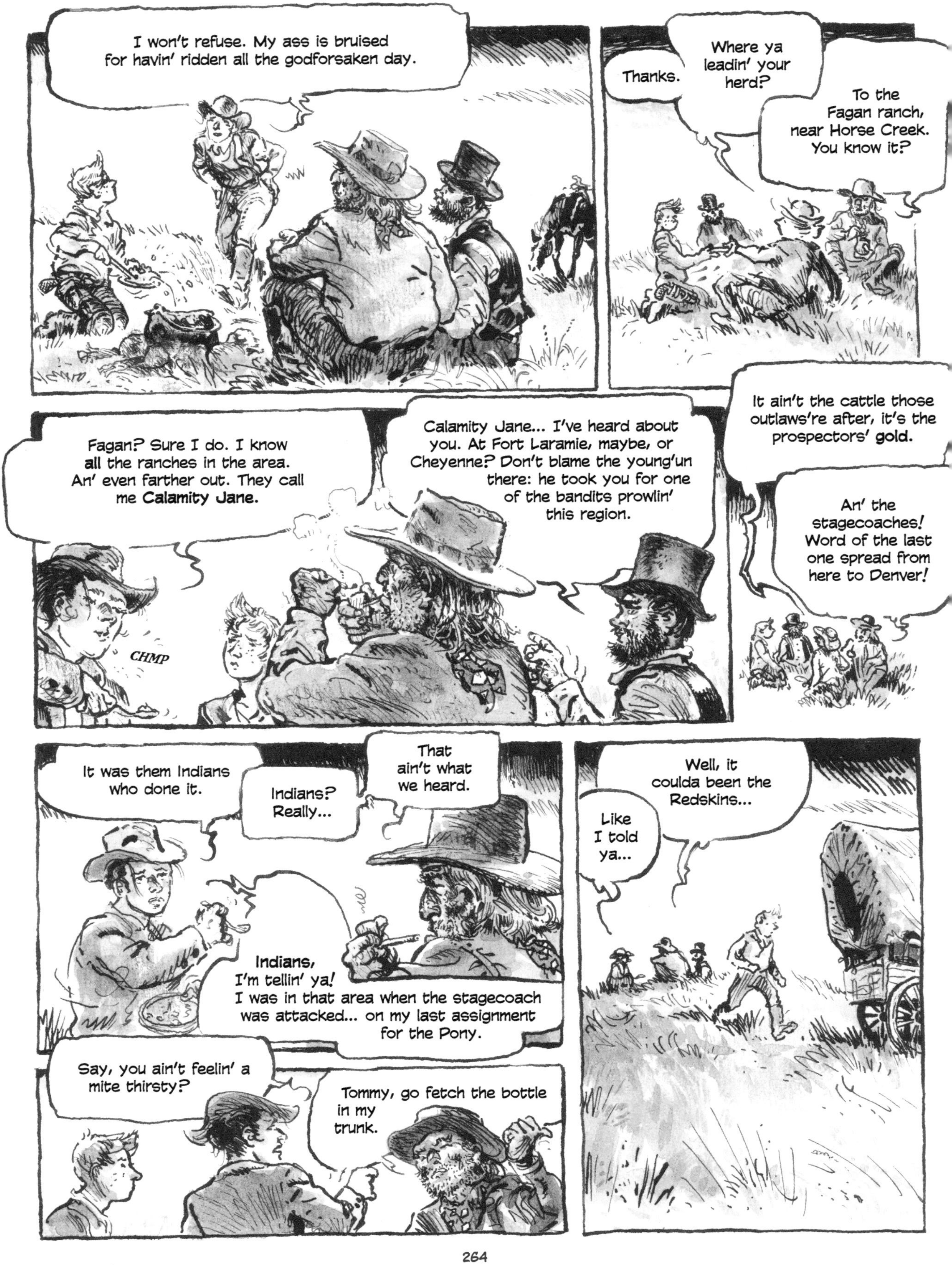
I won't refuse. My ass is bruised for havin' ridden all the godforsaken day.
Thanks.
Where ya leadin' your herd?
To the Fagan ranch, near Horse Creek. You know it?
Fagan? Sure I do. I know **all** the ranches in the area. An' even farther out. They call me **Calamity Jane**.
Calamity Jane... I've heard about you. At Fort Laramie, maybe, or Cheyenne? Don't blame the young'un there: he took you for one of the bandits prowlin' this region.
CHMP
It ain't the cattle those outlaws're after, it's the prospectors' **gold**.
An' the stagecoaches! Word of the last one spread from here to Denver!
It was them Indians who done it.
Indians? Really...
That ain't what we heard.
Indians, I'm tellin' ya! I was in that area when the stagecoach was attacked... on my last assignment for the Pony.
Say, you ain't feelin' a mite thirsty?
Tommy, go fetch the bottle in my trunk.
Well, it coulda been the Redskins...
Like I told ya...

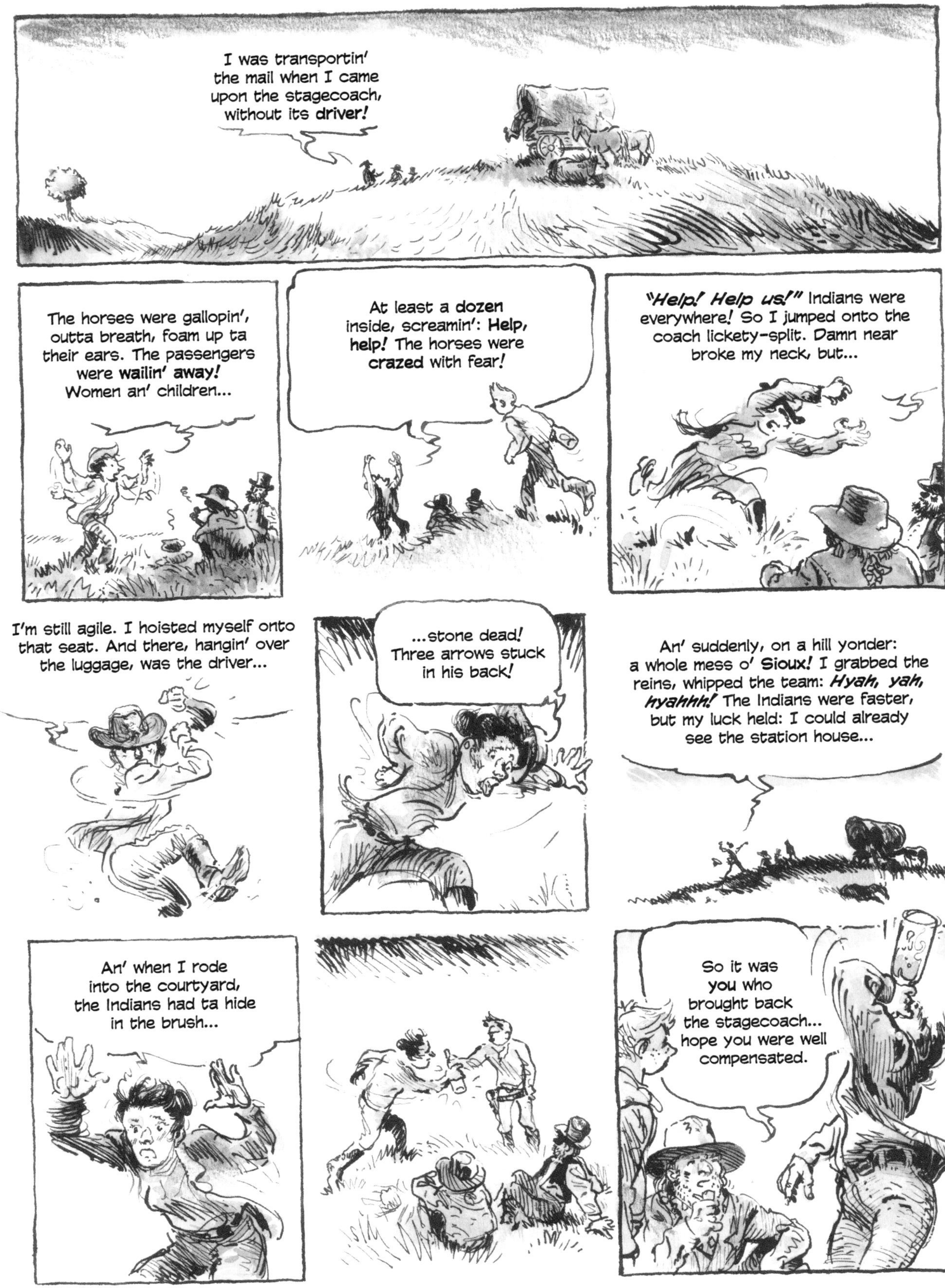
I was transportin' the mail when I came upon the stagecoach, without its **driver!**
The horses were gallopin', outta breath, foam up ta their ears. The passengers were **wailin' away!** Women an' children...
At least a **dozen** inside, screamin': **Help, help!** The horses were **crazed** with fear!
"Help! Help us!" Indians were everywhere! So I jumped onto the coach lickety-split. Damn near broke my neck, but...
I'm still agile. I hoisted myself onto that seat. And there, hangin' over the luggage, was the driver...
...stone dead! Three arrows stuck in his back!
An' suddenly, on a hill yonder: a whole mess o' **Sioux!** I grabbed the reins, whipped the team: ***Hyah, yah, hyahhh!*** The Indians were faster, but my luck held: I could already see the station house...
An' when I rode into the courtyard, the Indians had ta hide in the brush...
So it was **you** who brought back the stagecoach... hope you were well compensated.

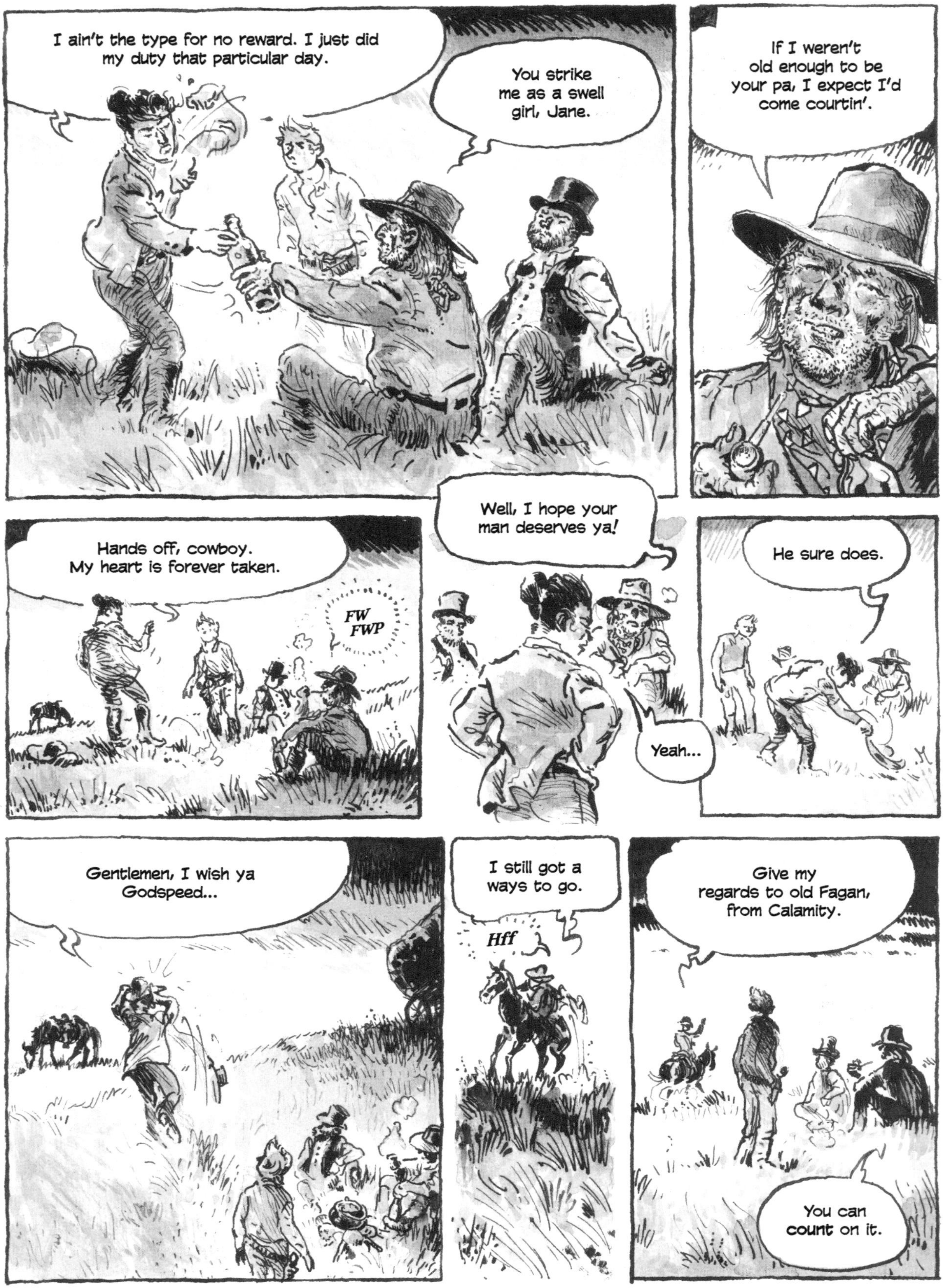
I ain't the type for no reward. I just did my duty that particular day.
You strike me as a swell girl, Jane.
If I weren't old enough to be your pa, I expect I'd come courtin'.
Hands off, cowboy. My heart is forever taken.
FW FWP
Well, I hope your man deserves ya!
Yeah...
He sure does.
Gentlemen, I wish ya Godspeed...
I still got a ways to go.
Hff
Give my regards to old Fagan, from Calamity.
You can count on it.

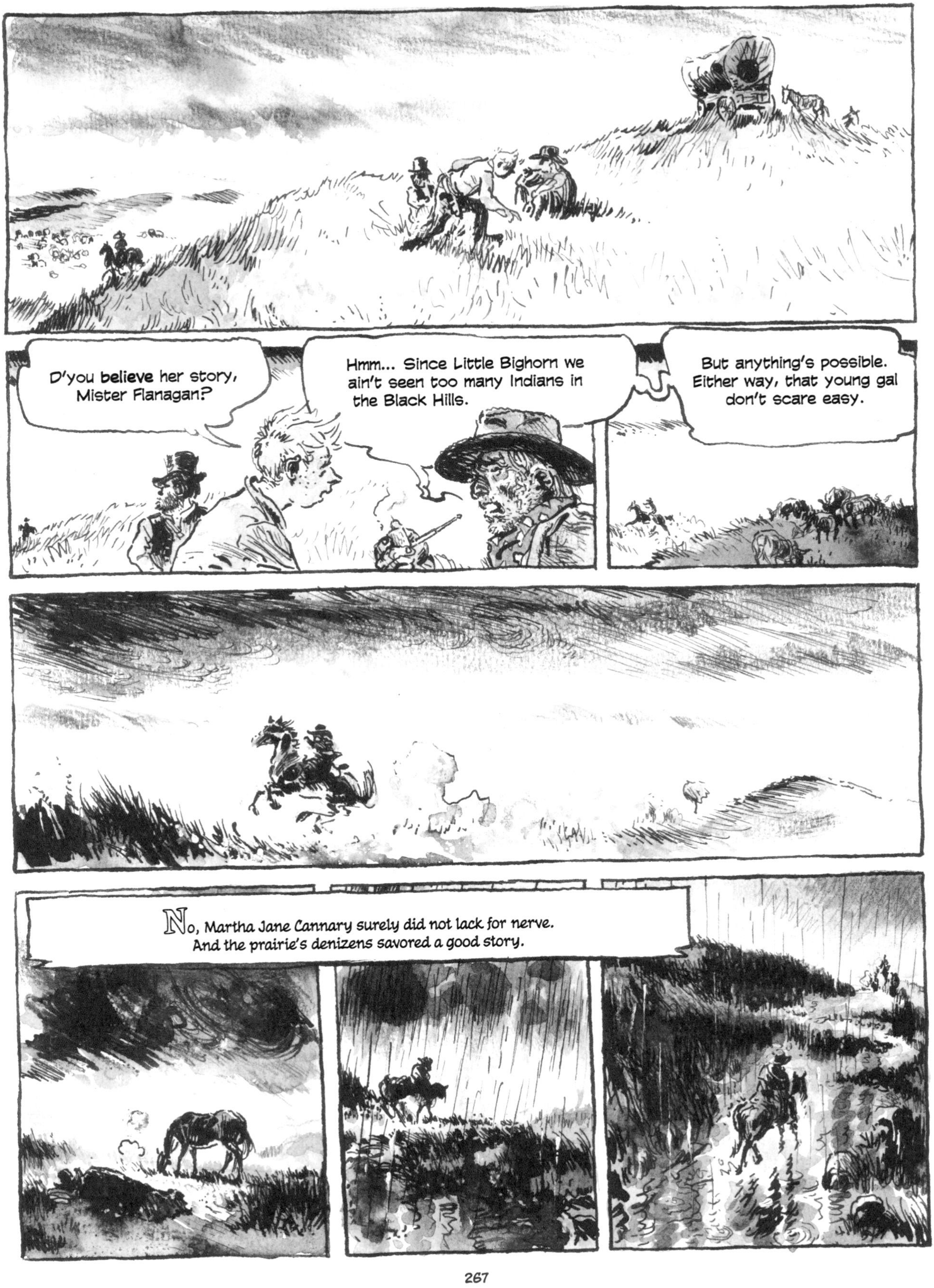
D'you believe her story, Mister Flanagan?
Hmm... Since Little Bighorn we ain't seen too many Indians in the Black Hills.
But anything's possible. Either way, that young gal don't scare easy.
No, Martha Jane Cannary surely did not lack for nerve. And the prairie's denizens savored a good story.

Entertainment opportunities were few, and good storytellers even fewer. So whenever talk drifted to the stagecoach attack, Jane jumped in to give **her** version of the events...

One way of remaining the center of attention.

I **vaulted** from my horse right as the stage began ta swerve!

I **just** managed ta grab hold. Three Indians were climbing up the side, but I brought 'em straight down!

BLAM! BLAM! BLAM!

I hauled myself up ta the driver's seat...

And there was Slaughter, stone dead... That sorry fella was **riddled** with arrows.

My god, the poor man...

Like I said, ma'am...

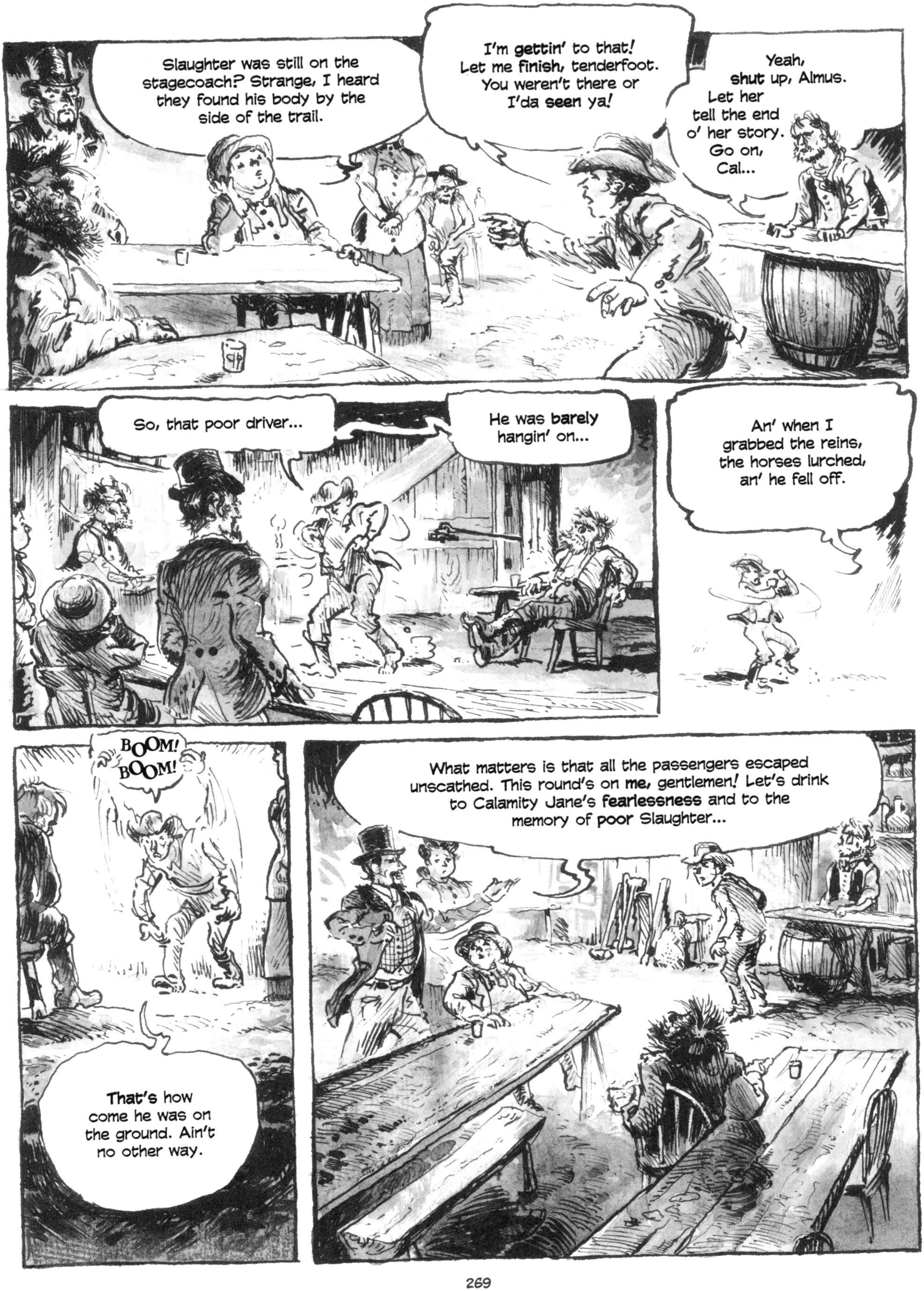
Slaughter was still on the stagecoach? Strange, I heard they found his body by the side of the trail.
I'm gettin' to that! Let me finish, tenderfoot. You weren't there or I'da seen ya!
Yeah, shut up, Almus. Let her tell the end o' her story. Go on, Cal...
So, that poor driver...
He was barely hangin' on...
An' when I grabbed the reins, the horses lurched, an' he fell off.
BOOM! BOOM!
That's how come he was on the ground. Ain't no other way.
What matters is that all the passengers escaped unscathed. This round's on me, gentlemen! Let's drink to Calamity Jane's fearlessness and to the memory of poor Slaughter...

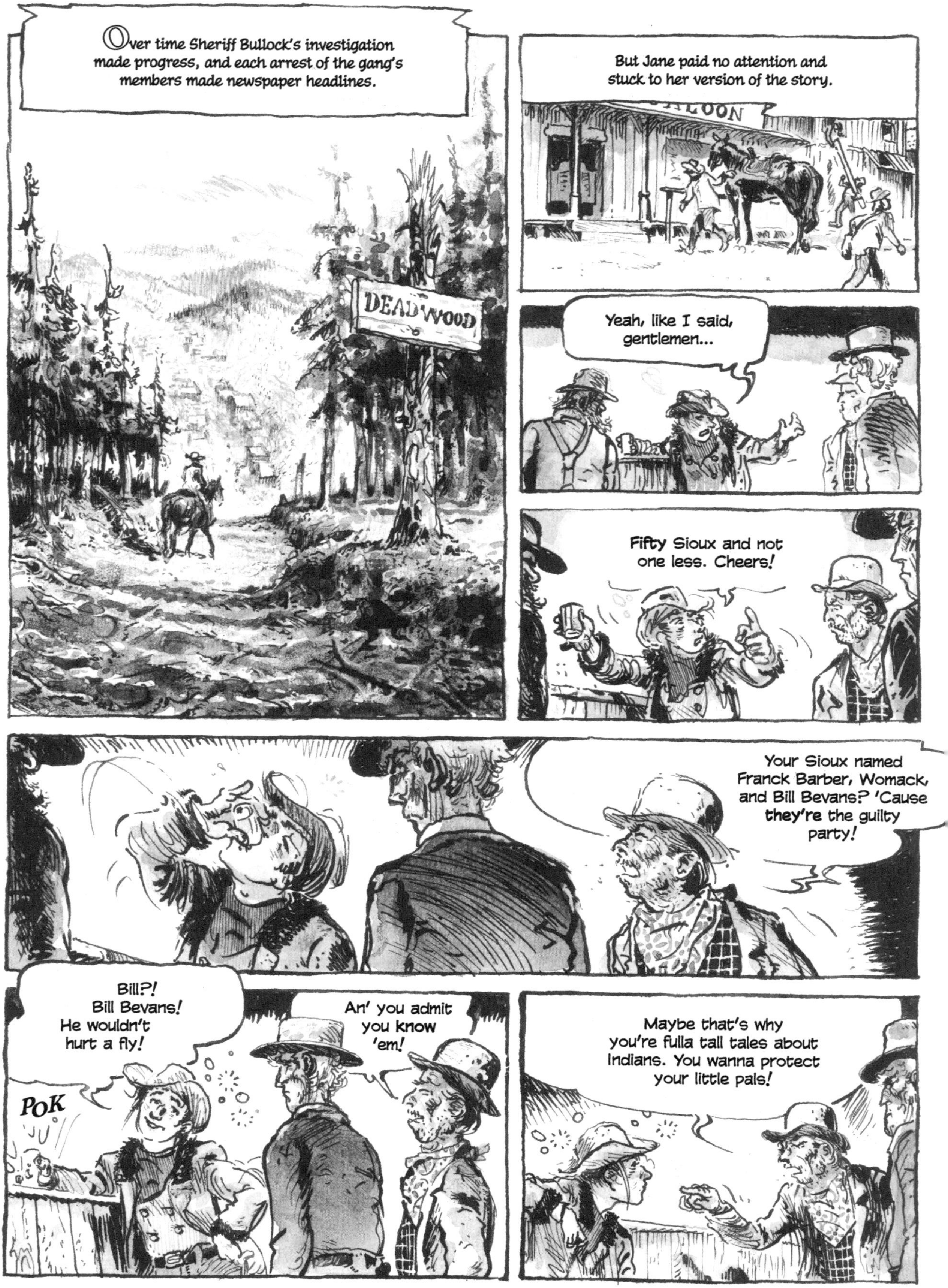
Over time Sheriff Bullock's investigation made progress, and each arrest of the gang's members made newspaper headlines.
DEADWOOD
But Jane paid no attention and stuck to her version of the story.
SALOON
Yeah, like I said, gentlemen...
Fifty Sioux and not one less. Cheers!
Your Sioux named Franck Barber, Womack, and Bill Bevans? 'Cause they're the guilty party!
Bill?! Bill Bevans! He wouldn't hurt a fly!
POK
An' you admit you know 'em!
Maybe that's why you're fulla tall tales about Indians. You wanna protect your little pals!

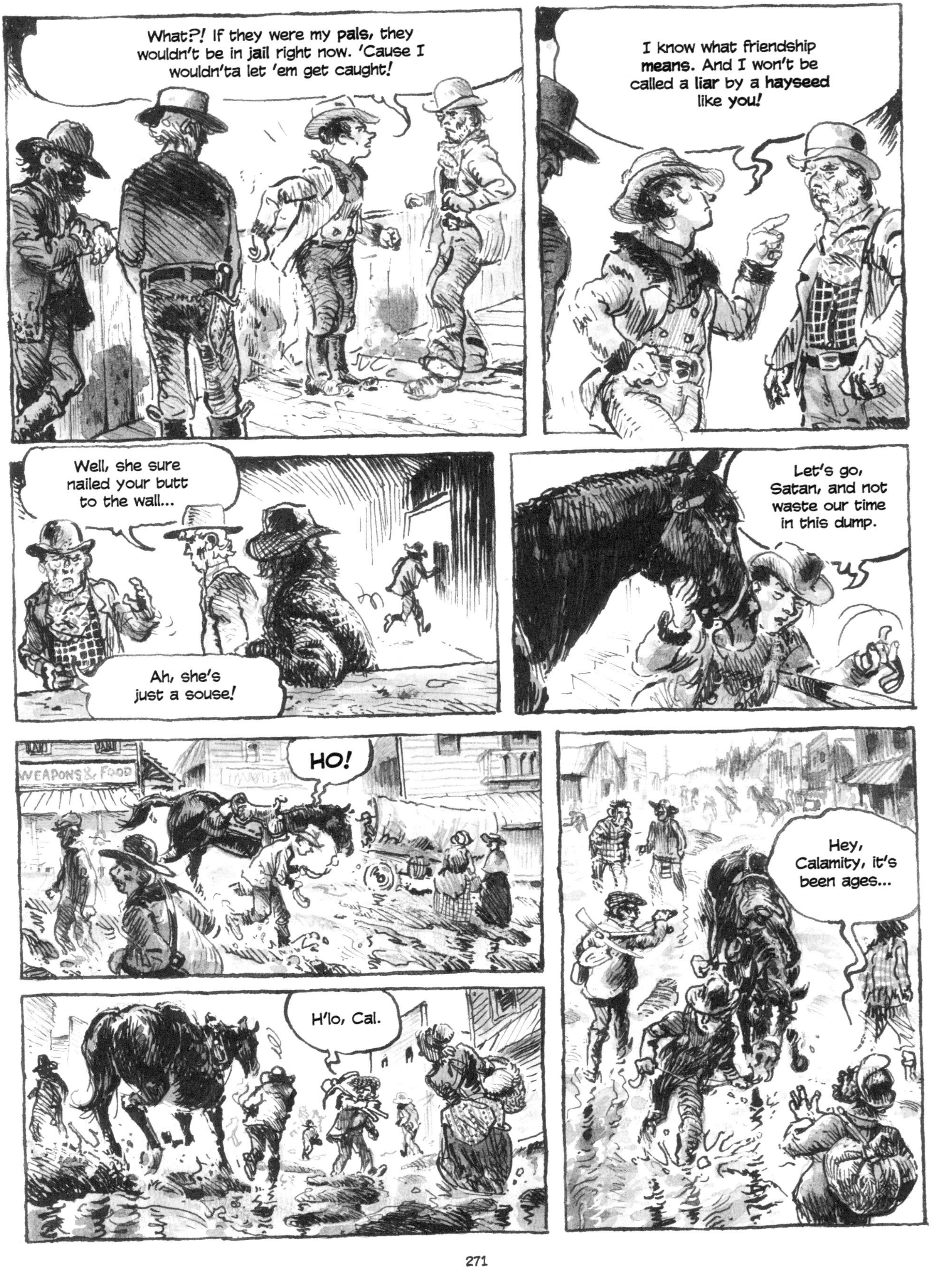
What?! If they were my pals, they wouldn't be in jail right now. 'Cause I wouldn'ta let 'em get caught!
I know what friendship means. And I won't be called a liar by a hayseed like you!
Well, she sure nailed your butt to the wall...
Ah, she's just a souse!
Let's go, Satan, and not waste our time in this dump.
WEAPONS & FOOD
HO!
H'lo, Cal.
Hey, Calamity, it's been ages...

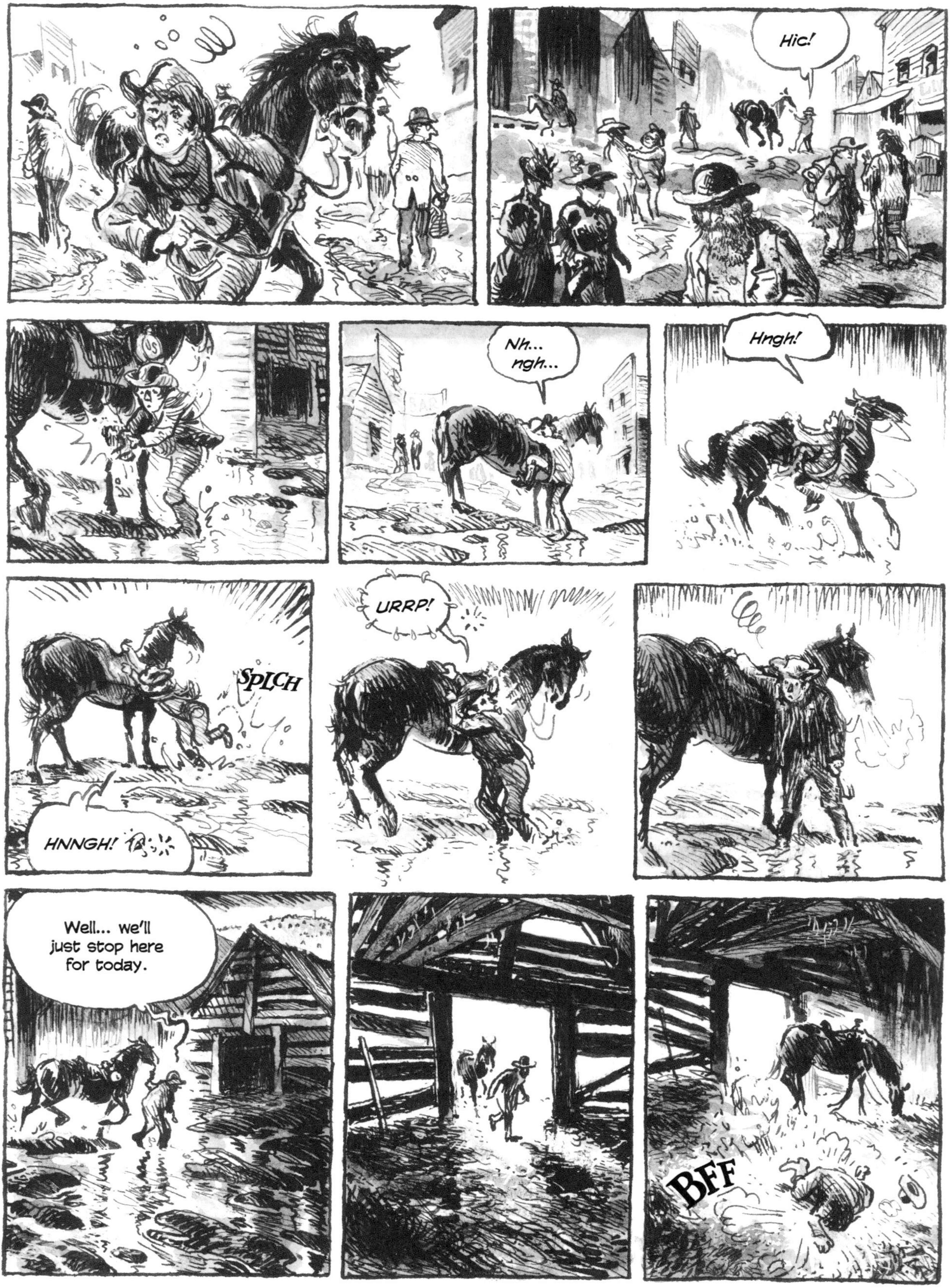
Hic!
Nh... ngh...
Hngh!
SPLCH
HNNGH!
URRP!
Well... we'll just stop here for today.
BFF

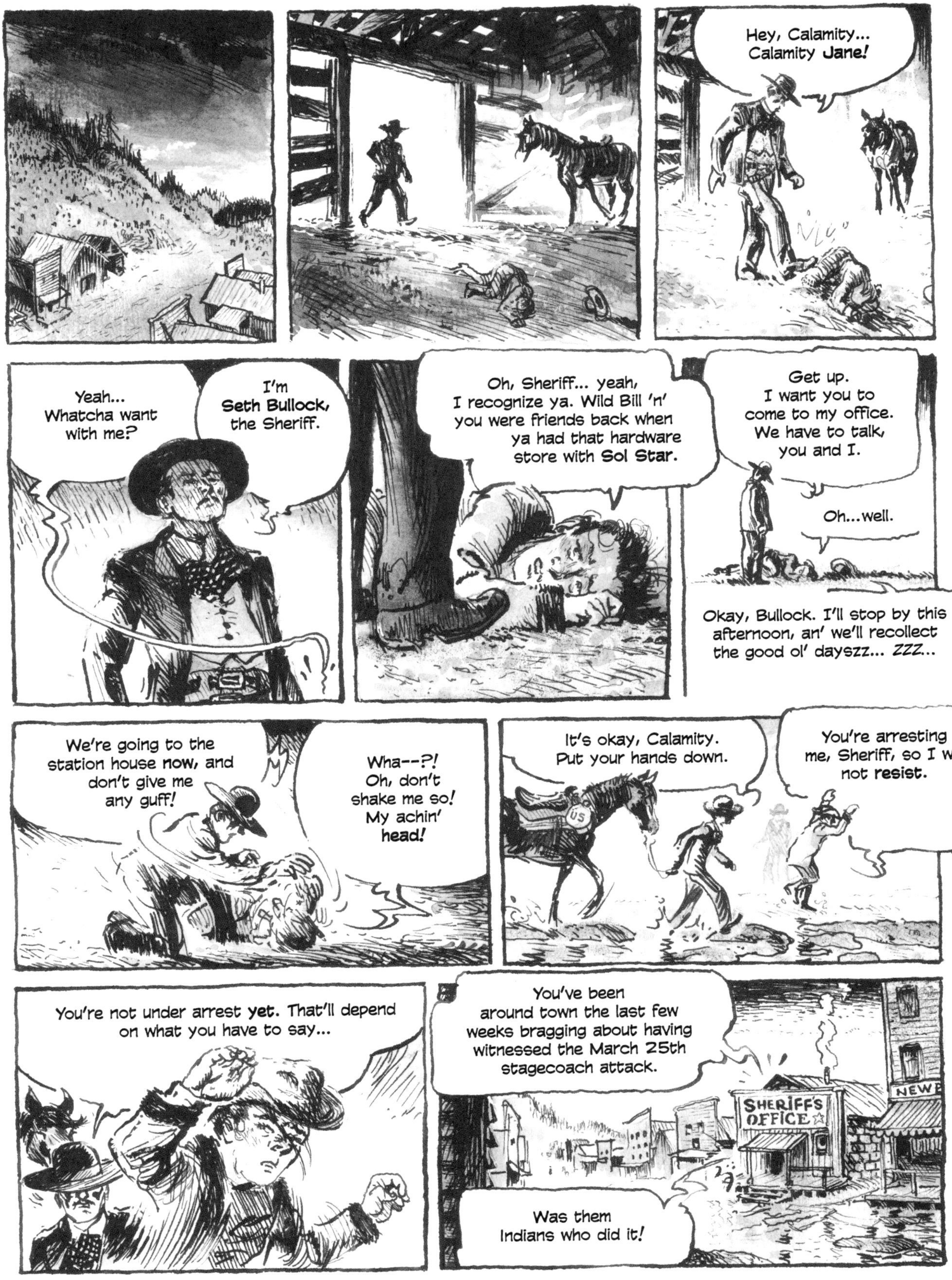
Hey, Calamity... Calamity Jane!
Yeah... Whatcha want with me?
I'm Seth Bullock, the Sheriff.
Oh, Sheriff... yeah, I recognize ya. Wild Bill 'n' you were friends back when ya had that hardware store with Sol Star.
Get up. I want you to come to my office. We have to talk, you and I.
Oh...well.
Okay, Bullock. I'll stop by this afternoon, an' we'll recollect the good ol' dayszz... ZZZ...
We're going to the station house now, and don't give me any guff!
Wha--?! Oh, don't shake me so! My achin' head!
It's okay, Calamity. Put your hands down.
You're arresting me, Sheriff, so I will not resist.
US
You're not under arrest yet. That'll depend on what you have to say...
You've been around town the last few weeks bragging about having witnessed the March 25th stagecoach attack.
SHERIFF'S OFFICE
NEWS
Was them Indians who did it!

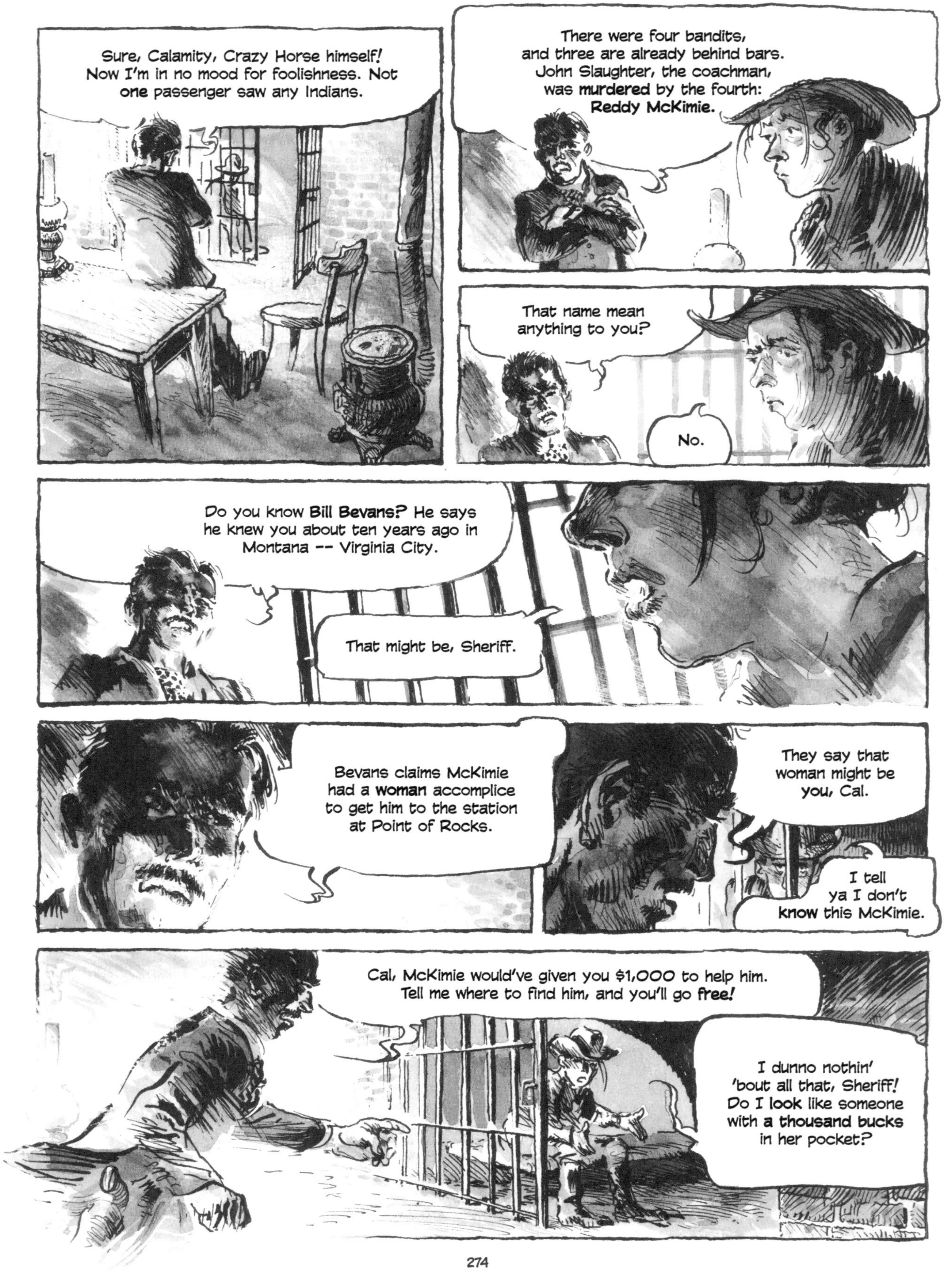

Sure, Calamity, Crazy Horse himself! Now I'm in no mood for foolishness. Not **one** passenger saw any Indians.
There were four bandits, and three are already behind bars. John Slaughter, the coachman, was **murdered** by the fourth: **Reddy McKimie.**
That name mean anything to you?
No.
Do you know **Bill Bevans?** He says he knew you about ten years ago in Montana -- Virginia City.
That might be, Sheriff.
Bevans claims McKimie had a **woman** accomplice to get him to the station at Point of Rocks.
They say that woman might be **you**, Cal.
I tell ya I don't **know** this McKimie.
Cal, McKimie would've given you $1,000 to help him. Tell me where to find him, and you'll go **free!**
I dunno nothin' 'bout all that, Sheriff! Do I **look** like someone with **a thousand bucks** in her pocket?

No.

There ya go! Shoulda started with that!

So, I can leave?

KLANG

SKLIIK KLIK

WANTED

Reddy Mc Kimie

2000 $

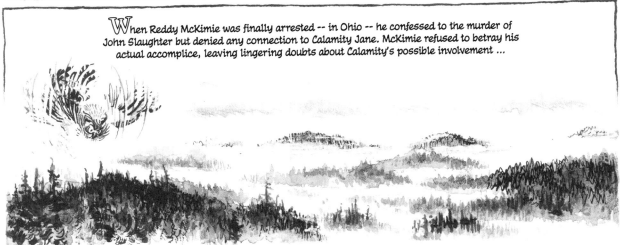

When Reddy McKimie was finally arrested -- in Ohio -- he confessed to the murder of John Slaughter but denied any connection to Calamity Jane. McKimie refused to betray his actual accomplice, leaving lingering doubts about Calamity's possible involvement ...

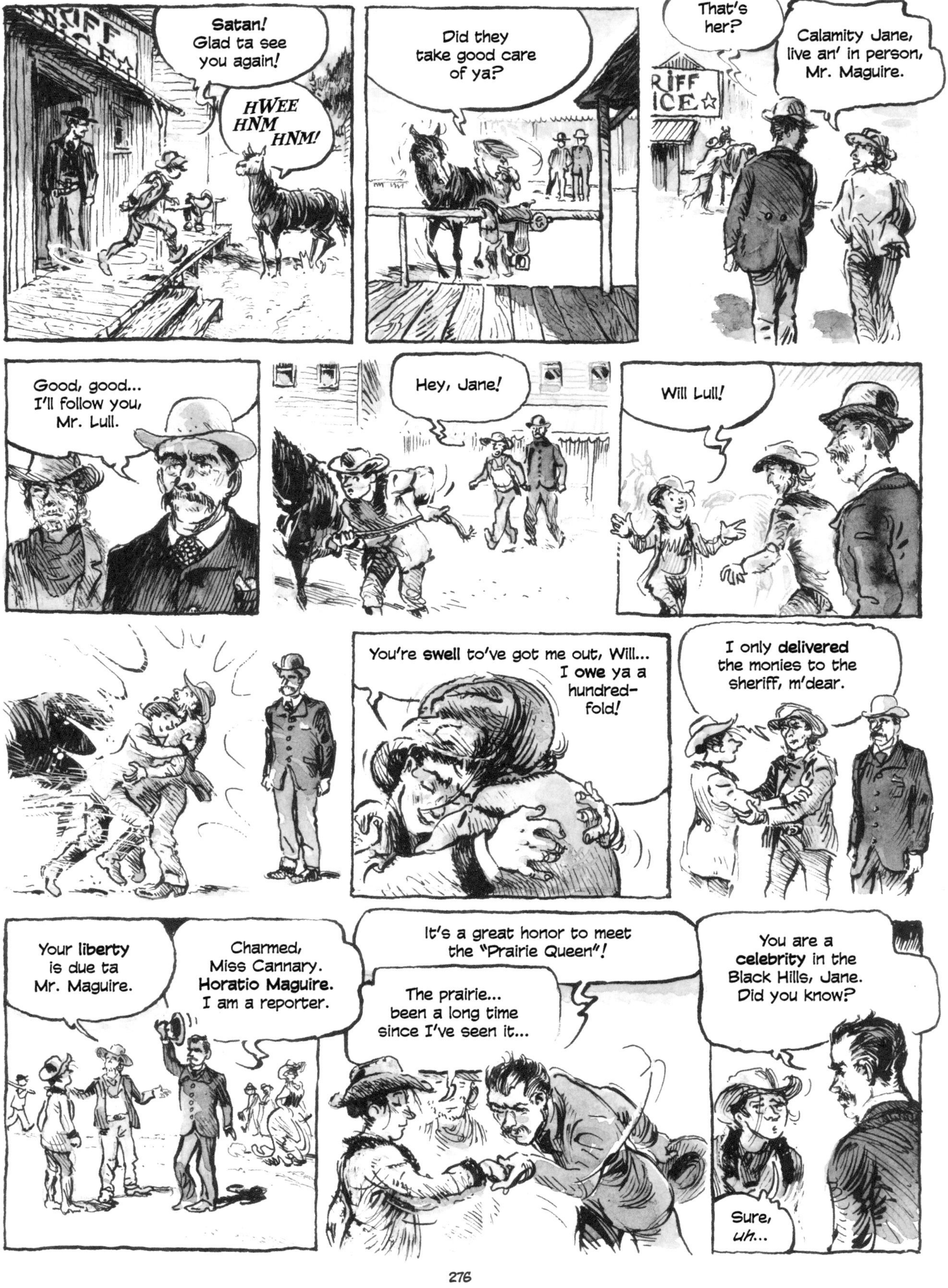

Satan! Glad ta see you again!
HWEE HNM HNM!
RIFF ICE
Did they take good care of ya?
That's her?
Calamity Jane, live an' in person, Mr. Maguire.
RIFF ICE
Good, good... I'll follow you, Mr. Lull.
Hey, Jane!
Will Lull!
You're swell to've got me out, Will... I owe ya a hundred-fold!
I only delivered the monies to the sheriff, m'dear.
Your liberty is due ta Mr. Maguire.
Charmed, Miss Cannary. Horatio Maguire. I am a reporter.
It's a great honor to meet the "Prairie Queen"!
The prairie... been a long time since I've seen it...
You are a celebrity in the Black Hills, Jane. Did you know?
Sure, uh...

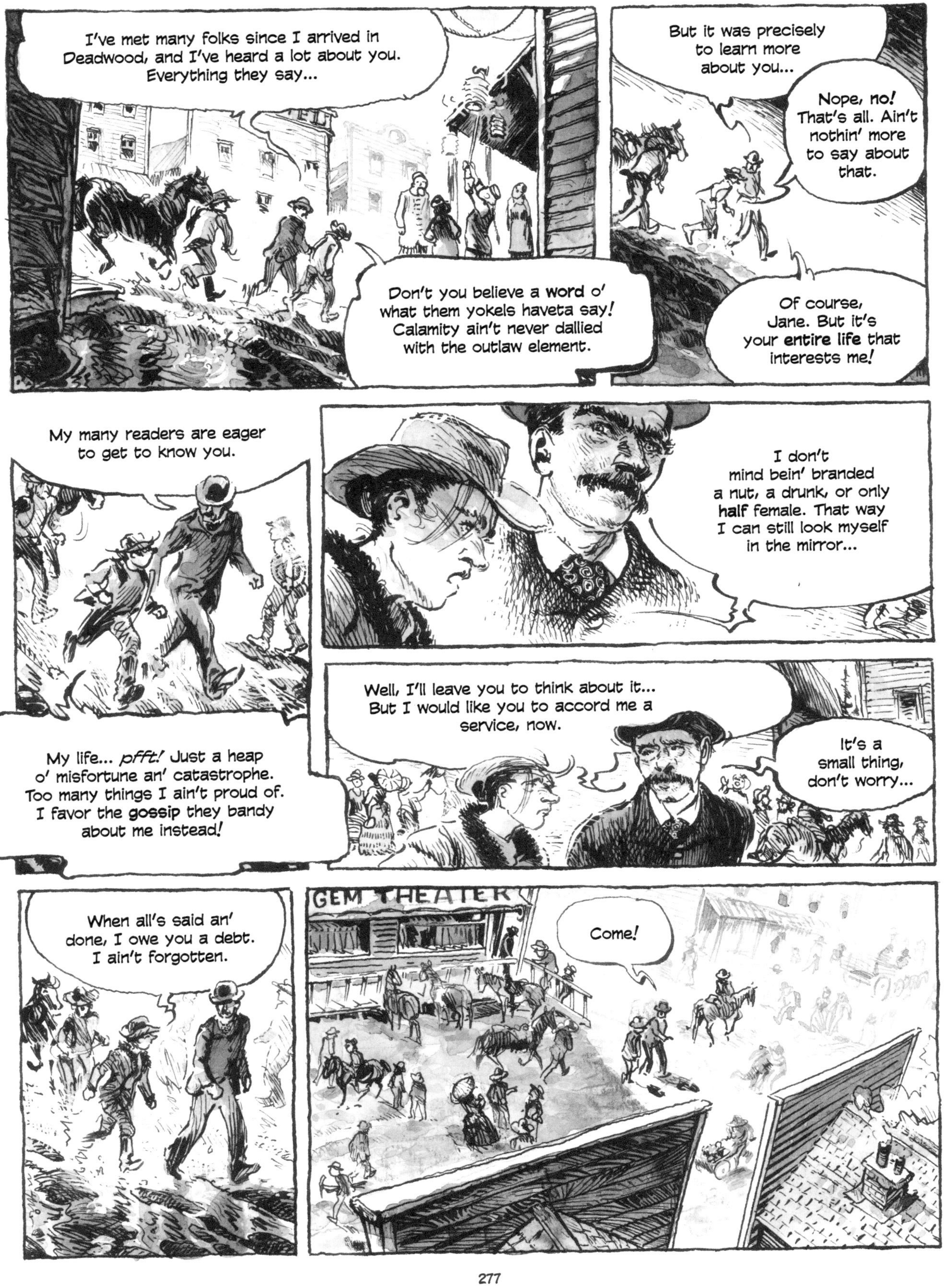
I've met many folks since I arrived in Deadwood, and I've heard a lot about you. Everything they say...
Don't you believe a **word** o' what them yokels haveta say! Calamity ain't never dallied with the outlaw element.
But it was precisely to learn more about you...
Nope, no! That's all. Ain't nothin' more to say about that.
Of course, Jane. But it's your **entire life** that interests me!
My many readers are eager to get to know you.
My life... *pfft!* Just a heap o' misfortune an' catastrophe. Too many things I ain't proud of. I favor the **gossip** they bandy about me instead!
I don't mind bein' branded a nut, a drunk, or only **half** female. That way I can still look myself in the mirror...
Well, I'll leave you to think about it... But I would like you to accord me a service, now.
It's a small thing, don't worry...
When all's said an' done, I owe you a debt. I ain't forgotten.
GEM THEATER
Come!

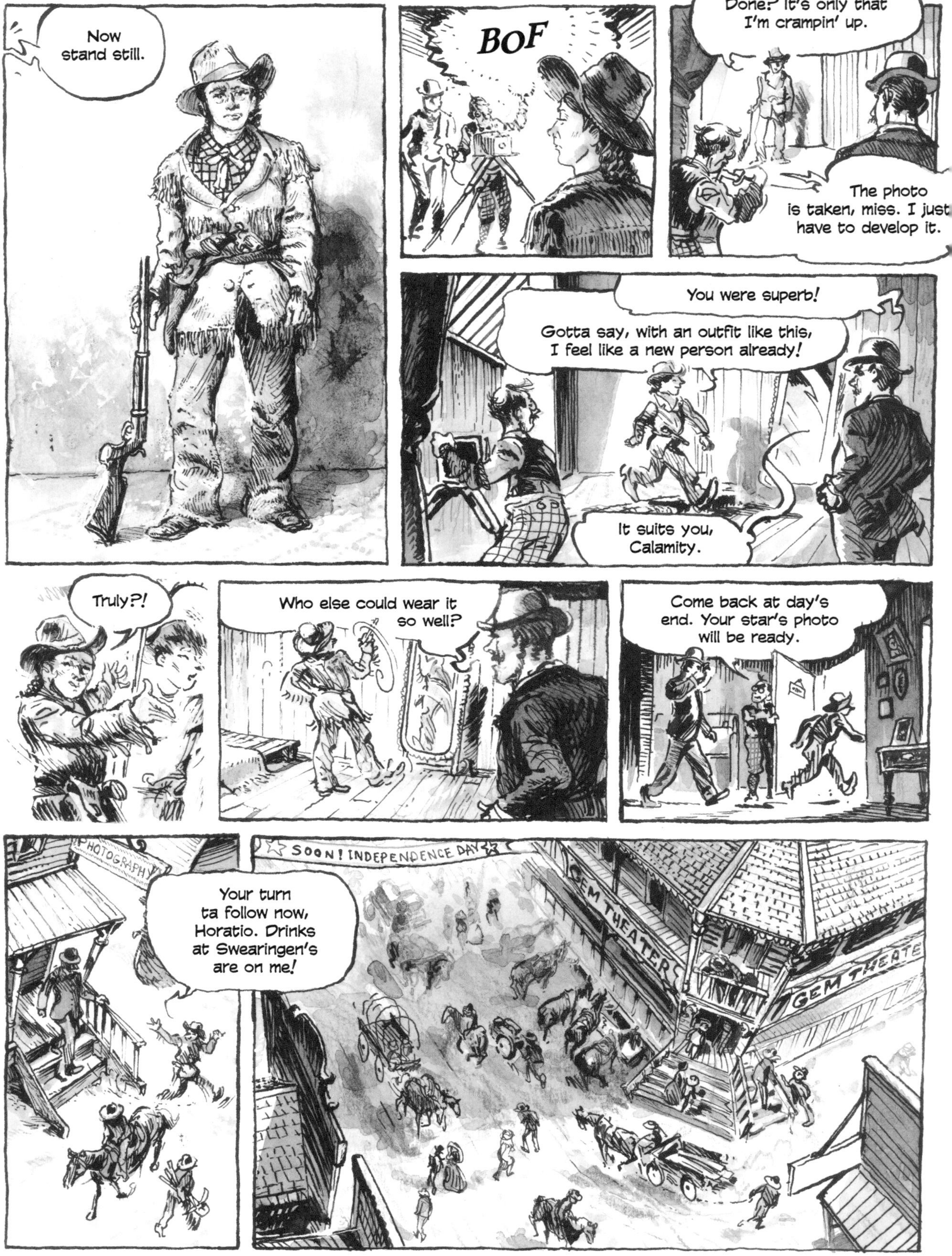
Now stand still.
BOF
Done? It's only that I'm crampin' up.
The photo is taken, miss. I just have to develop it.
You were superb!
Gotta say, with an outfit like this, I feel like a new person already!
It suits you, Calamity.
Truly?!
Who else could wear it so well?
Come back at day's end. Your star's photo will be ready.
PHOTOGRAPHY
Your turn ta follow now, Horatio. Drinks at Swearingen's are on me!
SOON! INDEPENDENCE DAY
GEM THEATER
GEM THEATE

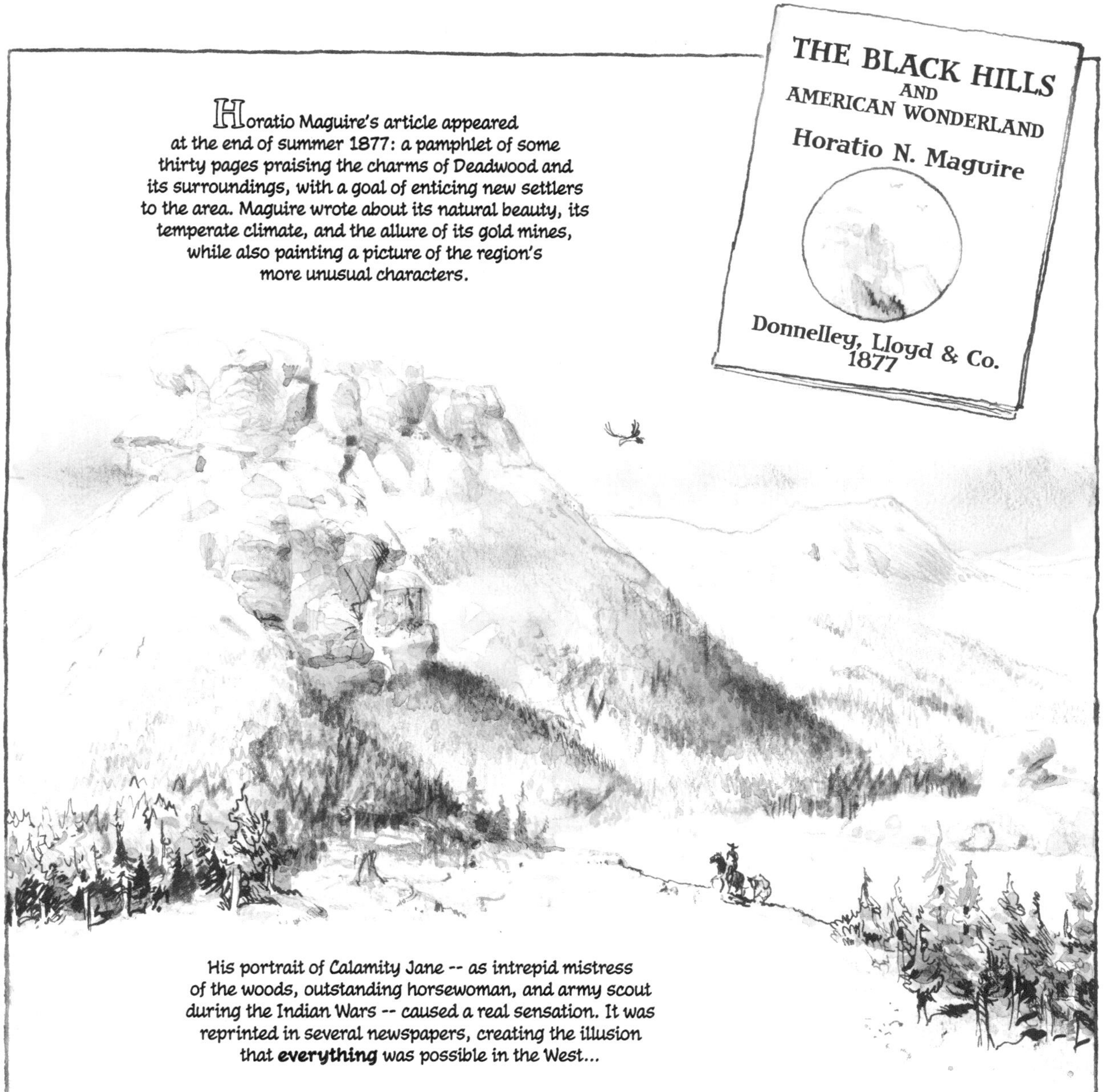
Horatio Maguire's article appeared at the end of summer 1877: a pamphlet of some thirty pages praising the charms of Deadwood and its surroundings, with a goal of enticing new settlers to the area. Maguire wrote about its natural beauty, its temperate climate, and the allure of its gold mines, while also painting a picture of the region's more unusual characters.
THE BLACK HILLS AND AMERICAN WONDERLAND
Horatio N. Maguire
Donnelley, Lloyd & Co. 1877
His portrait of Calamity Jane -- as intrepid mistress of the woods, outstanding horsewoman, and army scout during the Indian Wars -- caused a real sensation. It was reprinted in several newspapers, creating the illusion that **everything** was possible in the West...

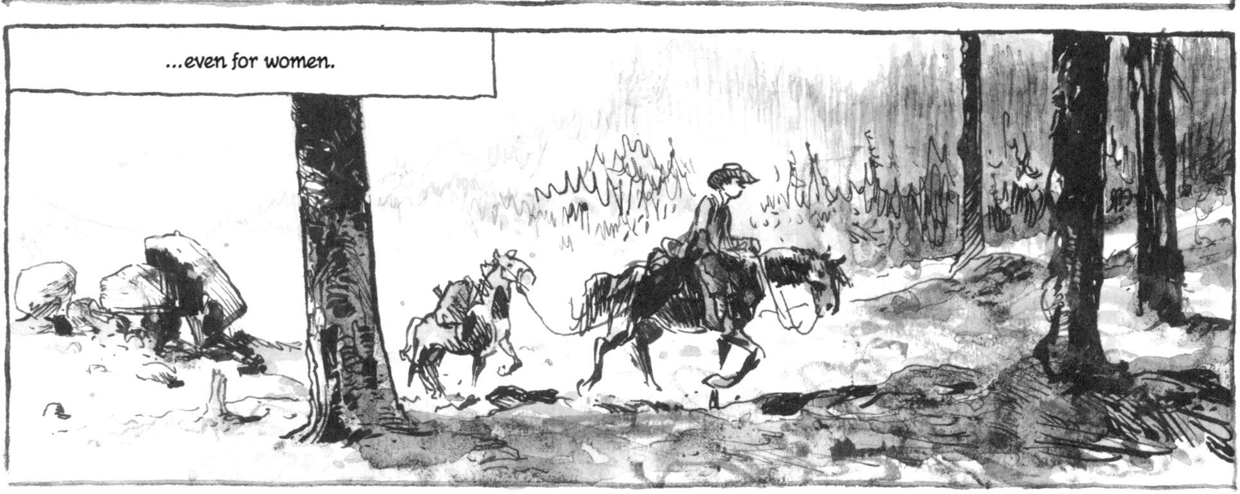
...even for women.

In the following months, Martha Jane Cannary became very popular, which did not forestall her precarious existence: eking out a living of constant small jobs.

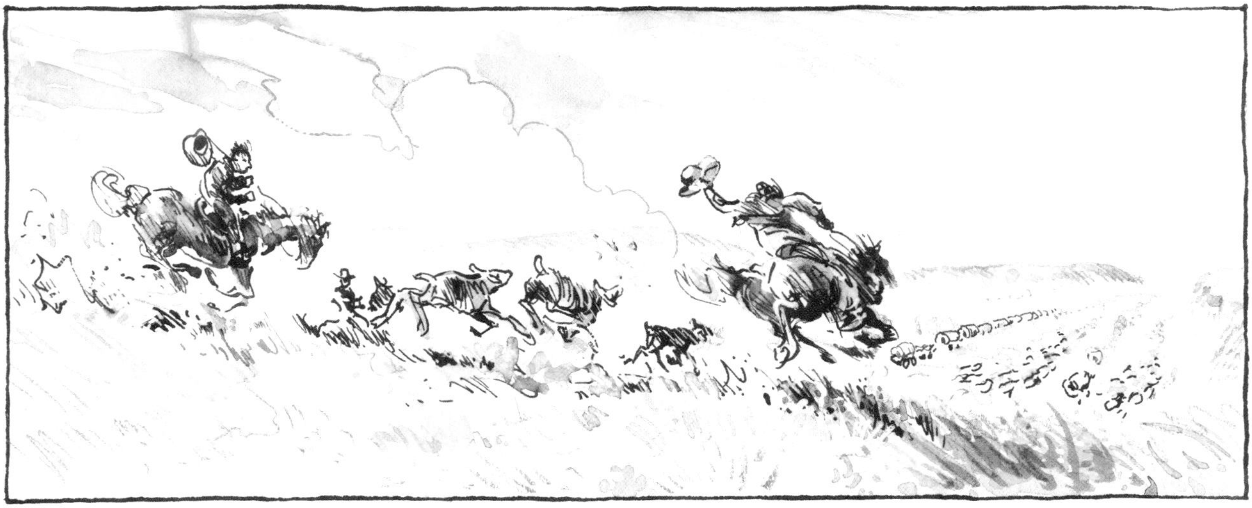

But wherever she went, the newspapers were quick to announce her presence, recounting her actions in a style as flamboyant as Maguire's.

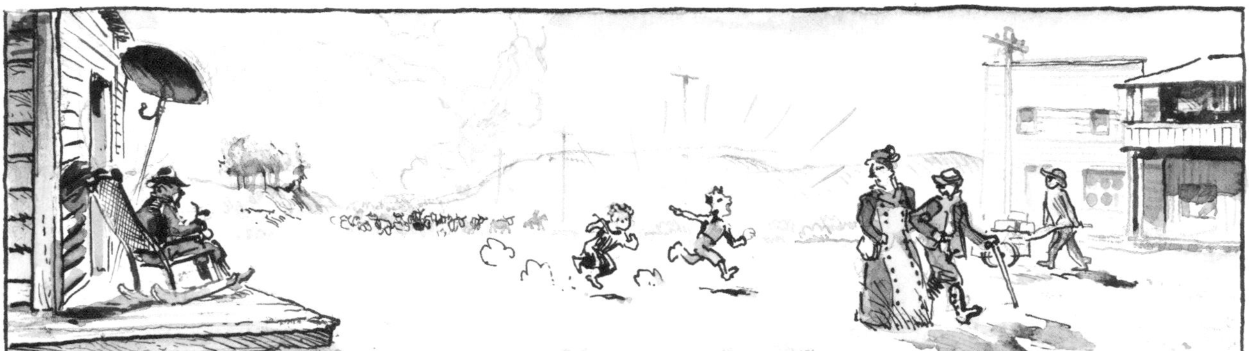

And so, on August 4, 1877, Nebraska's *Sidney Telegraph* headlined her arrival in town, alongside cowboy **"Teddy Blue" Abbott...**

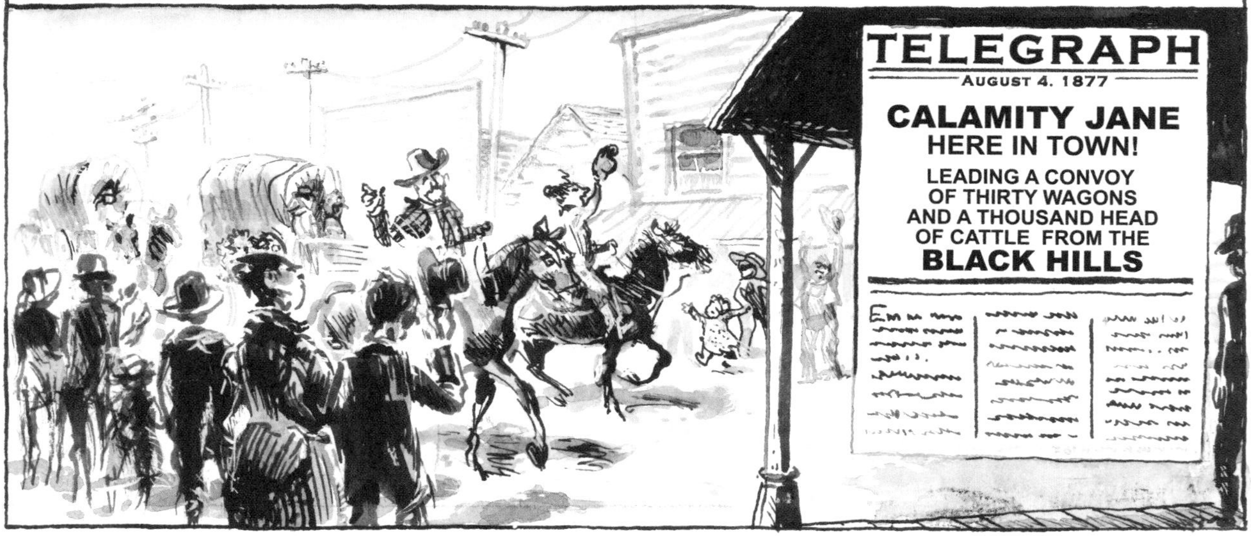
TELEGRAPH
AUGUST 4. 1877
CALAMITY JANE
HERE IN TOWN!
LEADING A CONVOY
OF THIRTY WAGONS
AND A THOUSAND HEAD
OF CATTLE FROM THE
BLACK HILLS

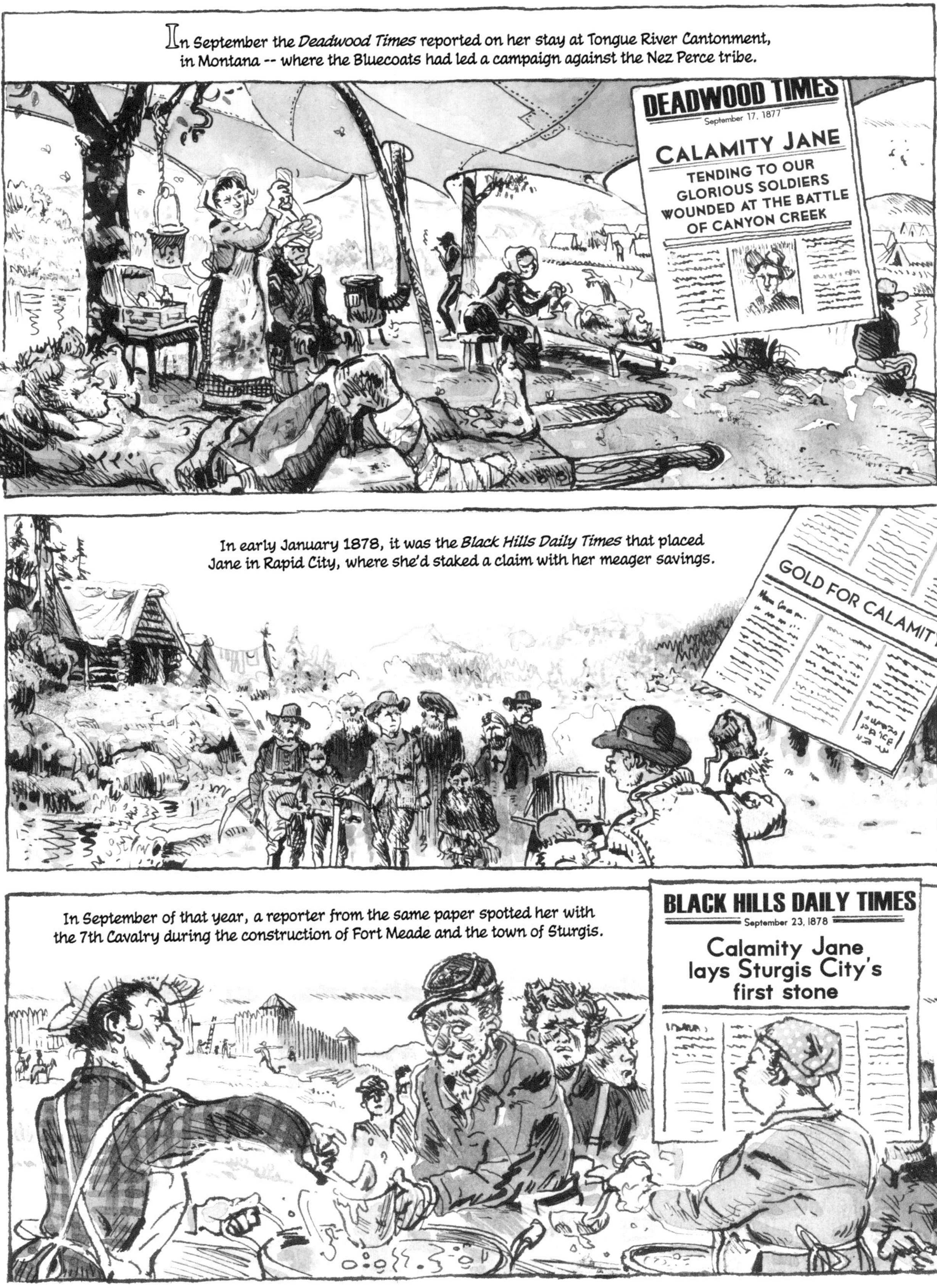
In September the *Deadwood Times* reported on her stay at Tongue River Cantonment, in Montana -- where the Bluecoats had led a campaign against the Nez Perce tribe.
DEADWOOD TIMES
September 17, 1877
CALAMITY JANE
TENDING TO OUR GLORIOUS SOLDIERS WOUNDED AT THE BATTLE OF CANYON CREEK
In early January 1878, it was the *Black Hills Daily Times* that placed Jane in Rapid City, where she'd staked a claim with her meager savings.
GOLD FOR CALAMITY!
In September of that year, a reporter from the same paper spotted her with the 7th Cavalry during the construction of Fort Meade and the town of Sturgis.
BLACK HILLS DAILY TIMES
September 23, 1878
Calamity Jane lays Sturgis City's first stone

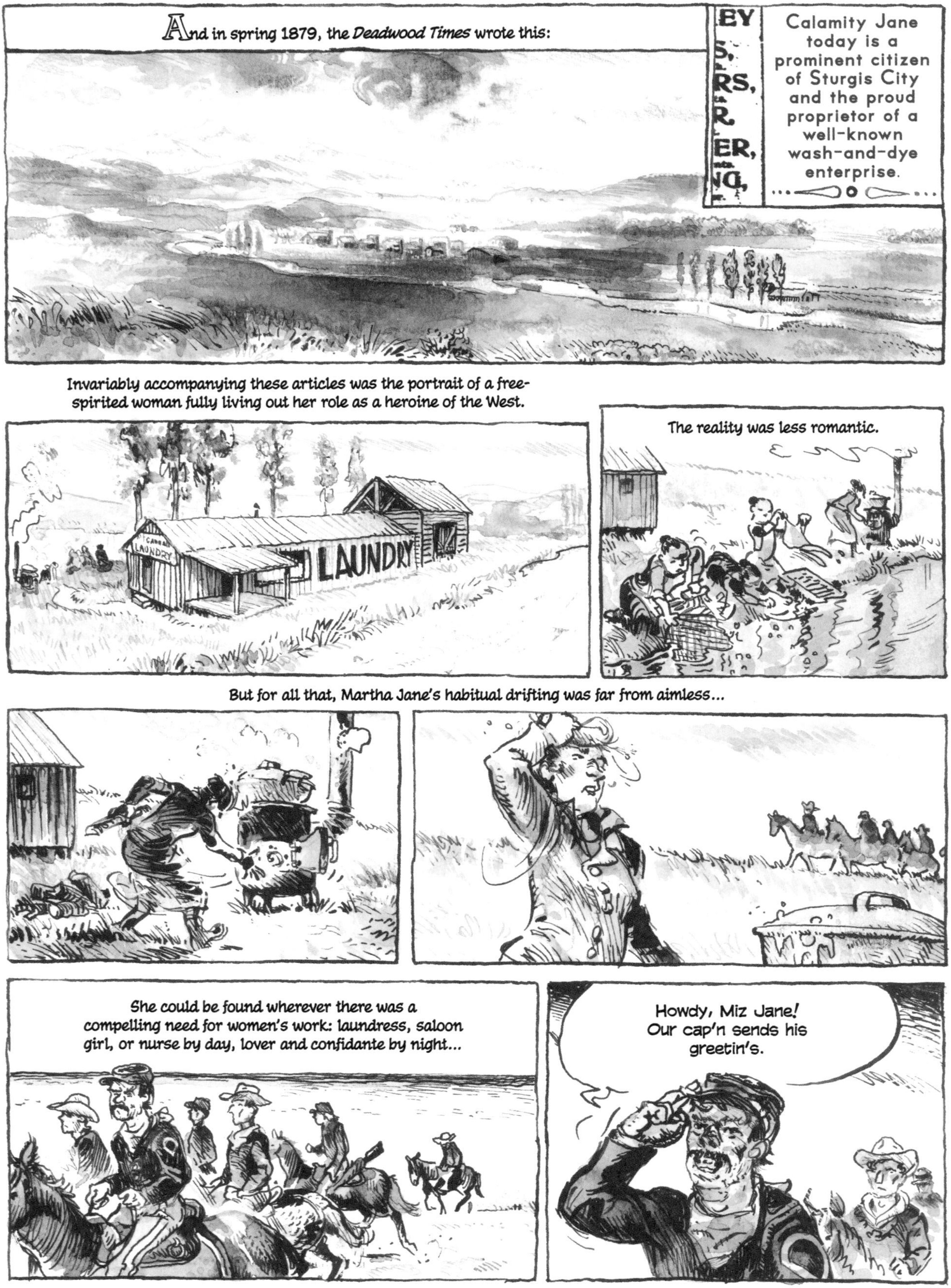
And in spring 1879, the *Deadwood Times* wrote this:
Calamity Jane today is a prominent citizen of Sturgis City and the proud proprietor of a well-known wash-and-dye enterprise.
Invariably accompanying these articles was the portrait of a free-spirited woman fully living out her role as a heroine of the West.
LAUNDRY
LAUNDRY
The reality was less romantic.
But for all that, Martha Jane's habitual drifting was far from aimless...
She could be found wherever there was a compelling need for women's work: laundress, saloon girl, or nurse by day, lover and confidante by night...
Howdy, Miz Jane! Our cap'n sends his greetin's.

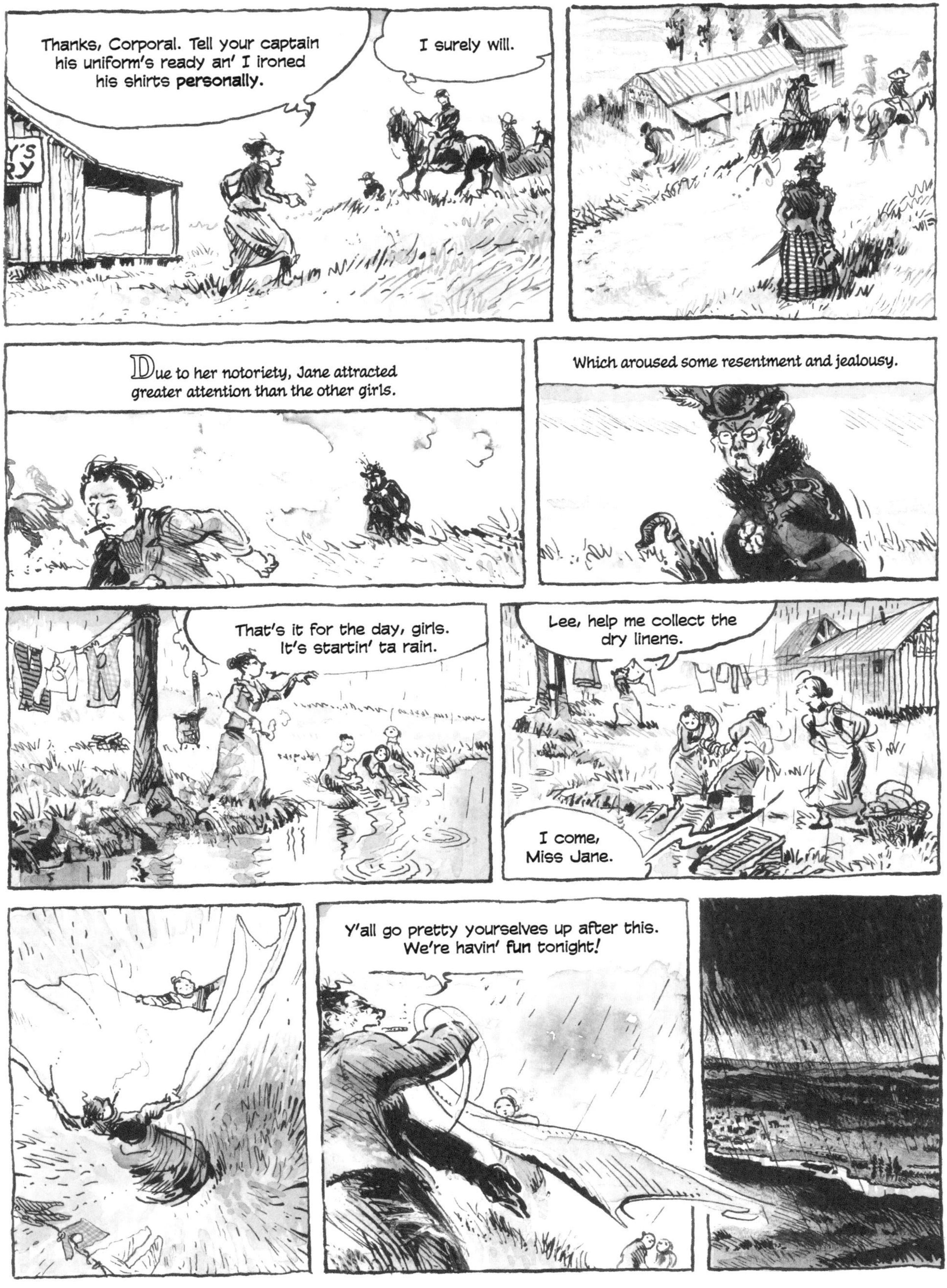
Thanks, Corporal. Tell your captain his uniform's ready an' I ironed his shirts **personally.**
I surely will.
LAUNDRY
Due to her notoriety, Jane attracted greater attention than the other girls.
Which aroused some resentment and jealousy.
That's it for the day, girls. It's startin' ta rain.
Lee, help me collect the dry linens.
I come, Miss Jane.
Y'all go pretty yourselves up after this. We're havin' **fun** tonight!

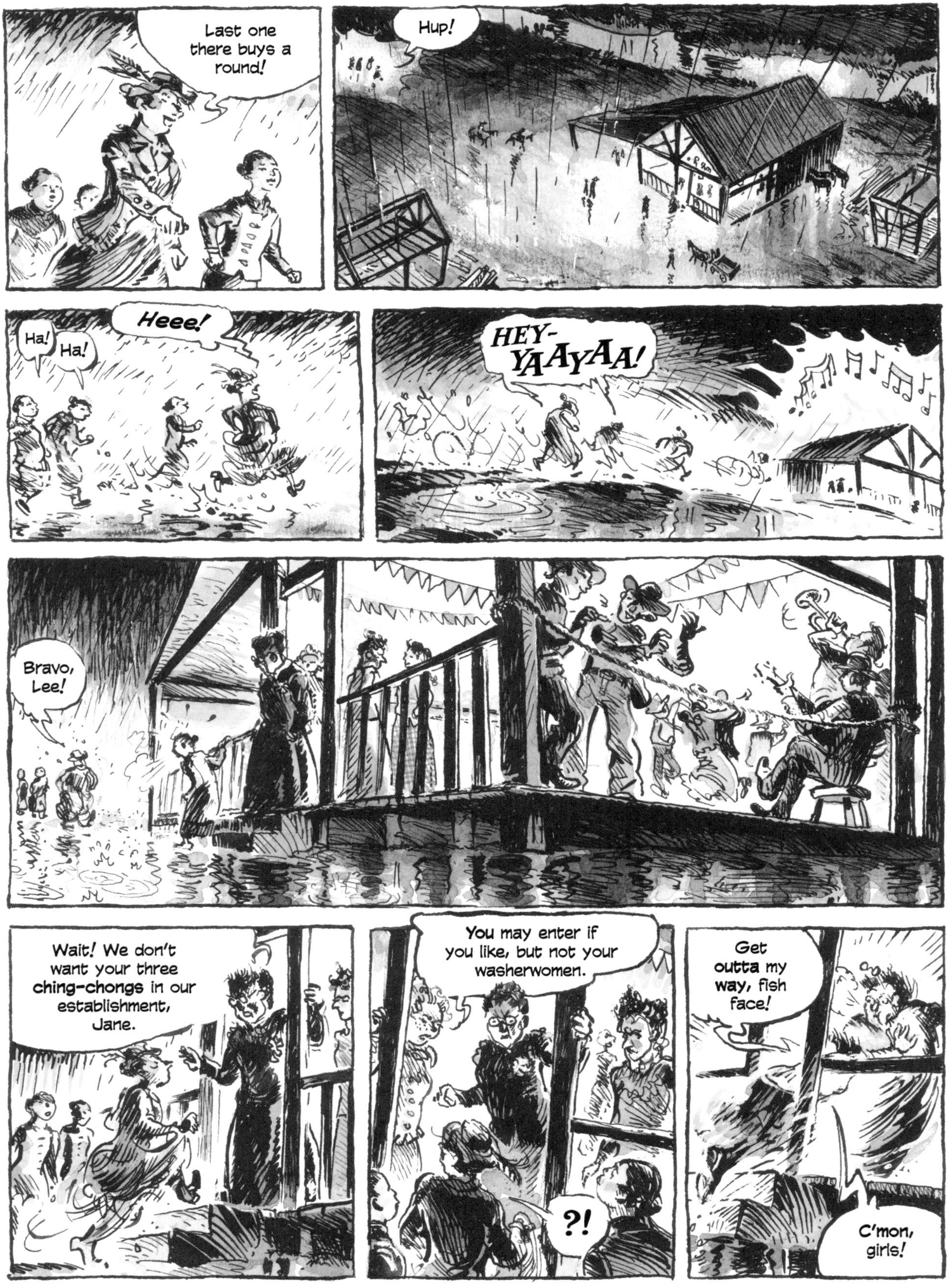
Last one there buys a round!
Hup!
Ha!
Ha!
Heee!
HEY-YAAYAA!
Bravo, Lee!
Wait! We don't want your three ching-chongs in our establishment, Jane.
You may enter if you like, but not your washerwomen.
?!
Get outta my way, fish face!
C'mon, girls!

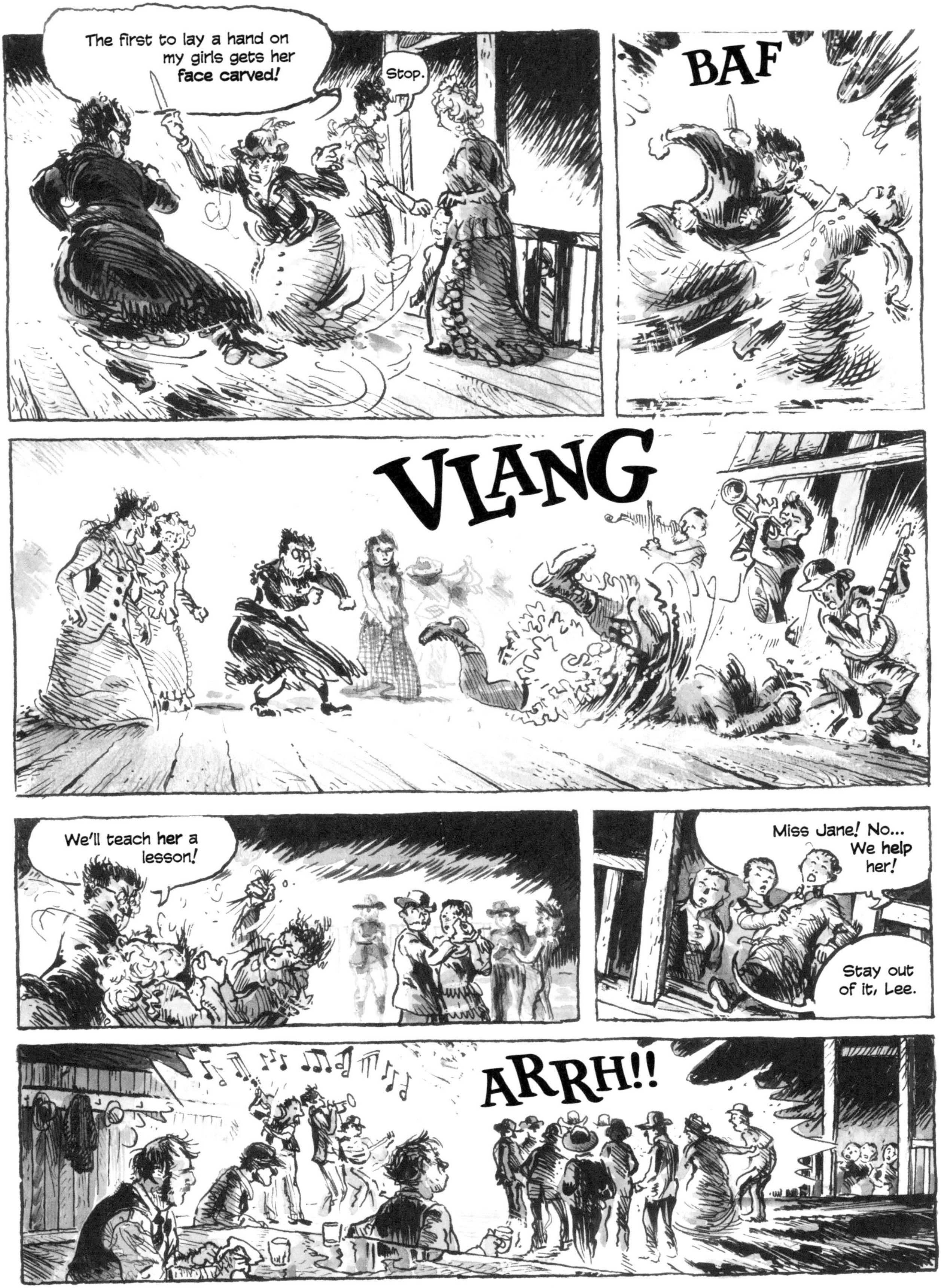
The first to lay a hand on my girls gets her **face carved!**
Stop.
BAF
VLANG
We'll teach **her** a lesson!
Miss Jane! No... We help her!
Stay out of it, Lee.
ARRH!!

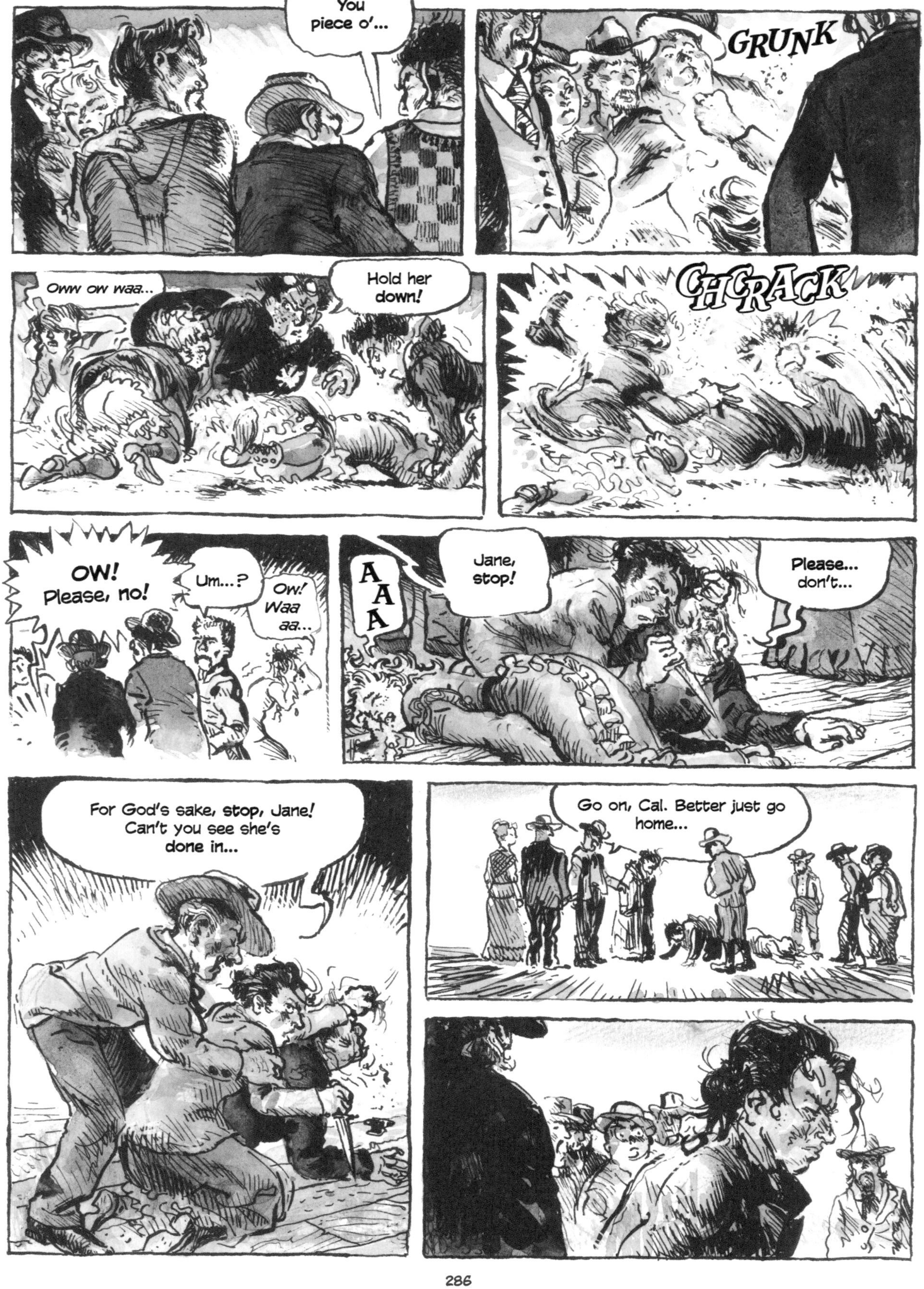
You piece o'...
GRUNK
Oww ow waa...
Hold her down!
CHCRACK
OW! Please, no!
Um...?
Ow! Waa aa...
AAA
Jane, stop!
Please... don't...
For God's sake, stop, Jane! Can't you see she's done in...
Go on, Cal. Better just go home...

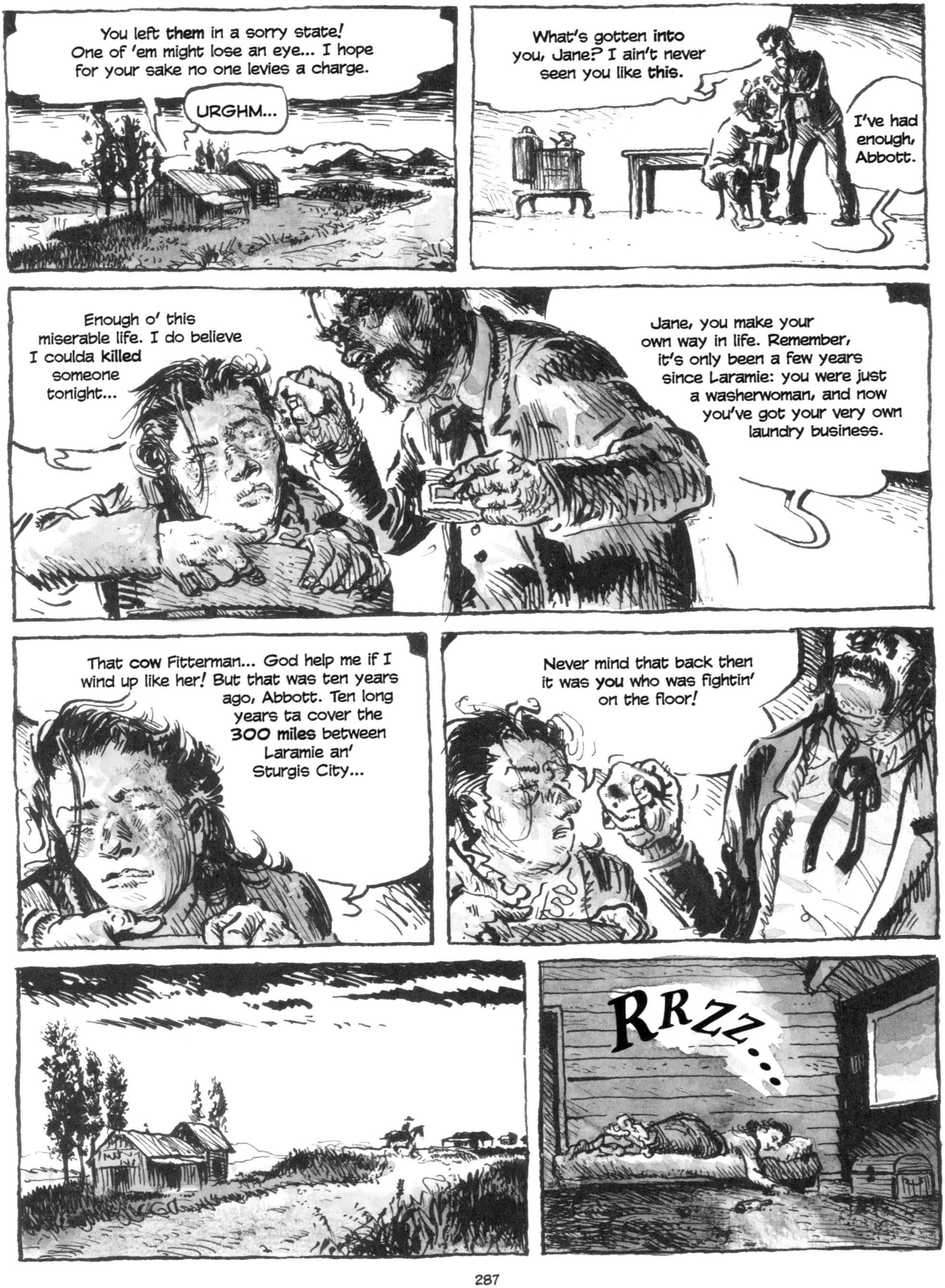

You left them in a sorry state! One of 'em might lose an eye... I hope for your sake no one levies a charge.
URGHM...
What's gotten into you, Jane? I ain't never seen you like this.
I've had enough, Abbott.
Enough o' this miserable life. I do believe I coulda killed someone tonight...
Jane, you make your own way in life. Remember, it's only been a few years since Laramie: you were just a washerwoman, and now you've got your very own laundry business.
That cow Fitterman... God help me if I wind up like her! But that was ten years ago, Abbott. Ten long years ta cover the 300 miles between Laramie an' Sturgis City...
Never mind that back then it was you who was fightin' on the floor!
RRZZZ...

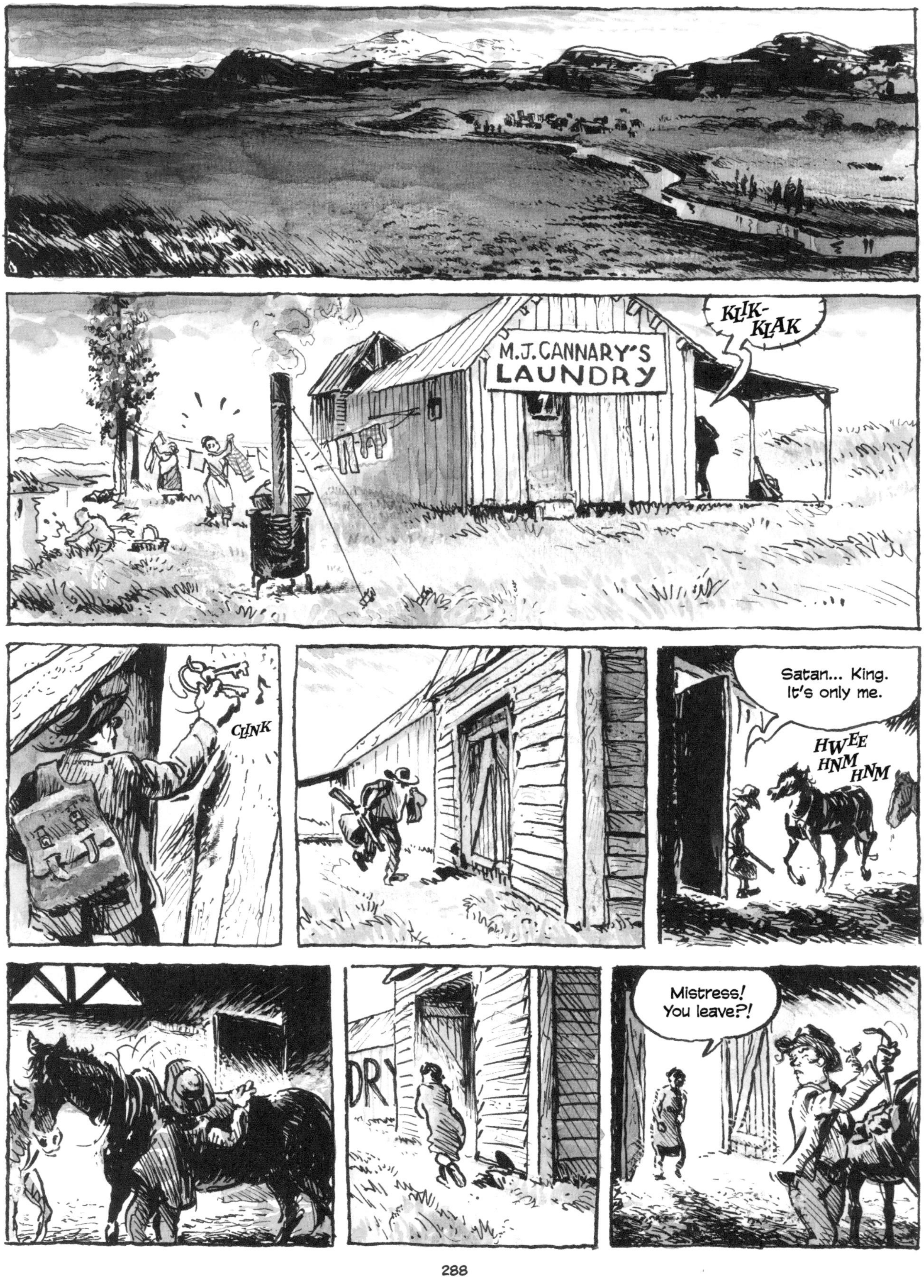
M.J. CANNARY'S LAUNDRY
KLIK-KLAK
CLINK
Satan... King. It's only me.
HWEE HNM HNM
DRY
Mistress! You leave?!

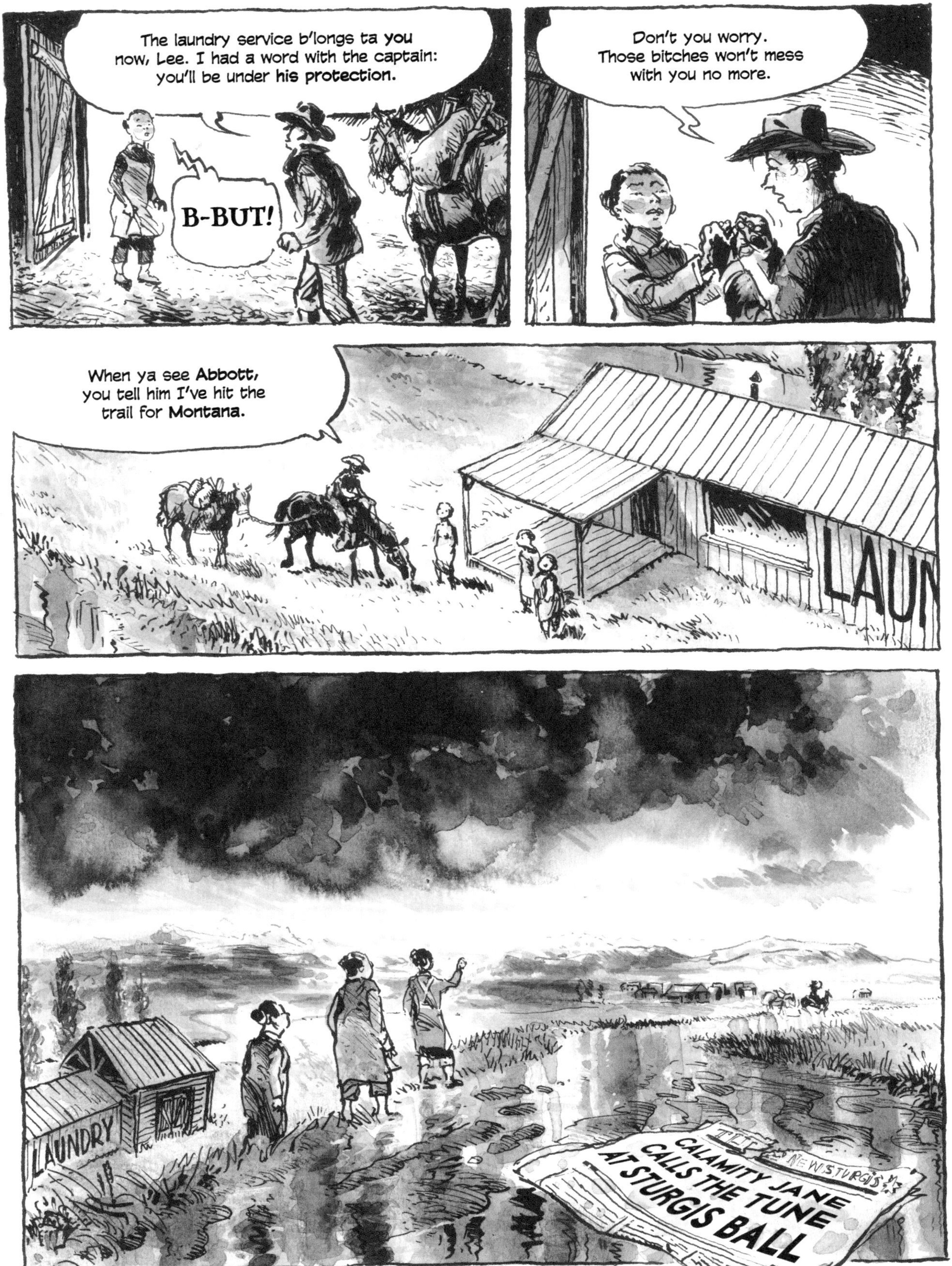
The laundry service b'longs ta you now, Lee. I had a word with the captain: you'll be under his protection.
B-BUT!
Don't you worry. Those bitches won't mess with you no more.
When ya see Abbott, you tell him I've hit the trail for Montana.
LAUN
LAUNDRY
CALAMITY JANE CALLS THE TUNE AT STURGIS BALL

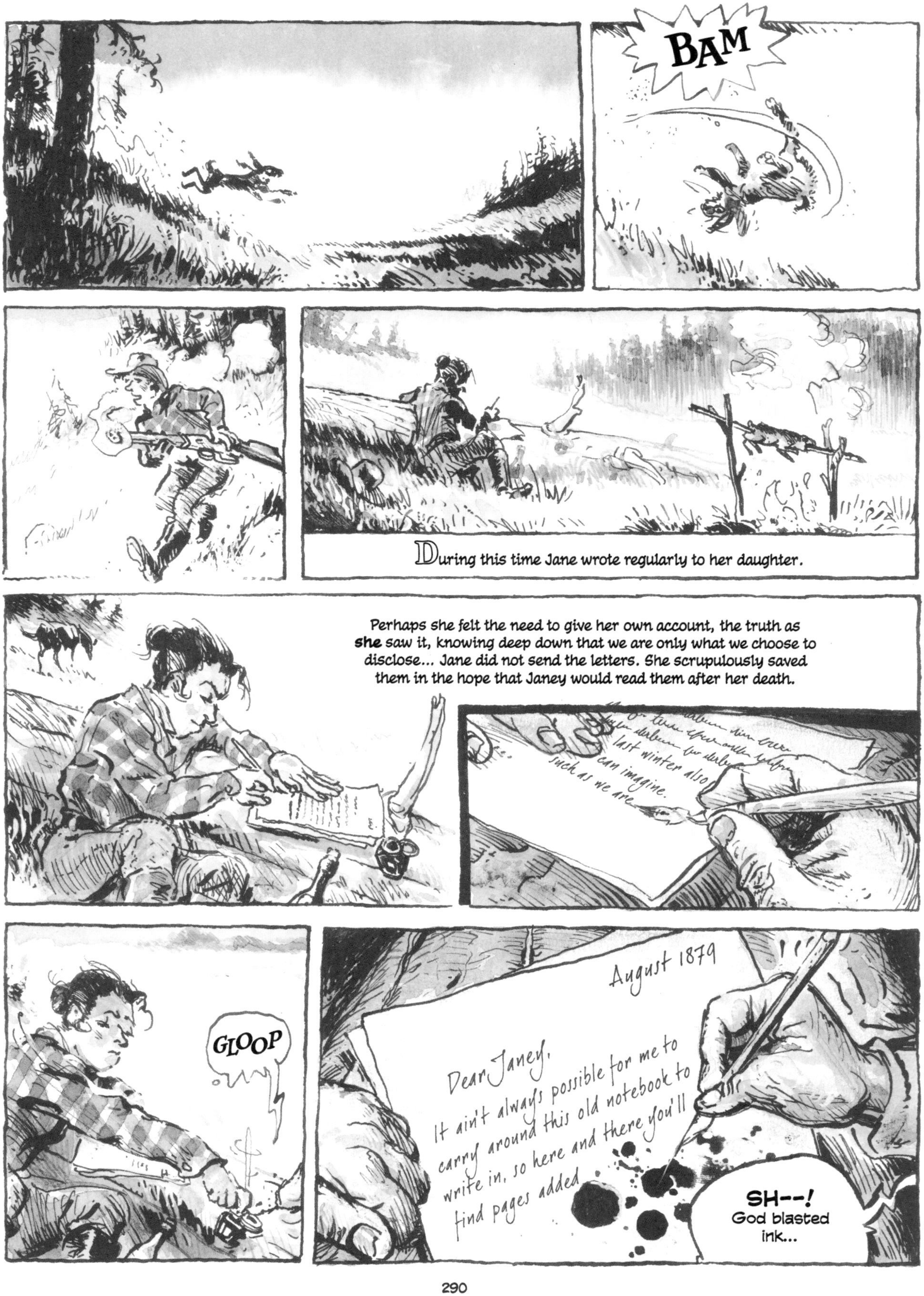
BAM
During this time Jane wrote regularly to her daughter.
Perhaps she felt the need to give her own account, the truth as she saw it, knowing deep down that we are only what we choose to disclose... Jane did not send the letters. She scrupulously saved them in the hope that Janey would read them after her death.
last winter also
can imagine.
such as we are.
GLOOP
August 1879
Dear Janey,
It ain't always possible for me to carry around this old notebook to write in, so here and there you'll find pages added
SH--!
God blasted ink...

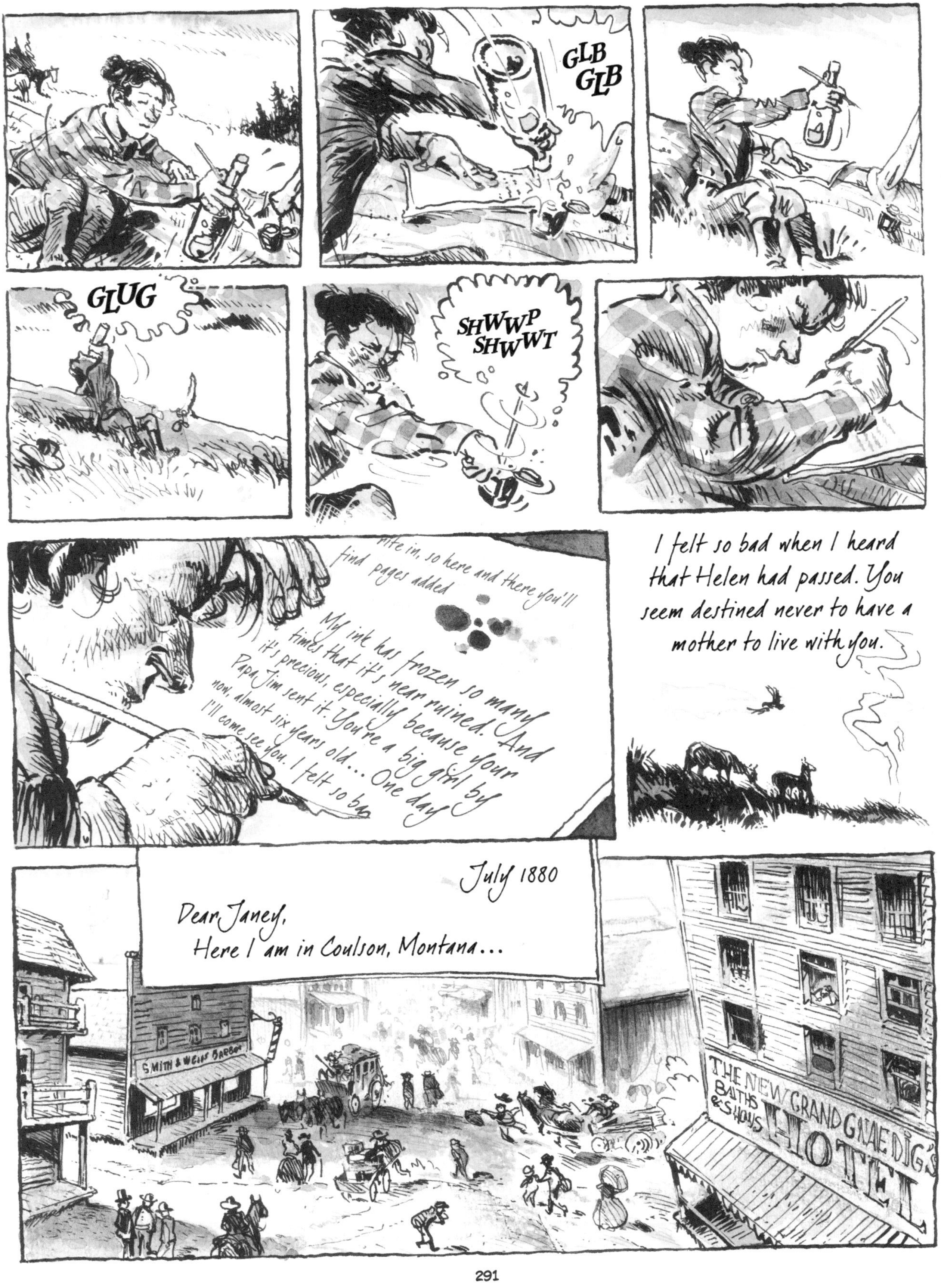
GLB GLB
GLUG
SHWWP SHWWT
in, so here and there you'll find pages added
My ink has frozen so many times that it's near ruined. And it's precious, especially because your Papa Jim sent it. You're a big girl by now, almost six years old... One day I'll come see you. I felt so
I felt so bad when I heard that Helen had passed. You seem destined never to have a mother to live with you.
July 1880
Dear Janey,
Here I am in Coulson, Montana...
SMITH & WELLS BARBER
THE NEW GRAND GRAEDIG'S HOTEL
BATHS & SHOWS

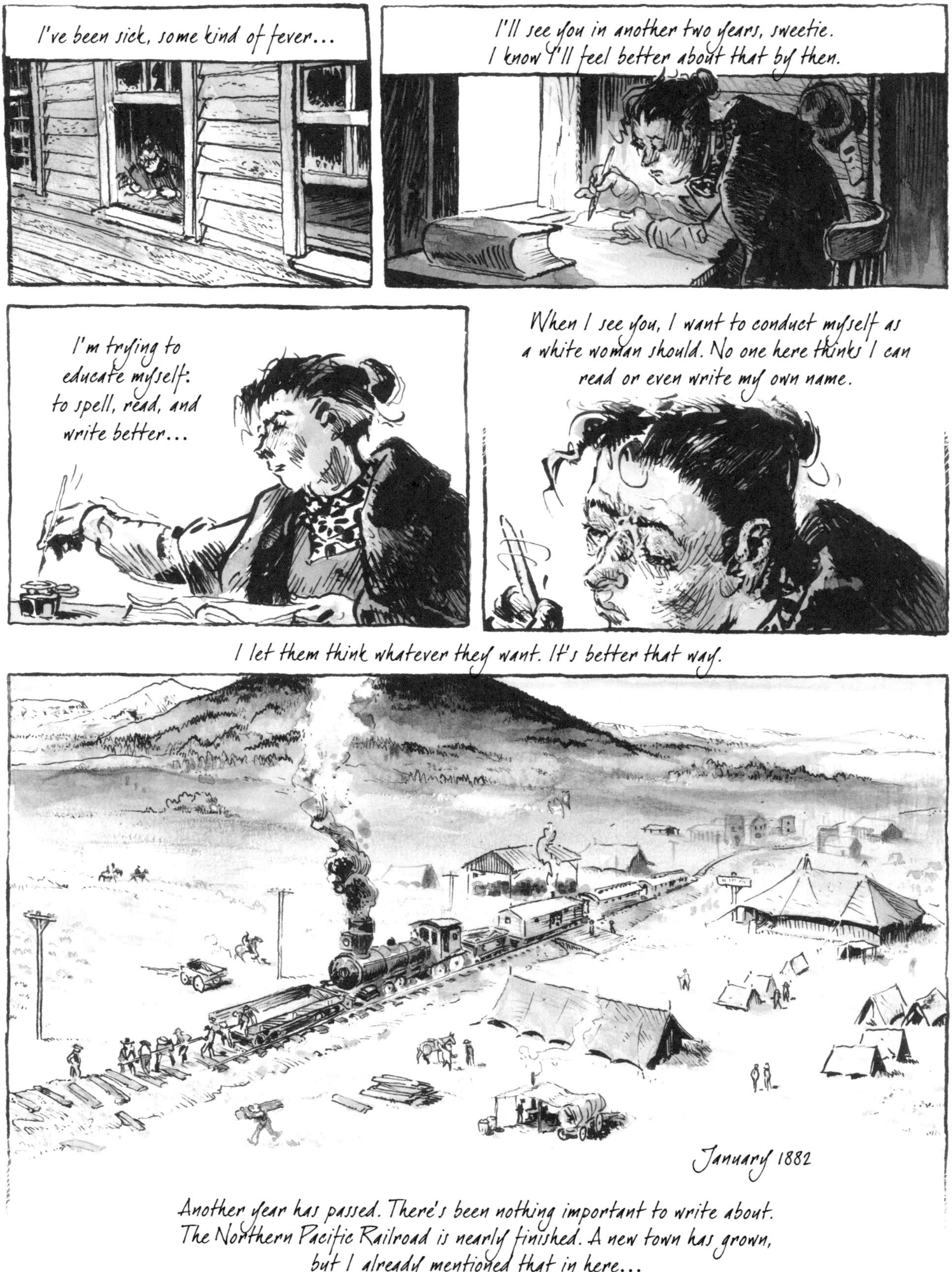
I've been sick, some kind of fever...
I'll see you in another two years, sweetie. I know I'll feel better about that by then.
I'm trying to educate myself: to spell, read, and write better...
When I see you, I want to conduct myself as a white woman should. No one here thinks I can read or even write my own name.
I let them think whatever they want. It's better that way.
January 1882
Another year has passed. There's been nothing important to write about. The Northern Pacific Railroad is nearly finished. A new town has grown, but I already mentioned that in here...

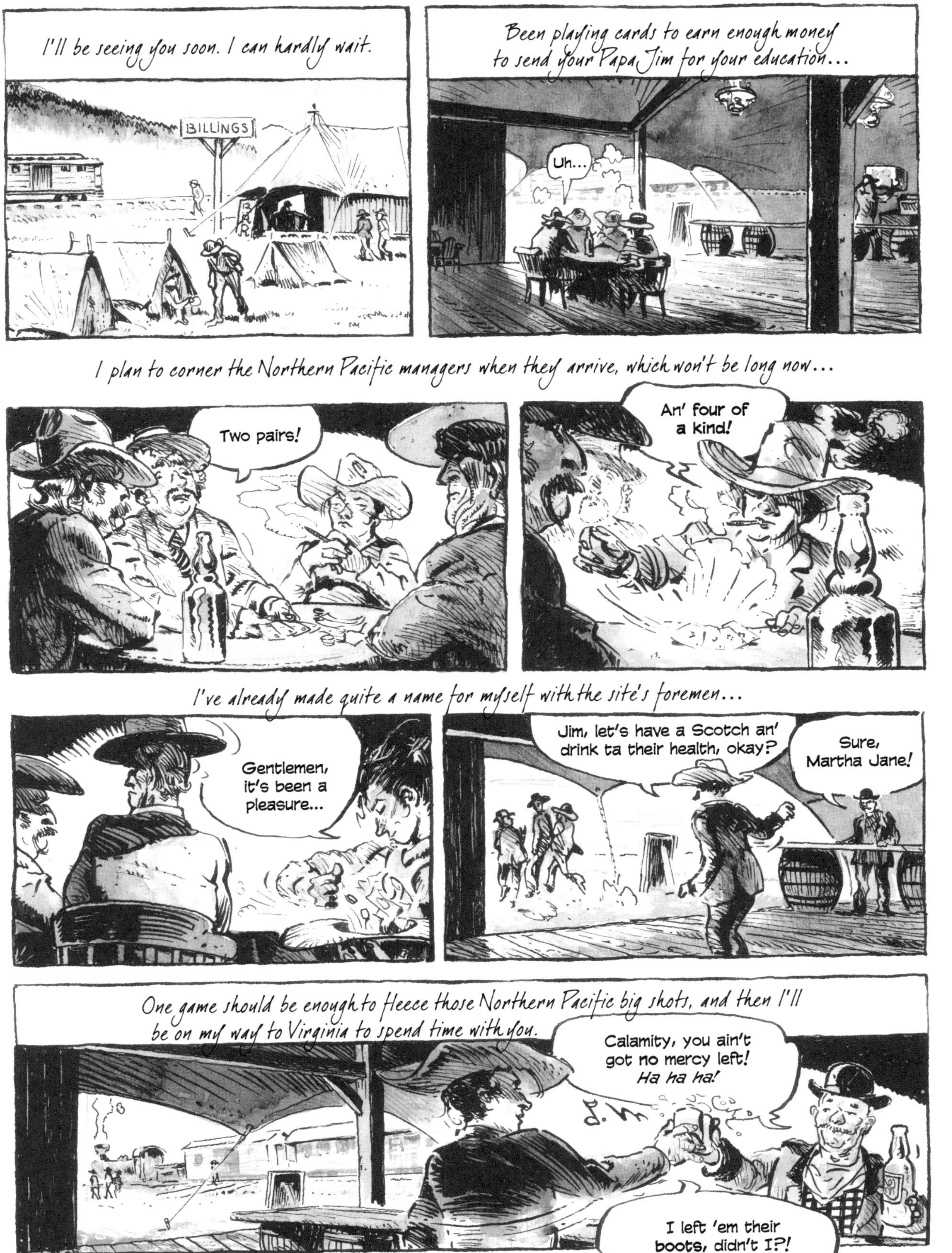
I'll be seeing you soon. I can hardly wait.
BILLINGS
Been playing cards to earn enough money to send your Papa Jim for your education...
Uh...
I plan to corner the Northern Pacific managers when they arrive, which won't be long now...
Two pairs!
An' four of a kind!
I've already made quite a name for myself with the site's foremen...
Gentlemen, it's been a pleasure...
Jim, let's have a Scotch an' drink ta their health, okay?
Sure, Martha Jane!
One game should be enough to fleece those Northern Pacific big shots, and then I'll be on my way to Virginia to spend time with you.
Calamity, you ain't got no mercy left! *Ha ha ha!*
I left 'em their boots, didn't I?!

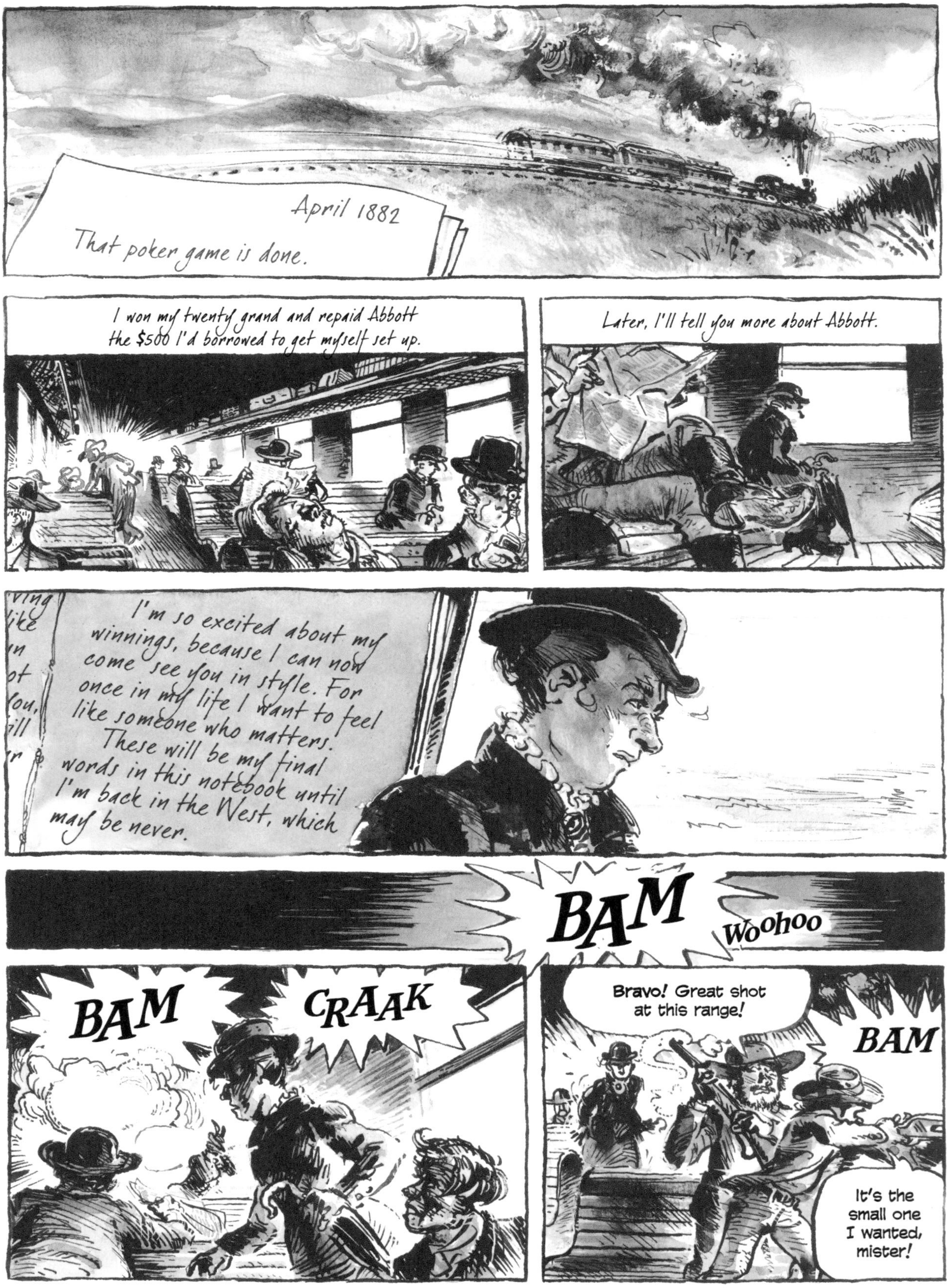
April 1882
That poker game is done.
I won my twenty grand and repaid Abbott the $500 I'd borrowed to get myself set up.
Later, I'll tell you more about Abbott.
I'm so excited about my winnings, because I can now come see you in style. For once in my life I want to feel like someone who matters.
These will be my final words in this notebook until I'm back in the West, which may be never.
BAM
Woohoo
BAM
CRAAK
Bravo! Great shot at this range!
BAM
It's the small one I wanted, mister!

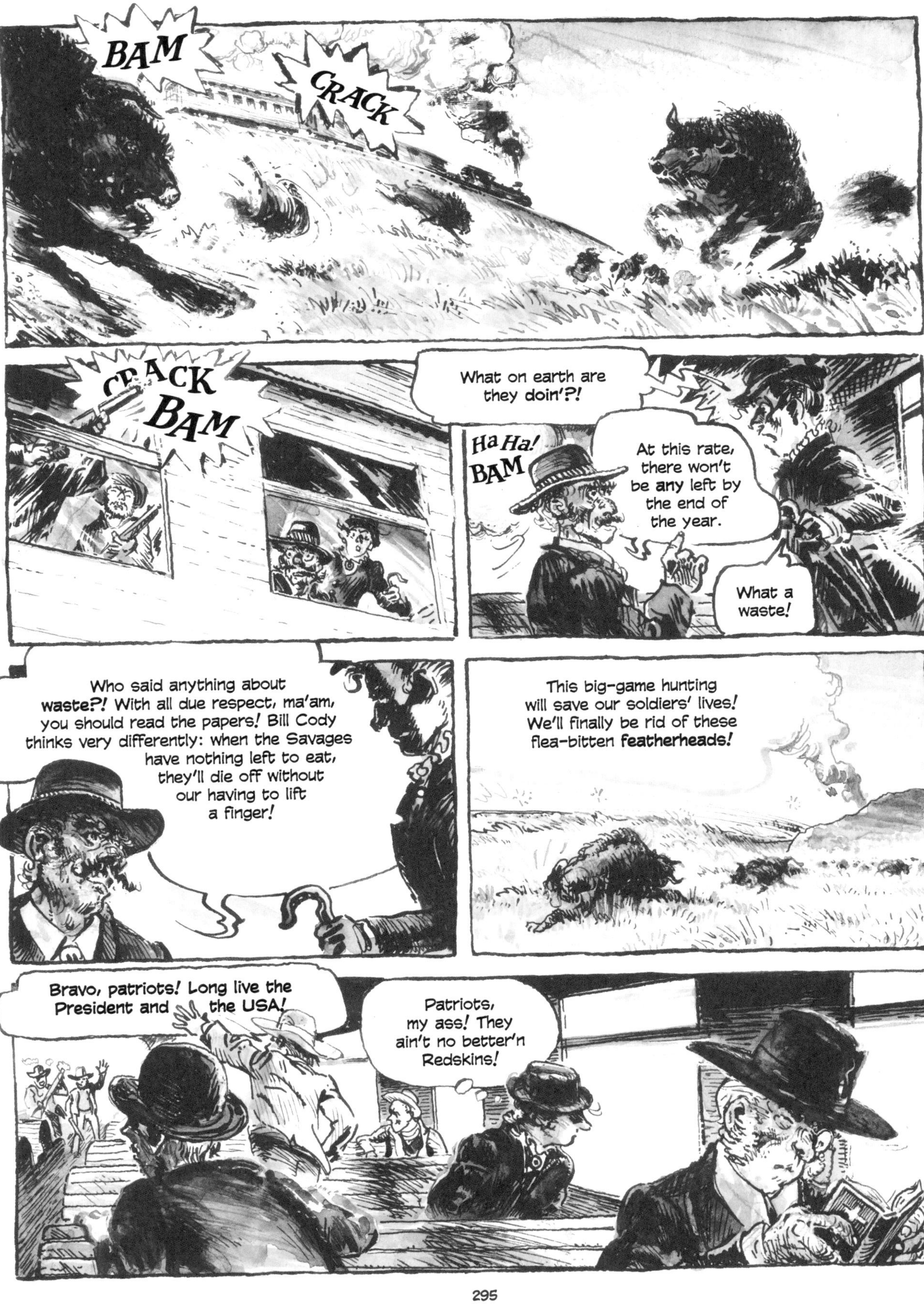
BAM
CRACK
CRACK
BAM
What on earth are they doin'?!
Ha Ha! BAM
At this rate, there won't be any left by the end of the year.
What a waste!
Who said anything about waste?! With all due respect, ma'am, you should read the papers! Bill Cody thinks very differently: when the Savages have nothing left to eat, they'll die off without our having to lift a finger!
This big-game hunting will save our soldiers' lives! We'll finally be rid of these flea-bitten featherheads!
Bravo, patriots! Long live the President and the USA!
Patriots, my ass! They ain't no better'n Redskins!

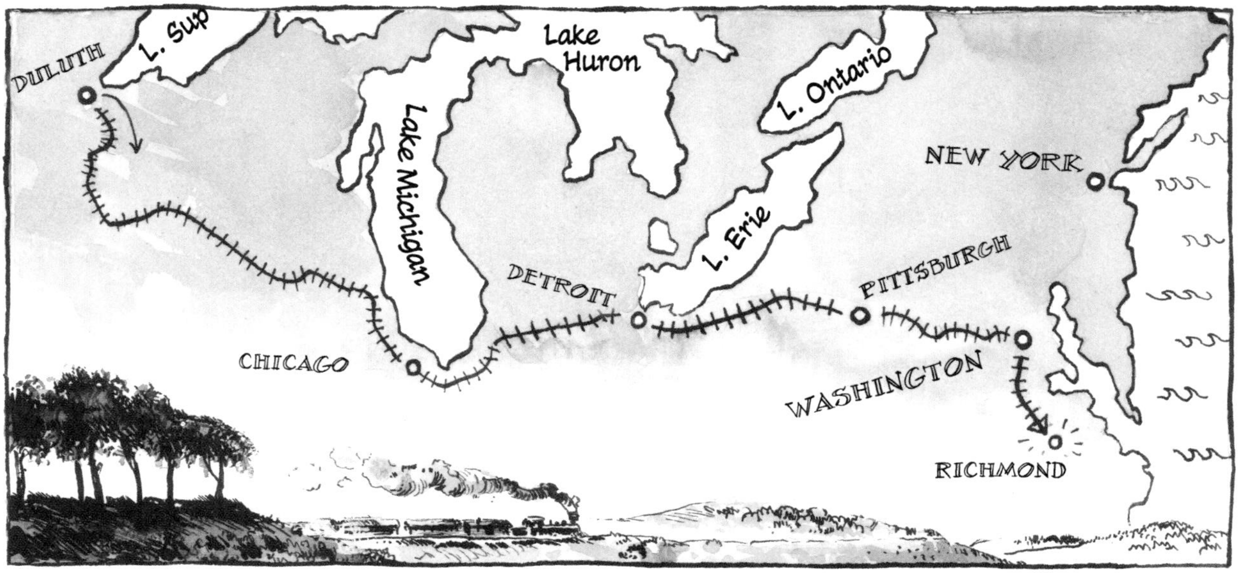
L. Sup
DULUTH
Lake Huron
L. Ontario
Lake Michigan
NEW YORK
L. Erie
PITTSBURGH
DETROIT
CHICAGO
WASHINGTON
RICHMOND

It was on her trip to Richmond that Martha Jane celebrated her 30th birthday.
She'd been knocking around the West for **15** years: an **eternity** for her...

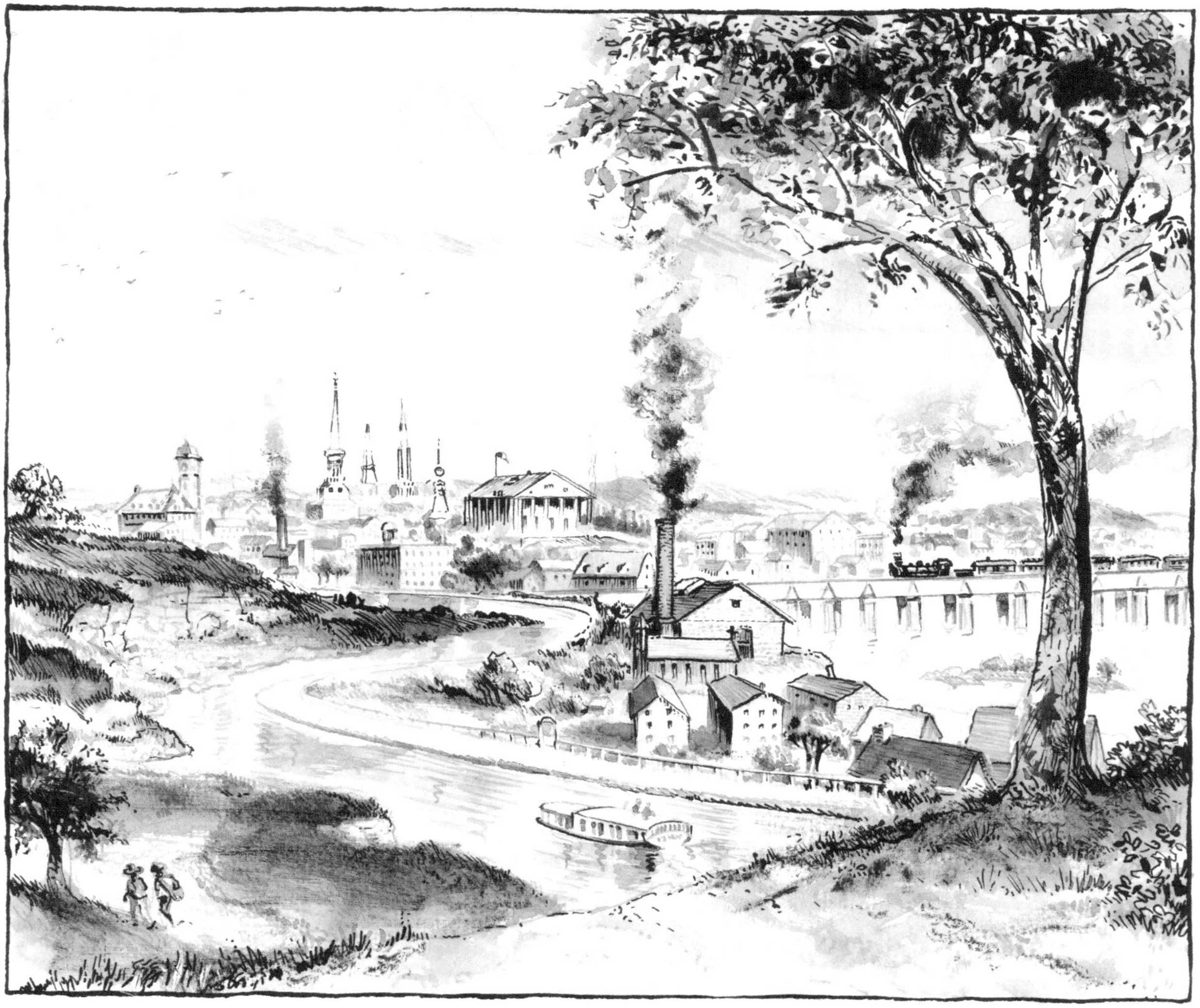

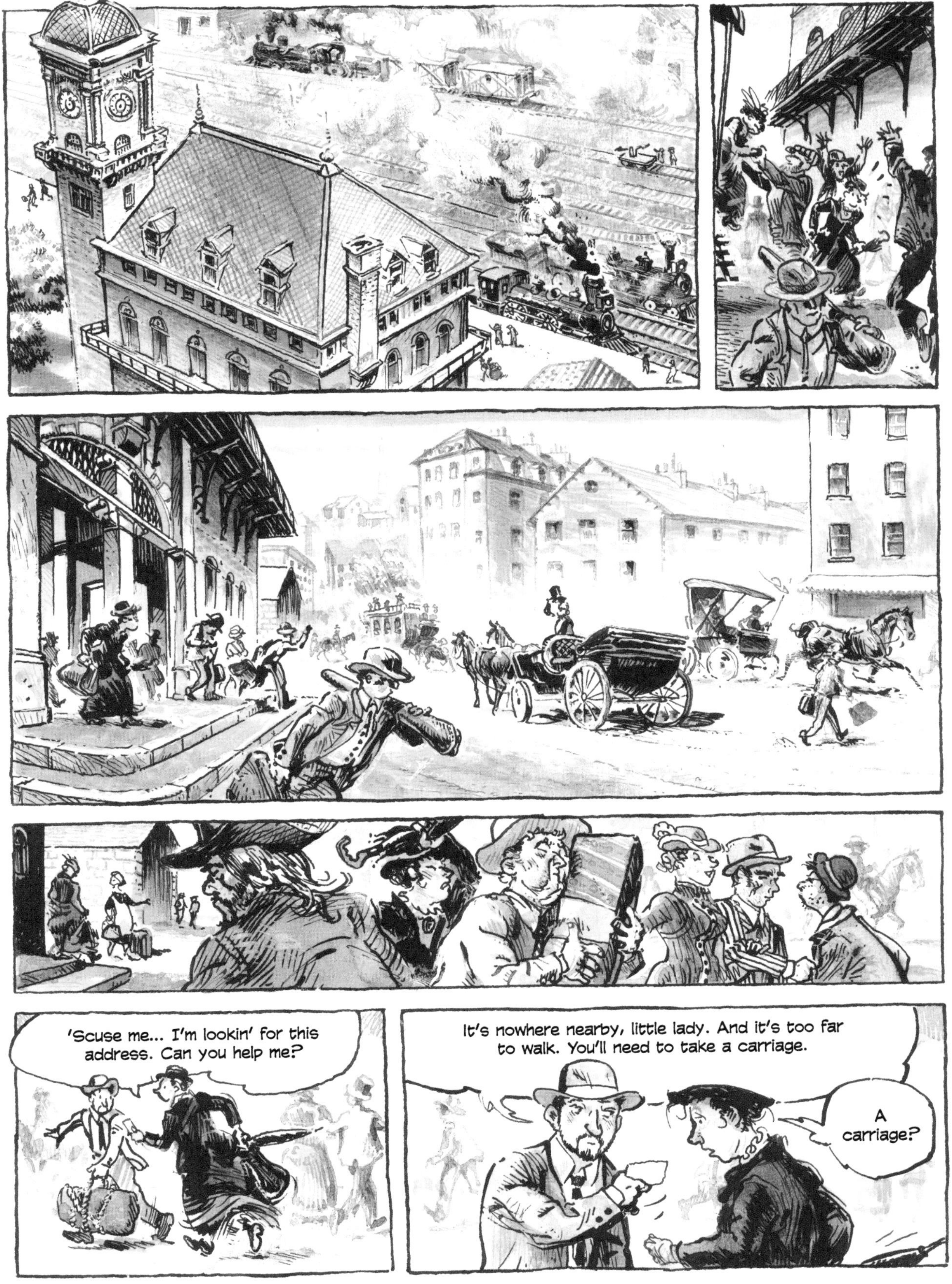
'Scuse me... I'm lookin' for this address. Can you help me?
It's nowhere nearby, little lady. And it's too far to walk. You'll need to take a carriage.
A carriage?

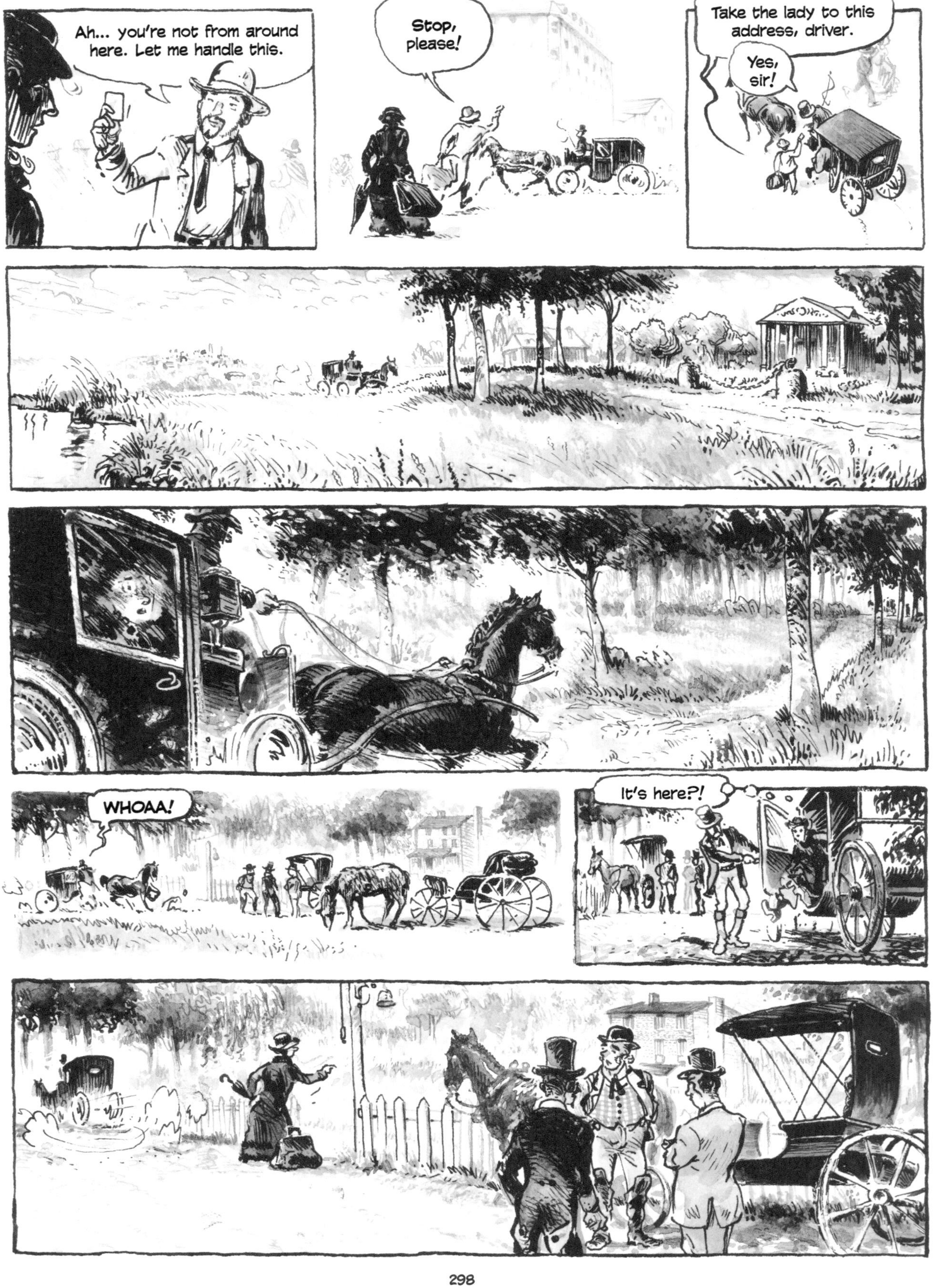
Ah... you're not from around here. Let me handle this.
Stop, please!
Take the lady to this address, driver.
Yes, sir!
WHOAA!
It's here?!

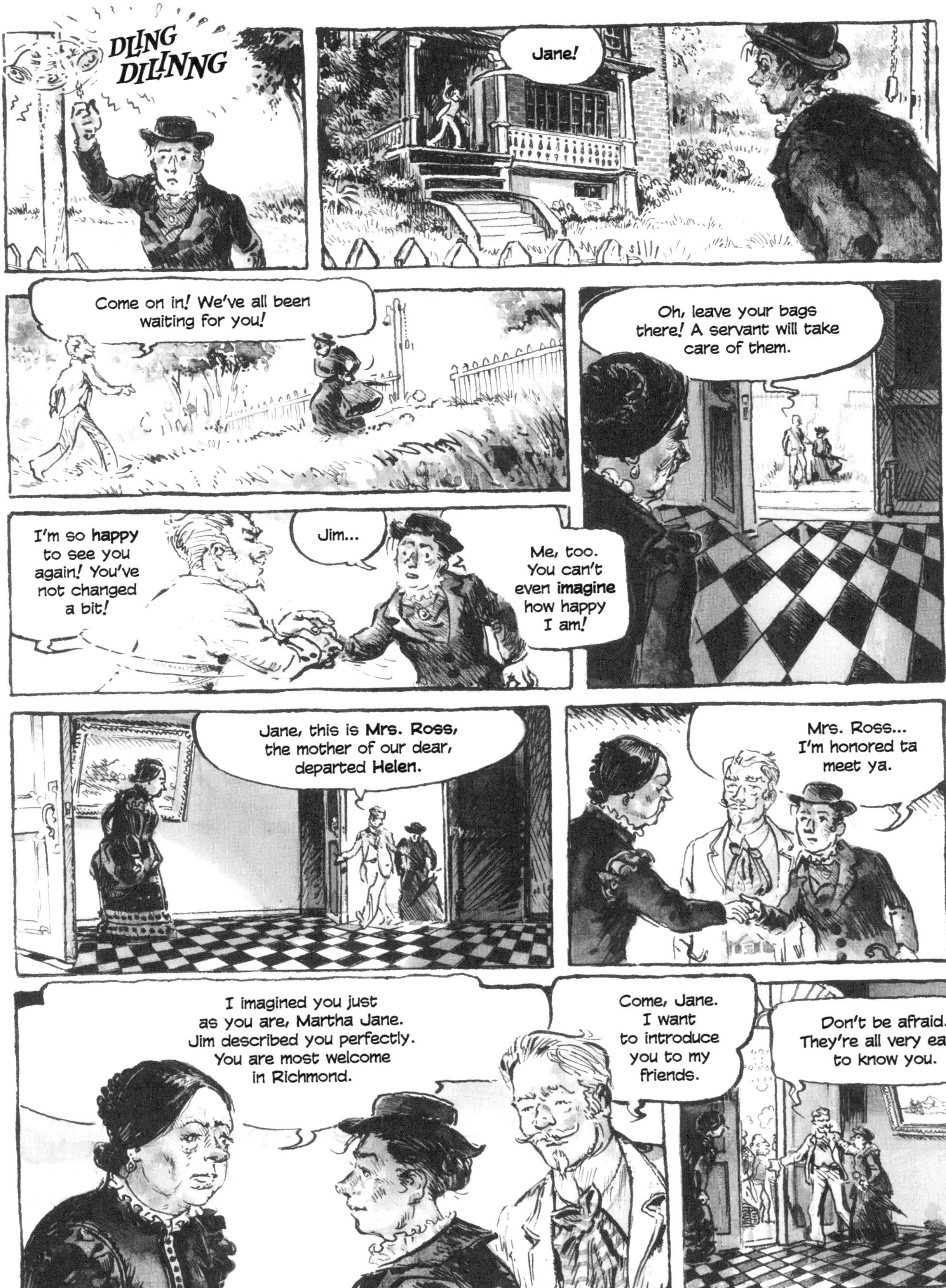
DLING
DILINNG
Jane!
Come on in! We've all been waiting for you!
Oh, leave your bags there! A servant will take care of them.
I'm so **happy** to see you again! You've not changed a bit!
Jim...
Me, too. You can't even **imagine** how happy I am!
Jane, this is **Mrs. Ross**, the mother of our dear, departed **Helen**.
Mrs. Ross... I'm honored ta meet ya.
I imagined you just as you are, Martha Jane. Jim described you perfectly. You are most welcome in Richmond.
Come, Jane. I want to introduce you to my friends.
Don't be afraid. They're all very eager to know you.

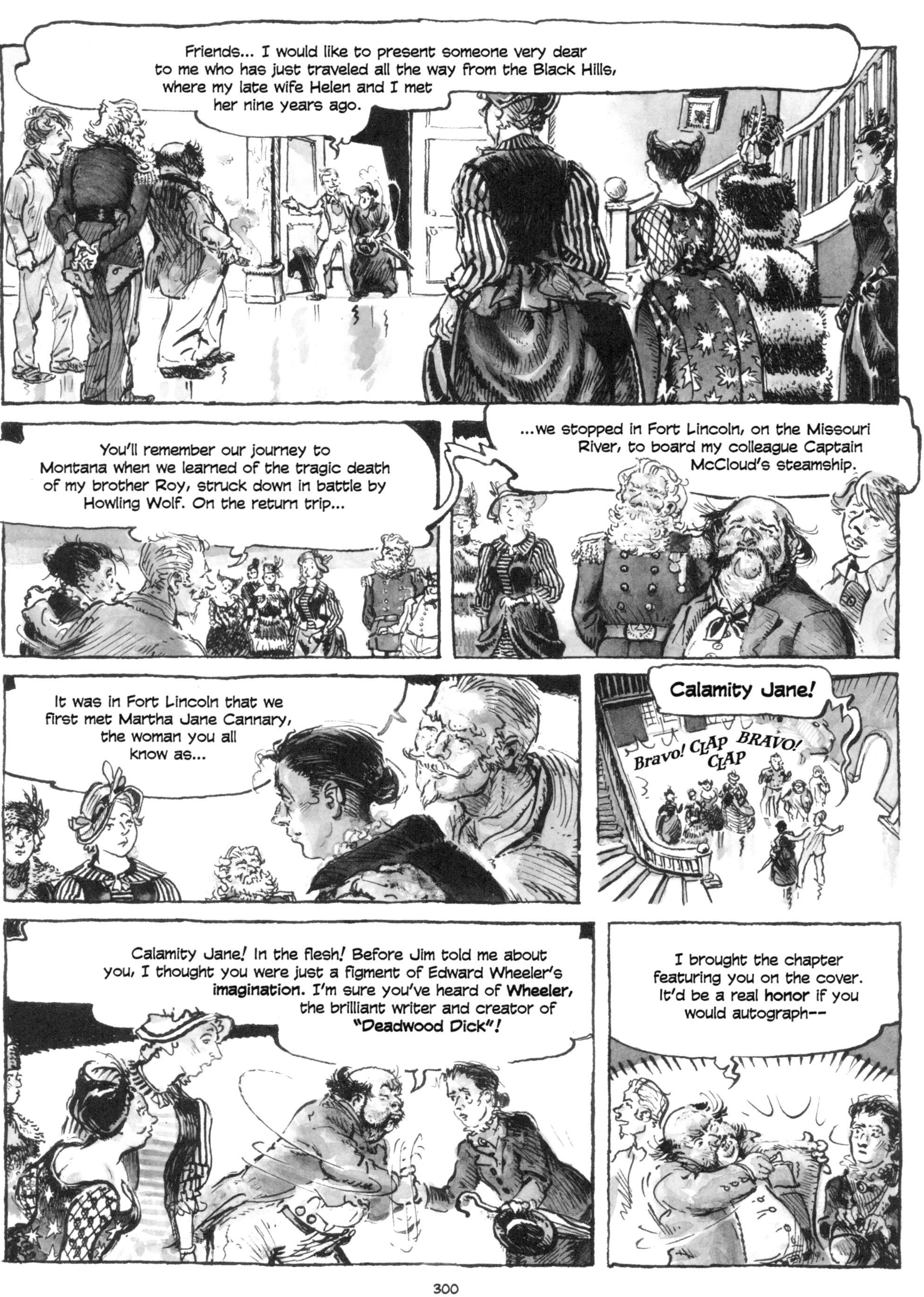
Friends... I would like to present someone very dear to me who has just traveled all the way from the Black Hills, where my late wife Helen and I met her nine years ago.
You'll remember our journey to Montana when we learned of the tragic death of my brother Roy, struck down in battle by Howling Wolf. On the return trip...
...we stopped in Fort Lincoln, on the Missouri River, to board my colleague Captain McCloud's steamship.
It was in Fort Lincoln that we first met Martha Jane Cannary, the woman you all know as...
Calamity Jane!
Bravo! CLAP BRAVO! CLAP
Calamity Jane! In the flesh! Before Jim told me about you, I thought you were just a figment of Edward Wheeler's **imagination**. I'm sure you've heard of **Wheeler**, the brilliant writer and creator of **"Deadwood Dick"!**
I brought the chapter featuring you on the cover. It'd be a real **honor** if you would autograph--

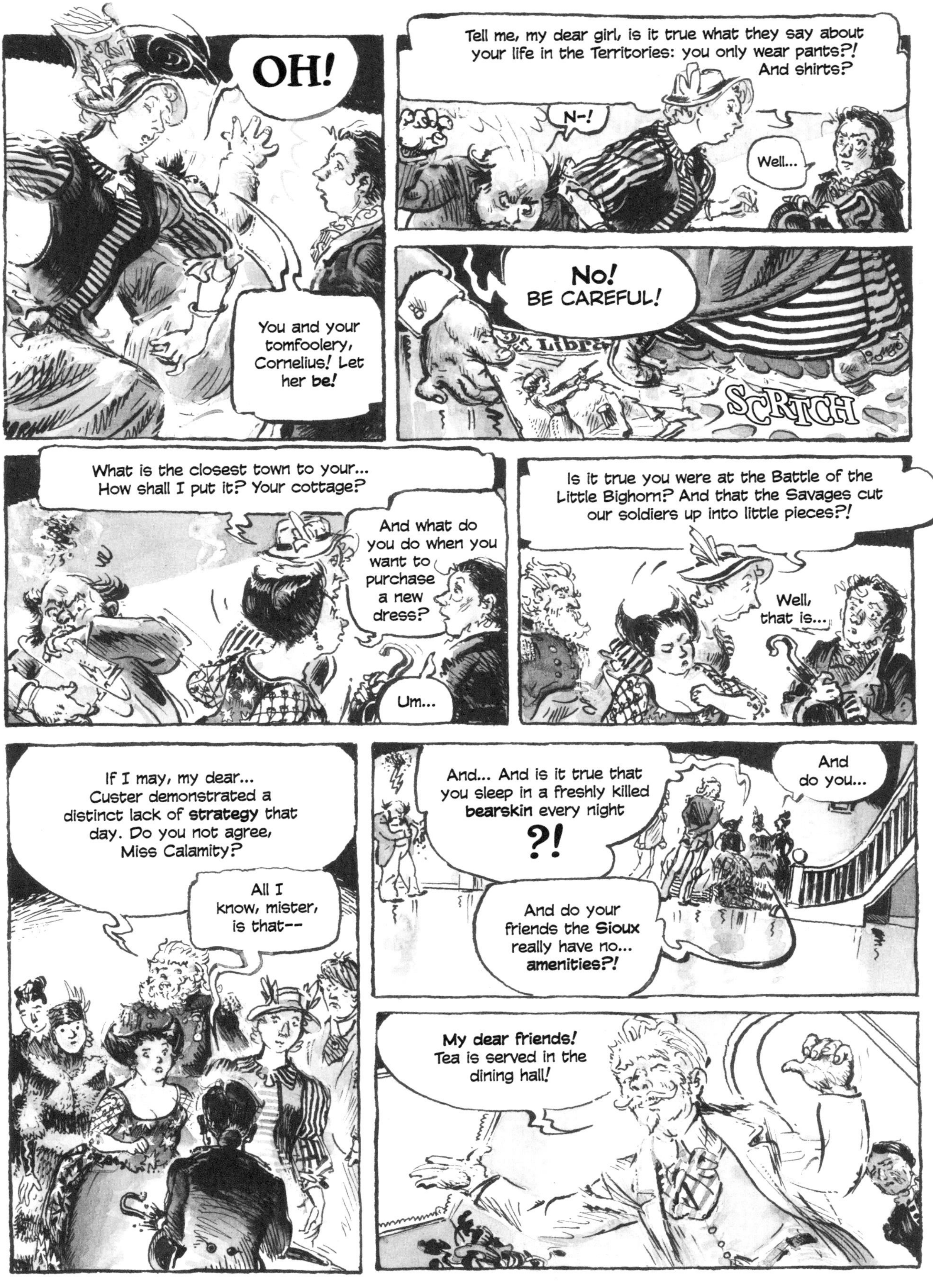
OH!
You and your tomfoolery, Cornelius! Let her be!
Tell me, my dear girl, is it true what they say about your life in the Territories: you only wear pants?! And shirts?
N-!
Well...
No! BE CAREFUL!
SCRTCH
What is the closest town to your... How shall I put it? Your cottage?
And what do you do when you want to purchase a new dress?
Um...
Is it true you were at the Battle of the Little Bighorn? And that the Savages cut our soldiers up into little pieces?!
Well, that is...
If I may, my dear... Custer demonstrated a distinct lack of strategy that day. Do you not agree, Miss Calamity?
All I know, mister, is that--
And... And is it true that you sleep in a freshly killed bearskin every night ?!
And do you...
And do your friends the Sioux really have no... amenities?!
My dear friends! Tea is served in the dining hall!

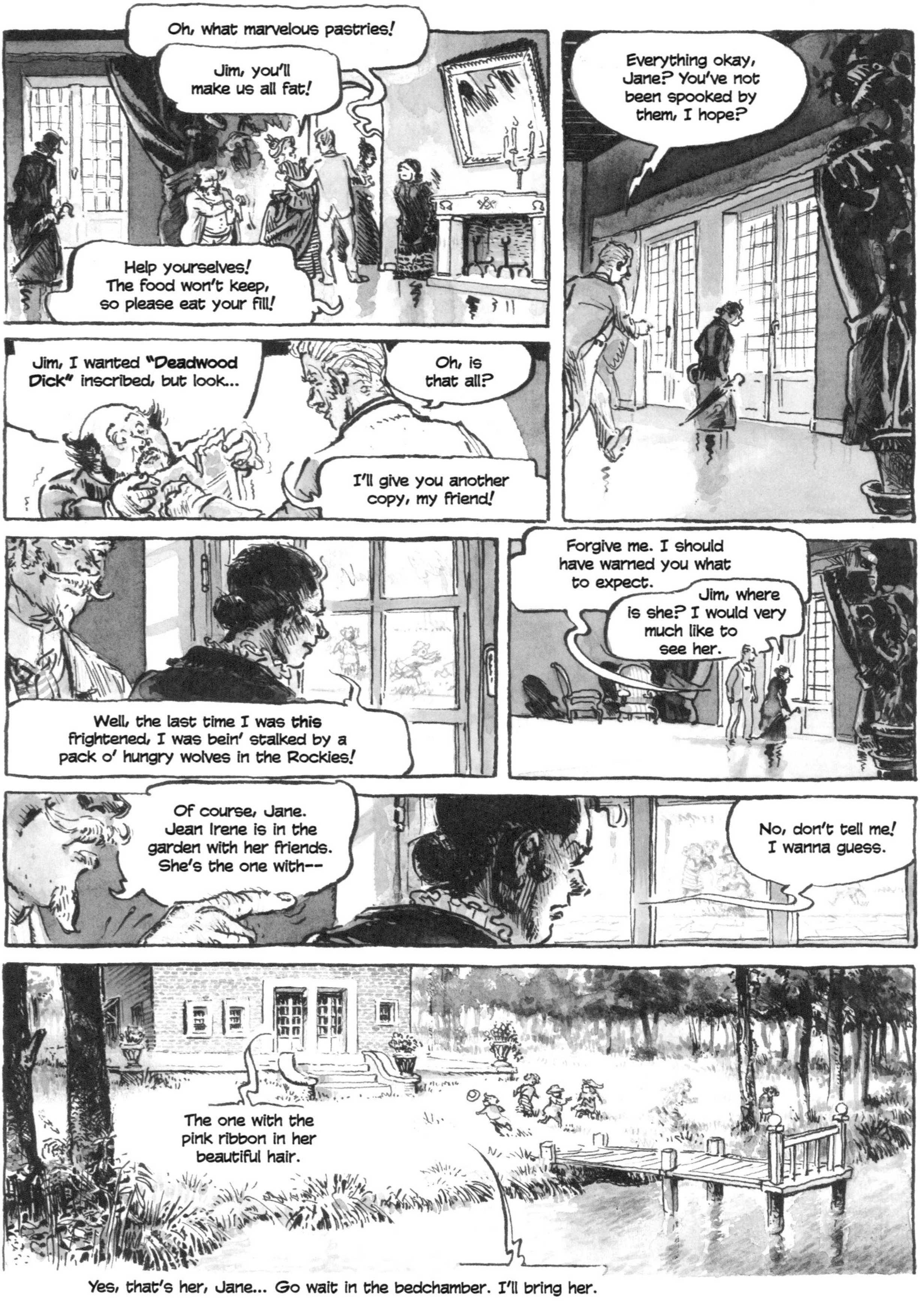
Oh, what marvelous pastries!
Jim, you'll make us all fat!
Help yourselves! The food won't keep, so please eat your fill!
Everything okay, Jane? You've not been spooked by them, I hope?
Jim, I wanted "Deadwood Dick" inscribed, but look...
Oh, is that all?
I'll give you another copy, my friend!
Well, the last time I was this frightened, I was bein' stalked by a pack o' hungry wolves in the Rockies!
Forgive me. I should have warned you what to expect.
Jim, where is she? I would very much like to see her.
Of course, Jane. Jean Irene is in the garden with her friends. She's the one with--
No, don't tell me! I wanna guess.
The one with the pink ribbon in her beautiful hair.
Yes, that's her, Jane... Go wait in the bedchamber. I'll bring her.

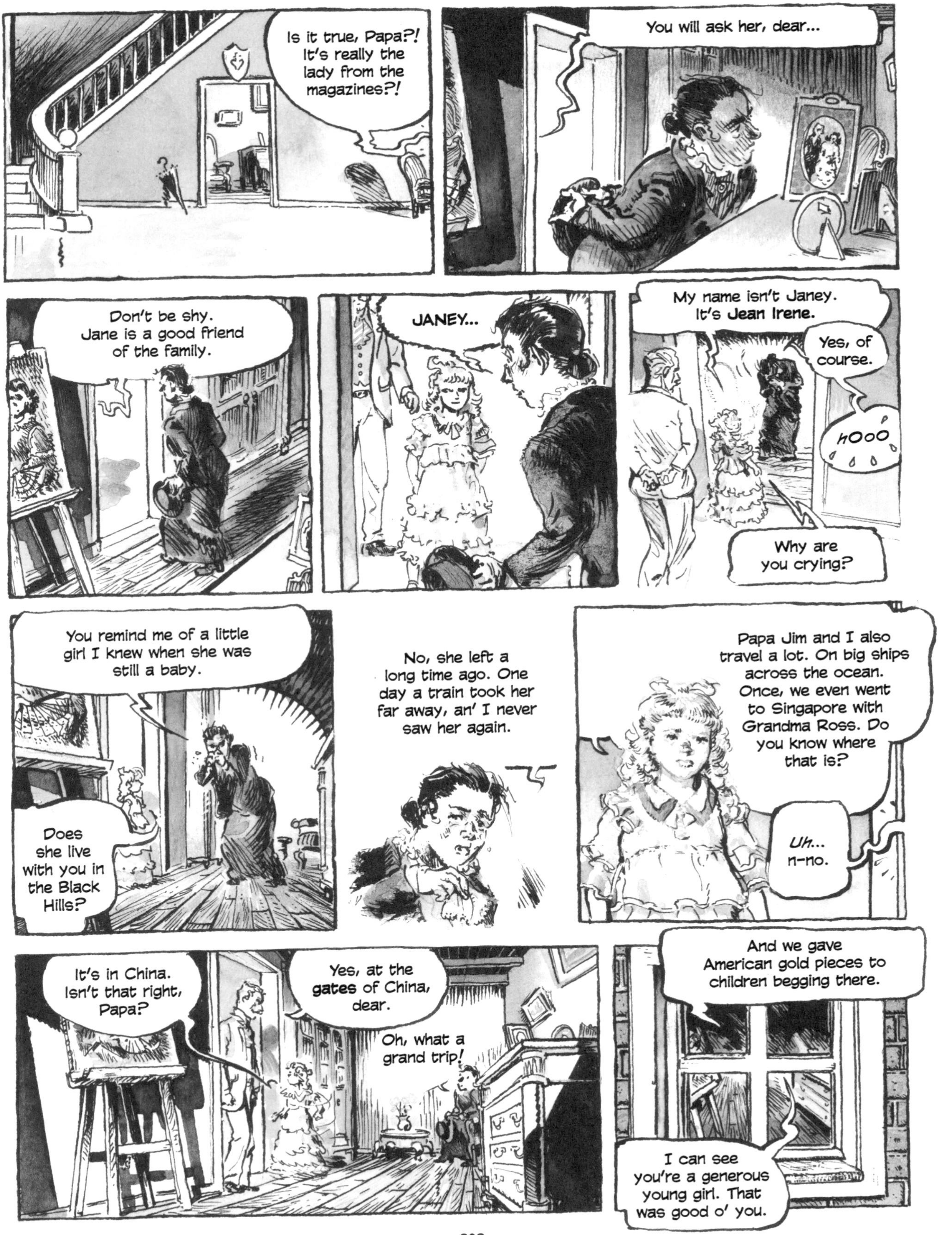

Is it true, Papa?! It's really the lady from the magazines?!
You will ask her, dear...
Don't be shy. Jane is a good friend of the family.
JANEY...
My name isn't Janey. It's **Jean Irene.**
Yes, of course.
hOOO
Why are you crying?
You remind me of a little girl I knew when she was still a baby.
Does she live with you in the Black Hills?
No, she left a long time ago. One day a train took her far away, an' I never saw her again.
Papa Jim and I also travel a lot. On big ships across the ocean. Once, we even went to Singapore with Grandma Ross. Do you know where that is?
Uh... n-no.
It's in China. Isn't that right, Papa?
Yes, at the **gates** of China, dear.
Oh, what a grand trip!
And we gave American gold pieces to children begging there.
I can see you're a generous young girl. That was good o' you.

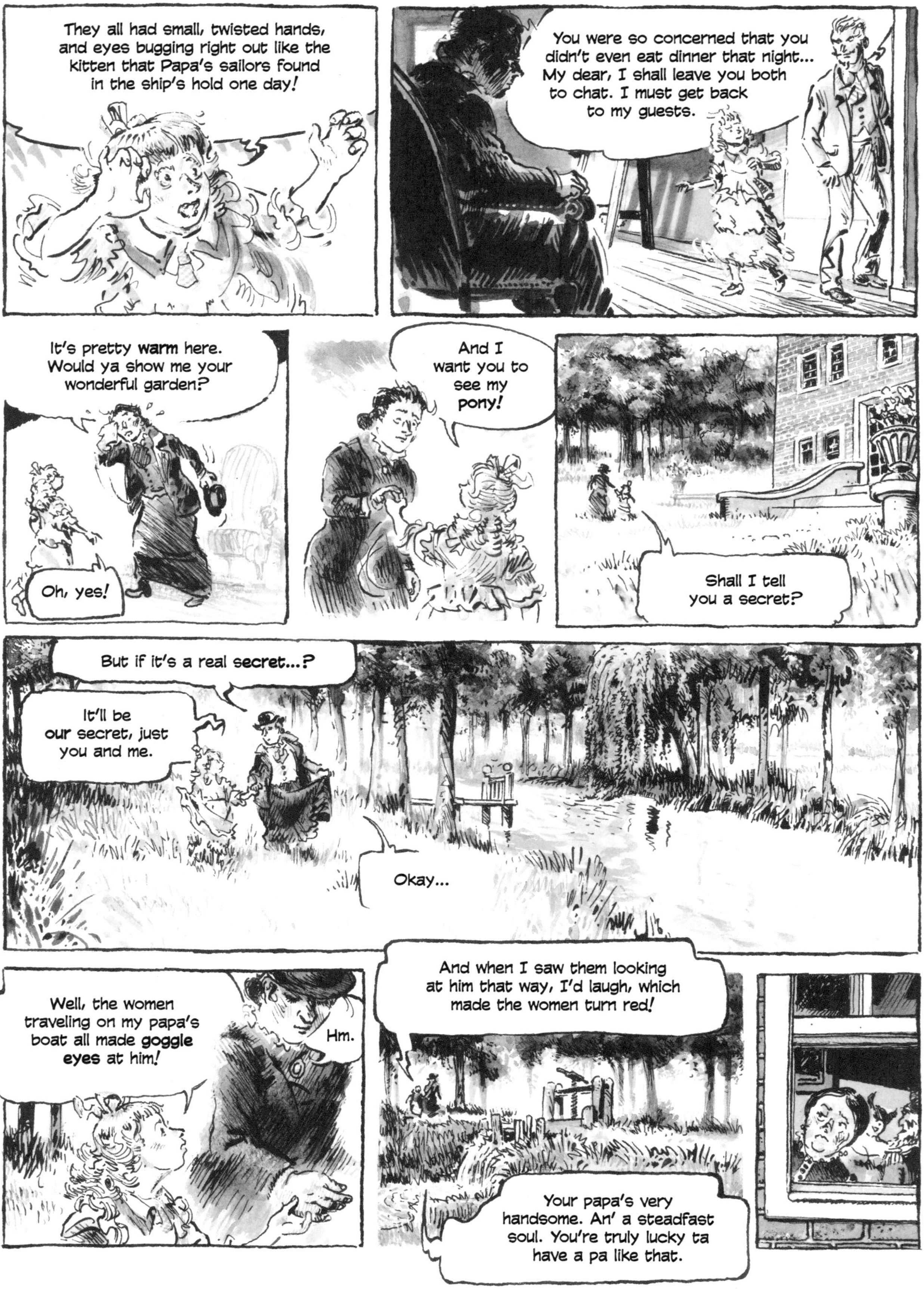
They all had small, twisted hands, and eyes bugging right out like the kitten that Papa's sailors found in the ship's hold one day!
You were so concerned that you didn't even eat dinner that night... My dear, I shall leave you both to chat. I must get back to my guests.
It's pretty **warm** here. Would ya show me your wonderful garden?
Oh, yes!
And I want you to see my **pony!**
Shall I tell you a secret?
But if it's a real **secret...?**
It'll be **our** secret, just you and me.
Okay...
Well, the women traveling on my papa's boat all made **goggle eyes** at him!
Hm.
And when I saw them looking at him that way, I'd laugh, which made the women turn red!
Your papa's very handsome. An' a steadfast soul. You're truly lucky ta have a pa like that.

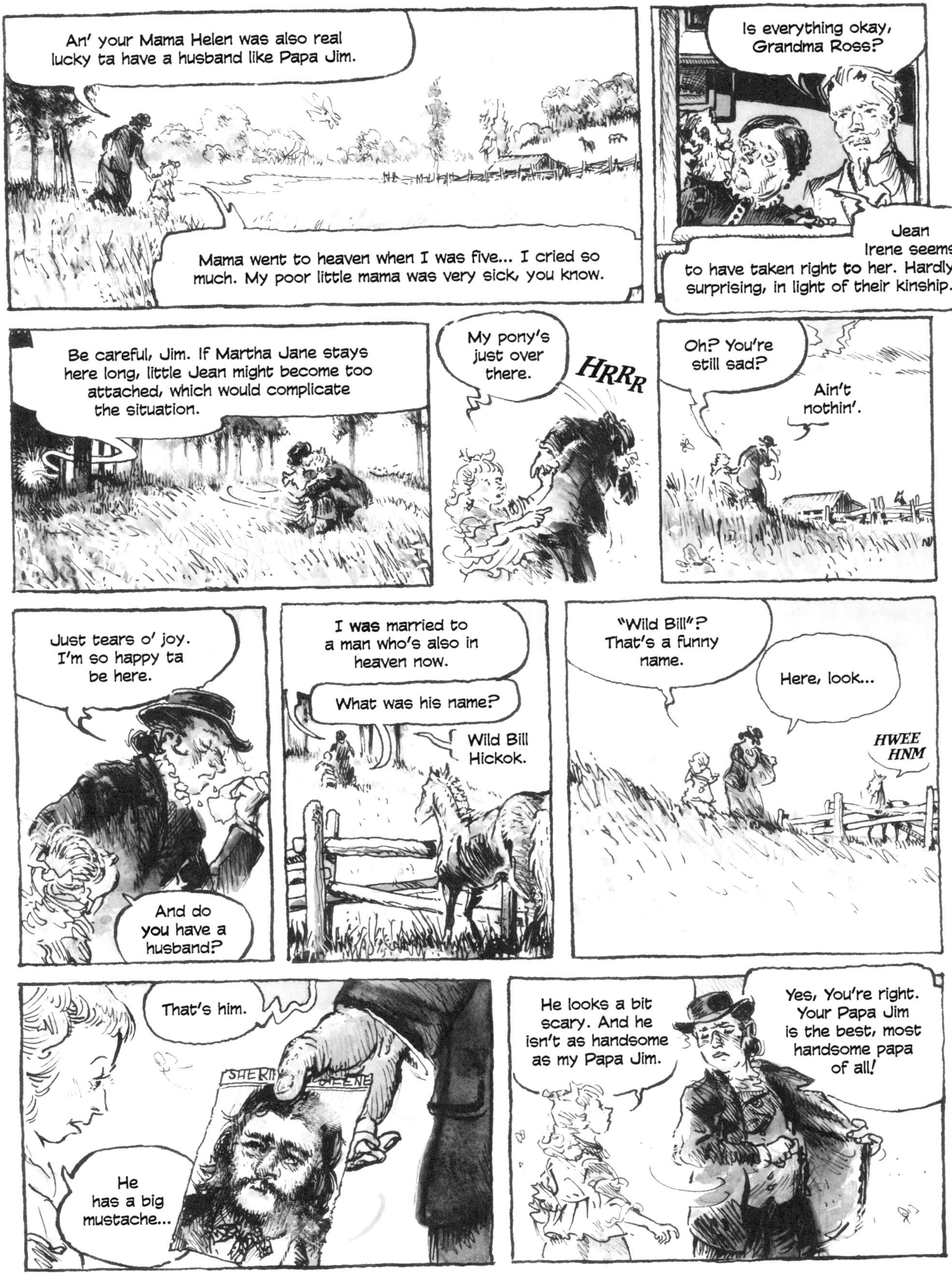
An' your Mama Helen was also real lucky ta have a husband like Papa Jim.
Mama went to heaven when I was five... I cried so much. My poor little mama was very sick, you know.
Is everything okay, Grandma Ross?
Jean Irene seems to have taken right to her. Hardly surprising, in light of their kinship.
Be careful, Jim. If Martha Jane stays here long, little Jean might become too attached, which would complicate the situation.
My pony's just over there.
HRRR
Oh? You're still sad?
Ain't nothin'.
Just tears o' joy. I'm so happy ta be here.
And do you have a husband?
I was married to a man who's also in heaven now.
What was his name?
Wild Bill Hickok.
"Wild Bill"? That's a funny name.
Here, look...
HWEE HNM
That's him.
He has a big mustache...
He looks a bit scary. And he isn't as handsome as my Papa Jim.
Yes, You're right. Your Papa Jim is the best, most handsome papa of all!

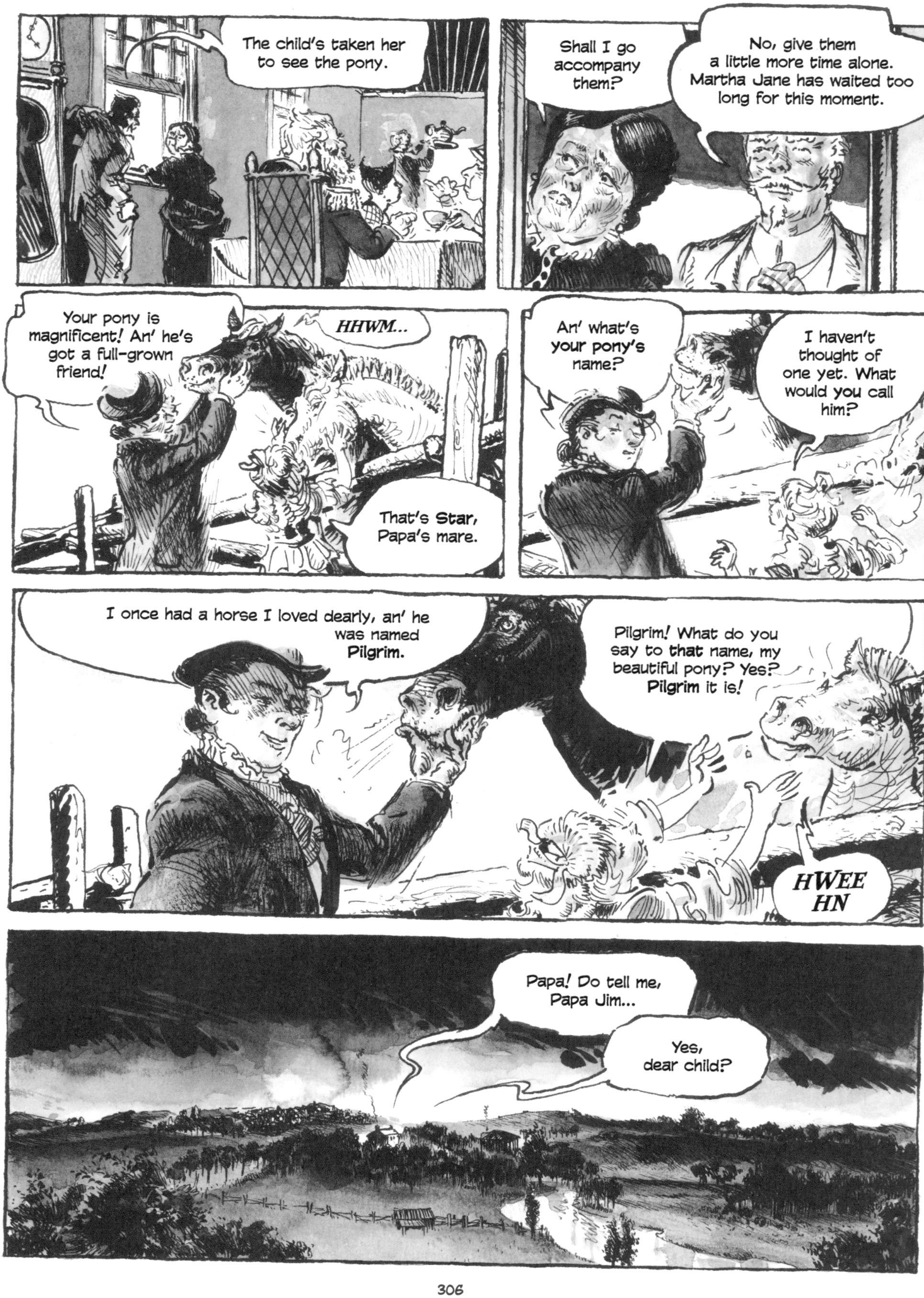
The child's taken her to see the pony.
Shall I go accompany them?
No, give them a little more time alone. Martha Jane has waited too long for this moment.
Your pony is magnificent! An' he's got a full-grown friend!
HHWM...
That's Star, Papa's mare.
An' what's your pony's name?
I haven't thought of one yet. What would you call him?
I once had a horse I loved dearly, an' he was named Pilgrim.
Pilgrim! What do you say to that name, my beautiful pony? Yes? Pilgrim it is!
HWEE HN
Papa! Do tell me, Papa Jim...
Yes, dear child?

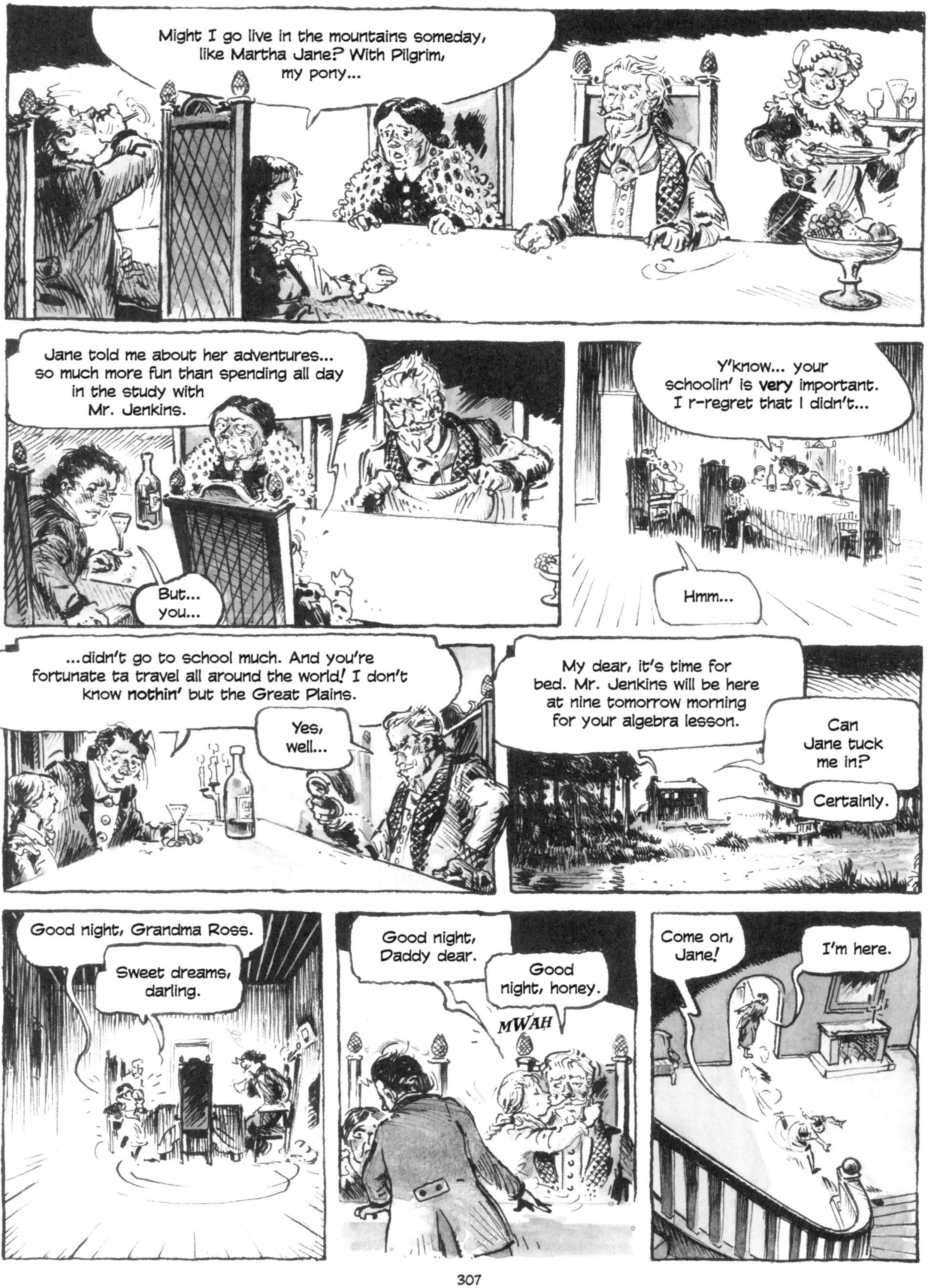
Might I go live in the mountains someday, like Martha Jane? With Pilgrim, my pony...
Jane told me about her adventures... so much more fun than spending all day in the study with Mr. Jenkins.
But... you...
Y'know... your schoolin' is **very** important. I r-regret that I didn't...
Hmm...
...didn't go to school much. And you're fortunate ta travel all around the world! I don't know **nothin'** but the Great Plains.
Yes, well...
My dear, it's time for bed. Mr. Jenkins will be here at nine tomorrow morning for your algebra lesson.
Can Jane tuck me in?
Certainly.
Good night, Grandma Ross.
Sweet dreams, darling.
Good night, Daddy dear.
Good night, honey.
MWAH
Come on, Jane!
I'm here.

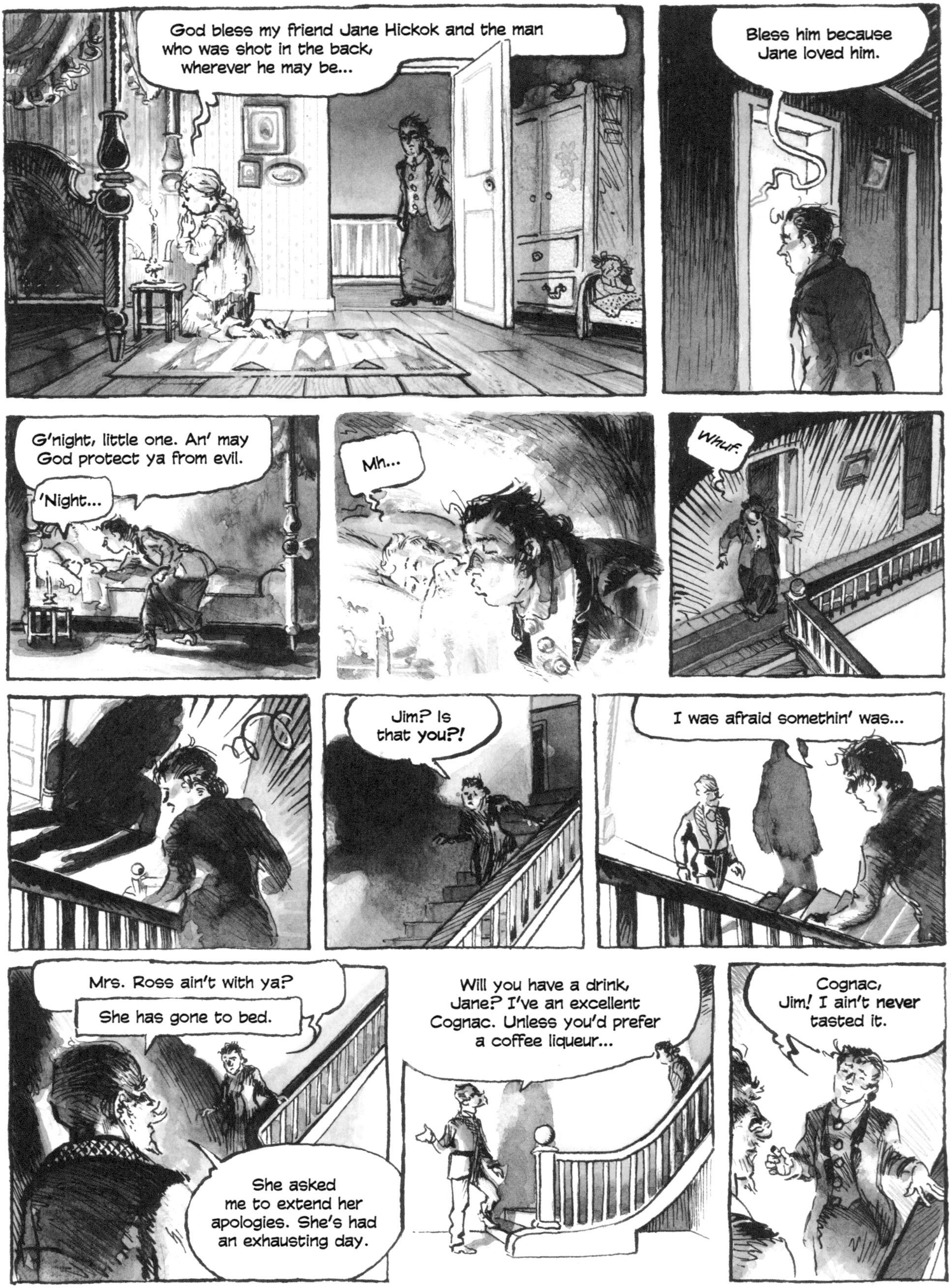
God bless my friend Jane Hickok and the man who was shot in the back, wherever he may be...
Bless him because Jane loved him.
G'night, little one. An' may God protect ya from evil.
'Night...
Mh...
Whuf.
Jim? Is that you?!
I was afraid somethin' was...
Mrs. Ross ain't with ya?
She has gone to bed.
She asked me to extend her apologies. She's had an exhausting day.
Will you have a drink, Jane? I've an excellent Cognac. Unless you'd prefer a coffee liqueur...
Cognac, Jim! I ain't never tasted it.

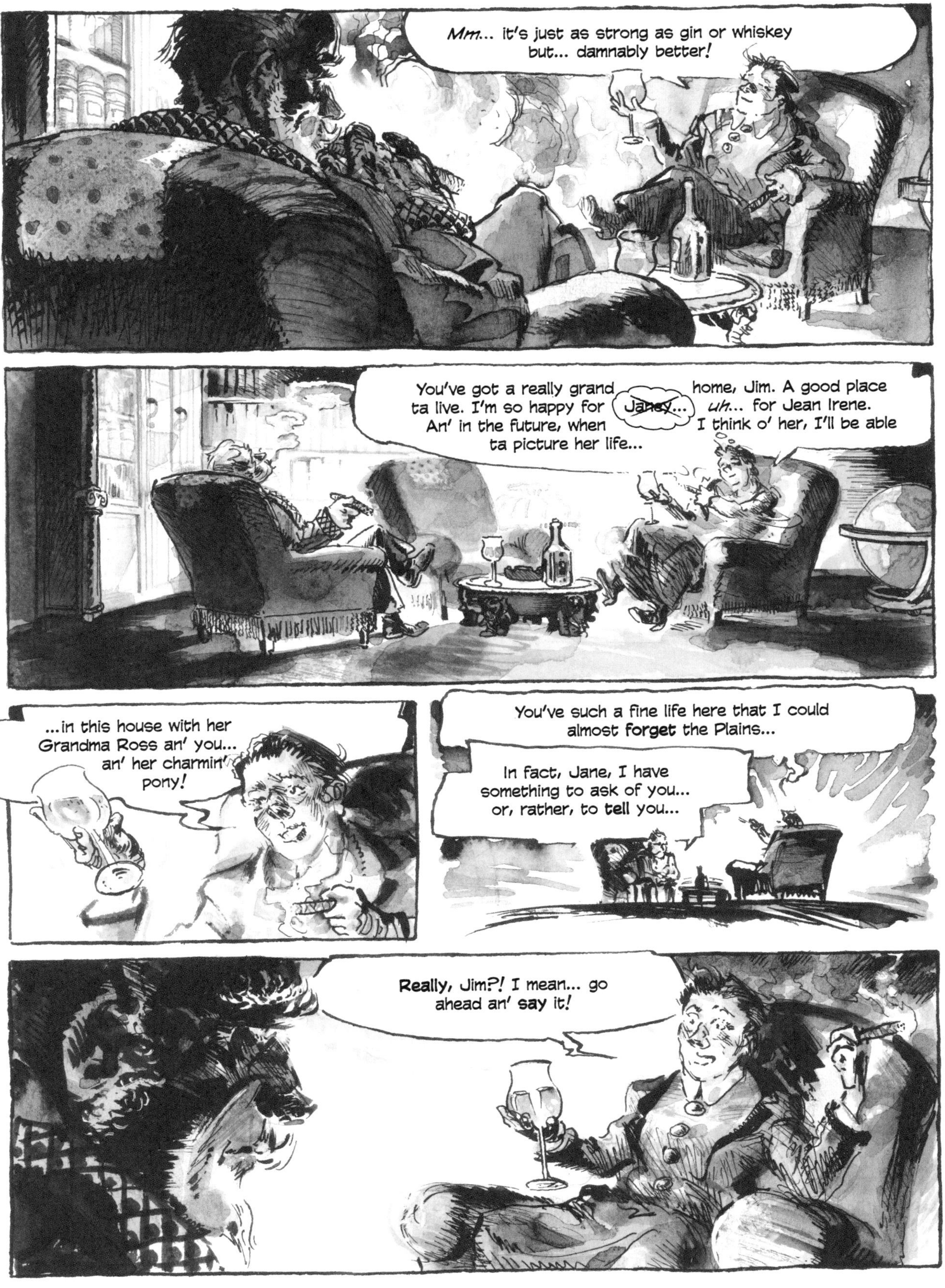

Mm... it's just as strong as gin or whiskey but... damnably better!
You've got a really grand home, Jim. A good place ta live. I'm so happy for ~~Janey~~... *uh*... for Jean Irene. An' in the future, when I think o' her, I'll be able ta picture her life...
...in this house with her Grandma Ross an' you... an' her charmin' pony!
You've such a fine life here that I could almost **forget** the Plains...
In fact, Jane, I have something to ask of you... or, rather, to **tell** you...
Really, Jim?! I mean... go ahead an' **say** it!

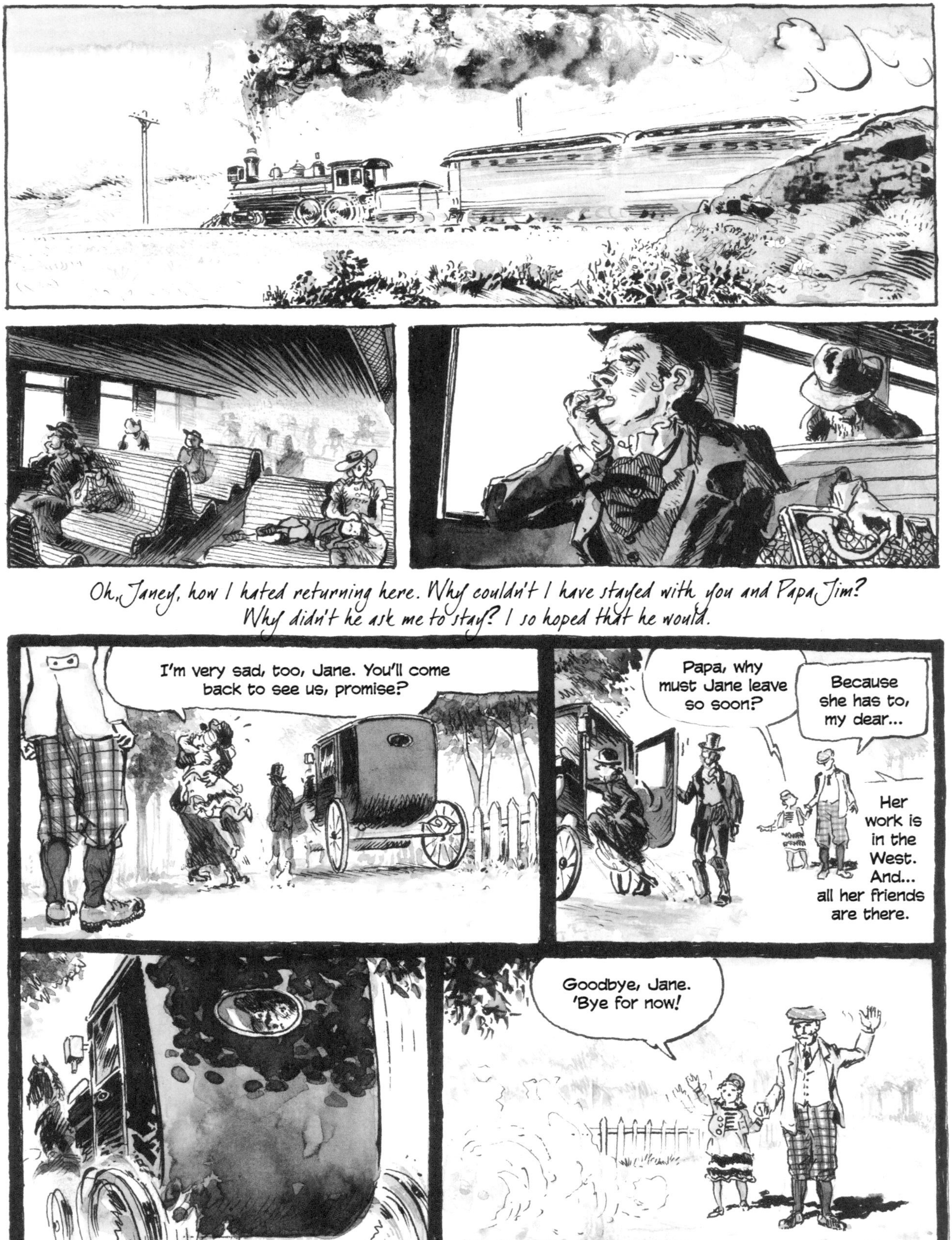
Oh, Janey, how I hated returning here. Why couldn't I have stayed with you and Papa Jim?
Why didn't he ask me to stay? I so hoped that he would.
I'm very sad, too, Jane. You'll come back to see us, promise?
Papa, why must Jane leave so soon?
Because she has to, my dear...
Her work is in the West. And... all her friends are there.
Goodbye, Jane. 'Bye for now!

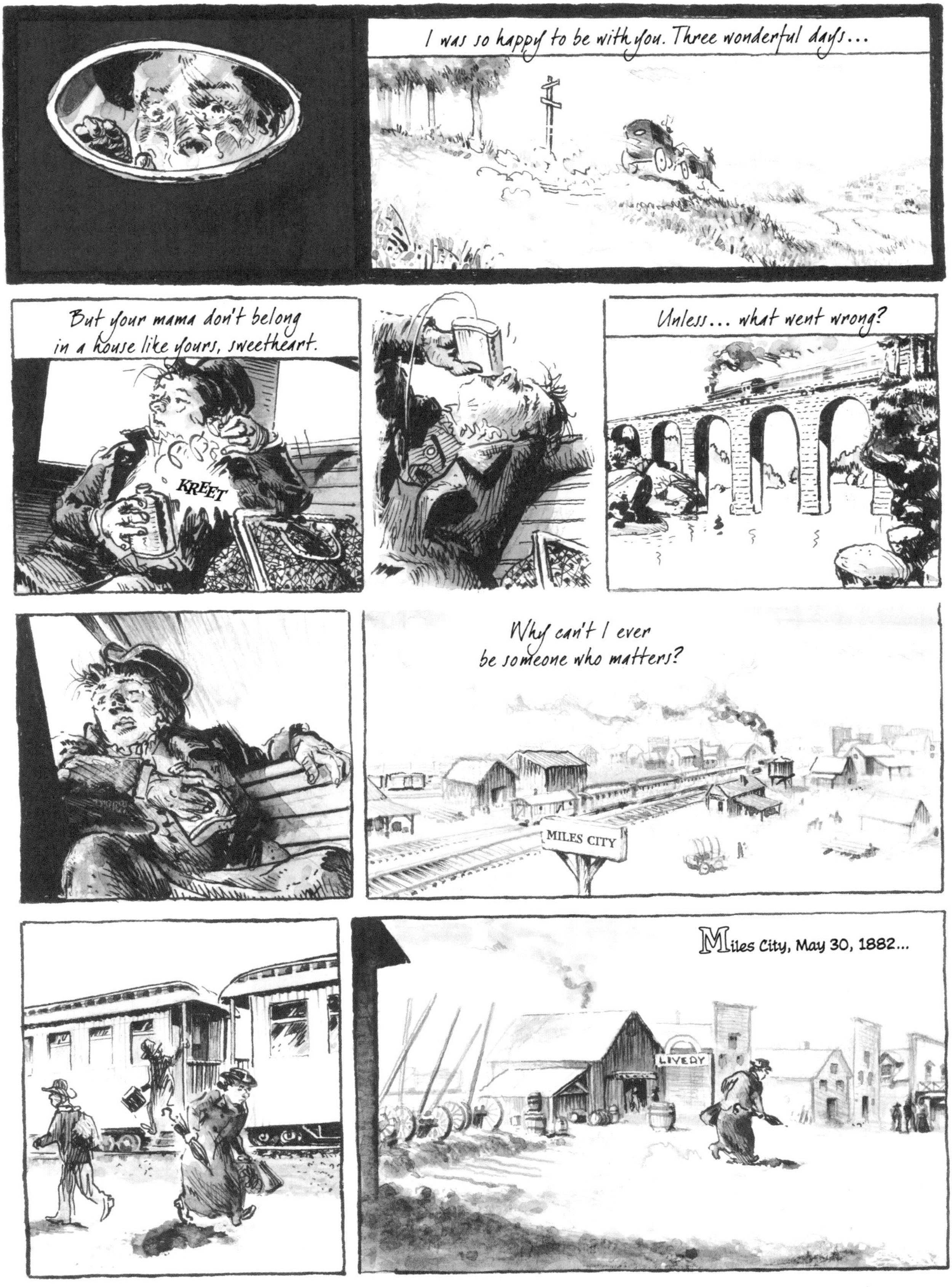
I was so happy to be with you. Three wonderful days...
But your mama don't belong in a house like yours, sweetheart.
KREET
Unless... what went wrong?
Why can't I ever be someone who matters?
MILES CITY
Miles City, May 30, 1882...
LIVERY

On The Road Again...

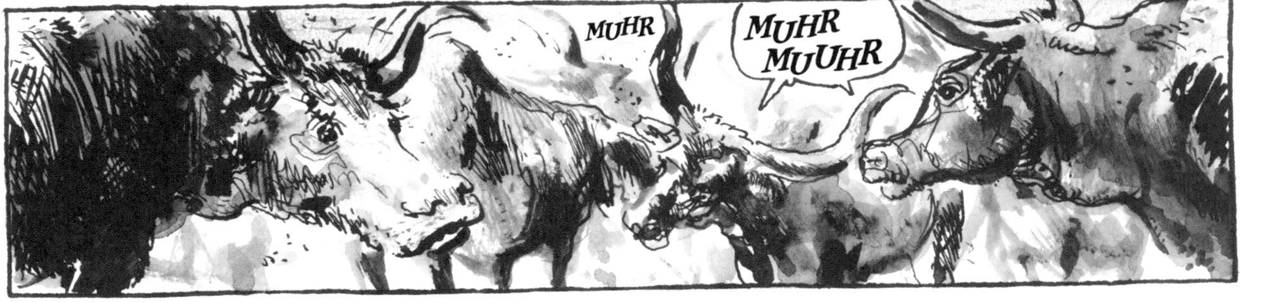
MUHR
MUHR MUUHR

The first Miles City houses were erected in the aftermath of the Battle of the Little Bighorn, when saloons and gambling halls began to be built near Fort Keogh, a new military outpost.

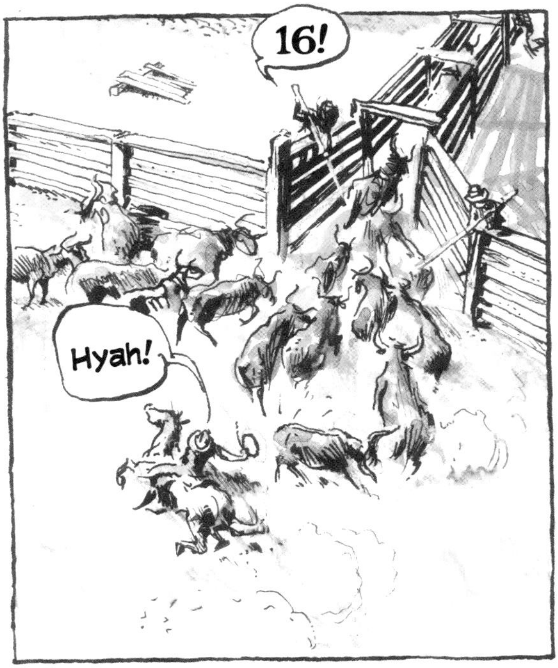
16!
Hyah!

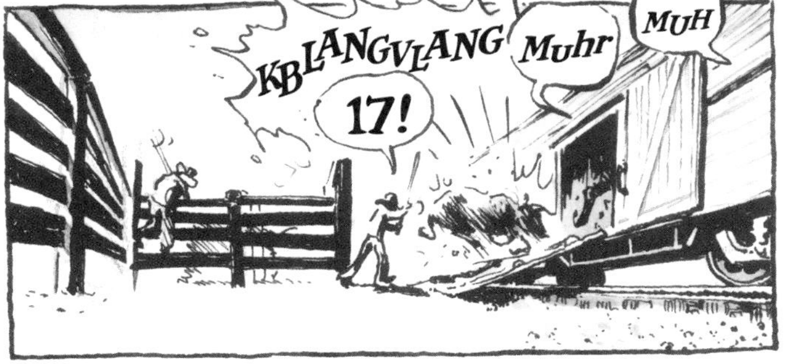
KBLANGVLANG
Muhr
MUH
17!

The town started growing with the arrival of Texas beef herds, driven each summer by throngs of cowboys through the rich and verdant pastures of the Yellowstone Valley.

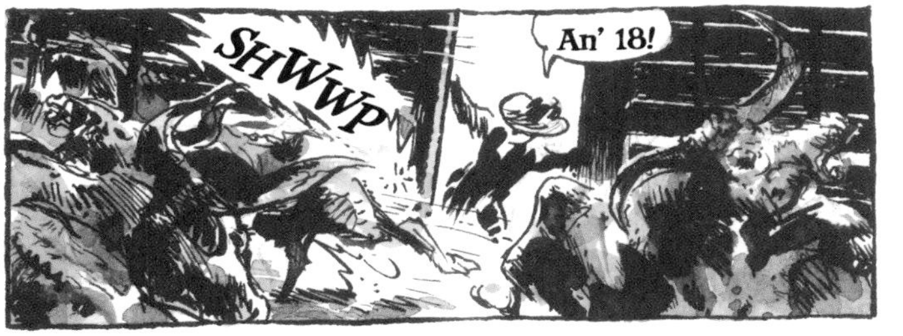
SHWWP
An' 18!

Miles City's real prosperity was due to the Northern Pacific Railroad engineers, who chose to route the line through it, much to the detriment of Coulson.

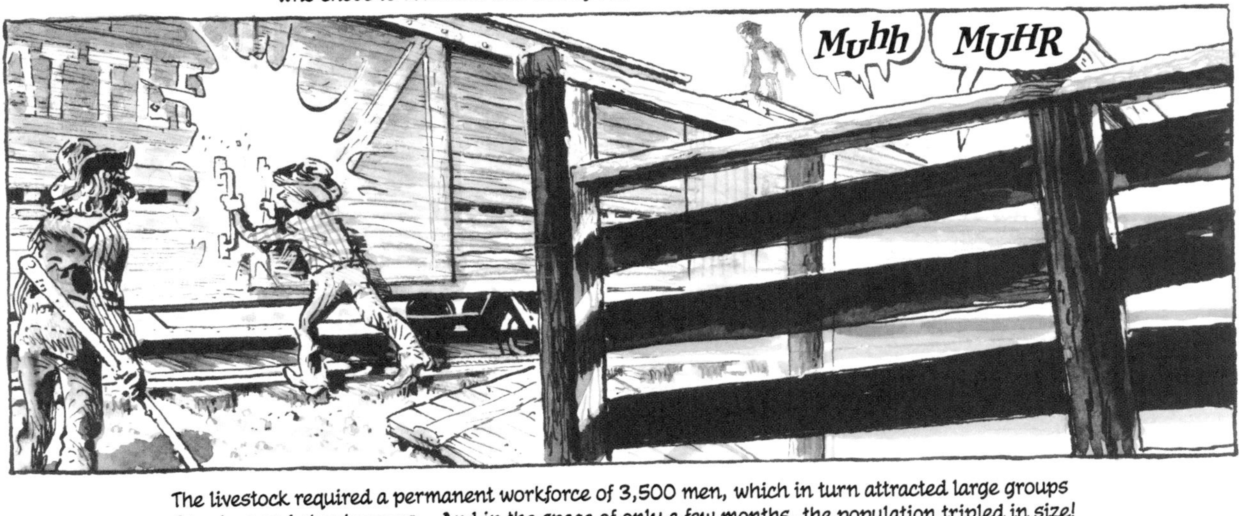
Muhh
MUHR

The livestock required a permanent workforce of 3,500 men, which in turn attracted large groups of traders and shopkeepers... And in the space of only a few months, the population tripled in size!

Efforts to connect Duluth to the major ports of Puget Sound had gotten under way in the early 1870s, but the Northern Pacific's progress was interrupted by the Panic of 1873.*

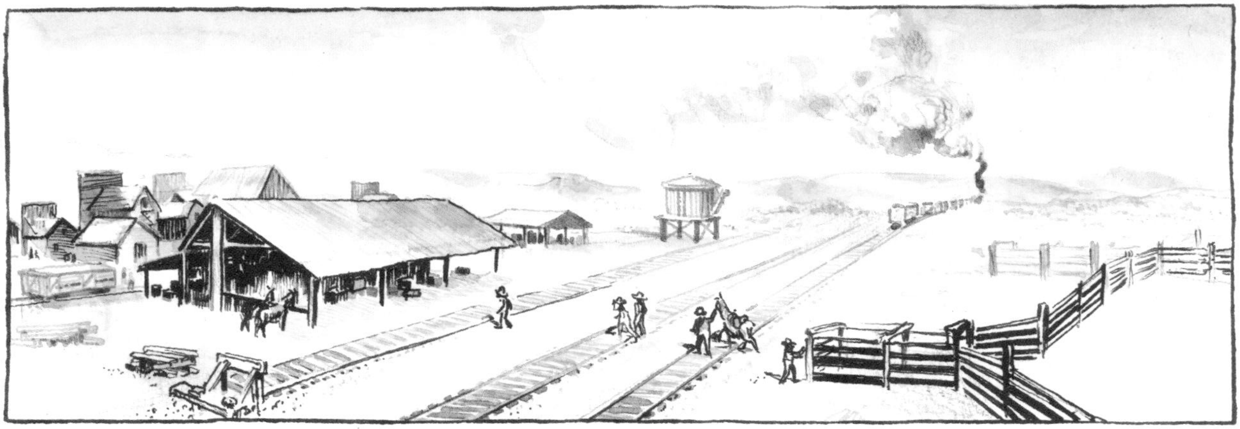

Work resumed in July 1881, linking the towns of Gladstone, Terry, Miles City, and Billings. By 1883, the line would continue through Livingstone, Bozeman, and Missoula, the goal being to reach Idaho before Christmas.

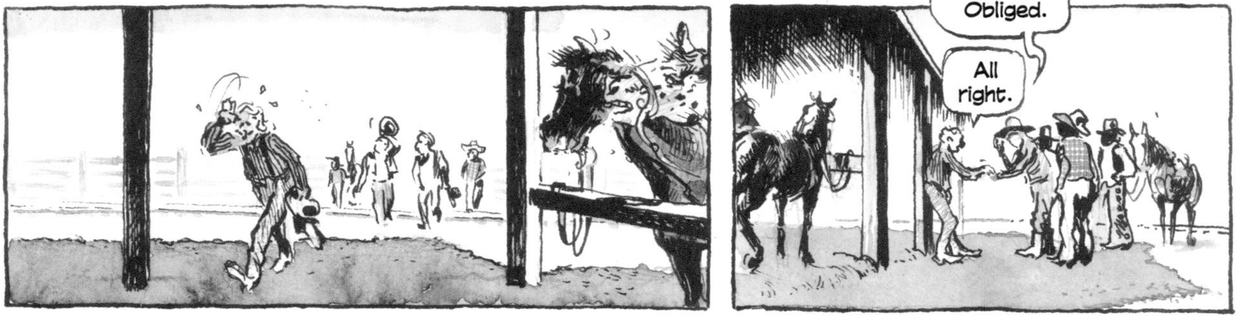

Obliged.
All right.

Now, thanks to the line's extension, once the cattle were fattened up, they were immediately dispatched from Miles City to the Chicago slaughterhouses.

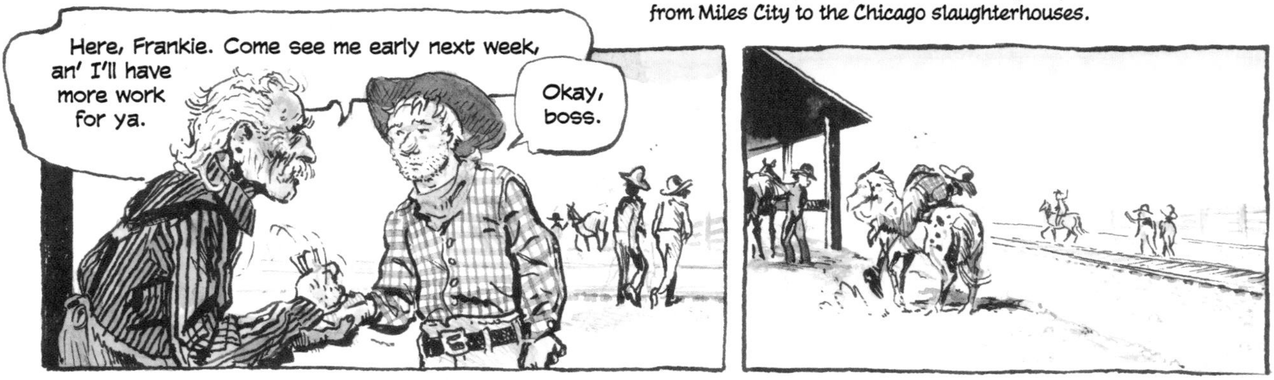

Here, Frankie. Come see me early next week, an' I'll have more work for ya.
Okay, boss.

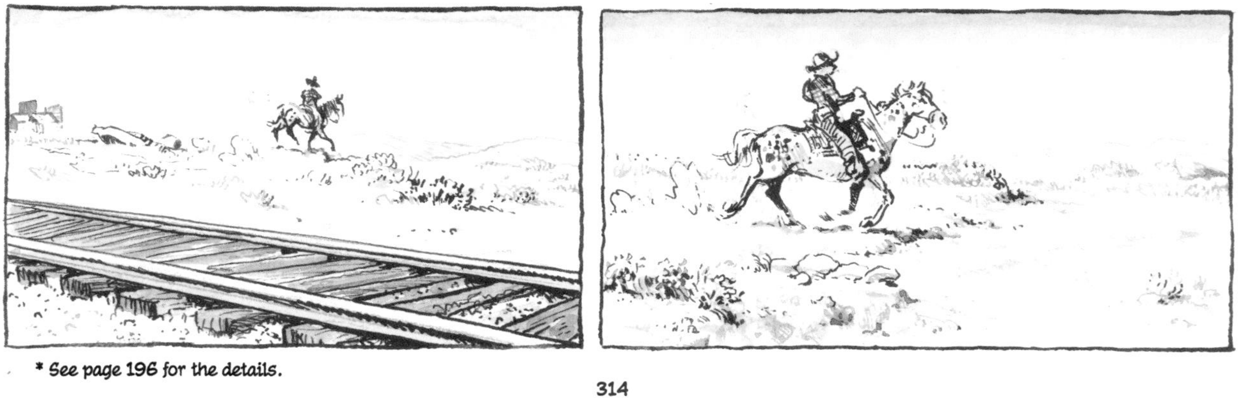

* See page 196 for the details.

At the start of 1883 Martha Jane took on a ranch in the Yellowstone Valley, twenty miles west of Miles City. There, she raised cattle and other stores for resale to Northern Pacific's employees, making an honest wage.

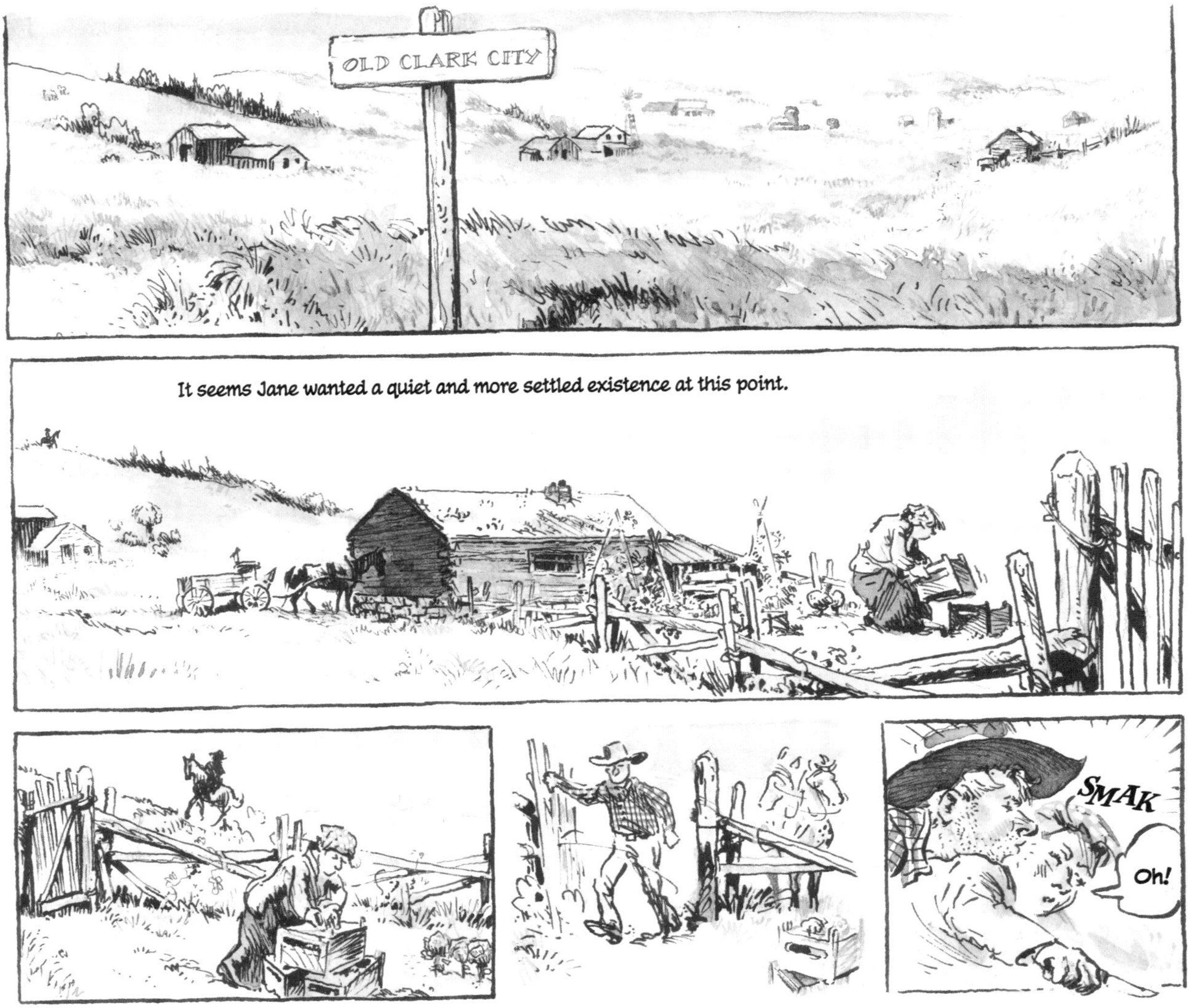
OLD CLARK CITY
It seems Jane wanted a quiet and more settled existence at this point.
SMAK
Oh!

She shared her life with a man named **Frank King,** a cowboy 15 years her junior... and for a time she called herself **Mattie King,** though the two never married.

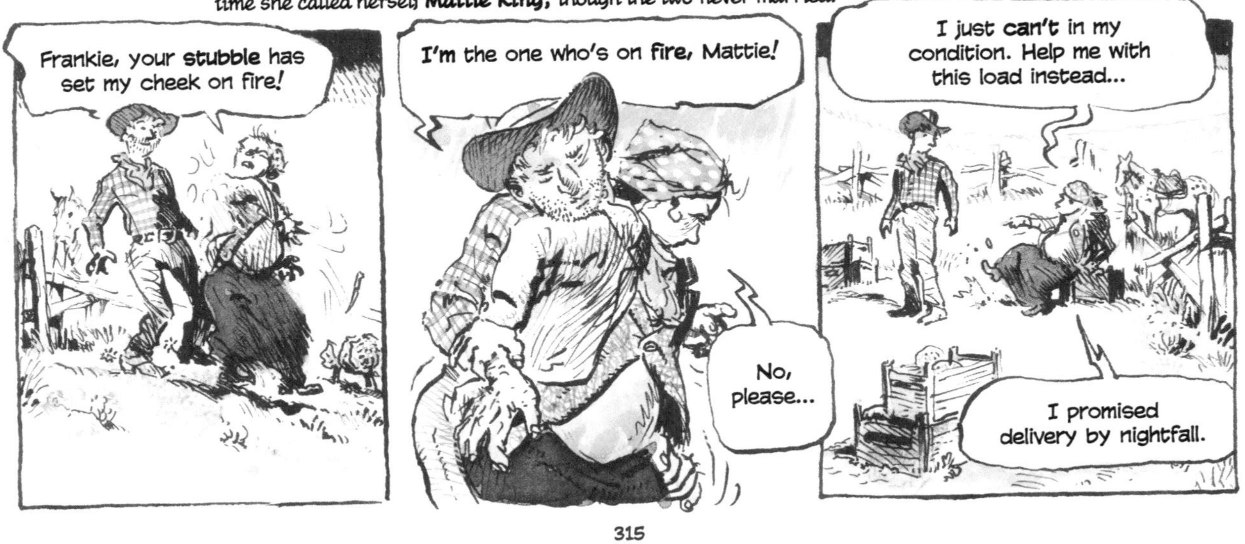
Frankie, your **stubble** has set my cheek on fire!
I'm the one who's on **fire,** Mattie!
No, please...
I just **can't** in my condition. Help me with this load instead...
I promised delivery by nightfall.

If y'want, I'll go with ya.

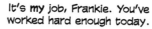

It's my job, Frankie. You've worked hard enough today.

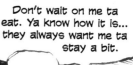

Don't wait on me ta eat. Ya know how it is... they always want me ta stay a bit.

But...

I don't mind waitin'.

Hey, Mattie!

?

R R M B L

Don't drink too much!

Don't worry.

R M M

Spring passed... and with the first summer storms, the grass began to yellow in spots.

BRRM

OW!

A A A

HF, HFF!

Nooo...

In August, Jane birthed a boy, probably premature.

He ain't a big one... but he's breathin'!

WHAAA...

Writing to Janey, she chose to conceal the truth:

I'm in Old Clark City, not far from where you were born. There's nothing for me here, but I'm taking care of a friend's baby...

I'll leave you two lovebirds.

See ya soon, Mrs. Alma.

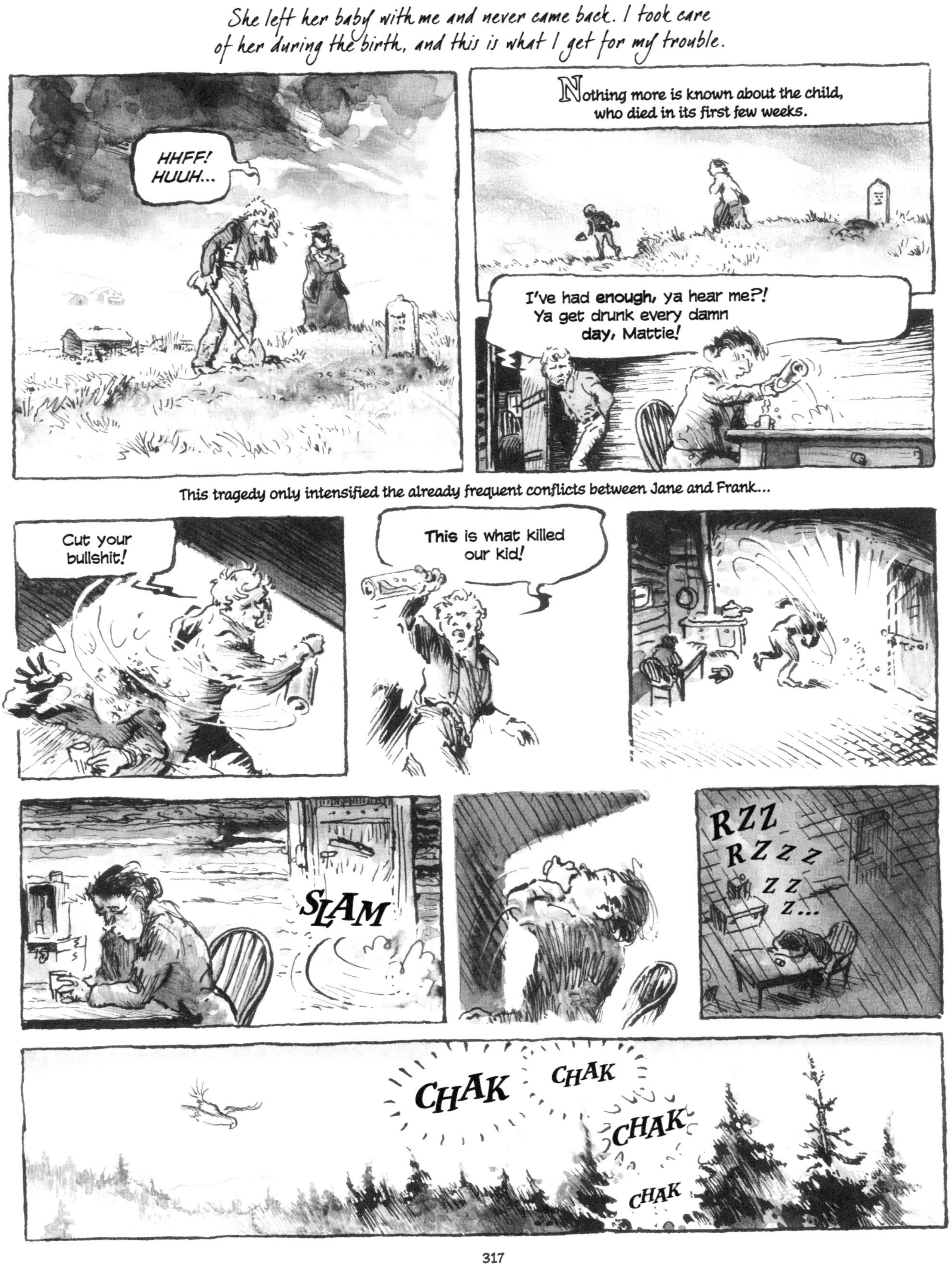
She left her baby with me and never came back. I took care of her during the birth, and this is what I get for my trouble.
HHFF! HUUH...
Nothing more is known about the child, who died in its first few weeks.
I've had enough, ya hear me?! Ya get drunk every damn day, Mattie!
This tragedy only intensified the already frequent conflicts between Jane and Frank...
Cut your bullshit!
This is what killed our kid!
SLAM
RZZ RZZZZ ZZ Z...
CHAK
CHAK
CHAK
CHAK

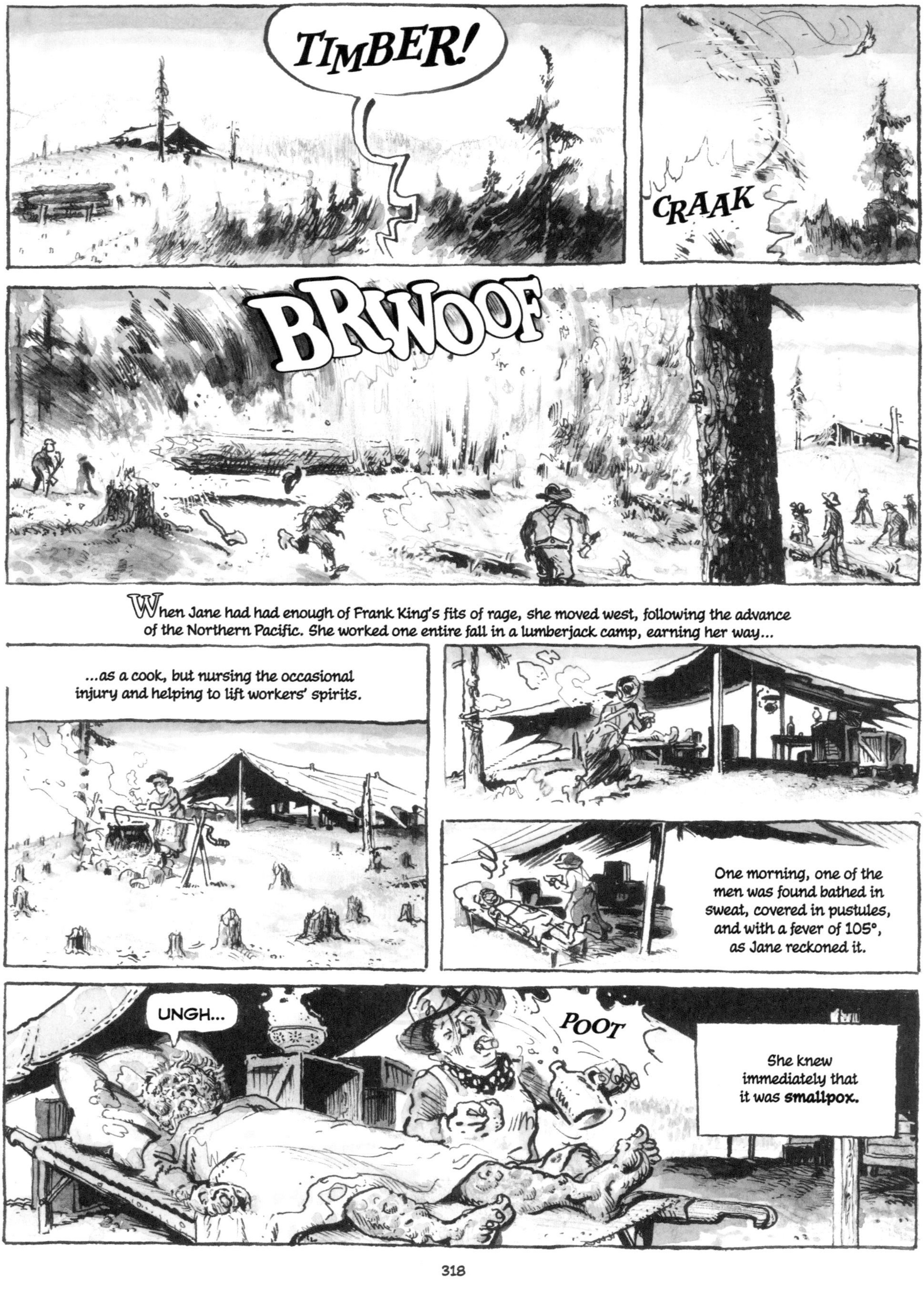
TIMBER!
CRAAK
BRWOOF
When Jane had had enough of Frank King's fits of rage, she moved west, following the advance of the Northern Pacific. She worked one entire fall in a lumberjack camp, earning her way...
...as a cook, but nursing the occasional injury and helping to lift workers' spirits.
One morning, one of the men was found bathed in sweat, covered in pustules, and with a fever of 105°, as Jane reckoned it.
UNGH...
POOT
She knew immediately that it was **smallpox.**

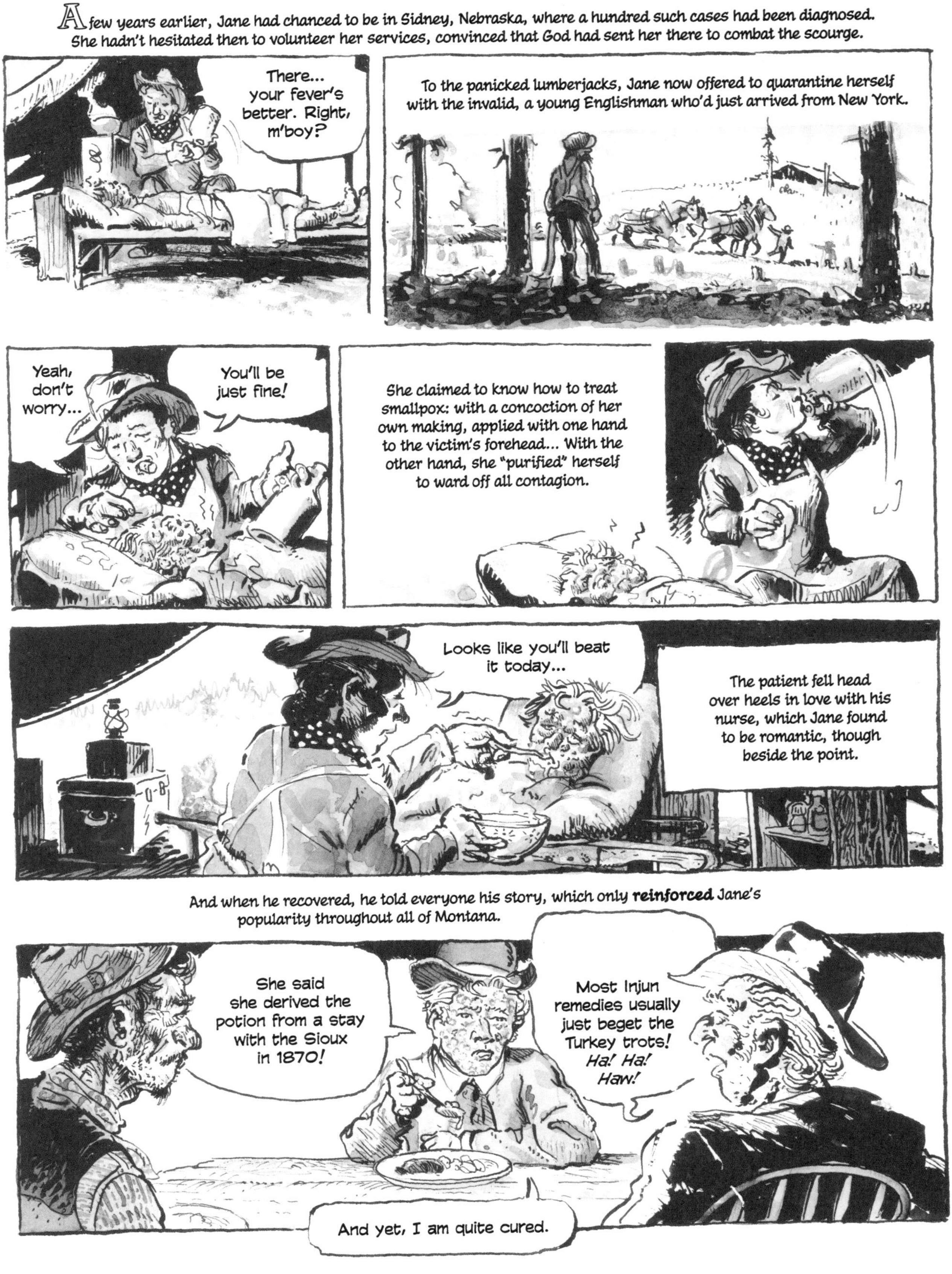
A few years earlier, Jane had chanced to be in Sidney, Nebraska, where a hundred such cases had been diagnosed. She hadn't hesitated then to volunteer her services, convinced that God had sent her there to combat the scourge.
There... your fever's better. Right, m'boy?
To the panicked lumberjacks, Jane now offered to quarantine herself with the invalid, a young Englishman who'd just arrived from New York.
Yeah, don't worry...
You'll be just fine!
She claimed to know how to treat smallpox: with a concoction of her own making, applied with one hand to the victim's forehead... With the other hand, she "purified" herself to ward off all contagion.
Looks like you'll beat it today...
The patient fell head over heels in love with his nurse, which Jane found to be romantic, though beside the point.
And when he recovered, he told everyone his story, which only **reinforced** Jane's popularity throughout all of Montana.
She said she derived the potion from a stay with the Sioux in 1870!
Most Injun remedies usually just beget the Turkey trots! *Ha! Ha! Haw!*
And yet, I am quite cured.

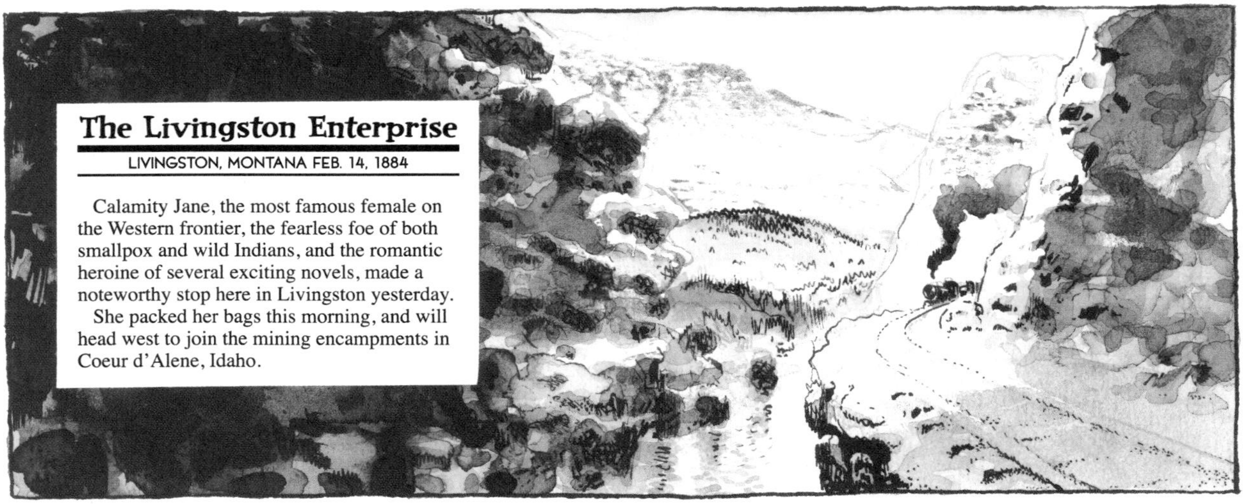
The Livingston Enterprise
LIVINGSTON, MONTANA FEB. 14, 1884
Calamity Jane, the most famous female on the Western frontier, the fearless foe of both smallpox and wild Indians, and the romantic heroine of several exciting novels, made a noteworthy stop here in Livingston yesterday.
She packed her bags this morning, and will head west to join the mining encampments in Coeur d'Alene, Idaho.

Gold was discovered in a remote corner of Idaho at the end of 1882. Other gold veins were confirmed in early 1884, and two hundred prospectors rushed to the region in one single day. The camp was soon home to 47 saloons!

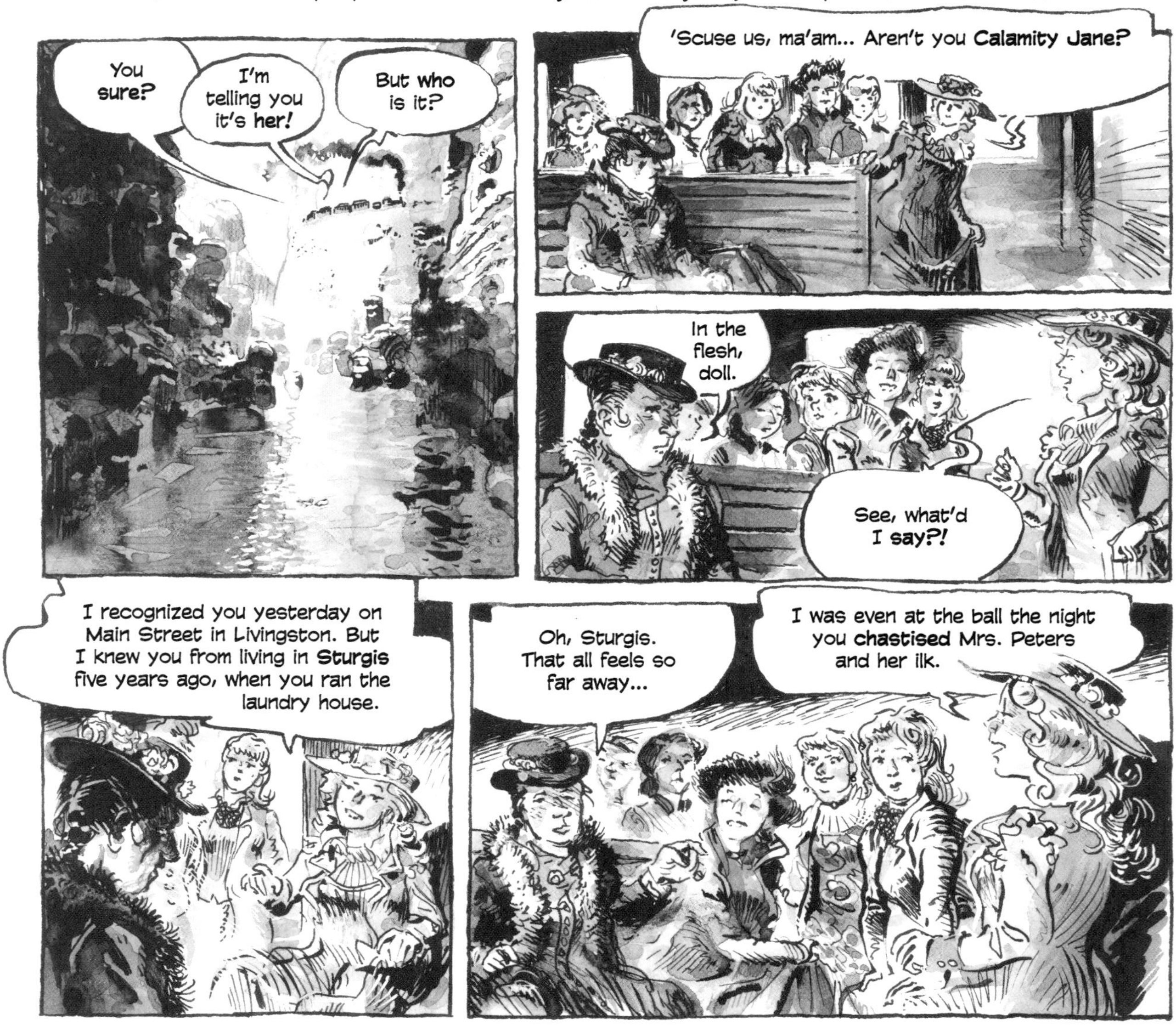
You sure?
I'm telling you it's **her!**
But who is it?
'Scuse us, ma'am... Aren't you **Calamity Jane?**
In the flesh, doll.
See, what'd **I say?!**
I recognized you yesterday on Main Street in Livingston. But I knew you from living in **Sturgis** five years ago, when you ran the laundry house.
Oh, Sturgis. That all feels so far away...
I was even at the ball the night you **chastised** Mrs. Peters and her ilk.

Nothin' ta brag about. I was some kinda **irritable** in those days.

Oh, no! You were **spectacular!** You should've seen it, girls! I swear, those old bitches really had it coming!

HA HAA! HOO...

Hee hee!

Ha haha!

What're you li'l darlin's doin' on this train?

We're the **Poopy Girls.** We're performing in Coeur d'Alene, but our singer just left us in the lurch...

Without her, we're not sure **what** sort of show we can give the miners.

Show your **legs,** by God! And your pretty little faces! Trust me, that's what those guys really wanna see.

We're on stage for **two** hours. How should we end the show?

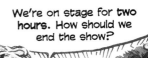

With your butts in the air! A big deal!

What about you, Miss Calamity?

Off ta the same place... but for poker, not dancin'.

Ha! Ha Ha Ha

Do you know how to sing, perhaps?

Ha! Ha!

KREET

Really? You hear **that,** girls?!

Like a crow! But I can tell a good story.

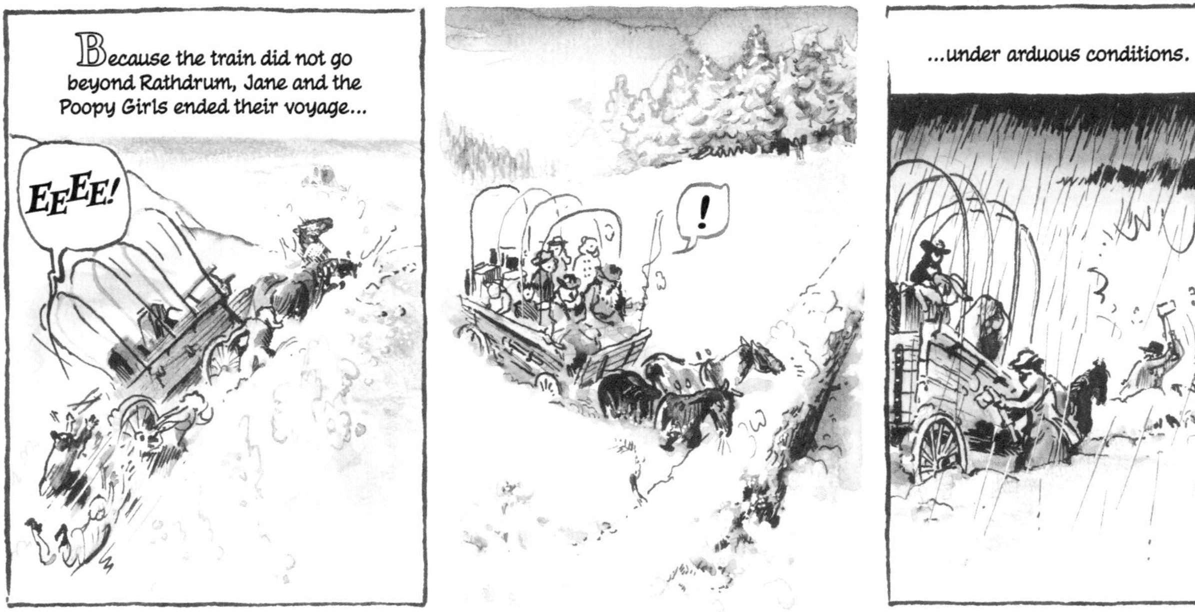
Because the train did not go beyond Rathdrum, Jane and the Poopy Girls ended their voyage...
EEEE!
!
...under arduous conditions.

"Hell! I coulda gone to New York and back in the time it took to travel the last few miles of this damn trail!"
--Calamity Jane quoted in the *Coeur d'Alene Sun,* February 23, 1884.

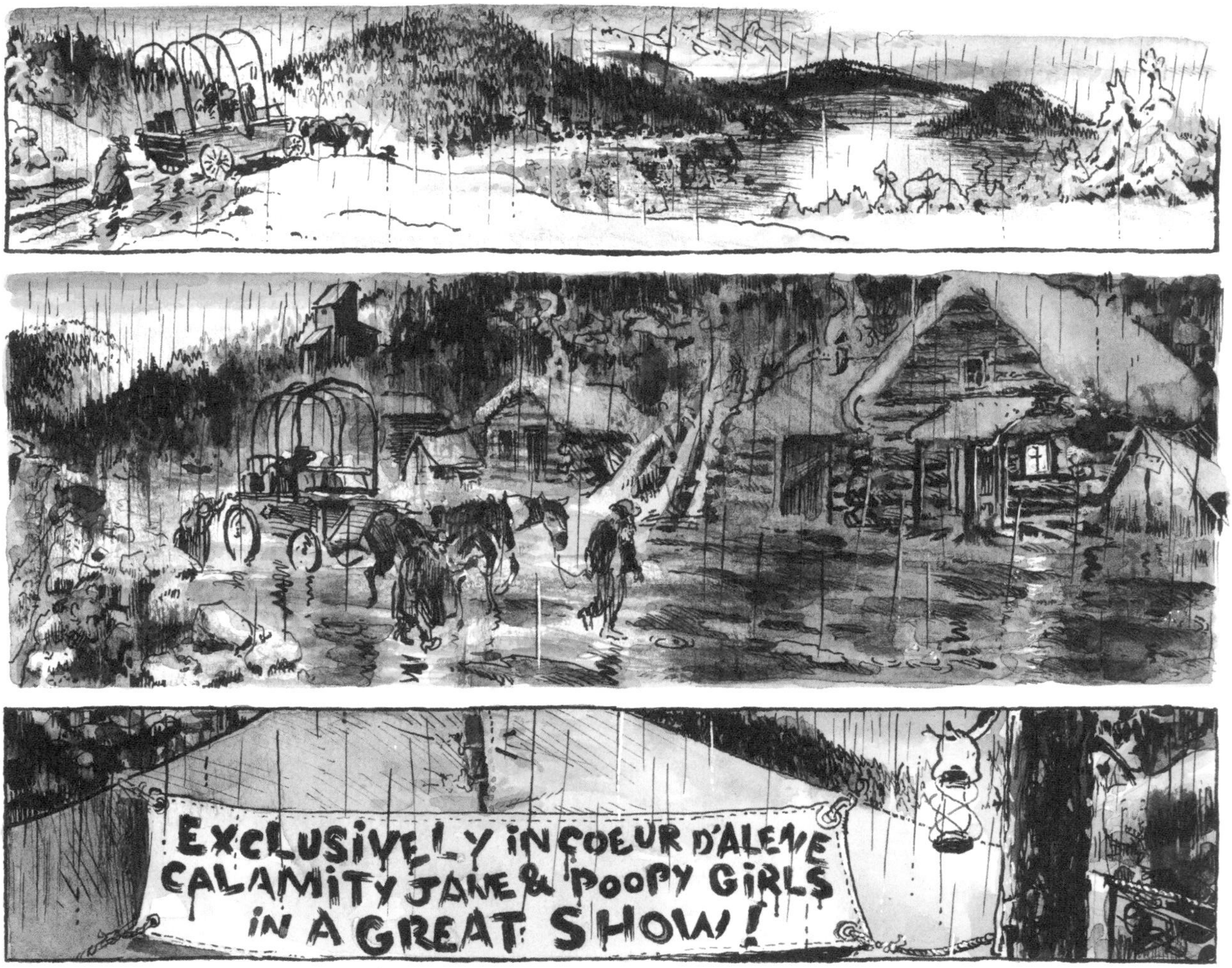
EXCLUSIVELY IN COEUR D'ALENE
CALAMITY JANE & POOPY GIRLS
IN A GREAT SHOW!

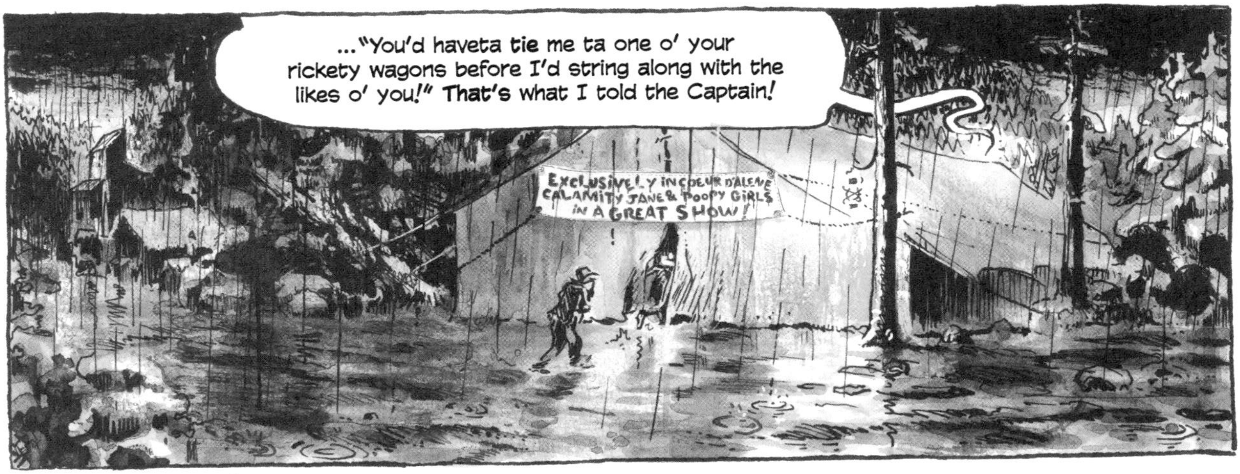
..."You'd haveta **tie** me ta one o' your rickety wagons before I'd string along with the likes o' you!" **That's** what I told the Captain!
EXCLUSIVELY IN COEUR D'ALENE CALAMITY JANE & POOPY GIRLS IN A GREAT SHOW!

On February 24, 1884, Jane first took to the stage, with the Poopy Girls and to the tune of an off-key fiddle. In front of 300 miners, she improvised a lengthy monologue about her life.

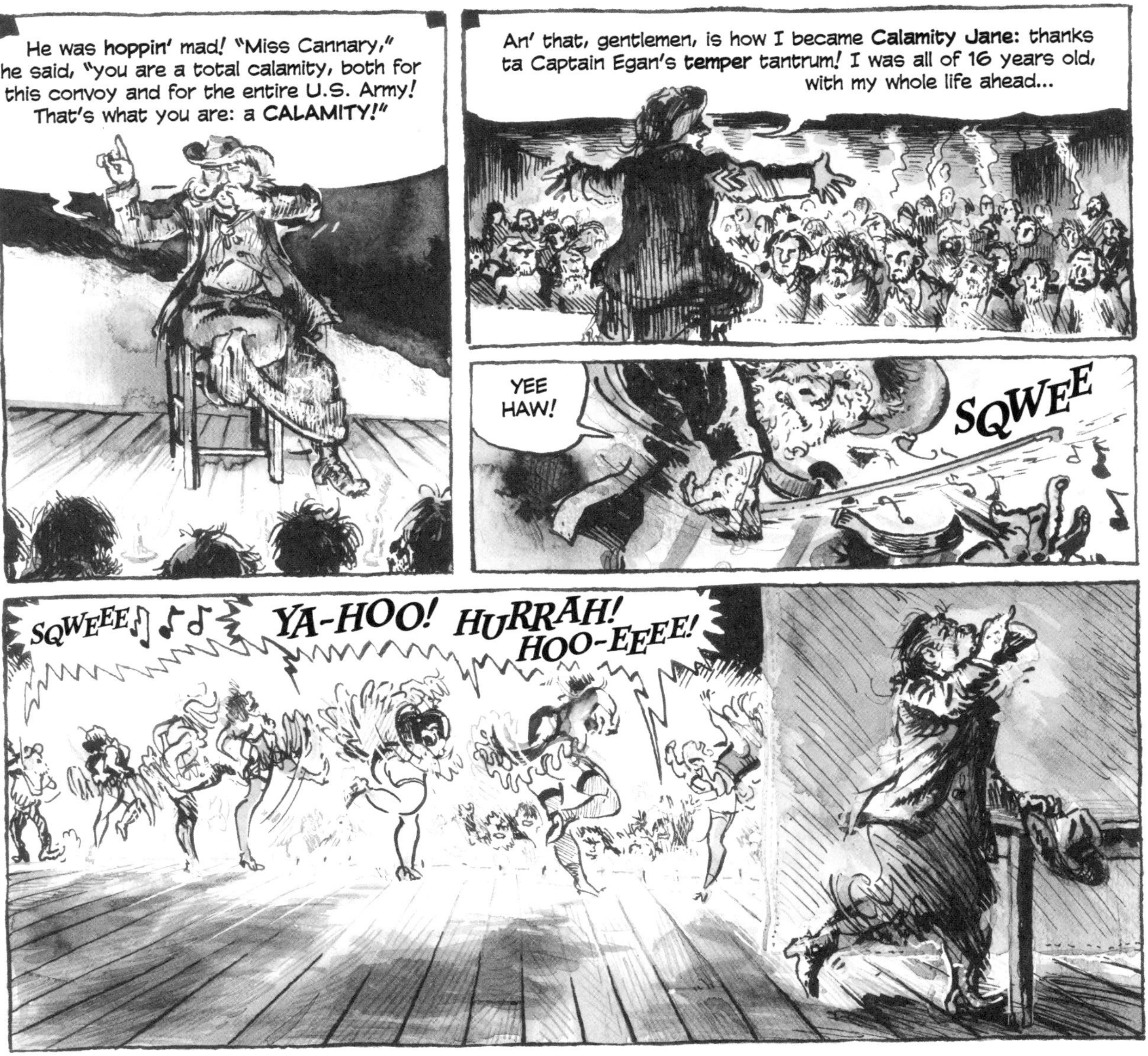
He was **hoppin'** mad! "Miss Cannary," he said, "you are a total calamity, both for this convoy and for the entire U.S. Army! That's what you are: a **CALAMITY!**"
An' that, gentlemen, is how I became **Calamity Jane:** thanks ta Captain Egan's **temper** tantrum! I was all of 16 years old, with my whole life ahead...
YEE HAW!
SQWEE
SQWEEE
YA-HOO! HURRAH! HOO-EEEE!

Night after night, Jane further embellished her tales, her "magic elixir" stirring her memories as she brought the house to laughter and tears.

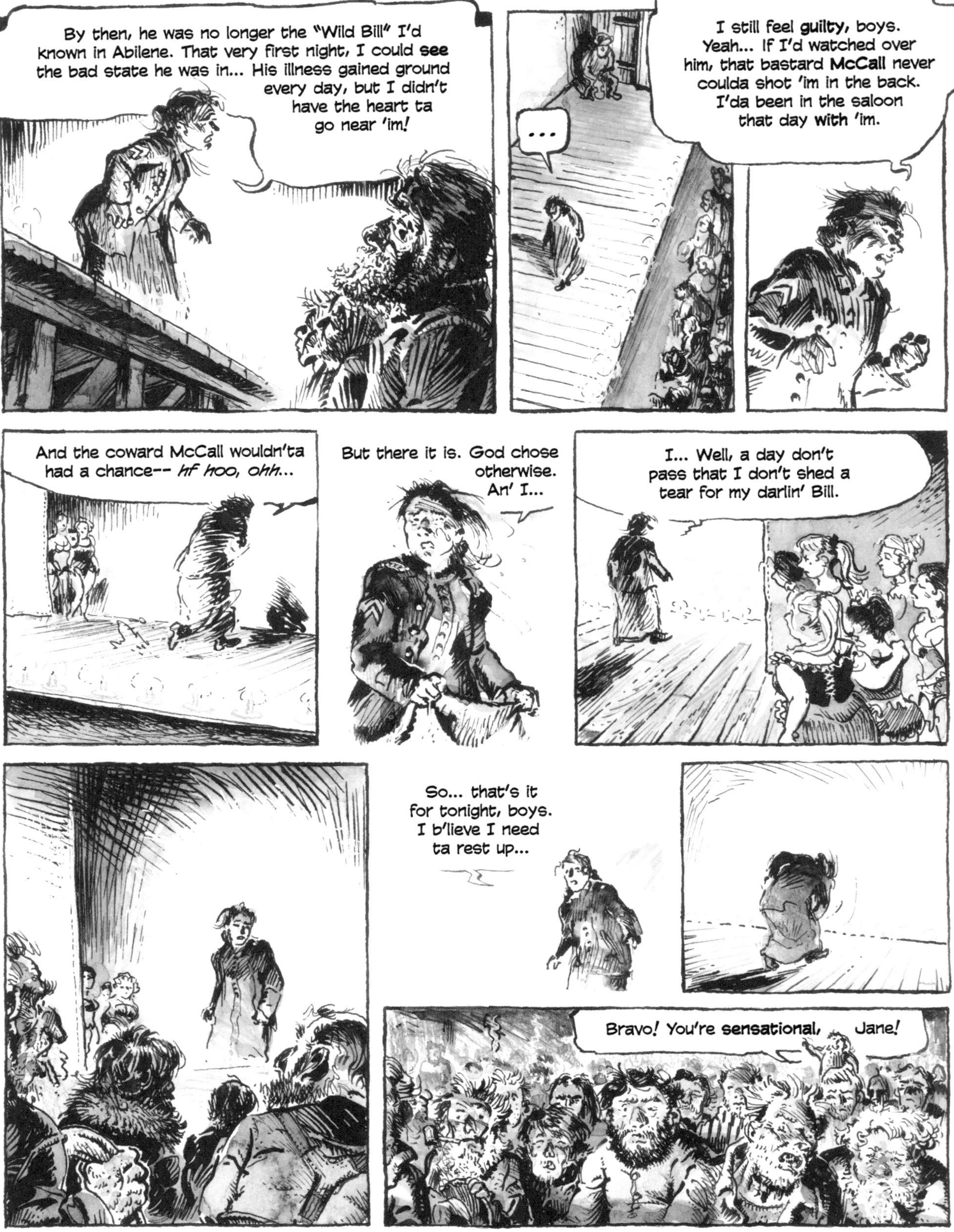

By then, he was no longer the "Wild Bill" I'd known in Abilene. That very first night, I could **see** the bad state he was in... His illness gained ground every day, but I didn't have the heart ta go near 'im!
...
I still feel **guilty**, boys. Yeah... If I'd watched over him, that bastard **McCall** never coulda shot 'im in the back. I'da been in the saloon that day **with** 'im.
And the coward McCall wouldn'ta had a chance-- *hf hoo, ohh...*
But there it is. God chose otherwise. An' I...
I... Well, a day don't pass that I don't shed a tear for my darlin' Bill.
So... that's it for tonight, boys. I b'lieve I need ta rest up...
Bravo! You're **sensational**, Jane!

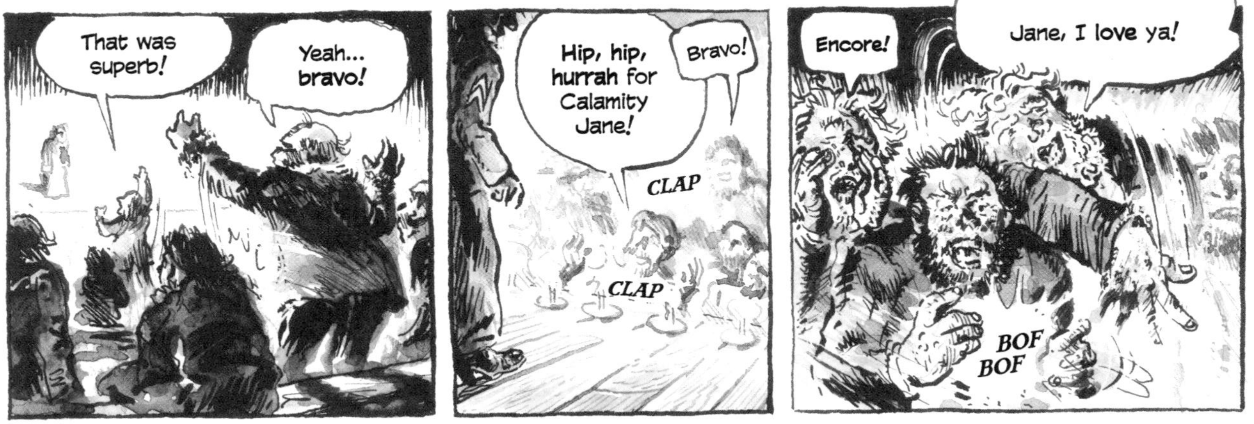
That was superb!
Yeah... **bravo!**
Hip, hip, hurrah for Calamity Jane!
Bravo!
CLAP
CLAP
Encore!
Jane, I love ya!
BOF
BOF

The show sold out for ten days running and ended with a standing ovation every night, leaving Jane speechless with emotion.

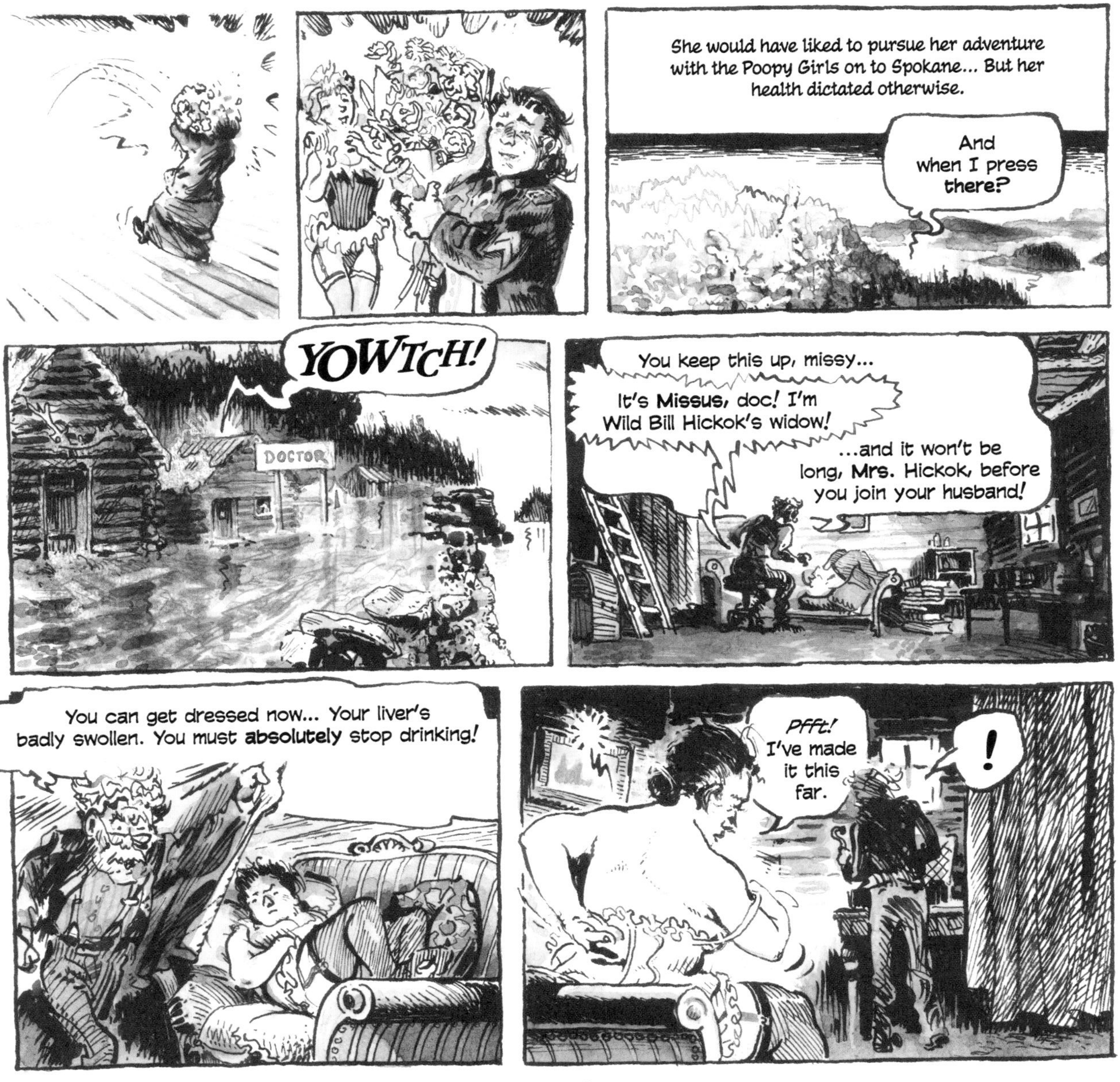
She would have liked to pursue her adventure with the Poopy Girls on to Spokane... But her health dictated otherwise.
And when I press **there?**
YOWTCH!
DOCTOR
You keep this up, missy...
It's **Missus**, doc! I'm Wild Bill Hickok's widow!
...and it won't be long, **Mrs.** Hickok, before you join your husband!
You can get dressed now... Your liver's badly swollen. You must **absolutely** stop drinking!
Pfft! I've made it this far.
!

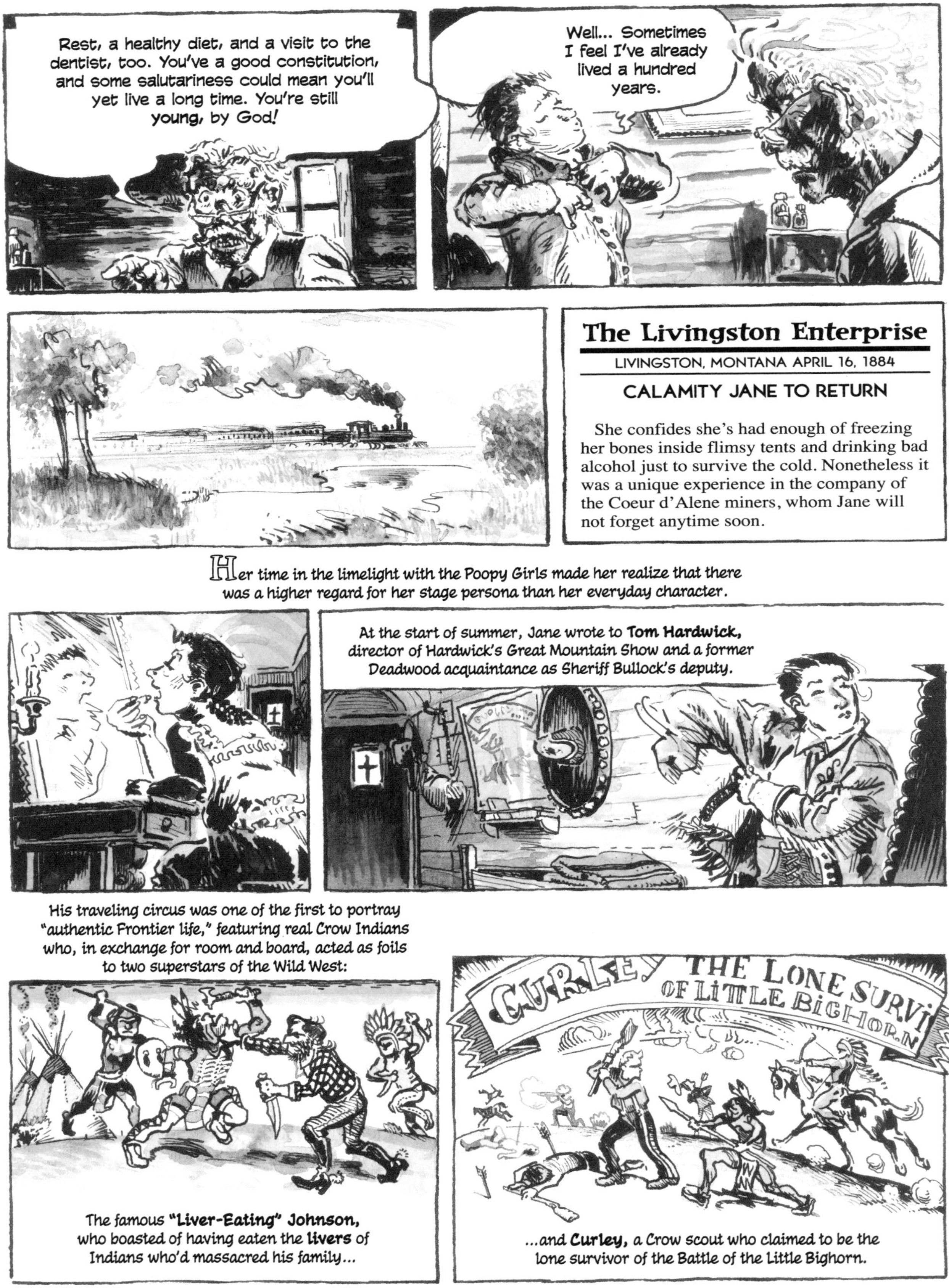
Rest, a healthy diet, and a visit to the dentist, too. You've a good constitution, and some salutariness could mean you'll yet live a long time. You're still **young**, by God!
Well... Sometimes I feel I've already lived a hundred years.
The Livingston Enterprise
LIVINGSTON, MONTANA APRIL 16, 1884
CALAMITY JANE TO RETURN
She confides she's had enough of freezing her bones inside flimsy tents and drinking bad alcohol just to survive the cold. Nonetheless it was a unique experience in the company of the Coeur d'Alene miners, whom Jane will not forget anytime soon.
Her time in the limelight with the Poopy Girls made her realize that there was a higher regard for her stage persona than her everyday character.
At the start of summer, Jane wrote to ***Tom Hardwick,*** *director of Hardwick's Great Mountain Show and a former Deadwood acquaintance as Sheriff Bullock's deputy.*
His traveling circus was one of the first to portray "authentic Frontier life," featuring real Crow Indians who, in exchange for room and board, acted as foils to two superstars of the Wild West:
The famous ***"Liver-Eating" Johnson,*** *who boasted of having eaten the* ***livers*** *of Indians who'd massacred his family...*
CURLEY THE LONE SURVI OF LITTLE BIGHORN
...and ***Curley,*** *a Crow scout who claimed to be the lone survivor of the Battle of the Little Bighorn.*

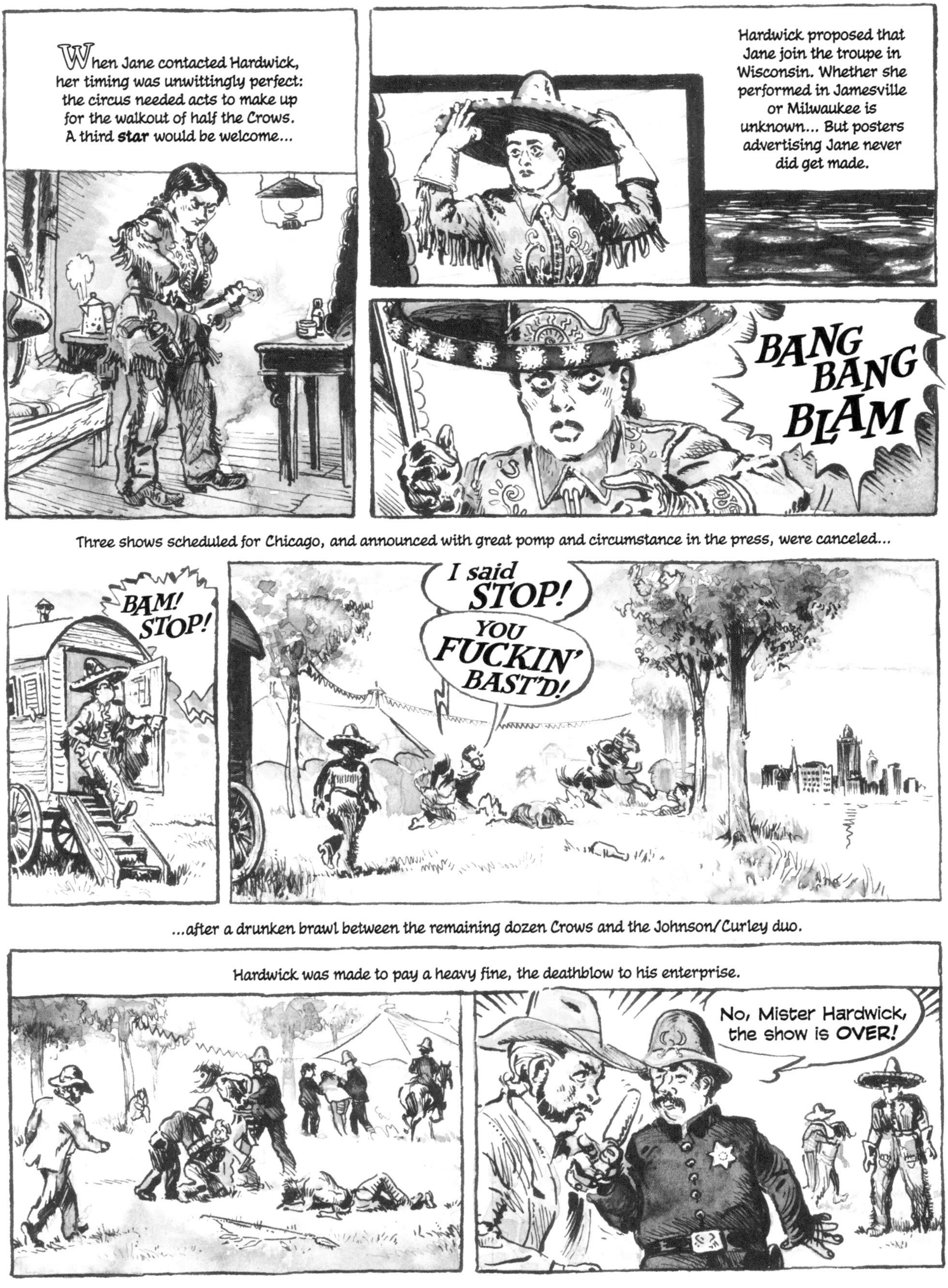
When Jane contacted Hardwick, her timing was unwittingly perfect: the circus needed acts to make up for the walkout of half the Crows. A third **star** would be welcome...
Hardwick proposed that Jane join the troupe in Wisconsin. Whether she performed in Jamesville or Milwaukee is unknown... But posters advertising Jane never did get made.
BANG BANG BLAM
Three shows scheduled for Chicago, and announced with great pomp and circumstance in the press, were canceled...
BAM! STOP!
I said STOP!
YOU FUCKIN' BAST'D!
...after a drunken brawl between the remaining dozen Crows and the Johnson/Curley duo.
Hardwick was made to pay a heavy fine, the deathblow to his enterprise.
No, Mister Hardwick, the show is **OVER!**

In the fall of 1884, Martha Jane returned to Wyoming, resuming her nomadic existence along the rail lines being built by both the Northern Pacific and the Union Pacific. For two years she lived out of a tent, traveling the territory in a chuckwagon.

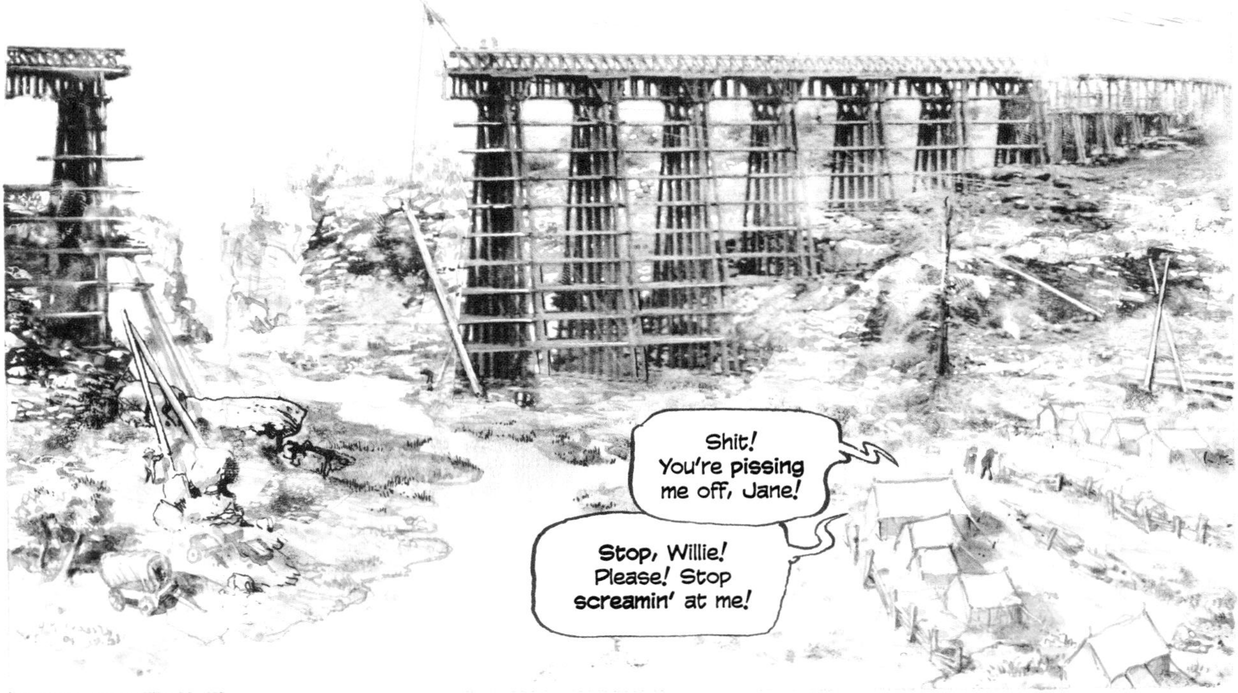
Shit! You're pissing me off, Jane!
Stop, Willie! Please! Stop screamin' at me!

In Rawlins, Jane took up with **William P. Steers,** a Northern Pacific brakeman. Nine years her junior, Steers so shocked his family by latching onto an "alcoholic of doubtful morals" that he was disowned, which made him bitter and contentious.

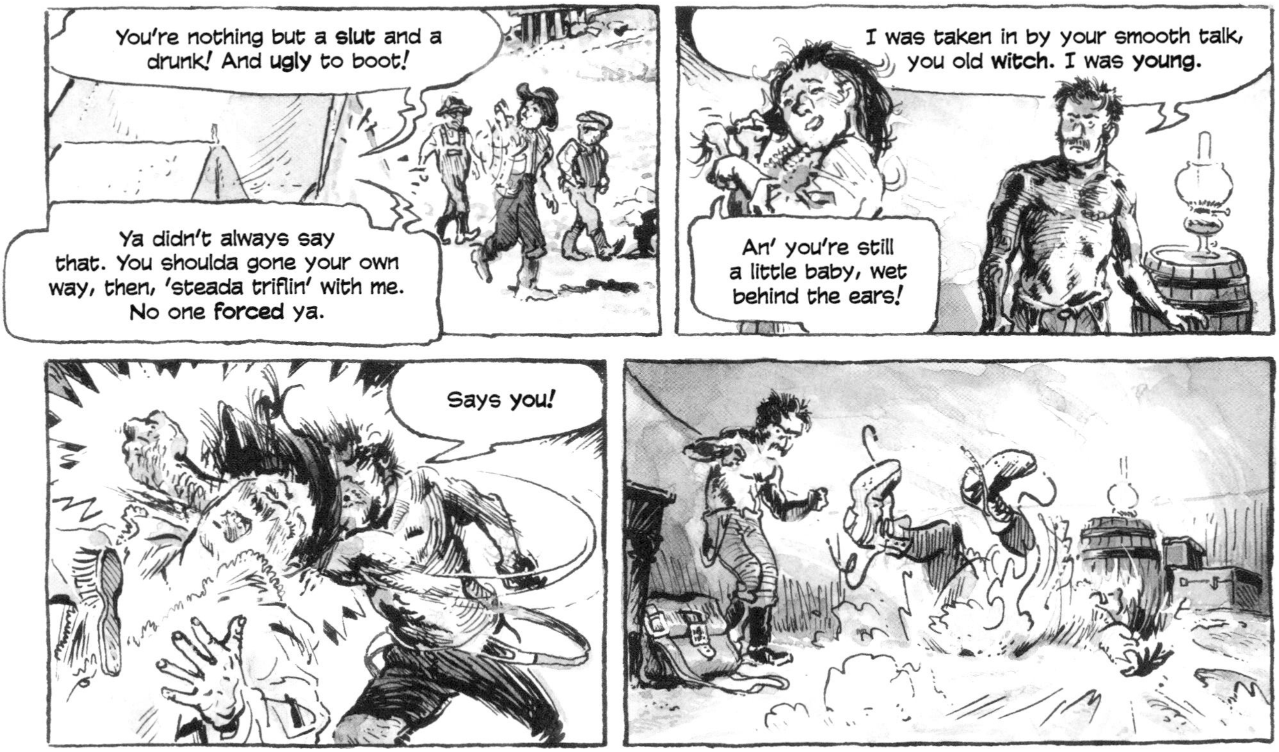
You're nothing but a slut and a drunk! And ugly to boot!
Ya didn't always say that. You shoulda gone your own way, then, 'steada triflin' with me. No one forced ya.
I was taken in by your smooth talk, you old witch. I was young.
An' you're still a little baby, wet behind the ears!
Says you!

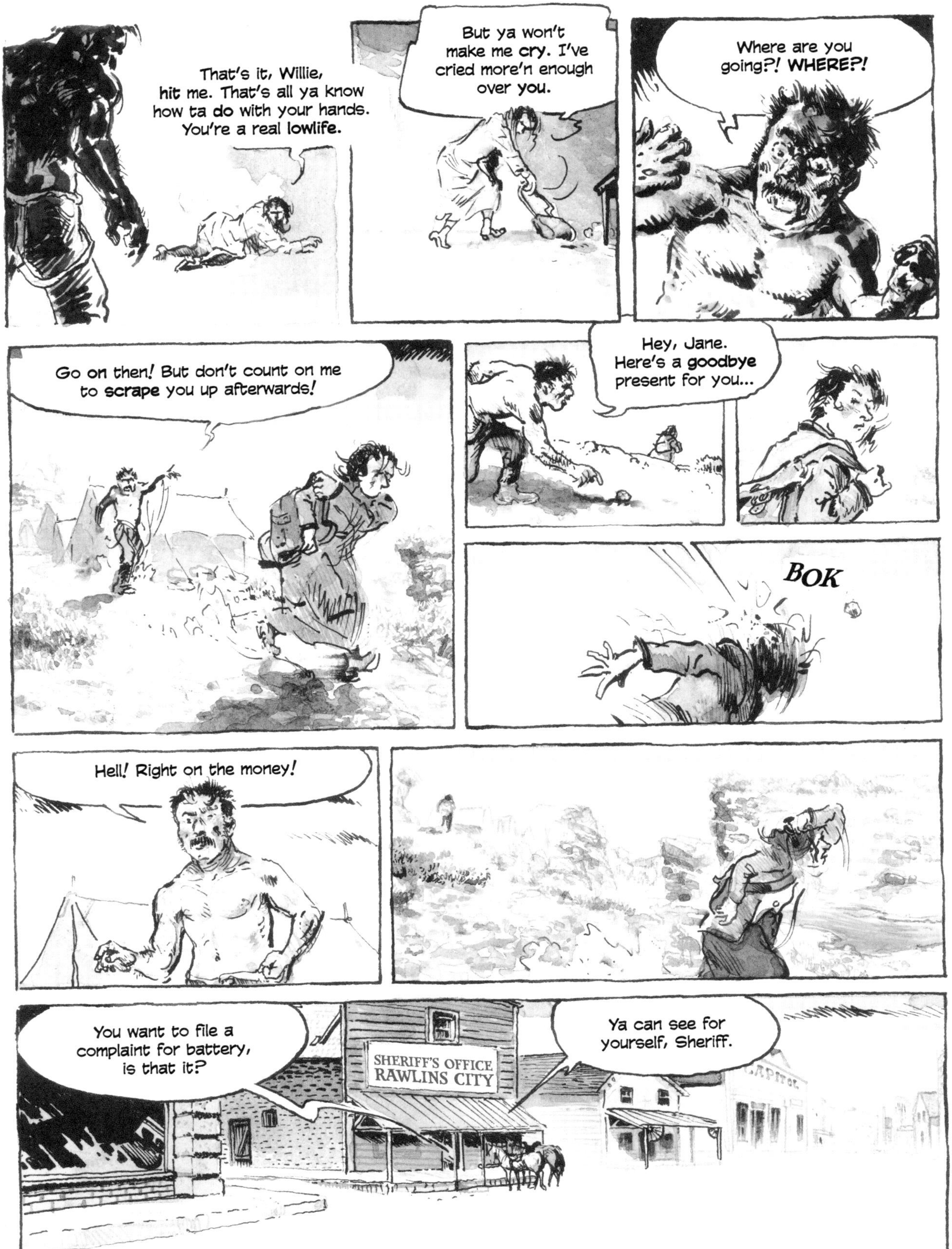
That's it, Willie, hit me. That's all ya know how ta do with your hands. You're a real lowlife.
But ya won't make me cry. I've cried more'n enough over you.
Where are you going?! WHERE?!
Go on then! But don't count on me to scrape you up afterwards!
Hey, Jane. Here's a goodbye present for you...
BOK
Hell! Right on the money!
You want to file a complaint for battery, is that it?
SHERIFF'S OFFICE
RAWLINS CITY
Ya can see for yourself, Sheriff.

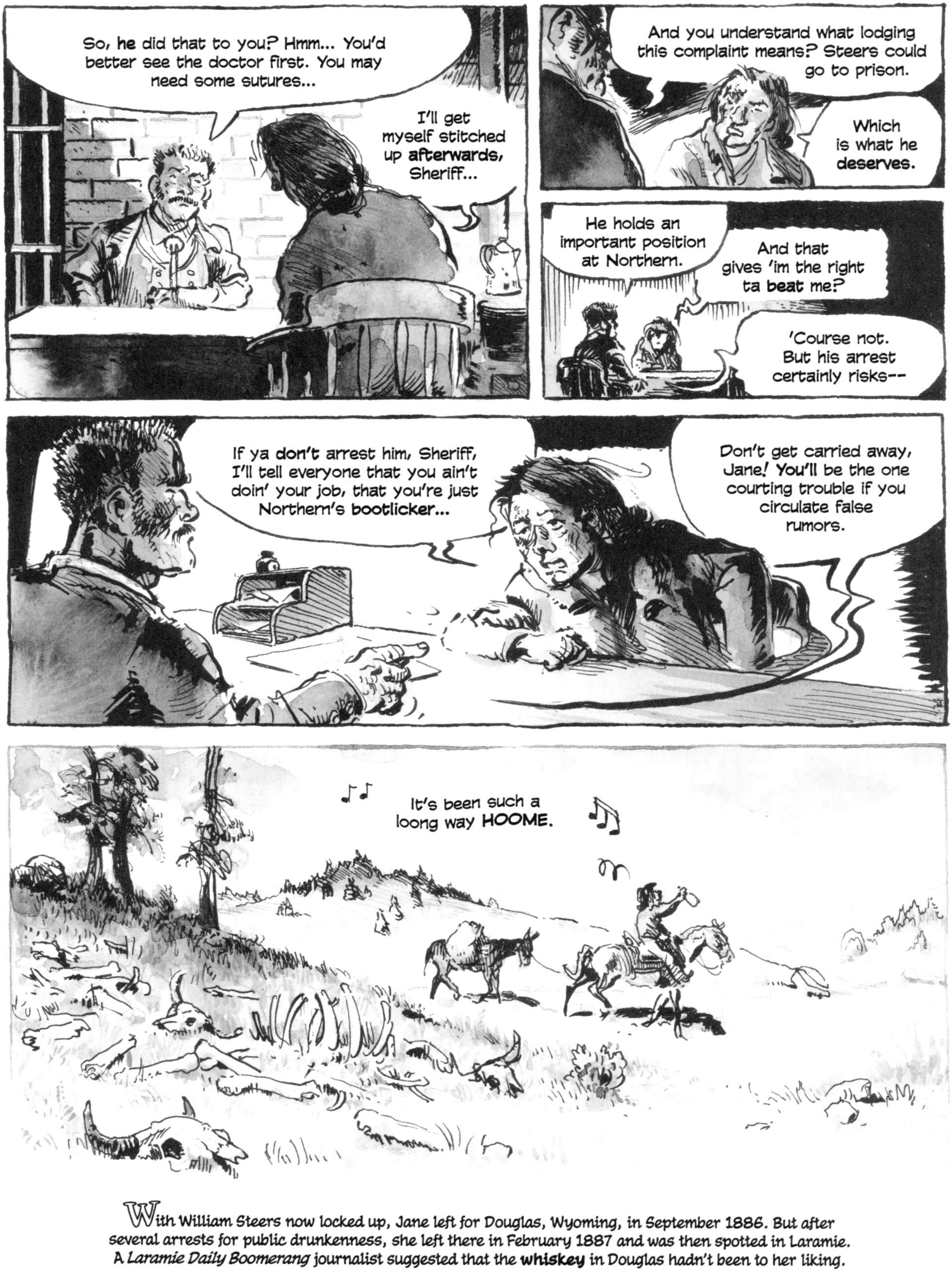
So, he did that to you? Hmm... You'd better see the doctor first. You may need some sutures...
I'll get myself stitched up afterwards, Sheriff...
And you understand what lodging this complaint means? Steers could go to prison.
Which is what he deserves.
He holds an important position at Northern.
And that gives 'im the right ta beat me?
'Course not. But his arrest certainly risks--
If ya don't arrest him, Sheriff, I'll tell everyone that you ain't doin' your job, that you're just Northern's bootlicker...
Don't get carried away, Jane! You'll be the one courting trouble if you circulate false rumors.
It's been such a loong way HOOME.

With William Steers now locked up, Jane left for Douglas, Wyoming, in September 1886. But after several arrests for public drunkenness, she left there in February 1887 and was then spotted in Laramie. A *Laramie Daily Boomerang* journalist suggested that the **whiskey** in Douglas hadn't been to her liking.

She next surfaced in Cheyenne, where she hadn't set foot in over ten years. There, she agreed to an interview with the Cheyenne Daily Leader...

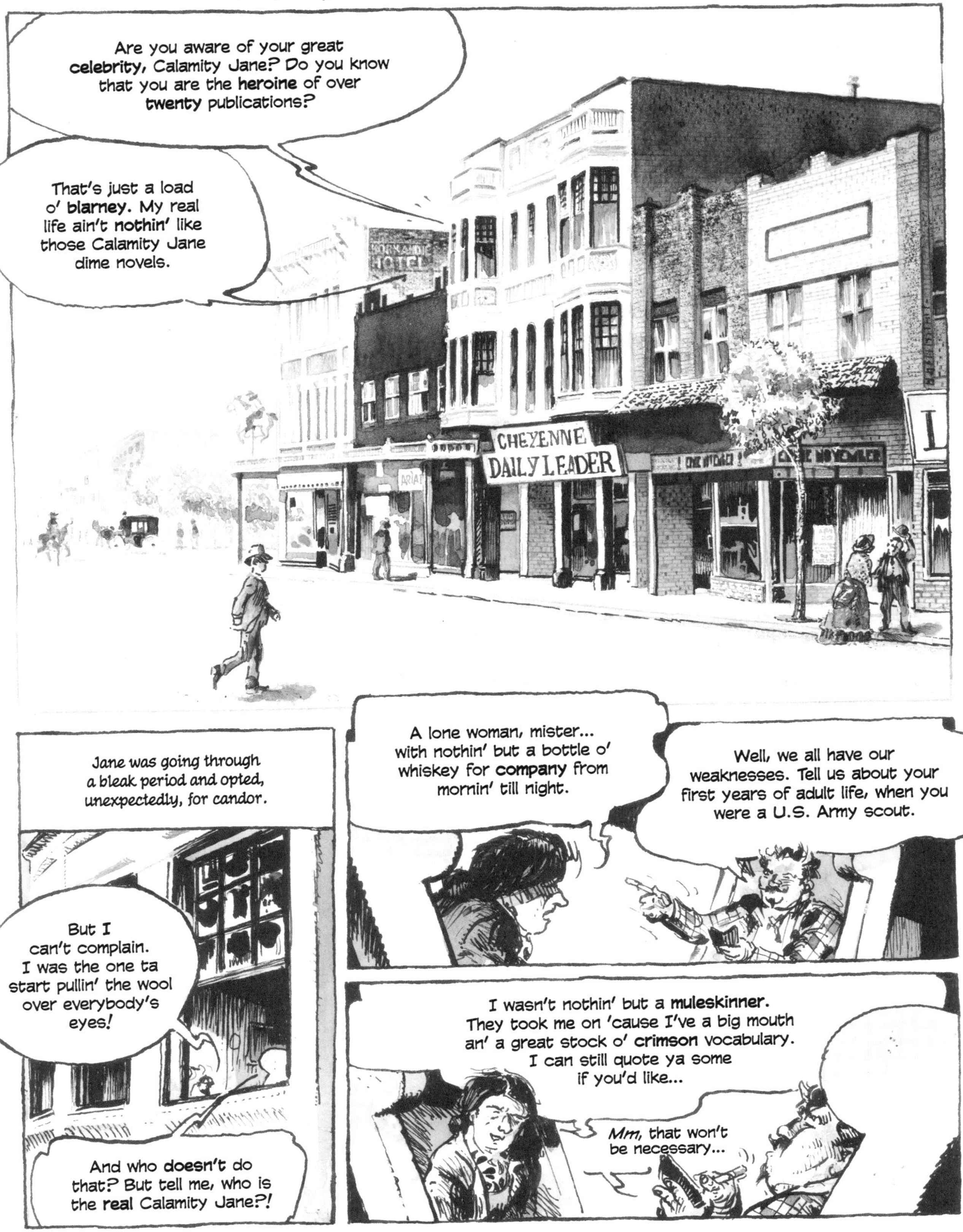

Are you aware of your great **celebrity**, Calamity Jane? Do you know that you are the **heroine** of over **twenty** publications?
That's just a load o' **blarney**. My real life ain't **nothin'** like those Calamity Jane dime novels.
CHEYENNE DAILY LEADER
Jane was going through a bleak period and opted, unexpectedly, for candor.
But I can't complain. I was the one ta start pullin' the wool over everybody's eyes!
And who **doesn't** do that? But tell me, who is the **real** Calamity Jane?!
A lone woman, mister... with nothin' but a bottle o' whiskey for **company** from mornin' till night.
Well, we all have our weaknesses. Tell us about your first years of adult life, when you were a U.S. Army scout.
I wasn't nothin' but a **muleskinner**. They took me on 'cause I've a big mouth an' a great stock o' **crimson** vocabulary. I can still quote ya some if you'd like...
Mm, that won't be necessary...

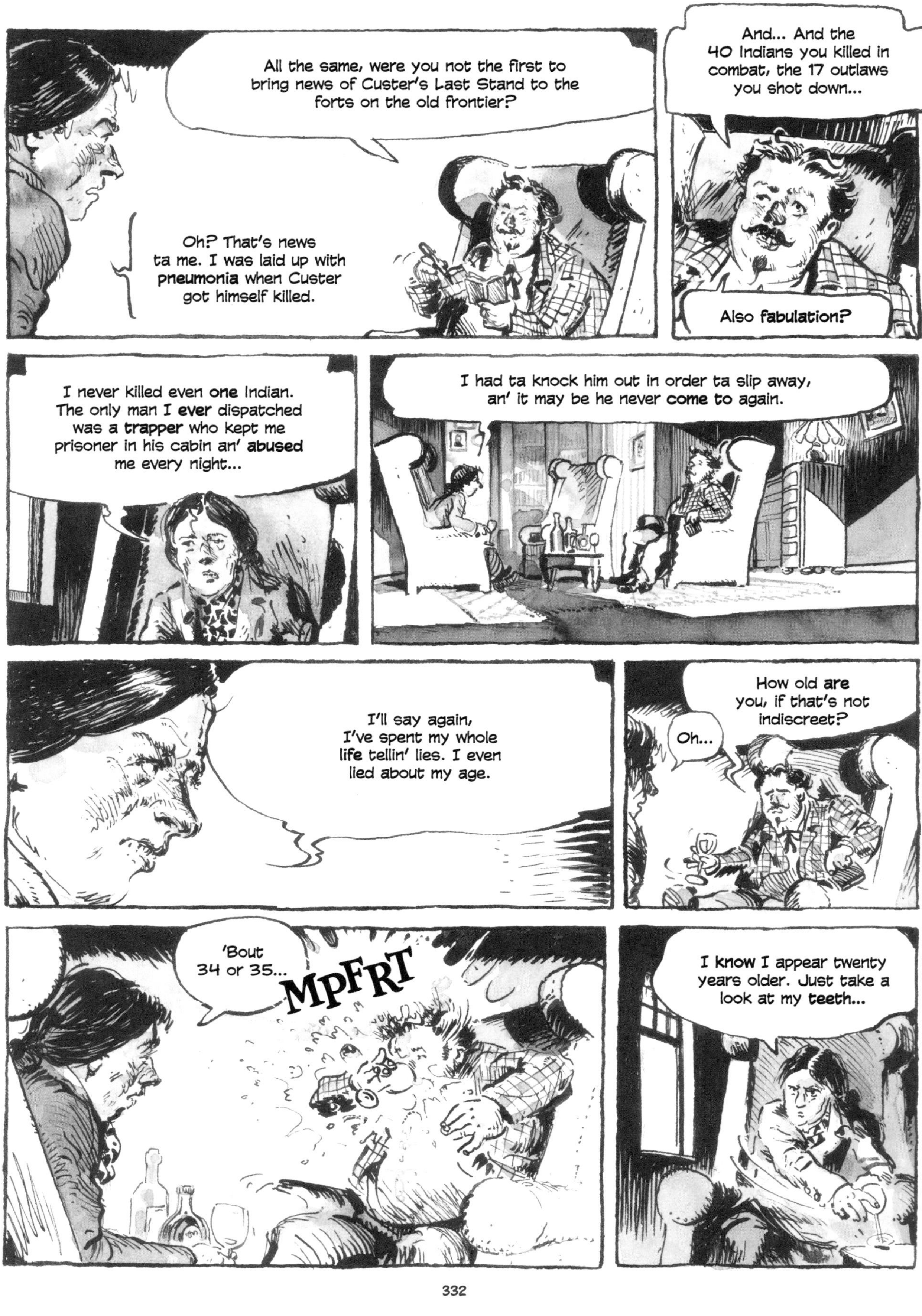
All the same, were you not the first to bring news of Custer's Last Stand to the forts on the old frontier?
Oh? That's news ta me. I was laid up with **pneumonia** when Custer got himself killed.
And... And the 40 Indians you killed in combat, the 17 outlaws you shot down...
Also **fabulation?**
I never killed even **one** Indian. The only man I **ever** dispatched was a **trapper** who kept me prisoner in his cabin an' **abused** me every night...
I had ta knock him out in order ta slip away, an' it may be he never **come to** again.
I'll say again, I've spent my whole **life** tellin' lies. I even lied about my age.
Oh...
How old **are** you, if that's not indiscreet?
'Bout 34 or 35...
MPFRT
I **know** I appear twenty years older. Just take a look at my **teeth**...

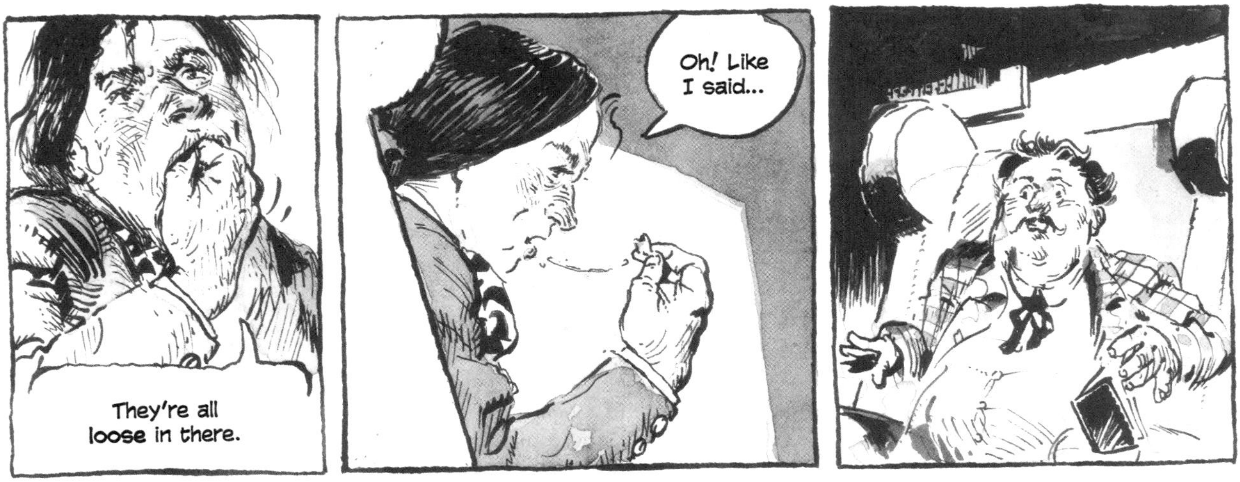
They're all **loose** in there.
Oh! Like I said...

The interview was published the next day with considerable **revision,** the *Cheyenne Daily Leader* management having deemed that its faithful readers might not be prepared to stomach the confessions of a human train wreck at breakfast...

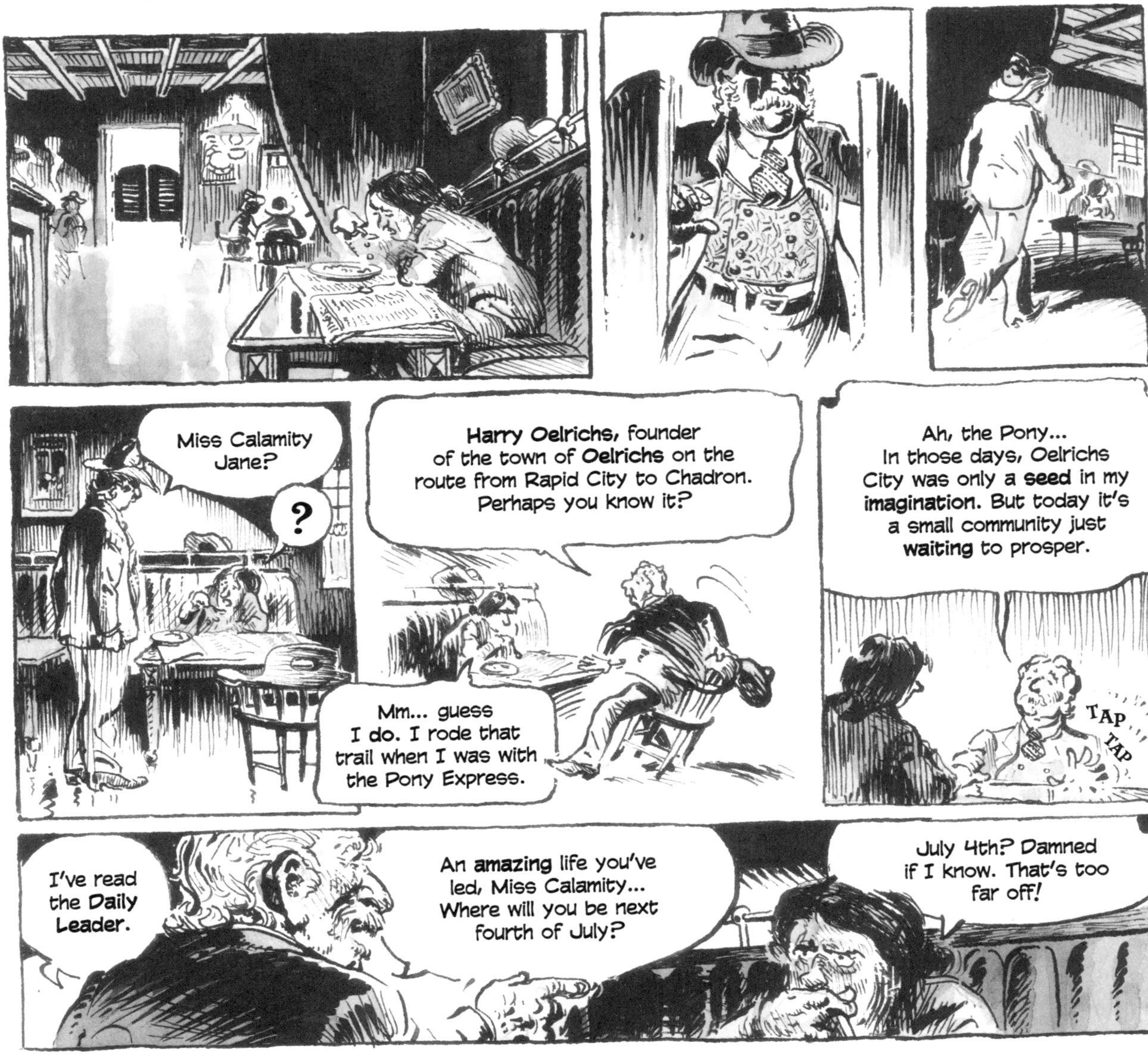
Miss Calamity Jane?
?
Harry Oelrichs, founder of the town of **Oelrichs** on the route from Rapid City to Chadron. Perhaps you know it?
Mm... guess I do. I rode that trail when I was with the Pony Express.
Ah, the Pony... In those days, Oelrichs City was only a **seed** in my **imagination.** But today it's a small community just **waiting** to prosper.
TAP
TAP
I've read the **Daily Leader.**
An **amazing** life you've led, Miss Calamity... Where will you be next fourth of July?
July 4th? Damned if I know. That's too far off!

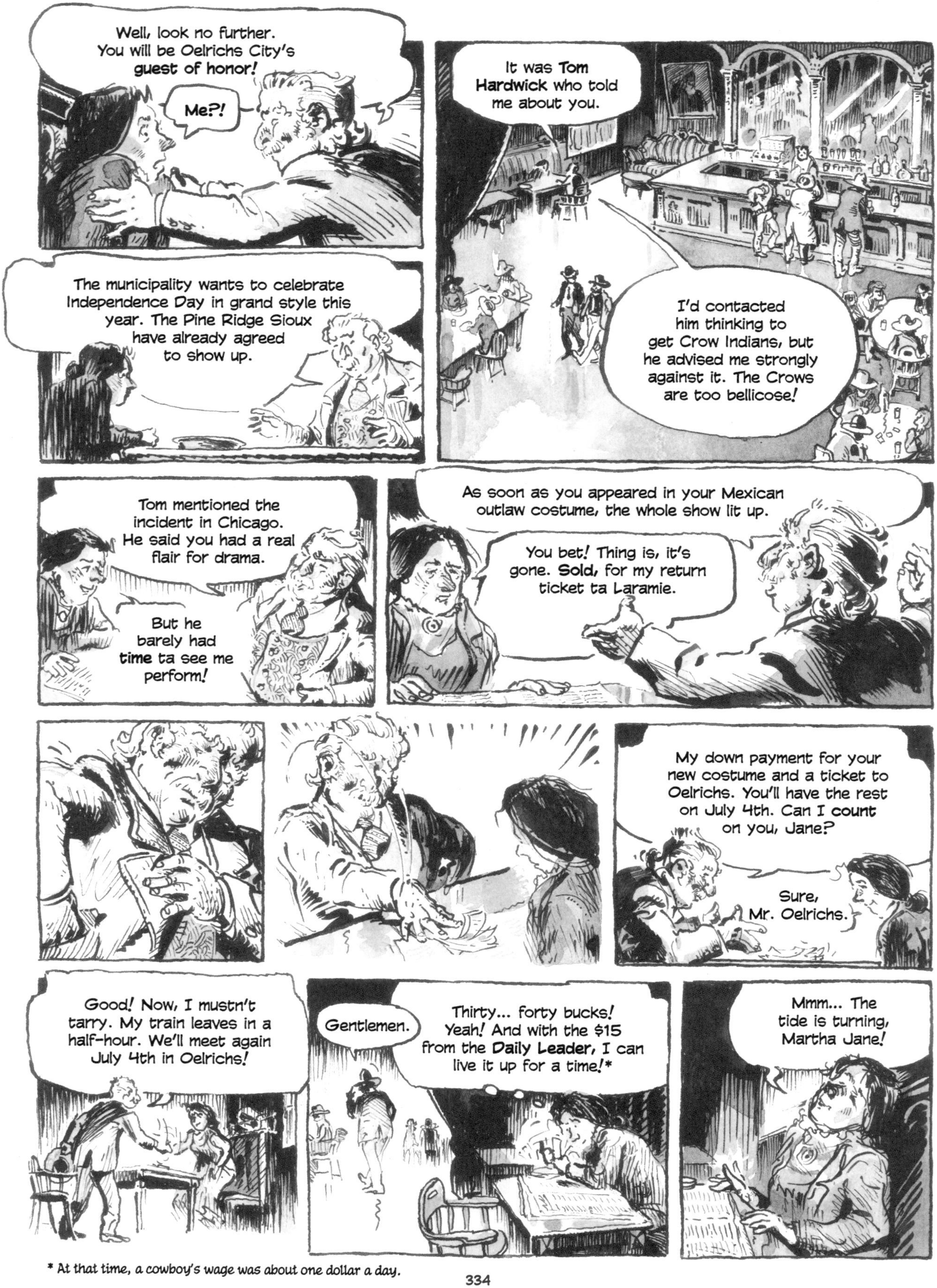

Well, look no further. You will be Oelrichs City's **guest of honor!**
Me?!
It was **Tom Hardwick** who told me about you.
I'd contacted him thinking to get Crow Indians, but he advised me strongly against it. The Crows are too bellicose!
The municipality wants to celebrate Independence Day in grand style this year. The Pine Ridge Sioux have already agreed to show up.
Tom mentioned the incident in Chicago. He said you had a real flair for drama.
But he barely had **time** ta see me perform!
As soon as you appeared in your Mexican outlaw costume, the whole show lit up.
You bet! Thing is, it's gone. **Sold**, for my return ticket ta Laramie.
My down payment for your new costume and a ticket to Oelrichs. You'll have the rest on July 4th. Can I **count** on you, Jane?
Sure, Mr. Oelrichs.
Good! Now, I mustn't tarry. My train leaves in a half-hour. We'll meet again July 4th in Oelrichs!
Gentlemen.
Thirty... forty bucks! Yeah! And with the $15 from the **Daily Leader**, I can live it up for a time!*
Mmm... The tide is turning, Martha Jane!

* At that time, a cowboy's wage was about one dollar a day.

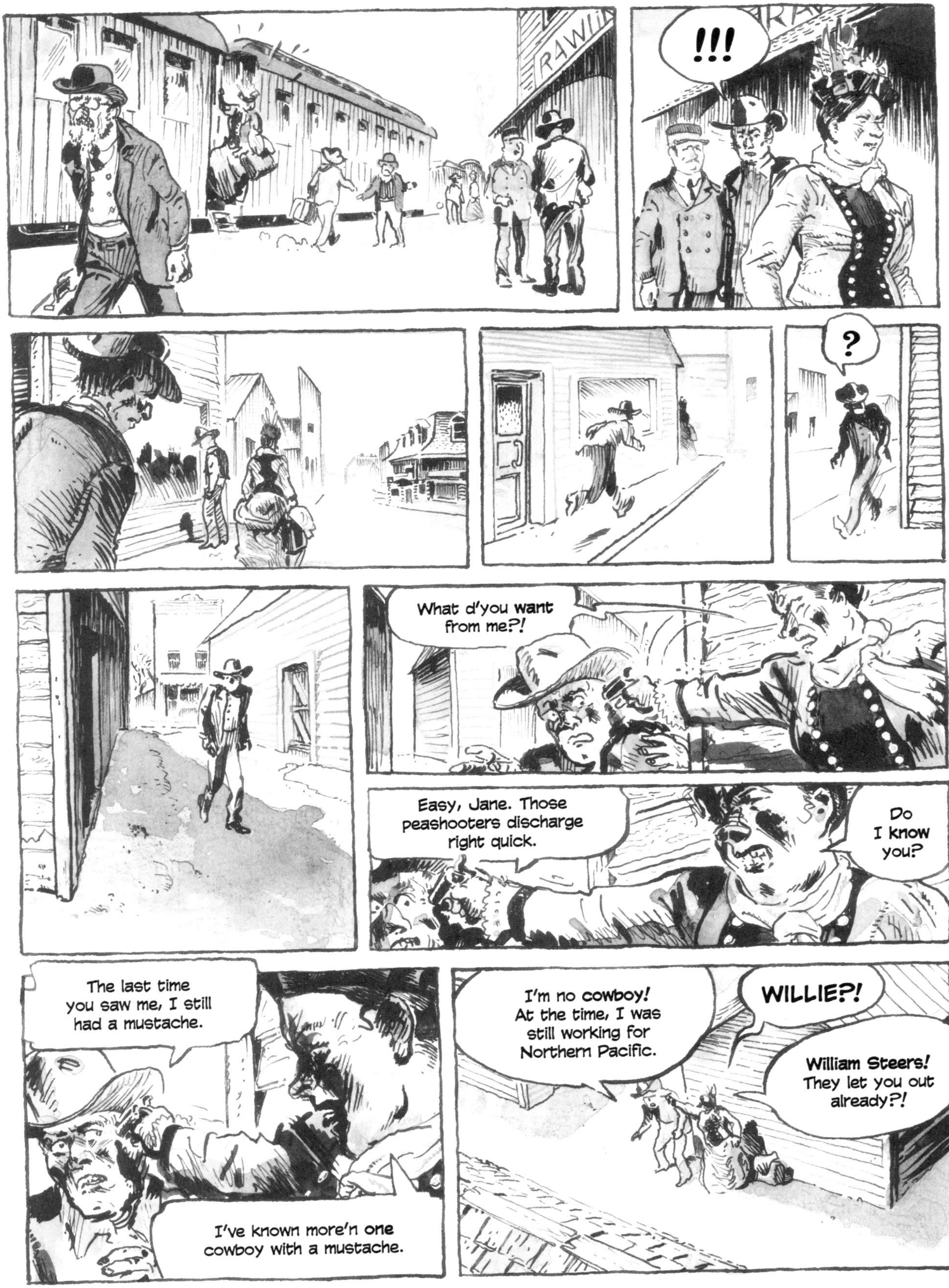
!!!
?
What d'you want from me?!
Easy, Jane. Those peashooters discharge right quick.
Do I know you?
The last time you saw me, I still had a mustache.
I've known more'n one cowboy with a mustache.
I'm no cowboy! At the time, I was still working for Northern Pacific.
WILLIE?!
William Steers! They let you out already?!

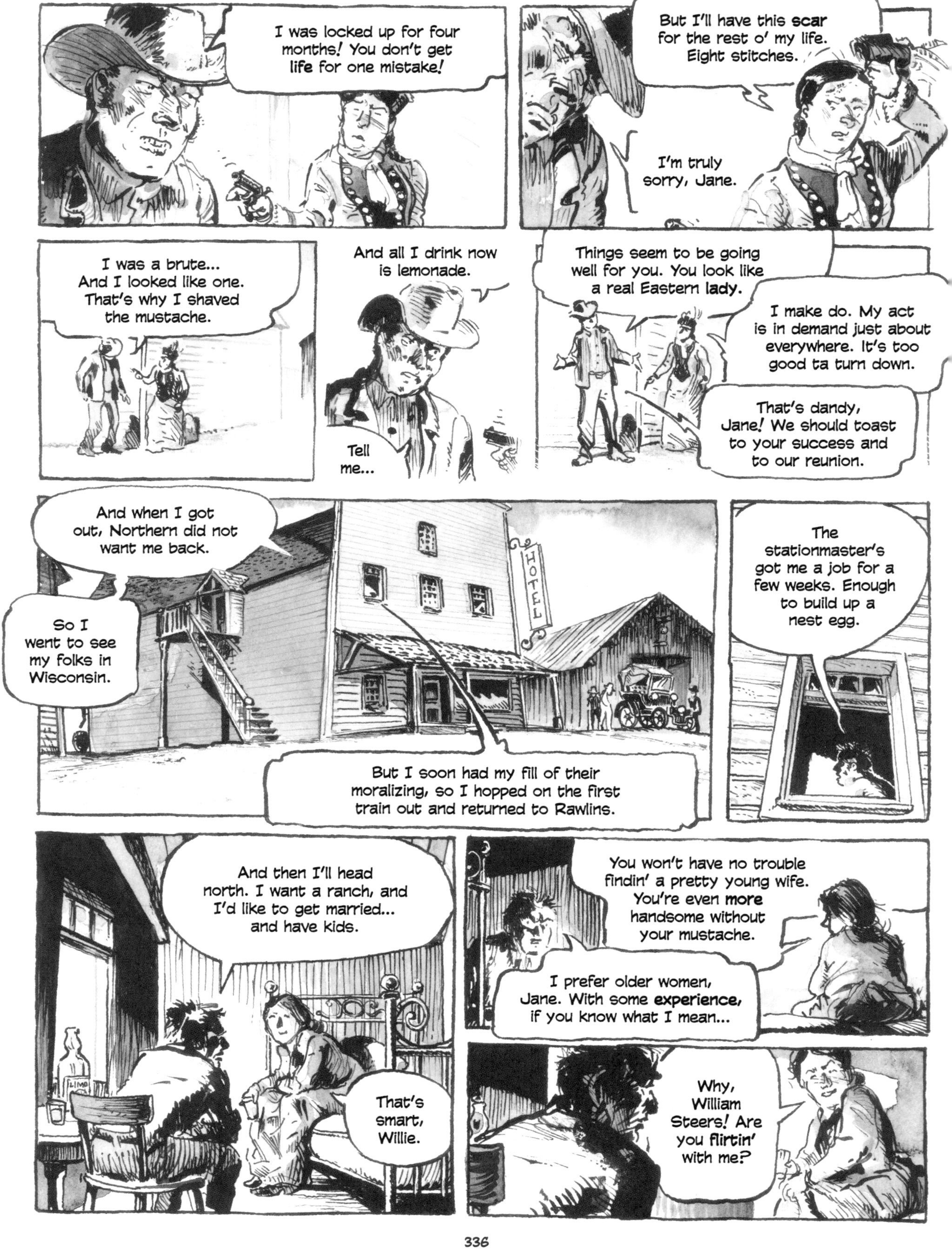

I was locked up for four months! You don't get life for one mistake!
But I'll have this scar for the rest o' my life. Eight stitches.
I'm truly sorry, Jane.
I was a brute... And I looked like one. That's why I shaved the mustache.
And all I drink now is lemonade.
Tell me...
Things seem to be going well for you. You look like a real Eastern lady.
I make do. My act is in demand just about everywhere. It's too good ta turn down.
That's dandy, Jane! We should toast to your success and to our reunion.
And when I got out, Northern did not want me back.
So I went to see my folks in Wisconsin.
HOTEL
But I soon had my fill of their moralizing, so I hopped on the first train out and returned to Rawlins.
The stationmaster's got me a job for a few weeks. Enough to build up a nest egg.
And then I'll head north. I want a ranch, and I'd like to get married... and have kids.
That's smart, Willie.
You won't have no trouble findin' a pretty young wife. You're even more handsome without your mustache.
I prefer older women, Jane. With some experience, if you know what I mean...
Why, William Steers! Are you flirtin' with me?

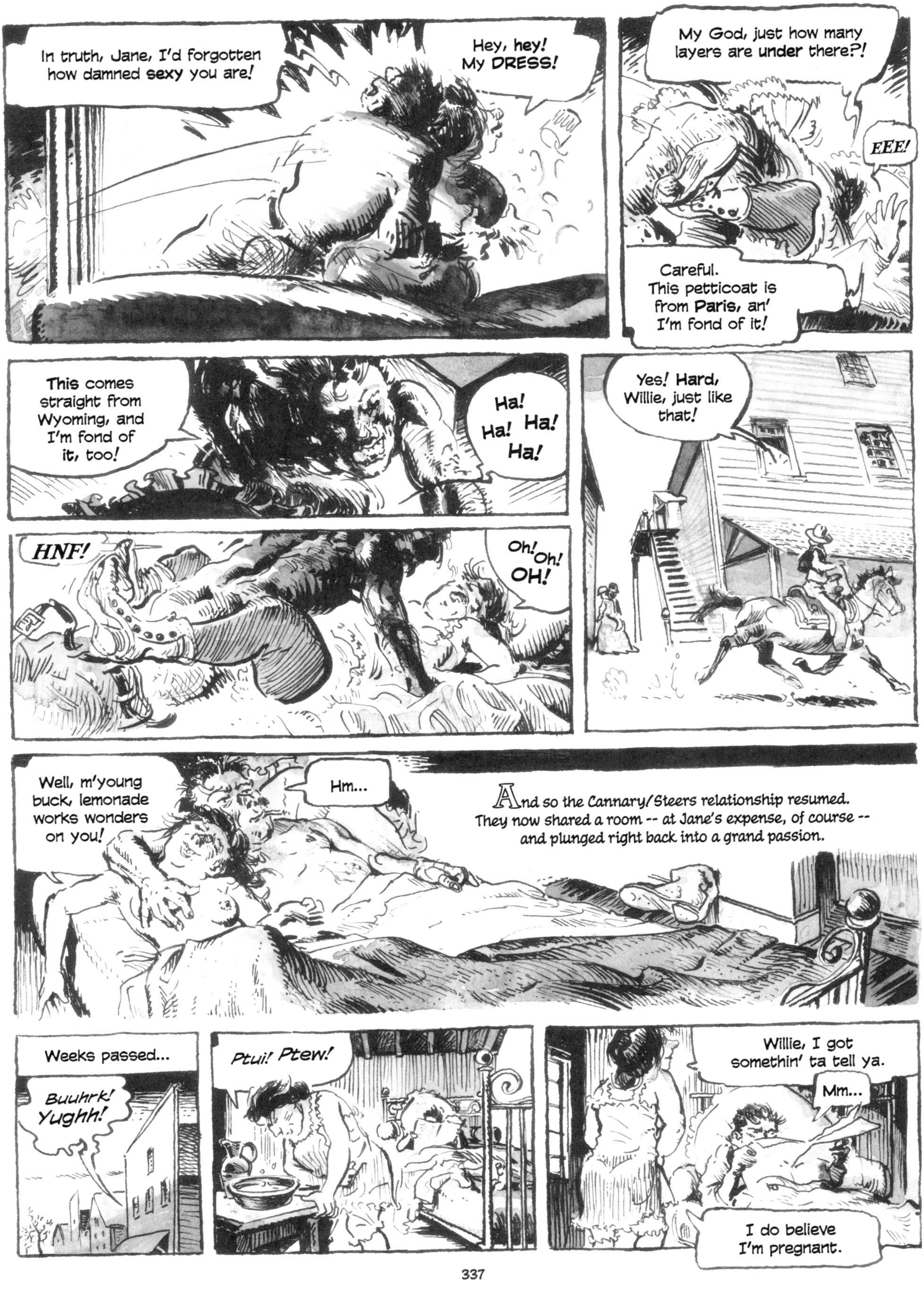
In truth, Jane, I'd forgotten how damned sexy you are!
Hey, hey! My DRESS!
My God, just how many layers are under there?!
EEE!
Careful. This petticoat is from Paris, an' I'm fond of it!
This comes straight from Wyoming, and I'm fond of it, too!
Ha! Ha! Ha! Ha!
Yes! Hard, Willie, just like that!
HNF!
Oh! Oh! OH!
Well, m'young buck, lemonade works wonders on you!
Hm...
And so the Cannary/Steers relationship resumed. They now shared a room -- at Jane's expense, of course -- and plunged right back into a grand passion.
Weeks passed...
Buuhrk! Yughh!
Ptui! Ptew!
Willie, I got somethin' ta tell ya.
Mm...
I do believe I'm pregnant.

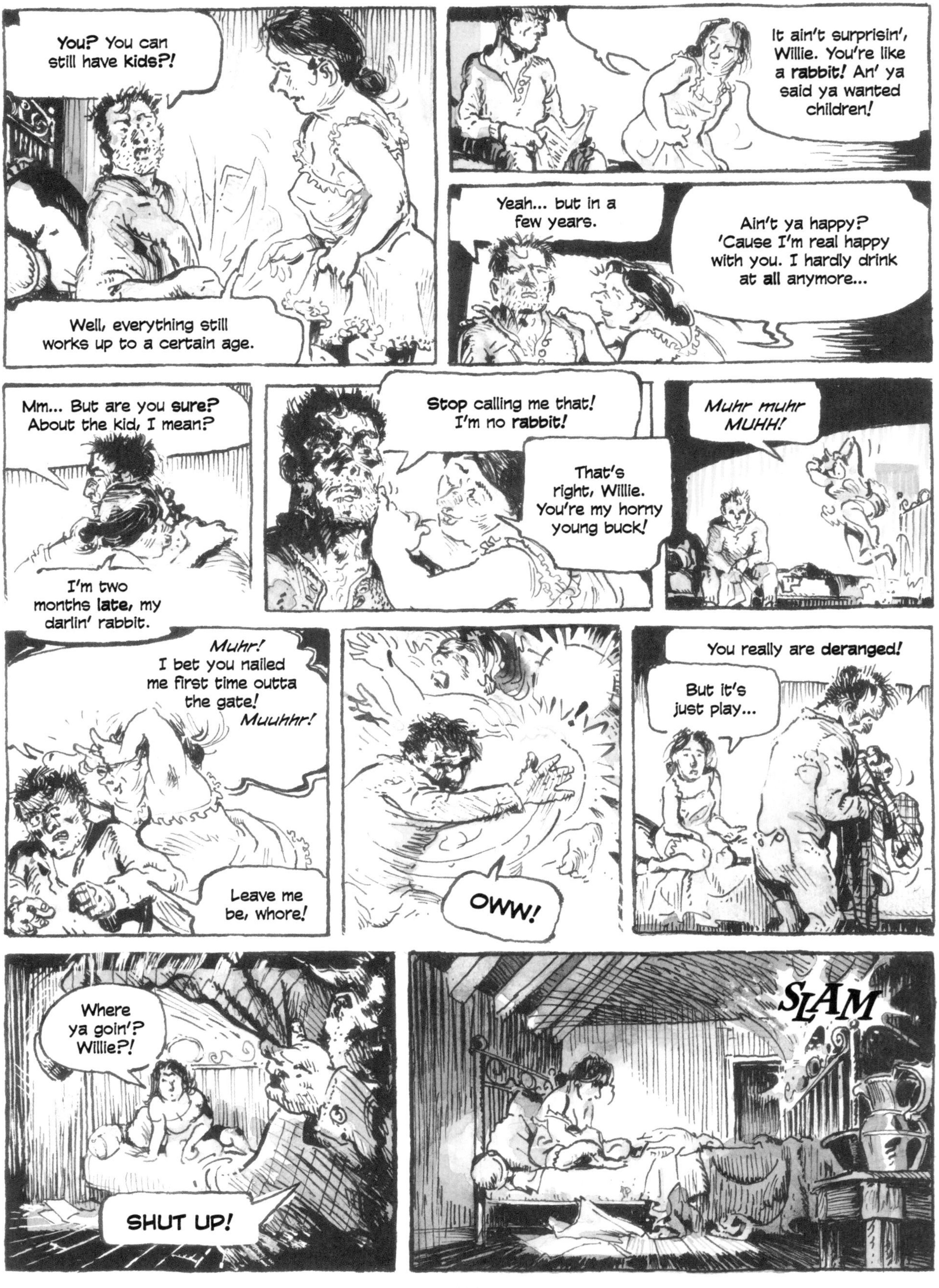
You? You can still have kids?!
Well, everything still works up to a certain age.
It ain't surprisin', Willie. You're like a rabbit! An' ya said ya wanted children!
Yeah... but in a few years.
Ain't ya happy? 'Cause I'm real happy with you. I hardly drink at all anymore...
Mm... But are you sure? About the kid, I mean?
I'm two months late, my darlin' rabbit.
Stop calling me that! I'm no rabbit!
That's right, Willie. You're my horny young buck!
Muhr muhr MUHH!
Muhr! I bet you nailed me first time outta the gate! Muuhhr!
Leave me be, whore!
OWW!
You really are deranged!
But it's just play...
Where ya goin'? Willie?!
SHUT UP!
SLAM

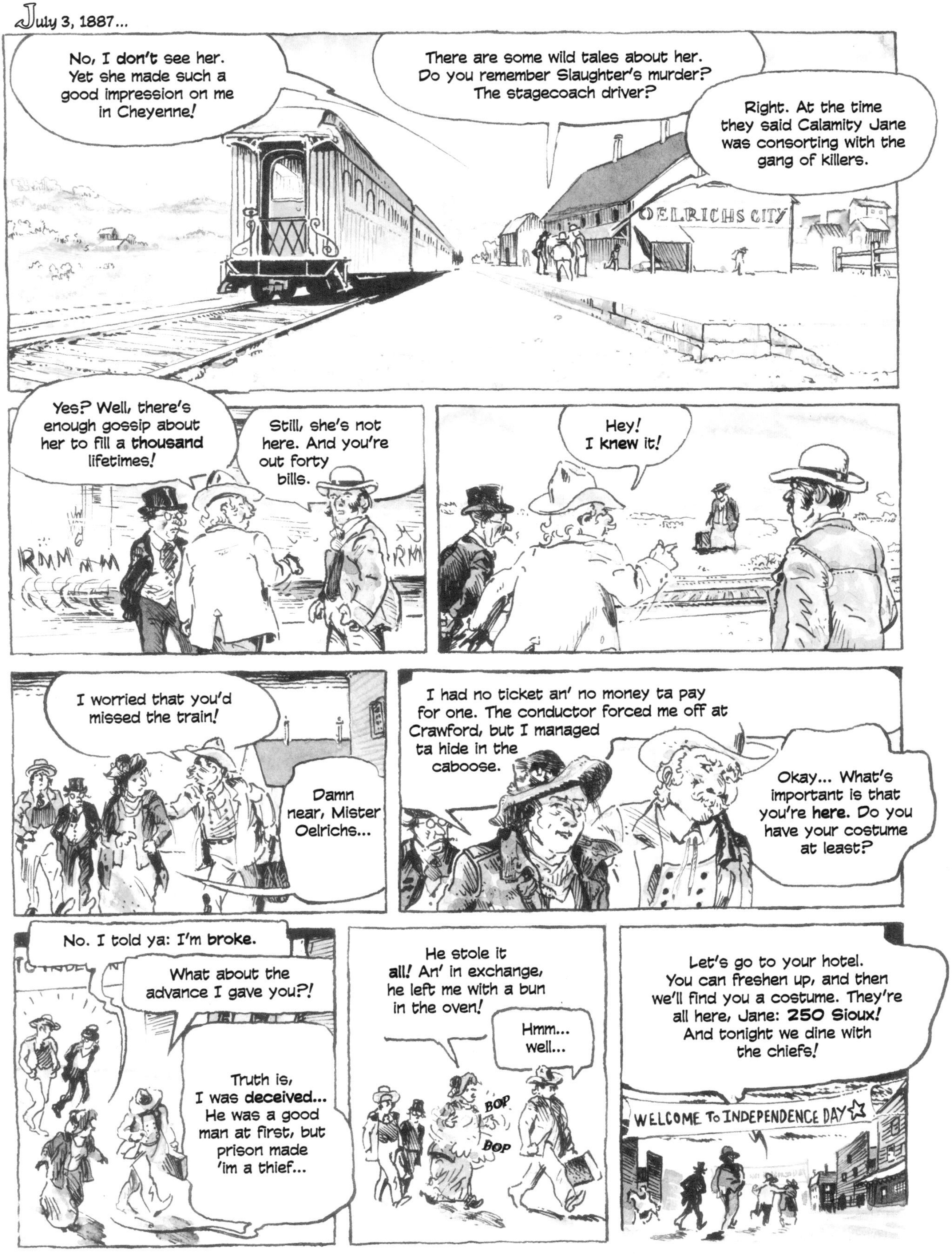
July 3, 1887...
No, I don't see her. Yet she made such a good impression on me in Cheyenne!
There are some wild tales about her. Do you remember Slaughter's murder? The stagecoach driver?
Right. At the time they said Calamity Jane was consorting with the gang of killers.
OELRICHS CITY
Yes? Well, there's enough gossip about her to fill a thousand lifetimes!
Still, she's not here. And you're out forty bills.
RMM MM
RM
Hey! I knew it!
I worried that you'd missed the train!
Damn near, Mister Oelrichs...
I had no ticket an' no money ta pay for one. The conductor forced me off at Crawford, but I managed ta hide in the caboose.
Okay... What's important is that you're here. Do you have your costume at least?
No. I told ya: I'm broke.
What about the advance I gave you?!
Truth is, I was deceived... He was a good man at first, but prison made 'im a thief...
He stole it all! An' in exchange, he left me with a bun in the oven!
Hmm... well...
BOP
BOP
Let's go to your hotel. You can freshen up, and then we'll find you a costume. They're all here, Jane: 250 Sioux! And tonight we dine with the chiefs!
WELCOME To INDEPENDENCE DAY

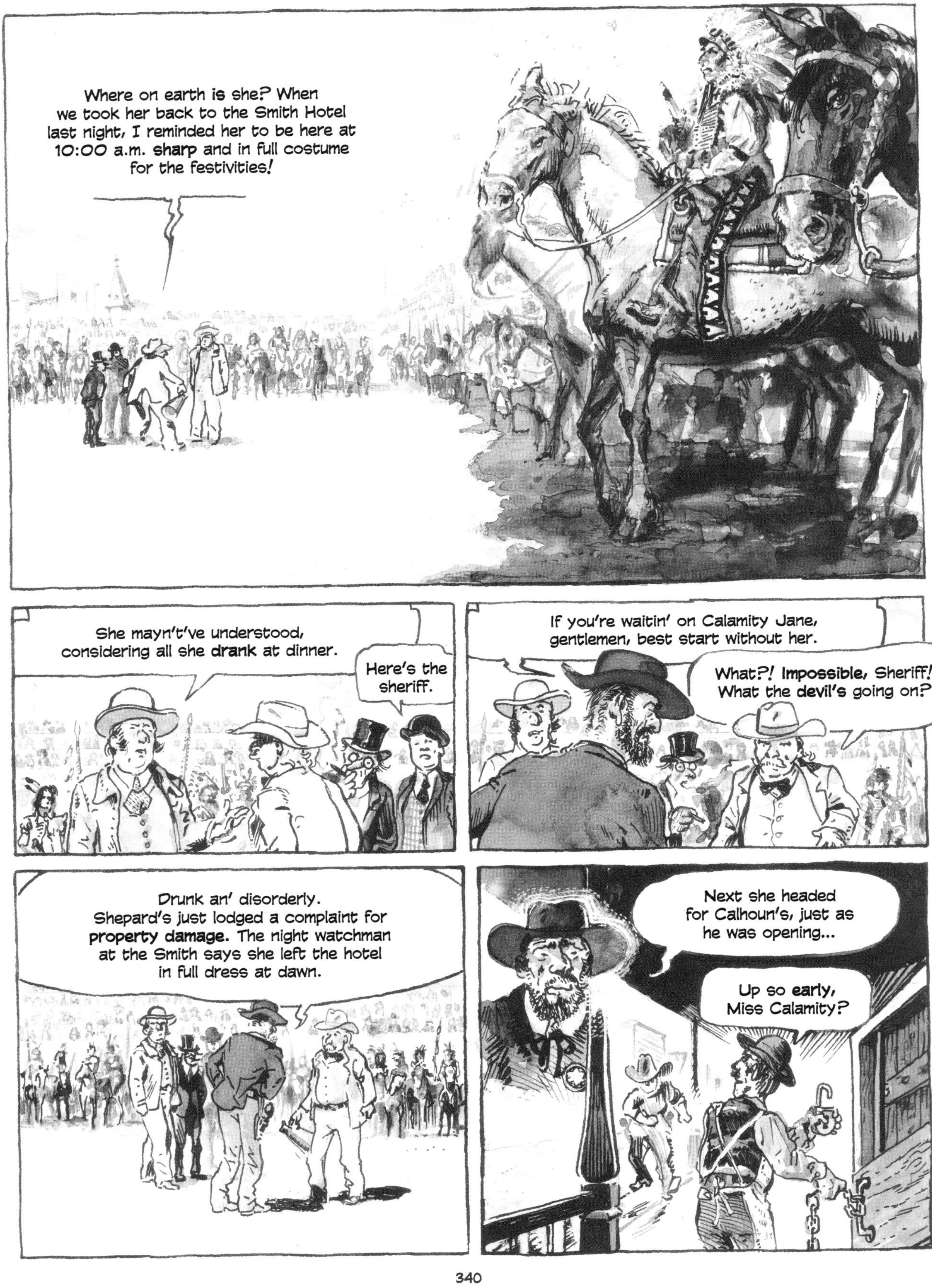

Where on earth is she? When we took her back to the Smith Hotel last night, I reminded her to be here at 10:00 a.m. **sharp** and in full costume for the festivities!
She mayn't've understood, considering all she **drank** at dinner.
Here's the sheriff.
If you're waitin' on Calamity Jane, gentlemen, best start without her.
What?! **Impossible**, Sheriff! What the **devil's** going on?
Drunk an' disorderly. Shepard's just lodged a complaint for **property damage.** The night watchman at the Smith says she left the hotel in full dress at dawn.
Next she headed for Calhoun's, just as he was opening...
Up so **early**, Miss Calamity?

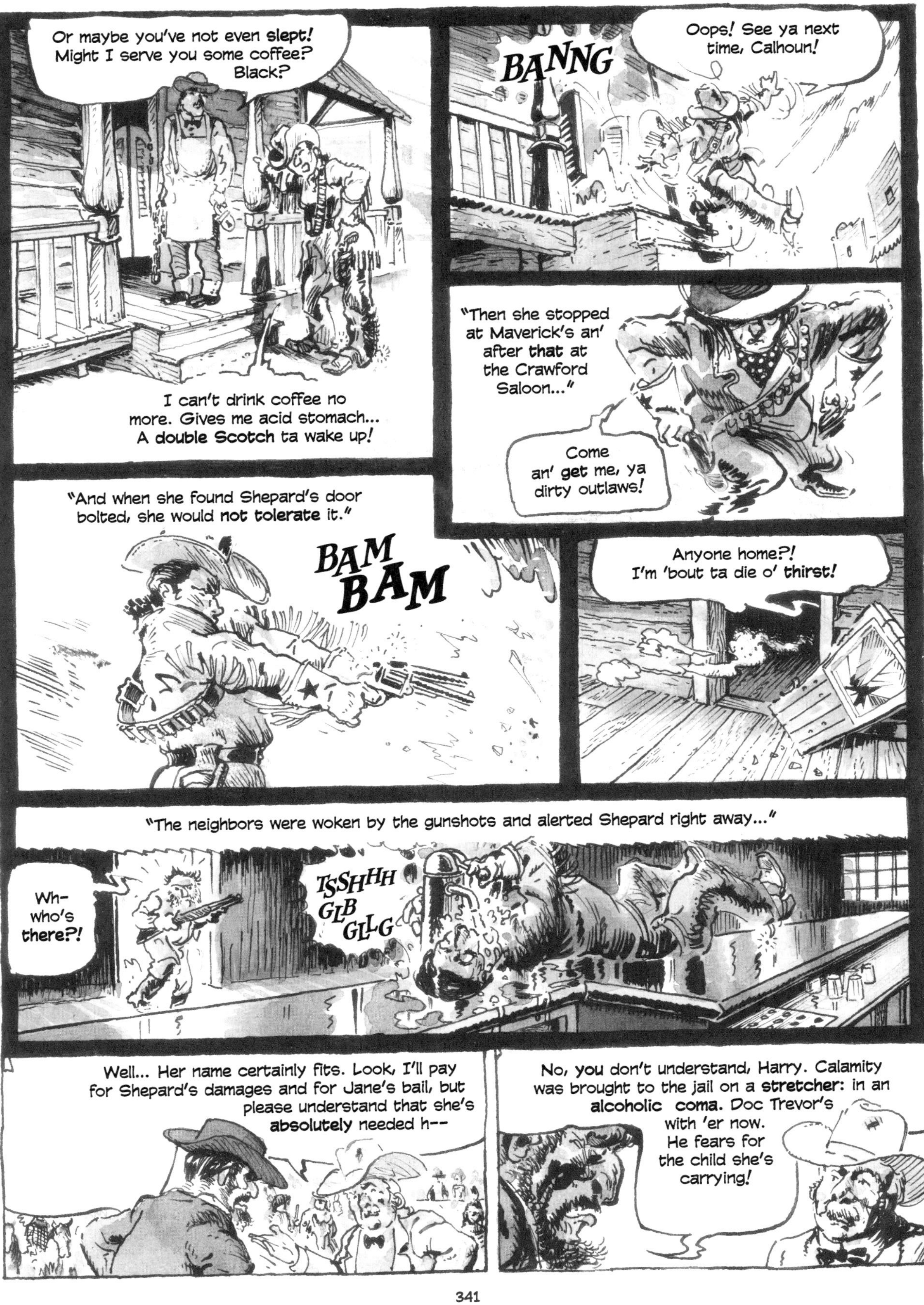

Or maybe you've not even slept! Might I serve you some coffee? Black?
I can't drink coffee no more. Gives me acid stomach... A double Scotch ta wake up!
BANNG
Oops! See ya next time, Calhoun!
"Then she stopped at Maverick's an' after that at the Crawford Saloon..."
Come an' get me, ya dirty outlaws!
"And when she found Shepard's door bolted, she would not tolerate it."
BAM BAM
Anyone home?! I'm 'bout ta die o' thirst!
"The neighbors were woken by the gunshots and alerted Shepard right away..."
Wh- who's there?!
TSSHHH GLB GLLG
Well... Her name certainly fits. Look, I'll pay for Shepard's damages and for Jane's bail, but please understand that she's absolutely needed h--
No, you don't understand, Harry. Calamity was brought to the jail on a stretcher: in an alcoholic coma. Doc Trevor's with 'er now. He fears for the child she's carrying!

Return To Deadwood

If there is some truth to Martha Jane's autobiography, which she dictated during the last years of her life to a man named Mulloy, her daughter was born on October 28, 1887. Martha Jane named the baby **Jessie.** Writing to Janey, Jane elected to conceal the truth once again:

Here I am in the town of Billings. That woman never came to collect her child. I've hired a nurse to take care of her, so that I can work. She's still just a baby.

Her father lives in Lewistown, but he's poor. The two of us do our best to pay for her keep.

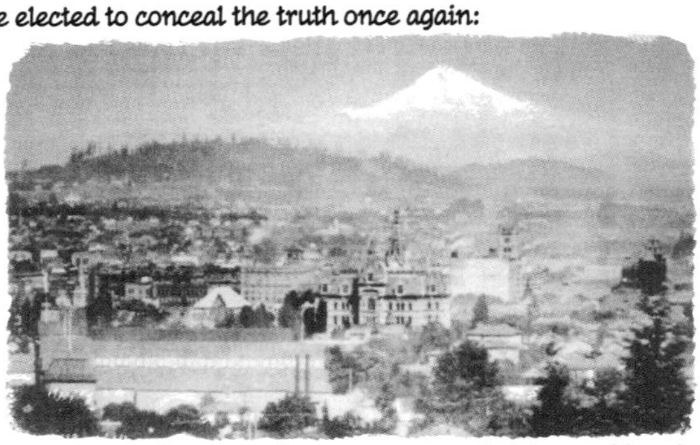

Portland, Oregon: Scenic view with Mount Hood

On a sudden whim, Jane decided to leave the area to tour the western part of the country. She traveled to Oregon first and then down the Pacific coast to San Francisco. From there, she crossed Arizona and New Mexico on her way to Texas, where she met a nice fellow: **Clinton E. Burke.**

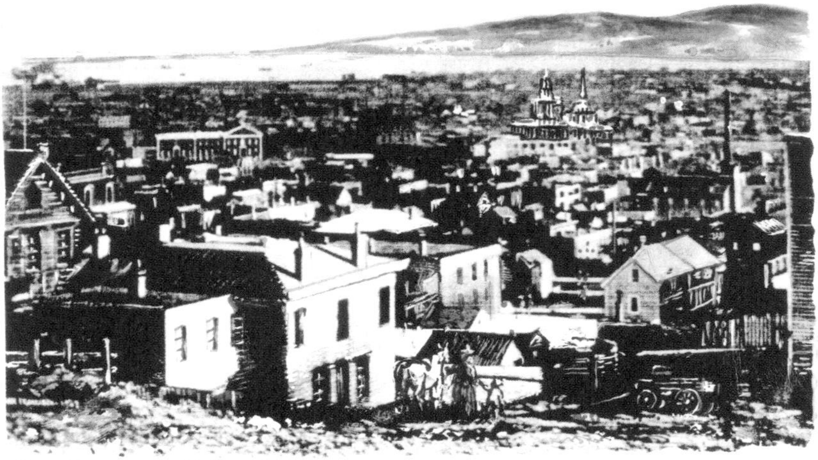

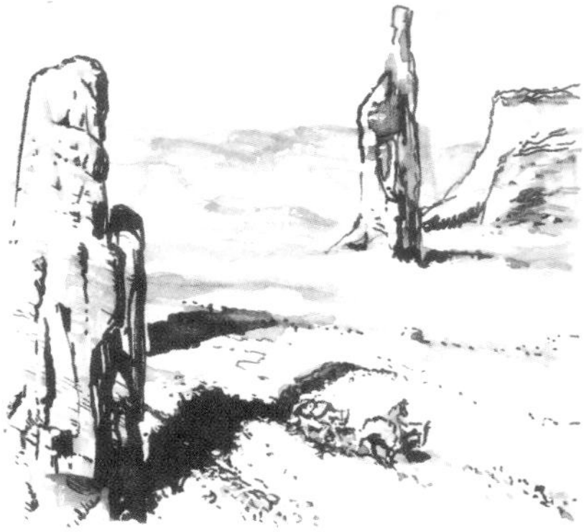

San Francisco, California

I did a foolish thing a while ago. I wed Clinton Burke. He caught me in a moment of weakness, and we married quickly. He's a good man, honest and straightforward, but I don't love him.

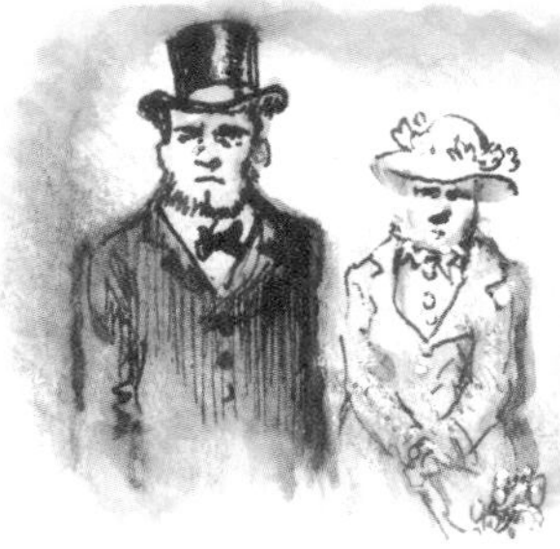

I still love your father, Bill Hickok. But Clinton is close to my age, with dark hair and blue eyes. The marriage ain't exactly a storybook romance.

The Burkes left to settle in Boulder, Colorado, where they ran a respectable hotel.

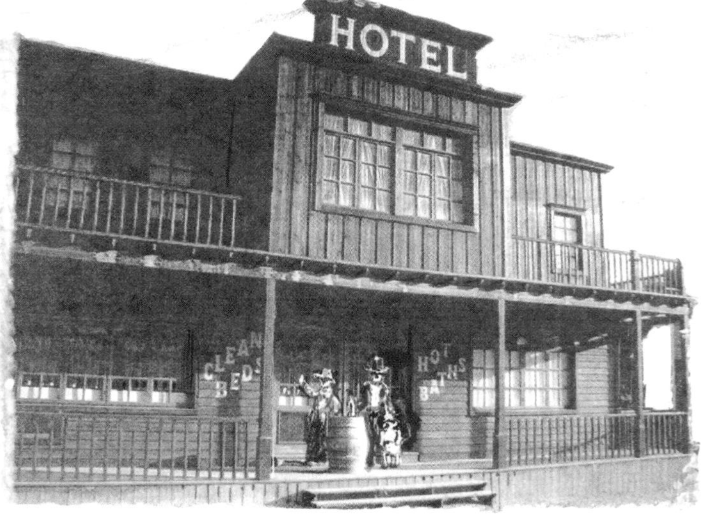
HOTEL
CLEAN BEDS
HOT BATHS

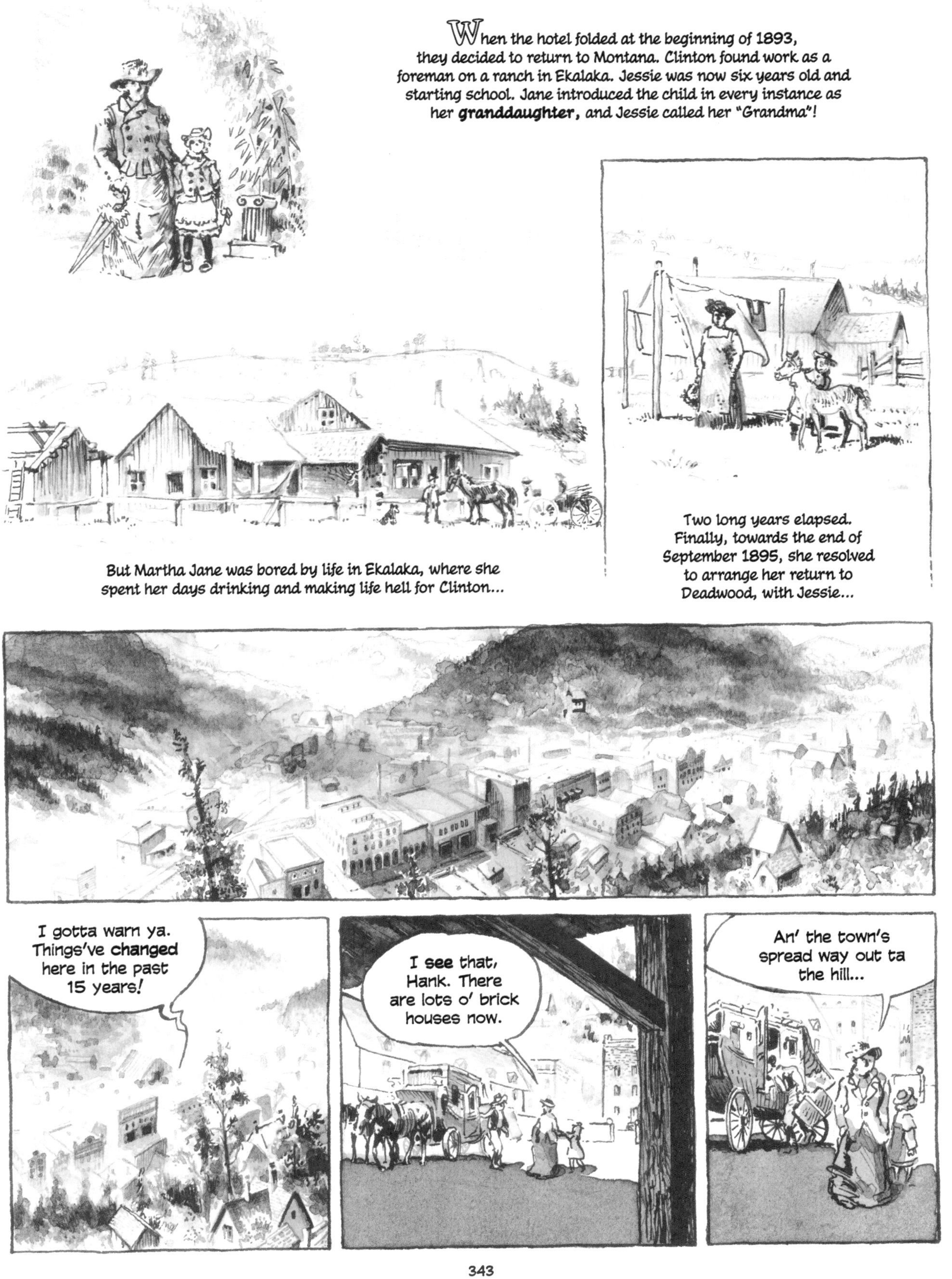
When the hotel folded at the beginning of 1893, they decided to return to Montana. Clinton found work as a foreman on a ranch in Ekalaka. Jessie was now six years old and starting school. Jane introduced the child in every instance as her **granddaughter**, and Jessie called her "Grandma"!
But Martha Jane was bored by life in Ekalaka, where she spent her days drinking and making life hell for Clinton...
Two long years elapsed. Finally, towards the end of September 1895, she resolved to arrange her return to Deadwood, with Jessie...
I gotta warn ya. Things've **changed** here in the past 15 years!
I **see** that, Hank. There are lots o' brick houses now.
An' the town's spread way out ta the hill...

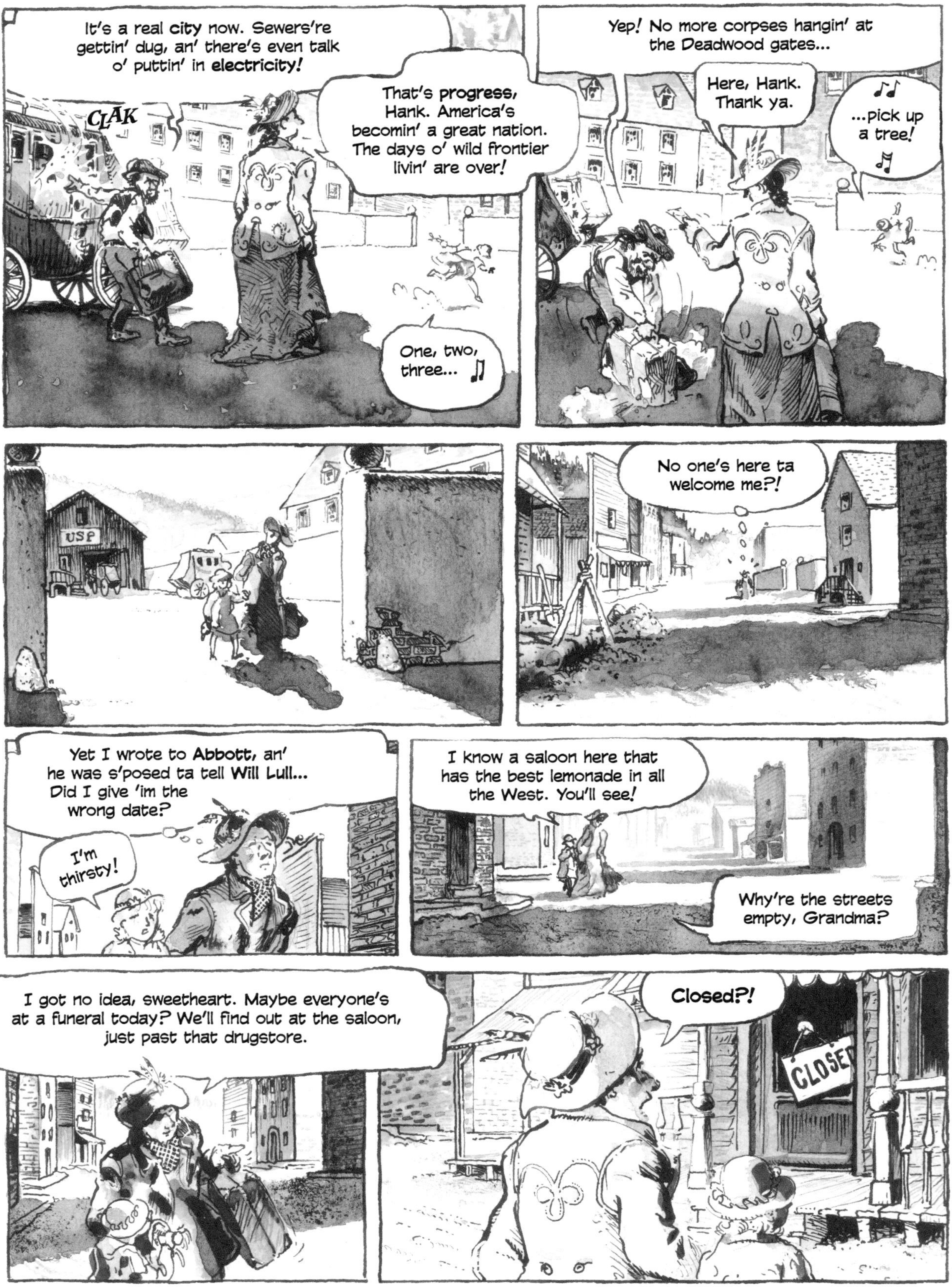
It's a real city now. Sewers're gettin' dug, an' there's even talk o' puttin' in electricity!
CLAK
That's progress, Hank. America's becomin' a great nation. The days o' wild frontier livin' are over!
One, two, three...
Yep! No more corpses hangin' at the Deadwood gates...
Here, Hank. Thank ya.
...pick up a tree!
USP
No one's here ta welcome me?!
Yet I wrote to Abbott, an' he was s'posed ta tell Will Lull... Did I give 'im the wrong date?
I'm thirsty!
I know a saloon here that has the best lemonade in all the West. You'll see!
Why're the streets empty, Grandma?
I got no idea, sweetheart. Maybe everyone's at a funeral today? We'll find out at the saloon, just past that drugstore.
Closed?!
CLOSED

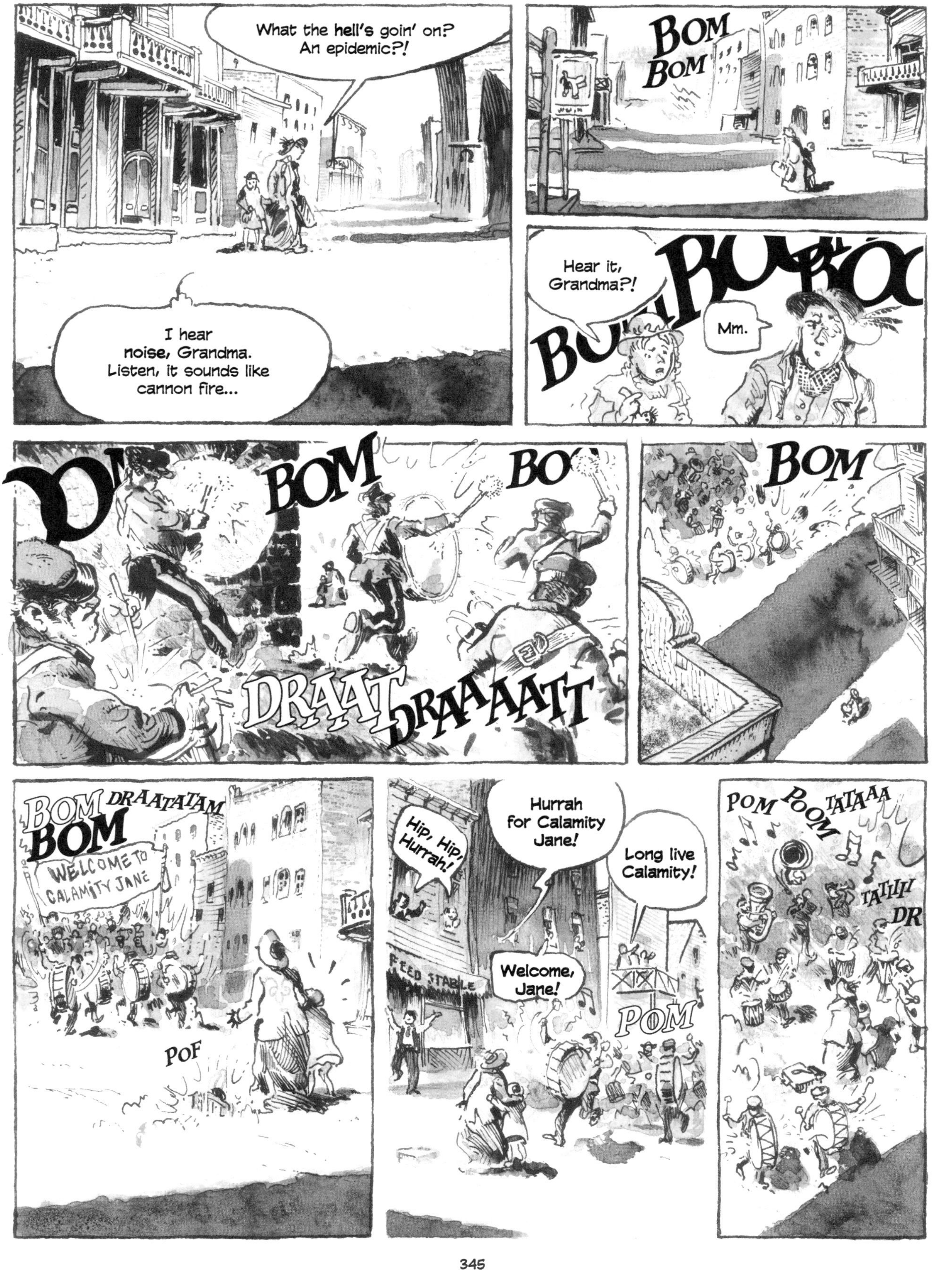
What the hell's goin' on? An epidemic?!
I hear noise, Grandma. Listen, it sounds like cannon fire...
BOM
BOM
Hear it, Grandma?!
Mm.
BOM
BOM
BOM
DRAAT
DRAAAATT
BOM
BOM
DRAATATAM
BOM
WELCOME TO CALAMITY JANE
POF
Hip, Hip, Hurrah!
Hurrah for Calamity Jane!
Long live Calamity!
FEED STABLE
Welcome, Jane!
POM
POM
POOM
TATAAA
TATIII
DR

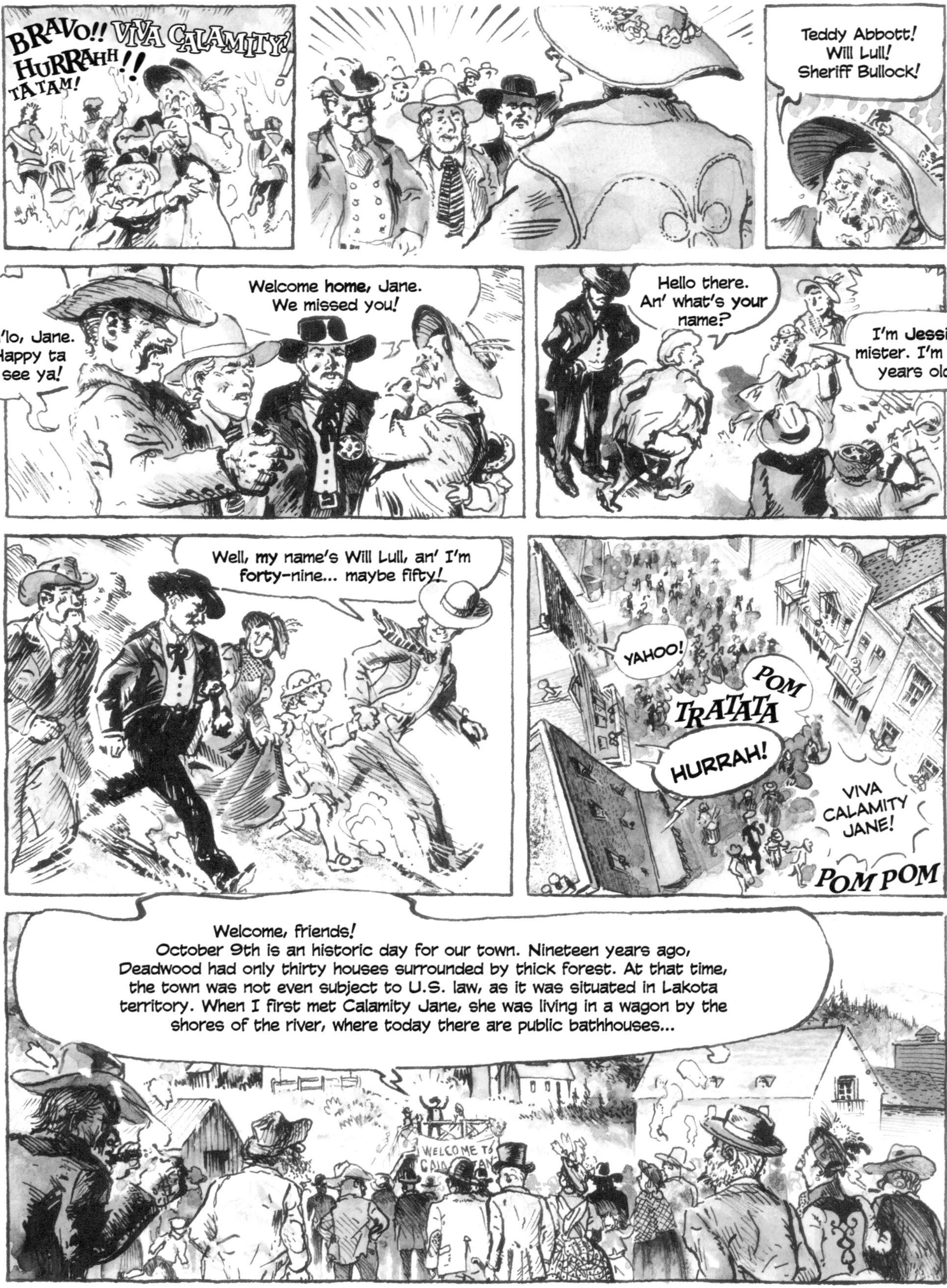
BRAVO!! VIVA CALAMITY!
HURRAHH!!
TA TAM!
Teddy Abbott! Will Lull! Sheriff Bullock!
H'lo, Jane. Happy ta see ya!
Welcome home, Jane. We missed you!
Hello there. An' what's your name?
I'm Jessie, mister. I'm nin years old.
Well, my name's Will Lull, an' I'm forty-nine... maybe fifty!
YAHOO!
POM
TRATATA
HURRAH!
VIVA CALAMITY JANE!
POM POM
Welcome, friends!
October 9th is an historic day for our town. Nineteen years ago, Deadwood had only thirty houses surrounded by thick forest. At that time, the town was not even subject to U.S. law, as it was situated in Lakota territory. When I first met Calamity Jane, she was living in a wagon by the shores of the river, where today there are public bathhouses...

Jane spent her time helping neighbors: treating injuries, feeding orphans, or running the mail all the way to Cheyenne... But Jane always came back to Deadwood, because of...

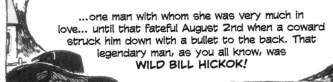

...one man with whom she was very much in love... until that fateful August 2nd when a coward struck him down with a bullet to the back. That legendary man, as you all know, was **WILD BILL HICKOK!**

Ya won't make me cry, Bullock. I'm tired o' tears, today anyway.

Jane, you are our very own! It would be our great honor if you'd rejoin Deadwood's original settlers as an official member of the **Society of Black Hills Pioneers!**

CLAP YES! BRAVO!! CLAP CLAP CLAP

Do... Do I haveta say somethin'?

Well, it's what a **celebrity** usually does... Just a few words.

But I didn't prepare nothin'.

C'mon, Jane. We all know you're the **queen** of improvisation!

HA HA!

Uh, well... Thank ya for such a reception. My head's swoonin'. *Uh*... I'm back in Deadwood with the intention ta stay put this time. It's true I'm more at home here than anywhere else, an' Lord knows I been around!

And I surely will live up ta... ta your fine welcome! Yeah, that's it, an' thanks again! C'mon now...

BRAVO, MARTHA!

Whoof!

The shortest speeches are always the best! Now, let's **party!**

Abbott! Will!

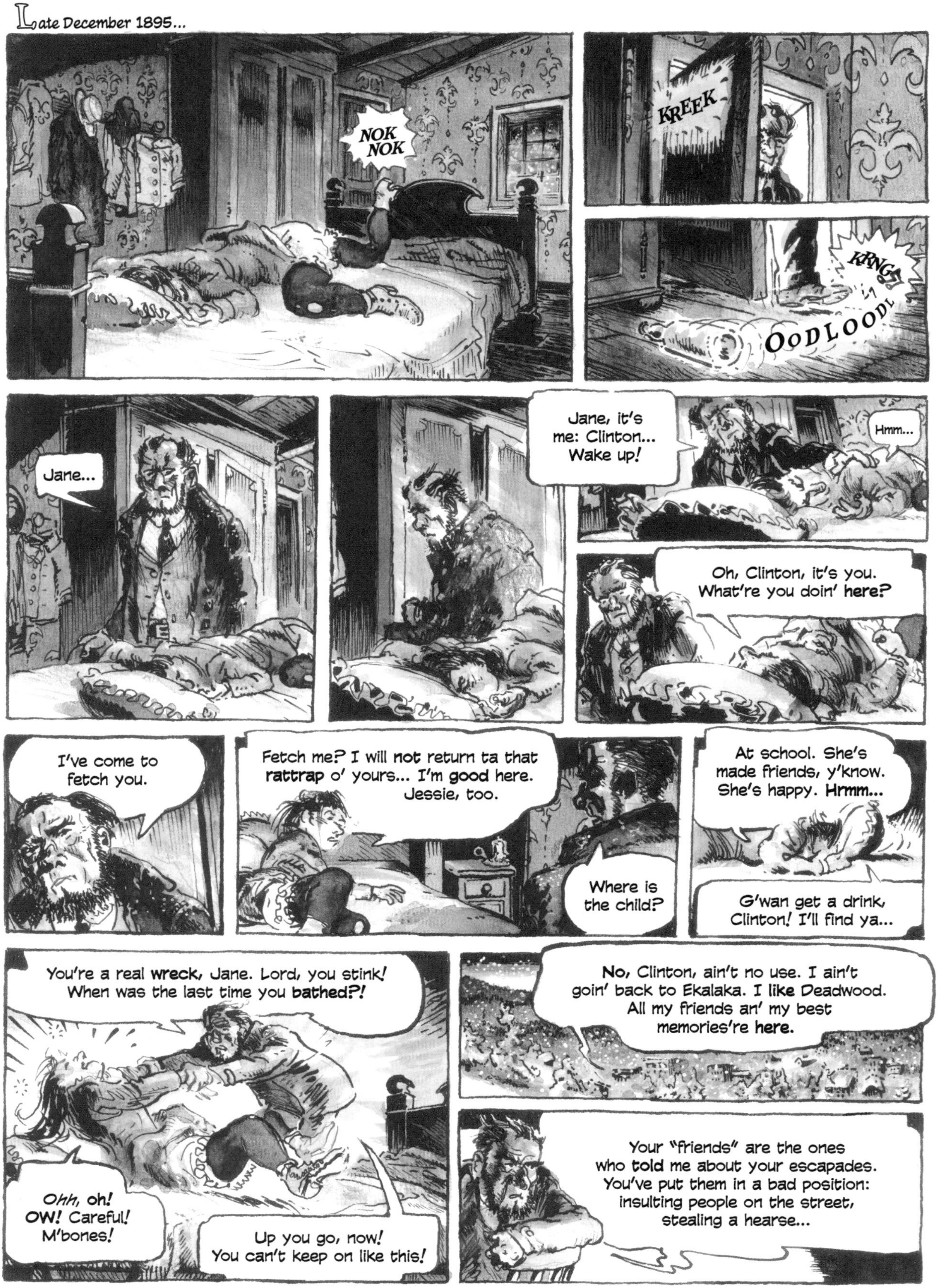
Late December 1895...
NOK NOK
KREEK
KRNG!
OODLOODL
Jane...
Jane, it's me: Clinton... Wake up!
Hmm...
Oh, Clinton, it's you. What're you doin' here?
I've come to fetch you.
Fetch me? I will not return ta that rattrap o' yours... I'm good here. Jessie, too.
Where is the child?
At school. She's made friends, y'know. She's happy. Hrmm...
G'wan get a drink, Clinton! I'll find ya...
You're a real wreck, Jane. Lord, you stink! When was the last time you bathed?!
Ohh, oh! OW! Careful! M'bones!
Up you go, now! You can't keep on like this!
No, Clinton, ain't no use. I ain't goin' back to Ekalaka. I like Deadwood. All my friends an' my best memories're here.
Your "friends" are the ones who told me about your escapades. You've put them in a bad position: insulting people on the street, stealing a hearse...

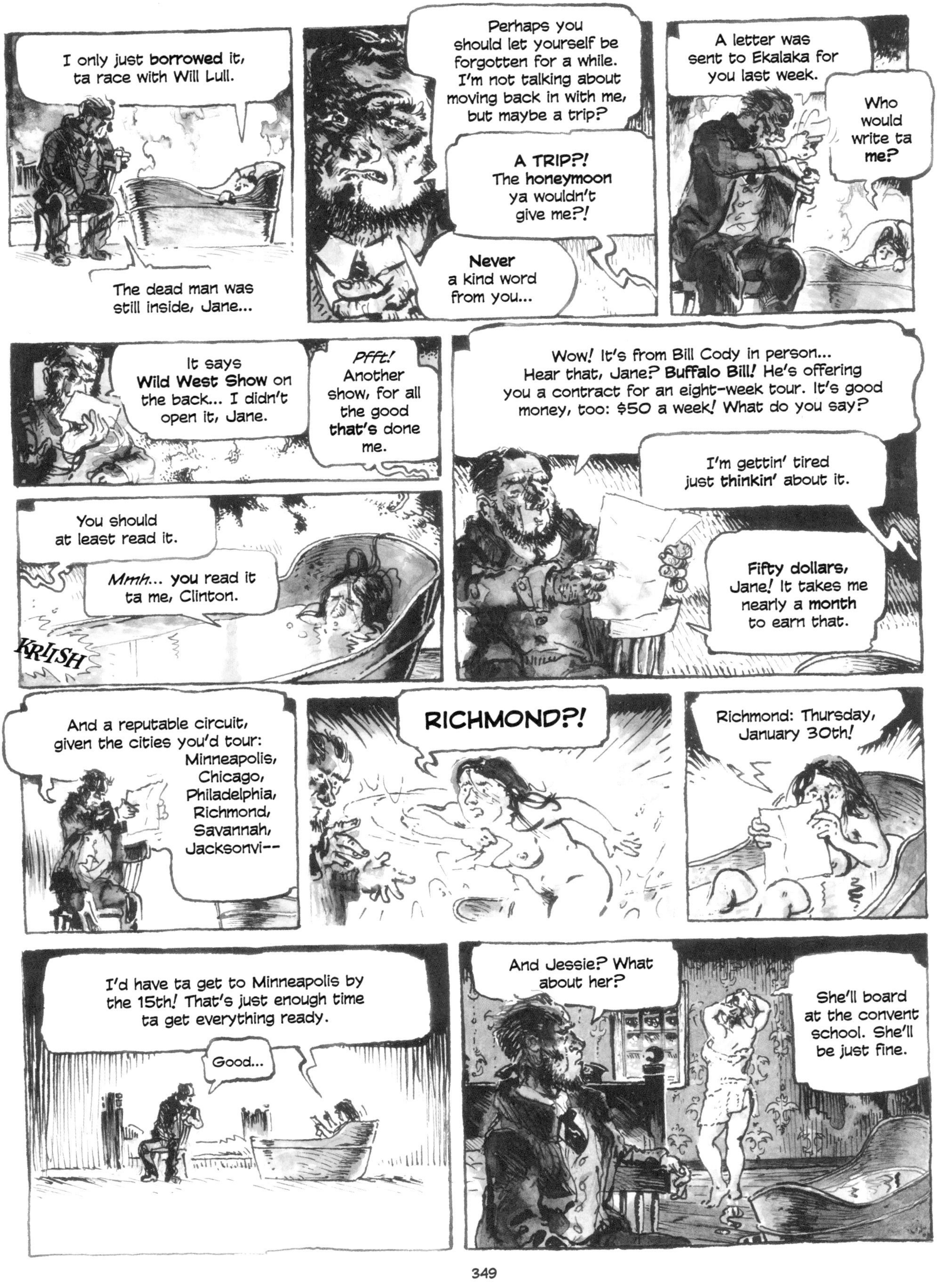
I only just **borrowed** it, ta race with Will Lull.
The dead man was still inside, Jane...
Perhaps you should let yourself be forgotten for a while. I'm not talking about moving back in with me, but maybe a trip?
A TRIP?! The **honeymoon** ya wouldn't give me?!
Never a kind word from you...
A letter was sent to Ekalaka for you last week.
Who would write ta **me?**
It says **Wild West Show** on the back... I didn't open it, Jane.
Pfft! Another show, for all the good **that's** done me.
You should at least read it.
Mmh... **you** read it ta me, Clinton.
KRIISH
Wow! It's from Bill Cody in person... Hear that, Jane? **Buffalo Bill!** He's offering you a contract for an eight-week tour. It's good money, too: $50 a week! What do you say?
I'm gettin' tired just **thinkin'** about it.
Fifty dollars, Jane! It takes me nearly a **month** to earn that.
And a reputable circuit, given the cities you'd tour: Minneapolis, Chicago, Philadelphia, Richmond, Savannah, Jacksonvi--
RICHMOND?!
Richmond: Thursday, January 30th!
I'd have ta get to Minneapolis by the 15th! That's just enough time ta get everything ready.
Good...
And Jessie? What about her?
She'll board at the convent school. She'll be just fine.

Dear Janey,

Here we are in New York City. The tour is a huge success: crowds cheering at the top of their lungs and applauding to bring the house down. Next week we'll be in Richmond. I look forward to seeing you there, sweetheart.

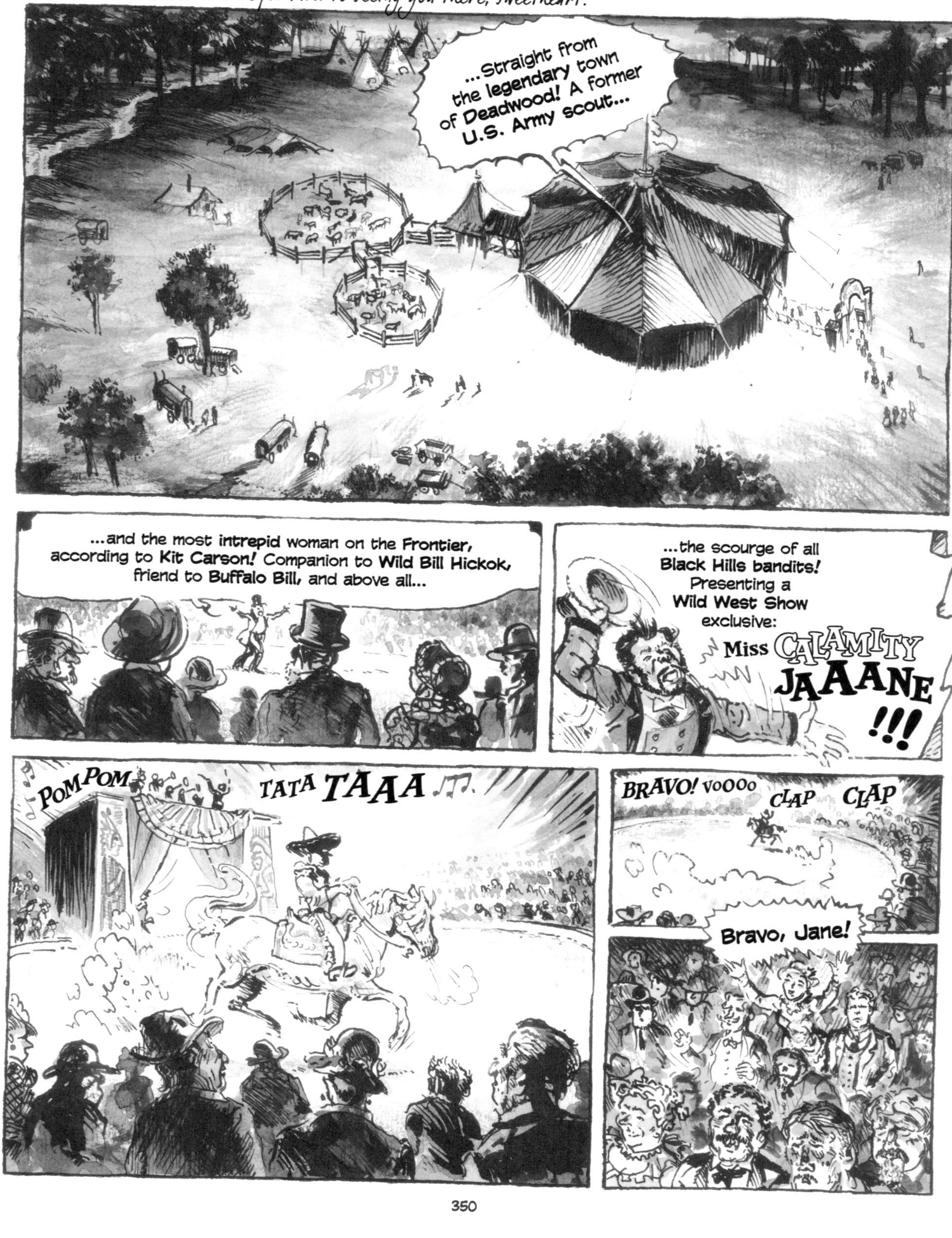
...Straight from the legendary town of Deadwood! A former U.S. Army scout...
...and the most intrepid woman on the Frontier, according to Kit Carson! Companion to Wild Bill Hickok, friend to Buffalo Bill, and above all...
...the scourge of all Black Hills bandits! Presenting a Wild West Show exclusive:
Miss CALAMITY JAAANE !!!
POM POM
TATA TAAA
BRAVO! VOOOO
CLAP
CLAP
Bravo, Jane!

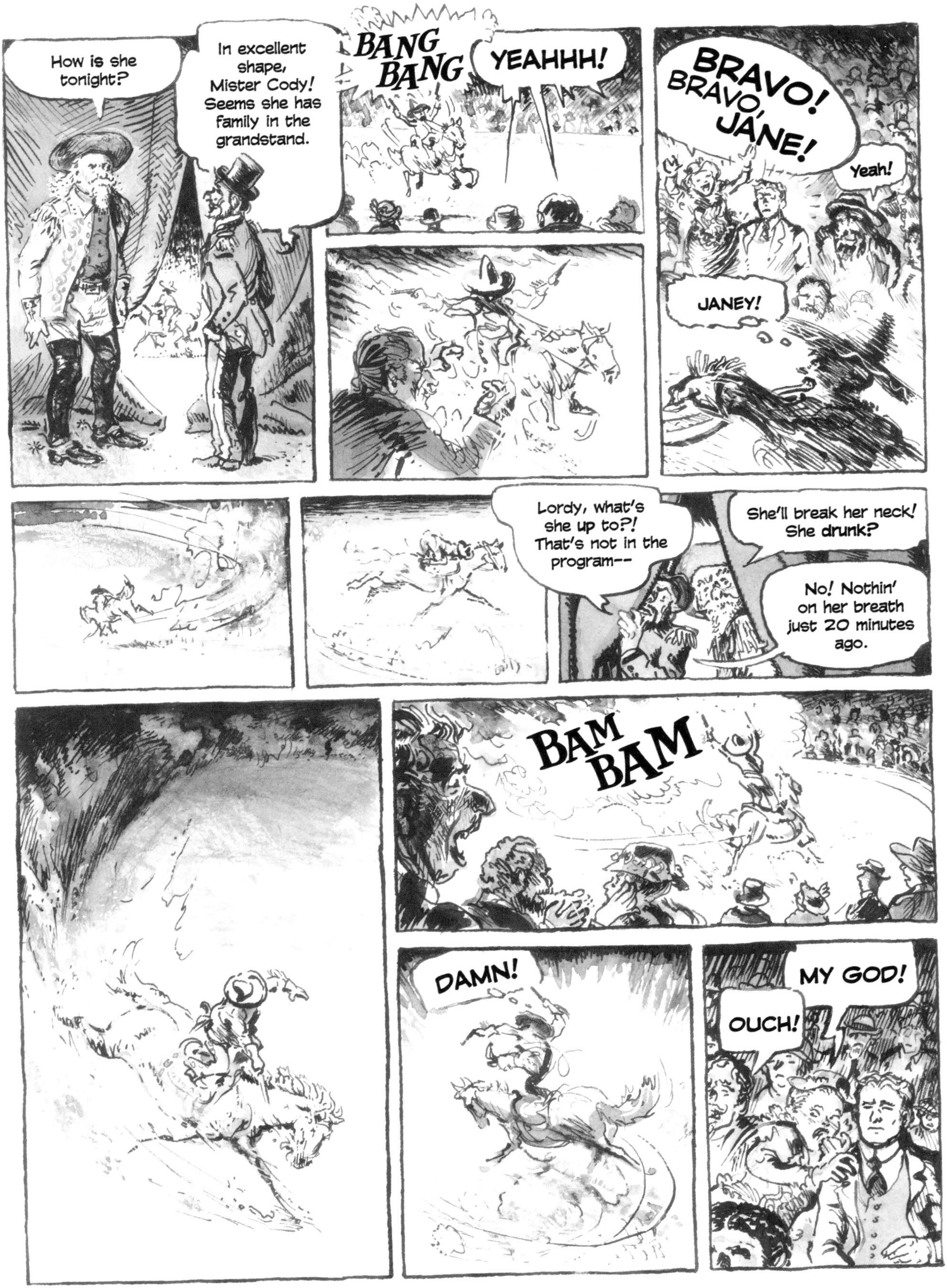
How is she tonight?
In excellent shape, Mister Cody! Seems she has family in the grandstand.
BANG BANG
YEAHHH!
BRAVO! BRAVO, JANE!
Yeah!
JANEY!
Lordy, what's she up to?! That's not in the program--
She'll break her neck! She drunk?
No! Nothin' on her breath just 20 minutes ago.
BAM BAM
DAMN!
MY GOD!
OUCH!

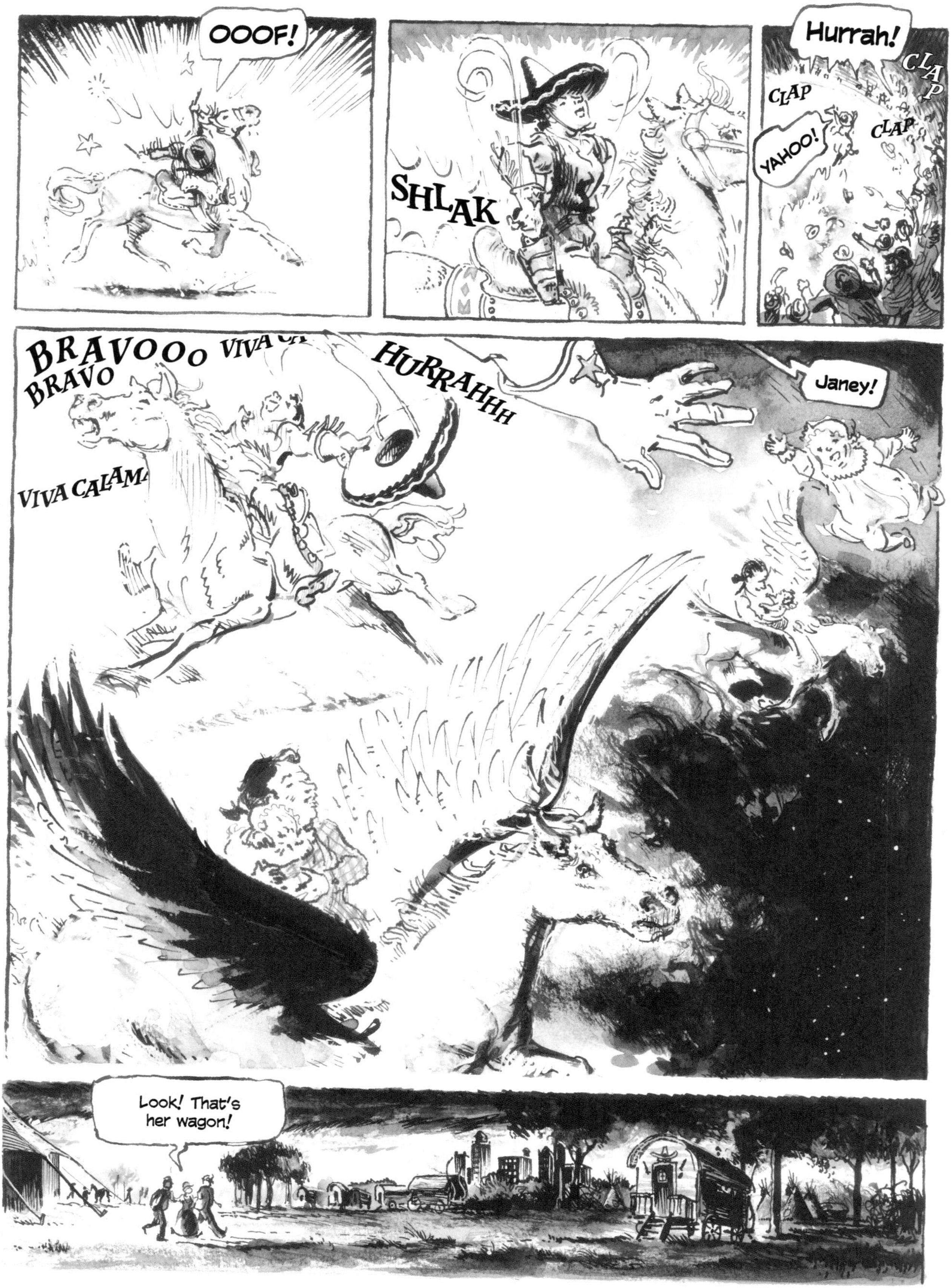
OOOF!
SHLAK
Hurrah!
CLAP
CLAP
YAHOO!
CLAP
CLAP
BRAVOOO
BRAVO
VIVA CA
HURRAHHH
Janey!
VIVA CALAMA
Look! That's her wagon!

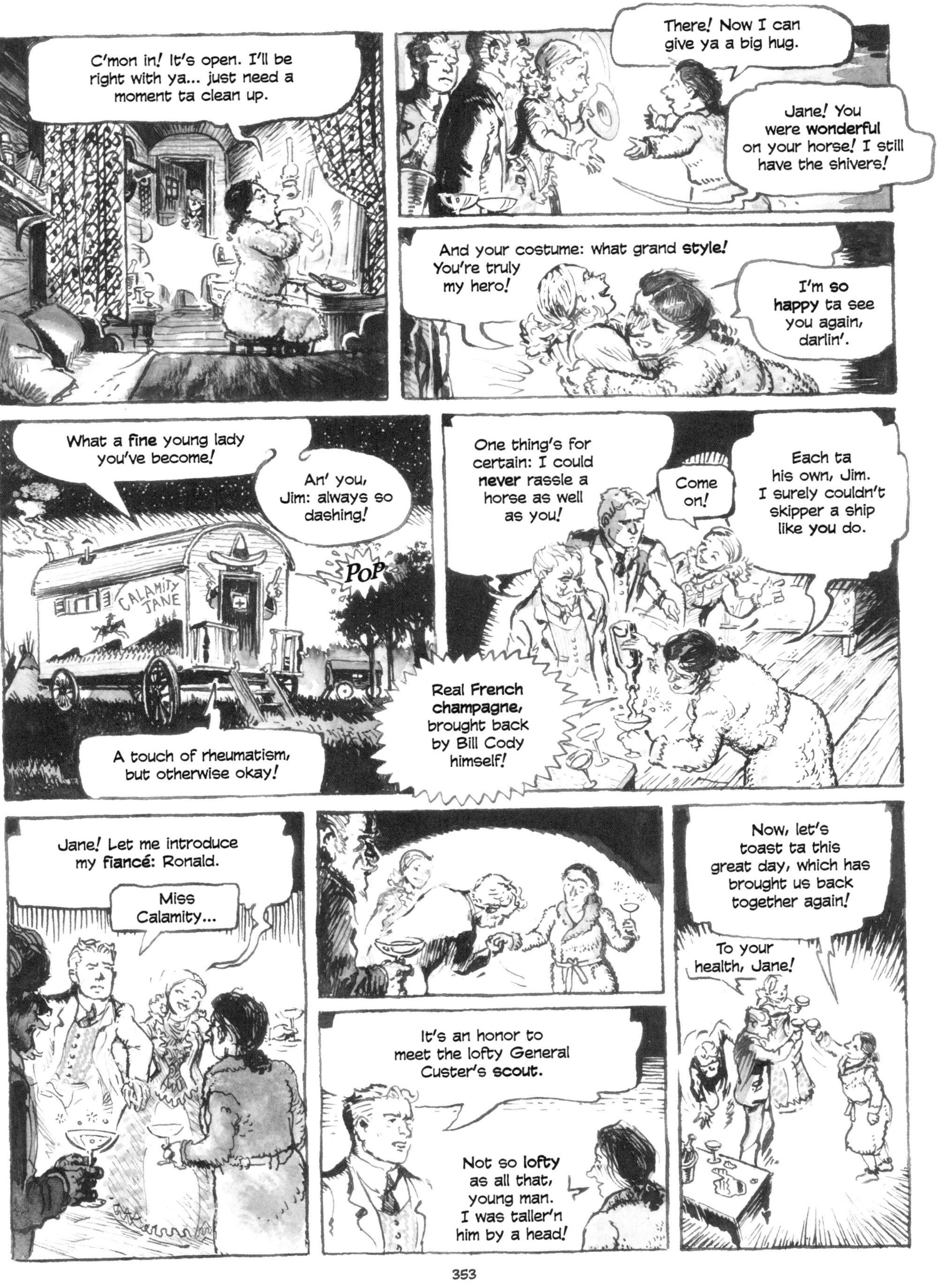

C'mon in! It's open. I'll be right with ya... just need a moment ta clean up.
There! Now I can give ya a big hug.
Jane! You were **wonderful** on your horse! I still have the shivers!
And your costume: what grand **style!** You're truly my hero!
I'm **so happy** ta see you again, darlin'.
What a **fine** young lady you've become!
An' you, Jim: always so dashing!
POP
A touch of rheumatism, but otherwise okay!
One thing's for certain: I could **never** rassle a horse as well as you!
Come on!
Each ta his own, Jim. I surely couldn't skipper a ship like **you** do.
Real French **champagne,** brought back by Bill Cody himself!
Jane! Let me introduce my **fiancé:** Ronald.
Miss Calamity...
It's an honor to meet the lofty General Custer's **scout.**
Not so **lofty** as all that, young man. I was taller'n him by a head!
Now, let's toast ta this great day, which has brought us back together again!
To your health, Jane!

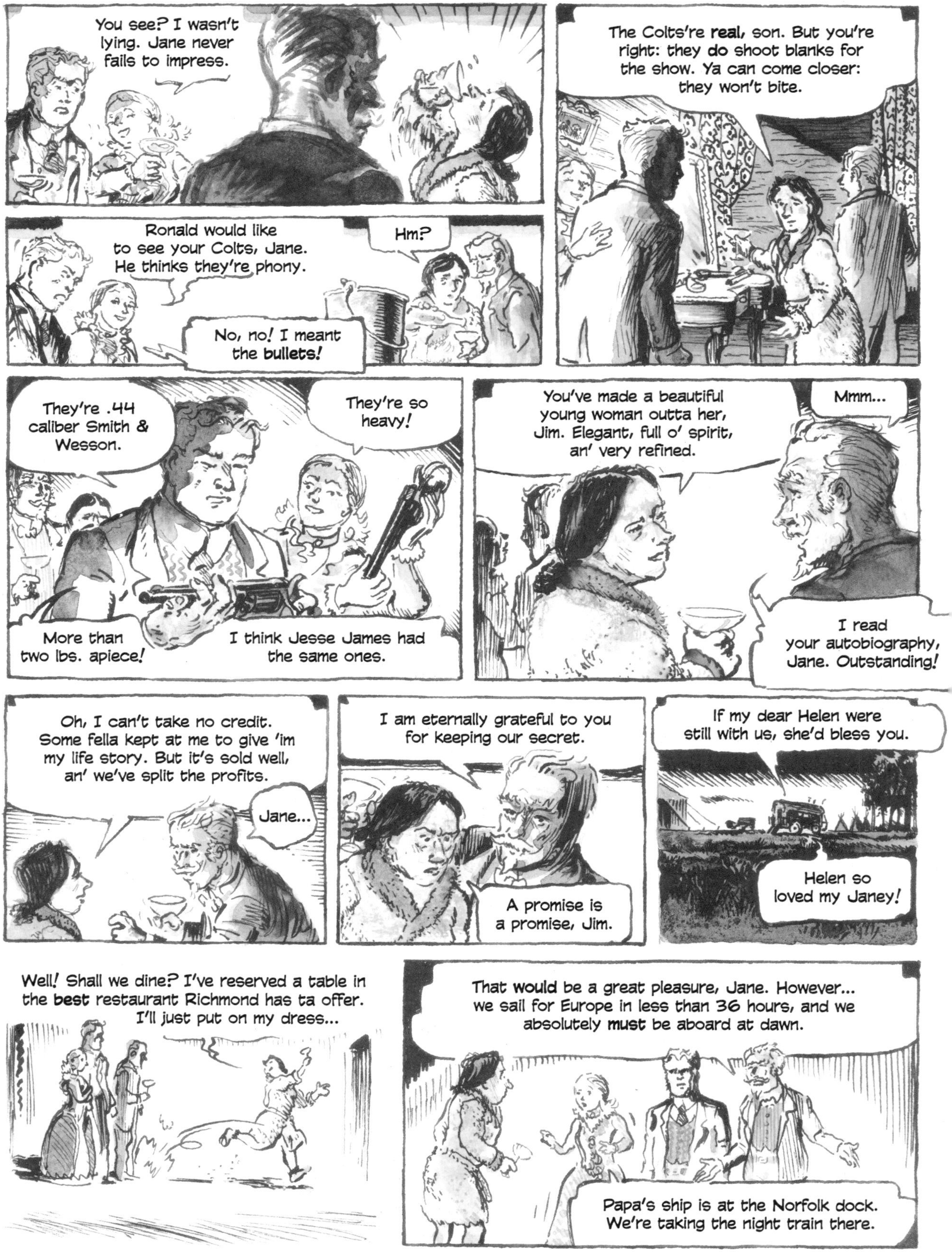

You see? I wasn't lying. Jane never fails to impress.
Ronald would like to see your Colts, Jane. He thinks they're phony.
Hm?
No, no! I meant the bullets!
The Colts're real, son. But you're right: they do shoot blanks for the show. Ya can come closer: they won't bite.
They're .44 caliber Smith & Wesson.
They're so heavy!
More than two lbs. apiece!
I think Jesse James had the same ones.
You've made a beautiful young woman outta her, Jim. Elegant, full o' spirit, an' very refined.
Mmm...
I read your autobiography, Jane. Outstanding!
Oh, I can't take no credit. Some fella kept at me to give 'im my life story. But it's sold well, an' we've split the profits.
Jane...
I am eternally grateful to you for keeping our secret.
A promise is a promise, Jim.
If my dear Helen were still with us, she'd bless you.
Helen so loved my Janey!
Well! Shall we dine? I've reserved a table in the best restaurant Richmond has ta offer. I'll just put on my dress...
That would be a great pleasure, Jane. However... we sail for Europe in less than 36 hours, and we absolutely must be aboard at dawn.
Papa's ship is at the Norfolk dock. We're taking the night train there.

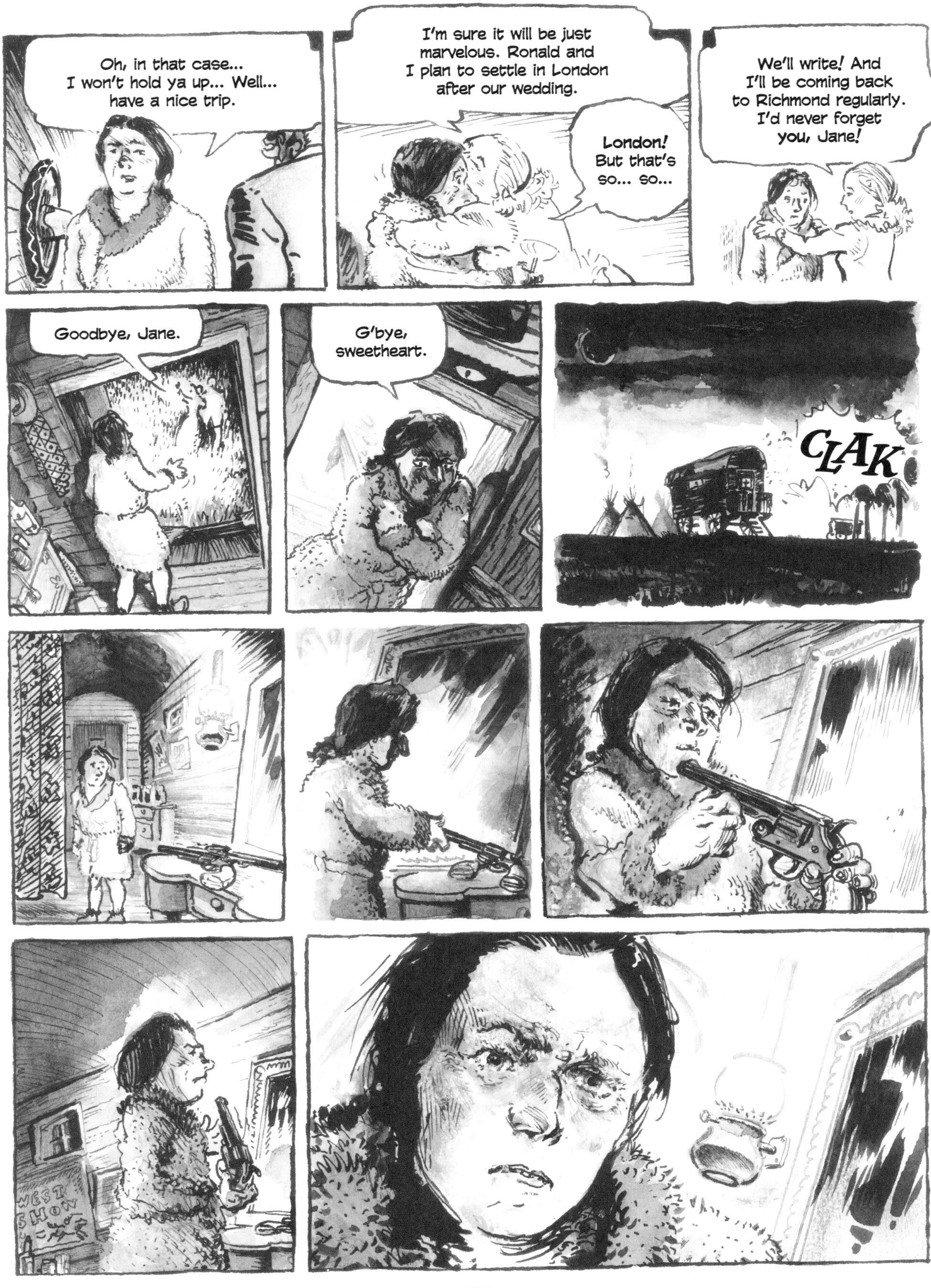
Oh, in that case... I won't hold ya up... Well... have a nice trip.
I'm sure it will be just marvelous. Ronald and I plan to settle in London after our wedding.
London! But that's so... so...
We'll write! And I'll be coming back to Richmond regularly. I'd never forget you, Jane!
Goodbye, Jane.
G'bye, sweetheart.
CLAK

Deadwood, July 1903...

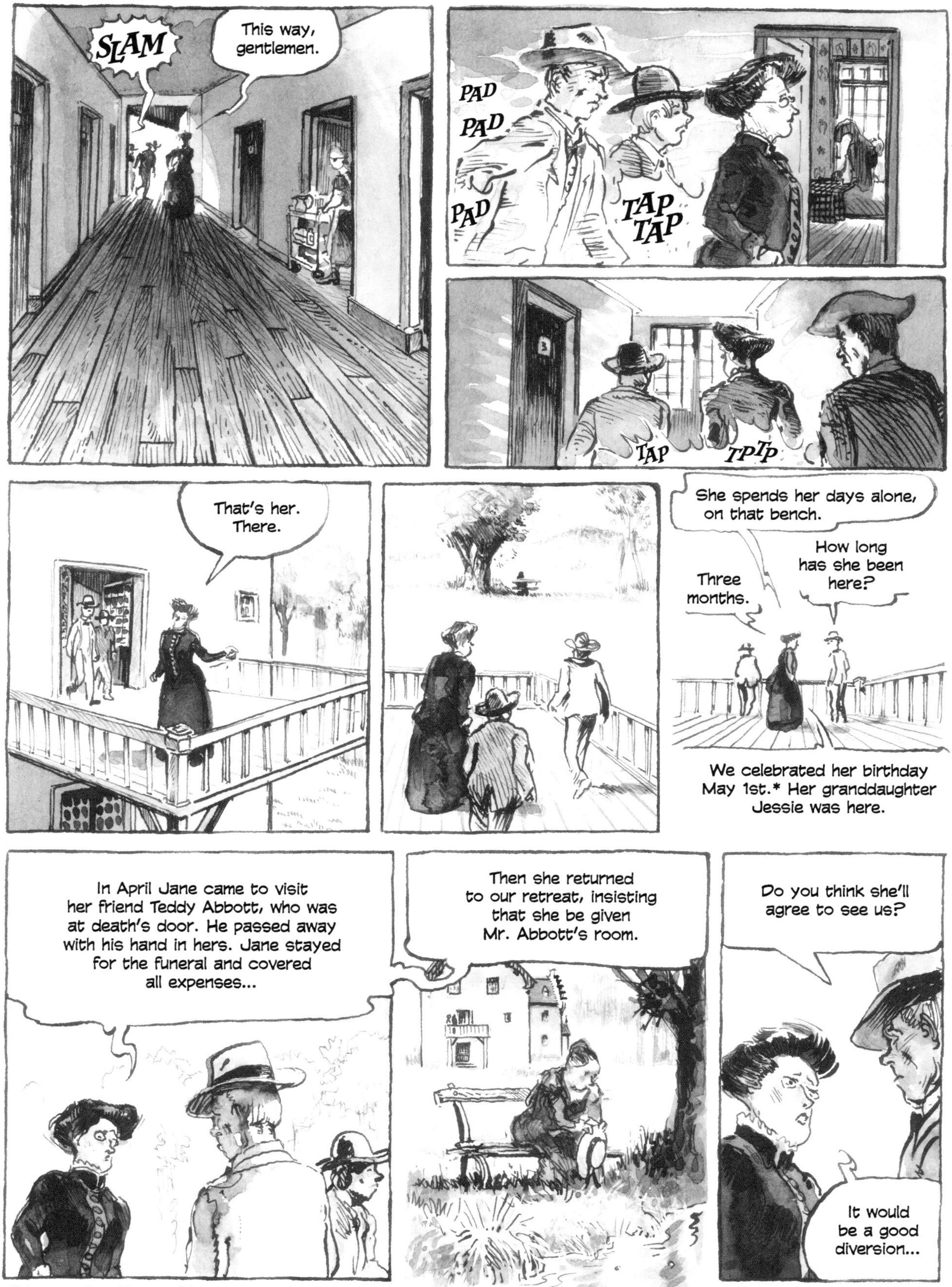
SLAM
This way, gentlemen.
PAD
PAD
PAD
TAP TAP
TAP
TPTP
That's her. There.
She spends her days alone, on that bench.
How long has she been here?
Three months.
We celebrated her birthday May 1st.* Her granddaughter Jessie was here.
In April Jane came to visit her friend Teddy Abbott, who was at death's door. He passed away with his hand in hers. Jane stayed for the funeral and covered all expenses...
Then she returned to our retreat, insisting that she be given Mr. Abbott's room.
Do you think she'll agree to see us?
It would be a good diversion...

* Jane was then 51 years old.

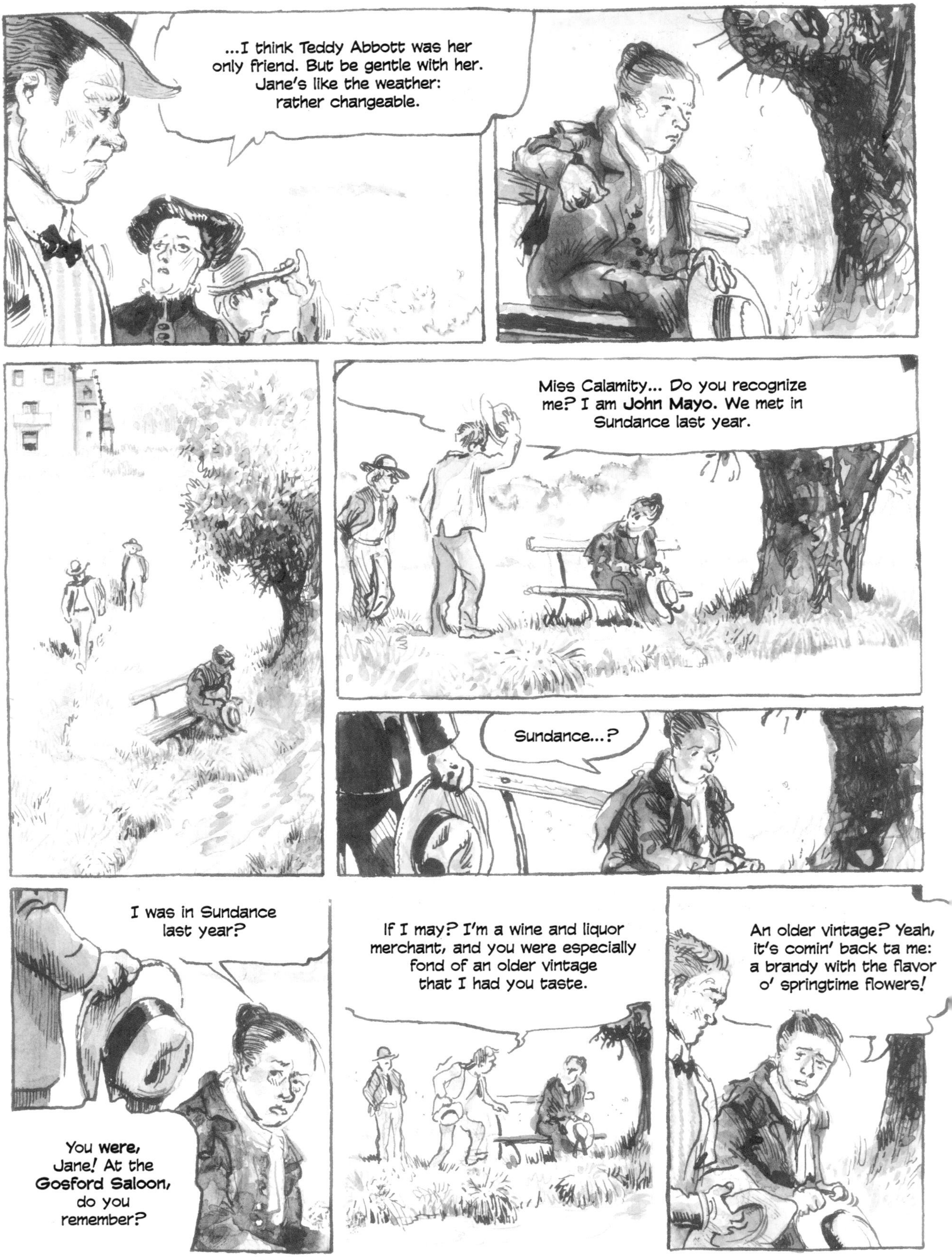
...I think Teddy Abbott was her only friend. But be gentle with her. Jane's like the weather: rather changeable.
Miss Calamity... Do you recognize me? I am **John Mayo.** We met in Sundance last year.
Sundance...?
I was in Sundance last year?
You **were,** Jane! At the **Gosford Saloon,** do you remember?
If I may? I'm a wine and liquor merchant, and you were especially fond of an older vintage that I had you taste.
An older vintage? Yeah, it's comin' back ta me: a brandy with the flavor o' springtime flowers!

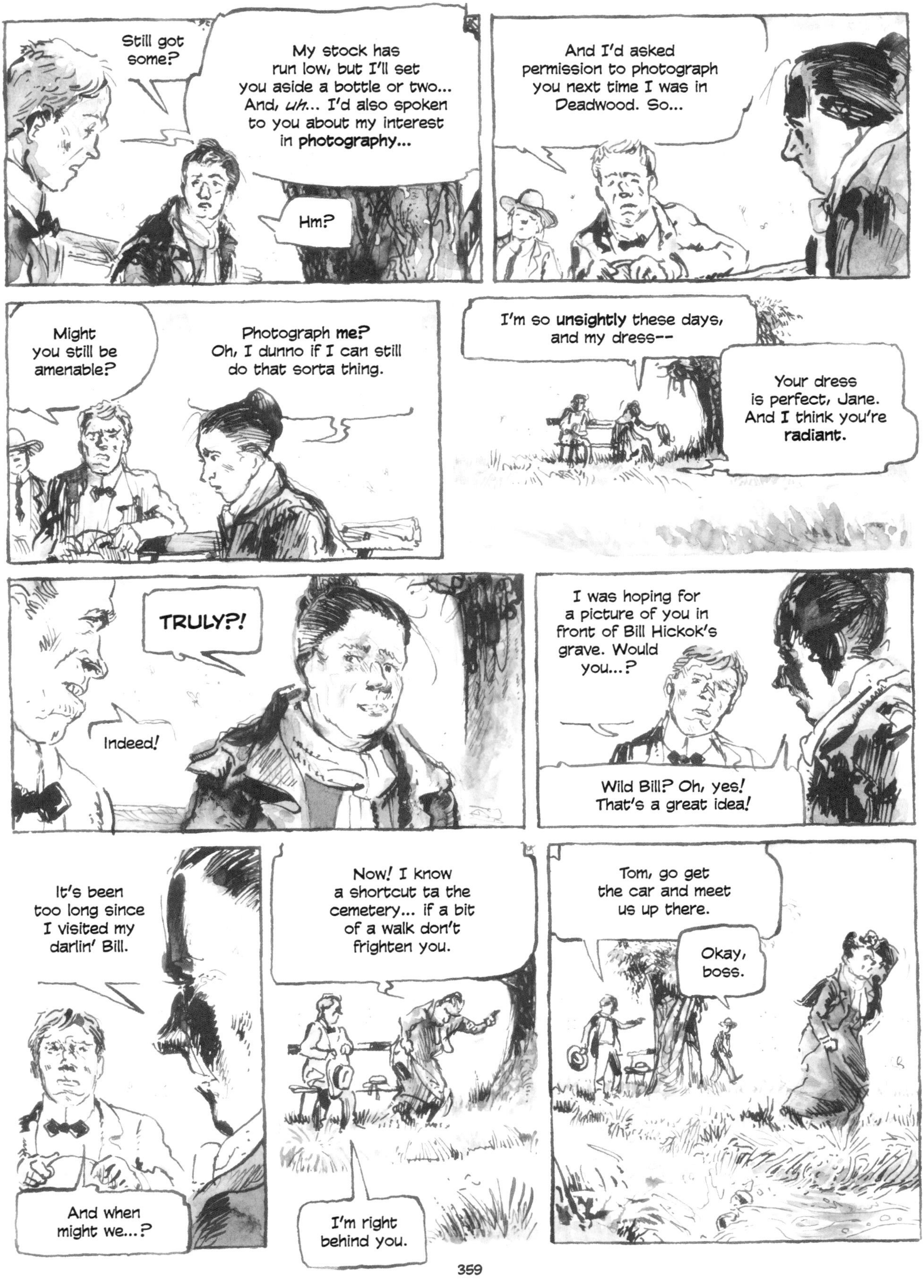

Still got some?
My stock has run low, but I'll set you aside a bottle or two... And, *uh*... I'd also spoken to you about my interest in **photography...**
Hm?
And I'd asked permission to photograph you next time I was in Deadwood. So...
Might you still be amenable?
Photograph **me?** Oh, I dunno if I can still do that sorta thing.
I'm so **unsightly** these days, and my dress--
Your dress is perfect, Jane. And I think you're **radiant.**
TRULY?!
Indeed!
I was hoping for a picture of you in front of Bill Hickok's grave. Would you...?
Wild Bill? Oh, yes! That's a great idea!
It's been too long since I visited my darlin' Bill.
And when might we...?
Now! I know a shortcut ta the cemetery... if a bit of a walk don't frighten you.
I'm right behind you.
Tom, go get the car and meet us up there.
Okay, boss.

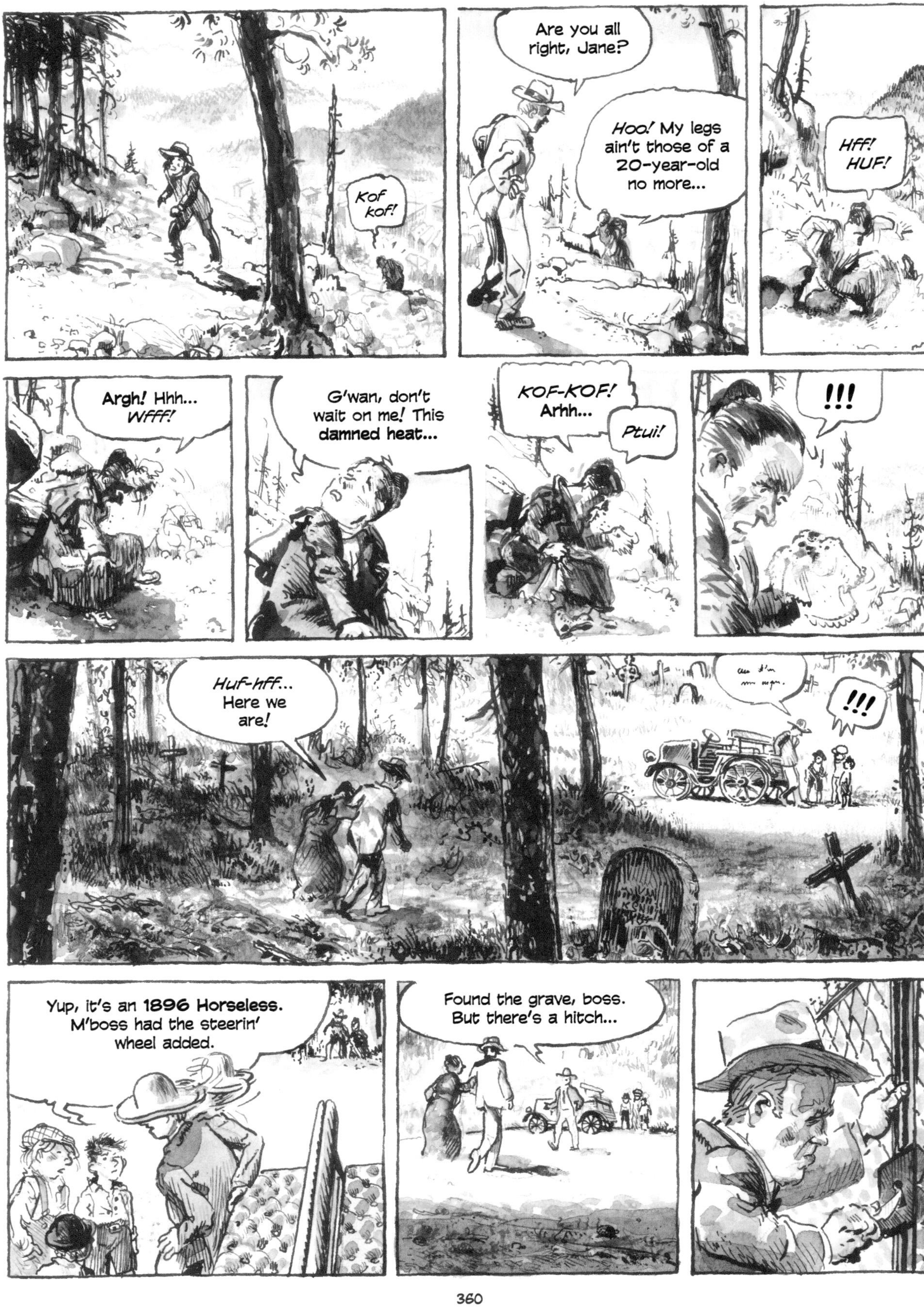
Kof kof!
Are you all right, Jane?
Hoo! My legs ain't those of a 20-year-old no more...
Hff! HUF!
Argh! Hhh... Wfff!
G'wan, don't wait on me! This damned heat...
KOF-KOF! Arhh...
Ptui!
!!!
Huf-hff... Here we are!
!!!
Yup, it's an 1896 Horseless. M'boss had the steerin' wheel added.
Found the grave, boss. But there's a hitch...

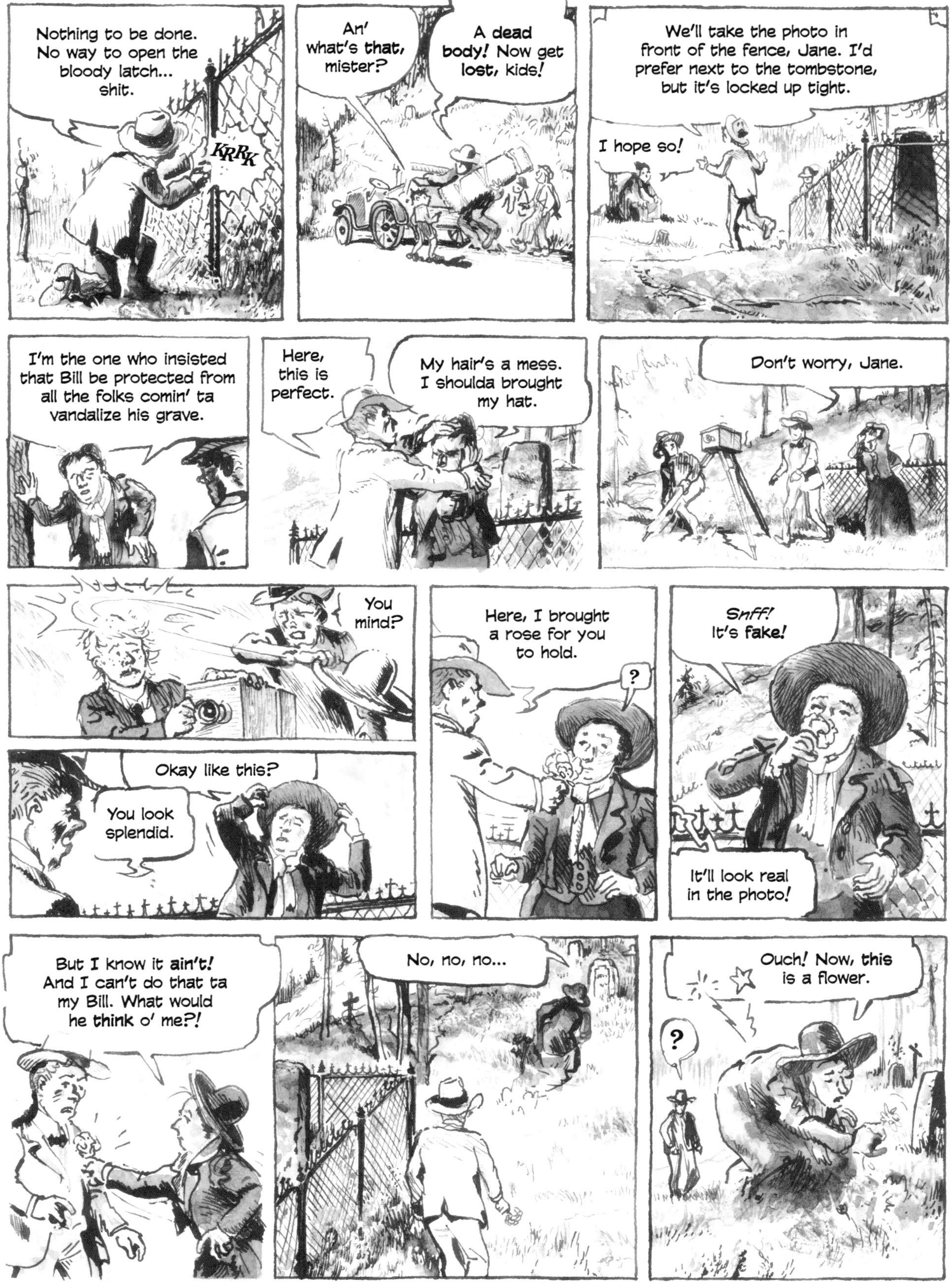

Nothing to be done. No way to open the bloody latch... shit.
KRRK
An' what's that, mister?
A dead body! Now get lost, kids!
We'll take the photo in front of the fence, Jane. I'd prefer next to the tombstone, but it's locked up tight.
I hope so!
I'm the one who insisted that Bill be protected from all the folks comin' ta vandalize his grave.
Here, this is perfect.
My hair's a mess. I shoulda brought my hat.
Don't worry, Jane.
You mind?
Okay like this?
You look splendid.
Here, I brought a rose for you to hold.
?
Snff! It's fake!
It'll look real in the photo!
But I know it ain't! And I can't do that ta my Bill. What would he think o' me?!
No, no, no...
Ouch! Now, this is a flower.
?

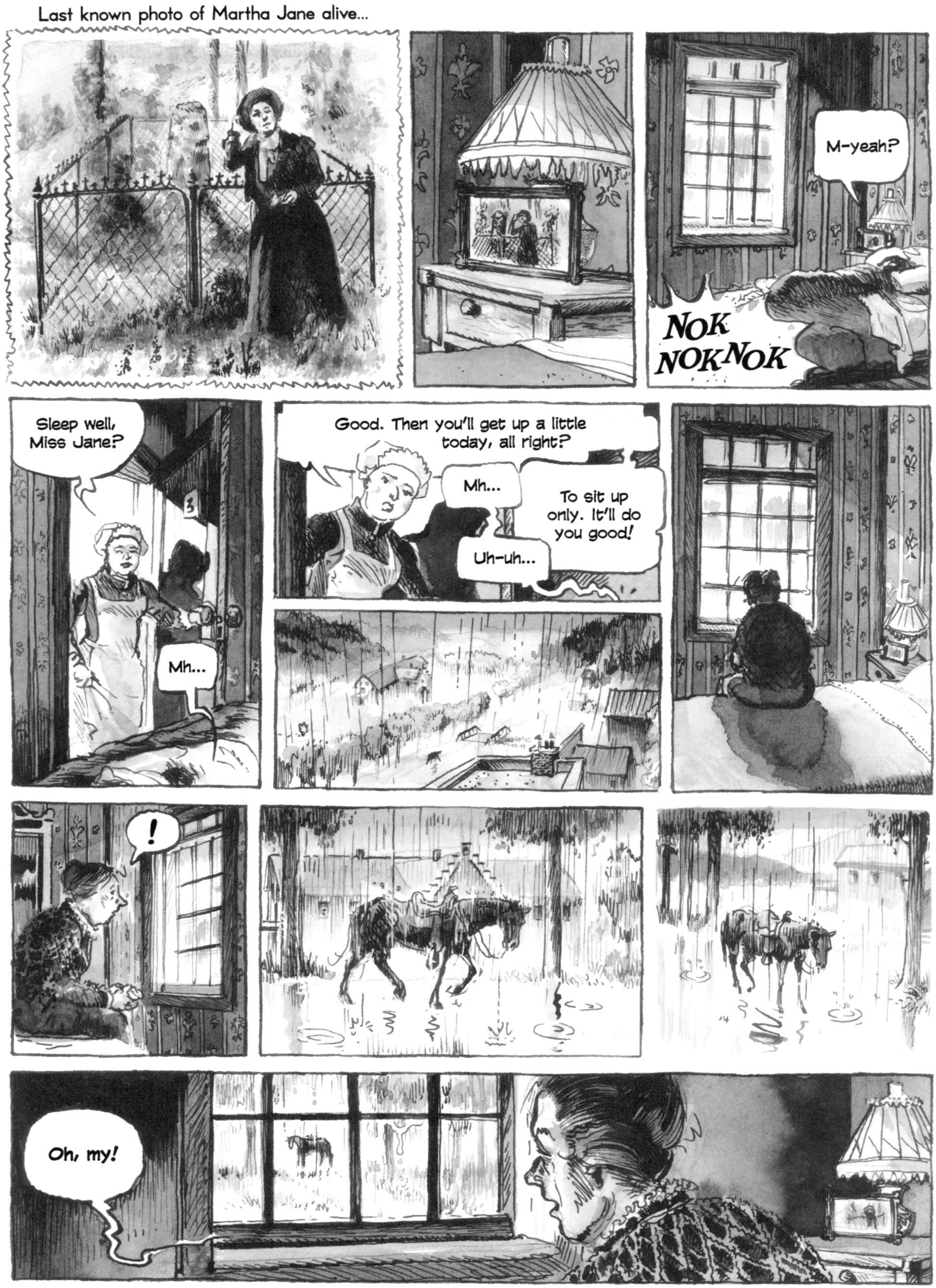
Last known photo of Martha Jane alive...
M-yeah?
NOK NOKNOK
Sleep well, Miss Jane?
Mh...
Good. Then you'll get up a little today, all right?
Mh...
To sit up only. It'll do you good!
Uh-uh...
!
Oh, my!

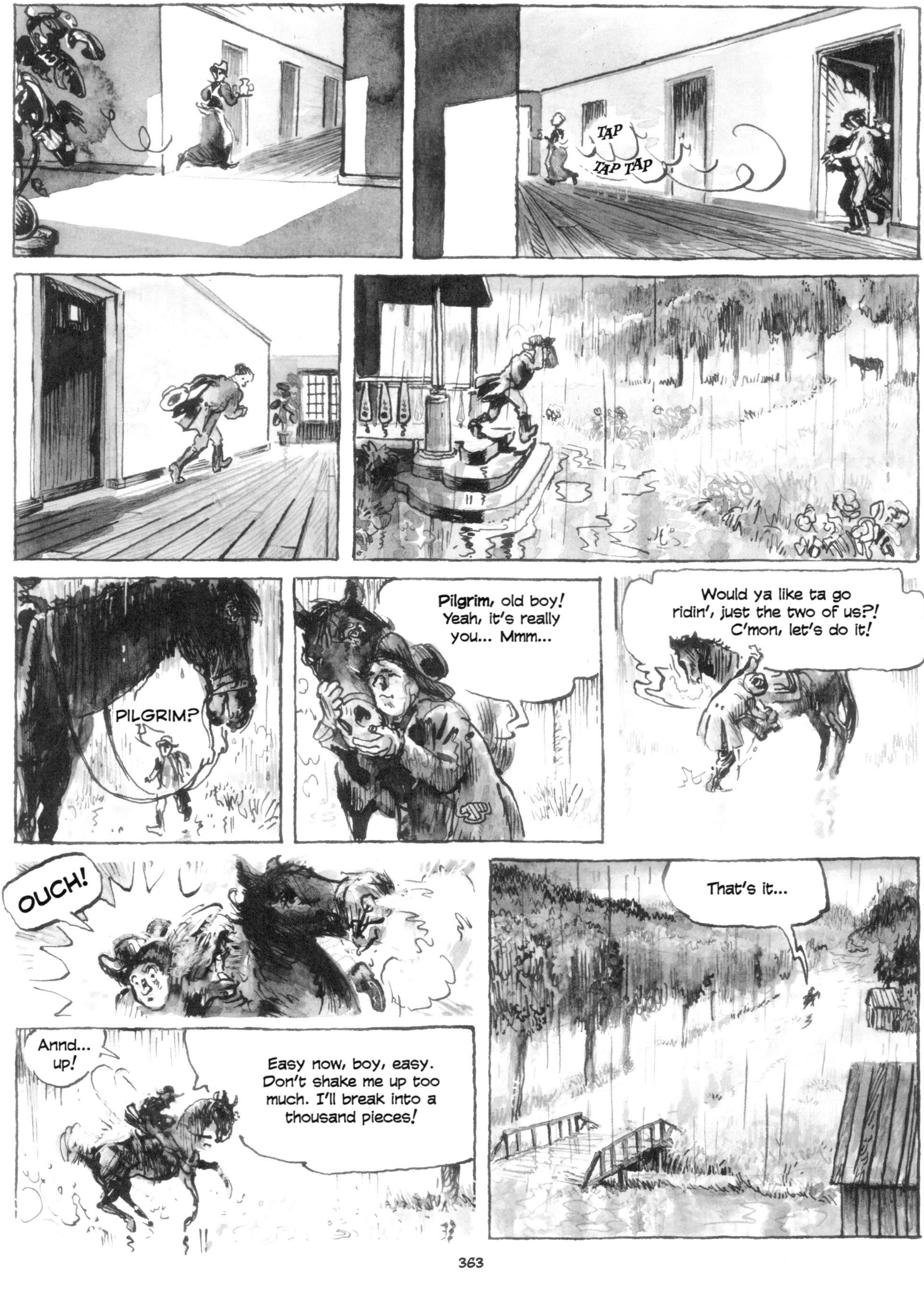
TAP
TAP TAP
PILGRIM?
Pilgrim, old boy! Yeah, it's really you... Mmm...
Would ya like ta go ridin', just the two of us?! C'mon, let's do it!
OUCH!
Annd... up!
Easy now, boy, easy. Don't shake me up too much. I'll break into a thousand pieces!
That's it...

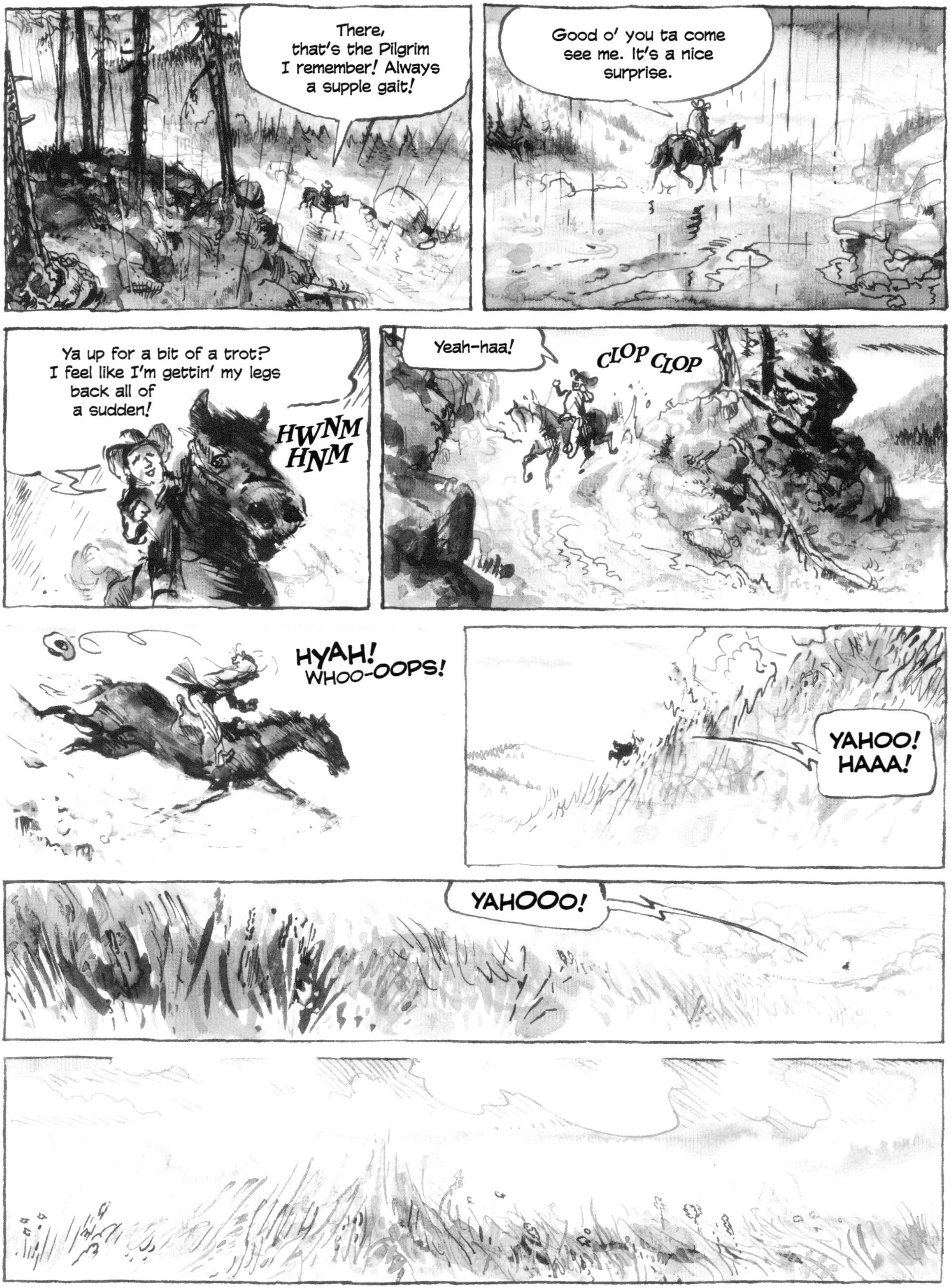
There, that's the Pilgrim I remember! Always a supple gait!
Good o' you ta come see me. It's a nice surprise.
Ya up for a bit of a trot? I feel like I'm gettin' my legs back all of a sudden!
HWNM HNM
Yeah-haa!
CLOP CLOP
HYAH! WHOO-OOPS!
YAHOO! HAAA!
YAHOOO!

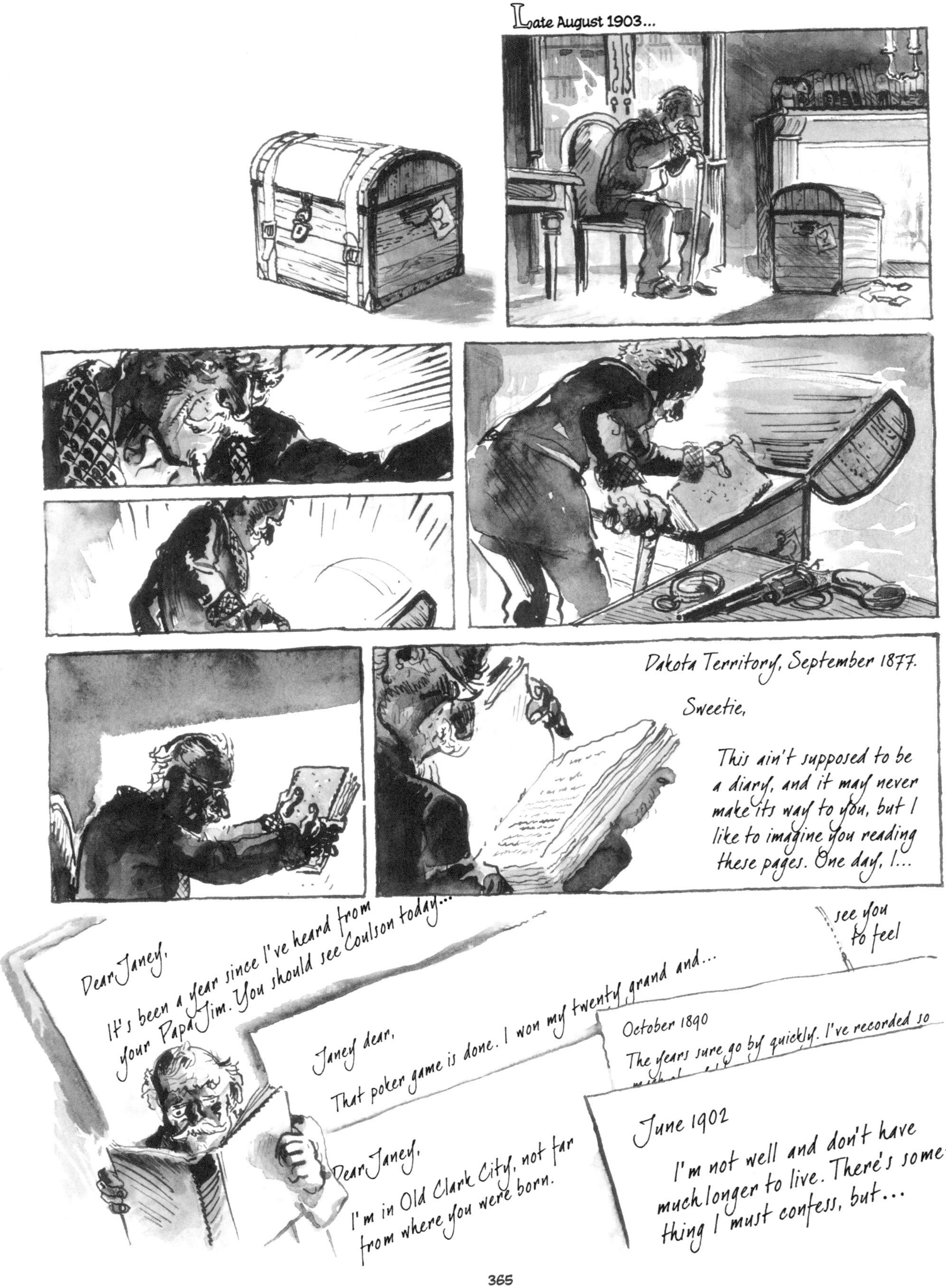
Late August 1903...
Dakota Territory, September 1877.
Sweetie,
This ain't supposed to be a diary, and it may never make its way to you, but I like to imagine you reading these pages. One day, I...
Dear Janey,
It's been a year since I've heard from your Papa Jim. You should see Coulson today...
see you
to feel
Janey dear,
That poker game is done. I won my twenty grand and...
October 1890
The years sure go by quickly. I've recorded so
Dear Janey,
I'm in Old Clark City, not far from where you were born.
June 1902
I'm not well and don't have much longer to live. There's something I must confess, but...

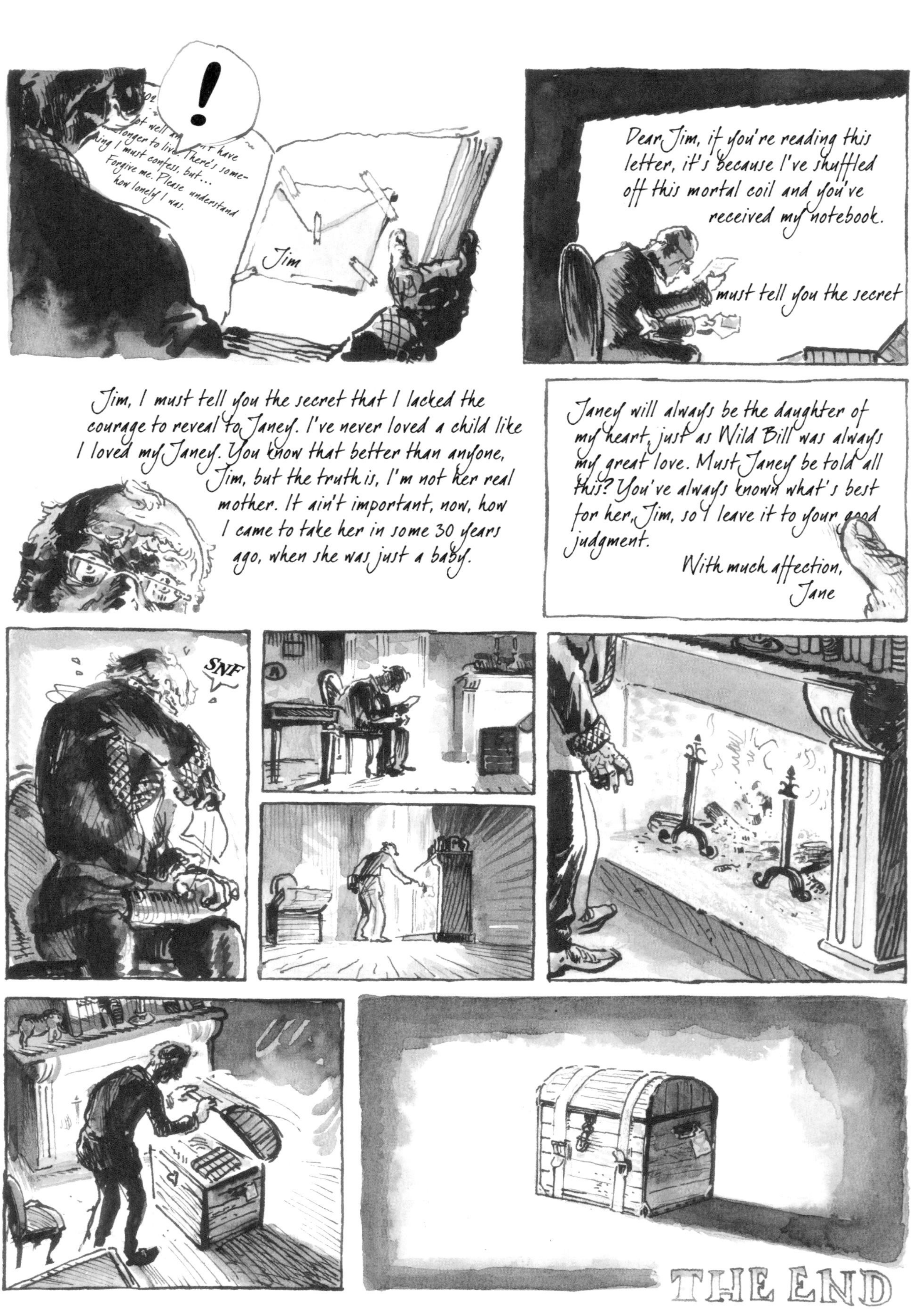

!
longer to live. There's something I must confess, but...
Forgive me. Please understand
how lonely I was.
Jim
Dear Jim, if you're reading this letter, it's because I've shuffled off this mortal coil and you've received my notebook.
must tell you the secret
Jim, I must tell you the secret that I lacked the courage to reveal to Janey. I've never loved a child like I loved my Janey. You know that better than anyone, Jim, but the truth is, I'm not her real mother. It ain't important, now, how I came to take her in some 30 years ago, when she was just a baby.
Janey will always be the daughter of my heart, just as Wild Bill was always my great love. Must Janey be told all this? You've always known what's best for her, Jim, so I leave it to your good judgment.
With much affection,
Jane
SNF
THE END